D0903685

Coronation Street: The War Years

Also available from Granada Media

Coronation Street: Keeping the Home Fires Burning
The Coronation Street Story
Who's Who in Coronation Street
The Rovers Return Pub Quiz

CORONATION STREET: THE WAR YEARS

The Complete Enthralling Saga of Coronation Street During World War II

Daran Little & Christine Green

CARLTON
BOOKS

This is a Carlton Book

Coronation Street is a Granada Television Production
Based on an idea by Tony Warren.
Coronation Street At War first published in 2000.
The Way To Victory first published in 2000.
This edition first published in 2001 by Carlton Books

In association with Granada Media Group

Text copyright © Granada Media Group Ltd, 2001

The right of Daran Little to be identified as the author of
Coronation Street At War and Christine Green to be identified as
the author of *The Way To Victory* has been asserted by them in
accordance with the Copyright, Designs and Patents Act 1988.

A catalogue record for this book is available from the British
Library.

ISBN 1 84222 601 0

Design by Jeremy Southgate

Typeset by
Derek Doyle & Associates, Liverpool
Printed and bound in the UK by
Mackays of Chatham plc, Kent, UK

2 4 6 8 10 9 7 5 3 1

CONTENTS

Coronation Street At War

CHAPTER ONE

3 September 1939 Britain declares war on Germany for invading Poland, and the Tanners invade Coronation Street.

The stench of rotting flesh from the back of the slaughter-house attracted rats, which scurried across the uneven cobbles to feast on remains. They passed unnoticed by the young woman making a short cut through Weatherfield's back alleys. The fiery tones of her hair were covered by the sheer headscarf tied tightly under her chin. Her pace was slowed by the weight of the battered suitcase she carried. Bought cheap from the pawn shop where it had been abandoned, it contained all her worldly goods – or, at least, all she was allowed to take with her from 16B Back Gas Street, the corner of Weatherfield where the sun never seemed to shine. The suitcase weighed her down and forced her to walk with a slight slump of her left shoulder.

As she emerged on to Canal Street at the side of the Leg of Mutton public house, she paused to rest. A customer, entering the public bar, leered at her and gave a low whistle. She stared him straight in the eye. She was used to his sort. There were plenty of them living in Back Gas Street. Out all day, scratching around for a living, then barging back to their hovels, demanding food, going off to the alehouse then back, swaying and singing bawdy songs, for a quick fumble under the bedclothes with wives who lay like statues, waiting for it to be over.

She picked up the case and went on her way, following the map pencilled for her on the back of an envelope. Not far to go, although it could have been Timbuktu as far as she was concerned. Girls from her side of the abattoir never ventured to the other side of Weatherfield.

The viaduct holding the Great Northern Railway, built in the 1830s, sliced the district into two distinct areas. She was used to the back-to-backs surrounding the old workhouse, the ragged school and the red-brick hospital for skin diseases.

Across the way stood neat terraces with bay windows and paved yards. Those houses even had their own toilet. That was class. It was four families to one WC in Back Gas Street. She smiled to herself: this was her lucky day, her chance to better herself. About time too. She just wished there'd been room in the removal van for her as well as the furniture. Still, she looked upon the trudge through the alleys of her childhood as a chance to wipe the slate clean and start anew. Even the air seemed fresher as she carried on her journey towards Coronation Street.

Unaware of how lucky she was to share a toilet with just her own family, another young woman, just a few years older than the one burning her bridges, clenched her fist and hammered on the wooden door for the fourth time. 'How much longer do you plan on being in there?'

The answer came in the form of a faint grunt.

'It's no flamin' joke, yer know. Get a move on!' Alice Hewitt was desperate for a pee. She gave the door one last bang, then stepped away into the body of the unkempt yard.

'Is that you, Alice, love?' A scraping of metal against stone was followed by a middle-aged face appearing over the brick wall separating the backyards of Nos. 7 and 9 Coronation Street. Vi Todd, an angular, plain woman in her forties who looked years older, wobbled on the upturned tin tub and scratched her hair through her scarf. 'Today's the day, love!'

'Aye', said Alice, glaring at the toilet door.

'What's up, love? Where's that bridal bloom?'

'It's him, our 'Arry; been locked in cludgy for last 'alf hour.'

'Well, that's men for you, no consideration.' Vi raised her voice, 'Do you hear me 'Arry 'Ewitt? It's yer sister's weddin' day. Show some consideration.'

There was no answer from the closet.

'Men,' said Vi, 'pig ignorant. Tell you what, love, nip round and use ours. The seat's nice and warm.'

Alice lifted the latch on the back gate, darted out into the entry, and emerged again in the Todds' backyard. There were no rats in the back alleyway that separated Coronation Street and Mawdsley Street, just weeds sticking up from cobbles and the odd rusting piece of scrap. Vi and Alice's deceased mother, Mary, had been sisters, and Alice was no stranger to the yard.

'Thanks ever so, Auntie. I'm nothing but nerves today.'

'Well, it's not every day you get married, love.'

'No, and it's not every day war's declared either.'

As Alice let herself into the toilet Vi stepped down from the tub. She tutted to herself and laughed, saying, 'There won't be a war, love.'

Alice lifted her nightdress and made herself comfortable. 'Isn't that what they said in nineteen fourteen?'

The one feature that both sides of the Weatherfield viaduct had in common was the public houses that nestled at the ends of most terraced streets. Coronation Street's own hostelry was the Rovers Return, named originally to commemorate the repatriation of a certain Lieutenant Philip Ridley from the Boer War then later in honour of all the heroes returning from the trenches of France. As alehouses went, it was quite a roomy establishment, boasting three bars – the public, which was the general bar area, the snug, which was traditionally the territory of the womenfolk, and the select, where waiter service added an extra penny to the price of a pint and which was mainly reserved for functions. It was from this bar that the comely figure of Mrs Annie Walker appeared, wiping her dusty hands on the edge of her flowered pinafore.

'Well, I still say it's most inconvenient.'

Jack Walker looked up from pulling the dregs of beer through the hefty bar pump, but his wife had already disappeared into the living quarters. There was no point in shouting after her; experience told him that she'd be back to carry on the conversation of her own accord. He didn't have to wait long.

'We're expected to change our arrangements at the drop of a hat,' she went on.

'It's 'ardly that,' protested Jack, but Annie barely drew breath.

'Folk have no idea the amount of preparation required in creating a finger buffet for forty. I know that crowd out there. They'll all appear at once and stuff themselves with my dainties, and all without a word of appreciation.'

Long-suffering Jack carried on drawing on the pump. 'That would have 'appened even if the weddin' 'adn't been brought forward.'

'A little consideration, Jack, that's all I ask.'

The howl of a baby filled the bar.

'That's our Billy awake now.' Annie sighed. 'You'll have to go to him, Jack, I've got the sandwiches to see to yet.'

'I'm not exactly standin' idle meself, love,' protested Jack.

'Don't be awkward, Jack.'

Annie retired through the big wooden doors that separated the bar from the Walkers' living quarters. Annie strove to maintain two separate identities: welcoming landlady, ready with a listening ear and a sympathetic nature, and the wife and mother, providing and caring for Jack and baby Billy. Her mother, miles away in Clitheroe, always referred to her as a saint living her life in turmoil upon earth. Annie was forced to admit she sometimes felt like a missionary sent to the heathen. She regarded the pub's living quarters as her inner sanctuary, a place where she fled the ravages of the uncouth and the unwashed. Her Vivaldi record sat upon the gramophone, her Stuart Crystal was displayed in the glass-fronted cabinet and plump cushions invited her to relax on the two-seater sofa. This was her haven, where Jack knew he had to put on the slippers that waited in the hallway before he entered, where she would only serve him breakfast if he'd put on his shirt collar, and where no customers were ever invited.

Annie's heart sank at the sight of the eight loaves stacked on the table. It simply wasn't done: weddings shouldn't be brought forward two hours simply because the Prime Minister wanted to address the nation.

*

The bony figure of Martha Longhurst lowered the last chair into position and sank down on it. She glanced up, following a wooden beam as it rose from the wall of the draughty old Mission of Glad Tidings and branched out along the ceiling. It wasn't exactly Manchester Cathedral but it was the highest ceiling in Coronation Street – step-ladders were dug out twice a year to allow for cleaning of the light fittings.

'You needn't think you've come 'ere for a sit down!'

Martha lifted a weary head to look in the direction of the voice but made no attempt to move. 'You can't brow beat me, Ena Sharples. I've put all the chairs out by myself and I'm 'avin' a rest.'

'You want to be careful. You're a young woman. You shouldn't be needin' rests at your age. You're not pregnant again, are you?'

'Am I 'eck! No, it's my Percy,' explained Martha. 'At it all night he were – 'ack, 'ack, 'ack.'

Ena closed the vestry door and walked across the stage to reach the stairs that led on to the floor, Martha's level. 'You want to keep an eye on that cough. Could turn nasty. TB.'

'It's not TB,' said Martha, 'I know TB. I lost both my parents to it.'

' 'Ave you seen the order of services?' asked Ena.

Martha gestured to the side of the hall. 'On top of the harmonium.'

Ena crossed the wooden floor, the soles of her shoes clanking as she walked. She passed the brass plaque, screwed into the side of the hall, which reminded the congregation that the building had been opened on 24 December 1902, its purpose to provide a place of worship for local believers and a shelter for the lost. Out of habit, Ena gave the plaque a rub with the sleeve of her cardigan.

'What 'ymns is she 'aving'?' asked Martha.

Reaching the harmonium, Ena picked up a sheet and scanned it. ' "Jesu, Heart of Man's Desire". Very nice.'

'Is that it? Not a Wesley? Only one 'ymn? That's a bit cheap. What's a weddin' without a lot of singin'?'

Ena sniffed in agreement. 'If you ask me, this whole circus is bein' done on the cheap. 'E 'asn't bought 'er an engagement ring, yer know.'

'Can you blame 'im? They've only been engaged five weeks. The lad's done right 'oldin' on to his money.'

'Why the rush, eh?' Ena gave Martha a meaningful look and started to fold the sheets before dropping one on each of the wooden chairs, set out in rows down the length of the hall.

'You don't think she's. . . ?'

'I'm not sayin' she is, am I? But you 'ave to agree it's a rushed do, i'nt it?'

'It's all this talk of war panickin' folk into speedin' things up. Folk are gettin' nervous. What do you think, Ena? Will we 'ave another war?'

'Well . . .' Ena paused and considered the question. 'There's always bin wars and I've no doubt there always will be. I never believed last lot were war to end all wars and I'll tell you why – it's human nature to covet, an' that's what this one will be about, if there is a war. 'Itler should be content wi' Germany an' not want more. I don't like war. I saw things in nineteen eighteen that I never want to see again.' Images of broken heroes, boys of seventeen and eighteen, returning home with shell-shock and limbs missing flashed through her head. Lads she'd been at school with, whose mothers wept in doorways, children left fatherless. 'But I'll tell you summat, Martha, I reckon a bit of a war would do that lot out there the world of good.'

'What lot?'

'My so-called neighbours. My mam always said war brought out the best in folk, an' I think she were right. If there is a war then Coronation Street'll never be the same again.'

Ena had been caretaker at the Mission since her husband's untimely death at the age of thirty-nine in the autumn of 1937. She lived in the vestry attached to the hall and had a separate entrance leading on to Coronation Street. It was a one-roomed affair, with a curtained-off area hiding the bed from visitors' gaze. Ena had never slept alone: as a child she'd shared with her sister, then with Sharples for seventeen years, and now her bedfellow was her eighteen-year-old daughter, Vera.

Ena's duties entailed keeping the Mission clean and setting up for meetings. For extra remuneration she also played the harmonium at weddings. Both she and Martha now darted into the vestry to exchange their hairnets for their best hats before taking their positions at the instrument as the wedding guests began to filter into the hall. They were greeted at the door by the tall, gaunt Sidney Hayes, tenant of No. 5 Coronation Street and local lay preacher.

The nervous groom, Samuel Edward Burgess, arrived early and sat on a hard chair with his best man, a fellow rambler who had been present the day that summer when Alice had won his heart by sharing with him her potted-meat sandwiches. Out of sentiment they'd asked Mrs Walker to include potted-meat in the buffet. He looked across to where Martha stood at the front of the hall, her fingers fidgeting with the three red berries attached to her hat. Ena nodded and Martha obligingly turned a page of music.

Ever the optimist, Martha calculated the likelihood of Alice jilting the pale-faced youth. There hadn't been a jilting at the Mission since 1923 when a local club-footed spinster had decided she wasn't prepared to be shackled to a man who whistled through his teeth as he spoke.

Martha wasn't the only one considering the possibility of a jilting. The bride's father, Thomas Hewitt, was fed up with waiting for the ceremony to start. Having witnessed his daughter starting to resemble his late nagging wife, he just wanted shut of her. Sam Burgess and Birkenhead were welcome to her. He sneered at her behind her back as she stood in front of her chest of drawers and propped her mirror against a jar of face cream. She rubbed at a dark smudge on the sleeve of her dress. Thomas pulled his watch from out of his jacket pocket for the third time that minute and sighed.

'No one will notice.' he said.

'I'll notice. And stop sighin'.'

'It's this collar; it's too tight.'

15

'I'll crown our 'Arry for this, Dad. First he spends best part of mornin' in lav, then he gets soot all over me dress.'

' 'E were only tryin' to 'elp.'

'Dressin' up as a flamin' chimney sweep an' gettin' his mucky hands on my wedding dress was not 'elpful!' She continued to rub.

'It's supposed to be lucky,' said Thomas.

' 'E's the one who's lucky! Lucky I didn't shove 'im down the stairs!' She squinted into the mirror. 'It'll 'ave to do, I suppose.'

She straightened her dress and glanced round at the bedroom. It was a poky hole but it was the only space in the world that had been hers, and hers alone. She'd painted the walls sunflower yellow in an attempt to brighten it, but the bedroom suite was made of heavy, dark mahogany, which seemed to soak up any brightness.

'Are you ready then?' Thomas asked, in a weary voice.

Alice looked at her father, noting his discomfort at dressing in his best suit, a new collar pinned tightly around his scrubbed neck. His face wore a pained expression, which she didn't notice – this was his usual expression. Gassed during the Great War, unemployed during the depression, married to a bonny lass who turned into a shrew and went pot-for-rags in the street, he felt as if life hadn't so much slapped him in the face as kicked him in the groin.

'You could have got a new suit. Those elbows are nearly worn through,' she complained.

'It's a good suit is this. It'll see me out. I'll be buried in this.'

'Not if I 'ave anything to do with it.'

Thomas flinched. She sounded more like her mother every day. He'd been surprised when Alice had booked the Mission for her wedding as he'd assumed the local parish church, St Mary's, would have been her choice. She'd said she didn't want to pass her mother's grave as she arrived to meet her intended. In a rare fond moment he smiled at the thought of Mary.

'What are you looking all soft for?' Alice demanded.

'I were just thinkin' of your mother.'

Alice picked up her bouquet. 'Waste of a good thought then.'

Thomas followed Alice out of the room, protesting weakly.

'She was your mother . . .'

'Yes, you're right, she was,' said Alice, without breaking her stride. 'She was also a ravin' loony who went for me and our 'Arry with the bread knife. I 'ope you've noticed I'm wearin' long sleeves. That's nothing to do with the weather, you know. I'll carry that scar till the day I die, and every time I see it I remember my mother.' At the bottom of the stairs she turned and looked up to where her father stood on the landing. 'Come on, we've not got all day, you know.'

The walk had been a long one and the suitcase handle cut into the young woman's hand. She was relieved to turn the corner and finally see her new domain. She walked past the doorway to the shop and glanced in. The lights were off inside, but she could make out the odd tin and package. It looked like every other corner shop she'd ever seen. Next to it stood the first house, brass numbers revealing it to be No. 13. She checked the scribbled note in her hand and moved on.

No. 11 Coronation Street had peeling paintwork and newspapers stuck in the front windows to thwart prying eyes. She tried the door. It was locked and he hadn't given her a key. She lowered her suitcase and perched on the edge of it, anticipating a long wait.

There was music coming from the large building opposite. Some sort of chapel, she supposed. Probably Sunday-morning worship. She hoped they weren't going to be a religious bunch. Further down a door opened, and her attention was drawn by the sight of a bride emerging from the house, followed by an older man. The white fabric of the dress seemed out of place in the dark, bleak Street. She watched with interest as the girl looked around disappointedly at the empty roadway. Shame: her big entrance and no bugger there to see it.

Alice grabbed her father's arm and set off across the cobbles. When she reached the middle of the street she drew parallel with the woman and her suitcase. She glanced in her direction.

'Good luck, love,' the woman called.

'Thank you,' replied Alice.

'Do you live down there?'

'Number five.'

The woman stood up.

'That makes us neighbours; I'm moving into number eleven. My name's Elsie – Elsie Tanner.'

Alice smiled a welcome. 'I'm pleased to meet you. I'm Alice and this is me dad. You'll 'ave to excuse us, only we're a bit late.'

'Don't let me 'old you up. See you around.'

Elsie pulled a cigarette packet out of her coat pocket and lit up while she watched Alice disappear around the side of the Mission. A few seconds later the music changed to the Wedding March.

'Ah,' said Elsie out loud, 'they're playin' my song.'

She was still sitting on her suitcase fifteen minutes later when the happy couple came out of the Mission as man and wife. After posing for a brief snapshot they led the bridal party back on to Coronation Street.

'She looks a picture,' commented Bessie Tatlock, a short, round woman with a head that darted from side to side adding to her overall resemblance to a hen. Her voice was as soft as her bosom.

'She's no oil paintin',' said Ena, overhearing her. 'The Hewitts have always had that dopey look around the eyes.'

'Nay, Ena,' protested Bessie, 'it's the bairn's weddin' day. She's meant to look bonny today.'

'I was a beautiful bride,' announced Ena, to anyone who was listening. 'My dress was made by a woman in Arkwright Street who did the guests' mendin' at the Midland Hotel. Smallest stitches you've ever seen.' She broke off as she caught sight of a van being driven down the Street. 'What's Piggott doin' deliverin' on a Sunday?' she said.

The red and white butcher's van came to a halt outside No. 11 and a burly man in his mid-twenties emerged from the driving seat. His bulky frame had dominated the small cab, and as he set foot on the Street he immediately cast shadows over the residents who, in comparison, suddenly seemed antlike. A huge hairy hand slammed the van door shut and the giant wandered around to where Elsie sat, unimpressed by his appearance. 'About bloody time an' all! I've bin sat 'ere like a stray cat for hours,' she said.

Ena and her friends stopped to look at the strangers. The man ignored the woman and opened the back doors of the van. Ena moved along the pavement to ensure she had a clear view of its contents.

'Throw us the key will you?'

Arnold Tanner dug a couple of fat fingers into his trouser pocket and pulled out a key, which he threw to his wife.

'Movin' in, are you?' Ena crossed the cobbles to get a better view of the proceedings. Years of practice had taught her the direct approach was always best: it was an art her neighbours had never mastered and of which they acknowledged her an expert.

'That's right love, I'm Elsie, 'e's Arnold.'

Ena smiled at the woman, her eyes instantly summing her up. Young, no more than eighteen, hand-me down coat, a wedding ring that proved nothing, and from the look of the coat's pull, about five months pregnant. 'I'm Ena Sharples. I look after the Mission. Are you chapel or church?'

Elsie laughed. 'I don't bother with either.'

Ena's smile froze. She turned her attention to the man and opened her mouth in surprise.

' 'Ere, I know you. You're Arnold Tanner!'

He looked at her without a trace of recognition. 'That's right. Do I know you?'

'I don't suppose you do, but I know you. By 'eck, it's comin' to summat when decent folk 'ave the likes of you movin' in next door to 'em.' She raised her voice and called to her neighbours. 'First empty 'ouse on the Street for years an' who gets it? The landlord's rent collector and bully boy.'

'Now, watch it, Mother,' warned Arnold.

'Don't you "Mother" me, you great ape. I'm not one of them as talk in secret. I speak my mind and call a spade a spade. You're a bully, Arnold Tanner. You might not collect down this street but we've all 'eard of you!'

Ena moved towards the man and pointed a finger at him.

'You 'ad old Mrs Crankshaw out on the street just because she were two weeks behind wi' rent. Two weeks! Her husband was still warm in his coffin but you wouldn't wait for insurance pay-out, would you?' Ena turned to her audience, 'She'd lived in that 'ouse all 'er life and 'e just turned up and stuck all she had in the world on the pavement. "Look after the widows and orphans," saith the Good Book, "look after", not kick when they're down.'

Arnold stepped forward so that his face was only a couple of inches away from Ena's. He admired her for not blinking or backing away and lowered his voice to make it as threatening as he could. 'Leave off, Ma.'

'You don't frighten me, Arnold Tanner!' she shouted in his face. 'I pay my rent to God, not to any man. What are you goin' to do? Raise your 'and to a defenceless woman? Strike me and be damned, Arnold Tanner, if you're not already!'

As Ena's voice rose her neighbours edged towards her. Arnold saw them and took a step away from her. He forced a laugh and smiled at his wife. 'The natives don't appear very friendly,' he said, as he returned to removing a table from the back of the van.

Ena stood her ground until she felt a tug on her sleeve. 'Come on, Mrs Sharples. There's a sherry waiting for you in Rovers. 'Appen there'll be sausage rolls an' all.'

It was Albert Tatlock who spoke. He was a short chap who worked as a clerk in the town hall, lived at No. 1 and was ruled by the demands of his appetite. Ena allowed Albert to walk her away from the scene leaving Elsie Tanner alone with her husband.

'Well, you've got us off to a right start, 'aven't you?'

Arnold ignored his wife and shoved past her as he carried the table through the open front door.

'Never mind that table,' she said. 'I'm the one you should be carryin' over the threshold.'

Arnold cast her a contemptuous look and grunted. 'I'm not carryin' you anywhere.'

'Charmin'.'

'Shut up and grab summat from the van. I married yer, didn't I?'

20

Elsie walked sadly around the vehicle. So this was married life, was it? A five-minute ceremony at the register office wearing a borrowed two-piece and no photos taken. A throw of confetti from her sister Fay and that was that. Married to a man she hardly knew, had barely spoken more than a sentence to. He'd been drunk the night she'd let him have her under the tenement staircase, among the cobwebs and a discarded pram. She remembered trying to interest him in conversation but, as she now knew, after a few bottles grunting overtook talking in his book. She'd lain back on an old blanket, in that dark poky hole, while he'd squeezed himself into her and, under his considerable weight, she'd struggled to keep breathing. Maybe he'd married her because he'd suffocated the rest of the local girls. But he was right: he had married her, and Elsie knew many a bloke in Back Gas Street who wouldn't have.

Annie Walker's eye kept wandering to the picture rail running around the select bar. She cursed herself for not having remembered to dust it. Just so long as no one else noticed.

Two tables away, Ena Sharples tapped Martha Longhurst's knee and made no attempt to lower her voice as she said, 'This room hasn't had a good bottoming since the Armistice.'

Martha hissed, 'Keep your voice down, she'll hear you.'

'I don't care. I speak my mind.' For Ena, passing comment on the state of people's lives and homes was second nature. From the moment the Walkers had arrived to take over the pub she'd sized Annie up. The sight of her clutching a linnet in a cage with one hand and holding a huge picture hat firmly in place on top of her head with the other had placed her firmly, in Ena's mind, as a misfit who would soon be swallowed by the levelling cobbles. Ena always maintained that a person had to be born in Weatherfield to survive the knocks and tragedies it threw at its inhabitants. Annie Walker was definitely not Weatherfield.

'I know but I don't see any point in fallin' out with the landlady. She could turn nasty and stop free drinks.'

'Free drinks? There's nowt free about these,' said Ena. 'It'll all be written down and given to Tommy Hewitt to pay for. Oh, yes, this'll set him back a tidy penny. And I bet you she charges for butter and not Maggie Ann.' Ena took a bite of her sandwich. She pulled a face. 'This paste's putrid. I'm 'avin' to force it down.'

On the top table the bride used a paper napkin to wipe her mouth and whispered into her husband's ear, 'What's the time?'

Sam slowly lifted his arm and pulled back his cuff to read his wristwatch. He seemed to do everything slowly. Even his words were delivered carefully, as if he feared they'd run away with him. 'Ten past.'

'No time for speeches, then,' said Alice. 'Just as well, judging by the amount of ale Dad's supped. We've only bin sat down twenty minutes and he's downed three pints.'

'And the sherry when we arrived.'

'No,' corrected Alice. ''E 'ad another pint instead, so that's four.'

'There's no 'arm done. It is a wedding.'

'Aye, 'is only daughter's. You'd think 'e'd have made the effort to stay sober till the cake were cut.'

Sam pushed his hand under Annie Walker's best linen tablecloth and gave Alice's thigh a squeeze. 'Don't worry, love,' he said. 'There's plenty of time before we catch the train.'

Alice smiled. 'It's not the train I'm bothered about, and well you know it. 'Ey up, Jack Walker's on his feet.'

The landlord excused himself from his table and squeezed his way past the backs of chairs to reach the Bakelite wireless set he'd carried into the room earlier that day. He turned it on and called for silence as it warmed up. 'Ladies and gentlemen, I know it's customary to have a speech or two from bride's father and the best man, but Alice and Sam 'ave decided to break with tradition. Their weddin' speech is gonna be made by the Prime Minister!'

Annie led the polite laughter, which died down as the residents turned their attention anxiously to the cultured voice coming from the wireless as Neville Chamberlain was introduced.

Everyone in the room sat in silence as the voice of their

leader crackled over the airwaves. 'I am speaking to you from the cabinet room of Ten Downing Street. This morning the British ambassador in Berlin handed the German government a final note, stating that unless we heard from them by eleven o'clock that they were prepared, at once, to withdraw their troops from Poland, a state of war would exist between us. I have to tell you now that no such undertaking has been received, and that consequently this country is at war with Germany.'

Ena felt shivers run down her spine and she sank her head into her hands as the Prime Minister continued to talk. She couldn't comprehend what she had just heard. War. Again. Once more to live through the pain of waving goodbye to strong young men only to see the few lucky ones return. Lucky? With broken bones, brains numbed by gas and limbs torn from their bodies? The knowledge that Coronation Street would once again experience the un-natural, unsettling life of a community without its men made her want to weep.

She glanced around at the ashen faces surrounding her. Sam Burgess, the groom. He'd go. Frank Barlow, with his wife full of child, him too. Young Harry Hewitt, the bride's cousin whom she'd known since he'd run bare-arsed around the Street. Would he survive Hitler's army?

No sooner had Jack snapped off the wireless than the wail of the air-raid siren cut through the air. Jack found eyes shooting in his direction and realised he'd have to take charge.

'Right. That sounds like kick-off. We'd best all go down the cellar.'

'But we haven't cut the cake,' protested Alice.

'Bring it with you,' suggested Jack, as he led the way out of the room.

The guests were quick to gather themselves and follow Jack through the empty public bar and down the cellar steps. Annie waited at the top of the stone flight, Billy asleep in her arms. Sam Burgess clutched the two tiers of wedding cake to his suit while Alice lifted her dress to ensure she didn't trip on it.

Bessie Tatlock eased her bulky frame down the steps, the panic in her voice ill-disguised when she asked her husband, 'Do you think there'll be gas?' The Tatlocks had chosen not to bring the ugly brown boxes to the wedding so the gas masks allotted to them, just days before, hung in the hallway of No. 1.

There was no electric light in the Rovers' cellar and shadows from the candles danced over the ceiling. Bessie held tight to Albert's arm and allowed him to guide her into a corner. He removed his jacket and rolled it into a cushion for her to sit on.

'How long do you think this'll go on?' she asked.

'I've no idea,' he replied.

'I hope it's not long. I need to pay a visit.'

Worried Bessie sat tentatively on the cushion and suddenly remembered her six-year-old daughter. 'Where's Beattie?'

'Over yonder, playin' with the Foyle girls,' answered Albert, attempting to make himself comfortable on the floor.

Alice looked about her at the dust and cobwebs in dismay. What was the point in worrying about a smudge of coal on her dress compared to this lot? 'It stinks of ale down 'ere,' she said to Sam.

'That's because it's a beer cellar.'

'Oh, thanks for telling me, Sam. I hadn't noticed.'

Seeing Alice glancing around, Jack Walker grabbed a blanket and thrust it at her. ' 'Ere you go, love, it's an old one, but it's clean. I keep it for puttin' over barrels when there's a frost.'

Alice received the blanket with gratitude and wound it around herself until her dress was covered. She lowered herself down and found herself sitting next to Ida Barlow from No. 3. Although only one of the narrow houses separated their homes, Alice knew hardly anything about the Barlows. They had moved into the Street just over a year before and were still regarded as newcomers. Alice, like many of her neighbours, had been born in Coronation Street and, although she'd never had admitted to it, shared Ena's views on outsiders. For her part, Ida would have made a perfect foil for Alice. They were roughly the same age but while Alice had developed a criticising tongue and a bitter personality, Ida was a quiet homebody, devoted to the young postal worker she'd married on 1 May 1938. Now she was seven months' pregnant and supporting her stomach with her hands.

'Are you all right, Ida?' asked Alice.

'Yes, love, I just need to get my breath back. It's all the excitement.'

Ida's husband Frank put his hand on her arm. 'Perhaps I could find a doctor.'

She smiled, enjoing Frank's concern. 'It's all right, love, honest. I just need to sit still for a while.' She turned her attention to the subdued bride. 'What a way to start your married life.'

'We'll miss the train now. So much for Morecambe.'

'There'll be other trains, don't fret. Morecambe'll still be there. There's worse places than this to spend your wedding day.'

'I know.' Alice's fingers pulled nervously at a thread in the blanket. 'It's just that it's so gloomy and I don't know what's goin' to 'appen.'

'Here, Jack Walker,' Ena's voice boomed in the darkness, 'I don't reckon to know much about licensed premises but I know enough to guess there's ale in these barrels.'

'That's right, Mrs Sharples,' Jack replied.

'Well, what are you waitin' for? Get one opened, lad. Then we can really get the party going.'

By the time the all-clear sounded a sing-song had started and the residents were passing round the two mugs and one chipped glass that were the only containers to be located in the cellar. Alice bit into a slice of wedding cake and sniffed back a tear.

'Come on, love,' said Sam, 'we can still catch the three o'clock.'

'I know,' she said. 'But I can't help thinkin' you're bound to be called up. I've only just become a bride, I'm not ready to be a widow.'

She started to cry and Sam awkwardly put his arm around

her. 'I'm not going to get killed, love. This war won't be like the last one. No more trenches and stuff. Everyone says it'll be over by Christmas.'

'I don't care what they say. It's just not fair.'

Overhearing remarks was a speciality of Ena Sharples and she startled Alice by looming suddenly out of the darkness. The candlelight hit her chin and mouth, casting a mask-like effect over the rest of her face. 'And whenever was life fair, Alice Hewitt?'

'Oh, shut up, Mrs Sharples. It's nowt to do with you. And my name's Burgess now. Mrs Burgess.'

'Well, *Mrs* Burgess. You'd do well to listen to someone wi' more experience of life than you. Life isn't fair. Mine hasn't been and neither's your dad's – or your mother's come to that, God rest her soul.'

'Save the sermons, Mrs Sharples, I'm not in the mood.'

Ena ignored her and carried on. ' "Man born of woman hath but a few days and is full of troubles." That's what life's about. You need to grab your 'appiness while you can. The banshee's stopped, so get yerself off on 'oneymoon. God alone knows when you'll 'ave chance to 'ave fun again.'

CHAPTER TWO

4 September 1939 The liner SS Athenia *is sunk in the North Atlantic by a German submarine. Albert Tatlock's hopes suffer a similiar fate.*

Ada Hayes was twenty-nine and a very capable woman. Everyone said so. It was a fact that in the Hayes household at No. 5 Coronation Street Ada's common sense was often put to the test as she mediated between the conflicting personalities of her family as they battled for space in the poky terrace. Her father, Sid, was a retired clerk who filled his days sitting on committee meetings and writing his sermons, which were delivered every other Sunday from the lectern at the Mission. He valued serenity and modesty as the two attributes to be most striven for but these did not come easy to his wife, christened Alice after her mother but always known by her middle name, Rose.

She was a woman sent easily into hours of anguish through worry over her family. The smallest of household chores was too much for her, and Ada had long since taken on the role of home-maker at No. 5. It wasn't that Rose was idle, but she was just as incapable as her eldest daughter was the opposite. At any sign of conflict in the family she retired to her bed and, out of fear of her husband, fought her natural inclination towards vanity.

The Hayeses had suffered a great deal at the start of their marriage: the outbreak of the First World War had found able-bodied Sid being marched off to prison for announcing he was a 'conscientious objector' to fighting. Rose spent the following four years being ignored and shunned by the neighbours, and struggled against being ashamed of Sid's actions – or lack of them.

The youngest Hayes children, Esther and Tom, were complete opposites. Esther was as shy as Tom was gregarious, as timid as he was brave, as quiet as he was loud. She was also a homebird, who enjoyed reading aloud to her mother while thirteen-year-old Tom ran amok in the maze of local terraced streets. Number five was a safe haven for the family. They rarely ventured beyond its front door, apart from Tom who only felt alive outside the confines of the house. Sid stood out from all the other men on the Street in that he had never entered the Rovers, and Rose chose to do her shopping at the corner shop when the other women were occupied with household chores. Not that she did much shopping: most of that fell upon Ada's shoulders.

On the morning of Monday 4 September when Ada broke the news of the evacuation, Rose didn't seem to take in the implications.

'I don't know how long I'll be gone, Mother.'

Rose stared at her elder daughter and said, 'You were back by four last time.'

'Yes, but that was just a practice. This is the real thing. I could be gone months.'

Rose chose not to hear what Ada was saying and looked around the room for her reading glasses.

'I'm sure I put them on the mantelpiece last night.'

'You did, Mother,' said Ada patiently. 'They're there, by the clock.'

She lifted her small suitcase on to the table and opened it. The neatly packed clothes filled most of the space but a gap was left beside her Bible. She opened the sideboard door and removed a jar from the shelf. 'I'm only taking the one jar. That should leave you plenty.'

'What's that?' asked Rose.

'The damson chutney. There's another five jars in the sideboard but don't go mad. Goodness knows when I'll be back to make more.'

'Where is it you're going, Ada?' asked Sid, from behind his newspaper.

'I'm not supposed to know but I think it's Blackpool.'

'That'll be nice for you, plenty of sea air.'

'Yes.' Ada sounded unsure as she eyed her mother. Either Rose had no idea what was happening or she was pretending not to.

For weeks now Bessie Street Infants and Juniors had been drilled in mock evacuations. There was great fear that as soon as war was declared the heavens would open and bombs would descend to destroy the cities. Like all schools around Manchester, the teachers at Bessie Street were prepared to gather their children, Pied Piper fashion, and lead them to the safety of the coast and the countryside. Parents had been given careful instructions explaining the whole nature of evacuation and Ada had left the government literature out for her own parents, but it seemed that, as always, if something didn't affect them personally they were not interested.

Ada closed the case and pressed each of the latches to make certain they were secure. She glanced at the living room clock. Five to eight. It would soon be time to go. She carried her case into the hall and put it down on the rug. She checked that her gloves and purse were in her coat pocket and decided to take the beige hat rather than the brown one.

She wondered if he was ready yet. Shouting was prohibited in the Hayes household so she ran up the stairs and pushed open his bedroom door.

Tom glared at her in defiance. 'I'm not goin' and you can't make me!'

'You've not got your coat on.' It was an observation, really: she wasn't in the least surprised.

'What's the use of puttin' me coat on? I'm not goin'.'

'Don't be stupid, Tom. You have to go. The whole school's going. It's not as if you're going to be on your own, is it?'

'I don't care about bein' on me own. I'd rather be on me own than stuck wi' that lot in some dump.'

'It won't be a dump. It'll probably be near the sea. You like the sea, don't you?'

There was no answer, just a hostile glare.

'Don't make it any worse than it has to be, Tom. Think of Mum and Dad.'

'It's all right for them, isn't it? They're not havin' to miss out on all the fun.'

'Fun? It's war, not a circus.'

'Yeah, with planes and bombs an' stuff.'

'Don't be daft, you don't know what you're talking about.'

'Yes, I do. I read *Picture Post* and I've talked to Billy Hibbert's brother who fought in Spain. That's why we've all got to go, 'cos Hitler's going to flatten all the cities. Only he won't get a chance because the RAF are gonna shoot his planes down and they've put a great big gun on top of Elliston's. It's the best thing ever to 'appen in this dump and you want to send me to the sea. Well, I ain't goin'!' He raised his voice in defiance.

Ada closed the bedroom door and advanced on her brother. She made sure her voice was too low to be heard downstairs and grabbed Tom's left ear. 'Listen to me, you little tyke. It's bad enough that I've got to go. Do you think I want to leave Mum like she is? Do you think I want to run off to the sea with thirty homesick nine-year-olds? Do you think I'm happy with the idea of taking responsibility for you on top of every-thing else? I'm not even *your* teacher. Now, I'd be perfectly happy to let you stay behind and be blown to kingdom come but for some reason Mum and Dad want you to be safe, all tucked up in bed while the bombs are dropping here. Think yourself lucky you've got an escape route. There's many who haven't.' She released his ear and straightened up. 'Now, I can frogmarch you down the street, into school and all the way to the railway station with one arm twisted behind your back for all your friends to laugh at, or you can come quietly and willingly. What's it going to be?'

Tom grabbed his bag and coat and glared at her. 'I 'ate you and I 'ate this war!'

Ada followed Tom down the stairs. In the hall she found Esther waiting with a paper bag.

'I bought you some humbugs for the journey.'

Ada thanked her and slipped the bag into her pocket.

Sid stood in the living room doorway and sucked at his pipe. 'Well, take care, then. Write when you can.'

'I'll let you know my address and the school where I'll be working. Don't worry about Tom. I'll make sure he doesn't get into mischief.'

'Of course you will.'

Sid smiled and walked back to his seat by the fire.

'Well, goodbye, then, Mum,' called Ada.

Rose stepped into the hall and kissed her three children. 'You'd better take your coat with you, Esther,' she said.

'But I'm not going, Mum,' the fourteen-year-old replied.

'Aren't you? Oh, I thought you were.' Rose shook her head and wandered into the living room.

Ada kissed her sister's cheek and picked up her suitcase. She pushed Tom through the open front door then turned and grasped Esther's hand. 'Look after them for me,' she said.

'I will. Don't worry. We'll be fine here and you'll be back soon. It'll all be over for Christmas.'

Elsie Tanner stood in her bedroom window, watching the lines of children and weeping mothers as they walked down the Street. She drew on a cigarette and pulled her dressing-gown closer around her. 'It's chilly in 'ere,' she said.

'It'll be all right when you've put some curtains up.'

Elsie skipped across the bare floorboards and slipped into bed, pulling the covers over her and exposing Arnold's bare flesh.

'Watch it! An' keep your feet to yourself. They're like ice.'

Elsie drew her foot up along Arnold's leg, rubbing the hairs the wrong way.

'Gerroff!'

She giggled and thrust her hand under the covers. 'My 'ands are cold an' all. I wonder where I could put them to warm them up?'

Arnold gave a jolt as Elsie's hand reached his thigh. 'Give us a drag,' he said.

She used her free hand to put the cigarette in his mouth. When he'd finished with it she placed her lips over his mouth and sucked in the smoke. He smiled and reached under her nightdress to grab her left breast.

'Arnold?'

'What?'

'Are you glad you married me?'

'Yeah. Sure.' His mind was on other things and he guided her hand to where he wanted it then groaned as she set to work, knowing what he needed. His head bent forward and he started to kiss her neck while his fingers fiddled with the tiny buttons of her nightdress. They were too small for his big hands and in frustration he ripped the material apart. She made no objection and he buried his head in her breasts.

She closed her eyes and, when he pushed her, fell backwards on to the mattress. Her hand worked its way round to his buttocks and squeezed encouragingly.

Ada Hayes counted her charges as she struggled to keep them together in the crowded playground of Bessie Street School. Parents had been asked to remain at home but many had flocked to see their little ones off. There was no mistaking this for one of the many rehearsals they'd had in the previous months. This was it. The real thing.

'Eric can't eat anything with currants in, Miss Hayes. You will make sure they know that, won't you?'

'I know the list said two pairs of shorts but Charlie's only got the one.'

'Rita gets sick on long journeys, Miss Hayes.'

'Miss, I need the toilet.'

'If you could tell whoever he stays with that he always has the cream off the top of the milk. He's a growing lad and needs it.'

'She's very susceptible to chills. Do you think I've got time to nip home and fetch her another jumper?'

'If you're going to Scarborough I need to know because my sister will meet you at the station and take the twins.'

Ada's jaw ached from smiling and trying to say the right reassuring thing to each child and parent.

On the other side of the playground she noticed her neighbours, Bessie Tatlock and Elsie Foyle, kissing their daughters goodbye. Beattie Tatlock and Hilda and Shelagh Foyle were sensible children and Ada wished she could have just one of them in her party.

32

Mrs Foyle pulled her fox fur around her neck and pressed sovereigns into the gloved hands of her two daughters. There would be no demonstrative actions or concerns from her: she had her position to think of. As proprietor of the Coronation Street corner shop she had social standing, and others, such as Bessie Tatlock, looked to her for a lead.

'Goodbye, Hilda. Hold Shelagh's hand and remember to stick together. Mr Carter has assured me that families will be kept together, but if anyone tries to separate you don't let them.'

The Foyle girls waved to their mother and disappeared into the crowd of children in search of friends.

Bessie Tatlock, who had been looking forward to a weepy scene with Beattie having to be pried from her loving arms, had been disappointed by the speed at which her daughter bade her farewell. She sniffed into her handkerchief and felt rejected by her only child. She decided that when Albert returned home at lunchtime she'd say Beattie had been hysterical at their departure. The idea cheered her.

Harold Carter, headmaster of Bessie Street, gave a shrill blast on his whistle and eighty-seven children immediately stood still. The eighty-eighth glared at his sister and shouted, 'I'm going to miss everythin'!'

In the public bar of the Rovers Return, Annie Walker regarded the government leaflet in her hand. Composition and literature had been her favourite subjects at St Joseph's Elementary School but the folded pamphlet might as well have been written in German for all the sense she could make of it. Jack had annoyed her by glancing through it and seeming to understand the instructions to the letter but, then, he always took things at face value. She prided herself on having a more a questioning nature and made a point of looking at situations from a variety of angles before committing herself to anything. She let out a heavy sigh and said, 'It just doesn't make sense, Jack. I understand about blacking out the windows but it's a public house, people come in and out all the time. If we can't show a light we're going to have to serve beer in pitch blackness.'

'We'll do nothing of the sort.'

'What's the alternative? Closing for the duration?'

Jack cut a length of tape and smoothed it down against the window. Annie watched in silence, as he taped a range of crosses over the pub's windows. She drew breath. 'You've gone crooked. It looks all one-sided.'

'Does it matter? Do you think anyone's going to mind if it's not bang on centre?'

'*I* mind, Jack. Goodness knows how long we're going to have to have these crosses up and they may as well look neat.'

'They're to stop glass shattering all over the place. It's nowt to do with neatness.'

Jack jumped down from the table he'd been standing on and admired his handiwork. 'Just the upstairs to do now.'

Annie viewed the taped windows with distaste. 'You've still not said anything about the door. What are we to do?'

Jack put his arm around her waist and gave her a hug. 'Give over worryin'. It's all sorted. I had a walk up to Swindley's first thing and ordered a length of black cloth. We'll hang curtains this side and folk'll just have to walk through them once they've shut the doors.'

'Well you might have told me,' complained Annie, 'instead of letting me carry on like that. I've got a lot to think about without wasting time on unnecessary problems. No doubt you'll be off soon to sign up. You'll go without a care in the world and it's me who's stuck here with a pub full of thirsty customers and our Billy to look after.'

'It's not as if I were goin' on holiday,' protested Jack, 'and, anyroad, chances are all those thirsty customers will be comin' with me. In last war neighbours all signed up together. Albert were telling me last night. The Weatherfield Pals, they called them.'

'There's another one eager for the off. Albert Tatlock. I bet he was up all night polishing his medals and doing drill practice with a broomstick . . .' Annie leant on the bar for support as her voice cracked and her eyes grew moist.

Jack put a hand on her shoulder and caressed her neck. 'Annie . . . love . . . 'Ave I said I'm going to sign up?'

She sniffed back a tear and faced him. 'No. But you will, won't you?'

Leaving him to ponder her question, Annie picked up the roll of tape and scissors from the bar and walked through into the living quarters.

Elsie coughed and lit another cigarette. She sat up in bed and pulled her nightgown over the toothmarks around her nipples. Her stomach was definitely showing more than before. She made a mental note to fight any sign of losing her figure and patted the bump.

As Arnold opened the wardrobe door, a coat-hanger banged against it, causing Elsie to look over to him. 'You won't find much in there. I 'aven't got round to unpackin' clothes yet.'

He reached in and pulled out a two-piece suit, the seams on the trousers crisp and neat.

'Blimey. Where did you get that from?' she asked in admiration.

'Cost a bit, this did. Quality. A mate in the know tipped me the wink. "Get some decent threads before the war," 'e said. So I did.'

He turned and grinned at her.

'Put some clothes on quick. It's not decent.'

He leered at her, and flexed his biceps. They were an impressive sight, as was the rest of his body. 'Too temptin', is it? Honest, you'll wear me out proper if you carry on like this.' He turned back to the wardrobe and closed the door. The movement caught the sunlight in the mirror and flashed into the Street.

Ena Sharples was closing the vestry door when she was momentarily dazzled. She looked up, seeking the source of the light, and found herself staring at Arnold's nude torso. She gasped.

He pulled up the sash window up and stuck out as much of his body as he could. 'Fancy a bit, Ma?'

Ena was lost for words and scurried away along the pavement, reddening with embarrassment.

'Arnold! You are a one!' said Elsie, and laughed as he closed the window.

'Gave 'er something to think about. Nosy bat.'

Elsie sighed in contentment and stretched out over the bed. 'I think I'll go into town later. Have a look round the shops. Fancy the flicks? There's a western on at the Luxy.'

'Can't. Won't 'ave time.'

'Why?' she asked, as she watched him climb into his trousers. 'What you doin'?'

'Said I'd go up to the town 'all with Ralph.'

'Oh. Wouldn't you rather come to the flicks with me than 'ang around with that great ape?'

'Some other time, eh?'

Arnold retrieved his shirt from the back of the chair where it had hung all night and slipped it on. He sat on the bed and offered Elsie one cuff while he did up the other. She inched closer, grasping the cufflink between her fingers.

'Look, doll, I should 'ave told you last night, but we 'ad other things on our mind, didn't we?'

'Tell me what?'

'I've decided to join the Navy.'

Elsie dropped the cufflink and stared at her husband. 'Why, for goodness' sake?'

'Because it makes sense. Listen, accordin' to Ralph it'll only be a matter of days before I get me call-up papers. Twenty-five, in me prime, I'll be one of first. This way I get to choose where I go. There's no way I'm goin' in the Army, nowt more than machine-gun fodder them lads are. I don't fancy flyin' and I've always been good on boats, so I'm going to offer meself to the lads in blue.'

'But . . . what about me?'

'I'm sure they'd want you more than me, darlin', but it don't work that way. I'm the bloke, you're the tart. I get to go, you stay behind.'

'But we've only just got married. Surely they won't call you up when you've just got married. Tell them about the baby! You'll be all right. There's plenty of others they can send.'

Arnold got up from the bed and put his suit jacket on. 'Don't be a nag about it, will yer? I've said I'm goin' and that's all there is to it.'

He strolled out of the room and on to the landing. Elsie

flung off the bed covers and started after him. 'No, that's not all there is to it, Arnold. I'm yer wife. You're meant to talk to me about things like this.'

He ignored her and carried on down the stairs.

'Don't walk away from me! Come back and talk to me. You can't just bugger off and join the Navy. I'm not staying here on me tod!' She ran down the stairs, her feet bare on the wooden floorboards.

Arnold put his wallet and cigarettes in his pocket and picked up his hat from the living room table.

Elsie arrived in the room and made an effort to stay calm. 'Arnold . . . love. Be reasonable. We only moved 'ere yesterday. I don't know anyone, I've no money, I can't pay the rent . . .'

'There's no rent, it's all seen to, an' you'll get me pay from the Navy. It'll keep you in fags and gin.'

'But there's other things. I want you 'ere with me, not off in a ship God knows where!'

'Do me a favour an' stop whinin' will yer?'

'I'm not whinin', I'm just sayin'–'

'Well, don't! All right?'

The slap caught her off-guard and sent her sprawling to the floor. She raised a hand to her cheek and stared at him.

'I told you to shut up. You should listen to me. Now get yerself dressed and put some makeup on and I'll take you out, buy you a frock – or summat to remind you of me.'

Elsie put her hand on her stomach and muttered, 'I've already got summat.'

Arnold shook his head and slammed out of the house.

Albert Tatlock left the office at a minute past one. He grabbed his coat and hat from his peg and ate his sandwiches as he ran down the stairs that separated Accounts from the town clerk's office. To date, the benefit of working in the town planning department had been a heated office and a week's holiday with pay. Now he had something else to add to the list: by keeping an ear cocked for passing conversation all morning he'd ascertained that the recruitment office was to open on the dot of one in the office immediately below his own.

Even so, a hefty crowd was still waiting in the foyer in front of the clerk's office. Its door had just been pulled back by the great man himself.

'One at a time, gents, please. Form a queue. His Majesty'll take you all, have no fear.'

Albert pushed himself into the throng and found his nose pressed against a familiar back. 'Jack Walker, is that you?'

''Ello Albert. Thought I'd see you 'ere.'

''Owever did you find out about it?'

'They've put posters up all over place.'

So much for insider knowledge.

'It were quiet in pub so I thought I'd 'ave a walk up and see what all fuss were about. Tommy Hewitt's yonder, wi' 'is 'Arry.'

More men joined the queue and Albert found himself being pushed from behind. As a short fellow he'd always hated queues.

'Name?'

'John Walker.'

'Age?'

'Thirty-nine.'

'Over there, table C.'

'Name?'

'Harry Hewitt.'

'Age?'

'Eighteen.'

'Over there, table A.'

'Name?'

'Albert Tatlock.'

'Age?'

'Forty-four.'

'Over there, door marked Exit.'

'I don't follow you.'

'You're too old. Stand aside, please, and let the next one in.'

Albert stumbled out of the room. Too old? He stared about him at the younger men pushing their way forward, and then forced a path through them to reach the street door. He stepped out into the daylight and gulped at the air. The queue to enter the town hall stretched down the pavement but he didn't notice it. He stood and blinked. A knot in his stomach tightened and he fought the urge to vomit in the gutter.

'Bit of a blow, that, Albert.'

He looked up and found Tommy Hewitt standing next to him. He managed, 'You too?'

'Aye. Seems we did our bit in the last lot an' they don't want us for this one.'

'I don't feel too old.'

'Me neither. But I suppose compared to some of those lads we're pretty decrepit. Oh, well, no use cryin' over spilt milk. Fancy a jar?'

Albert declined, so Tommy crossed the road and entered the Tripe-dresser's Arms – the ale wasn't Newton and Ridley but the barmaid wasn't as sour-looking as Annie Walker.

Dejected, Albert remained standing on the pavement, unaware of life carrying on around him. He was useless. Unwanted. Too old.

Elsie Tanner knew what they'd all say. Over-made-up tart. And they'd be right. But she had to hide her cheek somehow. Already it was beginning to swell and go purple. She'd stayed indoors for the best part of the day, scrubbing the walls with soapy water. She'd had no breakfast and no lunch. She was blowed if she'd have nothing all day.

She pushed the door open and a bell above it tinkled her arrival. The shop was empty but she heard the sound of raised voices coming from the living quarters, towards the rear. 'That's just typical, isn't it? Bloody typical. This has got your Amelia's name all over it, has this.' The woman's voice was shrill and carried remarkably well into the shop.

Used to neighbours airing differences in front of her, Elsie settled down in the chair provided for the infirm and hoped the argument would get spicy.

'Look, there's no need to carry on . . .' The man's voice was softer than the woman's and Elsie had to strain to hear him.

'No need? No bloody need? I did not marry you so I could be chained to that counter while you're putting your feet under your smug sister's table!'

'She's not smug.'

'She hates me, always has. Thinks I'm not good enough to be part of her family. Well, if you want to go and live with her you bloody well can! She's welcome to you and so's Lytham St Anne's! I'd rather look after things on me own anyway. You're useless you, bloody useless!'

'I'll be off, then.'

'Go. I shan't stop you. But go out the back way, I don't want Ena's hairnet twitching!'

Sensing that the free show was over, Elsie rose from the chair then opened and shut the door, making the bell clang loudly. She smiled in readiness as footsteps hurried in from the living quarters. A plump woman with beautifully curled peroxide hair stepped down into the shop and stood behind the counter. She smoothed down her apron with nervous hands and attempted to smile.

'Yes, love, how can I help you?'

'I've just moved into the Street. Next door but one.'

'Oh.'

The word spoke volumes. The nosy cow across the street had probably been spreading her evil lies.

'I just need a few bits and pieces.'

'Well,' said the woman, 'we are a shop.'

Elsie stared at her hair. It looked completely out of place in the dingy little room.

'Forgive me for commenting,' she said, 'but you don't seem much like a shopkeeper to me.'

'Don't I, love?'

'No. You look like you should be on the stage.'

Mrs Foyle smiled wryly. 'Does it still show?'

'What?'

She stuck out a hand and grasped Elsie's, pleased to be distracted from her domestic problems. If her husband wanted to evacuate himself to his butter-wouldn't-melt sister then so be it. He wouldn't be missed: the light had gone out of the marriage years ago. The young woman's arrival had revived happier memories, of her past life and the circumstances that had brought her to her current position.

'My name's Foyle but before I married it was Castleway.

Elsie Castleway. Maybe you've heard of me.' She launched into song, her mouth opening wide as she bellowed, ' "He'll break your heart if you let him . . . if you let him . . . so don't let him." ' She smiled and continued, 'I was quite something in those days. The Salford Sparrow they called me. Then I gave it all up for love, married Mr Foyle and swapped the stage for this counter.' She smiled wistfully as she remembered the applause.

'My name's Elsie as well. Elsie Tanner. I'm sorry I've never heard of you. You've got a lovely voice, though, and I adore your hair.'

'Save up and I'll do yours in the back room. I don't charge high street prices.'

'Thanks.'

'Now,' Mrs Foyle spread her hand and gestured around the shelves, 'what can I get you?'

'I want a couple of eggs and a loaf but I haven't any money because my husband went to work in such a rush this morning he forgot to give me any. Do you do tick?'

Mrs Foyle sighed. It was the old story. 'Go on, then, seeing as you're a neighbour. But don't make a habit of it.'

'Oh, thanks ever so,' said Elsie. 'I'll have a jar of Robertsons jam as well in that case. Strawberry if you 'ave it.'

Bessie Tatlock had moved into No. 1 Coronation Street the day she married Albert in 1919. She'd left service a week before the wedding, and as a present her employer, Mr Archibold, had given her a complete dinner and tea service. She'd cherished it over the years but sadly many pieces had been smashed or chipped while all-thumbs-Albert had washed them up. Now in her forties, no one would recognise the nimble house-parlourmaid who had darted along corridors with fine linen and silver tureens. The crowded living room at No. 1 suited her down to the ground as she was able to go about her household duties with the minimum of effort. She was pleased to have married a man dominated by his stomach: she'd much rather cook than clean and scrub, and so long as his plate was full he never moaned about the untidy state of the house.

She laid the table for tea and then, correcting herself, removed the third plate, knife and fork. She felt the tears welling as the front door slammed shut.

'Hello, love, it's only me,' called Albert, from the hall.

Bessie sniffed back the tears and reached into her pinny pocket for a handkerchief.

The living room door opened and there stood Albert in a navy-blue uniform and tin hat. He lifted a torch and shone it in Bessie's face. She flinched under the glare and jerked her head away.

'Stop it,' she protested.

He lowered the torch and grinned at her. 'What's that on yer 'ead?' she asked.

'It's me official 'elmet.'

'What are you chunnerin' on about, you fool?'

'I've got a job.'

'You've already got a job.'

'I mean another one. To 'elp fight the war.'

'In that 'elmet?'

'Yes. I'm an ARP warden. Air Raid somethin' or other. I forget just now. It's more important than bein' in the Army, because this time a lot of the fightin' 's goin' to be in the air and I've got the job of lookin' after the folk in the Street.'

'But I thought you wanted to join the Fusiliers like last time.'

Albert sighed impatiently. 'I've just said, this is more important. Hell's teeth, woman, I thought you'd be pleased. This way I'll still be 'ere with you as well as servin' the King.'

'Oh, well, that'll be nice.'

Bessie lifted the plate in her hand. 'Beattie's gone.'

'Aye, I saw her marchin' off to railway station this mornin'.'

Bessie sat and ran a finger around an empty plate. Albert sensed her loss and, feeling he should do something, removed his helmet. 'It won't be for long. She'll be back for Christmas. It'll all be over then.'

'Aye.' Bessie took a long look at Albert in his new uniform and tutted. 'I'll get me sewin' basket out later. Those trousers are far too long.'

CHAPTER THREE

9 October 1939 Food profiteering increases as does the population of Coronation Street.

Frank Barlow secured his bicycle to the chain hanging from the coal-hole and removed his cycle clips from his ankles. He looked up and saw that the back bedroom window light was on. He smiled at the thought of Ida fussing about, turning the room into a nursery for the baby. She'd been given a bag of old books and had carefully cut out pages with nursery-rhyme characters on them. She'd covered a light shade with them and stuck the rest on an old chest of drawers. Thinking of Ida brought to mind the problem he was dreading facing.

She had been born in 1916, six months after the death of her father in the battle of Loos. She'd been brought up to view war as an evil thing that stole husbands and fathers. Each morning, as the mail fell on the mat, she'd cast scared eyes in its direction, dreading the official envelope containing Frank's call-up papers. It was bound to happen: he'd served a year in the Navy cadets and had been on stand-by since the declaration of war.

Frank turned his bike light off and wondered how best to break the news. She'd been so relieved that the letter hadn't come but she hadn't thought that, with working in the sorting office at the post office, Frank often brought home their letters before they could be delivered. He felt for the envelope in his pocket and looked again at the window. The light was turned off. He let himself in by the back-door and hung up his clips on their hook over the enamel sink.

'Hello, love, busy day?'

Ida waddled into the living room and eased herself down into a chair. 'I'll just do another three rows and then I'll see to your tea.'

'No rush.'

He removed his gas mask from over his shoulder and undid his coat. As he shook it off he didn't notice the envelope fall on to the carpet. But Ida did. Her knitting needles stopped moving and she stared down at it. He turned and his eyes met hers. She didn't say a word but, after the shortest of pauses, bent double in sudden, intense pain. She leant on the table for support and tried to control her breathing. Her head spun and she cried out as the pain hit her again.

Frank looked at his wife and felt helpless. 'Who do I fetch? Shall I go on me bike for midwife?'

'Don't leave me!'

'You need someone, Ida.'

'Fetch Mrs Sharples, but be quick . . . please!'

Sally and Dot Todd didn't have far to walk home. They were employed as machinists at Elliston's raincoat factory which, although having its main entrance on Victoria Street, had a loading bay at the back, facing the terraced houses of Coronation Street. The sisters left the factory and strolled across the cobbles to their home at No. 9. They pushed open the front door – it was never locked. 'Mam, we're home!' called Sally.

At nineteen, she was the eldest sister by three and a half years. Dorothy Edith, or Dot for short, looked older than fifteen and was treated as such by family and workmates alike. The girls removed their headscarves, hung up their gas masks and entered the living room. Sally went into the scullery and out of the back door, calling back into the house, 'I'm dying for a pee.'

Dot kicked off her shoes and sank into a chair. 'Dad not back yet?' she asked.

Vi Todd looked up from kneading dough and blew flour off her nose. 'He's on lates all week.'

Dot grabbed a packet of cigarettes off the table and pulled one out.

'They're not yours, young lady. Your brother'll skin yer for takin' one of his.'

'He won't notice. 'Sides, I'm out of 'em just now. I'll nip to corner later and get some.'

'I had a caller earlier on.'

'Oh?'

Vi ripped the dough into four equal chunks and moved them on to a tin tray, which she placed on top of the range. 'The new woman from next door. Well, I say woman, turns out she's just sixteen. Only a few months older than you. You must 'ave seen her around the place.'

'Only in Street, not to talk to. What's she like?'

'Seemed all right. She's from Back Gas Street, on t'other side of canal. Rough lot over there. Dead common. But she seemed nice enough. Pregnant, so let that be a warnin' to you.'

'What do you mean?'

'Don't act innocent. You know what I'm talkin' about. Everyone likes a bit o' fun, I'm just sayin' don't take any chances.'

Sally entered the room. 'What you talkin' about?'

'Girl next door, sixteen with a baby on way. I were just makin' sure your sister took note. I saw the way she were looking at that lad at Alice's weddin'.'

'What lad was that?' asked Sally, picking up her *Picture Post* and falling into a chair beside the range.

'There were no lad. She's talkin' daft,' said Dot.

'I know what I mean. That lad who runs errands for Dirty Pol on Mawdsley Street.'

''Im?' Dot was outraged. ' 'E's got spots! I'm not interested in 'im!'

'That's what you say. I'm just glad 'e didn't come to the reception. Goodness knows what could 'ave 'appened in that dark cellar.'

'Mam, we were like sardines down there. You couldn't move for elbowin' someone you knew.'

Vi mopped down the table and wiped her hands on her apron. 'Just be warned.'

She carried her wooden board into the scullery and started

to fill a pan with water. When her back was turned Sally lowered her magazine and kicked Dot's leg. 'Was you really with that lad?'

'What if I was?' asked Dot. 'Ain't no crime in chattin', is there? He works the projector at the Bijou sometimes. Said he'd be able to get us best seats if we want them.'

'Sounds good.'

The back door opened, sending a chill wind through the living room. A young man wearing a grubby shirt and a heavy, threadbare jacket, let himself in and closed the door behind him. He removed the jacket, which had exaggerated his build. His features were sharp and pointed but his eyes were deep brown and he'd inherited long dark eyelashes from his mother, which drew the admiration of many local girls. His name was Jim. He gave his mother a peck on the cheek and gazed over her shoulder into the pan. 'Carrots again?'

'Stop mitherin' me and get from under me feet,' Vi said, prodding her son with a wet spoon.

He stepped into the living room and made for the fire. 'Budge up, Dot. Let dog see the rabbit.'

'Do you mind?' asked Dot, as he squashed into the chair beside her.

'No. Do you?'

'Mam, will you tell him!'

'Come on, move your fat bum, there's plenty of room for us both,' said Jim, leaning in towards the fire, which roared in the range.

'Who are you callin' fat? Sal, tell him!'

Sally buried her head in her magazine and ignored her siblings.

'My bum is not fat.'

' 'Course it is, but that's all right 'cos most fellas like summat to grab 'old of.'

Dot took a swipe at Jim's head but he dodged her hand and reached for his cigarettes. He opened the packet and looked inside. 'There was nine in 'ere earlier on.' He glanced at his sister's hand, bent forward and whispered into her ear, 'Fat, and a thief.'

She pushed him away. 'You stink of sweat.'

'Good job it's me bath night, then, isn't it? Wanna scrub me back?'

The game stopped at a knock on the back door. It meant a stranger or an official: anyone else would have just entered. Vi wiped her hands dry, cast a worried look towards her children and tentatively opened the door. 'Yes? Oh, it's you. Come in love.'

She stepped aside and Elsie Tanner bustled in. 'Sorry to intrude,' Elsie said, 'but I saw your son come home. It was your son, wasn't it?'

Without waiting for an answer Elsie looked into the living room and smiled at the threesome. Jim automatically got out of the chair.

'This is Mrs Tanner from next door. I told you I'd met her.'

'Please call me Elsie. Mrs Tanner is my husband's mother and I don't like her much.'

Vi gestured towards her children. 'That's Sally, Dot and Jim.'

'How do?' said Jim.

'I'm sorry to bother you when you've just come in. It's the range, you see. I can't get it to light and I wondered if your son might . . .'

Vi's sharp eyes took in the way Elsie was looking coyly at Jim. The ranges in the Street were all the same and any fool could light them. You certainly didn't need a man for the job.

Jim was quick on the uptake. He was in the scullery and holding open the back door before Vi could blink. She sighed. Just like his father.

Elsie followed Jim into her cold living room. Despite the chill she untied her coat and watched as he bent down and inspected the range.

'Where's yer coal?'

'It's in the scuttle. I thought I were best off starting with kindling.'

'No good in these old things. What you need is a load of coal and a fire-lighter. I'll have a roaring fire going for you in no time.' Jim looked around the bare, unhomely room. 'Where's yer 'usband?' he asked.

'Gone.'

'Gone?'

'Left for the Navy couple of weeks ago. At least, I think 'e did. He didn't leave a note or anything. Navy's welcome to 'im.' She lit a cigarette and watched Jim roll up his shirt-sleeves. He had nice long forearms.

Ena Sharples and Martha Longhurst stood looking at Ida. 'How pregnant did you say you are, love?' asked Martha.

'Thirty-seven weeks,' gasped Ida.

Ena removed her coat and sprang into action. 'Right, Frank Barlow, start boilin' water and I'll need some towels. Martha, you'd best fetch Minnie. She's too far gone to wait for midwife and we'll need all the 'elp we can get.'

Martha scurried off down the hall while Frank remained standing stock still in the room.

'Come on, man, snap to.'

Ena bent over Ida and put her arm around her. 'I'm goin' to 'elp you upstairs . . .'

Ida screamed and grasped the table with both hands. 'No . . . might be an air raid.'

'Nonsense, we 'aven't 'ad one since Alice Hewitt's weddin'.'

'I'm not going upstairs!'

Frank rushed into the room carrying a pan of water which he placed on the range. 'She's scared of bombs.'

'I'd figured that out for meself,' said Ena. 'Right, well, we'll 'ave to do the best we can down 'ere.'

'I'll fetch the eiderdown,' said Frank.

Jim regarded his handiwork with satisfaction. Elsie handed him a glass and said apologetically, 'It's only gin. I've no beer in.'

'That's all right,' he lied. He hated the stuff but he'd nurse it if it meant prolonging his visit.

'You must get lonely, in this 'ouse all by yerself all day.'

'Day's all right,' she said. 'It's the nights I mind most. Still, I'm not on my own, am I? I've got my bump.'

He looked at her stomach. 'It's amazin' to think there's a baby in there.'

'It kicks sometimes, and moves around. Would you like to feel it?'

He nodded, so she moved closer and pulled her blouse loose from her skirt. She undid enough buttons to reveal her belly button and to show the curve of her breasts. She took his shaking hand and placed it on her skin.

'Just leave it there a bit. Maybe you'll be lucky.' She smiled encouragingly at him and wished she'd made contact with the boisterous Todds weeks before. If she'd had known Jim was so easy to pull she'd have lured him into the house when she first saw him – the day she'd watched him swilling the backyard down. With his shirt off he'd been nothing to write home about, all angular shoulderblades, but when he'd turned round and she'd seen those gorgeous eyes she'd been smitten. He was certainly the best thing the Street had to offer. Harry Hewitt from No. 7 was the right age but he was too quiet for her: she liked a man who pushed himself forward not fumbled for loose change in his pockets. When Arnold had left she'd promised herself she'd be a faithful wife and she had, so far. There was no point in fighting nature, though, she mused. What Arnold didn't know wouldn't hurt him.

Frank sat on the bottom step and cursed himself for leaving his pipe in the living room. The hallway was dark and he knew he'd be more comfortable in the front parlour but he wanted to be here, near the living room door, to be as close to Ida as he could. Damn that letter and damn him for not having told her sooner, broken it to her more gently. He ran his fingers through his dark hair and cast an anguished look towards the closed door.

In the next room, a homely woman in her late thirties, with the pained expression of someone much older, stood over the pan of water and peered into it. 'It's not boiling yet, Ena,' Minnie Caldwell said slowly, as if treading a conversational minefield.

Martha bent under the table and spoke to Ida. 'Would you like some tea, love?'

Ida didn't answer, just grabbed her hand as the burning rushed up her again.

'Not another already?' asked Ena. 'Right, I think this is it.'
'But the water's not ready, Ena.' said Minnie.
'Well, let's 'ope we don't need nowt sterilisin'.'
Ena knelt down on the rug and peeled the blanket off Ida's legs. She'd never delivered a baby crouched on the floor before, but there was a first time for everything.
Ida let out a scream.
'That's it, love, you scream it out. Father, guide my hands I pray!'
Minnie stepped over Ena's legs and took her position on the other side of Ida. She lowered her head under the table flap and giggled. 'It reminds me of when I was little and played under the table while my mother did her sewing.'
Ida let rip another shriek.

Sid Hayes lowered his newspaper and glanced at the wall. 'Sounds as if Mrs Barlow's gone into labour,' he said.
'Should we say a prayer for a safe delivery?' asked Esther, laying aside her needlework.
Sid pondered the question. While he did so, another muffled scream came through the wall. Rose got up from the table and left the room. Esther heard her footsteps as she ran up the stairs to escape the noise.
'Good idea, Esther. Let's bow our heads for a moment.'
The tick of the mantel clock was the only noise in the room as the back door opened slowly. Esther lifted her head and cautiously opened an eye. She started as her brother Tom crept in.
Alerted by Esther's head movement, Sid lifted his own head and stared at his son. Ida screamed again and the startled Tom tried to work out where the noise had come from.
'You are supposed to be in Blackpool,' stated Sid.
'I never went.'
'What do you mean?' asked Esther.
'I decided against it so I never got on the train.'
'But where have you been?' Esther stared at her brother. 'It's been weeks.'
'I've been visiting Auntie Dolly in Bury, told 'er you'd sent me.'

Sid peered at him in disapproval, 'More lies.'

'Only she's 'ad enough of me so I thought I'd best come 'ome. Is there any bread? I'm starvin'.'

Esther got up but before she could go to her brother Sid lifted his hand. 'Have you forgotten our neighbour Esther? In her hour of need?'

'No, Father.' She sat again and followed his lead as he bent his head once more in prayer.

Tom stood shivering in the doorway. He eyed the fire longingly but knew his father's wrath too well to attempt to creep any closer. He hoped it wouldn't be a long prayer.

Sally Todd put her gas mask on the shelf behind the counter and looked round at the bar. 'Not many in tonight, Mrs Walker.'

Annie looked at the strap hanging from the gas mask with disdain. 'I don't think it's a good idea to keep it in the bar, love. We could easily trip over it there. Why don't you hang it in the hall with mine?'

'Oh, right.' Sally retrieved the offending item and took it through to the Rovers' hallway, annoyed with herself for giving Annie a chance to pull her up. She'd worked evenings at the pub for nearly six months, but felt Annie still didn't trust her and took the slightest opportunity to correct her manner, speech, bearing or attitude.

Annie opened a bottle of orange juice for herself. Sally was right: it was unusually quiet for a Monday night. The Tatlocks sat at a table, staring bleakly into their glasses, and Thomas Hewitt threw darts morosely at the board. 'Another pint, Mr Hewitt?' she asked.

Thomas stopped, dart in hand, and nodded slowly. 'Go on, then. Might as well stay a bit longer. Nowt to go back to. House is cold as grave since Alice went.'

Annie started to pull the beer pump and asked, 'How's she settling down with Sam?'

'All right. She popped over to see us yesterday for Sunday dinner.'

'I've not seen Harry for a while.'

'You won't. 'E's keepin' his 'ead down.'

'Why ever's that?'

' 'Cos he's bleedin' useless. Can't 'old a job down an' even the Army won't 'ave him. Medically unfit. Summat to do wi' his feet. It's all daft. You don't need yer feet to shoot a gun, do you?'

Annie put the pint on the bar top and picked up the coin Tom placed next to it. 'At least you won't have the worry of wondering if he's safe,' she said.

Tom picked up his pint and took a gulp. ' 'E's never done anythin' worthwhile,' he muttered into his glass.

Sally stifled a yawn and looked at the clock. Time had dragged something rotten since war had been declared. She kept waiting for it all to happen, the bombs, the gas, the Germans attacking. Instead all she got was boredom.

The pub door opened and closed, and the black-out curtain was pulled open. Elsie Tanner giggled as she led Jim into the pub and up to the bar.

' 'Ello Sal,' he said. 'Thought I'd bring Elsie 'ere in for a drink.'

He was holding Elsie tightly round the waist. They were both in high spirits and Sally noticed he had lipstick on his neck. 'Pint and a. . . ?' she was poised, waiting for Elsie's request, but she received the answer from her brother.

'Gin.'

'Take a seat, I'll bring it over.'

Annie eyed the new arrivals with disgust. Jim Todd might be twenty-one but the girl certainly wasn't. Still, it was a quiet night and fivepence for a gin was fivepence in anyone's money, twenty-one or not. Annie cast a look at the front door. She hoped Arnold Tanner wasn't going to turn up. She didn't want any trouble on Jack's night off.

Sally leant over the table at which Jim and Elsie had sat down and made a half-hearted attempt at wiping the top. 'It's dead in 'ere tonight. What a waste. Ernie Bradshaw wanted to take me into town.'

'Who's Ernie Bradshaw?' asked Elsie. 'Is he a neighbour?'

'Lives on Mafeking Street, works across the street in the packin' room. He's a bit of a reject, if you get me drift, but I wish I'd taken him up on his offer now.'

Jim glanced behind Sally's back and saw Annie staring at them. 'Look lively, Sal, she's watchin'.'

'Let 'er. Not as if we've got loads of customers waitin', is it?' She turned to Annie and called, 'Just takin' five minutes, Mrs Walker, while we're quiet.'

Annie sniffed and walked over to the till, so Sally drew up a stool and sat next to Elsie.

'Do you need a job?' she asked. ' 'Cos they're takin' on at our place. The pay's crummy but we 'ave a laugh.'

'What? Here?' asked Elsie.

'No. Over the street, raincoat factory.'

'Do you work there an' all?' Elsie asked Jim.

'No, I work at tram depot. I'm a mechanic. Started off as clippie but I'm 'appier with grease under me nails.'

'How about it, then, Elsie? Shall I put a word in for you?'

'No thanks, love. I'm doin' all right with Arnold in the Navy. Fourteen shillings a week and 'e's seein' as how it's paid straight to me. Mind you, I reckon by time this one's born I'll be crawlin' up the walls with boredom.'

'Push a bit more, Ida. You're nearly there.'

Ena tried to encourage her as much as possible but exchanged a worried glance with Martha. The contractions were coming too fast and Ida was worn out. Ena noticed that Minnie was no longer chatting to the young woman and instead was looking beyond the table to the sideboard.

'Minnie! What are you lookin' at?'

'That picture on the wall, Ena. Do you think it's Southport?'

Ida started to sob and dug her nails into Martha's hand.

'Come on, Ida Barlow,' Ena remonstrated, 'your 'usband wants to go to bed. 'E's got work in the morning. Now, push . . .'

Ida strained. Martha bit her lip. Ena lifted her head and urged Ida on. 'The 'ead's comin', you're nearly there. Push, Ida, push!'

Esther placed the bowl of soup in front of her brother. He grabbed his spoon but, catching his father's eye, paused to say grace before tucking in.

'If I didn't have to pay the fare you'd be on the next train out to Blackpool,' said Sid sternly. 'As it is, I'm not sure what to do with you.'

''Ow do you mean?' asked Tom, his mouth full.

'Well, your school has closed down, all your friends have been evacuated. You've become displaced.'

'But I live 'ere.'

'Did. You did live here. Before you were evacuated. You see, Tom, what you fail to understand is that you are, in effect, a missing person.'

'How can I be missin' if I'm at 'ome?' Tom giggled into his soup.

Sid ignored him and continued, 'I shall have to inform the authorities. See what they suggest.'

'I'm not goin' to Blackpool! You can't make me!'

'True,' agreed Sid, 'but I can make certain you don't stay here.'

Esther sat in her chair, her hands clasped on her lap. She glanced at her father, trying to work out what this was leading to. She wished Ada were here. She always knew how to read Father. She jumped when she heard her name mentioned.

'Shall we ask Esther her opinion?'

Esther loved her brother dearly but that love was overshadowed by her fear of her father's anger. At all costs she mustn't be seen to side with Tom against him or they'd both be out on the streets. She stammered, 'I think – I think that what Tom has done is very bad but I am glad that he had the strength of character to return home rather than wander in the cold.'

'Strength of character?' asked Sid.

'Yes.' She paused, trying to form the exact words she needed. 'A coward would have kept on the run. It took a great deal for him to come home. I'm certain he's ashamed of his actions.' She looked meaningfully at her brother, who stopped eating and lowered his eyes.

'Father, I think Tom's return is a great blessing as he'll be able to help me around the house and will be useful for fetching coal and such things.'

Sid considered his daughter's words but when he spoke it was not of his son. 'I wonder, in our debate upon Tom's future, if you've noticed something, Esther?'

She looked blank.

'Our neighbour has stopped screaming.'

Minnie opened the door and stepped into the hall. Frank was already on his feet, nervously clenching and unclenching his fists. 'You can come in now, Mr Barlow.'

Tentatively he walked past Minnie and entered the living room. His eyes searched out the bundle in Ena's arms.

'It was 'ard goin'. I've never seen such a quick baby until right up to the end. Then 'e seemed to change 'is mind.'

'He?'

'Yes, lad, you've got a son.'

Frank glanced down at the tiny person wrapped in a towel. The baby's eyes were shut fast but his mouth opened in a yawn.

'He's beautiful, isn't he, Frank?' Ida's voice was quiet, but as Frank knelt beside her on the floor he felt she'd never looked so radiant.

' 'E is that, love.'

'I've got a name,' she said.

Ena looked down at the baby and thought, 'He looks like a Herbert.' She prided herself on never being wrong.

'I want to call him Kenneth.'

Ena sniffed. What sort of name was that? Kenneth Barlow. He wouldn't go far in the world.

Sally let herself in and flung her gas mask on the floor. She pushed open the door to the living room and made for an empty chair beside the range.

Vi looked up from her mending. 'You're back early, love.'

'Hardly anyone in. Just Dad and a few of his mates. She let me go.'

'Nice of 'er.'

'She gets 'er pound of flesh out o' me often enough.'

Vi finished sewing a button on to a shirt and bit off the thread. 'That's Jim's shirt done for mornin'. I'll leave it out for 'im to put away when 'e comes in for his tea. Which looks a right mess, I might say. I expected 'im back from next door hours since. I suppose he went to see 'Arry or one of his mates from work. No thought to me keepin' 'is tea warm for 'im.'

Sally considered keeping her mother in ignorance but then decided there was no point. She might just as well find out from her than from one of the local gossips. 'Actually, Mam, 'e isn't out wi' a mate. 'E brought Elsie in to the Rovers earlier on.'

'You mean to say he's suppin' ale with 'er while there's best sausages and carrots waitin' 'ere for 'im? I've a good mind to carry 'is plate down to that Rovers and give it to 'im there to eat.'

'I wouldn't bother, Mam. They only had one drink and then left. 'E said as 'ow you weren't to wait up for 'im. I think they were goin' back to 'ers. If you know what I mean.'

'The brazen 'ussy!' exclaimed Vi. 'Talk about fast.'

'Don't take on so. Jim's a big lad now. 'E can look after 'imself. 'E'll be off soon, stood in some field with a rifle and a daft look on his face. Let 'im 'ave a bit of fun while he can. Look on bright side. At least 'e can't put 'er in family way, can 'e?'

Vi sighed and wandered off to the scullery to busy herself. The worn lino in front of the stone sink was her place for quiet contemplation. In her rowdy household there weren't many peaceful moments so she tended to grab them when they came her way. She looked out of the window, past the big taped X, which had been part of her provision against dropping bombs, and glanced at the brick wall that separated her boundaries from Elsie's.

No doubt her son was enjoying himself at No. 11 and she was glad of that. She'd always encouraged her children to take their pleasures while they could. She never had. The house Elsie now occupied had once been Vi's family home, dominated by her mother, Ivy Makepiece, who had been widowed at a young age with seven children to support. The harsh demands of life had turned her into a fighter, but often her aggression had been aimed at her children and their tender skin would carry the red, painful marks of her beatings. Vi now understood that her mother had only lashed out through frustration but, at the time, the children had hated her and planned their escape.

Vi had gone first, defying her mother by marrying Jack Todd at the age of twenty. Ivy had had plans to marry her daughters off for commercial needs and was waiting for the Rovers' landlord to be widowed, seeing him as the ideal catch for Vi. When Vi eloped to live in Mawdsley Street with Jack, Ivy refused to speak to her, even though their backyards faced each other. It was only after her other children had left home and Vi had children of her own that the cantankerous old woman admitted Vi had chosen her husband wisely and the pair had been reconciled.

Vi thought fate cruel indeed for taking her brothers and sisters from her and leaving her alone to shoulder the burden of her ageing mother as well as her demanding family. Her brothers, Frank and Ralph, had been killed during the Great War and pretty Susie had died a prostitute in London. Lil had been married off to Tommy Foyle at the corner shop, where Ivy had enjoyed an endless slate until Lil died, still in her twenties. William had escaped to Bury, without telling his family his new address, but her favourite sister Mary had married Thomas Hewitt from No. 7 and been driven insane by his inactivity during the depression.

Vi had inherited her mother's fighting spirit but refused to dominate her children's lives and had decided early on to let them make their own mistakes. She longed for her daughters to fall in love and settle down locally with men of their choice. Looking at Jack now, with his disgusting habits and idle ways, she could still catch glimpses of the good-looking bricklayer she had fallen in love with, the broad shoulders, slim waist, the chest like granite and the clear eyes Jim had inherited. They'd only been married a few months before he'd been called up and she'd waited, in his mother's home, for him to return. A man tormented by shadows and the screams of dying comrades that lived inside his head.

Her marital happiness had been short-lived, romance swapped for childbirth and the rigours of motherhood. The delights of sex had turned into a fearful experience with the savage thrustings of a man who had left his heart and feelings in a foreign field. She feared for Jim and what the new war would turn him into. As her only son, he occupied a special place in her heart and she had taken to praying each night that God would spare him, both from death and from the anguish that had soured his father. She was pleased he'd found comfort in Elsie Tanner's arms, and had no worries about her being married because the future, Vi knew, was so uncertain that anything could happen. Anything at all.

CHAPTER FOUR

October 1939 Half a million soldiers wait at the Allied front line, ready for action, while Ena and Albert man the stirrup pumps.

Albert Tatlock stood in the middle of Coronation Street and listened. No, he wasn't wrong, there was definitely no band. He scurried back to his front door where Bessie stood, leaning against the frame. 'It's not right,' he said, 'there ought to be a band. We had a band in nineteen fourteen for goin' and then another in nineteen eighteen for comin' back. We sang, 'It's a long way to Tipperary, it's a long way to go. It's a long way—'

'Oh, give over, Albert,' Bessie cut him off. 'It's bad enough without you carryin' on. Think about Ida next door. Do you think she wants you wakin' that bairn up with your caterwaulin'?'

Albert glanced up at the Barlows' front bedroom window. 'Eee,' he said wistfully, 'I wish I were Frank Barlow.' He shouldn't have said that. 'I didn't mean—' He was too late.

'Charmin',' said Bessie, and walked back inside, banging the front door after her.

Before Albert had a chance to follow his wife, the door to No. 3 opened and Frank Barlow emerged. He was wearing a green uniform and clutched a kit-bag.

'By 'eck, lad,' said Albert, 'you look a right bobby-dazzler.'

Frank attempted a smile and put his bag on the pavement.

'Mind you, you're wearing wrong colour for the Navy.'

'I transferred,' explained Frank. 'I'm in the 7th Cheshires.

59

Ida was worried because of me not bein' able to swim, you see.'

'I didn't know you could chop and change like that,' said Albert.

'It's with me bein' in reserves and just havin' the baby.'

Ida appeared at the door, clutching Kenneth to her. Her eyes were puffy and red from crying. She stared at her husband and the tears started to roll again.

'Come on, love, I've got to go.'

She bit her lip and nodded.

Albert stepped forward and touched Frank's arm. 'We'll look after her for you, lad. She'll not be alone much.'

'Thanks, Albert. My sister's goin' to come and stay with her.'

'Oh, that'll be champion, won't it, Ida?'

She couldn't bear to listen to them make arrangements. She wasn't a cat that needed feeding and letting out at night. She was a woman with a baby who needed her husband with her. How was she to cope? What if the raids started tonight? Or tomorrow? She was certain she wouldn't be able to get Kenneth into his special pram with the gas mask fitted over it. And the noise. How would they sleep through it?

Frank kissed her forehead and swung his kit-bag over his shoulder.

He was going.

He was going to get killed.

Just like her father.

Was this how her mother had stood? How she'd watched her husband join the column of men as they passed the end of the street?

Ida opened her mouth but there were no words.

Albert didn't have the same problem. He waved his hat and said cheerily, 'Ta-ra, Frank lad. Kill a Jerry for me!'

Ida had stopped crying. There were no tears left. She watched Frank as he marched carefully round the corner of the Rovers, falling in line with a group of soldiers setting off to goodness knows where. She'd heard people talking in the shops and in the Street, guessing at locations the men might be sent to. As in the last war, the men of Weatherfield had, on the whole, opted or been called up to join the Fusiliers. They didn't have seafaring legs and their hands, used to manual labour, naturally clasped a rifle. Years had gone past since Ida had heard the names of French towns spoken. Then it had been in connection with her father's fate in 1916. Now, she was convinced, one would prove to be the final resting-place of her husband. History was repeating itself and there was nothing she could do to stop it.

Elsie tried on Jim's cap and looked at her reflection in the mirror. She tilted her head to one side and pouted. 'What do you reckon?' she asked.

'You wanna be careful. That's Army property, that is.'

She turned round on the chair to face him as he lay in her bed smoking one of her cigarettes. She eyed the little tuft of hair on his chest, and suddenly noticed how skinny his ribcage was. Arnold was twice his size. In all departments, as it had turned out. But she told herself not to dwell on that. It had been fun while it lasted.

'What you thinkin'?' he asked.

'That it's been fun.'

'What 'as?'

'You and me.'

'It's not over yet.'

'Course it is. You're joinin' the flamin' Army in a couple of hours.'

'No. I mean I'm bound to 'ave leave, aren't I? An', anyway, it'll be over in a few weeks.'

'Jim, love,' said Elsie, in her sweetest voice, 'let's not plan the future. I'm a married woman. I'll be with Arnold after the war.'

'Oh, 'im,' Jim scowled.

'Don't go all sulky on me. We've 'ad a laugh. But, be honest, it was bound to come to an end eventually, wasn't it?'

The bedsprings creaked as Jim rolled over and reached for his discarded boots.

'What are you doin'?' she asked.

'Gerrin' dressed an' goin' to see me mam.'

' 'Ave I upset you?'

He looked at her sitting there, the swelling in her stomach larger than ever. She looked vulnerable and very, very beautiful. He smiled at her. 'No. You're right. It were fun while it lasted.'

Mrs Foyle finished weighing the thin slices of bacon.

Ena eyed the scales with suspicion. 'There's more fat than meat.'

Used to Ena's remarks on the state of her wares, Mrs Foyle took no notice and expertly wrapped the bacon. 'Anything else?'

'I'll take a couple of eggs and some scourin' powder.'

Mrs Foyle carefully lifted two eggs from a box and put them into a paper bag.

'Oh, yes,' said Ena, 'am I right in thinkin' I 'ave to register wi' you now I've got these things?' She produced a couple of ration books from her pocket and placed them on the counter.

'That's right, Mrs Sharples, if I am your chosen shop for groceries and provisions.

'Well, I'm blowed if I'm takin' me custom to Hetty Morris after all these years. Why? My custom not good enough for you?'

'I just wanted to make certain,' said Mrs Foyle, 'because in the past there has been unpleasantness.'

'I'm sure I don't know what you're talkin' about,' said Ena. Despite Elsie Foyle's insistence that her husband had left the marital home via the back door, she had learnt about his departure from Martha Longhurst, who had caught sight of him walking towards the station wearing his trilby and carrying two suitcases. She itched to enquire as to the situation but the jangling of the bell over the door announced the arrival of Vi Todd.

Vi walked into the shop and smiled at Mrs Foyle. 'Mornin', Mrs Foyle, Mrs Sharples.'

Ena inclined her head and scratched her cheek. 'Your lad off today, then?'

'That's right. I'm just gettin' him some chocolate for the journey.'

Mrs Foyle placed Ena's shopping on the counter and asked, 'Was that everything, Mrs Sharples?'

'Aye, chalk it up, won't you?' She'd get to the bottom of Mrs Foyle's husband's whereabouts some other time.

Ena moved away from the counter but made no attempt to leave the shop. She watched as Vi selected the chocolate. 'You'll not be the only one missing your Jim. Is Mrs Tanner comin' to station with you to see 'im off?'

From her vantage-point Mrs Foyle noticed the change in Vi's expression but her voice remained steady as she said, 'I don't think so, Mrs Sharples. They're sayin' their goodbyes right now, as a matter of fact.'

Ena snorted. 'I bet they are.'

Vi turned to look at the other woman. ' 'Ad you forgotten something, Mrs Sharples? Or were you stoppin' for the company?'

'I suppose that's what your lad sees Elsie Tanner for, is it? Company?'

'Meanin'?' Vi dropped all pretence of sweetness and advanced upon Ena.

'I've known you a long time, Violet Todd. I've known you since you was Vi Makepiece. You sat next to me sister Alice at school and I stood at church gate to see you wed Jack Todd. I've watched you 'old that family of yours together over the years and I've admired you for it.' Ena paused only to draw breath. 'But I never thought I'd see the day when you allowed that sort of carryin' on in your house. That lad o' yours 'as no right bein' shacked up with a married woman. 'Ave you no shame? She's 'eavy with her 'usband's child, or is your lad so thick he's kiddin' himself it's 'is?'

'Don't you call my lad thick. 'E wasn't dropped on his 'ead, nor does he spend days on end mutterin' to 'imself!'

It was a direct hit, and brought Ena's daughter into the conversation. Vi had a lot of time for Vera and felt for her, being bossed around by Ena all her life, but she wasn't going to let her own offspring be dragged through the dirt without getting in the odd swipe herself.

'My Vera's a decent girl, not like those two strumpets of yours, flashin' their legs to any fella who cares to see them. My daughter doesn't have men leering at her in the Street.'

'No,' said Vi, 'because she looks like her mother, like a ruddy great cart'orse. That's why!'

Mrs Foyle closed her eyes. Experience told her there was no point in attempting to intervene.

'I've seen some carryin's-on in this street over the years,' said Ena, 'but your lad jumpin' into bed with that whore while you just stand by and welcome in Sodom and Gomorrah takes the biscuit!'

'Will you listen to 'er?' Vi tried to win Mrs Foyle over to her side. 'Gettin' all bleedin' religious on us!' She turned to Ena and eyed her with disgust. 'You're nothin' but a hypocrite, Ena Sharples. Holier than God one minute, suppin' ale up to yer eyeballs the next. The only reason you're so against Elsie is that she knows 'ow to 'ave a good time. Not like your Vera. Soured before 'er time, that one. Like 'er mother. 'Ow did your 'usband die? Boredom, was it? Or did you lash him to pieces with that vicious tongue of yours?'

Ena glared at Vi, her face flushed with anger. ' 'Ow dare you?'

'I dare because I can, Mrs Sharples. You may well browbeat the rest of the spineless lot on this street, but you don't frighten me. Now, keep a civil tongue in your 'ead about my family or so 'elp me I'll pull your manky 'air out!'

Vi picked up the box of Fry's Assorted and slammed down six pennies. 'Thank you for the chocolate, Mrs Foyle. I 'ope you don't mind cash. Judging by some of your customers, I doubt if you see much of it.'

She pushed past Ena and left the shop, slamming the door behind her, which set the bell jumping around in its setting.

The men marched off to war. Some, like Frank, joined comrades as they walked down Rosamund Street, while others made their way to the railway station by themselves. Harry Hewitt watched schoolfriends trundle off happily under the weight of their kit-bags and cursed his luck at being medically unfit. His father continued to take it as a slight against the family and hardly spoke to him. The entire Todd clan, including Jack's mother Daisy from Mawdsley Street, turned out to wave Jim off. As a conciliatory gesture, Vi asked Elsie to join them for his farewell tea. She was touched by the invitation and was thankful that not all her neighbours were hostile towards her.

Jack Walker's departure from the Rovers Return into the unknown with the Lancashire Fusiliers left Annie alone at the pub. She refused an offer from a cousin to move away with little Billy: it suited her patriotic pride to see herself as soldiering on at the helm of the good ship Rovers.

Albert Tatlock made certain he saw off each man with a wave and a cheer. As they marched away his mind slipped back twenty years and he saw long-forgotten faces turn and call to him. Faces of his youth. Lads, little more than boys, excited by the adventure, thrilled by thoughts of battle, glory and honour. So few had returned.

Not everyone on Coronation Street shared Albert's longing for a bygone comradeship. Sid Hayes offended veterans of the First World War by standing up at the Mission and denouncing the tide of patriotism that seemed to be carrying the public along. He reminded his congregation of the carnage at the Somme, of the wounded and maimed boys who were brought home to be shut away in institutions. Make a difference, he urged his flock. Make a stand for Jesus the peacemaker.

Albert made a stand for himself, walking out of Sid's sermon and dragging an embarrassed Bessie with him. Old resentments resurfaced and he went to great lengths to find a white feather to stick on the front door of No. 5 Coronation Street.

Ida Barlow wasn't alone for long at No. 3. Her sister-in-law Marjorie arrived, with two suitcases and a canary in a cage. She was a tall, angular woman of twenty-seven, who had never married and had spent her pre-war evenings entering ballroom-dancing competitions. She had been Salford District Champion in 1937, and altogether had won fifteen cups and trophies. She had a passion for the tango and, inspired by the films of Carmen Miranda, embarrassed her conservative family by wearing flowers in her hair. By profession she was a sales assistant at Baxendale's huge department store in the centre of Manchester, where she handled the glassware. She'd never had much to do with Ida, seeing her as the timid mouse Frank had married and little more. It took several days of small-talk and heavy silences for the women to start to get to know each other.

'Don't you get a bit bored just sitting in of an evening?' asked Marjorie, in the cultured voice she copied from her manageress, who lived in South Manchester.

'I've never been one for goin' out. I like my home.' Ida sounded defensive.

'It's a very nice home. You keep Frank very comfortable.'

The silences were long, drawn out by the ticking of the clock and the atmosphere of waiting that hung around everybody. The waiting for something, anything, to happen. Marjorie was used to activity and had never been a homebird. She grew restless sitting about and longed to feel some french chalk under her heels. Ida, though, liked nothing better than to be in the heart of her home. She'd had only the one letter from Frank, telling her he was being sent overseas but the destination had been scored through with a thick black pen. She wrote every day, going into great detail about Kenneth's progress. She had no idea if he received the letters or not but just writing them made her feel closer to him.

Ena Sharples took possession of her ARP helmet and torch towards the end of October. As Albert had made a great fuss about his new position in society she couldn't resist calling on him in her new uniform. After knocking she didn't wait to be let in, but opened the door and found the Tatlocks in the living room, listening to *ITMA* on the wireless.

Bessie looked up from her knitting. 'Hello, Ena, love. Fancy a cuppa?'

'Not while I'm on duty, thanks all the same. I've come to see Albert.'

Albert turned in his chair and gave a start when he saw Ena.

'What you doin' with my 'elmet? Put it back. You can't lark about with that, you know. It's been issued by the War Office.'

'Oh, stop gettin' so aerated. It's not your 'elmet, it's mine.'

'Yours? Don't talk daft, woman. I'm the warden for Coronation Street.'

'Yes,' said Ena, slowly and deliberately, 'and I'm the warden for this side of Victoria Street, and the Mission of Glad Tidings. An' seein' as how the Mission is part on Coronation Street I've been told you an' me 'ave to join forces.'

Albert sat back in his chair. Suddenly all the shine had gone from his job. 'Oh,' he said, in a deflated voice.

'That'll be nice, Albert. A bit of company for you,' said Bessie.

'So,' said Ena, 'your body's required over at Mission. Some town-hall Johnny's comin' to show us 'ow to use stirrup pumps.'

'Right. I'd best get me 'elmet.'

As Albert rose from his cosy corner the door opened again and Martha Longhurst walked in, clutching a carpet bag.

'By 'eck, you're popular tonight, Albert Tatlock,' said Ena.

'No,' said Martha. 'It's Bessie I've come to see.'

'Well, you're welcome to 'er because me and 'im are off out on official business.' Ena eyed Martha's bag suspiciously. 'I 'ope you've got your gas mask in that thing.'

'Oh . . . no, I 'aven't.'

'And why not?' demanded Victoria Street's ARP warden.

'It gets in way and it's not as if we've 'ad any attacks or raids, is it?' Martha sounded disappointed. 'I don't see the point in carryin' it around all the time.'

'You will do when Adolf starts droppin' billy-doos on yer.'

Ena gave her friend a hostile glare and disappeared out of the house after Albert. Martha waited until they'd gone before taking off her coat and sitting down in Albert's chair. From her bag she drew out her knitting.

Bessie lifted up her own. 'What do you think, Martha? It's me second one today.'

'It's very nice, Bessie. What is it?'

'It's a . . . hang on.' Bessie lifted a folded-over copy of the

Evening News. She scanned the page and then said, 'It's a sea-boot stocking. I did the first one in blue but now I'm using up this yellow that was left over from Beattie's cardigan.'

'I've started a Balaclava 'elmet,' said Martha, with pride. 'It's for advanced knitters. It said so on that leaflet from the Admiralty. I'm all over the place with it, needle-wise, but I'm gettin' on in wi' it. I did think Vi Todd would be joining us. Her and his mother are very fast once they get goin'.'

Bessie sighed with contentment. 'I think I'm goin' to enjoy this war.' Then, despite her words, a worrying thought crossed her mind and she stared at Martha.

'What?'

'Ena won't want to join the knittin' circle, will she?' asked Bessie. She sounded panicky.

'No,' Martha reassured her. 'Ena's big on lots of things but she's not got the patience for knittin'.'

The two women settled down to a few minutes of solid clicking until Martha broke the quiet by asking, 'Bessie, these sea-stocking things? Who's going to want one blue and one yellow?'

Sally Todd leant over the bar and helped herself to a crisp. Her mother always chose to drink in the snug, where the beer was cheaper than in the public. Vi sipped her brown ale and listened to Sally's predicament.

'You see, I quite fancy nursin'. It's a very pretty uniform.'

'Nursin's all right for them as can stand sight of blood. You know what you were like when yer brother took up boxin' that time.'

Sally grimaced at the memory. 'He had a lucky escape with that eye socket. Yeah, you're right. 'Ow about Land Army? Lots of fresh air and farmers wi' big muscles.'

Vi took a glug of ale and belched. 'I 'ad an aunt who married a lad wi' a farm near Northwich. Your great-auntie Kelly, I've told you about 'er – fell out a 'ay-loft and landed on a pitch-fork. Mam took us to visit 'er once. I know they go on about the countryside bein' full of fresh air, but I couldn't stomach it. The stink o' them animals!' She shivered at the thought. 'Nasty, noisy things, peckin' around and snortin'.

'Orses are all right pullin' carts up and down Rosamund Street but when you get up close to 'em they're great 'ulkin' brutes.'

Sally munched another of Vi's crisps and said, 'We get cows an' sheep in Weatherfield.'

'On way to market. It's not as if we're used to 'em, is it?'

'Anyroad,' said Sally, 'it's not all animals, is it? It'll be mostly vegetables and pickin' fruit.'

Vi drained her glass. 'You're talkin' through yer 'at, Sally. Stick you in a field wi' a spade an' you'll end up a right mess be end of day. No dancin', no flicks, mud in yer hair, backache. They don't 'ave no hair salons in a field, yer know.' She chuckled at the picture in her head.

Sally sighed and ate another crisp. 'So it's forces or munitions. Can't say as 'ow I'm taken with either. Still, anythin' 's got to be better than spendin' any more time with Annie Sour-face Walker. Surprised she doesn't put the ale off.'

'She's missin' her husband.'

'She's missin' someone to nag,' said Sally, 'only she's not missin' because she's takin' it out on me.'

Vi peered into the public bar. 'Is yer dad still suppin'?'

Sally glanced into the main bar. Jack Todd stood by the dart-board with Thomas Hewitt.

'Yeah. He's still 'ere. 'Im and Uncle Tom are natterin' like a couple of old women.'

'I'll have another brown ale, then. Get the money off yer dad.'

Sally reached under the bar and produced a bottle. She used the opener that hung from a string beside the pumps to open it and placed it on the bar. 'Do you think I'd suit navy blue? There's a poster outside Luxy with a Wren on it. Nice little 'at. I fancy it meself.'

It wasn't really a question, just something to say. Talking seemed to be the only way to ease the boredom. Sally brushed a crumb off the bar and rested her powdered chin on her palm. She'd expected more from the war than this. The first few days had been deceptively busy with registrations and gas-drills, when policemen wandered round the place alarming everyone by waving football rattles in the air. Lorries had appeared full of bricks, and bare-chested men had built shelters at the bottom of some of the terraces. She'd watched the more affluent members of society, those with back gardens, being presented with sheets of metal to construct Anderson shelters and had been caught up in the initial widespread indignation at not being able to have a family refuge. She found the gas mask unflattering, and was relieved that she'd only had to wear it the once for the drill. In fumbling to tie the strap Sally had broken a nail and she held Hitler personally responsible for this.

Since that initial period of excitement and anticipation, though, each day of further inactivity brought fresh boredom. When was it all going to start? When were the heavens going to open and rain gas bombs down upon them all? The only good thing about the normality of the past month had been the reopening of the cinemas, which had been closed at the outbreak for fear of having hundreds of customers hit at once. Newsreels had shown Sally and Dot the delights of being a Land Army girl but Vi was right: Sally's legs were designed for dancing under a glitter-ball, not trudging through ploughed fields. She sighed afresh and mourned the passing of her dancing days. The Palais remained closed and, anyway, who was there to dance with? The only man her age in the neighbourhood was Harry Hewitt, and he was her cousin. She looked longingly at the Rovers' doors, willing them to open and reveal a handsome, available man who, miraculously, had escaped the draft.

In answer to her prayer, the black-out curtain was pulled aside and the Churchillian shape of Albert Tatlock appeared. Sally threw the last crisp into her mouth.

CHAPTER FIVE

December 1939 First RAF bombs dropped on Germany while Coronation Street suffers its first casualty of war.

Elsie Tanner opened the shop door and looked in dismay at the queue inside. Seeing her there, Mrs Foyle called, 'Come over here, love, and take the weight off.'

Grateful Elsie manoeuvred her way past the shoppers, who moved aside to allow her access to the wooden chair that stood beside the counter, and eased herself down. Mrs Foyle carried on serving Alice Burgess, née Hewitt. Having left the Street on her wedding day to live with husband Sam's family in Birkenhead, Alice's conscience had prompted her into paying a weekend visit to her father and brother. Typically she'd found the larder wanting.

'And a tub of Brylcreem for 'Arry,' said Alice, casting a look in Elsie's direction. 'Remember me do you?' she asked.

Elsie smiled and said, 'Sorry love, do I know you?'

'I saw you day you moved in. Only I was dressed in a big white frock an' had a veil.'

'Of course!' said Elsie. 'How's married life?'

'I've no idea, love. He were sent overseas after a fortnight. He signed up on the Monday, received orders on Wednesday and left on the Friday. I'm still findin' bits of confetti in stuff and 'e's goodness knows where.'

'What bunch is he in?'

'Fusiliers.'

'Like my son, Bert,' commented the woman behind Alice.

71

'You've grown since I last saw you,' said Alice, nodding towards Elsie's stomach.

'It's due in New Year but I wish it would just hurry up and come. I'm that sick of carryin' it around. I 'aven't seen me feet for months!'

Mrs Foyle placed the hair cream on the counter. 'That all, love? Three and six altogether.'

'Thanks.' Alice dug in her purse and handed over a selection of coins. She put the goods into her basket and moved aside as Bert's mother produced her shopping list. 'You want some company tonight?' she asked Elsie.

'Yes,' Elsie replied, 'that would be very nice.'

'Right, I'll knock on for you about eight. We'll go to Rovers.'

Before the First World War, Jack Todd had served his apprenticeship as a bricklayer. Afterwards he'd struggled to find employment as his experiences in the trenches had left him shell-shocked and incapable of stopping his hands twitching. Unable to lay any more bricks he had taken a job in the shunting yard, shovelling coal. That job had been snatched from him during the depression, long years during which he'd suffered the humiliation of seeing his family fighting over crumbs of food and having the house stripped bare to qualify for the means test. Six years of traipsing the streets in search of work had resulted in a job on the buses as a clippie. It was manageable now that the twitching was only sporadic, but it was short-lived: he was made redundant in favour of his own son. He took the only work left to him: digging up streets for the council. It was low paid, with no future prospects, and there was little to be proud of. He worked with a bunch of other no-hopers, ignored by passers-by, ill-treated by the elements and scorned by his neighbours in more secure jobs. He was forty-nine years old.

Sitting in his chair in the family home, Jack cleared his throat and spat phlegm into the fire. The coals sizzled and he started to cough.

Vi closed her eyes and tried to ignore her husband. It was the same every year: the cold always hit his chest and then it was hack-hack-hack all winter. Each time he acted as if he was going to die, and each year she wished he'd hurry up and get on with it.

'I shouldn't be surprised if I don't bring up blood.'

'Oh, you're bound to,' she agreed. 'Either that or your tripe and onions.'

Dot looked into the mirror over the sideboard. She held up the back of her hair and moved from side to side, gazing at her profile. 'I'm thinking of 'avin' a permanent wave,' she announced to the family.

'I'll do it wi' sugar and water, if you like,' offered Vi, 'only make yer mind up quick because goodness knows 'ow long sugar's gonna be available.'

'No. I mean a proper job. Thought I'd go to Mrs Foyle. She's very reasonable.'

Vi picked at a lump of food stuck in her back tooth. 'You want to watch 'er. I've seen her puttin' 'er finger on scales when she's measurin' out. And 'ave you noticed 'e's gone? That Tommy Foyle who was so devoted to the memory of my poor sister Lil that he upped and married a show-girl 'alf his age just three years after we buried Lil at St Mary's.'

Jack's mother, Daisy, stirred in her chair and opened an eye. She often spent the evening in front of the Todds' fire rather than lighting her own across the back alley in Mawdsley Street. She was a woman who lived for gossip and eagerly picked up the subject of the absent Tommy Foyle. 'Martha Longhurst sez she saw 'im luggin' siutcases to the station.'

'Perhaps he's run off with some tart,' offered Jack. 'Lucky sod.'

Vi looked at him with contempt and ignored him.

'He'll 'ave gone to live with that sister of his, that Amelia who refused to come to ceremony when 'e wed our Lil. Made 'er feelings known all right, she did. Thinks she's the Queen of Sheba, she does. I saw 'er once, she came callin' after the funeral. She 'ad a face as 'ard as that scullery sink. If 'e's gone to 'er you can bet that's the last we'll see of 'im for a while. She'll be puttin' all sorts into his head. I wouldn't be surprised if she doesn't get 'im to sell shop.' She laughed at a sudden thought. 'That would put that show-girl on her backside.'

'Who's that?' asked Daisy.

'Keep up, Mother, I'm talkin' about 'er at the shop. Thinks she's Jean 'Arlow with that 'air,' said Vi.

'I liked Jean 'Arlow,' said Daisy.

'So did I,' said Jack, grabbing his crotch. He spat again, this time missing the fire and hitting the wall.

'You're a dirty 'ound, Jack Todd,' said Vi, kicking him.

'Where's that letter from our Jim?' asked Dot. 'I thought I'd take it round to Elsie.'

'It's behind clock,' said Vi. She arched her back and rubbed her side before complaining. 'This corset's too tight. It'll 'ave to go back to Swindley's.'

' 'E won't tek it back if you've worn it,' said Jack.

' 'E'll 'ave to. 'Ow am I supposed to know if it 'urts or not unless I wear it? Trust you to say summat daft like that. Just because you've worn same clothes for best part of twenty years.'

'I look after my tackle. These trousers was made to last.'

Dot perched on the arm of her mother's chair and stuffed the letter into her pocket. 'Do you reckon I'll get more money now Elliston's gone over to making uniforms?' she asked. ' 'Cos that'll mean I can save up and go up town for me wave.'

'You can whistle for more money,' said Jack. 'You're doin' war work now, lass, and that means longer hours and basic pay.'

'Well, I think it's rotten,' said Dot.

'It won't be for long,' said Vi. 'It'll be over for Christmas.'

Daisy stirred in her chair and cackled. 'Will it buggery,' she said, and farted.

Jim Todd was hoping to be home for Christmas. It said so in his letter. To please Dot, Elsie showed a polite interest in the thin piece of writing paper. She supposed it would be nice to see Jim again, but she had no desire to have sex with him. That was in the past. Done with. She'd moved on. Not that there was another fella hanging around. There had been that blond sailor with the gorgeous blue eyes but he'd balked at her pregnant state. No, now it was the arrival of the baby that occupied her thoughts. It had taken on a dual personality

since Elsie had picked names. Clark, after Gable, or Linda
after glamorous Linda Darnell, whose appearance in the film
Hotel for Women had caused Elsie to weep and clutch the
hand of the stranger next to her. He'd been the blond sailor
with the blue eyes. Only it hadn't been until the light went up
that she'd seen the eyes.

The front door opened and Alice Burgess entered, calling,
'It's only me.'

Elsie handed the letter back to Dot and looked up from her
chair as Alice came into the room.

'Hello, Alice,' said Dot.

Alice looked surprised to see her younger cousin at No. 11
and hoped she wasn't bothering their new neighbour. 'Hello,
Dorothy. What are you doin'?'

'We've 'ad a letter from Jim. I were showin' Elsie.'

News of the affair hadn't reached Birkenhead, so Alice was
in the dark as to why Elsie might be interested in the letter.
She refused to give Dot the satisfaction of being asked for an
explanation. Instead she asked, ' 'Ow is 'e?'

'Says 'e' s learnin' French an' 'e's got leave soon.'

'That's nice.'

' 'Eard anything from your 'usband?' asked Elsie.

'Oh,' lied Alice, ' 'e writes every day.'

Elsie smiled. 'Just like my 'usband, then.'

Changing the subject, Alice pulled her coat closer to her
and asked, 'Are you fit?'

'Just need me coat and gloves,' said Elsie, easing herself up
from the chair.

'Where you goin'?' asked Dot.

'Rovers. Fancy it?' asked Elsie.

Alice butted in, 'She's too young, aren't you, Dorothy?'

Elsie was amused by the way Alice treated fifteen-year-old
Dot, whom they'd established was only seven months
younger than she. Being pregnant obviously put years on as
well as pounds.

Annie Walker and Ida Barlow hardly knew each other. Ida
had only entered the Rovers to attend two wedding recep-
tions in the select and had never joined the ladies of the snug.

75

They would nod when passing in the street and make small-talk if encountering each other in a shop but, if asked, they would have said they had nothing in common, other than their postal address. They would have been wrong in this: both were suffering in their husband's absence. Ida continued to pour out the details of her empty days into letters which she placed each afternoon in the pillar-box outside the corner shop. Annie also wrote letters, carefully written messages that would have surprised her customers if they'd read them. Annie was a romantic at heart and the war had given her the chance to cast herself in the role of Lady Hamilton. Her letters, which she scented with her own perfume, were written from the heart, sending intimate and fond words to her beloved. Words that her reserve prevented her from uttering aloud to Jack. In Annie's case, absence had certainly made the heart grow fonder.

Standing behind the Rovers' bar, she looked at the bottles of pale ale under the counter and calculated how many she would need for the evening. Ena Sharples was already in, and by the look of the way she was spreading herself out in the snug she was expecting her two friends. Bessie Tatlock was sitting with Albert at their regular table by the window. All four women had an endless appetite for pale ale. Annie beckoned Harry Hewitt over.

'Harry, love, could you go down the cellar and fetch me up a crate of pale ale? There'll be a drink in it for you.'

'Right you are, Mrs Walker.'

She watched him disappear down the cellar steps and felt it a shame that a young man as eager as the next to prove himself was considered unfit for service. True, he had taken a job at the housing office in town and, of course, Annie was the first to recognise how important his job would be when the bombs started falling. It was a shame that other people didn't see his war work in the same light.

Harry's sister entered the pub with Elsie Tanner. She dallied too long before pulling the curtains after her and from his table Albert shouted, 'Shut them drapes. You might as well draw 'Itler a map!'

Alice gave the curtains a tug and pulled a face behind

76

Albert's back, which he didn't see. However, he did notice the absence of boxes hanging from their shoulders.

'Alice 'Ewitt, where's your gas mask?' he demanded.

'Wherever it is, it's none of your concern,' she said.

He was up, out of his chair, and immediately at her side. 'It's got everything to do with me. I'm ARP warden for this street and as such it's my duty to make certain you carry your gas mask everywhere you go. Suppose there was an attack now?'

'I'd go 'ome and get it. I only live four doors down Street.'

Elsie laughed.

'What's so funny?' demanded Albert.

'You are. You take it all so serious.' she said. 'It's been as quiet as the grave since September. The only gas 'as come from you and Mrs Sharples, shoutin' at us to "Put that light out" and "Where's yer gas mask?". You need to relax, otherwise you'll be the one explodin', never mind bombs.'

Albert felt his face redden. The girls walked to the bar, turning their backs to him.

'Sit down, Albert,' said Bessie. 'Folk are starin'.'

'Two shandies, please, Mrs Walker,' asked Alice.

'I'll give you one shandy and a lemonade,' said Annie, with a look of dislike. 'Mrs Tanner's not old enough to drink alcohol.'

'Blimey,' said Elsie. 'There's nowt like a Coronation Street welcome, is there? First old Grumpy Pants then the stone maiden. All we need now is wind-bag Ena.'

Elsie jumped in surprise as Ena's head appeared over the snug counter on the opposite side of the bar.

'You want to show more respect for your elders, Elsie Tanner. This street is a decent street. We don't want none of yer Back Gas Street ways round 'ere. I've 'eard all about your father, Arthur Grimshaw. Am I right? I'm not wrong, am I? Throwin'-out time in his local means just that. Throw 'em out into the gutter. Mind you, 'e won't be in no gutters where 'e is now, will 'e? Not unless they've put a public 'ouse inside Strangeways.'

Alice looked nervously at her companion, wondering what she'd let herself in for in inviting her out for a drink.

'You know all about gutters, don't you, Mrs Sharples? Seein' as 'ow you spend most of yer time nosyin' about in them looking for muck to throw at folk!'

Annie arrived with the drinks and gave Elsie a cold stare. 'If you wish to drink in these premises I suggest you curb your tongue, Mrs Tanner. This is a respectable house and my customers are not used to being harangued.'

'She started it,' Elsie said, pointing at Ena.

'I hope I make myself clear,' said Annie.

The tension was broken when Harry appeared, carrying a crate in front of him. He slid it on to the floor behind the bar. Glad to be diverted, Alice questioned her brother. 'What you doin'?'

' 'Elpin' Mrs Walker.' His speech was slow, his voice quiet. He was a shy, clumsy lad with limbs that appeared too big for his body.

Annie set to, loading the shelf with the ale. Elsie picked up her glass and went to sit at a table under the dart-board. Alice invited Harry to join them but he didn't pick up on the desperate plea in her voice and declined. He waited for his free pint at the bar. Reluctantly she joined Elsie.

'I don't know how you stick it, livin' 'ere all yer life,' said Elsie.

'They're not a bad bunch,' said Alice, in defence. In actual fact she'd spent most of the last five years of her life complaining about the gossips and interfering biddies. But that was different. Elsie was still an outsider and people born on Coronation Street defended their own from strangers. It was something of an unwritten code.

'Mrs Sharples 'as been through a lot of 'ardship.'

'Wi' a face like that I'm not surprised,' said Elsie.

'Her husband died a couple of years ago. 'Im and me dad did a lot of marchin' when they were unemployed. Mr Sharples took cold and was dead within' the week. It could 'ave been me dad.'

Elsie drank some lemonade and decided against making flippant comments about Mr Sharples' death.

'And 'er Vera's been 'ard work.'

'What do you mean?' asked Elsie.

78

'She's a bit slow an' was 'eld back a lot at school. Thick as a brick she is.'

'I've never seen her.'

'She works at the bakery on Cross Street, puttin' sugar in Eccles cakes. When she's not there Ena keeps 'er in the Mission.'

'What a life,' said Elsie. 'Can you imagine bein' stuck in that place with Ena? No wonder she's a bit on the slow side. 'Er brain's probably addled wi' all that naggin'.'

Ena was joined by Martha and Minnie, who arrived together, muffled up against the cold. They walked through the public bar and let themselves into the snug, which was sectioned off by a frosted door. Traditionally the only place in the pub where women were welcome, ale was a halfpenny cheaper than in the public. After the Great War the womenfolk had been welcomed into the main bar but the widows and spinsters still levitated towards the snug for female-only company.

Ena looked up from her newspaper as her friends arrived.

'I thought we said eight o'clock. I've been sat 'ere like piffy bein' shouted out by that floozy from number eleven.'

'It were Percy,' said Martha. 'I 'ad to wait for him to come back from his shift. Our Lily's got a bad chest and I didn't like leavin' 'er alone.'

'Whose shout is it?' asked Minnie.

'It's yours,' said Ena.

'Are you sure?'

'Callin' me a liar, are you, Minnie Caldwell? Me, who's bin sat 'ere keepin' your seat?'

'No, Ena,' said Minnie, in haste, 'It's just that I thought I bought last night.' She went to the bar and waited patiently for Annie to attend to her. The public was filling up and Minnie noticed a man standing opposite her. He looked to be a few years older than her, in his late forties, tall with greying hair. He was smiling at her. She gave a nervous smile back, and tried to attract Annie's attention. When she looked back towards him he was still smiling.

'Cold outside,' he called to her.

'Yes,' she answered.

'Who are you talkin' to?' demanded Ena.

'A man, Ena.'

'What man?'

'I've not seen 'im before. 'E keeps smilin' at me.'

'Does he!'

Ena stood up and tapped Minnie's shoulder. 'Here, give us your coppers. I'll wait for Lady Walker to get round to us.'

Minnie sat down, used to having Ena boss her around.

Ena glanced at the man, and bared her teeth in a rare grin. If there were any strange men going around, she was going to make certain they knew she was available.

Back at the table Minnie sighed and looked unhappy.

'What's up?' asked Martha.

'It'll be Christmas next week.'

'So?'

'Well, everyone said war would be over by Christmas. It's just struck me, it's not going to be over, is it?'

'No. It's not even begun, really, has it?'

When Christmas came it seemed to take everyone by surprise. Mrs Foyle pinned a notice up behind the counter regretfully informing her customers that her supply of butter had dried up but that she'd had an extra delivery of bacon.

'Can't put bacon on my currant scones, can I?' complained Bessie Tatlock.

'I'm afraid you'll have to make do with what I've got,' said Mrs Foyle. 'There is a war on.' She seemed to be saying that a lot now. But behind her cheerful banter she was an anguished woman. Her husband, being waited on hand and foot by his devoted sister in Lytham St Anne's, had arranged for the children to join him, and Mrs Foyle objected to the snooty Amelia replacing her as their mother-figure. She realised she could easily shut up shop and join her family, even if it did mean living under Amelia's roof, but after nine years behind the counter, she'd grasped how much the shop had come to mean to her. She enjoyed the hustle and bustle – it reminded her of being on stage. Obviously the admiration of the audience had been replaced by the aggravation of annoying customers but, like the fans who had followed her theatrical circuit, they always came back. If she moved to the safety of Lytham she knew she'd die of boredom. At least here she was kept busy and, she had to admit, life was easier without Tommy under her feet. He was a good father but the spark had gone out of the Foyles' marriage after Shelagh's birth six years previously. Elsie Foyle had gone off sex and, after months of pestering, Tommy had stopped bothering her. She suspected he was looking elsewhere for intimacy and didn't want to pry. So long as he didn't make a nuisance of himself she didn't care.

Having opted to remain in Weatherfield, her biggest concern was the imminent rationing. Even during the hard years of '34 and '35 she'd kept her shelves stocked, sliding items across the counter to keep a family from starvation. She didn't like the idea of being authoritative with ration books. It was bound to cause hostility between her and the customers.

It was a Friday night when Albert Tatlock fell victim of his own infatuation with blacked-out light. Leaving the Rovers after his nightly half of mild, he'd been crossing Coronation Street to ensure that the loading-bay gates at the back of Elliston's were secure when he was hit by a van travelling with no headlights. The driver, Leonard Swindley, had covered them with card cut with a tiny slit to allow light through. The resulting beam was so thin that often, as on this occasion, he forgot to turn the headlights on. He only saw Albert at the last possible moment and braked hard, screeching to a halt. The noise alerted the neighbours to the accident but it had taken the arrival of Ena, with her regulation torch, before the victim could be identified. Leonard took Albert to the infirmary in the back of his van, which boasted the legend, 'Swindley & Son Emporium', of which Leonard was the son. The business was situated on the Queen's Parade on Rosamund Street. What had started life as a grand Edwardian shop had become a run-down dusty hole that stocked wing collars and whalebone corsets. It was rumoured not to have had a stock change since 1929. Young Swindley was mortified at having injured Albert, even if he wasn't a regular customer at the shop. He rushed him to the hospital and sat waiting until the nurse assured him all that was well except that Mr Tatlock's leg was broken.

Bessie was disappointed when Albert wasn't admitted for overnight observation, and made up a camp bed for him in the front parlour so that he didn't have to manage the stairs.

The next morning Swindley appeared before the local magistrate and was fined ten shillings for not having painted his bumper white.

Albert was furious when, because of his injury, he was temporarily relieved of his ARP duties. He suggested to Jack Todd that he might like to take over but Jack shied away from anything that hinted of effort or work, and Martha Longhurst's husband Percy took on the chore of looking after Coronation Street as well as its neighbour, Mawdsley Street.

Christmas Eve found the Todd household in more chaos than usual as the family prepared for Jim's homecoming. Vi's hoarding had proved fruitful and her larder boasted a turkey, plum pudding, a jug of cream, mince pies and sausages. She kept the larder key in her pinny pocket after she found her mother-in-law drooling over the cream.

Daisy took her usual spot in the most comfortable chair, while Dot and Sally set up the gramophone player in the front parlour and borrowed Annie Walker's collection of operatic 78s. Vi had planned a big tea for Christmas Eve and then a party down at the Rovers. She'd organised everything herself, not wanting to leave anything to Jack for fear of him ruining everything. Which he often did.

Vi had only just slipped into her best dress when there came a sharp knock at the door. She ran down the stairs but was beaten by Dot who flung open the door to welcome her brother.

The man standing on the doorstep was a soldier but he wasn't Jim. 'Hello, 'ave I got the right 'ouse? Todds?'

Vi reached the door and pulled it wide open. She pushed Dot aside and looked fearfully at the stranger. What did it mean? It had to be bad news. 'I'm Mrs Todd. Who are you?'

'Walt Greenhalgh. I'm a friend of your Jim's.'

'Jim? Where is he?' Vi demanded, looking up and down the Street.

'He sent me to see you. His leave's been cancelled.'

Vi stared at the youth. What did he mean? Cancelled? It couldn't be cancelled. She had a tin of peaches in the sideboard. Peaches were Jim's favourite.

'Do you think I could come in?' asked Walt. 'It's a bit parky out 'ere.'

Vi stood aside and closed the door behind him. He was a big lad and seemed to take up all the space in the hallway. He lowered his kit-bag from his shoulders and followed Dot into the living room.

Daisy opened an eye and stared at the visitor. 'By 'eck lad, the Army's put some meat on yer bones,' she said.

'It's not Jim, Granny,' said Dot.

Vi introduced Walt to the rest of the family and offered him a cup of tea. He took off his overcoat and sat at the table.

'Jim's dead sorry not to be 'ere and sends his love.'

'Why were his leave cancelled?' asked Jack.

Walt cast an eye around the room and said, 'I don't like to say . . . in the company of ladies.'

'Don't worry yerself, lad, we're all family. If Jim's done owt wrong just blurt it out.'

'Well, Sarge caught 'im at it with this tar – this woman from one of the villages.'

Jack chortled, 'Just like 'is old man.'

Vi snorted. 'In yer dreams. So, that's that, then, is it? 'E gets 'is leg over an' his family, them as love 'im, can whistle.' She looked ruefully at the spread laid out on the table. 'Well, thank you for comin' to tell us, Walt. I suppose you'll be wantin' to shoot off to your family. Where is it you live, love?'

'I'm from Openshaw. But me folks 'ave gone to me auntie in Formby for Christmas. I've missed the last train now.'

'Oh,' said Vi, 'you'd best stop with us for your tea, then. Do you like sardines?'

At the end of Coronation Street, next door to the corner shop, stood the last of the uniform terraced houses, No. 13. On the outside it looked identical to all the other houses in the district but inside was noticeably different as the lady of the house, May Hardman, used the front parlour as her living room. May did not socialise with the rest of the Street. In the nine years she'd lived in Coronation Street she'd never set foot in the Rovers Return and, as a regular attendee at St Mary's Church, viewed the Mission of Glad Tidings as an abomination.

A month before the declaration of war she'd given birth, in the infirmary, to a daughter, whom she had named Christine. The birth had left her exhausted and she'd put upon the nurses to look after the baby while she made the most of her stay in hospital. She was a woman who expected to be waited on. Lazy and self-centred, the nurses couldn't help but feel sorry for her downtrodden husband, George, whenever he visited.

May had rallied in time to take advantage of the evacuation of the local children. She had summoned her younger sister, Madge, from the family home, and demanded she house-sit for her at No. 13, fearing the authorities would billet a family in her home if it was unoccupied. Like most of the people in May's life, Madge was used to being bossed around by her and put up no resistance. On the contrary, while May pushed Christine's pram to the railway station, in preparation for moving to the coast, Madge waved her off with George and, glancing up at his profile, told herself that May was a fool.

May had been placed in a Blackpool boarding-house and was in her element ordering her landlady around. She never gave a thought to the husband she'd abandoned and he found, much to his surprise, that he didn't miss her. Just days after her departure he, too, left the Street, having enlisted with the Fusiliers. When the time came for him to go he was surprised to find that bidding farewell to his sister-in-law seemed harder than saying goodbye to his wife. Madge was a gregarious, cheerful soul who, it seemed to George, filled the house with light. He was amazed by the pleasant change in the atmosphere at No. 13 during the few short days they spent together. It was so pleasant to sit with her in the evenings, chatting and playing bezique, that he abandoned his place at the Rovers' bar, which had become his nightly place of solace.

For her part, Madge made the most of George's company and she struggled with the resentment she felt towards May for being his wife. She remembered the day May had brought him home to meet the family. It had been done very formally, very properly. Father had stood with his back to the fire, Mummy had served sherry in the crystal glasses. Poor George had been terrified and she'd seen his hands shake as he took the glass from Mummy. She'd thought at the time it wasn't fair on him. May was going through a rebellious stage, anything to cause ructions, to upset Father. George was meant to be her undesirable boyfriend, a back-street lad with no prospects, and an accent to cut glass. But he'd proved himself that first meeting, refusing to be intimidated, giving a good account of himself, talking about his dreams to work in an office rather than follow his father and brothers down the pit. May's face when Father commended him on his attitude!

Of course, as soon as May had introduced him, Madge had known they were ill-suited: her selfish, spoilt sister with this earnest young man, so eager to please, not believing his good fortune in having May even look in his direction. Yes, it had been at that first meeting that Madge had fallen in love with him.

But with May in Blackpool and George overseas, Madge lived a lonely existence. She made certain her days were filled with domestic chores and enjoyed chatting to the neighbours while queuing at Foyle's and Piggott's but they were wary of her. After all, she was snooty May's sister. Never having been one to drink, Madge never considered venturing into the Rovers, and on the rare occasion she didn't spend the evening by the fire she could be found sitting alone at the Luxy, watching a romantic film. The days passed slowly for her, until one evening, the night before Christmas.

That was the night George came home. He wearily opened the front door to No. 13 with his latch key and slid his kit-bag on to the floor. Alerted by the thump, Madge grabbed the poker from beside the fire and crept to the door. It was pushed open. He blinked in the light of the room and stood amazed at the sight of the cosy fire. 'May?' His voice was soft, full of disbelief and almost musical.

'George?'

He spun round in surprise. 'Madge? I thought you'd have gone back to your parents.'

'I wanted to stay. Is that all right?'

His weary face broke into a delighted smile. He nearly hadn't come home, not seeing the sense of taking leave while other chaps had stayed in France, but he'd decided in the end to come more for some peace and quiet than anything else.

'I've got forty-eight hours,' he said.

'Right. Let's make the most of it. Are you hungry?'

'I'd love a bath,' he said.

'Right.' She hurried into the scullery to fill the largest pan with water. 'Would you like me to go back to Mum and Dad? Let you have some peace?'

'No.' He spoke too quickly, causing her to look at him over her shoulder. He felt the need to say something else, to justify his position. 'I mean, I'd be grateful if you stayed. I haven't had any decent conversation lately.'

She brought the pan back into the room and placed it on top of the range. 'It shouldn't take long to boil. I'll fetch the tub.'

She disappeared into the backyard, her heart beating faster, leaving George to warm himself in front of the glowing coals.

Jack Todd and Walt Greenhalgh pushed the piano into the public from the select bar and positioned it near the black-out curtains. Mrs Foyle made herself comfortable on the stool and ran her fingers along the keys. 'By heck, when did you last have this tuned?'

Annie chose to ignore her and collected a tray of empty glasses.

Behind the bar, Sally Todd pulled at the beer pump and served a full glass to a young man in uniform. She smiled a winning smile as she handed it over and licked her finger when some beer spilt on it. He handed her some money, winked and said, 'Keep the change'.

Annie waited until Sally had walked to the till then said quietly, 'I pay you to serve beer, not yourself.'

Sally took the complaint on the chin. Annie had been

getting at her for a week, ever since she'd handed in her notice.

The pub was the fullest it had been in months. Uniforms mixed with shirtsleeves and jackets in the public while the snug was full of raincoats and hats.

The largest hat was perched on the head of a woman in her sixties with a hare-lip. She finished her milk stout and licked away her froth moustache.

'I'll 'ave another,' she said, banging her glass down on the table. Amy Carlton had developed the art of manipulating others into running around after her. It didn't cross her mind to offer to buy the drinks. She saw her function only as the gulper of ale. She looked longingly at the packet of Smiths' crisps open on the table and mourned the loss of her teeth. Crisps weren't the same sucked.

'You've never finished that already?' said Martha.

'Mother's always been a quick drinker,' said Minnie.

'Good job she doesn't often join us, then,' said Ena. She disliked having Amy Carlton included in the group as she knew she couldn't intimidate her. When it came to domineering, Amy could have given Bonaparte lessons.

'I'll 'ave another,' repeated Amy.

Minnie got to her feet and stood at the bar, trying to attract Annie's attention. She coughed politely but Annie, tapping her hand on the bar in time to the music, didn't hear her.

'Will you just look at 'er. 'Ave you ever seen such a wet weekend?' asked Amy.

'She's doin' her best,' said Martha.

'Well, as usual 'er best isn't use nor ornament to anyone.' Amy lifted her head and bellowed into the bar, 'Service, please!'

Sally and Annie both looked towards the snug and Minnie smiled apologetically at them.

Ena leaned over to Martha and said, 'I can't abide overbearin' women.'

Martha nodded her agreement.

The mirror hanging in the living room steamed over as George washed himself in the enamel bath. He squeezed the soap between his fingers, watching it squelch and change shape before he rubbed it into his skin. His shoulders ached from the weight of his troubles and the water cooled them as he used a jug to ladle it over his head. It wasn't until he started to dry himself that he wondered why he didn't feel self-conscious at being naked in the same room as his sister-in-law. He rubbed the towel down his legs and realised he'd put on weight eating army food. He'd never been bulky but in his youth had spent eighteen months training in a Salford boxing club.

The other side of the screen, Madge sat in an armchair. Arthur Askey was talking on the wireless but her ears heard only the splash of water coming from the tub. She wished she'd made more of an effort for Christmas. To save money and resources she'd decided not to decorate the house, or even buy in especially. There was no turkey, no trimmings, just a leftover chicken pie and a bag of sprouts. She hadn't even got a present to give him.

Walt Greenhalgh was thoroughly enjoying himself. After a hefty feed he'd started on the beer with Jack, and now the family had moved into the Rovers for the rest of the evening. It had already been agreed that he would spend the night in Jim's room and now he gave himself over to enjoyment.

'I don't like the way 'e keeps leerin' at me,' complained Dot.

'He's 'armless enough,' said Vi, her words beginning to slur after three sherries and a bottle of ale. 'I think 'e's a nice lad, an' 'e's our Jim's pal. Mind you, 'e is funny lookin', i'nt he?'

'Reminds me of that china pig's 'ead in front window of Piggott's,' said Dot grimacing, 'all podgy round the eyes and red cheeks. I'm lockin' me door tonight.'

'Bang on wall if 'e tries owt,' said Elsie. 'I'll rush round wi' me rollin' pin.'

The three women laughed, Vi's cackle rising above the others.

'It sounds a bit rough in the public tonight,' said Ena, screwing up her nose.

'It'll be that Elsie Tanner,' agreed Martha, ' 'Er sort lower the tone.'

Daisy Todd sneezed into her shawl then used the edge to wipe her nose, leaving a trail of snot on the wool.

'I used to like Christmas when I were a girl,' said Bessie Tatlock, 'an orange an' a 'andful of nuts in me stockin'. It weren't much, but we were 'appy.'

'Aye,' agreed Martha. 'I were in town the other day lookin' in the windows. Kids today don't know they're born. Dolls an' books an' train sets.'

'What 'ave you got your Lily?' asked Ena.

'I've run 'er up a dress for her doll and Percy's made some furniture for her little 'ouse.'

'A dress? The girl's fourteen, isn't she? What she want a doll's dress for?'

'She likes 'er doll,' said Martha defensively. 'I suppose you've bought your Vera something sophisticated.'

'I bought 'er a box of 'ankies from Swindley's. Plain white.'

'Is that it? Honestly, Ena, the way you treat that girl. She's eighteen. She doesn't want 'ankies. She wants a nice blouse or a bit of makeup.'

'No daughter o' mine's goin' about wi' a painted face!'

'I've sent Beattie a colouring book an' some crayons,' said Bessie, her eyes filling with tears.

The other women stopped glaring at each other. Ena patted her knee. 'She'll be 'ome soon, love.'

'I'm worried she'll 'ave forgotten who I am. Some nights I can't get to sleep so I go into 'er room and lie on 'er patch-work, 'ave a cuddle wi' 'er rabbit, Mr Flopsy –' She broke off and gulped at her ale.

'She's very lucky to get a colouring book,' said Ena. 'All I'll get this Christmas is a frozen lavvy.'

An hour later the atmosphere in the Rovers had cheered up. Mrs Foyle led the regulars in a chorus of 'Run Rabbit' and Annie delighted in the regular ping of the cash register as it opened its drawer to consume more and more coins. The Todd party was the most vocal, and Annie turned a blind eye when Dot stood on the table and started to dance. Walt cheered her on, whistling and stamping his foot. Elsie lifted her glass as Dot kicked out her foot. Annie's bar chairs were incredibly uncomfortable when you were full term, but there was no way Elsie Tanner was going to miss a good party.

Over at the bar, Thomas Hewitt and Jack Todd jeered at Dot. Thomas called out for her to lift her skirt higher, causing Sally to swipe at him with a cloth.

'That's your niece you're talkin' to, yer dirty 'ound!' she said.

'I'm only lookin',' he said.

'Well, don't.' She turned to serve someone and wished they'd all just go home. She hated being the only sober person in the room and was grateful that after tonight she wouldn't have to pull another pint. She couldn't wait to be on the other side of the bar watching Annie Walker run herself ragged.

Harry Hewitt stood next to his father at the bar and made eye-contact with his cousin. 'When you're ready, Sal.'

She smiled at him. He'd always been her favourite playfellow and for years she'd had a crush on him. She could still remember bawling her eyes out when she'd been told first cousins couldn't marry each other. When Auntie Mary had gone pots-for-rags with the carving knife she'd stayed up with him all night, comforting him. He was tall and gormless, completely harmless and amiable. He'd suffered the brunt of his father's criticism and disapproval for years. Thomas had wanted a boozy fist-fighter for a son and was disturbed at the way Harry always seemed to be shrugging his shoulders at life.

'Yes, Harry?' said Sally.

'I'll 'ave three pints and a kiss,' shouted Walt, barging in front of him.

'You'll just 'ave to wait, love,' said Sally, 'I'm servin'.'

'But I'm a soldier. I'm more important than 'im! 'E's in civvies!' Walt lurched into Harry and sneered at him. 'Why aren't you in uniform?'

'I don't mind if you serve him first,' said Harry.

'Can't you answer me? I said, "why aren't you in uniform?"' repeated the soldier.

Harry looked embarrassed and was nudged in the ribs by his father. 'Go on, tell 'im. Tell 'im how you're unfit. Tell 'im about yer feet.'

'You look fit enough to me,' said Walt, 'What's up? You a coward?'

'I think you've 'ad too much to drink,' said Sally.

'Belt up an' give me three pints.'

'Don't talk to 'er like that,' said Harry, glaring at him.

'Why? What you goin' to do? Yer coward!'

Walt surprised everyone by lunging at Harry and hitting him across the face. Harry staggered and received another blow as Walt punched him in the stomach.

'You bastard!' shouted Sally.

Harry went down on the floor and Walt kicked him in the gut.

'Do something!' Sally screamed at her father.

Jack Todd looked around, trying to work out what was going on.

Harry groaned as Walt got in another kick. Sally opened the bar flap and made a grab for Walt's arm but she was beaten to it by Ena who, alerted by screams, rushed when others stood still. She grasped Walt's raised arm and twisted it. 'I reckon it's time you went 'ome, son.'

He glared into her eyes, weighing up the possibility of striking the woman. She stared back at him defiantly. Slowly he lowered his hand and allowed himself to be led from the bar. Sally bent to attend to Harry and frowned at her father and uncle. 'Call yerselves men!' she said. ' 'E's worth six of you!'

In the front bedroom of No. 13, down the street from the gossipy old biddies and the brawling men, two lovers gave themselves over to the pleasure of exploring each other's bodies for the first time. George arched his back and gasped. His pelvis shuddered and he fell against Madge. She stroked his hair and kissed his cheek. They lay in silence for a few moments, with Madge pulling the sheet over them.

'I can't believe we've just done . . .'

She silenced him with a kiss and glanced down to where his nipple rubbed roughly against hers. The clock at St Mary's chimed midnight. They lay together, listening to the sounds of the night. On the twelfth stroke Madge whispered in his ear, 'Happy Christmas.'

CHAPTER SIX

January 1940 Food rationing starts, Elsie christens Annie Walker's carpet.

It had happened. Christmas had come and gone and the war hadn't ended. The residents were resigned to living under the dark cloud of war. The men were gone and it was time for the women to take on their jobs. Sally and Dot transferred from Elliston's raincoat factory to Lewinsky's uniform factory on Monday 1 January 1940. Both girls had been looking forward to a change but found themselves manning identical machines to those they'd left behind. They sat side by side, seaming arms on to heavy jackets. The hours were longer at Elliston's, for the same pay and the girls cursed the rush of patriotism that had caused them to sign up for war work.

After Walt's visit, having gleaned information on what her son was doing in France, Vi refused to let her daughters grumble about their lot. 'There's the likes of our Jim and Walt guardin' the Siegfried Line, 'angin' about in all sorts of weather and then there's you two, sittin' down on yer backsides all day in the warm, moanin' and carryin' on. You want yer legs slappin'.'

It was the coldest January for years. The harsh tones of the cobbles disappeared under a thick blanket of snow, which gave no comfort to the residents as their houses turned into ice-boxes. Draughty windows, ill-fitting doors and bare floorboards forced them to huddle close to their fires and worry about the future now that the coal merchant had imposed rationing. Rationing was a word on everyone's lips, and the morning of the eighth found Mrs Foyle preparing for battle as she followed government instructions and started rationing her supplies of bacon, sugar and butter. She propped up notices explaining the allocations: four ounces of bacon per person, per week, twelve ounces of sugar, four ounces of butter. She used wax crayons in an attempt to make the notices as jolly as possible, reckoning on enough abuse without appearing too official.

All went well until half-way through the morning when Vi Todd burst through the door. Pushing past the couple of customers waiting, she marched up to the counter. 'What do you mean by refusin' to serve my mother-in-law?'

Mrs Foyle carried on serving. 'Just the luncheon meat, is it, Mrs Earnshaw?'

'I'm talkin' to you!' shouted Vi. 'Just because you've been on the stage don't mean to say you can get all hoity-toity with me, madam.'

Mrs Foyle placed the tinned meat on the counter and looked at Vi. 'I am busy with a customer, Mrs Todd. If you'd like to wait, I'll see you when I'm able.'

Vi ignored her and carried on, banging on the counter with her fist. The women behind her mouthed their disapproval.

'My mother-in-law's been shoppin' 'ere from the day this shop were built in nineteen hundred and two. Years before you arrived on the scene. She's been a faithful customer, a loyal one, all these years. Never let her slate run into the next week –'

'Mrs Todd, please. There is a queue.'

The three other women in the shop glared at Vi but she ignored them, in the same way she ignored everything and everyone that threatened to put her off her stride.

'Just ask your 'usband. 'E'll tell you. She's spent every bit of money she's 'ad in this shop an' now you turn round and throw 'er out, tellin' 'er she's no longer welcome.'

'Mrs Todd,' said the shopkeeper, struggling to keep her temper, 'I don't know what tales Mrs Todd senior has been telling you but I can assure you I have not thrown her out. She came to see me earlier on with her ration book for some sugar and I pointed out that I could not serve her sugar as she hasn't registered with me. I'm not expecting her, haven't sugar for her, and therefore can't serve her.'

'Like she said, then, you've refused 'er custom! She's at my 'ouse now, sobbin' into 'er shawl.'

Vi turned to her unsympathetic audience. 'A woman of seventy-one, who's worked all 'er life on looms, a mother, grandmother. All she wanted was 'er twelve ounces, like what the paper says we're entitled to. She 'asn't got many pleasures in life. A spoonful of sugar in 'er tea. That's all she's asking for. Some people,' she glared at Mrs Foyle, 'can be as petty as 'Iter. Give 'em a little bit of power an' it goes to their 'eads!'

'Right, that's it. Get out of my shop!' Mrs Foyle stormed round the counter, taking Vi by surprise. She pulled open the door with such force that the bell was nearly knocked off its casings.

'Come on, get out. Go to Hetty Morris an' see if she'll take you on. I don't need your custom – I'm always having to chase you to settle up.'

The shoppers exchanged glances, their suspicions concerning the idle Todds confirmed.

'You can't throw me out,' said Vi.

'Why not?' demanded Mrs Foyle.

'Well . . .' Vi searched for a reason but couldn't find one.

At that moment Ena Sharples arrived on the scene. She was struck by the rarity of seeing Mrs Foyle not only out from behind the counter but also holding the door open. 'What's goin' on?' she asked. 'Is there bother?'

Vi wasn't prepared to have Ena witness her discomfort. She walked out with as much dignity as she could muster.

'Now then, Mrs Earnshaw. Just the luncheon meat, was it?' Mrs Foyle brushed her hands down her apron, feeling pleased with herself.

Bessie Tatlock saw no point in keeping her daughter in Blackpool any longer. Obviously it was all a hoax: no bombs, no gas. Hitler was too busy in France to bother with England. Beattie should be at home, with her parents, not stuck in some squalid seaside shack.

She sat in the Barlows' living room and let the shawl drop from her shoulders. 'It's ever so good of you, Mrs Barlow, only I've never been one for writin' and my Albert's only good wi' figures.'

'That's all right, Mrs Tatlock. I had the writing paper out anyway. I generally write to Mr Barlow this time of day.'

'Oh,' said Bessie, interested in the chance of gleaning a titbit. 'How's 'e gettin' on?'

Marjorie, Ida's sister-in-law, smirked behind her magazine. It made it sound as if Frank were away at boarding-school. 'His last letter was just before Christmas and he said the officers were going to be serving Christmas dinner to them in a big barn. Fancy that, all them stripes doshing out turkey and bread sauce.'

'Did they have turkey?' asked Bessie. 'We could only afford chicken.'

'Well, Frank's been stationed near a farm so they probably killed one of their birds.'

'Sounds very cosy. 'Asn't he done any fighting yet?'

'No.'

'Oh.' Bessie was disappointed.

Ida pulled a sheet of paper loose from her writing folder and asked, 'What shall I put?'

Bessie bit her lip in concentration. Ida waited patiently, pen in hand. Then: 'Dear Beattie,' she wrote, as Bessie dictated, 'yer dad says nothin's 'appening so come 'ome, Mum.'

Ida paused and smiled at her neighbour. 'Don't you think that's a bit short? Perhaps we could say something about how much you're missing her, how lonely it is without her.'

'Yes,' said Beattie, 'that sounds lovely. Tell you what, you write what you think's best.'

While Ida bent to her task Bessie eyed Marjorie with suspicion. She'd seen little of the tall woman since she'd moved in and hadn't had a chance to figure her out. Ena Sharples had said she didn't trust any woman who had got to her age and didn't have a wedding ring on her finger. Bessie was inclined to agree. She'd heard that Marjorie Barlow enjoyed her job so much that she had little interest in men, but that couldn't be right.

Sensing the older woman's eyes on her, Marjorie lowered the *Picture Post* and forced herself to smile.

'Settlin' in are you?' asked Bessie.

'Yes, thank you.'

'Must be a weight off Mr Barlow's mind to know someone's keepin' his wife company.'

Marjorie smiled.

Kenneth stirred in his cot, attracting Bessie's attention. 'Ah,' she said. 'Children are such a blessin', aren't they?'

'Yes. I've not got any myself.'

'No, 'cos you're not married, are you? Still, don't worry, Mr Right's bound to turn up sooner or later. I met Mr Tatlock when I was nineteen. But we can't all be blessed so early on, can we?'

Marjorie grimaced at the thought of being landed with anyone like dull Albert.

At the other end of the Street another unmarried woman was thinking of her Mr Right, only in her case she knew she'd found him. The two days Madge and George had spent together had been the most wonderful of her life. They'd passed most of their time in bed, only emerging to raid the larder. She couldn't remember how it had happened, just that it had seemed the most natural thing in the world. To cling so tight to someone you had loved in secret. To give yourself over to just a few precious hours of passion. Behind the net curtains, where people wandered up and down the Street, she knew it would seem sinful, but that was because their minds were grubby and they only saw what they wanted to. She knew different. She knew that the Hardman marriage was a farce, that May was a cold, distant woman who treated George worse than a dog. She couldn't work out how Christine had ever been conceived and George had told her that as soon as she'd discovered she was pregnant May had put a ban on lovemaking that had never been lifted. He deserved better than that. He needed warmth and affection. He was a good man and now, finally, he was hers.

George had returned to duty a different man. He walked taller, smiled more and had promised he would write to May and tell her their marriage was over. They'd have to run away somewhere, where no one would know them, where no one would be able to point a finger and condemn. They'd go far away, somewhere safe.

Her letters held no caution as she wrote of what he meant to her and how it would be. 'How long must we be apart? How long until I can hold you again in my arms, stroke your hair and whisper of my love? I have a pain inside me, a void that fills the pit of my being since you are not with me.'

He received them greedily. George Hardman wasn't a man to take advantage of a desirable woman purely for the sport of it, and Madge reminded him of how May had once been. She laughed, listened intently and her eyes shone with love when she looked at him. He hadn't told anyone about their love, hadn't boasted of his conquest. It wasn't like that. She was no casual fling. She was the real thing.

His letters were as unguarded as hers. 'You talk of a pain inside, I also have that, but more, much more. I lie in bed at night, listening to the snores and I think of you, of your smile and your eyes, and I long to kiss them. To kiss all of you and never to stop . . .'

While the letters crossed the Channel, May Hardman strolled along the seafront at Blackpool, pushing Christine in her pram. For the first time in years she felt content, away from prying eyes and small minds. Away from the confines of a back-street terrace. Away from her husband, who looked at her as if he were a wounded puppy. So easy to push around, forever under her feet, bothering her. The one letter he'd sent her had said he was in France. Well, the French were welcome to him.

Annie had enlisted the help of Martha Longhurst as an emergency barmaid. She rose to the occasion by digging her best dress out of the wardrobe and applying rouge to her normally bare face. The effect reminded Annie of an Aunt Sally doll she'd seen on a fairground in Morecambe. Normally she would have worried about customers being put off their beer by the sight but since beer was a precious commodity perhaps that would be a good thing.

Vi Todd was still smarting over her run-in with Mrs Foyle, even though two days had passed. She sat with her daughter and continued on her well-trodden road. 'I think she ought to be reported. There 'as to be some code or other these shop-keepers must keep to. An' if keepin' a civil tongue in yer head isn't one of their rules then it bleedin' well ought to be.'

'Oh, Mam, will you stop chunnerin'on about Mrs Foyle?' said Sally. 'I've been 'ard at that machine all day, listenin' to all them women goin' on about their problems. I want some peace an' quiet.'

'Charmin',' said Vi, with a sniff. 'Just you think of all them times you've gone on about some fella or other, carryin' on, weepin' and wailin'. You've never stopped to think I might want some peace an' quiet, 'ave you? Oh, no, use me like a convenience all of you! But when I've got something to moan about, when I've been attacked and shouted at in public, it's a different story.'

'Mam, will you shut it? You're always bein' shouted at in public. You like bein' shouted at in public. It gives you chance to 'ave a good bust-up. What's annoyed you this time is that she threw you out, you didn't walk out.'

'Think you know it all, don't yer?' said Vi, before drinking from her glass. 'Well, you know nowt.'

Sally turned in her chair and decided to let her mother sulk. It was a shame that all the soldiers and sailors had gone again. They'd brightened things up over Christmas. She'd been caught by a tall Geordie under the mistletoe and had kissed him until her jaw ached. She closed her eyes and remembered the sensation against her thigh as she'd felt him stir beneath his trousers.

The black-out curtain was pulled open and Dot appeared, clutching a bundle of newspapers to her coat. She joined her family. 'There was ever such a long queue and I 'ad to wait until Mr Jackson put more chips on.' She unwrapped the package, to reveal three smaller bundles, which she handed round. Vi opened hers and started to eat her fish and chips.

'Excuse me,' called Annie, from behind the bar, 'what do you think you're doin'?'

''Avin' us tea,' replied Vi, sticking a chip into her mouth.

'Not in here you're not. This is a public house, not a works canteen.'

'Don't blame us,' said Vi. 'If you wanna moan get on to Mr Chamberlain. 'E's the one who said we 'ad to watch our coal. Well, no one can say the Todds don't do their bit. We're savin' our coal by spendin' more time in 'ere.'

'Mrs Todd, I can't have the smell of fish and chips assaulting my customers. This is a public house.'

Vi interrupted, 'Yes, an' we're the public, an' we eat in our 'ouse so why can't we eat in 'ere? You sell crisps an' stuff. There's no difference, an' to show you I don't mind you interrupting us tea I'll 'ave two lemonades an' a brown ale. These chips could do wi' a good swill down.'

Annie walked away from the bar. What was the point in trying to maintain any sense of normality? She might just as well give up. If they wanted to live like animals, then why should she bother to refine them? As soon as the war was over, she told herself, she and Jack would sell up and move to a quiet country pub with bare beams and horse brasses.

In the snug, Bessie showed Ena the letter that had come in the morning post.

'It's from this Mrs Forsythe, her that our Beattie's stayin' with. She says that Beattie were upset by my letter and doesn't want to come 'ome, seein' as 'ow she's 'avin' such a nice time.' Her voice was strained as she asked, 'She can't stop us from fetchin' our Beattie 'ome, can she? She's our daughter.'

'Course she is. You want to take this letter down to Bessie Street School and demand–'

Ena broke off as a loud bang came from the public bar.

The pub door flew open and the curtain was pulled roughly aside. Chill air blasted in through the open door, Annie turned in alarm. 'Who on earth . . .'

She stopped as her eyes fell upon the shape of Elsie Tanner, clinging to the table nearest the door. She was panting and Thomas Hewitt, at the table, lifted his pint pot in alarm.

'I need 'elp!' cried Elsie.

Sally was on her feet and at Elsie's side, 'What is it, love? 'As it started?'

Elsie squeezed her eyes shut and nodded.

'They're comin' one after the other,' she said.

Thomas jumped away from the table.

' 'Elp me!' pleaded Elsie.

Ena emerged from the snug and clicked her tongue against her teeth. 'Hurt, does it? Well, you should 'ave thought of that nine months ago when you were 'avin' your pleasure.'

'I don't need a lecture from you.' Elsie glared at her.

'Don't you? Well, from where I'm standin' I reckon you're wrong there. You know, I'm surprised at you, Elsie Tanner. I always thought alley-cats crawled off to be on their own to give birth, not interrupt folk suppin'.'

'Mrs Sharples,' objected Sally, 'I don't think this is the time for that. Elsie needs 'elp.'

' 'Er? Need 'elp?' Ena laughed. 'That's rich. I'd 'ave thought she were beyond salvation, meself.'

Elsie glanced around the room. 'Won't anybody 'elp me?'

Vi stood up and made towards the bar. Annie saw where she was going and sprang forward. 'Out of me way, Annie Walker. Sally, bring Elsie through.'

'Where do you think you're goin'?' asked Annie.

'Into your livin' room,' said Vi. 'Or would you rather she had the baby in the select?'

'You can't bring her into my living room.' Annie was aghast at the idea of customers entering her sanctum.

'What's up? Bit of a mess, is it? Don't be proud.'

Vi barged past Annie and helped Sally support Elsie, who cried out in pain as she passed through the bar door. Ena finished the last of her stout then followed the procession.

'Where are you goin', Ena? I thought you didn't like Elsie Tanner,' said Martha.

'I don't, but I'm not passin' up a chance to see Annie Walker's doin's. Besides, I'm the best midwife round 'ere. That bairn'll be in safe hands with me to guide it into the world.'

As always, Annie's living room was spotless. The only threat to the white linen tablecloth and thick carpet was little Billy but, as Annie found it most convenient to place his playpen in the hallway next to the bar, even his grubby fingers seldom came to rest in her haven. Following the group through the pub, Ena tutted to herself at the sight of Billy sitting forlornly on the hall lino, sucking a building brick. Pausing only to tell herself what an ugly child he was, she hurried into Annie's living room. Her eyes darted around the ornate room: on the polished top of the sideboard stood a photograph of the Walkers' wedding day, surrounded by a silver frame. Jack Walker was handsome and Ena felt certain he was too fine a man to be wasted on Lady Annie. Apart from the frame, all the other ornaments and furniture appeared aged and worn. Good quality but no sign of the finery that Ena had come to imagine filling Annie's nest. She was disappointed.

Annie looked on anxiously as Vi and Sally lowered Elsie to the floor.

Ena stood in the doorway and rolled up her sleeves.

'Go away, Mrs Sharples,' said Elsie.

'I'm goin' nowhere until that baby's born. Vi Todd might look as if she knows what she's doin' but she's more used to gettin' rid of babies than birthin' them.'

Vi glared at Ena. 'What do you mean by that?'

'What I say, deny it if you dare, but I've seen them poor girls knockin' at yer door at night.' Ena turned to attend to Elsie. 'Besides, she stinks of vinegar.'

'Put one finger on me, Mrs Sharples, an' I'll bite it off!' warned Elsie, before screaming and clutching hold of Ena.

'Comin' fast, are they, lass?' Ena asked quietly.

Elsie nodded and started to cry. 'I'm scared, Mrs Sharples.'

'There's no need to be. I've delivered 'undreds of babies, and I'll look after you. For sake of bairn, mind, not you.'

'Do you think you can make it upstairs?' she asked.

'I'll try —' Elsie broke off as she felt wetness between her legs.

Sally drew away as the fluid hit the carpet.

'My Wilton!' exclaimed horrified Annie.

'It's comin'!' shrieked Elsie.

'We've not time to get 'er upstairs, we'll just 'ave to make do 'ere.' Ena turned to Vi in wonder. 'What is it about war babies wantin' to get out quick? It's another Kenneth Barlow, is this one.'

In the pub, Dot picked at the remains of her mother's fish and crossed to the bar. 'Give us a gin, will you?' she asked.

Martha folded her arms. 'I'm not that green,' she said. 'You're under age. You can 'ave another lemonade.'

'Oh, go on,' said Dot, 'no one's lookin'. You can 'ave some chips.'

At the mention of the word Martha felt her stomach rumble. She checked to make sure Annie wasn't in sight then lowered her voice: 'Go on then.'

The exchange was made and Martha stuffed a handful of chips into her mouth, savouring the taste. 'Oh,' she said, with her mouth full, 'they've no salt on them.'

'Open some crisps an' nick the blue packet,' suggested resourceful Dot.

Before Martha had chance, Sally wandered into the bar from the back room. 'It's a girl,' she announced. 'Mrs Walker said I could take Elsie a double gin.'

A few days after the arrival of the new baby, Albert leant out of his back bedroom window and shouted down into the yard at No. 5.

'Hey, Tom Hayes, 'ang about!'

The boy looked about him in alarm. He was playing truant from school and was wary of policemen, who had a habit of materialising from thin air.

'Up 'ere, lad.'

Tom looked up and saw Albert waving from his window. ' 'Ello Mr Tatlock. What's to do?'

'Come round to my backin'. I'll be down in a tick.'

Several ticks later, after hopping down the stairs with his leg in plaster, Albert opened his back door and let the lad in. 'Now then, Tom, 'ow do you fancy doin' yer bit for the war?'

Tom looked at Albert with distrust. 'I'm not doin' owt wi' Mrs Sharples,' he said, warily.

'No. It's men's work I need you for. Are you doin' owt this after?'

Tom remained suspicious. 'I'm not sure.'

'Look, lad,' said Albert, 'I wouldn't ask if it weren't important, would I? It's vital war work I need you for. Surely you can spare a few hours for the sake of your country.'

Tom's mind spun with possibilities. 'Is it top secret? Like spyin'?' he asked hopefully.

'Summat like that,' said Albert, avoiding Tom's eyes.

Ten minutes later the unlikely couple stood side by side in a corner of the park. During their walk through the streets Tom had convinced himself that Albert was a cunning spy who had carefully crafted a secret identity for himself. Who would ever suspect little Albert of being anything but a boring, blustering clerk? It was really clever how the government chose covers for their agents. As they neared the park Tom worried briefly if Albert was one of those perverts his father preached against and that he was going to be led astray in the shrubbery. But he told himself that with one leg in plaster Albert would be a pushover if he had to fight his way to freedom.

Walking past the bandstand Tom saw a group of men standing looking at the grass. Perhaps one of them was a contact Albert needed him to meet.

' 'Ow do, Albert,' said a man with a pipe.

Tom felt certain this was a password and that Albert would say something about red cows being hard to milk.

'Fair to middlin',' was Albert's disappointing reply. He turned to Tom and pointed to an area of grass cornered off by string. A post in the middle bore a piece of paper with '16' written on it. 'Right, 'ere we are, lad.'

Tom looked at the plot in bewilderment. 'Where are we?'

'At my allotment. I've been given this to 'elp grow spuds an' stuff.'

Tom stared at him in dismay. 'You said it were important war work!'

'So it is. We've been told to dig for victory.' He thrust a spade at Tom. 'Only with this leg I can't do much diggin'. It won't take you long, just dig it all over. It'll keep you warm anyroad.'

Tom refused to take the spade. 'Get lost,' he said. 'I'm not your slave.'

'Now then, lad,' said Albert. 'We've all got to do our duty. You dig this lot for me an' I'll forget my duty as to tellin' your dad about you waggin' school. I'm right, aren't I? You should be behind your desk now, shouldn't you?'

Tom glared at him and grabbed the spade. 'Where shall I start?'

'Wherever you like, lad. It's all got to be done.' Albert chuckled as Tom stepped over the string and drove the spade into the ground. It didn't go far.

'It's rock 'ard!'

'Aye, lad, that's because there were a ground frost last night. Keep at it, you'll soon make 'ead-way.'

Albert fumbled in his waistcoat pocket for his tobacco paper. It was going to be a long job.

Elsie stood in the vestry doorway and handed the bunch of flowers to a surprised Ena. 'Just by way of a thank-you,' she muttered in embarrassment.

'That's very nice of you. Mind, I'll still be charging my usual ten shillin's.'

'I know. I just wanted to give you something extra.'

'How is she, little Linda?'

'She's got 'ealthy pair of lungs on 'er!' laughed Elsie. 'Just like 'er mother!'

' 'Ave you written to her daddy yet?'

'Doesn't seem much point, Mrs Sharples. 'E's not written since 'e went away. Doesn't care for either of us.'

'Don't go writin' 'im off like that. There's many a fella who's been licked into shape by the sight of his first baby. You write and let him know. It could make all the difference.'

Elsie pulled the shawl around her child. 'I'd best be off. It's still cold out an' she should be wrapped up warm.'

Ena saw her visitor out and smiled to herself as she settled down again in front of her stove. Despite being cast as the demon king by her residents she loved babies. Their vulnerability appealed to her and each new delivery caused her to wonder anew at the work of the one who crafted them inside the womb. She could never understand people who refused to believe in God. Who else could bring forth such a miracle? All those little identities, those fresh slates waiting for the world to etch misery and delight upon them. Ena had had three children: two girls and a boy. Little Ian had been born in the lean years when her malnourished body had not been able to sustain him. Just hours after birth he'd died in her arms. They'd not been able to afford a burial but the grave-digger at St Mary's had been a pal of Sharples and had placed the tiny body in a box under one of the oaks in the churchyard. No gravestone marked the plot but each year Ena laid a bunch of bluebells under the tree on the anniversary of his birth and death.

Her daughters, Madge and Vera, had both survived. Madge had left home as soon as she'd been able and lived on the other side of Manchester but for all Ena saw of her she might as well have emigrated to Australia. Her departure had taken place after a blazing row, during which Ena had screamed that she never wanted to set eyes on Madge again. That had been four years ago and she hadn't. Vera, the last of the children God had blessed her with, was neither use nor ornament. Ena viewed the unfortunate girl as her own cross, which she bore without complaint. She knew the neighbours felt she made more of Vera's backwardness than was necessary but they saw her as a sturdy young woman with a vacant expression. To Ena she would always be the vulnerable child.

Having set Vera to work in the Mission, counting hymn books, Ena savoured a few precious hours alone with her thoughts. She closed her eyes and shifted her body on the horsehair sofa. The ticking of the mantel clock brought her a feeling of security, as it had when it had stood in her family home in Inkerman Street. Pawned each Monday morning, her mother had always striven to have it back on the mantel the following Friday, when Dad was paid. Like the smell of carbolic and freshly baked bread, its ticking always put the world to rights.

She was disturbed by a knocking on the door that separated her snug vestry from the draughty Mission hall. She got up and walked cautiously to the door but didn't open it. Instead she called out, 'Who's there?'

'It's me, Mrs Sharples, Percy Longhurst.'

Ena opened the door and admitted the scrawny fellow. 'Whatever are you doin' creepin' round my Mission at this time of night?'

'I was just checkin' on the boiler room. Vera said you were in.'

After having received orders to turn the basement of the Mission into an air-raid shelter for the residents of Coronation Street, Ena and Percy had spent three days clearing out decades' worth of junk and erecting the bunk-beds issued by the town hall. Albert had got under their feet by standing about, making suggestions, and after a while Ena had sent him off to mither someone else. She'd been surprised to find Percy such a help in lifting and carrying as she'd always had him down for a wet streak of a man, especially in the days when her Alfred had been alive and they'd stood together at the Rovers' bar. Alfred had been twice the man Percy was, but they'd been best friends so Ena always tried not to speak harshly to him. 'Why were you checkin' down there?' she asked.

'It's a clear sky,' explained Percy. 'Just the sort of night Jerry'll strike. Best to be forewarned.'

Percy was a thin, weak-looking man, who had given the best years of his life to the railway and was now employed as a station porter. Ena had known him since before he'd married Martha and although she didn't know much about him she realised he was lying. He looked more shifty than normal and kept his eyes downcast. She decided she didn't want him in her vestry, whatever his reasons for visiting.

'Good to know you're on top of things,' she said, holding open the door for him to leave.

He cleared his throat. 'I don't want to go just yet . . . Ena,' he said. 'There's something I've been meanin' to say to you.'

'Oh, aye?' She eyed him suspiciously.

'Yes. These last few weeks, workin' alongside you, well . . . I've enjoyed meself.'

She nodded.

'I've always liked you, Ena . . .' he stammered, looking at his feet. 'You've a very caring nature. Oh, I know you try to hide it. But it's there.'

'Is it?'

'Yes. You're a woman with a big heart.'

She laughed nervously. 'Well, that's a nice thing to say. Thank you.'

'I've not finished. My Martha, she's a very cold woman. She doesn't understand a man needs more than a hot dinner to keep him going. If you follow my drift.'

Ena didn't just follow, her mind was galloping ahead and she grew anxious to stop him. 'I'm not sure you should say anything else, Percy. Martha's been a good friend to me over the years, aye, and a good wife to you.'

'You only think she's your friend. She calls you something rotten behind your back. I stand up for you all the time, but you know Martha, she's got a very cruel tongue.' He moved towards her and she instantly shrank back from him. There wasn't much to him and she knew she could fend him off if necessary but his presence was still alarming. 'I just want you to know how I feel, Ena. Just in case.'

'In case of what?'

'In case anything should 'appen to Martha. When the bombs start fallin', as they're bound to. Any day now. Well, if anythin' did 'appen to Martha, I'd be a free man again.' He placed his hand on her arm, making her flinch. 'And I'd be ready to be *your* man.'

The smell of his breath so close to her face gave Ena the strength she needed. 'You've been drinkin'! You don't know what you're sayin'.'

'I – I only 'ad a couple, for Dutch courage,' he slurred.

'I think you'd better leave. Vera'll be in here any minute and questions'll be asked.'

He nodded and crossed to the door. 'I'll call tomorrow. In uniform. That way folk'll think it's ARP business. Goodnight.'

She bolted the door behind him and shuddered. Nasty little man, with his nasty ideas. As if she'd look twice at him. Not a patch on her Alfred. Still, it made a change to have a chap stuttering his love for her. She looked in the small mirror on her bookcase and regarded her reflection. She'd just had her fortieth birthday and found her first grey hair but she knew she was still a handsome woman, and her waist was only a few inches wider than it had been on her wedding day. She hadn't let herself go like Martha Longhurst. Yes, Percy had been right, Martha did have a tongue on her that could cut steel. And whatever did he mean about Martha calling her behind her back?

CHAPTER SEVEN

Spring 1940 The Phoney War ends and bombs fall on Weatherfield.

'Now Churchill's leadin' us, you watch, it'll all change. 'E'll soon have 'Itler on the run.' World authority on strategy and politics, Thomas Hewitt beat out his pipe on the Rovers' bar and dug in his pocket for a pipe-cleaner.

'Oh, yes,' agreed Albert Tatlock. 'Our lads'll be 'ome in no time. I never thought much of Chamberlain. 'E's a keen fisherman you know, I read about it in paper.'

'I've never seen the point to fishin',' said Thomas. 'Stood there with a rod in yer 'and waitin' for some minnow to tek a bite. I don't reckon it meself.'

'No,' agreed Albert.

' 'Ow's yer leg?' asked Thomas.

'It's bin all right since they took the cast off. Doctor said I were lucky. Could 'ave bin worse.'

'I remember a chap in the trenches with me. There was this bang and we was knocked to ground. When we got up he pointed to a leg beside us on ground and said, "Is that yours or mine?" I 'ad a count and said, "I've both mine still," so 'e looked down and said "Bloody 'ell, it's mine." Never felt a thing, straight off.'

'I've got floatin' shrapnel,' said Albert proudly.

'Oh, aye? Where is it?'

'I've not felt it for a while. Sometimes I feel it in me side, then in a day or two it moves on.'

'Fancy that,' said Thomas.

'It don't 'urt or anythin'. I got it when a mine exploded near me dug-out. That were on Somme. Fella next to me was there one minute then, whoosh! gone, and all I got were a piece of shrapnel. Amazin', really.'

'Aye.'

'Have you two quite finished?' asked Annie.

'Nay, lass, mine's only 'alf drunk,' said Thomas.

'I wasn't referring to your drinks. I was referring to your appalling choice of conversation. Do you think I want to listen to tales of legs being blown off and people being killed when my husband is goodness knows where staring danger in the face?'

Albert shifted uncomfortably. 'Nay, lass, we weren't thinkin', sorry.'

'If you don't know where 'e is,' asked Thomas, 'how do you know 'e's starin' death in face?'

Annie looked at him with contempt and marched off to the snug, where Ena was tapping on the counter with a sixpence.

'Mrs Sharples. How would you like it if I took to knocking on your woodwork over at the Mission with coins of the realm?'

'If that's what it took to get me attention I reckon you'd be justified. I've bin stood 'ere for nearly five minutes,' Ena exaggerated. 'You've bin ignorin' me.'

'I have not. I've been run off me feet.'

'Well, now you're 'ere I'll 'ave a milk stout.'

'Just the one?' asked Annie, bending down for a bottle.

Ena glanced at the table where Minnie and Martha sat, staring into their glasses. 'Aye, I'm lookin' after me money careful now. If them two want another they can dig into their own purses.'

'That'll be fivepence,' said Annie.

Ena paid her and resumed her seat.

'I think it's very nice of Mr Churchill to give us meat,' said Minnie.

'What do you mean?' asked Martha.

'Mrs Foyle said I could 'ave one shillin' and sixpence worth once a week. That's more than I normally get. Me mother says we should register with Piggott because 'e 'as the best cuts. What do you think, Ena?'

'I think she's right for once in 'er life. I wouldn't go to t'other place, that's for certain. I wouldn't trust anythin' 'e passed on as chicken for a start. There's too many cats go missin' round 'is way.'

'Oh, Ena!' Minnie put her hand to her mouth, 'you don't think ...'

'I do. And 'appen he's got the right idea. There's folk eatin' 'orses in France, yer know. It's that or starve.'

'Well, no one's eatin' my pussy!' said Minnie.

'Oh, give over,' said Martha. 'Your mangy tom would be no more than a mouthful.'

' 'E's beautiful, is my Stinker.' Minnie had named her cat after a character in her favourite wireless programme, *Band Wagon*.

'I see Albert Tatlock's on 'is feet again,' said Martha.

'Aye, and back in uniform too,' said Ena.

'My Percy's very disappointed. 'E'd hoped to continue workin' wi' you, Ena. 'E said as much over breakfast.'

'Did 'e?'

' 'E did.'

'Did 'e say owt else while 'e was at it?'

'Whatever do you mean, Ena?'

'Just wonderin'.' Ena smiled to herself and drank from her glass.

Jack and Vi Todd entered the pub together. While Vi made her way to the snug, Jack nodded to Albert and Thomas and attracted Annie's attention. 'Pint of best and a pale ale for missus. 'Ave you not got wireless on?'

'No,' said Annie, pulling his pint. 'Should I have?'

'Evenin' news says there's goin' to be an important broadcast at nine.'

'By Mr Churchill?' asked Annie, suddenly interested.

'Don't know.' Jack looked at the pub clock, 'It's nearly five to. Can we listen?'

Annie nodded towards the set, which stood in its place beside the snug. 'You'll 'ave to get it warmed up.'

There was a wave of feminine protest when Jack opened the snug door and entered the female sanctuary. 'Beggar down, lot o' you,' he said gruffly, and started fiddling with the wireless.

'We're 'avin' no Sandy McPherson in 'ere, Jack Todd,' said Ena.

'Give over, woman. It's important news.'

The pub was hushed as the customers and Annie drew near to the set as it crackled into life. The BBC news was just coming to an end when the announcer said that the new Secretary of State for War, Mr Anthony Eden, would address the nation.

The women made no objection when Albert and Thomas edged into the snug. Mr Eden sounded earnest, and as he spoke about German tactics there was no other sound from his audience in the Rovers Return. 'We want large numbers of such men in Great Britain who are British subjects, between the ages of seventeen and sixty-five, to come forward now and offer their services in order to make assurance that an invasion would be repelled. The name of the new force which is now to be raised will be the Local Defence Volunteers. This name describes its duties in three words. You will not be paid, but you will receive uniforms and will be armed. In order to volunteer, what you have to do is give your name at your local police station, and then, when we want you, we will let you know . . .'

Albert clapped his hands together, making everyone jump. Without listening to any more of the broadcast he headed out of the bar. 'Right, this is what I've been waitin' for. I'm off to sign up. Who's comin' with me? Thomas?'

'Aye, and if you 'ang on I'll get my 'Arry to come as well.'

'I'm with you too,' said Jack, grabbing his hat from the bar.

The pub emptied of men, leaving the women looking at each other. Annie switched off the wireless.

'By 'eck,' said Ena, 'for a short 'un, Albert moves fast when 'e wants to.'

'Local Defence,' pondered Martha. 'I wonder what it means.'

'It means that if 'Itler gets past RAF, Army and Navy and actually sets foot on British soil we can all sleep safe in our beds because Albert Tatlock and Jack Todd will be defending us.' Ena shook her head in disbelief. 'Why should England tremble?'

Two hours later, unhappy Albert slowly opened his front door. As he closed it behind him he heard his friends singing in the Street. They were drunk. He was sober.

'That you, Albert?' called Bessie.

Who did she think it was? Goering? He opened the door to the living room. Bessie sat in her rocking chair, knitting. It was the same every night. Knit, knit, knit.

'You're late in. Was there a good crowd at the Rovers?'

'I've been down at Tile Street police station.'

She stopped knitting. 'Whatever for? You've not been 'ad up for 'ittin' another policeman, 'ave you?'

'Blimey, woman, that were five year since. We was marchin' for jobs, for goodness sake.'

'What, then? Why 'ave you been to police station?'

'Did you not 'ear on the wireless?'

'I turned it off 'alfway through news. Borin', it were.'

'Mr Eden were on, callin' for volunteers. Men to defend England. 'E said we 'ad to go to the police station.'

'So, you're goin' to be defendin' England, are you?' she asked.

'As it 'appens, no I'm not.'

'But you said –'

'I know what I said!' He sank into a chair and ran his fingers through his thinning hair. 'It's not bleedin' fair. I'm too old to be a regular an' now I can't join this new lot because I'm an ARP warden. Apparently I'm vital to operations.'

'Well,' said Bessie encouragingly, 'that's nice.'

'No, it's not nice. I want a rifle. Not a torch.' He looked pathetic and rejected.

She felt sorry for him. The Great War had been such a big part of his life. He'd been looking forward to another war for years. 'Never mind, love, I'll make us some cocoa.'

'And do you renounce the devil?' Sid Hayes' voice boomed around the Mission hall.

'I renounce the devil,' said Elsie.

Ena sniggered and bent forward to whisper loudly in Vi Todd's ear, 'That'll be news to 'im.'

Elsie glared at Ena then handed Linda to Sid. He supported the baby carefully in one arm, its christening gown hanging over his shoulder.

'Will the godparents please step forward.'

Sally, Dot and Harry Hewitt edged nervously on to the stage.

'Repeat after me –' Sid's words were cut short dramatically by a loud wailing. The congregation looked at each other in bewilderment until Tom Hayes shouted, 'Air raid!'

Ena took charge as the residents started to scramble about, sending chairs in all directions. 'Into the basement. Gas masks on!'

'I haven't got mine with me!' Minnie spun round in terror. Why had she left the blasted thing hanging on the banister today of all days?

Ena rushed into her vestry and grabbed her ARP helmet. Albert had already opened the door leading to the boiler room and was shining his torch down the steps. 'Come on, shake a leg,' he called.

Sid handed Linda back to Elsie while the Todd girls struggled into their gas masks. In the distance there came the sound of a loud boom.

Rose Hayes screamed, 'They're coming! They're coming!'

Esther grasped her mother by the elbow and pushed her towards the basement.

Marjorie Barlow jumped on to the stage and shouted to Ena, 'Is there anything I can do, Mrs Sharples?'

Ena gestured into the vestry. 'Get them blankets off my bed. It'll be chilly down there and those babies will need coverin' up.'

Marjorie ran into the vestry.

'Minnie, get down below. Stop goin' on about your gas mask, I've got a couple of spares down there. Hurry!'

The residents filed down the stairs, running below and emerging into a large bunker running the length of the Mission. Albert went straight to the antiquated stove in the centre and bent to light it. In couples, family groups and singles, the residents entered the room and looked about them for somewhere to sit.

Ena and Percy had done a good job in clearing the place up and, viewed in the light of flickering oil lamps, it looked hospitable. Ida Barlow fell upon one of the bunk beds, cradling Kenneth to her. This was it, she was certain. The building was old and wouldn't stand up to a direct hit. With her helmet and gas mask, Ena looked like an alien from one of Tom Hayes' comics. She followed Marjorie down the stone steps and asked, 'Are we all 'ere?'

No one could understand what she was saying as the mask distorted her words so Ena shone her torch around the group, counting them off in her head.

Jack Todd, Vi, Sally and Dot, Sid Hayes and his hysterical wife Rose, nervous Esther and Tom the tearaway, Albert and Bessie Tatlock, Marjorie Barlow, Ida and her baby, Elsie Tanner and hers, Annie Walker and young Billy, struggling to free himself of the Mickey Mouse gas mask, Thomas and Harry Hewitt, her Vera and Minnie Caldwell. 'Where's Elsie Foyle?' she asked.

Annie Walker must have understood her as she answered, through her own gas mask, 'She's visiting her husband for the day.'

Dust fell from the ceiling as another boom shook the building.

'Carpet bombing, I bet,' shouted Tom, in excitement. 'We should count. There'll be a bomb after each six, I bet.'

Esther hugged the sobbing Rose to her while Sid stood away from his family. He'd been distracted for too long and needed to ignore the situation to continue with his work. 'Would the godparents step forward?' he asked calmly.

The group goggled at him.

'. . . four . . . five . . six . . . BOOM!' said Tom, as the building shook again.

Elsie handed Linda to Sid for a second time while Dot and Sally broke ranks to stand beside her. Their eyes darted round the dimly lit basement as the noise above blocked out all other sound apart from the loud beating of their own hearts. Without being aware of their actions, the Todd sisters grasped each other's hands.

'Do you renounce the devil?' asked Sid.

'. . . two . . . three . . .' counted Tom.

'We renounce him,' repeated the girls, without conviction, eyeing the ceiling warily, as if their original denouncement had caused him to start dropping the bombs in the first place.

'. . . four . . . five . . . six . . .'

A loud crash filled the air and Ena caught sight of the wild panic in her neighbours' eyes, frozen in time before the lamps fell from the wall and they were plunged into darkness. The foundations of the Mission jumped, and one of the bunks jolted from the wall then crashed down on to the stone floor. It caught Dot on the shoulder as it fell and she cried out in pain and sank down. In total darkness, the residents clung to each other in an attempt to remain standing. Dust and masonry fell from the ceiling. Rose's screams filled the air until Ena, guessing at where she stood, slapped her hard across the face.

After the dust had settled, Albert produced his warden's torch and shone it around the shelter. He located one of the lamps and gingerly lit the wick. The flame roared into life, casting light around the basement.

'Linda Tanner, I welcome you to the family of God,' continued Sid, as if nothing had happened, 'May the Lord be gracious unto you, may he cause his face to shine upon you, now and for ever. Amen.'

'Amen,' repeated Ena.

The other residents remained silent.

'. . . three . . . four . . . five . . .' As Tom counted, they all stared up at the ceiling. Ena mouthed a silent prayer.

This time the boom was distant.

'They've gone!' shouted Tom. 'It's all right, Mam, they've gone.'

Rose Hayes looked at her son as if she had no idea who he was. Esther hugged her close and rocked her gently.

Ena looked around at the group. 'No one leaves here until we get the all-clear.'

The residents emerged slowly from their shelter. They were a dishevelled lot, their hair and clothes grey from plaster and mortar dust. In the daylight they blinked and shaded their eyes from the sun, which shone as if nothing was amiss. No one spoke because it didn't seem there was anything to say. Those who had complained of being bored by the war now cursed their stupidity. Dust filled the air outside the Mission as well as inside. Inside mouths it tasted dry and pieces of grit made eyes raw. The sound of fire-engine bells mixed with the wail of the all-clear and a tide of people appeared, some in uniforms, running past the group, along Viaduct Street.

'What's been hit?' asked Albert, grabbing a policeman as he raced past.

'Mawdsley Street chapel's gone.'

Ena felt a shiver run down her spine. The sister chapel to the Mission! Identical down to the wooden chairs. Then, remembering who lived in the house next to the chapel, she cried out, as if stabbed by one of the shards of glass that littered the cobbles. Vera looked at her in alarm, but before she could question her, Ena started to run across the cobbles. As if frightened of losing sight of her, the others followed. She sped past the corner shop and into Mawdsley Street. The chapel was ablaze, the heat overpowering. Glass and bricks were everywhere. She shielded her eyes and searched for the house that was as familiar to her as her own vestry. It wasn't there.

She scrambled over the hoses that lined the street and pushed past a fireman, shouting, 'Mind out of the way.' She stumbled over bricks towards the chapel and caught sight of a familiar figure throwing bricks out of his path. She rushed to him as fast as she could and clutched his arm. 'Percy, lad, where's Martha?'

He turned his face towards her. It was blackened and smeared with blood. His shirt hung off his shoulders in tatters. 'I don't know, Ena! She went to lav and then the siren went. I can't mek out where the backyard used to be!' He dropped a brick and collapsed on a pile of rubble.

She inched forward and bent, cradling him to her. 'She'll be all right, lad, we'll find 'er.'

'She's dead, Ena, an' it's all my fault!'

'Nay, lad.'

'Those things I said to you about 'er? Wishin' 'er gone!'

117

'You'd bin drinkin' . . . I've forgotten all about it.'

'I killed 'er, Ena! She's gone and I'm still 'ere!' He clung to her. 'What am I goin' to do without 'er?'

The blast on Mawdsley Street had blown out some windows at the back of Coronation Street. Elsie returned from the christening to find her net curtains blowing in the wind and glass all over the living room floor. The scullery was in an even sorrier state, with the back door hanging off its hinges. She stepped out and looked at where her wall had once been. There was nothing now between her yard and the half-ruined backs of the Mawdsley Street houses. The fires burned brightly and illuminated the sky dramatically. Elsie looked at the sky and thought it beautiful, like the most glorious of sunsets.

'Amazin', isn't it?'

Elsie turned to acknowledge the voice. It came from Harry Hewitt, who less than an hour before had been standing in for Jim Todd as Linda's godfather. 'I know I shouldn't say it, Harry, but it's almost worth all this to see such a marvellous sky.'

'How's Linda?' he asked.

'She slept through it all, would you believe! Keeps me awake all the night an' then sleeps through that lot!'

Harry gestured towards the blaze. 'I'd best see if I can help.'

'Aye.'

Elsie turned to go back indoors when something caught her eye. 'Harry!'

Alerted by the anxiety in her voice he rushed to her side and looked where she pointed. The wall separating the backyards of Nos. 11 and 13 was no longer in place. The bricks lay on the ground in a heap, and sticking out from underneath was a pair of female legs.

Elsie buried her head in Harry's shoulder.

He called out down the terrace to where his father stood watching the damage with Albert.

'Mr Tatlock! Dad! Over 'ere!'

The men came running and summed up the situation. Albert pulled at the bricks to free whoever was beneath them.

118

Elsie kept a tight hold of Harry. 'Who is it?'

Grimly Albert pushed his helmet out of the way and stood up. 'It's May Hardman's sister. She's dead.'

Elsie gasped and clung to Harry. 'Madge? She said she wouldn't come to the christening but was going to pop round later . . .' She burst into sobs.

'Harry lad, you'd best take 'er indoors. Get the baby and take them to my house. Mrs Tatlock'll know what to do with them.'

Daisy Todd sat shivering in front of the range. Dot picked up her shawl from where it had fallen on the floor and covered her grandmother's shoulders. 'You're safe now, Gran,' she said.

'Good job you went into the shelter, Mam,' said Jack, unsure how he should comfort a woman who had seen her home disappear, worse that she was his own mother.

'I've never known owt like it,' said Daisy. 'I were expectin' gas, nowt like this.'

Sally put her hand on Daisy's bony knee. 'You'll be all right,' she said. 'You can 'ave Jim's room. We'll do it up nice for you.'

Vi pushed open what was left of the back door and entered her house. 'It's all gone, Mam,' she said, 'all your furniture and stuff.'

'I only 'ad a few sticks,' said Daisy in a small, quavering voice. 'We bought it all from second-'and shop the day we got married.'

Vi bent down and produced a framed photograph from beneath her cardigan. 'They tried to stop me but I managed to climb into the living room. Bert's picture was still 'anging on the wall. 'E's not scratched or anything.' She handed the photograph to Daisy. It was of a young man in uniform, smiling for the photographer.

'Bert!' Daisy traced the face of her dead husband and said, 'Oh, thank you, God, thank you for lettin' me 'ave this picture, if nothing else.'

Vi smiled at her, thrilled that she'd brought some consolation.

Daisy turned the picture over and pulled at the nails that held the back of the frame in place.

'What are you doin'?' asked Jack.

'It'll be delayed shock,' said Vi. 'Shell-shock.'

Daisy freed the back of the frame and pulled off the cover to reveal a piece of paper. 'Thank you, God,' she shouted, letting the photograph fall from her lap. The glass cracked across Bert's features as Daisy unfolded a pound note and kissed it.

Ena stroked Percy's head as he sobbed into her neck. With her free hand she hugged fourteen-year-old Lily Longhurst to her. She'd never liked the girl, but death made her generous and Lily was the only child of her best friend.

'I really loved 'er!' wailed Percy.

Ena shifted uncomfortably on the rubble. Folk were starting to stare at him and his outbursts. 'Pull yerself together, man,' she hissed in his ear. 'Think of Lily.'

Percy looked at his daughter and burst into new tears. 'What's she going to do without 'er Mam?' he asked, through the sobs.

'Whatever are you scrikin' for?'

Three heads turned and three pairs of eyes stared at Martha.

'It's a ghost,' said Percy.

'Give over, man, she's flesh and blood, all right,' said Ena, clambering to her feet. 'Where the bloody 'ell 'ave you been?' she demanded of Martha.

'I've been at Jubilee Terrace with Minnie's mother.'

'What were you doin' down there?' asked Ena.

'When that siren went I were out back and by time I'd finished 'e,' she pointed at Percy, '' 'ad scarpered with Lily. There was all this noise an' I knew I 'ad to make sure Minnie got to the shelter.'

'Minnie was already at the shelter,' said Ena.

'Well, I know that now, don't I? Anyroad, I went to 'er 'ouse and 'er mother told me where she was so I went wi' her to their shelter. It were very nice, we 'ad a sing-song.'

'Sing song!' said Percy. 'We thought you was dead!'

'You daft –' Martha broke off to stare behind Ena. ' 'ere, where's my 'ouse gone?' she demanded, her mouth falling open as she viewed the open space where No. 16 Mawdsley Street had once stood. She could see right through from where her front door had once stood to the barrels in the backyard of the King's Arms on Canal Street. As she looked, a wall identified by its familiar printed paper as having once belonged to her front parlour, gave way and crashed on to the heap of bricks and timber. As the dust settled the sun broke through to catch itself on a brass flower-pot, which still contained Martha's prized aspidistra.

Days after the bomb fell on Mawdsley Street, wireless sets brought the news of the Allies' retreat and defeat at Dunkirk. For those with menfolk fighting in France, anxious hours followed, scanning newspapers and dreading visits from strangers. The newsreaders told listeners that hundreds of thousands of men had been trapped in Dunkirk and many had been rescued by a fleet of ships and boats of all sizes. They had been pulled from the beaches and the Channel, and were slowly being brought home. Thousands had been rescued but how many had been lost during the rescue attempt?

'No news is good news,' said Dot, as she raked the fire over.

The atmosphere was heavy in the Todd household, as it was in the Barlows' and in Annie's living room. Albert spent hours poring over his map of France, trying to work out how the troops could have been so cut off that their only escape was the beaches. He wished he lived on the south coast and had been able to man one of the little boats the newsreader had spoken of.

Life had to carry on as normal. Shopping had to be bought, machines worked, food prepared, and at evening time, those who dared leave their own firesides huddled together in the Rovers. Annie welcomed their custom – anything to stop thinking or looking at the clock. No matter how many pints she pulled, she couldn't take her mind off Jack's fate. She'd known he'd been in France, along with the rest of the Fusiliers. He would have been forced to retreat, of that much she was certain. But what would have happened then? Her concentration slipped and so did the glass she was holding. It fell to the floor and shattered. She bent to retrieve the pieces and cut her finger.

'Bet you're glad they wouldn't 'ave your 'Arry,' Albert said to Thomas, receiving a grunt in reply. 'I mean,' he bumbled on, 'I know your Alice's chap is out there but 'e's not yer own, is he?'

In the snug Minnie sipped her ale and said quietly, 'I saw Mrs Norris at the market today. She's got three lads in the Fusiliers. She'd been cryin', you could tell.'

' 'Arry Moss,' said Ena.

'Pardon, Ena?'

' 'Arry Moss. 'E were a lad I were goin' to marry. His auntie was caretaker at the Mission before me. I used to go and 'ave me tea wi' them. 'E were a lovely lad, used to make me laugh. He died at the Somme. They never found 'is body.'

'Aye,' said Martha. 'There's many a good man lyin' in a foreign field.'

'I always 'oped it would never 'appen again,' said Ena. 'Look at Annie Walker's face, see the pain.'

Suddenly Annie's facial expression changed as, standing up with the broken glass, she let out a scream. Ena, Minnie and Martha jumped up and craned over the counter, following Annie's eyeline to the pub doorway.

'Well, don't I get a hug?' asked Jack Walker, as he lowered his rifle to the ground.

'Jack! Oh, my Jack!' Annie ran from behind the bar and threw herself at her husband. His blackened hands reached round her and drew her softness towards his bloodied uniform.

Beside him stood the weary figure of Jim Todd. 'Is me mam in snug?' he asked.

'Nay, lad, your lot are at 'ome,' said Albert, excitedly clapping Jim on the back. 'Welcome 'ome lad, welcome 'ome!'

Annie clung to her husband and sobbed into his dirty uniform.

'Are you all back, lad?' asked Ena, coming out of the snug. 'Frank Barlow, is 'e with you?'

'Don't know, missus, 'e's not with our lot. It's just me and

Mr Walker, and George Hardman. Only he went straight 'ome. Can I 'ave a pint?' he asked hopefully.

'Jim Todd, your mother's goin' mad at 'ome waitin' for word of you. Get down that street!' Ena pushed him out of the pub and watched as he moved off slowly down the pavement. She waited until he'd let himself into No. 9 and heard the delighted howl of his mother before she started to follow him. At the open doorway she leant in and pulled the door shut before continuing her walk to the end of the Street. At No. 13 she stopped and pushed open the front door.

'Madge, is that you?' Despite the pain from the bullet lodged in his leg, George scrambled to open the door. His smile faded when he saw Ena in the hallway. 'Oh, I thought . . .'

'Welcome home, George 'Ardman,' said Ena. 'You look as if you could murder a cup of tea.'

'The fire's out in the range,' he said, gesturing back into the house.

'I meant over at my vestry.'

He stared at her. 'I don't understand . . .'

'She's gone, lad.'

'Gone? Where?'

'I mean, she's dead.'

Ena moved forward, thinking he was going to faint, but he managed to catch hold of the doorknob and straightened up. He winced in pain.

'Who's dead?' he asked.

'Your sister-in-law,' she said. 'It happened a week back. Stray bomber droppin' its load on us. She were out in the back. Doctor said she wouldn't have known anything. It was a piece of glass, went straight through 'er heart.'

George sank on to a chair, barely listening to Ena.

'I've bin lookin' out for you,' she said. 'I wanted to be the one to tell you.'

'Why? What business is it of yours?' he demanded.

'I were the one to lay 'er out, lad. And I found these in 'er pocket.' She produced three letters from her handbag and handed them to him. 'No one's seen them but me, 'er and the chap who wrote them. I've shown them to no one else.'

George looked at the letters in his hand and traced his own handwriting. 'You've read them?'

Ena nodded.

'I suppose you think I'm a dirty sinner? Livin' with my wife's sister like that. Well, you're wrong, we love . . . loved each other.'

'I'm not judgin' you, lad. Only God can do that.'

George turned away from Ena. 'Why did this happen? Why now, when we'd finally found each other?'

Ena sat in the chair opposite him and leaned forward. 'God works in mysterious ways. I don't know 'ow long you and Madge 'ad been seein' each other, but knowin' what I do of you and your wife I'd guess it started after she left wi' the kiddie.'

'Spyin' on us, were you Mrs Sharples?'

She ignored him and pressed on, 'All I'm sayin' is that folk reach out for tenderness in wartime. It's only natural. These things 'appen. It's important to put them in context. You're a married man.'

'Oh, shut up!' he shouted, and tried to stand but the pain in his leg caused him to fall back into the chair. 'What do you know, Mrs Sharples, of love? What do you know? You know nothin' I want to 'ear. Nothin'!'

'I'll tell you what I know of love. I'll tell you where I found them letters.'

He looked at her. 'She 'ad them letters in a pocket in 'er slip, 'ere,' she patted her chest, 'next to 'er 'eart.'

George's eyes swam with tears and his face crumbled. 'I – loved – her,' he sobbed.

Ena put a hand on his shoulder. 'I know, lad, I know.'

George spent the night sleeping on Ena's sofa in the warm vestry. In the morning he was woken by Vera as she crept off to work. Once dressed, he followed Ena down the Street towards the cemetery at St Mary's, where she showed him the fresh grave that was Madge's resting-place.

The doctor Ena sent for told George he was lucky the bullet had missed the bone. George didn't share the doctor's enthusiasm for his good fortune. What was the point of anything without Madge? He couldn't even remember when he'd been shot.

True to her word, Ena kept her knowledge of the affair to herself, and the residents wondered why, in the days following his return, she had taken to calling upon George Hardman. Perhaps his experience at Dunkirk had led him towards religion. They didn't have chance to question him as he locked himself away at No. 13 and admitted only Ena.

Ena made the most of her privileged position and adopted an air of mystery concerning George. Always one who wanted to lead with the gossip and be involved in everything of interest, Martha found the subterfuge infuriating. 'I think she's only doin' it to annoy me,' she said to Percy, as they waited in line at the town hall. Since losing their house the Longhursts had camped in Minnie Caldwell's cramped bedroom. It was a far from ideal situation, made worse by Minnie's mother finding fault with all Martha did. When Martha found Amy Carlton helping herself to the Longhurst family's rations she decided they would have to move out. This prompted the couple to seek official help and found them sitting on a cold bench outside a door marked 'Housing Officer'. The door opened and a young woman came out, propelling a small child in front of her. She clutched a yellow sheet of paper and looked pleased with herself.

'Next.' The voice was distant but clear.

Martha nudged Percy and picked up her bag. After forty minutes on the bench Percy was glad to get up and wondered how many had got piles from the cold slab during the winter months.

Entering the office Martha was startled to find Harry Hewitt's familiar face smiling at her from behind a desk. 'Are you the 'ousin' fella?' she asked.

'I'm the housing clerk, Mrs Longhurst.' His dealings with Martha had been minimal but from a young age she'd featured in his life, as much as the bricks and cobbles of the street. Always there, part of the landscape.

Martha's spirits rose. There was nothing like having friends in high places. Amy Carlton could stick her draughty cludgy.

'How can I help you?' asked Harry.

'Well,' said Martha, sitting opposite him and pulling reluctant Percy down to join her, 'we want an 'ouse.'

Harry referred to a file in front of him. 'Your home being sixteen Mawdsley Street?'

'That's right. It were flattened a week last Tuesday.'

'Where have you been living since then?' asked Harry.

'At Minnie Caldwell's. She's a good friend.'

Harry scanned his notes, aware that he had to toe the official line but knowing that Martha wouldn't like it. He hoped she wouldn't shriek at him. 'I see,' he said. He sucked his pen to give himself a moment's thought then dived in. 'I'm sorry, but as far as this office is concerned you don't qualify for a house as you already have accommodation at . . .' again he referred to his notes, '. . . nineteen Jubilee Terrace.'

'Minnie Caldwell's,' repeated Martha, as if talking to a small child, 'like I say, but we're not suited.'

'Whether you're suited or not, you still have accommodation.'

'But there's three of us in one bedroom.'

'I could point out 'ouses where there are five or six in each room.'

'But our Lily shares with us.' She reddened slightly as she said, 'It's not right, she's fourteen and very advanced for her years.' She nudged Percy. 'Say summat.'

He looked blank and then said, ' 'Ow's yer dad, Harry? I've not seen him down Legion of late.'

'Oh, he's all right, Mr Longhurst.'

Martha stared at her husband in amazement. ' 'Ow's yer dad?' she echoed, with contempt. 'I'm tryin' to find us a billet an' all the support I get is " 'ow's yer dad?"'

'Mrs Longhurst, I know, ideally, every family should 'ave it's own 'ouse but I'm afraid you're low priority. You're one of sixteen families made homeless a week last Tuesday. I'm still dealin' with reallocation for those in temporary accommodation before the war. And you 'ave a roof over your 'eads. You're not 'omeless.'

Martha glared at Harry. 'What about that lass who was in 'ere before us? She looked 'appy enough.'

'That lady had a two-year-old child and was pregnant.

She's higher up the scale than you are. All I can do is put you on the waiting list.' He leaned across the desk and lowered his voice so that it wouldn't be heard by his superior in the next room. 'Unofficially, Mrs Longhurst, I suggest you ask amongst your friends. Your very *close* friends. I had one asking questions about lettin' a property this mornin'.'

Never one for subtlety, Martha asked, 'Who was that, then?'

'I suggest you try the Mission of Glad Tidings,' said Harry, and closed the file.

Harry Hewitt's walk home at night from the town hall took him past the shops on Rosamund Street and St Mary's Church. During the winter it had been a question of dodging the trams and other vehicles and trying not to bump into anyone in the blacked-out streets. In spring and early summer, the park-keepers normally put on a good show, flowerwise, but this was the first June of the war and the park was unrecognisable. The bandstand, erected in 1906, had been removed, its wrought-iron castings going towards the making of Spitfires. The park railings had also disappeared and the lawns had been given over to local gardeners to grow their own produce. Harry carried on, past the park and the church, crossed Rosamund Street and turned left at the corner of the Rovers Return. He'd lived in Coronation Street all his life, born and bred in No. 7. As a child he'd swung by a rope from the lamp-post, pushed by Alice or one of his cousins. Grandma Makepiece, his mam's formidable mother, had lived at No. 11 and had seen her three daughters married and settled into the street before her death in 1938. Lil had been the first Mrs Foyle, and Harry remembered his aunt slipping him sweets over the counter before bronchitis took her in 1927. Vi had married Jack Todd against her mother's wishes and moved into No. 9, while Mary had wed returning war hero Thomas Hewitt from No. 3 and settled at No. 7, the middle house in the terrace block.

Surrounded by family, Harry's childhood had been happy and secure. He knew everybody and lived in the pockets of his neighbours. But all that was changing: Grandma and

Auntie Lil were dead, his own mother was buried at St Mary's after her death in the asylum, Alice was married, his cousins were growing up, soon moving on, no doubt. For himself, Harry was content to stay in Coronation Street. It had all he wanted.

He opened the front door and immediately heard the sound of sobbing. Quietly he closed the door and walked into the living room.

Auntie Vi looked up as he entered. She had on the floral pinny she always wore and was sitting with her arm around Alice. Harry couldn't remember a time when he'd seen Alice cry before. Even when their mother had attacked them both with the carving-knife she'd been angry rather than upset, and had fought back instead of crying. The sight disturbed him and made him feel vulnerable. 'What's up?' he asked, in a quiet voice.

His father shook his head and turned his back to him.

'We've 'ad bad news, love,' said Vi. 'It's Sam.'

Harry shifted his weight from one foot to the other, unsure what to say.

Alice lifted her tear-stained face and said, 'My 'usband's dead, 'Arry.'

He wanted to rush to her, comfort her with an embrace, but his feet wouldn't move. Displays of affection were alien at No. 7.

Thomas Hewitt cleared his throat and said, ' 'E died a 'ero's death.'

'He died a fool's death!' shouted Alice.

Vi eyed Thomas nervously.

'Why did he go and volunteer?' demanded Alice, 'If 'e'd 'ung around 'e'd only just 'ave been called up. 'E wouldn't 'ave been anywhere near Dunkirk!'

' 'E signed up because 'e was proud to be English,' said Thomas.

'Proud to be English?' Alice sneered at her father. 'You don't 'alf talk a load of rot! 'E signed up because you got 'im drunk and pushed 'im into it. All yer talk about a man's duty! What about a 'usband's duty? I was only a wife for a week. I'm goin' to be a widow for the rest of me life!'

Thomas glared at his daughter. He muttered, 'You should be proud of 'im.'

'Proud? Proud that 'e's left me alone?'

'Proud that 'e did something with his life, not like others.'

Harry realised the remark was aimed at him and flushed. 'I were unfit,' he said, to his father's back.

'Don't drag our 'Arry into this,' warned Alice.

'It's not my fault, it's me feet,' said Harry.

'Yer feet!' sneered Thomas. 'You sound like an old woman. I tell you now, I wouldn't let feet stand in *my* way. You let them put you off. Yer should 'ave stood there and refused to leave until they accepted you. You don't need feet to 'old a gun, do you?'

'Dad, stop it,' warned Alice. 'Shut up now, or I'm done with you.'

'Thomas,' said Vi, 'leave lad alone.'

'It's nowt to do wi' you, Vi. Keep out of it,' said Thomas.

'I know what you're tryin' to do, Dad. Sam's dead, you need someone to be proud of so you're pushin' 'Arry to sign up.'

'Why shouldn't I 'ave someone to be proud of?' challenged Thomas.

'You've two children, Dad. Be proud of us! Of who we are!'

Thomas laughed to himself. He stood in silence, as did Harry, while the women looked from one to the other.

'Would it mean that much, Dad, if I did join up?' asked Harry.

'Harry, don't listen to him,' pleaded Alice.

'Aye, lad, it would. It made a man of me, did the Army. I reckon it'd make one of you too.'

'Don't you dare go!' Alice was on her feet and rushed towards Harry. 'Take no notice of 'im, 'e's just a bitter old man. You've your whole life in front of you, as Sam 'ad 'is. Don't listen to 'im, 'Arry. You're more of a man than 'e'll ever be!'

Harry looked beyond Alice to his father. Thomas puffed on his pipe and smirked at his son. He'd issued a challenge and knew he wouldn't have to wait long.

Harry glanced at the clock. Nearly a quarter past six. 'I reckon recruitin' office'll still be open.'

129

He walked out of the room as Alice screamed, 'No!' She turned to Thomas with hatred drying the tears in her eyes. 'I'll never forgive you for this, Dad. If our 'Arry signs up, I'm warnin' you, I'll walk out of this 'ouse and I'll never set foot in it while you're alive!'

Vi spoke up, her voice urgent: 'Alice, don't say owt you'll regret later.'

'I won't regret a word, Auntie Vi. 'E drove my Mam mad, my husband to his death, and I'll not stand by and let 'im send 'Arry off!'

The front door slammed shut.

'Looks like you're too late, love,' said Vi.

Jack Walker's embarkation papers arrived while he was out visiting his brother Arthur, who ran the Nag's Head down by the canal. Annie contemplated losing them under some newspapers but common sense made her realise that it was better if Jack returned voluntarily than under the guidance of the Military Police. He made light of the news that his holiday had come to a premature end, but Annie knew her husband well enough to see the flicker of pain that crossed his eyes.

He hadn't spoken of his experiences in France, hadn't told her of the anxious hours he'd spent with his fellow Fusiliers, waiting day and night on a beach with nothing to eat and little to drink. Driven to this position by the advancing German army, he'd prepared himself for the inevitable capture or certain death. The company leader hadn't known if they should surrender or fight it out. Personally, Jack favoured a prisoner-of-war camp to a grave. It weighed heavy on his mind that he'd volunteered to leave his wife and baby son for a snatch at glory. He'd come to the conclusion that he must be a selfish man to leave Annie holding the fort at the pub while he'd sat about waiting for action. He was the oldest recruit in his section and as such had been made corporal. He was proud of his position, but during those hours of waiting in the chill of the sea air, he had realised the stripe meant nothing. They would all be machine-gun fodder. The lads had looked to him for guidance. He hadn't known what to say or do. During the last sleepless night when the bombardment was at its worse, he'd decided to make it his duty to get at least one of his lads to safety. Familiarity had caused him to select young Jim, and he'd put a fatherly arm around the boy as he'd sobbed against him. They didn't want to die but during that night death seemed a welcome alternative to the uncertainty of the future. Relief had come early in the morning. It had been fast, and bloody. He didn't remember much of the scramble into the water or the boats. Men's cries had merged with shouts of encouragement and the rat-a-tat-tat of the guns. He'd been pulled inside a tub and yanked Jim in after him. He must have passed out soon afterwards, his soaking boots and trouser legs clinging to him. Bombs had been dropped on the makeshift armada and he'd seen the sky light up with flames.

His recuperation at home was short and the demands of running a business meant that the Walkers had little time to be alone together. By the time they climbed into bed Annie was exhausted. Despite days of thinking of little else, Jack couldn't muster the energy for lovemaking.

Jim was more active. He wasted little time in dwelling on his experience at Dunkirk. Guessing that the Fusiliers could do little without him, he threw himself into activities, intending to make the most of what few precious hours were left to him. He played football, went to the cinema, drank in the Rovers and creaked Elsie's bedsprings. Despite her vow not to let him between her sheets, she took just one look at his battered, exposed soul and opened her arms. It wasn't until he'd returned to war that she remembered the rumours concerning Jim and various French women and a few days after that she discovered he'd left her a present. Not a baby, thank God, but a nasty little infection, which led to a visit to the clap clinic on Lower Edward Street.

Elsie's ties with the Todd family were strengthened when she started work at Colbolt's Engineering. Sally and Dot had swapped their machines at Lewinsky's for machines at the armoury, making bolts to be riveted on to rifles. The pay was marginally better and the firm had a large canteen, where food was served free of charge. Sally had to work twelve-hour shifts, but Elsie and Dot were both under eighteen and left after nine hours. There were three breaks a day and the atmosphere was cheerful, the girls able to chat as they worked.

Ida Barlow had been anxious that she would be ordered into munitions work herself and had readily agreed to look after Linda to free up Elsie. Now she was an official child-minder and was saved from the draft. Having two babies to care for took her mind off Frank's whereabouts. Since Dunkirk she had not heard from him and had no idea if he was still alive.

Working on the construction line with the Todds, Elsie enjoyed her new-found freedom. The only hitch was the management's idea of maintaining community links by plac-ing the workers in sections depending on where they lived. As a result Elsie worked alongside not only Dot and Sally but also Ena, Minnie and Martha.

Vi Todd had laughed all evening when her girls had told her who their workmates were. The thought of the six women sitting facing each other, each at their own machine, reaching over the same bench for discs of metal to grind into bolts, keeping up conversation and supporting each other to reach targets, was just too much.

Ena wasn't too impressed either and kept a sharp eye on the girls. She itched to find fault with their work, but Elsie and the Todds were conscientious. There was always the chance that Jim might have to use one of the rifles made at Colbolt's and they ensured that their bolts were the perfect shape.

It took a long time for Elsie to get used to the noise of the machine room. Older hands, like Ena and Martha, who had served time in Victorian cotton mills, found themselves returning to forgotten skills of mouthing and lip reading. In this way whole conversations could take place with work-mates. As anyone could attempt to work out what was being said in this way, more personal or private conversations were reserved for breaks or lunch.

Martha lowered her tray on to the table and slipped on to the bench, squeezing between Ena and Minnie. 'Budge up, Minnie, you're spreading out.'

After checking that everyone around them was occupied with their own thoughts or conversations, Martha bent towards Ena and said, 'I've been told you might know of a property for rent.'

'Oh, you 'ave, 'ave you?' said Ena, chewing a piece of fish.

'Harry Hewitt mentioned it in passing. Only I'd be very interested.'

'But, Martha,' said Minnie, butting in, 'you're suited at my 'ouse.'

Annoyed by the interruption Martha attempted to shut her up. 'Let's face it, Minnie, it's not the perfect situation, is it? You've only got the two bedrooms and I don't think it's fair asking your mother to share her bed, not at her age.'

'She doesn't mind. It reminds her of harder times.'

'We slept seven to a bed at 'ome,' said Elsie, coming to sit opposite the women. 'What we talkin' about, girls?'

'Nothin',' said Martha.

'Yes, we were,' said Minnie. 'You were askin' Ena if she 'ad somewhere to live because you don't like it at my 'ouse.'

'I'm very grateful, but it's time we found somewhere of our own.'

'I see.' Ena paused to pull a fishbone out of her mouth. ' 'Er mother playin' up, is that it? I wouldn't think she's the easiest woman in the world to live with.'

'No,' said Minnie ruefully, 'she's not.'

'Do you know of somewhere, Ena?' asked Martha.

Ena nodded, and took a swig of tea from an enamel mug. 'Number thirteen. George 'Ardman wants tenants while he's overseas and his wife's in Blackpool.'

'Next to me?' asked Elsie.

'That's right. Be nice for you, knowin' you only 'ave to bang on wall an' someone you know'll be there.'

Elsie and Martha exchanged looks, neither of them happy with the idea. Martha forced herself to smile at Ena, realising it was the best offer she'd get.

'Should I talk to 'im about it then?' she asked.

'Nay, lass, 'e's left, and 'e doesn't plan on comin' back till after war. I've got the keys. If you like, we can come to some arrangement.'

'George 'Ardman's given you keys to number thirteen?' Elsie couldn't keep the surprise out of her voice.

'And why shouldn't 'e? We're old friends, me and the 'Ardmans.' Ena looked down at her plate, disappointed at having come to the end of her lunch. She stabbed the remaining pea and popped it into her mouth. They never gave enough food. It was a good job she had her humbugs to see her through till the tea break at six.

On the day Harry Hewitt gave up his office job and went to war, his sister Alice packed her suitcase, took one last look around the living room of her youth and left Coronation Street, without speaking to her father. She dropped her front-door key down the drain grid outside the Rovers and ran to catch the Stockport bus. Vi Todd watched her go, and wondered at the stubbornness of Thomas Hewitt. 'There's no one left in that 'ouse for 'im to drive out now,' she said to Jack, as she served up his tea.

He looked at his plate with disgust. 'What's this?'

'Tater pie.'

'What's it got in it?'

'Taters. Don't blame me. Government says eat more taters.'

'If Government told yer to stick yer 'ead in gas stove, would yer?'

Vi ignored him and picked up her knitting. 'Give it a rest and get it down yer. I've nearly finished this scarf. I'll not do another, though. Garter stitch is a right bugger.'

'So's this muck,' said Jack, flicking pieces of potatoes around on his plate. 'I've got patrol tonight, I need some meat inside me.'

'We've 'ad it all for this week,' said Vi.

'Well, I'm not eatin' this. It's pig's swill, is this.' He scraped his chair back and reached for his jacket. 'Where's me armband?'

'Where it always is.'

Jack opened the sideboard drawer and pulled on his LDV armband. Until the uniforms arrived it was all he had to distinguish himself from mere civilians. 'I'll get some fish on me way,' he said.

She carried on knitting. 'You on with Thomas Hewitt?' she asked.

'Aye.'

'Well, think on, I don't want you invitin' 'im back 'ere after you've done playin' at soldiers. It's his own fault he's on his own. Drivin' everyone out o' the house. When I think of my poor sister, 'ow she put that house together, what she went through in childbirth just to 'ave 'im see them off like that.'

'I wish I could drive you lot off,' mumbled Jack to himself, as he left the house.

Tom Hayes stood in Albert's scullery with a potato sack in his hand. It hung, weighed down, at his side. Tom kept twitching as it jerked and sharp beaks popped out near his bare knees.

Albert looked at the sack with suspicion.

'Where did you say you got 'em?'

'They're on the level, Mr Tatlock, honest.'

' 'Ow much do you want for 'em?'

'Bob apiece, Mr Tatlock. There's six birds, all great layers.'

'I'll give you a dollar for the lot.'

'Oh, Mr Tatlock!' complained Tom, twisting to avoid another beak. He used his free hand to pull his grey flannel shorts lower.

'Tek it or leave it.'

Tom pushed the sack at Albert, secretly glad to be rid of the chickens. 'It's daylight robbery, is that, Mr Tatlock. Them birds are worth a bob of anyone's money.'

'You don't 'ave to sell 'em to me, lad. Try someone else. I've survived this long without chickens, I reckon I can last out a while longer.'

'But they're bound to start rationin' eggs soon, Mr Tatlock.'

'Bah! They can't ration eggs.' Albert laughed at the thought. 'A dollar I say and a dollar I'm stickin' to.'

Tom dropped the sack on the floor and held out his hand for the money. His skin was covered in scratches.

'Nay, lad, you don't think I 'ave that sort of money in 'ouse, do you? You'll 'ave to wait till pay day. I'll not run away.'

Tom sighed and slammed out of the house.

135

After he'd gone, Albert bent down and untied the sack. Six curious heads emerged.

' 'Ello my beauties, who's goin' to be layin' nice warm eggs for Uncle Albert, then?'

He lifted a grey hen out of the sack and stroked it as it clucked in alarm.

The scullery door opened and Bessie looked in. 'What's all that . . .' She stopped at the sight of the chickens. 'Get them things out of my scullery, Albert Tatlock. Nasty dirty vermin!'

'Chickens aren't vermin, woman, rats is vermin!'

'I don't care. Nasty things they are,' she squealed and pointed to the bird in Albert's hands. 'Look at it, starin' at me.' She retreated into the living room. From behind the safety of the door she shouted, 'I mean it, Albert, if you want any tea you'll 'ave to get them out of my scullery!'

Vera Sharples' job at the bakery came to an end when she was informed that she should be gainfully employed for the good of the nation rather than the few who ate her Eccles cakes. After reading a poster that told her she was needed to be ready with a hosepipe she dreamt of a career in the fire service. When she dared to speak of her dream Ena dismissed it immediately and told Vera she'd get her a job in the machine room, where an eye could be kept upon her. As always, Vera submitted to her mother's wishes. At first she dreaded the thought of spending all day under Ena's gaze but then remembered what she had said about sharing a bench with Elsie Tanner. For months she'd sat on the lumpy and uncomfortable vestry sofa biting her fingernails and looking through the leaded window on to Coronation Street. Unlike her mother, Vera wasn't interested in the lives of her neighbours. She didn't use her position to spy on them, merely in the hope of catching sight of Elsie Tanner.

Her mother's hostility towards the girl had caused Vera to become interested in her. She'd seen quite a lot of her as Elsie generally went out at night. Most nights she went out alone but sometimes she returned with a man. Vera would look longingly as the front door of No. 11 closed behind Elsie. How she envied her her freedom to come and go as she pleased. She knew, from her mother's investigations that Elsie was only seventeen, two years younger than Vera. It might as well be twenty years' difference when she compared herself with Elsie. Elsie always looked nicely dressed and her hair was beautiful. Vera wore Ena's cast-offs and hated her mousy locks. Life wasn't fair. At night, faithfully saying her prayers, she'd found herself adding a new line. Now she asked the Almighty to make her more like Elsie Tanner. She'd never built up the courage to talk to her. She nodded in the Street if passing – but actually to talk to the owner of that lovely red hair, to the girl who didn't seem to care what anyone thought of her . . . It was just too much and she longed for Elsie to become her friend.

Elsie never had any trouble in making new friends. After only one day at Colbolt's she came across a girl she vaguely knew from Back Gas Street. Like Elsie, Mary O'Malley was a redhead, but while Elsie's hair verged on the edge of brunette, Mary's was bright ginger and stuck out from her head like a wire brush. Her face was freckled and she had a runny nose, which left the skin above her top lip red and sore.

Elsie bumped into her in the rush to clock off at the end of the day. 'Mary O'Malley!'

Mary turned and smiled in recognition. 'Elsie Grimshaw!'

The girls pushed their way out of the factory and sought the security of a brick wall, away from the swarm of workers.

'Actually it's Elsie Tanner now.' She thrust her wedding ring under Mary's nose.

Mary looked at the ring in envy. 'I'm married as well, but I 'ad to pawn me ring. The name's Mrs Patrick Lynch.'

Elsie opened her mouth then shut it quickly. Patrick Lynch was renowned around Back Gas Street for preying on young girls. A big Irish docker, he'd seen more knickers than the scrubbers at the wash house. If Mary had married him, Elsie was certain he'd never remain faithful.

'You still living down Back Gas Street?' she asked, 'I'm in Coronation Street.'

'Aye. I heard you'd gone up in the world,' said Mary. 'I'm not in Gas Street any more. Not since the bomb.'

'Bombed out, were you, love?' asked Elsie sympathetically.

'We're sleepin' wi' me auntie,' said Mary.

'Patrick not fightin' then?'

'Oh, he is. No, I meant me and me baby, little Elizabeth Theresa.'

'How old is she?' asked Elsie. 'I've got one five months old. Linda.'

'Elizabeth's just six weeks. She came early during the air raid. I were that scared!'

Elsie looked at the backs of the retreating workforce. 'I'd best be going – got to pick Linda up from a neighbour. I'll see you around the place, maybe?'

Just two hours after saying goodbye, Elsie was surprised to open her front door and find Mary standing outside, holding a bundle.

After putting the kettle on the range and inviting Mary to lay down the sleeping Elizabeth, Elsie questioned the reason for the visit.

'I didn't think you'd mind,' said Mary, 'but me auntie's 'ad enough of Elizabeth cryin' and I 'ad nowhere else to go.'

'She's chucked you out?'

Mary nodded and looked around the living room. 'Nice place you've got 'ere. How many do you share with?'

'It's all mine, love.'

'A whole 'ouse to yerself?' Mary was amazed at the luxury.

Elsie eyed her and decided to make the offer before being asked. 'You can 'ave one of the back bedrooms. There's no beds in there but you can use the cushions from the chairs in the parlour. It's warm an' it's dry. But you can't stay for long, just till you get sorted.'

Mary beamed. 'Thanks ever so, Elsie. I'm ever so grateful.'

Within a week Elsie couldn't remember a time when Mary and little Bet hadn't been around. The latter screamed half the night, often setting Linda off, while Mary was soon uncovered as a slovenly article who failed to lift a finger to help Elsie.

On 22 June France surrendered to Hitler, and the residents waited for the imminent invasion. Ena slept with the bread-knife under her pillow and feared for Vera once the inevitable raping started. She felt that the likes of Elsie and the Todds would be able to cope with the conquerors' demands, but Vera was another matter. The Local Defence Volunteers patrolled in earnest and prepared lines for action. Jack Todd stored ammunition in his coal hole and drilled Vi on how to use his rifle. In the event of him being shot she would have to take his place.

Ena wasn't alone in fearing rape. Dot Todd took the tram into Manchester, visited the central library and looked up the German for 'I've got a venereal disease.'

Any stranger to the area was viewed with the utmost suspicion. The regulars at the Rovers vowed that if any foreigners arrived asking for directions they'd be bundled into the pub and thrown down the cellar steps. The mood was no longer carefree: anxiety and fear took over. There was much glancing over shoulders and the residents shut themselves away in the evenings and listened to the wireless.

Suddenly it seemed very important to do all one could for the work effort. Jack Todd and Thomas Hewitt organised the collection of all aluminium pans and tubs to be melted down and turned into Spitfires. At No. 5, Rose Hayes panicked at the thought of surviving with just one saucepan and hid the largest she had in the coal shed. The bus company caused chaos by removing all numbers from its vehicles and replacing them with the names of public buildings and well-known parks.

'That'll confuse 'Itler,' remarked Ena Sharples. ' 'is whole invasion plans'll be up the spout now he won't know which is the number four!'

Annie Walker was not pleased to discover that the name of her home was being used to identify the end of Rosamund Street. 'It's bound to attract the wrong sort of customer,' she said. 'Can you imagine getting on to a bus which says its destination is the Rovers Return?'

The thought of German boots marching down the cobbles caused more trivial matters to be swept aside. Vi and Mrs Foyle were relieved to make the peace and Vi was welcomed back to the shop as a faithful customer. The shopkeeper was bombarded with ration books and pamphlets from the War Office. There was an outcry when sugar was cut from twelve to eight ounces a week and Albert Tatlock faced a future of sugarless tea.

Dot Todd waited twenty minutes outside the Bijou cinema for her sister, but in the end decided to see the film without her. It was *Gone With The Wind* and she'd already seen it twice before, but the sign outside the cinema said it was moving on at the end of the week and this was her last free evening. Without giving her absent sister another thought, Dot sat in a seat in the stalls and unwrapped a toffee. The cinema was crowded and, just as the newsreel was about to start, she was forced to stand up as a couple squeezed past her to find empty seats. As she stood up, Dot was nudged and her bag of sweets fell from her hand, scattering on the floor. Bending to pick them up, her hands were joined by another, larger hand with hairs on the back of it. Having retrieved them, Dot sat back and smiled her thanks to the man sitting next to her.

'Don't mention it.' He had white teeth and spoke with a strange accent. She froze at the sound of his voice, and when he smiled again she decided to put her studying to the test. *'Ich habe eine Geschlechtskrankheit.'*

He carried on smiling and, unsure if he had understood or not, she pointed to herself and slowly said, 'I am English.'

He nodded and said, 'You are very beautiful as well. I am French.'

On second hearing, the accent was no longer threatening, just caressing. She offered him the bag and he selected a toffee.

By the time Atlanta was burning Dot's mouth was wrapped around his, her eyes tight shut as his tongue explored her cavities.

His name was Jean, which Dot found amusing, and he was from Lyon. Having escaped his native land at Dunkirk, he'd been billeted in Manchester and was awaiting the chance to rejoin his countrymen. He was over six foot tall, with jet black hair and a sunburnt face.

'He looks just like Tyrone Power,' was Dot's description to

Sally. 'He's twenty-three, he's got three sisters and he knows a lot about tractors.'

Sally screwed up her nose. 'Who wants to talk about tractors? What sort of a kisser is he?'

Dot flushed. 'He uses his tongue a lot.'

Sally sighed. 'I've read about them French in that book me dad said were dirty and took off me to 'ave a crafty read in cludgy.'

'He's ever so good-looking and I think I love him.'

In the weeks following her meeting with Jean Dot's world changed. Munitions stopped being a chore, family life was no longer a drag. She thought of him all day and counted the hours until she could be with him again.

He had no money and was reliant upon the goodwill of his landlord in Cheetham Hill. Dot dug deep into her purse to entertain him, and didn't resent spending her money on him. It was on their third outing, just days after their first meeting, that he stammered in his broken English that he loved her. They were standing in the doorway of Swindley's Emporium and Dot had her back to the window display of cotton nightwear. Considerably shorter than Jean, her neck ached from the kissing as he forced his mouth down on hers. He broke off long enough to whisper his love into her ear then started to kiss her neck. Her heart beat faster as he loosened her blouse and ran a rough hand over her brassière. He pulled up her skirt and, when she didn't object, worked a hand into her knickers. She cried out and he rammed his tongue into her mouth, his free hand pulling at the buttons of his flies. It was dark in the blackout and Dot had a rush of excitement. Something new was happening and she was certain it wasn't the sort of thing good girls did on the doorstep of the local haberdashery. Her mind flicked back to an image of herself, sitting in a pram outside the shop waiting for Vi to finish her shopping.

She staggered back against the glass as he raised her leg and thrust into her. He moved her up and down, rubbing her thigh against the edge of the wooden window-frame. She felt splinters entering her skin and wanted to complain, but he was muttering words in French and she liked the feel of him inside her. He started to pant then suddenly relaxed, squashing her against the window. His hands lowered her to the tiled floor of the doorway and she felt something wet and slimy rub against her thigh. Whatever had happened was to do with the fact that he loved her. Dot wanted to cry with happiness.

CHAPTER EIGHT

July 1940 RAF and the Lutwaffe fight over Dover. Sally and Dot fight over a six-foot Frenchman.

It was a mild night in early July. Elsie was walking home down the Street after half an hour spent in the company of a friendly seaman in the Rovers. She was humming to herself and was startled to hear her name hissed from behind her.

'Mrs Tanner!'

It came again. She stood in the Street and tried to work out where the voice was coming from.

The front door of No. 3 opened slightly and the same voice said, 'Over here.'

Elsie hesitated before slowly walking back towards the door. It opened and Marjorie Barlow smiled nervously at Elsie.

'Have you a minute, Mrs Tanner? she asked, drawing back slightly.

Elsie followed her into the hall and stood in the shadows. Marjorie was at least a foot taller than Elsie and took on the appearance of a grandmother clock as she stood tall in the lobby. She opened the door to the front parlour and ushered Elsie into a comfortable room with large padded armchairs and a china display cabinet. Elsie's own parlour was bare, apart from an old sideboard she'd inherited with the house. She thought the chairs looked welcoming but, as Marjorie remained erect, she felt she couldn't sink into one.

'I'm sorry to drag you in like this, Mrs Tanner.'

'Please, call me Elsie.'

Marjorie gave a half smile and carried on in the same hushed tones. 'I'm whispering because I don't want Ida to hear us. She's in the scullery washing up.'

Elsie nodded.

'It's about Ida. I need to speak to you. She'd be very upset if she knew I was, though.'

'Is it something about Linda?' asked Elsie, in concern. 'Is she too much of a 'andful?'

'No, nothing like that. Ida loves having Linda during the day, I think it takes her mind off Frank.'

'Still no news?'

'Ida's convinced herself he's dead. I think it's for the best, really.'

There was a silence while Marjorie thought of her missing brother and Elsie wondered why she'd been dragged in off the Street.

'So. . . ?' she asked.

Marjorie was jolted back to the present. 'So . . . yes, well, you see it's about your friend, Mrs Lynch.'

'Mary?' asked Elsie in surprise.

'It's a bit awkward but she's been coming round and borrowing money off Ida. Apparently they were both in the shop the other day and your friend didn't have enough cash on her and, well, you know how soft-hearted Ida is. She stepped in and gave your friend a shilling. Well, since then, it turns out Mrs Lynch has borrowed over a pound from Ida. Now, please don't take this the wrong way, Mrs Tanner, but I've seen Mrs Lynch's sort roaming round Baxendale's and filling their pockets. I don't believe Ida will see that money again and, unless something's done, I think your friend'll be round asking for more.'

'I see,' Elsie said. 'Thank you for telling me. I'll make sure Ida isn't bothered again.'

'I hoped you'd say that, Mrs Tanner.'

Elsie left the house and returned thoughtfully to her own home.

The wireless was blaring and Mary was pouring tea. Ash dangled from her cigarette and she sang along with the big band booming out of the Bakelite. ' "Chew, chew, chew your bubblegum . . ." '

Elsie looked about the room with fresh eyes. It had never been tidy: she was the first to admit she was a slut when it came to housework, but there was clutter and there was pigsty. There was no doubt about it, since the arrival of Mary and Bet, Elsie had allowed her standards to be dragged down to Mary's level.

'I reckon I can squeeze another cup out.' Mary held up the teapot as an offering.

Elsie sat down. There was something hard under the cushion. She dug about and produced a wedge-heeled shoe.

The wall surrounding the range shook suddenly as three sharp bangs came from the other side. In response Mary shouted, 'Shut up, you four-eyed ferret!' She laughed and said to Elsie, 'She's bin bangin' on that wall for best part of an hour.'

'Well,' said Elsie, 'it is rather loud.'

'Oh.' Mary crossed to the table and turned down the volume.

Upstairs a baby started to cry.

Mary looked daggers at the wall. 'That's that cow's fault, wakin' Elizabeth up.'

Elsie glanced in the direction of the hall. If Bet wasn't attended to, she'd end up waking Linda. Mary gave no sign of moving. She just stood drinking tea, her toe tapping in time to the music. Elsie sighed and pulled herself up from the chair. As she passed the squares of towelling drying in front of the range, she pulled one off to take with her, just in case.

Dot looked at her father with distaste as he scratched his stomach through his string vest. In the chair opposite him her grandmother broke wind and sighed contentedly. Dot turned to her mother and begged, 'Please let me use the parlour. I can't bring 'im in 'ere.'

'Why ever not? Don't Frenchies sit around the fire of an evenin' as a family?'

'Yes, but, Mam . . .' Dot looked at her family tableau and wanted to cry. Why couldn't her family resemble the ones she saw in the *Sunday Pictorial*? This was like the ape house at Belle Vue Zoo.

Vi's fingers ached from knitting so she wasn't in the best frame of mind. The lass had a boyfriend and wanted to show him off. Fair enough, but why should she go to the trouble and expense of lighting a fire in the parlour? It hadn't been aired since her own mother's laying out and funeral nearly two years before.

'You can't use the parlour. There's a funny smell in there.'

' 'E'll be used to funny smells, will the Frenchie,' said Jack.

Dot stared at her father. 'How do you work that one out?' she asked.

' 'E's French ain't 'e? Stands to reason.'

'I don't trust the French,' said Daisy, chewing on a piece of paper.

'I don't know why I'm botherin' bringin' 'im round, I don't, honest. It were you lot as said you wanted to meet 'im.'

'We do,' said Vi, 'course we do. Blast! I've dropped a bloody stitch now!'

'What you worryin' about, love?' asked Jack. 'Not told 'im you live in a palace, 'ave yer?'

'No,' replied Dot, 'but I did let him think I lived with a family of 'uman bein's and not a load of gorillas.'

A rap at the front door caused Dot's eyes to dart to the clock. He was early!

Sensing her daughter's discomfort, Vi put aside her knitting and knocked Jack's feet off the table. 'Right, we'll 'ave no more talk about Frenchies. If Dot likes 'im 'e's good enough for me.' She nudged her daughter into the hall. 'You'd best let him in before Elsie Tanner claps eyes on him.'

There was just time to side the pots before Jean's big frame entered the room. Dot stood nervously beside him as he stuck out his hand to shake with Jack, who noted his firm grip and found himself dwarfed by his huge bulk.

' 'Ow do, lad?' he asked, feeling vulnerable in his own home. He struggled to gain control of himself. 'Do you smoke?' He offered Jean one of the roll-ups he'd been working on but Jean declined and instead pulled out and handed over a packet of his own.

'They're French,' said Dot, enthralled by Jean's every movement.

Jack took a cigarette and nodded to Jean to sit opposite him in front of the range. 'I were in France meself, when we bailed you out last time.'

Dot rolled her eyes and sat on the arm of Jean's chair, putting a protective arm around his bulky shoulders.

Daisy clicked her top plate up and down in her mouth and stared at him. He smiled at her but she grimaced in return.

'Grandma's living with us now that her house has been bombed,' said Dot apologetically.

' 'Ow do you take yer tea, love?' asked Vi.

Jean said, 'I do not drink tea. Some water, perhaps?'

Vi blinked. She'd never met anyone who didn't drink tea. It was like finding someone who didn't breathe air.

'Water?' she repeated.

'In the tap, Mam,' said Dot.

Vi hurried off to the scullery and poured water into a cup. It just didn't seem right without the tea leaves.

Jack took a puff of his cigarette, and started spluttering and coughing. Daisy leant forward and thumped him on the back. 'By 'eck, lad,' he said, after coming up for air, 'these fags are bleedin' powerful.'

Jean grinned and showed off his teeth. Vi made a mental note to ask Dot if the teeth were real.

The door opened and Sally walked in, fresh from the factory. She shook her hair loose from her scarf and stuck out a hand in Jean's direction. ' 'Ello, I'm Sally. No need to ask who you are.' She winked at Dot. 'Nice goin', kid.'

Dot beamed and relaxed, squeezed closer to Jean. He placed a hand on her thigh and stroked her suspenders through the thin material of her dress. Vi, Daisy and Sally noticed the gesture, while Jack coughed on the cigarette again.

Later, once Sally and Dot had taken Jean to the Rovers and Jack was on LDV duty, Vi and Daisy stood at the scullery sink together, looking out into the backyard. Tufts of grass poked out among the flagstones and the odd dandelion added colour to the scene.

' 'E was very friendly,' said Vi.

' 'Is 'ands were all over 'er,' said Daisy, 'an' by way she didn't stop 'im I reckon it weren't for first time.'

147

Vi sighed. 'I 'ope she's not done nothin' she'll regret.'

'Course she 'as,' said Daisy with a chuckle, 'an' if I were 'er age I'd 'ave done same. I've not seen shoulders that wide in years.'

'Give over.' Vi nudged her mother-in-law and handed her a cup to dry. 'He seemed nice enough,' she said, trying to calm her own anxieties.

'It won't last,' said Daisy. ' 'E's got rovin' eyes, you can tell.'

Down the street, in the Rovers, Jean's eyes roved over Sally's backside as she bent to chat to a friend sitting at table. His face was locked into a smile and Dot felt content that he was happy to be with her.

Sally returned from the bar with the drinks and sat down next to Jean. Dot didn't notice the way she brushed against him or the way she hitched her skirt higher as she crossed her legs, but Jean did. He took a gulp of beer and glanced down at Sally's white skin, peeping out from the top of her stocking. She saw the look and joined in the smiling. 'So, Jean,' she said, running her tongue over the edge of her teeth, ' 'Ow do you like England?'

'It is full of beautiful ladies,' he said.

Sally laughed. A little too loudly, thought Dot.

'Jean's taking me to the Bijou. We're going to see *The Old Maid*.'

How appropriate, thought Sally.

'Why don't you come with us?' asked Jean.

Behind his back Dot urgently shook her head to put Sally off and was relieved when Sally said, 'No, I've got things to do. Besides, I saw it in town earlier in the year. It's not that good.'

'Then perhaps we should not go,' said Jean to Dot.

'Oh, don't let me put you off,' said Sally. 'I'm sure you'll 'ave a great time. It meks all the difference goin' to flicks wi' someone you love.'

'You do not 'ave someone to love?' he asked.

'No,' Sally said, casting her eyes down. 'No one.'

Elsie Foyle longed to close the shop and bathe her aching feet. She'd got as far as turning the sign to 'closed' when

Elsie Tanner had arrived on the doorstep, looking weary after a long shift on munitions. 'I think I'll treat meself tonight,' she said, casting her eye along Mrs Foyle's top shelf. 'Go on, give me some dried figs. I've not 'ad figs since before the war.'

Mrs Foyle climbed her small step-ladder to reach the packet. 'Goin' to Bijou, are you? There's a Bette Davis on, I'm thinkin' of goin' meself.'

'Not tonight. I just want to soak me feet and eat me figs.'

'Blimey! Whatever 'appened to the lively young thing that moved in day war broke out?' joked Mrs Foyle, stepping back behind the counter.

'She got bored rigid sat starin' at Ena Sharples' ugly mug all day listenin' to *Workers* flippin' *Playtime* on Tannoy.'

Elsie picked up her purchases and said, 'I'll settle up while I'm 'ere.'

Mrs Foyle produced the slate book from below the bacon slicer and flipped it open. 'Right, that's one pound ten and elevenpence ha'penny.'

Elsie stared at the shopkeeper. ' 'Ow much? It can't be.'

'It's down 'ere Elsie, that's with what you've just bought, the figs and the pilchards.'

'There must be some mistake.'

Mrs Foyle handed the book over for her to read. She scanned the neat handwriting then laughed. 'I thought so. I 'aven't 'ad 'alf the stuff on that list.'

Mrs Foyle glanced at the book and said, 'Well, not you personally, perhaps, but the young woman livin' with you. She puts 'er shoppin' on the slate as well. She said it was all right with you.'

'She what?' cried Elsie.

'I thought, with her living with you –'

'The cheeky cow!'

'Oh, Elsie, I'm sorry. She said it were all right.'

Elsie emptied her purse on to the counter and pushed a note and some coins towards Mrs Foyle, 'There's all but 'alf a crown there. I'll 'ave to owe it you, and do me a favour, if anyone else wants to buy stuff on my tick tell 'em to throw themselves in the cut!' She stormed out of the shop, leaving shamefaced Mrs Foyle counting the coins. She'd lied: it was three shillings short.

After an evening spent brooding, Elsie had worked herself up into a state by the time she'd retired to bed, alone. She sat in bed and pondered her dilemma. Mary was homeless, bombed out with no one to turn to. She had a baby, and her husband was goodness knows where. It made sense to have her stay at No. 11; Elsie had plenty of room and enjoyed the company. Or, at least, she had thought she enjoyed the company. Mary did have a way of spreading herself around the place and she was hardly in of an evening. Elsie looked at her alarm clock. Nearly midnight and Mary was still out. Elsie had babysat for the third night in a week. She spent more time with tetchy Bet than she did with Linda, who seemed to be flourishing under Ida's care and attention and just wanted to sleep whenever her mother was around.

Elsie felt too young to to tell a mate to stop borrowing money and running up bills. That was grown-up stuff. Tedious. When was it she'd stopped being a child? Was it when Arnold had slipped the ring on her finger, or had it happened earlier when she'd lain with her knickers round her ankles while he drooled over her breasts?

The front door slammed and Elsie heard giggles. She got out of bed and stepped out on to the landing.

'Ssh. You'll wake the dead,' said Mary.

'Come 'ere, then,' said a man's gruff voice.

Elsie edged closer to the top of the stairs and peered down. Mary's back was against the front door and a man was pressed against her, nuzzling her neck. She pushed him away when she saw Elsie looking at her. 'Hello, love. We didn't wake you up, did we?' she asked.

Elsie walked down the stairs.

The man turned to look at her. He was in his early fifties, balding, and even from the distance between them Elsie could smell the booze on his breath.

' 'Ello darlin'. Is this yer sister?'

'It's me mate, Elsie.'

He leered at Elsie. 'Nice legs, love. 'Ave you come to join the party?'

Elsie ignored him and spoke to Mary, 'Don't you think you ought to be in bed? We're on at eight in the mornin'.'

'Yeah, we're just goin' up.'

Mary pushed the man towards the stairs but Elsie blocked their way. 'Where the 'ell do you think 'e's goin'?'

'To me room.'

'What for?'

The man laughed. 'For a fuck, darlin', what do you think?'

'Not in my 'ouse you're not!'

'Oh, come on, Elsie, don't act like a nun. We'll keep the noise down and 'e'll be gone in the mornin'. You won't know he's been 'ere, honest.'

'Suppose Bet wakes up?'

'Well, you can see to 'er can't you?' Mary grabbed Elsie's elbow and whispered, 'Look, I'll split whatever he gives me with you.'

Elsie stared at her. 'You mean 'e's payin' you?'

' 'Ere, tell you what, darlin',' the man put in, licking his lips, 'I'll mek it worth your while if you join us.'

'Get out!' Elsie screamed in his face, pushing him so that he tumbled backwards down the stairs. She turned to Mary, her eyes blazing. ' 'Ow long 'as this bin goin' on? You takin' money off fellas?'

'Everyone does it, Elsie.'

'No, they don't. I don't.'

'It's no big deal. It's just sex and I get a few bob as well.'

'Not in my 'ouse, you don't.'

The man lay at the bottom of the stairs and rubbed his head. He groaned.

'Get 'im out of 'ere, and in the mornin' you can clear off yerself. I've 'ad enough.'

Elsie ran up the stairs and went into the children's room. Both girls slept peacefully. She picked up Linda and carried her into her bedroom. She laid the baby on her bed then bolted the door behind them.

If sex wasn't on offer at No. 11 Coronation Street it was in the bomb-site that was the remains of No. 7 Mawdsley Street. In what had at one time been the back room where she'd visited

Daisy for Sunday dinner, Sally lay on a three-legged sofa while Jean made a ham-fisted attempt at removing her knickers. She gave a cry and pulled away. ' 'Ang on. I've got me dress caught.'

'Take it off.'

'Give over,' she said. 'If we're caught I'm not running starkers down Rosamund Street!' She laughed at the thought.

He'd been waiting for her when she'd left the Rovers. He'd had time to walk Dot home, kiss her tenderly against the front door then wait under what would normally have been the street lamp, if the blackout hadn't been in operation. She hadn't been surprised when he'd softly called her name. She had led him here to her love-nest next to the tallest wall in the remains of the house. The back half had been blown off completely but the living room could still provide adequate cover. Sally looked up at the stars above them, through the roofless house.

He tugged impatiently at the buttons on her dress.

'Slow down.' She tried to make herself more comfortable and allowed him to guide her hand down to his naked buttocks. She giggled as he licked her ear and wrapped her legs around his waist.

Less than eight hours later, Sally suppressed a yawn as she sat with the rest of her unit at their shared bench, lowering levers and turning handles. The drone of the machines filled the air and ears.

Martha glared at Elsie round the side of her machine and tossed another bolt into the trough in front of her.

Ena noticed the look and sucked on her humbug. 'Gettin' on all right with your new neighbours?' she asked Martha, with a chuckle.

Martha turned her glare on Ena.

Ena shrugged and looked at Vera, who sat next to her, twisting a bolt in her fingers.

'It's no good,' Vera said, 'I can't get the thread right.'

Ena tutted and asked, 'How many 'ave you done in the last 'alf-'our?'

'Three.'

'Three! I've done thirty odd. For goodness sake, look lively.'

'I can't do it,' wailed Vera.

'How many more times do I need to show you? Just put it in, bring lever down and twist slow but firm. Are you puttin' it in far enough?'

'I don't know.'

Ena looked at her daughter. Where had she come from? Was it really all down to that knock on the head she'd had as a baby?

'It is 'ard, Ena,' said Minnie, from the far end of the bench. 'It took me a while to get the 'ang of it.'

Ena sucked her humbug and stared at Minnie. She was another who was soft in the head.

Martha yawned.

'Your Percy coughin' again, is 'e?' asked Ena.

Martha glared at Elsie. 'No, it was 'er and 'er lodger. Doors slammin' all night.'

Elsie tossed a bolt into the trough and said, 'Well, you can rest easy from now on 'cos she's gone.'

'Why?' asked Martha, interested. ' 'Ave you had a fallin' out?'

'Don't you know? I'd 'ave thought you'd have had a glass up to the wall.'

Sally looked at her sympathetically. 'Give you a 'ard time?'

Elsie shrugged. 'She's moved on.'

'Where?' asked Dot.

'Said she were off to Oldham or somewhere.'

'Damn,' said Dot. 'She owed me two bob.'

Elsie laughed. 'You and 'alf Weatherfield.'

'Shouldn't be so trusting,' said Sally to Dot. 'That's your trouble. You're an easy touch.'

Dot glanced at her sister, hurt by the edge in her voice. Sally swung her legs out from under the bench and stood up.

'Where do you think you're goin'?' asked Ena, the self-appointed section leader.

'Lav break.'

Sally stalked off to the toilets, reaching into her pocket for her cigarettes as she went. It was no good, she couldn't sit next to Dot and carry on as normal. She was so infantile, chatting about Jean all the time. It was boring.

Back at the bench Dot wondered what she'd done to annoy her sister so much.

Albert Tatlock was a man of simple pleasures and the concept of 'make do and mend' appealed to him. The chickens were a great boost to his vision of himself as the provider in his family. He had used wood stored at the back of his coal shed to construct a run for the birds. In the weeks he'd had the allotment it had been transformed by the early summer growth and compared favourably to Jack Todd's meagre offerings on the next plot. Albert prided himself on the amount of care and attention he devoted to his new found hobby and thought Jack foolish for letting such a ripe source of production go to waste. The only way Jack's allotment stood out was in that it contained a small wooden shed, acquired by Jack from a friend in the shunting yard. It was made from an old signal box and was just the thing to store tools and sit in when it rained. Albert had coveted the shed since its arrival and had finally struck a deal with Jack, which enabled him to use it in exchange for a part share in the chickens.

Each day, as soon as he finished work, Albert rushed to the park to view his farmland. He'd already set Bessie to finding the best way to make the most of his carrots, green beans and peas, and was pleasantly surprised to find that Tom had been correct in saying the birds were good layers.

He'd grown fond of the fowl and given each a name. That had made his discovery of the empty run even more painful. He'd arrived as normal, with the bits of crusts he'd torn off his sandwiches to feed his 'girls' as titbits, only to find them all missing. Jack wasn't as sentimental as Albert. He put the disappearance down to a fox and insisted on making the run more secure for when the chickens were replaced. He'd grown accustomed to his eggs and was determined that no fox was going to get the better of him. To validate his claim on half the birds, he'd coughed up half the cash to pay Tom Hayes for replacements. Tom's price had risen, and the coins he collected jingled in his pocket. He was saving up to buy a bicycle he had his eye on in Rushton's window: red with a chrome bell and a leather saddle.

Albert peered into the run and nudged Jack. 'Don't that black one remind you of anything?'

Jack looked at the scrawny bird. 'My Vi?'

'No,' said Albert, looking at all six chickens. 'They all look just like the last lot we 'ad.'

Jack took a closer look. 'Chickens are chickens, Albert. They all look same.'

Albert shook his head. ''Appen you're right, Jack. But they do seem identical to last lot.'

The houses in Coronation Street were associated with different tones and volume levels. The Tatlock, Barlow and Hayes homes tended to be quiet, the Todds and Tanners rowdy. Generally, the passer-by who knew something of the occupants took it for granted that raised voices at No. 9 and No. 11 were commonplace. However, on the night of 22 July an all-time high decibel level was reached in the Todd household. Passing on her way to the Rovers, Ena slowed down to listen as the shrieking voice of Dot reached the Street at large.

'You tart!'

Inside the house, in the living room, Dot slapped Sally around the face. Sally caught her breath and then, with a yell, launched herself on Dot. The girls pulled each other's hair and lashed out with their nails. Vi jumped out of her chair and tried to separate her daughters.

'You dirty tart!' Dot screamed at Sally, and punched her shoulder.

Sally yanked Dot's hair again and shouted, 'I didn't mean for you to get 'urt!'

Vi succeeded in prising Sally's hand off Dot and pushed the pair apart. 'That's enough!' she shouted. 'This isn't getting us anywhere! We need to talk this through.'

'I told you 'e 'ad rovin' eyes,' said Daisy smugly.

'Shut up, Gran!' said Dot.

'Don't talk to yer grandma like that,' said Vi. 'Now, you, sit 'ere, and you,' she pointed at Sally, 'you sit on t'other side of the table.'

Both girls sat and glared at each other.

'Right,' said Vi, 'let's get this straight. Sally, 'ave you or 'ave you not bin with Jean?'

'What do you mean "bin with"?'

'Don't get smart wi' me or you'll feel the back o' my 'and. You know what I mean.'

Sally smiled, causing Dot to burst into tears.

'She 'as! She's a dirty tart!'

'Who are you callin' a tart? From what Jean tells me you dropped yer knickers before you asked him 'is name!'

'I never! 'E told me he loved me.'

Daisy cackled in the background.

Sally patted down her ruffled hair. 'Look, kid, as soon as your back were turned 'e was all over me. I didn't encourage 'im.'

'Why?' demanded Dot, 'when I told you 'ow much 'e meant to me? Why did you 'ave to do that wi' 'im?'

'Because I could.' Sally leaned across the table. 'There's a war on and there aren't that many decent fellas around. 'E said you didn't mean anythin' to 'im. 'E also said 'e'd never done anything wi' you, 'cos of you bein' so young.'

'Well 'e's a bleedin' liar!'

Sally sighed.

Vi looked from one sister to the other. 'What a mess. The pair of you no better then that tart Elsie Tanner took in. Well, I 'ope he used protection, wi' both of you.'

'I'm not stupid,' Sally said.

Vi looked at Dot. 'Well?'

Dot started to cry. 'I don't know.'

'What do you mean, you don't know? Did he put anything on 'is thingy?'

'I don't know. We only do it in dark.'

'Same 'ere, but I make sure,' said Sally.

'That's because you're a bleedin' tart!' roared Dot.

Sally got up from the table and said, 'I'm not listenin' to any more o' this. I'm sorry, Dot. All right? I didn't know he was fuckin' you.'

Vi leapt up and slapped Sally round the face. 'Don't you dare use words like that in this 'ouse!' she yelled.

Sally put her hand to her cheek. 'I don't 'ave to put up wi' this. I'm twenty, not some little kid like 'er.'

'While you live under my roof you'll keep a civil tongue in yer head.'

'I pay my way. I give you more than most would. I carry this family. You, me dad –'

'You do not go with yer sister's boyfriends!' yelled Vi.

' 'E told me it were all over between 'em.'

'You should 'ave said, Sally. If you thought that you could 'ave asked me,' wailed Dot, 'but you knew it wasn't true so you didn't bother. You just sank yer claws into 'im and lured 'im away from me and I'll never forgive you! You've ruined my life!' She burst into tears and fell upon the table.

Sally sighed and made to leave the room.

'Where are you goin'?' demanded Vi.

'Out. With Jean.'

'No you're not. You're goin' up to your room and you'll stay there until I've sorted this mess out!'

'An' you're goin' to stop me, are you?' Sally laughed in her mother's face.

Vi raised her hand and smacked her again across the face. Sally gasped and turned to run to the front door, but Vi was after her and grabbed the back of her dress. There was a rip as Vi pulled it from Sally's back.

'You bitch!' screamed Sally. 'My new dress!'

Vi hit her about the head, pushing her up the stairs. Sally tried to fend off the blows but made no attempt to lash out herself.

'You've done some low-down things in your time, Sally, but this is too much. You've broken yer sister's 'eart!'

'Mam, please stop it,' begged Sally. 'I didn't mean to 'urt Dot, I swear. I wanted 'im so much. There's no one left to dance with, Mam, no one to 'old you and say nice things. I just wanted to feel alive again.' She collapsed on the stairs, hugging the banister as she cried.

Vi felt exhausted as she looked at her daughter. Dot carried on crying in the front parlour.

There was a knock on the door. Sally looked up, her face red and swollen.

'Don't let 'im see me like this, Mam,' she pleaded.

Vi nodded for her to run upstairs. She closed the living

room door and composed herself, straightening her pinny before opening the door.

Jean's smile froze on his face as Vi kicked him hard between the legs. He doubled up and cried out as he hit the pavement. She leant over and spat on him. 'I don't know 'ow to say it in French but I reckon you'll get me drift when I say stay away from my girls or I'll cut your dick off and feed it to me 'usband's chickens.'

The door slammed as Jean crawled off over the cobbles.

CHAPTER NINE

21 December 1940 In Geneva the Swiss government cuts off diplomatic relations with the USSR. In Weatherfield the water supply is cut off.

The second autumn of war was harsher than the first. At the end of July incendiary bombs had dropped on Weatherfield's neighbouring town, Salford, and the air raids had sent the residents flying for cover. The smell of fear, mixed with dust and smoke, filled the air. Newsreels had shown the horrified residents the devastation of Coventry and Southampton. The grey images of broken communities, together with the sombre, clipped tones of the newsreader, caused every wife and mother in the Street to contemplate the reality of losing the security of her home.

Houses taken for granted before were now cherished, as if national treasures. Albert Tatlock arranged for a lorry-load of sand-bags to disappear from a town hall spread-sheet and reappear, as if by magic, at the end of Coronation Street. The residents turned out in force to form a human chain and the bags were unloaded at great speed and stored in backyards. For the briefest time the residents went along with Albert's plans and covered their back walls with the bags but, as Vi Todd put it, she wasn't going to live like a rabbit in a burrow, and they were removed.

During those late-summer raids Ida Barlow had refused to leave her home and had lain in her makeshift shelter, constructed beneath the living room table, her saucepan

159

rammed on her head. However, apart from that one summer night, Weatherfield remained untouched by the blitz that rained down for two solid months on the people of London and other cities. Although unscathed the residents remained ever alert. Albert and Ena wore their ARP uniforms at all times, and people tended to run rather than walk when outside. Black-out precautions took on more importance.

Thomas Hewitt, Jack Todd and the other men in their LDV division were no longer ridiculed by the residents. Tom Hayes received a smack round the head from a passer-by when he shouted, 'Look, Duck and Vanish,' at the men as they drilled in the park.

Rationing took its toll. What at first had been greeted as 'fairness for all' now turned into a chore. Rations were being cut, and arguments flared up at the smallest hint of favouritism from a shopkeeper. Mrs Foyle considered closing the shop and going to stay with her husband and daughters in Lytham. The occasional letter she received from them told of countryside walks, bracing air and endless supplies of seafood. It was the feeling of obligation that kept her hand on the bacon slicer, that and the knowledge that she'd rather be living alone than in the company of her husband twenty-four hours a day. Still, the hordes of complaining shoppers that she faced every day finally got to her and she sank into depression.

Ena Sharples was always on the lookout for a shift in behavioural patterns, and when she looked out of her vestry window and saw the queue of anxious women waiting impatiently outside the corner shop she knew something was wrong. Saturday, 8.45 a.m: the corner shop door should have been dangling. It wasn't. It remained shut, the blinds pulled down.

Ena left the vestry and strolled across the cobbles.

At the front of the queue stood Martha. She banged on the glass panel of the door and called out, 'Yer late, get this door opened!'

The other women joined in, encouraging Martha to bang again.

Ena nodded to familiar faces and walked up the line, passing Martha. She carried on into Viaduct Street and nipped into the back entry that separated Coronation Street from Mawdsley Street. She opened the latch on the shop gate, and a few seconds later let herself in at the back door.

Elsie Foyle sat in her kitchen, smoking. Her hair was still in curlers under a hairnet, and she wore a dressing-gown over her nightdress. As Ena entered the shop's living quarters she looked up, startled by the intrusion.

'Who said you could let yourself into my home?' she demanded.

'You poorly?' asked Ena.

Mrs Foyle laughed. 'You're a nosy article, aren't you? I might have known you wouldn't be out there with the rest of them hammering on my paintwork.'

Ena put her hands in her coat pocket. The room was cold, the range unlit. She nodded in the direction of the shop, 'Martha Longhurst would 'ave made a champion knocker-upper.' Without waiting for invitation, Ena pulled up a chair and sat next to Mrs Foyle at the table. 'Why don't you tell me what's to do?' she asked.

'It's nowt to do wi' you, Mrs Sharples. Just shut the door after you, eh?'

'It's all right,' said Ena. 'I can guess, you don't 'ave to tell me.'

'Oh, know everythin' do you?'

'King Solomon asked for wisdom and the Lord gave it to 'im. I like to think 'e's given a small amount to me too.'

'Well, come on, then, Mrs Sharples, what's up with me?'

'Yer lonely.'

Mrs Foyle let her cigarette dangle from her lips and clapped her hands. 'Oh, well done, Mrs Sharples. What a genius you are. I'm lonely.'

Ena clasped her gloved-hands together and looked at Mrs Foyle. 'Don't make light of it, lass. You put on a good performance out there six days a week, you shouldn't push yerself too much. It's natural, I suppose. I've never bin one for Gaiety theatres, but I reckon you get to enjoy all that applause.'

Mrs Foyle smiled fondly, recalling the clapping that had washed over her as she stood on the stage and sank into a deep curtsy. 'The Prince of Wales came to see me once, Mrs Sharples. Him that gave up the throne. I sang "There's A Light In My Heart For You". I've still got the dress I wore.'

'Royalty's never 'eard me sing,' said Ena, 'not that I know of anyroad. Must be nice.'

'It is.'

'You can't live off memories, yer know. I've tried it. Seventeen years I 'ad with Sharples before 'e were took and I 'ave seventeen years of memories up 'ere.' She tapped her head with a finger. 'When he died I didn't know what to do wi' meself. My eldest, Madge, she'd already left 'ome, but I 'ad Vera to think of. I remember I couldn't bear six thirty in the evenin' because that was when he'd come 'ome from work. When 'e 'ad work that was. Six thirty.' She sighed. 'Now it comes and goes an' I hardly notice.'

'My husband's not dead,' said Mrs Foyle quietly.

'He might as well be, love. He doesn't turn up a right lot, does 'e?'

'No.'

Elsie Foyle closed her eyes and saw herself as a bride, entering the shop for the first time. Tommy had explained the stock and ordering to her. They had laughed, as if it were all a game. He'd let her shift all the tins and packages around, put framed copies of her music around the shop. They'd been happy. Shelagh and Hilda had been born. The shop started to drive them. She wasn't a natural mother, and had had the girls mainly to please Tommy. He'd doted on them. They seemed to prefer his company. She'd given the shop all her energy, all her focus. Tommy had got in the way. They'd drifted into a different sort of marriage from their neighbours. The shop was hers, childcare was for him. He seemed to enjoy himself, and the shop counter became her stage.

Martha's banging brought her back to reality. She put a hand to her hair and felt a curler.

'My hair . . . I'm not ready to open up.'

Ena placed a woollen hand on hers and said reassuringly, 'It's all right. You go upstairs and sort yerself out. I'll tek care of that lot.'

Mrs Foyle smiled in gratitude and disappeared.

Ena opened the door and stepped down into the shop. The figures of the women were silhouetted behind the blind. She took off her coat and gloves and stored them under the counter. Noticing the black book that kept a record of what people owed on the slate, Ena opened it and scanned the names. She chuckled. Fancy Annie Walker owing that much.

Bessie Tatlock grated potato into her mixing bowl, her chubby elbows moving in time to the rhythm of the music playing on the wireless. Albert lowered the newspaper and stared suspiciously at the potato. 'I thought you were mekin' us Christmas pud,' he said.

'I am.'

Albert laid aside the paper and watched Bessie pick up a carrot to start grating it into the bowl. 'Stop lookin' so worried, lad, it'll be all right. I jotted recipe down off wireless this morning. They wouldn't get us mekin' stuff that weren't nice, would they?'

Albert thought back to the last two meals Bessie had prepared from the radio. 'Aye, they would. I wouldn't feed a dog some of the stuff you've laid in front of me.'

'I'm doin' me best, Albert. There is a war on.'

'There's not, is there?' Albert got up and walked over to her. 'By 'eck, I never knew that.'

She gave him a cold stare. 'Sarky bugger.'

Albert picked up the scrap of paper with the recipe scrawled on it and read Bessie's spidery handwriting. ' "Flour, breadcrumbs, suet, mixed fruit . . ." This is gonna be some pud, i'nt it?' He smacked his lips and peered into the bowl.

Bessie picked up another carrot.

'No, lass,' said Albert, 'it only says one carrot.'

'It's instead of mixed fruit. I've no fruit but plenty of carrots.'

Albert turned up his nose and jingled the change in his trouser pocket.

'Why don't you go to allotment 'stead of gettin' under me feet?' she asked.

'Not much to do up there. I picked the sprouts on Thursday.'

'Well, go an' chat to yer pals.'

Albert wandered round to the other side of the table and picked up a card from the mantelpiece. It was a snow scene. 'Don't seem like Christmas somehow,' he said, with a sigh.

Bessie stopped grating and said, 'Why don't you show Beattie your chickens? I reckon she'd like to see them.'

Beattie Tatlock had returned home the previous day, brought back as it had been judged safe enough for the children to return for Christmas. All but Beattie had been delighted to be reunited with their parents. She resented that she had had to give up her comfortable home with her cheerful foster parents to live in the cramped conditions of Coronation Street.

Bessie had been thrilled by her return and fussed around her until Beattie shut herself away in her bedroom, refamiliarising herself with old toys and books, all far too young for her now. Her parents still expected her to be a contented six-year-old. Instead, at eight, she was sullen and made no attempt to disguise the contempt she felt for her native surroundings. Both Albert and Beattie were at a loss as to how to treat her.

'Four days to go till Christmas,' Albert said. 'We should buy 'er summat more than that picture book.'

'Albert,' said Bessie thoughtfully, 'it bein' Christmas, I thought we could treat ourselves.'

''Ow do you mean?'

'Well, it's not going to seem very jolly sittin' down to a pile of carrots an' spuds, is it?'

Albert's stomach groaned in protest. He wished he hadn't been so enthusiastic when planting the carrots.

'A bit of bird would mek all the difference,' Bessie said, avoiding his eyes.

'Aye,' said Albert.

'I'll pluck it if you kill it.'

Albert stared at her. 'Kill what?'

'One of yer chickens. Think about it, love, Oxo gravy, bread sauce. I could do a nice bit of stuffin'. It'll seem like a proper Christmas then.'

Albert smiled, 'You're right. I'll do it. I'll still 'ave five left for eggs, won't I?' Less than an hour later he stood among the Brussels sprouts on his allotment, grabbed hold of a struggling chicken and stuffed it into his sack.

Jack Todd watched him carefully. 'She's a plump bird,' he said, 'like your missus.'

'She is that,' said Albert, with a chuckle.

'I fancy the brown one meself, an' the one with the dodgy eye.'

Albert looked at Jack in confusion. 'What you talkin' about?'

'For us Christmas dinner. That's what you've got that one for, i'nt it?'

'Aye. But I paid for these birds, they're mine.'

'Albert,' said Jack in annoyance, 'who 'elps you feed 'em? Who brings scraps an' stuff? Who lets you use his shed?'

Albert shifted uncomfortably. 'Go on then, 'ave one.'

'Two. I need two.'

'Whatever for?'

'There's five of us, i'nt there. Stands to reason I need two. There's only three of you to your one.'

'If you tek two I'll only 'ave three left,' complained Albert.

'You'll get more,' said Jack dismissively. 'Can I share your sack?'

Albert sighed but was then struck by a thought. 'Hey, we're goin' about this all wrong.'

'Do you reckon?'

'Aye. Perhaps we should club together and share two birds, instead of eatin' three.'

Jack pondered the suggestion and chewed his lip. ' 'Ow would we work that out?'

'Well, there's me and my Bessie, Beattie, you and Vi, the girls an' your mother. Eight of us, all told. Now, with careful carvin', you've got four legs an' wings and a load o' white meat.'

'I don't like white meat,' said Jack.

'Well, you can 'ave one leg. It still leaves us with three more to go round.'

'And would we all 'ave to eat together? It's a bit of a squeeze round table at best of times.'

'Well, no, just cook birds and cut meat up.'

'Go on, then,' said Jack, 'meks sense, does that.'

Albert bent down to the run and lifted the roof. The chickens ran into the hen-house. Jack placed a hand on Albert's shoulder. ' 'Ang on. Seein' you lift that off 'as got me worried.'

'What about?'

'What's to stop any other bugger comin' along at night an' stealin' the rest? It's 'appened before.'

Albert realised Jack had a point. The chickens had now been stolen twice but luckily Tom Hayes had managed to replace them both times.

'What should we do, then?' he asked.

'We'll 'ave to tek them all back to Coronation Street for safe-keepin'. Just till after Christmas.'

Elsie Tanner handed the badly wrapped packet to Ida. 'It's just a little thank-you, for bein' so good wi' Linda.'

Ida blushed and pulled off the paper. It was a small bottle of scent. 'It's lovely.'

'It's more than lovely,' said Marjorie. 'We sell them on the ground floor at Baxendale's. Very nice smell.'

Elsie smiled. 'I'm glad you like it. I wanted to give you somethin'. Linda's too young to understand about Christmas an' I wanted to give someone a present. It makes it seem more like Christmas.'

'Well, we've no presents to give you, Elsie, but we've a drop of sherry if you're interested,' said Marjorie, moving towards the sideboard.

Elsie sat in an armchair and put Linda on to the rug where Kenneth lay, sucking his fist.

'Bless 'em,' said Ida.

Elsie looked round the room. 'I see you've not put any decorations up yet.'

Marjorie poured three sherries and passed one to Elsie. 'There doesn't seem much point, does there?'

'Oh, I don't agree. I'm putting paper chains up tonight,' said Elsie, excited by the thought.

'You needn't bother,' said Ida. 'I've seen the photographs in *Picture Post*. When the bombs drop there'll be nothing left.'

Elsie pulled a face and sipped her sherry, wondering if Ida had been hitting the bottle before she arrived.

166

'Now, then, Ida,' said Marjorie, too brightly, 'let's not think of things like that.'

'But we must,' said Ida. 'It's goin' to 'appen soon.' She got up and went into the scullery.

Marjorie grinned apologetically at Elsie and sat next to her. 'She's been like this for weeks now. It started when she heard about Frank being missing. She's convinced he's dead and she's going to follow him. She has this dream where she's running with Kenneth and God stands on a cloud throwing bricks at her until she's buried by them. I keep trying to cheer her along but it's a losing battle. At least Kenneth's too young to understand it.'

'Is there anythin' I can do?' asked Elsie.

'Just act like everything's normal.'

Ida returned with a plate of home-made biscuits. She offered them to Elsie and sat beside the fire.

The flames were comforting.

Elsie lifted her glass and said, 'Happy Christmas.'

Sunday, 22 December, was another cold day. The residents went about their daily business. Ena was up early, warming up the Mission hall for the ten o'clock service. Across the Street, at No. 5, Sid Hayes put the finishing touches to his sermon, pleased with himself for another job well done. Esther polished his shoes and reminded herself they'd need doing again that afternoon as Sid was giving a talk at the Bold Street Mission on the other side of the canal.

Bessie's preparations for Sunday worship were spoilt by the presence of the six chickens. Seeking security, Albert had housed them in the spare bedroom and Bessie was disturbed by the sight of a persistent beak pecking the wood at the bottom of the door. She felt certain they were bound to escape and attack her.

Elsie Tanner had her normal Sunday lie-in, telling herself that the best thing about the war was that church bells had stopped ringing on Sunday mornings. It was a thought shared by Annie Walker who likewise lay in bed, not wanting to emerge from beneath her warm covers. Both women were blessed with infants who slept late.

167

Dot and Sally were talking to each other, just. Since Vi had seen off Jean he hadn't returned to the Street, and Sally had bounced back by finding herself a young man who had managed to dodge the call-up. His name was Derek, and he had a way of getting his hands on luxury items such as matches and fruit. He wasn't as good a lover as Jean, but as long as he kept her in Wright's Coal Tar Soap Sally wasn't bothered.

Annie dug out the paper chains from the Rovers' cellar and made a half-hearted attempt to add some festive cheer to the pub. The dark brown paintwork in the bar was peeling and looking in desperate need of a new coat. She knew Jack would say it didn't matter and that no one would be bothered in wartime, but that wasn't the point. It bothered her. She was not going to make excuses for her standards and didn't see why they had to be compromised. She had conversations in her head by the hour with Jack, who always put up the arguments she expected but, as in real life, she tended to win each point.

As if rising to the challenge of the paper chains, the Rovers hummed to the chatter of customers and the clink of glasses. Annie herself was in an unusually good mood as she'd persuaded Sally to help behind the bar for the day. 'I can't tell you what a joy it is to see you here where you belong,' Annie said, smiling at Sally.

Sally beamed back and thought, You can grovel all you like 'cos this is a one-off.

It seemed as if everyone had selected that afternoon to let their hair down and forget the war. Christmas had come early to Coronation Street, and Annie beamed as her cash register pinged.

Mrs Foyle sat next to Ena in the snug and drank some stout. She leaned closer to Ena and said, confidentially, 'I've had a crate of oranges delivered. I'm going to put them in the shop tomorrow. One per person, first come first served. I'm not shouting about it, though, so keep it to yerself.'

Ena smiled. She liked an orange to suck.

The little bar was crammed full of women. Bessie Tatlock had brought her knitting and her wool kept jumping down off the bench where she sat. Minnie looked at the wool and sighed. 'I wish I were a knitter.'

'Why don't you give it a go?' asked Martha.

'She can't,' said Amy, scornfully. 'She 'asn't got the fingers for it for a start an' she can't count for another.'

Ena looked at her dejected friend and felt sorry for her, living with a mother like Amy. Never a kind word for her, criticising all the time.

Amy finished drinking and, as usual, licked off her frothy moustache.

'Shall we 'ave a sing song?' suggested Minnie.

'No,' said Amy.

'I think that's a champion idea, Minnie,' said Ena in defiance of the old woman.

Amy frowned at her.

' 'Ow about some carols?' suggested Martha.

Ena opened her mouth to start off with 'God Rest Ye Merry, Gentlemen' but she stopped as she heard singing coming from the public bar. She spun round in her chair to see who had dared start the carols without her knowledge.

A trio of nervous singers stood in the doorway, holding song-sheets for protection. Leonard Swindley stood in the middle and rattled a collection box. 'O come all ye faithful . . . joyful and triumphant . . .' he sang, sounding anything but.

Albert and Jack edged away to the bar, avoiding the collection box.

Ena dodged back into the snug. She resented this on her territory. Since Mawdsley Street Congregational had been hit the Mission squad had been hanging around Coronation Street a bit too much for her liking. She liked lay preachers like Sid Hayes, who kept themselves hidden away at home and only emerged for services.

Leonard rattled his box and cleared his throat, 'Donations kindly received. All donations will be put towards the children's party.'

Annie leant across the bar and offered him a pound note. 'On behalf of the Rovers Return,' she said, making certain the customers saw how much she was donating.

'She can afford it,' said Ena, with a sniff, 'I've seen her darting back and forth from that till all afternoon.

Mrs Foyle agreed. 'Aye, it's funny that folk have money for

beer and not for groceries. I can't see Mrs Walker giving tick as freely as me.'

Ena smiled to herself, remembering the piece of ammunition she'd stored in her mind concerning Annie and the credit book.

The door opened and Swindley appeared with his box.

'Good afternoon, ladies, I wonder if I might pass my box round you.'

'Pass that round 'ere an' you'll not get it back, Leonard Swindley,' said Ena.

'Here,' said Martha, dropping a coin into the box. 'We're not all as dishonest as Mrs Sharples would 'ave you believe.'

'I'm sure you're not, madam,' said Swindley, inclining his head.

'You want to check that box soon as you get out o' 'ere. She'll 'ave given you a button from her top. It's an old trick.'

As soon as Swindley had left Ena mimicked him, ' "I wonder if I might pass my box." '

'Goodwill to all men,' Minnie reminded Ena.

'Who said Leonard Swindley was a man? Ena guffawed. ' 'E's as spineless as his father.'

It was six thirty in the afternoon when the laughter and singing in the Rovers was cut dead by the wail of the air-raid siren.

Ena sobered immediately and got to her feet, shouting over the wail, 'Right, ladies, quick as you can. Mission basement's nice and warm.' She made a dash for the door and found herself fighting against people's backs. 'Let me through! ARP warden! Let me through,' she bawled, over the confusion. The customers poured out on to the Street, carrying Ena with them.

Annie ripped off her pinny and pushed Sally's coat into her hand. 'Off you go, Sally, join your mother if you can. I'm staying here with Billy though, and you're welcome to join us in the cellar.'

'I'd best go wi' others. Mrs Sharples will be expecting me.'

'Right you are.'

Sally didn't move. Her lip quivered. 'Mrs Walker, you don't think . . . I mean, Coventry and . . .'

Annie put up a hand. 'Don't think it, Sally. Even if it's Manchester's turn, we're not in the city centre, are we? Now, come on, or your mother'll be worried.'

She pushed Sally out of the empty pub then bolted the door behind her. She ran back behind the bar, opened the till and grabbed the notes. Upstairs, Billy had started to cry, bothered by the sirens. 'I'm coming,' she called, and ran into the hallway.

Ena ran across the cobbles, her coat flying wide behind her in the wind. Vera stood in the vestry doorway, clutching her mother's helmet and torch. She cried out in relief at the sight of Ena and thrust the helmet at her. 'Put it on. It'll be all right if you put it on.'

Ena pushed her back into the vestry. 'Get the boiler room door opened. I'm sending them round the side entrance.'

Albert already had his helmet on and was busy banging on the door of No. 5.

Esther's petrified face peered round the net curtain in the bay window. Albert saw her and shouted, 'Come on, lass, get down shelter!'

He ran on to the next house.

Esther ran into the living room, where Rose was busy bundling family photographs into her handbag. 'I can't find the ration books,' she said.

Esther grabbed them from the shelf and thrust them at her mother. 'Come on, Mam!'

A boom filled the air and Esther's eyes shot upwards. 'Come on! Dad said I was to get you to the shelter straight away.'

Rose looked around her in panic. 'Where is your father?'

'He's at Booth Street tonight. He set off half-hour ago. Come on!'

Elsie Tanner ran across the cobbles, clutching Linda in a shawl with a pillow tucked under her arm. She looked up at the sky and saw the searchlights on top of Elliston's factory illuminating the darkness. She stopped and shouted up, 'Put that light out!' She laughed at her own joke and carried on towards the Mission entrance where Ena stood, swaying her torch from side to side. She found herself next to Mrs Foyle and said, 'Just like 'Itler eh? Anythin' to spoil our Christmas!'

Vi appeared at her doorway clutching a pillow-case. Feathers floated down from it as she turned and called into the house, 'Come on, mother!'

Dot followed Daisy out into the Street and shut the door behind her. 'Don't see why you 'ave to bring them chickens wi' you,' she said.

'They're our Christmas dinner, that's why. I'm blowed if Adolf's deprivin' me of me parson's nose.'

Dot let out a scream as the street shook and a deafening noise assaulted her. The group of women staggered then ran across the cobbles.

Ena pushed people through the Mission door, counting her regulars. Percy Longhurst appeared at her side in his own ARP helmet. 'It's gettin' crowded down there. How many more?'

'Not many. It's because of us 'avin' your lot an' all.'

A crash made her jump back. Percy instinctively put an arm around her. 'It's all right, Ena, it'll be all right.'

She shook off his hand and felt annoyed with herself.

The bombing came closer and closer. The drone of the engines filled the air and the sky was a blaze of colours.

Esther dragged a screaming Rose out of the house. Ena saw that the girl was losing the battle to steer her mother towards the Mission. She ran over to meet them and, without pausing, gave Rose's face a hard slap. Immediately Rose stopped screaming and allowed herself to be dragged inside.

'Well done, Ena,' shouted Albert, but she didn't hear him. He kept close to Elliston's back wall as he ran towards the Mission.

'That's the lot. Mrs Walker's staying put.'

Ena turned to enter the shelter but noticed a light appear in the Street.

The front door of No. 3 was flung open and Marjorie Barlow appeared, waving to attract attention. 'I need help, Mr Tatlock!'

Albert rushed back over the street. 'Come on, love, they're getting nearer.'

'It's Ida. She says she's going to die and I can't get her to leave the house. Oh, Mr Tatlock, I'm scared.'

Albert followed Marjorie into the house, the wind blowing the doors shut. Ida sat in a chair shaking, with Kenneth beside her feet, crying. Albert knew he only had seconds in which to act. He ordered Marjorie to pick up the child and to run to the shelter, saying he'd drag Ida by her hair if he had to. 'Come on, Ida!' he shouted in her face, 'Frank told me to look after you, an' so 'elp me that's what I'm goin' to do!'

Ida looked at him, tears forming in her eyes. 'Frank always wanted the best for me. He was such a worrier.'

'If he were here he'd want you down that shelter, safe.'

Ida nodded. 'Yes, you're right. But he's not here, he's dead. And I'm going to die as well, I've dreamt it.'

'Rot!' said Albert. 'Frank would want you safe. Now come on!'

He grabbed Ida's hand and pulled her up from the chair. She put up no resistance as he dragged her through the house.

As they reached the hall they were shaken by a thunderous noise that echoed around them. The front door flew off its hinges and a beam of white light blasted them. Albert felt the skin on his face sink inwards and shielded his eyes. Ida opened her mouth to scream but no sound came out. They staggered backwards but kept their footing. As soon as the blast died, Albert pulled Ida over the door and out on to the Street.

Ena stood at the end waving her torch frantically and shouting, 'This way!'

Albert set off with Ida, heading towards the torchlight.

'Ida, is that you?' called Marjorie, from the darkness.

'Yes, is Kenneth all right?'

'Oh, thank God,' said Marjorie, 'I thought –'

It happened in slow motion. Suddenly Ida saw Marjorie illuminated by the whitest light imaginable. Then the sea of bricks descended in a rush, like a great Niagara, hitting the pavement, the cobbles, the wall. Albert shoved Ida back towards the terrace. The roar was deafening. The whole street seemed to lift up and turn round, upside down, as Ida's head hit the cobbles.

The dust settled and Ena staggered to her feet. A whole section of Elliston's back wall had fallen into the street below. Seven storeys of bricks and mortar. She stood still, staring at the scene. Percy ran up behind her.

'Ena, are you all right?'

'Yes. Get help! We need help!'

Ena ran forward as Percy disappeared into the shelter. She tried to remember where they'd been standing. How far from the wall had Marjorie been? Was Albert this side of No. 7 or the other? As she pulled at the bricks others joined her, hands digging, pulling. The shelter emptied as the residents risked their lives to help. The bombing continued in the distance, sirens and shouts mingled with the cries of the injured.

Tom Hayes stumbled upon Ida. She lay where Albert had thrown her, clear of the bricks but covered in glass from broken windows. Percy Longhurst felt for a pulse and found it beating weakly. Elsie Tanner ran into Rosamund Street and jumped in front of an ambulance on its way to the city centre. She begged the driver to stop and help. By the time a stretcher emerged for Ida, Albert had been heard calling for help, his leg trapped beneath timber beams. Bessie embraced him where he sat on the cobbles.

It took another half-hour's digging to find Marjorie's body. Once she was lifted out, fifteen-month-old Kenneth was revealed safe and sound, protected by his dead aunt's torso.

Coronation Street still stood, but it was battle-worn. Its windows had blown in, showering glass and dust over every inch of living space. The corner shop had suffered a hit, with half the building demolished. Mrs Foyle's stock, including the oranges and the residents' Christmas boxes, was ruined by glass splinters and rubble. A gaping hole was all that was left of the shop floor and counter. The Street's gas supply had been cut off at the mains and the water pipe had been fractured. The Todds' dinner was safe but they had no means of cooking it.

Albert's leg, broken once more, was set in a cast but he still managed to help Jack board up the windows with wood and lino. Ida was released from hospital with shock and bruises, the nurses explained that her bed was needed for worse cases. Elsie took her in at No. 11.

Annie emerged from her isolated shelter to find her shelves had been looted by rescue workers in search of refreshment. As her living quarters were at the back of the pub, her furniture and belongings were relatively unscathed, apart from one of her china shepherdesses, which had fallen off the mantelpiece.

Manchester had been devastated by the bombs. The city centre stood in ruins, fires burning into the night and the next day as the initial raid had lasted twelve hours. The same night as Marjorie Barlow died her beloved Baxendale's was burnt to the ground.

It was Leonard Swindley who performed the dreaded duty of knocking on the door of No. 5 and telling Rose that Sid had been killed, along with sixteen others in a brick shelter on Back Gas Street. It had taken a direct hit and Sid's body had been one of the few found. Rose had to be sedated.

Christmas Day brought a rest from the raids and the homecoming of a resident. Frank Barlow jumped down from the lorry that had given him a lift from the station and rushed into the Street with his kit-bag balanced on his back. His smile faded as he took in the battered sight before him. His front door was missing, as were his windows. All were boarded up from the outside. He hammered on the wood and called, 'Ida!'

Albert Tatlock appeared in what had once been his front window and looked out. He peered at the soldier in front of him, and it took a few beats for him to associate the sunken-faced man with the jovial lad who had left for war.

'Frank lad!' He leant out and grasped the young man's arm. 'It is you, you're alive.'

'Where's Ida, Mr Tatlock? What's 'appened?'

'She's down the Street at No. 11, lad. We've had a rum do.'

Before Albert had finished talking Frank ran down the

pavement and hammered on another piece of wood, this time a makeshift door.

Elsie opened the door, a sprig of mistletoe in her hair. 'Hello, soldier,' she said, eyeing him up and down.

'It's me, Frank Barlow. Where's Ida?'

Elsie stepped backwards and gestured into the house. Frank pushed past her and entered the living room. Ida sat in a chair with Kenneth on her lap. The hair on the right of her head had been shaved off and she had stitches along a cut. Kenneth was giggling as she jiggled her knees up and down. Frank took off his cap and smiled. ' 'Ello, Ida.'

His voice startled her. She looked at him in disbelief. 'It can't be you. You're dead.'

He opened his arms wide. 'I'm not, love.' He rushed across the room and embraced his family. Ida put a hand to the back of his head and fingered his hair. She smelt his eyebrows as he rubbed against her and felt his bristles against her skin. Suddenly she started to cry, great loud sobs that broke like waves over him. Standing by the side of the range and watching his mother cry, Kenneth felt isolated and suddenly afraid. His lower lip started to tremble and he let out a wail.

Frank looked over Ida's shoulder to his son and let out a cry. 'That can't be Kenneth.'

Ida beamed with pride and wiped away a tear as Frank bent down and opened his arms again. Kenneth took one look at him, stumbled backwards and sat down heavily on his nappy.

Elsie stood in the doorway and found herself crying. She pulled the mistletoe from her hair and said, 'I'd put kettle on, only we've no water!'

CHAPTER TEN

January 1941 British advances loosen Mussolini's grip on Africa. Sid's death loosens Rose's grip on reality.

Elsie Tanner slammed her front door shut and shivered. She turned up the collar on her coat and noticed that the fraying in the sleeve was getting worse. While she was inspecting her clothing Vi Todd came out of No. 9, also wrapped in her warmest clothes. She nearly bumped into Elsie. 'Hello, love,' she said. 'If it snows any more I'm not gettin' out of me bed.'

Elsie smiled back and said, 'My lav seat's like an iceberg. I'm 'angin' on until I get to work.'

'You're up early, aren't you?'

Elsie nodded to the end of the Street. 'Wi' Foyle's out of action I thought I'd best catch that woman on Victoria Street. Mrs Walker says she opens at seven.'

'Hetty Morris?' asked Vi. 'She'd open in middle of night if someone knocked on 'er door. Watch 'er when she measures out for you because she's been up in front of beak for it.'

'Thanks. Do you want owt? I shan't be long – I've left Linda on 'er own.'

'You run along then, love. I'm off to start me new job in Rovers.'

'At this time?'

'It's Annie high-and-mighty Walker. Said she wanted me in at crack o' dawn to give the pub a good scrub out. Dust in her knick-knacks, I reckon.'

Elsie stepped tentatively off her doorstep and on to the

177

pavement. The snow crunched beneath her shoes. They looked worn too.

Annie blearily wandered into the bar in her dressing-gown. She yawned as she approached the front doors and pulled back the black-out curtain. 'Who is it?' she asked.

'Me, Mrs Todd, bright an' early as requested.'

Annie pulled back the bolt and opened the door to admit her new cleaner. 'Whatever time is it?' she asked, stifling a yawn with the back of her hand.

'Ten past seven. Sun's not up yet but I thought that seein' as how you was so keen on early start you wouldn't be waiting till the cock crowed.'

Annie felt very underdressed in Vi's presence. She was annoyed with herself for being caught out in her night attire and wished she'd had the foresight to remove her curlers. She could tell by the way Vi was clicking her teeth that she intended to give a full account of Annie's appearance to her cronies later in the day. To grasp control of the situation Annie gestured towards the select.

'I suggest you start in there, Mrs Todd. You'll find a mop and everything else you'll require in the cupboard under the stairs. I've tidied the living room to my satisfaction and it's the three bars that require your attention. I'll be upstairs if you need anything, bathing Billy.'

After Annie had swanned off, Vi tugged off her raincoat, unwound her scarf and dropped them on a table. She wandered over to the door leading to the select, opened it and peered into the darkness. The smell of stale ale and cigarette smoke assaulted her nostrils. It wasn't a part of the pub she'd had much experience of. It was aired for weddings and such-like, but generally Vi couldn't see the point in using it, especially as Annie charged an extra penny a pint for table service.

Mrs Foyle knocked on Ena's vestry door and glanced over her shoulder to make certain no one was watching her. The door opened and she was ushered in.

'I'll not keep you long, Mrs Sharples,' she said. 'I know you've to clock on at eight but I wanted to catch you before you left.'

'Well, you 'ave done.'

Vera appeared at the curtain that kept the iron bedstead from view of visitors. 'Who is it, Mam?'

'Never you mind who it is. Get yer boots on and mek sure you've got an 'anky, I'm blowed if I'm listenin' to you sniffin' all day.' Ena looked at the basket in Mrs Foyle's hand. 'Goin' shoppin'?' she asked, laughing at her own joke.

'No. It's just a few pieces that were left on shelves after looters had taken their pick. Some tins and stuff. It's all covered by the insurance so I thought you could find a home for it all.'

'By 'eck, insurance, eh? All right for some. Martha Longhurst lost 'er home an' no one's said owt about insurance to 'er.'

'I've lost my livelihood, Mrs Sharples. There is a difference.'

'So there would seem,' said Ena, with a sniff.

Mrs Foyle placed the basket on the floor next to the door. 'If you don't want it, give it to Mrs Caldwell. I just thought you might like first pickings.'

Ena laughed. 'You're right there, Elsie Foyle. What about you? What are you goin' to do wi yerself now there's a gapin' hole in yer shop? Off to throw yerself on mercy of council, are you?'

'No. As a matter of fact I'm catching the ten past ten to Blackpool. I'll be in Lytham just after lunch.'

Ena raised an eyebrow. 'Will you?'

'I think it's time I saw summat of my family and I think I deserve a holiday.'

'For duration?' asked Ena.

Mrs Foyle shook her head. 'I've my livelihood to think of, Mrs Sharples. I said holiday, not retirement. Builders are going to make do over the way while I'm gone. I'll look to you for progress reports.'

'And you'll get 'em, 'ave no fear o' that.'

The door closed behind Mrs Foyle and Ena picked up the basket to peek inside then noticed Vera staring at her. 'I suppose you've been stood there listenin' to everythin'. Well you know listeners never 'ear good of themselves.'

'But, Mam, I only thought –'

'And you know what thought did, don't yer? Followed a muck-cart an' thought it were a weddin'!'

Beattie Tatlock skipped down the stairs at No. 1 carrying her rag doll. She ran into the front parlour and dived on to the sofa, giggling to herself. In the living room Bessie sighed and folded a yellow cardigan to place in the small case that sat open on the kitchen table.

'She's walked round wi' a face like a funeral since Christmas an' now she's goin' again she's like a sunbeam.' She pulled a handkerchief from her rolled-up sleeve and blew her nose loudly. 'I keep fillin' up.'

Albert shuffled his feet. 'She's just excited about the journey.'

'I must admit all that sea air's done her the power of good,' said Bessie begrudgingly. 'She looks very healthy.'

'She's bin well fed,' agreed Albert.

The tears started to fall again while in the parlour Beattie bounced on the sofa and sang to her doll, 'We're going home, we're going home.'

Bessie waved Beattie off from the doorstep. She'd wanted to go to the station with her but her daughter had refused to let her and accused her of being an embarrassment. Instead Albert had taken her on his way to work. They'd trundled off through the snow together, and he'd made her stop at the end of the Street and wave. That had been nice.

Rose Hayes sat staring into her cup. The tea was untouched. Esther crept around her, as she had since Sid's death two weeks previously. The doctor had given the family pills to keep Rose sedated, saying it was in her best interest to be as calm as she could be. Her eyes were dull and empty, her shoulders hunched.

Esther glanced nervously at the living room clock. It was nearly ten to two and while her supervisor at work was understanding she knew she couldn't afford to be late back again. 'Aren't you going to drink your tea?' she asked, forcing herself to sound cheerful.

There was no reply.

'I wonder how many forms I can process this afternoon? Perhaps I'll break my record. I've got sausages for tea. You like them, don't you? We'll have mashed potatoes as well. It'll just be the two of us, because Tom's going round to his friend.' Esther waited a beat, knowing there would be no response. 'Mrs Barlow said she'd call in about three, make sure you're all right. She said if you needed something you were to bang on the wall. She's really cheered up since her husband . . .' Esther realised talk of marital partners might not be a good idea and changed tack, 'so just bang on the wall if you need anything.'

She started to pull on her gloves and wondered how long she could carry on.

Elsie threw a bolt into the trough and yawned. 'I've had enough of this,' she said. 'How many more weeks are we goin' to 'ave to sit 'ere pullin' bleedin' levers?'

'There's worse jobs,' said Ena.

'You should count yerself lucky you're not one of them look-out girls, standing on top of buildin's with binoculars starin' up at the sky all day,' said Martha, pulling her handle up sharply.

'I saw a picture of one of them in *Picture Post*,' said Minnie. 'She was called Irene and it said she was very 'appy. And she was educated as well. Her father was a dentist.'

Ena threw a bolt into the trough and pointed at Elsie, 'Well, *'er* father were a ringer at Shafto's.'

'Blimey,' said Elsie. 'Is there no bit o' dirt you don't pick up, Mrs Sharples?'

'My father was a tackler,' said Minnie, 'and Mother used to sell clothes pegs.'

'Like a gypsy?' asked Dot.

Ena gave her a cold stare. 'No, like a woman who struggled to make ends meet. You three should show a bit more respect to the likes of Mrs Caldwell's mother.'

'Why?' asked Sally, 'because she's so old?'

'Because it was Mrs Caldwell's mother and her pals that got you the vote.'

Minnie nodded gravely. 'Ena's right, you know. I 'eld 'er banner once in Albert Square. We was moved on.'

'Me gran talks about stuff like that,' said Dot. 'It don't mean much to me, I'm too young to vote.'

'I can't wait till I'm old enough to vote,' said Elsie.

Ena stopped turning her lever and stared at her in surprise. 'Why?' she demanded.

'Because it's true what you say, about the likes of Mrs Caldwell's mother, chaining themselves to railin's and throwin' themselves under horses.'

'She did lie down in front of a cart once. It were to stop the bailiffs,' said Minnie.

'That Anthony Eden, he'd get my vote,' said Elsie.

'Why?' asked Martha, 'what are his politics?'

'Bugger his politics.' Elsie chortled. 'It's his voice on the wireless, dead deep and sexy.'

Ena threw another bolt in the trough. 'You've got sex on the brain, Elsie Tanner.'

'So what if I 'ave, Mrs Sharples? God gave me my sex drive, didn't he?'

Ena opened her mouth in amazement. She turned to her daughter, who was listening to the exchange. 'Vera, go and wash yer 'ands.'

Vera looked down at them. 'Why?'

'Don't ask questions, just do it.'

Ena waited until Vera had slunk off to the washroom before turning on Elsie and a giggling Dot. 'Never 'ave I 'eard anythin' so blasphemous in my life. To mention the Almighty and sex in that way. You should get down on your knees and beg forgiveness.'

Martha tutted in agreement. 'Shocking.'

'Oh, come off it, Mrs Sharples,' said Sally. 'If God didn't give Elsie her sex drive, then, who did?'

'It's a wonderful thing, Mrs Sharples,' said Elsie.

'It's for begetting children and that's all,' said Ena.

Minnie sighed. 'I never 'ad any children and it's too late now.'

'Is it 'eck,' said Elsie. 'You want to get yerself dolled up one night and come on the town with us. We'd find you a willin' fella, Mrs Caldwell.'

Ena's face went red and she stood up. 'Minnie, Martha, it's nearly teatime. Let's be first in queue for a change.' She looked down on the three girls laughing at the other side of the bench. 'Laugh all you like. You might think you're funny but I'm tellin' you now, you know nowt about it. I know you think you know all there is to know but there's more to keepin' a man than what you're talkin' about.'

'I've been married twenty-two years,' said Martha smugly, 'and you don't find me chunnerin' over the details of my marital bed all the time.'

The thought of scrawny Martha in the midst of sexual ecstasy sent the girls off into fresh peals of laughter.

Ena grabbed her bag and said, 'Come on, or we'll miss the buns.'

Sex was on Elsie's mind when she jumped into bed that night. Not because of her conversation in the factory, but because of the thirty-six-year-old Polish airman who lay naked under her covers. They'd met at a dance held at the Alhambra. It was held to raise funds to help displaced servicemen from overseas. Elsie had no money to put in the collection tin so had done her bit by giving the best-looking foreigner a bed for the night. That had been over a fortnight ago and he hadn't been back to the shelter since. He didn't speak much English, but his hands had a language all of their own. He hadn't shaved for a couple of days and his dark growth rubbed harshly against her inner thigh as he explored beneath the candlewick. She kneaded his thick hair with her fingers and moaned in satisfaction, hoping that Linda wouldn't wake up in the next bedroom.

His name was Peter and he was Jewish; that much she'd established while putting the sheath on to his penis. Lying back while his tongue darted over her flesh, she decided she didn't need to know any more than that.

The news that a foreign serviceman's cap was hanging over Elsie Tanner's bedknob was quick to reach Ena's sharp ears. She kept a special guard at the vestry window and caught sight of the man as he came and went at unsociable hours. Ena had read about women in France collaborating with the Germans and felt certain that if ever Hitler did manage to break fortress Britain Elsie wouldn't hold out for long. She pulled her shawl tightly around her shoulders. Vera was snoring in the bed and the thought of Elsie fornicating across the cobbles upset Ena. It wasn't right: she was a married woman. Even if her husband was a villain. Vows had been exchanged and they should be kept. She knew what it was like being lonely. Hadn't Sharples been taken when she was still in her prime? But you needed respect for yourself. You needed to keep yourself clean.

Ena sat in her chair and picked up her Bible. She hugged it to her and muttered aloud, 'Help me, O Lord, guide me I pray. Tell me what I must do to help that poor child save herself before it's too late.'

Three-year-old Billy Walker ran laughing into the bar in his pyjamas, a one-eared rabbit in one hand.

'Ah, don't 'e look bonny,' said Bessie Tatlock.

Annie picked up her son and looked apologetically at her customers. 'I'm sorry,' she said, 'I'm going to have to settle him down again.'

'It's all right, Mrs Walker,' called Sally from her table, 'I'll look after the bar for you.'

Annie smiled her thanks then disappeared with Billy into the hall.

'Right, Uncle Tommy, were you next?' asked Sally, lifting the bar flap.

Thomas Hewitt banged his pint pot down on the bar. 'I'll 'ave another in there,' he said. He glanced nervously to his side as Ena Sharples appeared from the snug.

'Don't look so worried, I'm not cadging ale from likes of you Thomas 'Ewitt. You want to get out of yer pit more often on a Sunday mornin', like most of 'em round 'ere. No, it's Albert Tatlock I want.'

Albert gulped down his beer and looked at Ena. 'Is it official business?' he asked.

'Does it 'ave to be?'

He shrugged his shoulders.

'Well, it isn't, but that don't mean to say it's not important.'

Bessie looked intrigued as Albert left her side and crossed to Ena. She held open the snug door and ushered him in. Once on the other side of the door Albert fingered his cap nervously. The snug being women's territory, it was unnerving for a lone man to be in it.

'Sit down,' invited Ena.

'I'd rather stand, if it's all same,' he said.

'Suit yerself.'

She sat. After a couple of seconds he joined her, feeling foolish. 'What's to do?' he asked.

On the other side of the bar curious eyes were fixed on them so Ena shifted her chair round so her back blocked their view into the snug.

'I need a man,' said Ena.

Albert gulped. 'Do you?' he asked, in a small voice.

Ena nodded. 'And I reckon you'll do.'

Albert stammered, 'Will I?'

'I thought of Jack Todd but seein' mess he's made of his two I changed me mind.'

Albert looked bemused.

'No, I reckon you've more sense than a lot of 'em round 'ere. And you're a God-fearin' man.'

He continued to stare uneasily at her.

'It's Elsie Tanner,' she said conspiritorially.

'Is it?' he asked.

'She's in need.'

'Is she?'

'And you're the one who's goin' to 'elp 'er.'

Albert felt his palms getting sweaty. 'Mrs Sharples,' he cleared his throat, 'what is it you're talkin' about?'

'Elsie Tanner carryin' on with every fella who winks at her, that's what I'm talkin' about.'

'I've never winked at Elsie Tanner,' protested Albert.

Ena stared at him, 'Of course you 'aven't. You're not sort.'

Albert didn't know whether to be pleased or insulted.

Ena pressed on, 'She needs someone to give 'er a talkin' to. A father figure who'll point out the error of her ways and pull 'er back on to the good path. A bit of plain talkin's all that's needed and you're the man for the job.' Ena stood up and towered over the startled Albert. 'Just put it to 'er straight. Tell 'er about men who take advantage of girls and say as how she should be savin' 'erself for 'er 'usband.'

Albert stared at her in horror. Him? Tell Elsie Tanner to save herself?

Elsie and Dot sat at the living room table flicking through an issue of *Picture Goer*.

'Don't you just love Clark Gable's eyes?' said Dot.

'They're better than his ears,' said Elsie, 'I'll give you that, but I prefer his shoulders. I like a man with shoulders.'

'Has Peter got shoulders?' asked Dot.

Elsie smirked, 'He's got shoulders on top of his shoulders,' she said.

'Elsie, you're so lucky,' said Dot. 'I've not found anyone after Jean. I reckon I've been spoilt. He was the best.'

'Give over, he was giving your Sal one, he can't 'ave bin that good.'

Dot looked at a photograph of Clark Gable's face and traced his profile with her finger. 'I wish I were Carole Lombard,' she said. 'I bet he's a brilliant lover.'

'As brilliant as brilliant Jean?' asked Elsie with a laugh. She pulled a cigarette out of her bag and got up from the table. Holding her hair back with one hand she put her head towards the fire in the range and lit the cigarette.

The front door opened and closed and someone cleared his throat.

'Who's there?' demanded Elsie, reaching for the poker.

'It's only me, Albert from number one.'

Elsie put back the poker and called, 'Well, come in, then, it's draughty in that lobby.'

Albert entered the room and removed his cap. At the sight of Dot he backed against the door and said, 'You've company, I'll call back.'

'Don't be daft,' said Elsie. 'It's only Dot, she won't bite yer.' She smiled to put Albert at his ease. 'What can I do for you, Mr Tatlock? I've no milk if you're on the borrow.'

'No, it's nowt like that. I just thought to meself, it's a while since I saw Elsie and 'ad a chat with her, so I came down Street.'

Elsie looked bemused. She could hardly remember saying two words to Albert in months. 'That's very kind, Mr Tatlock – isn't that kind, Dot? Mr Tatlock's come for a chat.' She sat on a chair and gestured to a vacant one. 'Sit yerself down, Mr Tatlock, we was just talkin' about film stars. Do you reckon Carole Lombard much, Mr Tatlock?'

'Who?'

'Carole Lombard, married to Clark Gable.'

Albert shook his head, 'I'm not one for pictures.'

'Oh, you'll 'ave to come wi' us sometime, won't 'e Dot?'

Albert went red as Dot laughed.

'We could sit on back row,' continued Elsie, 'and share a box of Maltesers. There's an art to eatin' Maltesers, you know. I nibble all the chocolate off then suck middle until it melts in me mouth. 'Ow about you, Mr Tatlock? Do you do that or do you just bite into them?'

'I don't know,' he said uncomfortably. 'I suppose I just crunch 'em.'

'Oh, you're wastin' 'em if you crunch 'em,' said Elsie. 'You want to savour 'em. That way they last longer.'

'I prefer gums,' said Dot. 'Do you, Mr Tatlock?'

Albert sat straighter in the chair and said, 'I've not come to talk about gums.'

' 'Ave you not?' asked Elsie, her eyes wide open in surprise. 'What 'ave you come to talk about, then?'

The directness of the question took Albert by surprise and he struggled to think of a reply. Eventually he opened his mouth and found himself saying, 'Men.'

'I beg your pardon, Mr Tatlock?'

'Men.' He looked from Elsie to Dot then back again, frantically trying to form the words he'd rehearsed in his mind. The girls smiled encouragingly and he blurted out, 'There's some strange men about and you should be careful.'

'How do you mean?' asked Dot.

'Men that take advantage of young women.'

'In what way?' asked Elsie innocently.

'By . . .' The words were replaced by a blind panic.

'Stealing their purses?' suggested Dot.

'Makin' them darn the holes in their socks?' suggested Elsie.

Albert knew he'd lost any nerve he'd built up to enter the house. He knew they were mocking him and he was frustrated that they embarrassed him so much. They were little more than children and they made him feel so foolish. He got to his feet and made his excuses then rushed from the room and the house. Behind him Elsie and Dot erupted in laughter.

'What was that all about?' asked Dot.

' 'E just wanted a chat,' said Elsie and wiped a tear from her eye.

Sunday afternoon found Ena banging on Elsie's front door, her jaw set, determined to succeed where Albert had failed. She should have dealt with Elsie herself in the first place.

Elsie opened the door in her dressing-gown and gave Ena a hostile glance. 'Yes, Mrs Sharples? Collectin' for Salute a Soldier week, are you? I've already given.'

Ena looked past Elsie and noticed the pair of men's boots in the hallway. 'Aye, lass, I'm sure you've done your bit.'

Elsie straightened her back and glared at Ena. 'Come on, spit it out. I'm catchin' cold 'ere.'

'Aren't you going to invite me in?' asked Ena. 'I thought you were more hospitable than this, or is it that I'm not wearing trousers or in uniform?'

Elsie went to close the door but Ena placed her foot in the way. 'I'm come to say my piece and I intend to say it,' she said, raising her voice.

The net curtain at No. 13 twitched as Martha, alerted by Ena's voice, struggled to see what was going on.

Elsie opened the door again and sighed. 'Come on, then, get it said.'

'You've a man up there.' Ena gestured up the stairs.

'So?'

'So you don't deny it? Brazen, aren't you?'

'There'd be no point in denying it, Mrs Sharples. I've seen you with yer nose rammed against your window. You want to watch it, else someone'll report you for being an enemy spy. Talk about Mass Observation.'

' 'Ave you no shame?' asked Ena. 'Standing there in yer nothin's with a strange man sleepin' in yer 'usband's bed?'

Elsie scratched her lip and smirked. ' 'E's not sleepin' love. Far from it.'

Martha appeared at her doorway. 'Oh, Ena,' she said, 'what a surprise.'

Ena beckoned her over. 'Come 'ere Martha, I might need you if she cuts up rough.'

Martha flinched, but Elsie said, with a grin, 'Mrs Sharples, I can assure you I 'ave no idea of cuttin' up rough. Now, will you say your piece and let me get back to bed?'

'I'll say my piece all right, Elsie Tanner. You're a dirty blackguard and I'm 'ere to tell you to change your ways before it's too late.'

'Too late for what?' asked Elsie.

'For your soul!'

Elsie laughed. 'Well, thanks, Mrs Sharples, but I reckon the state of my soul is of no concern to you.'

'It is when you drag the rest of us down to your level,' said Ena. 'This is a decent street, not some back-street Sodom and Gomorrah, which is what you're turnin' it into.'

'Hear hear,' said Martha. 'I can 'ear you, you know. Comin' through walls. I've 'ad to move my Lily into back bedroom because of the stuff coming from yours. I don't know where you learnt words like that but it wasn't at Bessie Street School, I'm sure. Oh, Ena, I couldn't begin to tell you.'

'You mean you 'aven't already?' asked Elsie. She turned her back on Martha and addressed Ena, 'Look, Mrs Sharples, I'm not doin' anyone any 'arm. I'm not stealin', or murderin' no one, I'm just gettin' on wi' my life.'

'Them's just two of the Lord's Commandments. Another's "Thou shalt not commit adultery," or does that one stick in yer throat?'

'It's got nothin' to do wi' you, Mrs Sharples!'

'I'll not stand by and see you ruin yer life.'

'That's right, Mrs Sharples. It's my life. *My* life. Not yours, not 'ers, not anyone else's. And don't talk to me about adultery. Wherever Arnold Tanner is you can bet there's some tart tucked away nearby.'

She turned to go into the house but Ena put out a hand to stop her. Elsie spun round. Her voice was no longer so light-hearted as she said, 'Go away, Mrs Sharples. Go and take your evil-minded friend and get off my doorstep. If I want to 'ave a bit of fun I'll 'ave a bit of fun. With the whole flamin' Navy if I want to.'

'You're man mad,' said Ena in disgust.

'So what? I like men. Are you jealous? Is that what all this is about? Because if you are, you only have to say. I'm sure my friend can fix you up. He must 'ave a pal who isn't that choosy.'

Ena glared at her then stepped back on to the pavement.

Elsie pulled her dressing-gown around her and lowered her eyes. 'Whatever you think of me, Mrs Sharples, I'm not some little tart who's desperate. I'm just lonely, and some-times . . .' her voice cracked. '. . . I need someone to hold me.'

Ena rasied her eyebrows. 'Don't give me loneliness, lass. You surrendered quicker than France. Go on, get back upstairs to whoever it is you've got up there. I've said me piece, you've not listened, but I didn't think you would. Just think on this, though. I'll be writing to Arnold Tanner, care of 'Is Majesty's forces. I'm sure 'e'll be interested in what I 'ave to say even if you're not.'

Elsie stared at her in defiance. 'Do what the hell you like,' she said, and slammed the door in Ena's face.

CHAPTER ELEVEN

July 1941 Germany has invaded Russia. Elsie experiences some domestic violence.

Elsie had picked up quite a few Polish words and expressions. She wasn't entirely sure what they meant but as most had been learnt to the accompaniment of twanging bedsprings she guessed they weren't to be used in polite company. Not that she mixed much in polite company: immediately after her row with Ena, the older woman had applied for a bench transfer and had dragged her friends and daughter with her to the other side of the factory. Their places had been taken by three young women from Kitchener Street.

Ena wasn't satisfied with the atmosphere at her new bench. The women there were more sober and industrious than Elsie and the Todds so rather than leading the section's production output Ena found she had to concentrate to keep up. At first break Martha complained that her fingers were already aching from twisting and pulling the lever so quickly. Ena knew she could cope and that Minnie would plod along in her own fashion, not at all bothered by the amount she produced, but she worried about Vera. She could not get the hang of the machine at all, and her work was shoddy and unacceptable. At the old bench Ena had covered for her, but now she couldn't turn out enough bolts to share with her and the old lags were quick to complain. Their spokeswoman was a tight-mouthed woman in her thirties whose fingers darted in and out of the bolt trough at an incredible speed.

'We've always been fastest section,' she complained to Ena,

'I've a husband and three brothers in Cheshires. They're doin' their bit, I'm doin' mine.'

'We're all doin' our bit, otherwise we wouldn't be sat here twelve hours a day, would we?' replied Ena.

'It's your daft daughter who's draggin' us down. We never had complaints from foreman before you lot arrived. I tell you now, next time he comes looking for someone to blame I'm pointin' 'er out. She shouldn't be 'ere.'

'Don't you tell me where she should or shouldn't be,' warned Ena. 'I don't tek kindly to that sort of talk.'

Before the morning was over the foreman had moved Vera off the bench and had put her on broom duty. She was content to wander the pathways between benches pushing dirt around, but Ena wasn't at all happy with the idea. How could she keep an eye on her? How would she know if she sought out the company of unsuitables, such as their neighbours on the other side of the huge room? Ena bit her lip and watched Vera as she disappeared into the sea of bent backs.

The grand reopening of Foyle's Provisions and Groceries took place on a sunny morning and was heralded by the residents as a sign of the change of tide in the war. The air raids had continued throughout the first half of the year, with damage being done to the streets down by the docks. Coronation Street wasn't touched after the Christmas blitz and its residents fell into an almost nightly ritual of gathering possessions and wandering over to the Mission at the wail of the siren. Some had taken to leaving bedding in the boiler room to save time and effort.

Mrs Foyle had returned from her holiday refreshed and ready to face the moans and complaints of her customers. Cheese and preserves had been rationed since she'd last stood behind the counter and she was certain the likes of Mrs Longhurst would have plenty to grumble about. While in Lytham she had made a resolution not to work so hard. In order to implement this one of the first things she did back in Weatherfield was to put a card in the window advertising for a shop assistant. At least, she had written the card. Before she'd had a chance to lean it against the display of Spam

Esther Hayes had walked past, read it, applied and had been taken on. It meant a cut in wages for her but she felt the need to be closer to Rose during the day.

As well as a new face behind the counter, the shop had a new sign, painted in brown and yellow. Mrs Foyle had wanted gold, but paint was in short supply so yellow had had to do. Inside it was pretty much the same, but all the dusty old display boxes had been replaced with crisp new ones. It was like starting over and she was grateful for the opportunity. She decided to rid herself of one headache by prominently placing a card on the counter. In big black letters it read 'Sorry, no tick'. Vi Todd stared at the notice as if it wasn't written in English. ' 'Ow do you mean, no tick?'

'What I say. Cash only. You can't buy drinks in the Rovers on tick, can you? Well, in future if you want my goods I want to see pounds, shillings and pence.'

'I've never 'eard the like, it's disgraceful –' began Vi.

Mrs Foyle interrupted the flow: 'Mrs Todd, we're not going to fall out over this, are we? You're a sensible woman. Think about how helpful this new arrangement will be to you.'

'How do you mean?'

'Well, if Mr Todd came in and asked for cigarettes he'd put them on your slate, wouldn't he? Probably without you knowing about it. Then at the end of the week it's a surprise when you come to reckon up. This way he'll have to pay before he gets his fags. It'll save you money in the long run.'

Vi couldn't help admire the logic. She sniffed and said, 'That sea air's been a tonic for you, hasn't it?' She dug in her purse and pulled out some coins. 'I reckon I've enough for what I need.' She placed the coins on the counter before producing her ration books. 'You still want these, I tek it?'

Mrs Foyle smiled as she took the books.

Elsie wasn't sure if Ena had kept her threat to write to Arnold or not. She'd learnt that generally Ena's threats weren't idle, but it seemed a spiteful thing to do and her gut feeling was that Ena wasn't malicious.

Sally didn't share her generous opinion of Mrs Sharples and told her so. 'You want to be careful Elsie. There's no point in rubbin' 'er nose in it. If your Arnold finds out 'e could stop the Navy sendin' you 'is pay. That two quid keeps you in gin and fags. 'Ow are you gonna cope without it?'

'She 'asn't written. If she 'ad I'd 'ave 'eard from 'im by now.'

'That's not to say she won't write if you carry on with Peter. I saw 'er twitchin' in snug the other night when you two were in there. And Sour-face Walker was lookin' down 'er bony nose an' all.'

The girls were sitting on the grass outside the factory gates, soaking up the midday sun and sharing Elsie's packed lunch of potted-meat sandwiches. A noise in the sky caused them to look up, shielding their eyes from the sun.

'It's one of ours,' said Sally, identifying the plane.

'Why can't I be allowed to enjoy meself?' asked Elsie, returning to her theme. 'It's not as if it's a different fella every night. I've been seein' Peter for nigh on six months now. It's like we're goin' steady.'

'I think it's amazin' you've got the energy. I can 'ear you through bedroom wall, at it all night. Then you come 'ere all day. You must be fit to drop some days.'

Elsie giggled and bit into her sandwich. 'I've never known owt like it.'

'How many fellas 'ave you 'ad?'

'Blimey, what sort of question's that?'

'Come on, I've been with three, what about you?'

'I can't remember. More than you, anyroad. It's like that in Back Gas Street. As soon as you get your monthlies they're sniffin' around. I got mine when I were twelve.'

'So Arnold wasn't the first?'

Elsie shook her head.

'And Peter's the best?'

'So far.' Elsie chuckled.

Sally munched on a crust and then asked, 'What was our Jim like?'

'I'm not tellin' you!'

'Better than Arnold?'

Elsie shivered. ' 'E's a brute. I don't want to talk about 'im, an' I don't care if Ena's written to 'im. Perhaps it'll get 'im out of me life.'

*

Tom Hayes stood at the shop door, keeping an eye open for customers. None were around so he staggered into the shop carrying a heavy suitcase and asked the curious shopkeeper, 'Is my sister about?'

'She's out back, stock-taking. Shall I get her? Is it your mother?'

'No,' he said quickly. 'It's you I've come to see.' He lifted the suitcase on to the counter.

Mrs Foyle looked at it suspiciously. 'What's it about, Tom?' she asked.

He lifted the catch on the case and opened the lid. Mrs Foyle looked inside and saw neat rows of square cans looking up at her.

'Best 'am,' said Tom. 'Bet you've not seen the likes since nineteen thirty-nine.'

Mrs Foyle glanced at him. 'Where are they from? I don't want no trouble.'

'Kosher goods, honest. They're part of a shipment come in down the docks. This warehouse was hit by bombers the other week an' I've been asked to take these round the community, offer them to shopkeepers such as yerself.'

'Why be so secretive about it, then?'

'You can't let everyone know you're walkin' streets with a case full of 'am, can you? 'Ow about it, then? Two bob a can. I bet you can mark 'em up at four easy. A little extra ration for your regulars, eh?'

It went on, everyone knew it did. Why shouldn't she believe him? Everyone knew the docks were a prime target and it wasn't as if she was going to hoard them for herself. She'd share them out, like he suggested. She knew she had to act fast. There was no point in letting any of the customers witness the exchange. She opened the cash register.

Ena Sharples looked suspiciously across the bar to where Annie, thinking no one was watching her, wiggled her backside. Ena's brow creased. Something was definitely going on inside that tightly permed head.

'Yes, Ena. Do you want another?' During one of her occasional shifts behind the bar, Martha always looked after her friends in the snug. She knew too well the frustration of slow service.

Ena kept her voice low as she nodded towards Annie, 'What's up wi' Fanny By Gaslight?'

Martha folded her arms across the bar and leant confidentially towards her friend.

'She's joined an Am Dram. You know, the lot down at St Joseph's. They did *Hamlet* before the war and Slow Doris wi' the cleft chin played the ghost. You remember, that bloke in front kept glaring at us and saying as how it weren't a comedy.'

'What's she doing that wigglin' for, with her backside? Not doin' Salome, is she?'

'*Desert Song.*'

'Fancy.'

The snug door opened and Minnie entered from the public. She walked slowly and looked dejected. Instead of sitting at the table she joined her friends, pulled a handkerchief out of her sleeve and blew her nose.

'What's up with you?' demanded Ena. 'Lost yer cat again?'

'I were just 'avin' a think, Ena,' she said defensively.

'There's no need to snap,' said Martha. 'Ena were only concerned for you.'

'What is it, lass, what's to do?' asked Ena, sympathetically.

'I've just been down Tile Street. Past the police station.'

'You've never had men exposing themselves to you again, have you?'

'No, Ena. I just wanted to see it. Armistead was born there. His mother lived there all her life. Number twenty-three, it were a lovely 'ouse. There was some grassland at the back and Armistead's father had fenced a piece off. 'E grew vegetables. First time I went for my tea I got a shock because he'd put up a scarecrow and I thought it was a man lookin' in the back window. When we wed his mother wanted us to live with 'er, but my mother 'ad one of 'er turns so we ended up wi' her instead. The 'ouse is gone. Just a big 'ole. Even the bit of grass at the back. Just a big 'ole. It could 'ave been my 'ome.' She sniffed again.

'Well, my 'ome on Mawdsley Street's the same, you know. I lost everything when that bomb 'it it,' said Martha bitterly.

Ena waved for Martha to shut up, and put an arm around Minnie's shoulder. 'You're missin' 'im aren't you, love?'

Minnie nodded.

'It's all right to miss 'em, you know. It's what love's all about.'

The noise of the public door banging open made the three women jump. A huge man in uniform stood in the doorway. With a couple of strides he was at the bar and banging on it for service.

'Can I 'elp you?' asked Martha, as if it were the last thing she wanted to do.

'Pint of best.'

'We're only servin' 'alves, I'm afraid.'

She pulled the drink while he cast his eye around the bar. 'Quiet tonight,' he said.

'It's the same most nights.'

' 'Ow much?'

'Fourpence, please.'

He threw coins on to the bar and sank the beer in one. Banging down the glass he wiped his mouth with the back of his hand then walked out of the pub. Martha was still holding his money when the door shut behind him. She turned to the snug, where Ena and Minnie still stood, watching.

'So,' said Ena grimly, 'he got my letter, then.'

Down the Street, at No. 11, Elsie Tanner was coughing over a cigarette. Smoking had become a luxury and the fags she could get her hands on were rough. The wireless was on in the background. Henry Hall was conducting his orchestra and 'Manchester's Own' Betty Driver was belting out a number, but Elsie wasn't listening. She rubbed the sole of her aching foot and exclaimed at the state of her skirt. She'd been reading in a magazine how to make a new skirt out of a pair of men's trousers. Sounded perfect. Unfortunately, the men in Elsie's life took their trousers with them when they left the house.

The slam of the front door made her jump. It was a strange time for visitors.

'Who's there?' she demanded.

No one answered but the living room door swung open and Arnold Tanner sauntered in. Elsie gasped. ' 'Ello, doll, I'm back.' He opened his arms, as if expecting a fond embrace.

'Where 'ave you come from?' Her voice was little more than a whisper.

'Italy. Nice and warm. Got a bit of a tan. Want to see? From what I 'ear you've got a thing about Continentals,' he sneered.

She felt sick.

He looked round the room and nodded his approval. 'Very 'omely. You've made a good job of it.'

'Thank you.'

'Aren't you gonna offer me a cuppa?'

'It's rationed, or doesn't that affect you lot in the Navy?'

'Something a bit stronger then?'

She produced a half-empty bottle of gin from the sideboard and threw it at him. He caught it, undid the lip and drank straight from the bottle. She sat on the other side of the table, hating him. 'Jumped ship 'ave you?' she asked.

'Where is 'e?'

'Who?'

'Don't play games. Your friend. I've heard all about him. Course, I might be behind the times. Moved on, 'ave you? Found someone else to give you a seein' to?'

She sat bolt upright, watching him pace round the room.

'I don't know what you're talking about,' she said. 'There's no one else 'ere. Just me and Linda.'

'Linda?'

'Our daughter.'

'What sort of name is Linda?' He stopped and bent his head down so his nose almost touched hers. 'Linda?'

'I – I like it,' she stammered.

'Well, I don't. You should 'ave asked me. I wanted a name like Amy. That was my mother's name. Course, that's if she is my kid.'

'She is. You know she is.'

'I know you're a tart who needs teaching a lesson.'

She flinched as he raised his hand but he stopped when he

198

heard the distant sound of a toilet flushing. It wouldn't have meant anything if Elsie's eyes hadn't darted to the back door.

Arnold smirked. 'So, that's where 'e is.'

'Please, Arnold. I don't want no trouble . . .'

He put a finger to her lips then backed away to stand behind the back door. Elsie's mind raced. What could she do? What would Arnold do? Who could help her? Inside, she began to cry but her eyes remained dry and she forced herself to stay calm. She knew she could manipulate the situation somehow. She'd always been able to twist Arnold round her little finger. She stopped thinking when the door opened and Peter walked in. He looked straight at her and smiled.

'What you look at?' he asked.

Arnold hit him from behind: a strong, powerful blow to the head which sent the tall Pole falling to the floor as if he were a pile of building bricks toppled by a child.

Elsie leapt to her feet as Arnold's own foot made contact with Peter's side. Again and again. 'Stop it, Arnold. You'll kill 'im!' she screamed.

'Yeah,' he said, with a laugh. 'Then I'll kill you.'

She made a bolt for the hall, running as fast as she could with only one shoe on. He gave Peter's limp body another kick and followed her, his face flushed, his eyes shining. In the hall he reached out a hand and grabbed her ankle. He gave it a pull and she fell on her face on the stairs. His eyes took in her slender body and he gazed longingly at the outline of her backside. She tried to get up but he refused to release her ankle. He moved closer and ran his free hand up her leg. She tensed and caught her breath. When his hand reached the hem of her summer dress he slipped it under the fabric.

'Arnold . . . not 'ere, not on the stairs . . .'

Her words took him by surprise and he released her. Quickly she scrambled up the stairs. It took him a second to realise what had happened and his reflexes were slow as he clambered after her. She stumbled at the top of the stairs and fell, ripping her last pair of stockings on a stair track. They reached the bedroom door at the same time.

She wasn't able to grasp the lock and found herself being pushed backwards on to the bed. It groaned under their weight. She hit out at his head and felt the sudden, sharp blow as he smacked his hand across her face. Her body went limp as he ripped the dress off her and started to unbutton his flies.

On the other side of the wall Sally lay in bed listening to the hammering of Elsie's bedsprings. She smiled to herself.

'Peter's really goin' for it tonight,' she said to Dot.

Dot stepped out of her dress and sat at the dressing table. 'Lucky cow.'

Downstairs Peter slowly came to. One eye swam with blood and he vomited on the scullery floor before crawling into the backyard.

Upstairs, on the other side of the other adjoining wall, Martha Longhurst sat up in bed and thumped the bedroom wall with the heel of her shoe.

'There's decent folk tryin' to get to sleep in 'ere!' she shouted.

Next to her, Percy turned over in bed and muttered, 'Leave 'em be. Just because you've gone off the boil don't mean to say other folk 'ave to.'

Elsie hugged herself and looked down on Arnold's comatose body. It shuddered as he snored. She could hear Linda stirring in the next room and, slowly, she moved off the bed, stepped over his discarded clothes and ran from the room. She let herself into Linda's bedroom and gently stroked her daughter's head. When Linda had stopped fretting she looked around the room, at the cut-out pictures pasted on the walls, the few toys scattered about the place. There wasn't much, but it was enough. She loved No. 11 Coronation Street. It was her home, hers and Linda's. It was nothing to do with the bastard snoring in the front bedroom.

Tom Hayes lifted the sash window and silently crept into his bedroom. Taking care not to knock over any of his model planes, he fell upon his bed. It was an entry into the house he had practised on many nights. Leaving his bedroom via the window, when he was certain the rest of the household had gone to bed, he'd shin down the drainpipe and land on the sacking he'd placed on the coal-hole. Weatherfield at night was an Aladdin's cave. Bomb-sites offered up treasures, and it was amazing how many people still left their doors unlocked, despite all the police warnings about looters. There were always pickings to be had from the gullible, like his own neighbours. That night he'd successfully rounded up a couple of chickens from Albert's allotment and delivered them to a butcher on Tile Street. On his way back he'd stumbled upon a jewellery box under a load of rubble where Pear Street had once stood. A nice hoard for a night's work.

Elsie watched the sun rise at five o'clock. As the house filled with light she saw herself in the mirror for the first time. Her cheek was red and swollen, her lip cut and her eye half closed. Her slip hung in tatters from her shoulders and the bruises on her body were turning purple. She listened for the back door of No. 9 to open, as she knew it would, as Vi left for her latest job, cleaning up at the abattoir.

Hearing the click, she picked up the sleeping Linda and carried her out into the backyard, stepping over the mixed stains of blood and vomit without a thought for Peter's whereabouts.

'Vi,' she called.

On the other side of the yard wall, Vi stumbled over a crooked flagstone. 'Elsie? What's to do?'

'Vi, I need your 'elp. Can you take Linda in and put 'er in with the girls? She's asleep.'

There was the sound of footsteps as Vi left her yard then appeared in Elsie's. She was shocked to see the state of Elsie and exclaimed in alarm, 'What on earth –'

'I'm all right, Vi. I just need Linda taken care of. I don't want 'er in the house when 'e wakes up.'

'Who is it?'

'Arnold.'

Vi nodded and took the sleeping bundle. Linda muttered as her arms sought Vi's neck and hugged her in her sleep.

'Do you want my Jack?' asked Vi.

'No. I can take care of him meself. It was Linda I was worried about.'

'You can come and stop wi' us, you know.'

'Thanks, but this is my 'ome and I'm not runnin' away because of 'im.'

' 'Ow long's 'e back for?'

'Not long,' said Elsie.

The cold water hit Arnold's face with force. He spluttered and jumped out of bed. Elsie lifted the second bowl of water and poured it over his head as he sat on the floor. He shrank back from the water and opened his eyes wide with alarm, focusing on his wife's determined face.

'You're a stinkin' animal, Arnold Tanner, and that's the last time you do that to me!' she screamed. She threw his clothes across the floor. 'Get dressed and get out!'

She was out of the room and down the stairs before he could stop her. Then she stood panting in the living room and listened to the creak of the floorboards as he pulled on his trousers and followed her.

He blinked in the sunlight when he entered the living room and held out a hand to her. 'Elsie, darlin', don't be like that. I got carried away, that's all. I 'ad to teach you a lesson.'

'You raped me!'

He laughed. 'Don't be stupid, love, we're married.' He stepped forward but stopped moving when he noticed the rifle.

She picked it up, forcing herself to steady her arms as she aimed it at his bare chest. 'Don't come any closer, just get out and don't come back!'

'Where did you get that from?' he asked.

'Mr Todd next door. Home Guard. It's loaded and I reckon I can hit you at this range. Now go! And if you come back I'll not give you any warnin's, I'll shoot yer balls off!'

She was hysterical, no mistake. He eyed her carefully and decided she was capable of pressing the trigger. 'You're not worth it.'

'Neither are you,' she said with contempt, 'I don't want you comin' back 'ere. I want a divorce . . .'

He didn't reply, just spat on the floor and swaggered out of the house.

Elsie lowered the rifle and started to cry. Her shoulders heaved as the tears fell.

After she'd finished at the abattoir Vi brought Linda home. She could tell from the cheerful music bellowing from the radio that Elsie's mood had lightened.

'Was the gun any use?' she asked.

'Better than the bread-knife I were plannin' on usin'.'

Vi looked at her face in concern. 'You should see a doctor.'

'No. It'll mend. I'll just stay indoors for a week.'

'Sally was going to tell supervisor you were poorly.'

Elsie nodded her thanks. 'I shan't be seein' him again. Some marriage, eh?'

'Was 'e always 'andy with 'is fists?'

Elsie puffed on her cigarette before answering. 'Not like last night. I suppose he 'adn't 'ad a woman for a while and got upset because I didn't fancy it.'

'Don't go defendin' 'im,' said Vi. 'He should be locked up for doin' this to you.'

Elsie shrugged. 'My mother put up with worse from me dad. She 'ad me and then six other girls. I think she were relieved to die in the end. When he wasn't fuckin' her he was usin' her as a punch-bag. What a life.'

'If Jack ever lifted 'and to me . . .'

'What? What would you do?' Elsie leaned across the table and pointed at her face. 'I tried to stop him, you know. I tried to run away. I didn't just stand there like me mam did, tellin' me it was part of married life, saying as how it was the drink. And then, when he started lookin' at me, pawin' me, she never stopped him, said it was because 'e was a man. All that muck he'd come out with. I always said no man would treat me like he treated my mother.'

Vi stared at her and said, 'You're talking about your father, aren't you?'

Elsie shrank back into her chair. 'Let's talk about something else, eh?'

Vi didn't know what to say. She saw the rawness in the young woman's eyes and wished she could help, think of something to say that might ease the pain. But that was just it. There was nothing to say.

*

Ena eyed the tinned ham before putting it back on the counter. 'I don't think so, thank you all the same,' she said to Mrs Foyle.

'It's all right, Mrs Sharples, it's just bombed stock.'

'I won't tek it 'cos I don't want the bother of it on my conscience.'

Mrs Foyle removed the tin from the counter and looked annoyed. All her other customers had been thrilled with the bounty. Trust Ena to kick up a fuss.

'I'll not ask you where you got it from,' said Ena, 'but if you take my advice you'll get shut of it quick. Your shop's only just opened and it'll be a shame to see it closed down so soon.'

'I hope that wasn't a threat, Mrs Sharples.'

Ena shook her head in disbelief. One minute best pals, the next deepest suspicion. Still, that's what came from having a guilty conscience. 'I'll just take the cocoa and a canister of Vim.'

Mrs Foyle fetched the items and placed them on the counter. 'That's elevenpence.'

Ena handed her a shilling and waited for her penny change. 'Think on, get shut, and stop foolin' yerself it's bombed stock.'

An hour later a man stood in the spot Ena had occupied. He wore the uniform of a special constable. Mrs Foyle was thankful Esther had gone home and that no one else was in the shop when he opened the door and blocked out the light with his dark suit. 'Are you Elsie Foyle?' he asked.

She grabbed hold of the counter for support.

'We've received a report, Mrs Foyle, that you have been selling rationed goods over the counter. Do you mind if I inspect your stock?'

As he walked round the shop she glanced out of the big glass window that overlooked Coronation Street. Across the way, Ena Sharples walked along the outside of the Mission and peered into the shop window.

He found the ham straight away and piled the remaining tins on the counter. 'Would you mind telling me where you acquired these items, Mrs Foyle?' As he opened his notebook, she felt sick.

After he had made his report, Elsie Foyle showed him out. She felt drained and annoyed with herself for having been caught out. They'd all be pointing the finger now. Her neighbours loved seeing other folk dragged down to the gutter. It passed for entertainment in Weatherfield. Her eye caught the familiar shape of Ena standing in her own doorway across the Street. She didn't want a scene and hated it when the customers started on each other in the shop but she couldn't just bite her tongue. 'Proud of yourself, are you?' she called.

Ena didn't reply.

'It was only a bit of ham, when all's said and done. Do you think it's easy running this place and keeping this lot round here happy?'

Ena stepped out of the shadow. 'There's other ways of 'elpin' folk.'

'By reporting them to police? What harm have I done you, Mrs Sharples? Tell me.'

'Someone has to make a stand.'

'That's you, isn't it? Judge and jury. Well, now we know and just so you know, you'll not be welcome in my shop any more.' She closed the door.

Ena turned to go back to her vestry but stopped when another loud voice called across the cobbles. 'Makin' more enemies, Mrs Sharples?'

Elsie stood on her doorstep, clutching Linda to her.

'Fancy a cup of tea, Mrs Sharples? You can sit and count my bruises, if you'd like. Or would you like me to tell you first hand how my loving husband showed me who 'ad top 'and?' She stepped into the Street and screeched at Ena. 'Who gave you the right to sit in judgement, you old bitch? I wasn't doing anyone any 'arm. I was only lookin' for a bit of affection. Now I'm a punch-bag and some poor bloke out there, who's already lost every single member of his family – his parents, his wife, his children, everyone – well, God knows what state 'e's in because I'll be surprised if 'e's still alive. And it's you that's done that.' She pointed a finger at Ena. 'It might 'ave bin Arnold's boot that kicked his 'ead in but you're the cow that guided it there! I just 'ope you can live wi' yerself!'

Ena made no reply. She told herself she'd nothing to reproach herself for. They were the guilty ones, the fornicators and cheats. It wasn't easy being an upstanding member of that community when that community was Coronation Street.

CHAPTER TWELVE

*11 August 1941 Churchill and Roosevelt sign the Atlantic Charter,
saying they seek no territorial gains in the war while Tom Hayes'
material gains land him in deep water.*

Martha Longhurst clocked herself in and hurried through
the benches of busy workers to find her own section, in the
far corner of the room. She attracted hostile glances from the
women opposite as she sat at her bench and immediately
reached for a piece of metal to turn into a bolt.

'Feelin' better, are you, Martha?' said Ena loudly. 'Usual
trouble, was it?'

Martha nodded and bent her head to her work.

When the others had resumed their activities Ena leant
close to her friend and said, 'Well?'

'Forty shillin' fine and a warnin' from magistrate about
underminin' the war effort.'

'Is that all? Forty shillin's? She'll 'ave made more than that
sellin' the stuff in first place.'

'Yes, but she gets her name in paper. I saw newspaper fella
jottin' it all down in 'is notebook. An' she looked that upset.'

'So she should, draggin' Coronation Street through the
courts for all to read about. Hetty Morris'll be livin' off this
for years. What did bobbies say,' she asked innocently, 'about
'ow they'd found out?'

'They didn't. It were all over in two shakes. She just got up,
said 'er name and address, said she was guilty and then
listened to magistrate. She looked like she were goin' to cry.'

'Folk say she were always a good actress.'

'Oh, no, Ena, I think she were proper upset. Her ears were red.'

Minnie leant towards the two women and asked, 'What are you talkin' about?'

Ena straightened up and started to turn her lever. 'Nowt for you to worry about, I were just askin' after Martha's ailments.'

Returning from the court, Elsie Foyle closed and locked the shop door behind her. The blinds were still pulled down and she had no intention of opening up. People had paid to see her on the stage and she was blowed if she was giving free performances to all and sundry to gawp at just because she stood behind a counter. She was angry with herself for going against her better judgement and jumping at the chance to make an easy profit.

Her thoughts were disturbed by a banging on the door. 'Mrs Foyle, are you opening?'

She recognised the voice. Vi Todd. She should have guessed because she'd seen Daisy Todd keeping watch from the front parlour as she'd walked down the Street to get home.

'Mrs Foyle, I need some ciggies.'

Vi knew she was in the shop so there was no point in pretending otherwise. She couldn't hide herself away from them. She slipped the bolt and opened the door.

Vi darted in and closed the door behind her. ' 'Ow are you, love?'

Mrs Foyle smiled bravely and said, 'Fine. Cigarettes, was it?' She moved behind the counter but didn't bother taking her coat off.

'Yes, ten Capstans.'

'Plain or corked?'

'Plain.'

The packet of cigarettes was placed on the counter. Mindful of the request from the government to save paper and packaging, Vi opened the packet, removed the cigarettes then slid the empty box back to Mrs Foyle.

'Ninepence, please.'

'They didn't send you down?' Vi asked, putting the cigarettes into her pocket.

Mrs Foyle laughed. 'Hardly.'

'It'll 'ave been a fine, then.'

'That's right.'

Vi counted out the exact money. 'I suppose you'll be more careful in future.'

'We'll all have to be, won't we?'

Vi's brow creased and she asked, 'What do you mean?'

'Well, I was in wrong for selling the stuff but there was plenty round here that bought it, knowing it wasn't part of ration. I reckon they're as guilty as me, don't you?'

Vi stepped back from the counter. 'Don't try and get clever wi' me, Elsie Foyle. It's folk like me that look to likes of you to set us an example. You told me that 'am was bombed stock. I believed you. You led me astray, not other way round, so don't start preachin' at me. I came 'ere offerin' support. I can see now I shouldn't 'ave bothered. Whoever reported you to bobbies did us all a favour, I reckon. Least you won't be able to shove any more black-market goods at us.'

As Vi stormed out, Mrs Foyle pressed 'sale' on the till and threw in the money. The coins hit the wooden tray with a thud, causing her to look inside. It was empty. She went to call for Esther, before remembering she'd given her the morning off to avoid customers questioning the girl. She'd put nearly two pounds' worth of change in the till that very morning. Where was it? Unable to cope with a mystery without a cup of tea to steady her nerves, she pushed the bolt across again and rushed into the living room. If anyone else knocked on the door they could starve, as far as she was concerned.

Annie Walker opened the Rovers' back door and let Billy run into the living room while she removed her hat and gloves. She'd had no intention of ending up in the courtroom: she'd only been passing and looked in. Pure coincidence that her fellow retail trader had been standing in the dock. She looked at her reflection in the hall mirror and patted her hair, making sure all the pins were in place.

Billy trotted up to her, proudly holding a green apple. He lifted it up to show her and said, 'Apple for me.'

She looked at him and smiled encouragingly, before realising what he was holding. The apples were kept in the Dartington Crystal bowl on the sideboard, pushed close to the wall so he couldn't reach it. She frowned and walked past Billy, who sat on the bottom step and dug his teeth into the fruit.

The living room was wrecked. The Luftwaffe couldn't have made a better job of it. It seemed to Annie that every single one of her possessions had been thrown on to the carpet. Drawers had been ransacked, tables overturned, every surface cleared. She stumbled into the room and felt something give beneath her feet, accompanied by the sound of crunching. She looked down and found she'd trodden on her wedding photograph, bereft of its frame but still united with the glass that covered it. There was no sign of the fruit bowl but the apples lay among letters and table linen. She couldn't speak. It was as if she were watching herself in a nightmare. It couldn't have happened. She'd only been gone an hour. She didn't have to look for the petty cash tin: the sideboard drawer she kept it in had been forced open, the lock broken, the polished wooden surround ruined.

Her sole birthday card, received that morning, lay to the side of the table. It was open and she could read the greeting, 'Happy Birthday, fondest wishes from Mother'. To think that an hour before her only complaint had been that there'd been no card from Jack. Billy had watched her open the card and admire the painting of lilacs on the cover. He'd grinned and said, 'Billy's birthday.' She'd said, no, not Billy's but hers. Billy's was another month and maybe Daddy would remember his.

She tipped up her wedding photograph and watched the broken glass slide from it. The picture beneath, taken in black and white, then hand-coloured by the photographer, was scratched from contact with the broken glass. She hoped it wasn't an omen.

Elsie Foyle and Annie Walker weren't the only local victims of theft. Over the road, across the tram-lines, in the park, Albert Tatlock had turned detective to solve the mystery of the disappearing chickens. He and Jack had tried rebuilding the chicken run, had draped it with chains and padlocks, but the birds kept disappearing at the rate of one or two a month. Other allotment holders complained of similar thefts. Albert had replenished his livestock twice and now refused to buy more. He became obsessed with the safekeeping of his remaining birds. Bessie refused to have the fowl anywhere near the house and although Jack offered to keep them in his backyard Albert didn't like the way Daisy eyed the birds. She looked like a woman whose hands itched to twist necks.

Albert took down the calendar from its nail in the shed and brought it out into the light to show Jack.

'There you go, I reckon tonight's our night,' he said.

' 'Ow do you mek that out?'

'It's a pattern, see? 'Arold Cartwright's been 'it three times in last three months, we've been got twice but always a week after 'Arold. His prize layer went last Tuesday. Tonight's our night.'

'Are you sure?' Jack sounded doubtful.

'It's a system. I've made notes. I'm tellin' you, tonight someone's gonna try and nick one of me 'ens.'

' 'Ow do you mean try? We've not managed to stop 'em yet, 'ave we?'

'Ah, but this time we won't be tekken by surprise, will we?'

Jack scratched his head and thought for a few moments, 'I'm not with you.'

Albert grunted and waved the calendar in his face. 'Tonight's the night, an' we'll be ready for the bugger. Even if we 'ave to stay 'ere all night.'

'All night!' Jack screwed up his nose. 'I don't fancy that, Albert.'

'An' I don't fancy bein' made a laughin' stock or losin' another bird!'

Esther was disturbed by the news of her employer's missing money. She'd tried to ignore her brother's nocturnal activities and the sacks he stored in the coal-hole one day then removed the next. There was the question of how he'd raised enough money to buy the new bicycle and how, very suddenly, he seemed older than her. He'd grown tall, inheriting his

211

father's build, and Esther was ashamed to realise she was frightened of him.

Teatime in the Hayes household was a quiet affair. Esther placed the food on the table and then, after removing her pinny, sat down with her mother and brother. She closed her eyes to say grace, knowing that the others would not be closing theirs, Tom because he didn't believe and Rose because she only ever closed her eyes to sleep, these days.

'What's this?' asked Tom, looking suspiciously at the food on his plate.

'Kippers and mash.'

'They don't go together,' he complained.

'It should have been kidneys but I didn't 'ave time to queue at Piggott's.' Esther looked at her brother as he flicked his fork through the potato. 'If you don't want it don't muck about with it. I can turn that into fishcakes.'

Rose lifted a forkful to her mouth in silence. Esther watched her chew, hoping she'd removed all the bones. 'I saw Mrs Todd early, she was asking after you.' Esther waited for her mother to make some acknowledgement but none came. 'And Mr Swindley was telling me he'd booked his week's holiday. I saw him outside the shop, he's going on a walking trip in Wales. I told him about the holiday we had in Conway. Do you remember that, Mother?'

Tom snorted and said, ' 'Course she doesn't remember it. She doesn't even remember her own name.'

Esther glared at him across the table.

'It's true. It's all them pills you keep giving her.'

'Dr Lewis says she must have them. They're to calm her.'

'That was in December, Esther. Eight months she's been on them. Surely she's calm enough by now.'

Esther shifted uncomfortably in her chair. Tom was right. Here they were, having a conversation about Rose when she was sitting between them and not hearing a word they said. Maybe it was time to take her off the pills, but who knew what she'd be like without them? Esther's day might be tiring and hectic but at least it had routine. If Rose wasn't so full of pills she might start wandering about and hurting herself.

Tom got up from the table, his tea untouched.

'Where are you going?' demanded Esther.

'Out.'

'I thought we could spend an evening in together, listen to a few records . . .'

Tom laughed. 'You must be joking. I'm not seven any more, Esther. You can't keep me trapped in this 'ouse.' He slammed out of the room.

Rose continued to feed herself and Esther pushed her own plate aside. She rested her head on her arms and stared up at her mother. Perhaps the pills had had their day. She wanted to talk to her about Tom, seek her advice. But she couldn't. Rose didn't even seem to know she had a son. Esther felt a tear roll down her cheek and let it fall on to her plate. She missed her dad. She was little more than a child herself, and shouldn't have to shoulder the responsibilities of the whole family. It was all right for Ada, sunning herself in Blackpool for the duration.

Her letters were full of educational dilemmas and of the sweet male teacher she was working with. When did Esther get chance to meet a man? Over the bacon counter? She couldn't go out like the Todd girls, showing their thighs and making eyes at servicemen. She had to stay in, night after night, watching Rose. She'd taken to locking the knives away all day and only made food that could be eaten with a fork. What had happened to the happy family environment she'd grown up in? Had it even existed? She knew all her friends at school had shied away from calling at No. 5 Coronation Street in case Sid lectured them, but every family was quirky in some way. Wasn't it? Something had to change. Soon.

It was quiet in the bar so Annie turned on the wireless and listened to a piano concerto as she polished glasses. It helped take her mind off the intrusion. She'd called in Vi Todd and tidied up as best she could but her heart hadn't been in it and she'd soon tired of Vi clucking and saying over and over, 'It's criminal.' In the end Annie had shut the door on the living room and told herself she'd sort out the rest in the morning. When it wasn't her birthday. The police hadn't held out much chance of retrieving anything: with houses standing empty and others turned into bomb-sites there was a roaring trade in second-hand goods and no one would question a couple of German shepherdesses and a load of assorted glasses being on the market. At least she'd been insured.

Billy sat on the floor behind the bar, playing with a ball. The warmth of summer was fading fast and Annie had shut the front doors to avoid turning on the heat. She looked around the bar. Five customers. Thomas Hewitt and Percy Longhurst throwing darts at the board, Ena, Minnie and Martha nursing their drinks in the snug. She sighed. What a birthday.

In the snug, Ena noticed that Minnie was staring into the public. 'What are you so interested in?' she asked.

'Nothing, Ena.'

'She were watchin' my Percy playin' darts,' said Martha. ' 'E's very good, you know. Used to be on the works team.'

Not to be outdone Ena said, 'My Alfred always said darts was too easy. 'E was a rugby union man. Played for St Thomas's first team. Used to come 'ome filthy. The state of 'is knees!'

'Anyroad, why are you lookin' at my 'usband? I hope you're not 'arbourin' any ideas, Minnie Caldwell. You've always bin a sly one.'

'Oh, Martha, 'ow can you say that?' said Minnie, in a hurt voice. 'As a matter of fact I'm not watchin' your Percy. I was thinkin' 'ow sad Mrs Walker looked.'

Ena and Martha observed Annie as she continued to polish glasses.

'She's not exactly burstin' wi 'appiness, is she?' said Ena. 'It's not nice, knowing someone's had a rummage through yer drawers. Then again I don't suppose they'd bother if she weren't always goin' on about her bits and pieces bein' so valuable.'

'I reckon it's more than that mekkin' her sad,' said Martha knowingly.

Ena waited but as no explanation was forthcoming said, 'Come on, then, what are you waitin' for? Fanfare on trumpets?'

'It's 'er birthday.'

'How do you know that?' asked Ena.

'Because I remember last year, she 'ad them flowers and she remarked that it were 'er birthday and it were the eleventh, same day as my 'Arold.' Martha smiled as she thought of her son who had drowned in Mosley's Flash when he was only three years old.

Ena, also remembering the cheeky-faced lad, patted her friend's knee. 'Who wants another?' she asked, getting to her feet and coughing to attract Annie's attention. 'Three milk stouts, please.'

Annie moved to find the bottles. As she did so Ena leaned over the bar and said, 'I understand congratulations are in order.'

'I'm sorry, Mrs Sharples?'

'Many 'appy returns, and may you 'ave many more in front of you.'

Annie forced herself to smile as she placed the bottles on the bar. As a rule she tried to keep the customers in the dark as to her personal life.

'Did you get a card from Mr Walker?'

'No,' Annie opened the bottles. 'It's probably caught up in the forces mail.'

Ena nodded and said, 'Well, 'appy birthday from the snug. We'd buy you a drink but munitions pay doesn't run to treats.'

'Of course not,' said Annie, a forced smile on her face. 'Please have these on me, and thank you for your kind wishes.'

The ladies all raised their bottles in thanks and settled down to drink.

'What side of thirty-five do you reckon she is?' said Ena.

'It's 'ard to tell,' said Martha, 'wi' all that powder she puts on 'erself.'

Ena nodded in agreement. 'No makeup or powder 'as ever touched my face. I believe in natural beauty. My skin's always been radiant. Soap and water, that's all I've ever used. My Alfred used to say I could 'ave been one of them mannequins wi' my face and figure.'

Martha bit her tongue and glanced down at Ena's body. It

wasn't worth saying anything, she thought. Let her have her moment of glory.

Bessie watched Albert pull on his coat and handed him his Thermos. 'I don't like it,' she said, 'I've not slept alone since nineteen nineteen. I don't like it.'

'It's just one night. That's all. And in morning I'll tell you who the tyke is who's been doin' away wi' my chickens.'

'I reckon it's Tom Hayes from number five.'

'Don't talk daft, woman. He wouldn't dare nick them birds. It's 'im I bought 'em off in first place. No, I reckon it's someone from t'other side o' canal.'

He stuffed the Thermos into his pocket and picked up his ARP helmet.

'You're never tekkin' that,' said Bessie, in surprise.

' 'Course I am. There might be a raid. I 'ave to be prepared.'

She looked him over. His helmet was, and always had been, a size too big, his old trench coat covered most of his body, bicycle clips kept the bottoms of his trousers tight and his black boots were done up with brown laces. 'You look prepared all right,' she said, 'but I don't know what for.'

He grunted and left the house.

Fifteen minutes later, Jack propped up his rifle inside the shed and threw his blanket down beside it. Albert had already nabbed the deck-chair, leaving him the wooden stool with the cracked seat.

' 'Ow long do you reckon we'll 'ave to wait?' he asked.

Albert shrugged. 'Dunno.'

'My missus didn't believe I were spendin' night up 'ere you know. I reckon she thought I 'ad a woman on go.' Jack reached into his trousers and rearranged himself. 'These new combos Vi bought on market don't 'alf pull on yer privates.'

Albert winced.

'Mind you,' continued Jack, warming to his theme, 'I could 'ave a woman on go. There's plenty round our way in need of a good seein' to.'

'Like who?' asked Albert.

'That Elsie Tanner's a dirty scrubber.'

'You're old enough to be 'er dad,' said Albert, disdainfully. 'She wouldn't look twice at you.'

'All right, then, what about 'er at the shop? Anyone with 'air that colour must be a goer.'

'She's married.'

'Where's 'er 'usband then? Blimey, if I 'ad a nice bit of cracklin' like 'er at 'ome you wouldn't find me wastin' time in Blackpool or wherever 'e's meant to be.' Jack grinned to himself, 'Yes, I fancy 'er all right. 'Ow about you?'

'Don't talk daft, Jack. I'm 'appy enough wi' my Bessie.'

'No, come on,' said Jack, pulling his stool closer to Albert. 'Just for a laugh. Ena Sharples?'

The men guffawed together at the impossible thought of finding Ena attractive.

'I'd rather go five rounds wi' Jackie Brown,' said Albert. 'Mind you, 'er friend's all right.'

'What? Four-eyes Martha?'

'Nay, t'other one, Minnie. Nice plump bird, she is. I don't like skinny women. I like something to cuddle up to at night.'

'Aye,' said Jack with a sigh. 'So do I.'

'Your Vi's as thin as a rake,' said Albert.

'Aye, I know, don't stop you dreamin', though, does it, Albert? Oh, yes, I can see meself behind that shop counter weighin' out 'umbugs.' He got up and wandered around the allotment. He looked around and muttered, 'Come on, whoever you are. I'm not spendin' all night waitin' for you.'

The sun set at half past eight. Two hours later, Albert heard footsteps approaching and reached for the stick he'd brought with him for protection. He glanced round for Jack but couldn't see him in the darkness. The footsteps came closer, then stopped. Suddenly a hand came down on Albert's shoulder. He jumped up in alarm and spun round, his stick raised.

'Steady on, Albert, it's only me,' said Jack.

'What do you think you're doin?' Albert bellowed. 'Creepin' around like that!'

'I was just 'avin' a piss.'

'You could 'ave told me!'

'I did. You didn't 'ear because you was asleep.'

'I wasn't!'

'You was!'

The two men glared at each other but the effect was spoilt as neither could make out the other's features in the darkness.

Jack took advantage of Albert standing to sit in the deckchair. 'Your turn to keep watch,' he said.

The blackout folded around Coronation Street like a well-worn blanket. The residents were used to it now but still resented the intrusion after enjoying the long sunlight of the summer. Annie locked the pub doors and decided to leave the washing of glasses to Vi in the morning. It had been a quiet night and she calculated she'd given out on returned bottles nearly as much as she'd taken over the bar. If things carried on so bleak she'd have to consider closing the Rovers and moving back to her family in Clitheroe.

Next door, at No. 1, Bessie had a restless night, missing Albert. Ida Barlow had grown used to sleeping alone and was content, so long as the sirens didn't start up. Her gas mask sat in its box under her bed, just in case Hitler tried a sneak gas attack. Next to it lay a bag containing her mother's engagement ring, her identity papers and ration books.

Her neighbour, Esther, was wide awake as she listened to Tom's shoes scraping down the brickwork as he escaped into the night.

Thomas Hewitt snored away at No. 7, his teeth keeping guard on the table beside his bed.

Vi Todd sat up knitting by the dying embers of the fire, while Sally and Dot cut out photographs from film-star magazines.

At No. 11, Elsie Tanner turned off the wireless and finished a generous slug of gin. She'd never been one for early nights, even if she did have to clock on at eight a.m.

Martha and Percy both attempted to outdo each other in a snoring contest at No. 13 while above the shop Mrs Foyle sat

at her dressing-table and looked out through her net curtains
to the roof of the Mission of Glad Tidings. She sighed heavily
and wondered if it was worth keeping the shop going. She
had no friends, just customers who viewed her in the same
way they did the bacon slicer. But, then, if she went to live in
Lytham she wouldn't be welcome there either. She'd
neglected her family for the shop and now the shop had
turned its back on her. She started to cry.

The piercing wail of the air-raid startled Albert and Jack. It
was still dark but Albert automatically swung his torch on to
the run. The door was open and all the chickens were gone.
He shone the torch on Jack's face and shouted, 'You fell
asleep!'

'So did you,' said Jack, 'and it was your turn to keep watch!'

They gathered their belongings and their wits and ran
through the park, Albert trying to illuminate the way with
his torch.

'Put that light out!' called a voice from one of the houses
that backed on to the park. Albert switched off the torch and
ran straight into a bench. He cursed as his groin smashed
into it.

Ena yawned and pulled on her ARP helmet as she opened the
Mission doors. Vera lit a candle and went off down the steps
to the cellar. Ena looked out into the darkness searching for
sight of Albert. By now he should be knocking on front doors
urging residents to leave their homes. He was nowhere to be
seen.

Ida Barlow was the first to arrive with young Kenneth.
She wore a long overcoat, had a blanket over her shoulders
and clutched a vanity case. She moved automatically. It was
all routine now and the horror of Marjorie's death had moved
to the back of her mind. 'Mornin', Mrs Sharples,' she said,
stifling a yawn.

Ena nodded and handed her a piece of yellow chalk. It was
her system for ease of identification. Each household had its
own coloured chalk and drew a circle on the stone floor in

which were placed the family's belongings. It avoided confusion once the cellar became crowded.

Mrs Foyle appeared next, along with the Longhursts.

Lil Longhurst was complaining. 'Bet it's another false alarm. I were in the middle of a great dream. Me and Ray Milland were on a desert island together, countin' coconuts.'

Her mother prodded her forward down the steps while Percy remained with Ena at the door. 'Where's Albert?' he asked.

Albert and Jack ran across Rosamund Street. Just before turning into Coronation Street Jack caught Albert's arm and stopped him. 'What are we gonna tell folk when they ask if we caught thief?'

'I don't know,' said Albert, aware that he hadn't fulfilled his ARP duties.

'How about we say it were a huge dog and it took us by surprise.'

'We could 'ave shot it.'

'Aye, that's no good.'

'Look, let's just say nothin'. We don't 'ave to say chickens were taken, do we?' Without another word Albert ran into the Street to assess the situation.

Ten minutes later all the residents were shut up underneath the Mission hall. Ida lay on one of the bunks with the sleeping Kenneth. Thomas Hewitt slumped in a corner. Ena moved round offering cups of warm water. Bessie pulled out her knitting and the Todd girls huddled together for warmth. 'We could be 'ere for ages and never know if it were day or night,' said Dot mournfully.

Esther tucked a blanket round her mother and wished Tom was with them. Since Sid's death in an alien shelter she only felt content during a raid if the whole family were together.

Jack laid his rifle on the floor and sat down next to his wife.

'Well?' she asked, her voice heavy with accusation. 'What 'appened?'

He avoided her eye and muttered, 'Nowt.'

She snorted. 'Of course nothin' 'appened. I've never 'eard of anythin' so daft in all me born days.'

To Jack's embarrassment she called, ' 'Ere, Martha, 'ave you 'eard what my 'usband's bin up to? Sittin' up all night in park waitin' to find a chicken hustler.' Her loud cackle filled the cellar.

'Shurrup,' he said.

'I can just see you and Albert Tatlock, listenin' out for stray tom-cats an' courtin' couples, wi' your pop gun at the ready. Why should England tremble?' She laughed again.

Jack's embarrassment turned to annoyance. He turned on Vi and said, 'You think it's funny, do you? Funny that me and Albert 'ave only just escaped death!'

Albert looked up in alarm, others looked up in interest.

'Oh, aye,' said Percy, 'what's this, then?'

Thinking on his feet, Jack stammered, 'We found thief, if you must know. We decided not to tell anyone in case it frightened the women.'

Ena asked, 'What would frighten us?'

Bessie dug Albert in the ribs. 'Yes, come on Albert. We want to know now.'

Albert opened his mouth but Jack butted in. 'He was dead quiet. Walked like a cat, 'e did. We didn't know 'e was there until he was upon us.'

'Who?' asked Sally.

'A German.'

There was an intake of breath.

' 'E was a big fella,' continued Jack, ' 'ad a wild look in his eyes. 'E shouted at us and pointed 'is gun at us. I 'ad me rifle in the shed but I couldn't get to it. I wanted to, but thought if I moved Albert would get it through the 'eart.'

Bessie gasped and grabbed her husband.

'So we just stood there. 'E still 'ad part of 'is parachute attached. He opened the run and grabbed a chicken in his big 'and and with one twist of his wrist he killed it, dead. Then the siren started and that must've shocked 'im 'cos 'e looked around to see where noise were comin' from. I ran for me rifle and Albert dived for cover.'

Albert grunted, not liking being cast in the coward's light.
'What 'appened then?' asked Martha.

'By time I'd got my rifle up I looked for him but 'e'd fled.
Scared of me shootin' 'im, I expect.'

'So, he's still out there!' Martha's eyes shot to the door. ' 'E
could 'ave followed you, intent on killin' all of us in our beds.'

Dot screamed as a sharp knock sounded on the cellar door.

Bessie clutched Albert. Jack dropped his rifle but Thomas
grabbed it and stood, raising it to his shoulder. Vi pulled her
daughters to their feet.

'No one move!' warned Percy.

The knock came again, followed by a broad Lancashire
voice saying, 'Are you down there?'

'Don't sound German to me,' whispered Martha.

'It'll be a trick,' said Percy.

Ena broke away from the tableau and climbed the steps to
the door. 'Who is it?' she called.

'Police. Open up.'

It certainly didn't sound like a German, so Ena carefully
opened the door. Behind her the others shrank back into the
cellar.

'Is there a Mrs Hayes in there?' asked the policeman.

Rose cried, 'It's Sidney, isn't it? But he's dead. He's dead!
Dead!'

Mrs Foyle leapt forward, took Rose's shoulders and gave
her a firm shake. 'Mrs Hayes! Stop it! Stop it, I tell you, you're
upsetting the babies.'

Esther got to her feet and walked to the bottom of the
stairs. 'I'm Esther Hayes, Officer. Can I help?'

The policeman moved aside and pulled the struggling
figure of Tom Hayes into the light of the cellar. As he tried to
free himself from the firm grasp of the law a chicken fell from
beneath his jacket, fluttered down the steps and into the
cellar.

'Do you recognise this lad, miss?' asked the policeman.

'He's my brother,' Esther said.

'I found him runnin' down Lower Edward Street with a
sackful of chickens.'

'Get your 'ands off me!' shouted Tom.

Ena turned to Jack and Albert and said, 'For a German 'e speaks good English, don't 'e?'

Albert had the grace to look sheepishly at Bessie while Vi swiped at Jack with her handbag.

CHAPTER THIRTEEN

October 1941 Hitler nears Moscow. The Rovers' pumps run dry.

Ida beamed with delight as she looked through the viewfinder of her box Brownie and snapped a photograph of Frank gingerly holding Kenneth. It was the little boy's second birthday and he hadn't stopped crying since his father's arrival the night before. He resented the presence of the large man with the booming voice who demanded so much of Ida's time and kept stroking her thigh. The house seemed full of him and his belongings. His big kit bag stood in the hallway; his uniform hung over the back of chairs. He seemed to have an awful lot of stuff, and none of it birthday-present-shaped. Since Frank had arrived Ida had turned into a silly woman, giggling and flapping her arms around. Kenneth kept staring at her. She wasn't being very much like his mother. He struggled free of his father's grip to dash forward and yank his toy train out of Linda Tanner's hands. She howled in protest and was picked up by Elsie.

It was a small gathering consisting of the Barlows, the Tanners and the Walkers, and Ida had laid on a birthday tea with candles stuck into a bowl of Kenneth's favourite mashed potatoes. She was having a wonderful time, with her family all together, and was too happy to notice how preoccupied the other guests were. Elsie would normally have thrilled to some activity to break up the monotony of her day but she felt uncomfortable being part of such a domestic, family scene and sat staring out of the back window into the yard. Annie gave up trying to make small-talk and instead played her favourite game of evaluating other people's belongings. No. 3 Coronation Street was not Chatsworth and the Staffordshire pot dogs seemed to be the only items of any note.

Billy Walker wandered off into the hall only to re-emerge holding Frank's service rifle. He stood in the doorway and shouted, 'Bang, bang, you're all dead!'

Annie froze and Ida dropped a tea-cup in alarm. Frank jumped out of his chair and prised the rifle from Billy, who burst into tears when Frank shouted at him, 'Don't ever touch a gun. It's loaded! You must never touch a gun!'

Linda and Kenneth, frightened by Frank's tone, joined in the crying.

The next day, Frank returned overseas, refusing to tell Ida anything about his movements in the interest of national security. After he had left she decided never to wash the pillow on which his head had lain during the two nights he'd been home. She held it to her at night and smelt the mixture of Gold Flake tobacco and Brylcreem.

In October Jack Walker and Jim Todd also came home on leave. The Fusiliers had seen action in Egypt and were weary and in need of the basic pleasures of life. Unfortunately they found their womenfolk too preoccupied to offer welcoming arms. Annie's thoughts seldom ventured further than the Rovers' cellar. Her supply of best bitter had already run dry and the mild was down to half a barrel. She'd been thankful that the government hadn't raised the price of beer since the previous April. Even so, barrels were costing her fifty shillings more than they had before the war. She'd been alarmed to hear of pubs closing down through lack of profits and feared that she'd be driven the same way. Either that or the pumps would run dry.

As soon as he'd dumped his kit-bag at No. 9, Jim knocked at Elsie Tanner's door. Despite seeming pleased to see him she'd pulled away when he'd tried to kiss her. 'No, Jim, I'd rather not.'

He lunged forward, ignoring her words, eager to feel her softness. She allowed him a kiss but when he squeezed her breasts she again moved backwards. 'I mean it. I'm sorry but you can't just come in 'ere and jump on me.'

'Oh, come on, Elsie. It's been ages,' he whined.

She turned her back on him and fumbled in her bag for a cigarette. There weren't any. 'Blast it.'

'What's up, love?' he asked.

'I need a fag and I've run out. She's not got any at the corner so I'll have to get some cork-tipped at the Rovers.'

He dug into his pocket and pulled out a full packet of Players. He tossed them across the room to her. 'Keep 'em. I've got loads. Me pal don't smoke so 'e gives me his ration and I give 'im my chocolate.'

She smiled. 'Fair swap, I reckon.'

He stepped forward and lit the cigarette for her. She drew in the smoke, savouring the luxury of a decent fag for a change. He lowered his hand and moved it down to her waist. She recoiled at his touch. 'Thank's for the fags, Jim, but I mean it. I'm off men just now.'

He couldn't mask his disappointment, and she felt sorry for him but her resolve didn't weaken.

'How long a leave 'ave you got?'

'Long weekend.' He was sullen.

'Why don't you go into town?' she suggested. 'Good-lookin' lad like you, they'll be queuin' up. Take yer pick. Blonde, redhead, brunette. Try the Palais, that's where Sally goes.'

'Sally goes there, does she?' he asked. 'Not you?'

'Not for a while.'

'Look,' he stepped forward and held out his hand, 'I don't want to go into town. All the way back I've been thinking of you, Elsie. It's you I want. Not some scrubber from the Palais.'

'Jim, love, you only think you want me but any girl would do for what you want me for. I'm handy, that's all. I'm sorry, love, but like I say, I'm off men just now.'

He decided not to waste any more time on her and left. After he'd gone Elsie slipped the cigarette packet into her bag and snapped it shut. She blew out a stream of smoke and hoped he would have better luck elsewhere.

Later that evening, after watching Jim and his father head down to the Rovers, Elsie left Linda asleep and knocked on the Todds' back door. She opened it before anyone could answer.

Vi looked up as she stepped into the living room. 'Hello, Elsie, love,' she said, laying aside her mending.

'I waited till I saw Jim and Jack go out.'

Vi eyed her up and down. The girl looked pale and drawn. 'I've nowt to offer you to drink, love,' she said, 'but yer welcome to take the weight off yer feet.'

Elsie sat in the armchair opposite Vi. 'Is Mrs Todd out?'

'Daisy? Yes, she's gone to the Rovers with her cronies.'

'What about Sally and Dot?'

'I'm all on my own love. Why?'

Elsie bit her lip and looked down at her hands. When she spoke she was so quiet that Vi had to lean forward to catch what she said. 'I'm in trouble, Vi. I need 'elp an' I've 'eard folk say it's the sort of 'elp you can give me.'

Vi sank back into her chair and folded the dress she was hemming. 'I see. Like that, is it?'

Elsie nodded.

'How far gone are you?'

'Just over two months.'

'Arnold?'

Elsie nodded again and fingered the slim silver chain round her neck. 'It's 'is all right,' she said, 'I know I'm not short of company but I always make sure they take precautions. Arnold never gave me chance to object.' She looked at Vi with pleading eyes. 'Can you 'elp me?'

Vi sighed and leant forward in her chair. 'You did right comin' to me. I might be able to if you're certain. Are you?'

Without hesitation Elsie said, 'Definitely. Linda's more than a 'andful for me.'

'You get seven pints o' milk a week on ration when you're pregnant, you know.'

'I'm not desperate for milk. No, I want rid.'

'It's a dangerous business – and not just for me if I were to get caught. I've known plenty of girls like you not make it.'

'You can't put me off, Vi.'

Coronation Street: The War Years

Vi glanced at her watch. 'Are you workin' tomorrow?'

'No, it's my Saturday off.'

'Come round after lunch an' bring a towel wi' you. An'
think on you don't tell anyone about it. It's been a while since
I 'elped out. I stopped when a woman I knew were sent to
prison, but seein' as it's you . . .'

'Oh thanks Vi,' Elsie grasped the older woman's hands and
squeezed them. 'Tomorrow, then.'

Billy Walker sat on his father's knee cheerfully tucking into
the chocolate Jack had brought home for him. Annie bustled
about making tea but her progress was broken as she kept
stopping to smile at the scene. She made a mental note to
borrow Ida's camera and felt pleased with herself for having
hoarded a packet of biscuits.

Jack rubbed the sole of his foot against the hearth and
sighed. 'Annie, love, it's grand to be 'ome.'

'It's grand to have you home. It's been over a year since I
last saw you. You look older. Are you eating properly?'

'Yes, I am.'

'Well, make sure you do. You want to take things easy, get
the young lads like Jim Todd to do all the running about.' She
poured tea into a mug and mourned the heap of smashed
china that had once been her Duchess tea service.

Billy rubbed a dark brown hand down his bare legs and
continued to munch as Jack tried to put a finger through the
dainty cup's handle.

He had wanted her to close the pub for the evening, insist-
ing that the customers would understand, but she'd resented
his coming home and taking charge. She'd kept the pub
running on her own and wasn't going to let her customers
down. Instead of locking the doors, she was proving to herself
just how versatile she was by juggling her family and her
work, darting backwards and forwards between the bar and
the living room.

The sound of a telephone ringing in Coronation Street was
a rarity. The only one in existence was in the Rovers' hallway
and the Walkers made it available to regulars for the price of
a local call. If more privacy was required there was a call-box

at the end of Rosamund Street but as most of the residents didn't know anyone with a telephone to call they remained unaccustomed to the instrument.

Not so Annie Walker. Since her telephone's installation in the summer before the war she had mastered a telephone manner to make any switchboard operator jealous. When the telephone rang that Friday evening, interested drinkers broke off from conversations to listen to it while Annie wiped her hands on her apron before walking into the hallway to take the call. 'Hello, the Rovers Return Inn, Mrs Anne Walker speaking.'

She waited until the caller had identified himself, holding the handset away from her ear as the broad voice boomed down the line. 'Is that the Rovers? It's Archie Manders 'ere, ringin' from brewery.'

'Mr Manders, did you say?'

'Aye, 'ead drayman.'

Annie screwed up her nose in disgust. A call from the brewery normally meant one of the Ridleys or the Newtons or at least their secretary. Never a drayman. She cleared her throat and asked, 'I'm expecting you in the morning, I believe?'

'That's right.'

'Good.'

'Only we're not comin'.'

'I beg your pardon?'

'We've no ale for yer, missus.'

Annie raised her voice and a dozen customers in the bar looked troubled as she repeated, 'No ale?'

'That's right, missus. We've run out. Sorry.'

'That's not good enough. I demand you put me through to Mr Ridley –'

Annie stopped when she realised she'd been cut off. She dialled the brewery's number.

The living room door opened and Jack peered out into the hall. 'Who were that? Were it for me?'

Annie continued dialling and said, in an agitated voice, 'Some drayman with no sense and no idea. Saying there was no ale for me. Ridiculous –' She broke off as the telephone was answered. 'Good afternoon. This is Mrs Anne Walker from the Rovers Return Inn, Coronation Street. I wish to speak to Mr Ridley, please.' She clasped her hand over the mouthpiece and said, 'I'll soon have this sorted, love. You go and put your feet up.'

Jack shrugged but rather than return to the comfort of his sofa he strolled into the bar and helped himself to a nip of whisky.

' 'Ey up Jack lad,' called Albert.

Jack crossed to where a group of men stood at the bar.

'I 'eard you was back,' said Percy. 'Seen 'Itler off, 'ave yer?'

'Aye, and Rommel as well,' said Jack, sipping the whisky.

' 'Ow long you got, lad?' Albert leaned over the bar, pleased to see someone he knew in uniform.

'Long weekend, but by looks of it I'm not goin' to see much of Annie. Between you lot and our Billy she's run off 'er feet.'

'Well, she won't be for much longer,' said Annie, walking into the bar.

Jack spun round in surprise, 'What do you mean?'

'I managed to get some sense out of Moira Kendall. Do you remember her from that dance? Christmas nineteen thirty-eight? Had a blue chiffon dress that sparkled when she did the fox trot. Well, I always say it takes a woman to speak plain. Apparently the brewery has run out of beer.'

'Never!'

Annie ignored Albert's interruption and continued, 'It turns out I'm not getting my delivery tomorrow, after all. Goodness knows when I'll get any in. Moira tended to think it might be a week or a fortnight.'

'A fortnight!' Albert's voice was faint and his mouth hung open in shock.

'Pint for Albert,' ordered Percy Longhurst, 'and make it snappy.'

Annie started to pull the beer and said, 'Make it last, Mr Tatlock. This could be the last one you get in here for a while. Perhaps you'd be interested in cider? It can be very palatable.'

'I'm not drinking apples,' said Albert. 'I'll just 'ave to see if they've ale at Flying Horse.'

Annie placed the full glass in front of him and sighed. Jack placed his hand on her shoulder and said, 'Now then, love, it won't be for ever.'

'I wish I shared your optimism.'

'Come on, this 'as given me an idea. Seems daft openin' when we've no ale. 'Ow about you and me closin' shop and 'aving us a little 'oliday. Remember Llandudno? The Happy Valley?'

Annie smiled at the memory. 'Do you think we could?'

'Aye, love. Leave it to me.'

Early the next morning, Jack and Annie caught the tram to the railway station. He carried a suitcase, she carried a troubled frown. She had no qualms about leaving Billy with Jack's brother and his wife but the pub was a different matter. There was no telling what would happen if the local thieves got to hear about it standing empty all weekend. 'I should have locked the spirits in the larder,' she said, causing the woman opposite to shift on the bench and stare at her. Annie saw the look and thought, She probably thinks I'm an alcoholic.

Three hours later the tram and Weatherfield were miles away as the couple stood on the promenade and breathed in the sea air. The journey, like everything else in wartime, had dragged on: a carriage crowded with servicemen and their girlfriends, smoking and chatting; endless stations with their names deleted by thick black paint; buffet rooms that sold only weak tea and powdery scones; field after field of pastures turned into arable land, with tractors that seemed to move faster than the train and scarecrows that looked better dressed than the farm workers. The Walkers' carriage was at the front of the train and the steam rising from the engine billowed in through the cracks around the window-frame whenever the train limped through a tunnel. Jack seemed to enjoy the journey and told Annie it was luxurious after being bounced around in an army lorry. She wasn't impressed and arrived in Blackpool in a bad mood.

Jack beamed and gestured out towards the sea. 'How about that, then, Annie?'

'I thought you said we were going to Llandudno. If I'd known we'd end up in Blackpool I'd have stayed at home.'

'You 'ave to go where the trains are goin'. You 'eard station fella sayin' there were no trains to Llandudno. Anyroad, what's wrong wi' Blackpool?'

'Nothing, if you're on a chara and it's just for the day, but for a weekend?' She pulled her hand out of her pocket and waved towards the sea. 'We can't even go for a walk along the beach.'

Jack followed her gaze, taking in the barricades and line of barbed wire, which ran the length of the Golden Mile. 'There's other things to do. We can go to Fleetwood.'

'Kippers make me bilious.'

He picked up the case and grabbed her arm. 'Come on, let's find a B-and-B somewhere. 'Appen we won't be goin' out much anyroad, not when I get you into bed.'

'Jack Walker!' She sounded indignant, but he recognised the twinkle in her eye. He hadn't seen it since before Billy's birth but it was definitely there.

Elsie decided there was no point in greeting the new experience with a gloomy outlook. She walked Linda into Vi's living room and grinned as if she was embarking on a works outing.

Vi was feeling less cheery. In the past she'd come close to being investigated by the police and knew what she was risking in aiding Elsie. She held out a hand and guided Linda into the front parlour, where she'd already laid out the remains of Sally and Dot's childhood. A doll with an eyelid missing, a box of scraps for cutting and pasting and a storybook with half the pages coloured in. With the promise of biscuits to come, she left the little girl to her own devices and returned to Elsie, who was standing in the cluttered room looking warily at the zinc bath tub, which Vi had already filled with water.

'She'll 'ave to stay the night,' said Vi. 'I'll tell the others you're poorly.'

'Won't I be able to look after 'er, then?' asked Elsie.

'Not in the state you're goin' to be in.'

The false brightness faded from Elsie's face. Her stomach clenched and she felt dangerously close to tears. She couldn't really believe she was going through with it.

Vi wasted no time. She moved swiftly into the scullery and locked the back door. 'We've got a good two hours. Try and relax. No one's goin' to know.'

Elsie felt numb and vulnerable. Her head was full of questions but she was too scared to ask them. Instead she ran her hand over the side of the bath, as if it was made of marble.

'Take yer clothes off,' said Vi, crossing to poke the fire into action. 'I'm sure you want to ask but I reckon you're best off kept in dark. Forget all you've 'eard about pills and bits off trees. This is best way I know.'

She bent down and pulled two full bottles of gin from behind Jack's armchair. 'This is your tipple, i'nt it?'

'Yes,' said Elsie, stepping out of her dress, 'are we goin' to 'ave one?'

Vi chuckled and poured herself a generous measure. 'I'm 'avin' one, to steady meself, you're 'avin' the rest.'

Elsie stood in the room completely naked and tested the water with her toe. She quickly drew back as pain rushed up her leg. 'It's boilin'!'

'Stop complainin' and get yerself in.'

'In that?'

'Yes love, in that. You'll soon get used to it.'

Panic was setting in among the group assembled in the Tatlocks' living room. Albert shifted his weight from one foot to the other. After all he'd lived through: bombardments, near starvation during the depression and gunshot wounds, he should have been able to put the latest crisis in prospective. But he couldn't.

'This is a fine to-do,' he said, agitated and confused.

Percy agreed. 'I didn't think they'd start on beer. I can't understand it! It's not as if we get it from overseas, is it?'

'Beer's made from 'ops,' said Martha helpfully.

'I know that,' said Percy.

'Well, I were only sayin'.'

'Now then, you two,' Albert butted in, 'we don't want arguments among ourselves. We need to think 'ard.'

'So far is it just Rovers and Flying Horse without ale?' asked Jack Todd.

'Tripe-dressers' Arms 'ave closed,' Percy reported.

'The Laughing Donkey's only serving regulars,' added Albert, 'and then only one pint of mild.'

The group looked glumly at each other. The fire crackling in the grate cast orange shadows over their faces.

In the silence Daisy Todd, sitting forgotten in an armchair, got to her feet and said, 'If you want beer that much you can 'ave it. At a price.' Without giving any explanation she barged through the neighbours and shuffled out of the house.

Later, while the council of war continued to bemoan its fate, the hunched figure of Daisy Todd crouched over the wasteland next to the canal. Her thick black shawl covered her head and shoulders and hung low over her arms as she carefully snipped the stem of a nettle. She straightened up as much as she could and showed the nettle to her companions. 'You want ones like this,' she said.

'I know,' said Amy Carlton impatiently. 'Why are you tellin' me?'

'I'm not, I'm tellin' yer daughter.'

Minnie glanced at the greenery in Daisy's hand. She'd allowed herself to be bullied into joining her mother and her friend and was now wondering why she always allowed people to boss her around. She corrected herself: it wasn't people, it was women. Her father had been a gentle soul, seeking solace from his nagging wife in the company of his clock collection, which filled the house. He had each one set to a different time, according to which country they represented. Minnie might never have excelled in composition at school but she always knew what the time was in Sydney, Australia.

Her own husband, Armistead, had been another gentle person, totally devoted to her. She'd been blissfully happy during their ten-year marriage and having him in her life helped her cope with her mother's criticising tongue. Now it was just the two of them, and in Amy's eyes Minnie wasn't a woman of forty-one but still the pathetic little girl who clutched her apron and got under her feet. Ena and Martha were Minnie's oldest and closest friends but they were just the same: they never asked her opinion, but patronised her and rode roughshod over her feelings. They cared for her, though, and she was grateful for their friendship.

She'd first met Ena when they'd attended Silk Street School together. A bigger girl had stolen the hot potato she'd kept in her apron pocket for food and warmth. Ena had sought out the thief, thumped her nose and retrieved the potato, winning Minnie's undying gratitude. Martha had come into their lives when they were full-timers at Hardcastle's Mill. Thirteen years of age and in charge of three looms, Martha was older by four years and again Minnie had been grateful when she'd shown her the ropes and warned her against going into the storeroom alone: the storemen took young girls by surprise and had their way with them on the sacks. Minnie had been a Carlton then, Ena a Schofield and Martha a Hartley. They'd married but clung to their friendship. It was the one consistent thing in their lives.

'She's not payin' any attention! Minnie!'

Her mother's voice brought Minnie back to the harsh reality of standing in the marshy ground beside the dirty canal. She bent over reluctantly, clasped the underside of a nettle with her gloved hand and pulled at it.

Jack Walker supported himself on his side and ran a finger over Annie's nightgown.

'Stop it,' she said, with a giggle, 'you're tickling.'

He sighed with contentment and pulled the sheet up to cover her. She looked fondly at his face and remembered the first time she'd seen it. It was a blur as he'd been running towards her at the time. She'd been standing on a pack-horse bridge looking down at the canal, watching the oil in the water making patterns. She'd heard a yell and suddenly he'd grabbed her from behind then forced her down on the cobbles. She'd screamed for help and kicked out but he'd held her down until other people arrived, drawn by the commotion. She'd wanted him arrested for assault before he'd explained he'd thought she was planning to throw herself into the water. He'd wanted to save her life, and the romantic in her leapt for joy. That had been four years ago. Four years during which time they'd become immersed in childcare, running the pub and battling through the war. Love had turned into familiarity. She looked at his thin nose and shallow eyes, and wished she could be more loving for him, but it just wasn't in her nature.

He got up and pulled on his pyjama bottoms. He wanted a cigarette but knew Annie didn't like the smell in the bedroom so instead he contented himself with looking out of the bay window at the waves crashing on to the pebbled beach. Only in wartime could you find a hotel that boasted a sea view and actually delivered what it promised.

Annie left the bed quietly and padded across the carpet to join him. She slipped her hand around his waist and rested her blonde head on his bare shoulder. 'What are you thinking?' she asked.

'I were just wonderin', will it ever end? Will we ever be able to stand at this window in peacetime and see donkeys carryin' children up and down beach?'

'It can't go on for ever, love.'

'Sometimes it feels like it is.'

She closed her eyes, sensing his pain. She knew he'd made the decision not to tell her about the things he'd seen, the battles he'd fought and although she was grateful she was aware that his experiences made a void she could not bridge. 'I do love you, Jack,' she said.

'Annie, love, my flower.'

Her eyes moistened and she hugged him closer. He kissed her and rested his hand on her shoulder.

Elsie's skin had turned salmon-red. Beads of sweat ran down her face and splashed into the water. Vi held out another glass of gin and Elsie slowly, painfully, shook her head. 'I can't. No more.'

Vi held the glass to Elsie's mouth and forced the liquid down her. Elsie spluttered and it ran down her chin. Her eyelids fell and her voice was slurred as she cried, 'Don't want any more!'

Vi slapped her face hard. 'Don't go to sleep! More water.'

'No!' Tears fell down Elsie's flaming cheeks.

Vi grabbed Elsie's nose, forced her head back and poured gin straight from the bottle into her mouth. Elsie gagged and wrenched her head free. She spat into the bathwater and clutched her mouth.

'You can't be sick,' shouted Vi, anxiously fanning Elsie with her pinny. Then she ran a cold flannel around the back of the girl's neck and cradled her head. 'Deep breaths, love. Come on, it's nearly over.'

Vi had no idea if it had worked. She never had until a few hours had passed. The hardest part was over and she just had time to bundle a weeping Elsie into bed at No. 11 before her own family got home. Hearing movement in the backyard she unlocked the door and found Minnie Caldwell outside with a battered coal cart piled high with nettles. Daisy had noticed Vi turning the key and pushed past her to stare suspiciously into the living room. 'You got a fella in here?'

Vi set about clearing the table of the lunch things and snapped, 'Don't talk daft.'

Daisy's foot hit an empty gin bottle as she saw the bath in front of the fire. It normally appeared on a Monday night. Gin and a zinc tub added up to one thing. Hearing Amy arrive, she kicked the bottle under a chair. There was no point in broadcasting the fact that Vi had slipped back to her old ways. 'Come in, Amy, Vi's got the bath ready for us,' she said.

Vi looked at her mother-in-law in alarm and stood back while Daisy squeezed into the scullery.

Once Amy had moved into the living room Daisy hissed, 'Where is she?'

'Who?' asked Vi.

'Whoever you've bin seein' to.'

Vi sighed. 'She's back in 'er own bed. I was goin' to empty the tub then see to 'er.'

'You can leave water, I've a use for it.'

Vi decided not to enquire further. Instead she threw her apron on to the worktop and slipped out of the back door, avoiding Minnie who was carrying in an armful of nettles.

'Where do you want these?' asked weary Minnie of the old woman.

'In tub,' said Daisy.

Amy glanced into the bath and pulled a face. 'Bit mucky this water. Bin washin' yer smalls in it 'ave yer?'

'Water's water,' said Daisy. 'My mam made this once in a bucket straight from Irwell. A bit o' muck gives it a kick.'

Any thought Minnie still had about tasting the brew once it was finished disappeared from her mind at that point. She threw the nettles into the bath and went to fetch more.

Daisy removed her gloves and spat on her palms. 'Right, let's get poundin'.'

If residents walked down Coronation Street, turned right at the Rovers and travelled along Rosamund Street they crossed Mawdsley Street then found themselves at a small parade of shops. Built in 1887, the lettering on the brickwork under the roof line named it the Queen's Parade. It consisted of seven shops with large windows framed proudly by wrought-iron. The middle shop of the seven had always borne the sign 'Swindley's Emporium'. This draper's shop had remained untouched through the blitz, which had destroyed larger stores in the centre of Manchester. In fact, it had remained untouched since 1927 when Thomas Swindley had sold off half the original double-fronted premises during an economic slump. His staff had also been halved and Thomas had begun to train his only son in the art of commerce. That son, Leonard, now managed the shop with the help of an elderly retainer, Miss Bull, whose build resembled her name. Leonard himself was not a slim man and often space behind the mahogany counter was at a premium. Unmarried and twenty-six years of age, Leonard had avoided joining the forces by standing in front of a tribunal and declaring himself a concientious objector on religious grounds. He had volunteered his services for the Ambulance Corps, which had appeased the tribunal, but no one had contacted him since his offer sixteen months before.

Leonard greeted the morning of Monday, 13 October, with the same optimism he mustered at the start of every week. He changed the sign on the door to read 'Open' and ran his finger along one of the shelves. Miss Bull, whose duties included the cleaning of the premises, watched him, her mouth set in a grim line. He caught her eye and lifted his finger guiltily. 'Spotless as usual, Miss Bull.'

She sniffed and munched on a boiled sweet.

The door opened and Ena rushed up to the counter.

'Good morning, madam.'

Ena interrupted him: 'Don't madam me, I want none of your sales patter. Me daughter's clockin' me in and I need to be behind a weldin' machine in fifteen minutes. I want a corset for a mature figure and there's three coupons to cover it.'

She slapped her coupon book on the counter and glanced around the shelves at the stock on display. Yellowed pieces of card held buttons and pins, and a bank of wooden drawers protruded from the shelves bearing labels written with anti-quated neatness: 'collar studs', 'elastic, black', 'elastic, white', 'gents collars, various', 'black crêpe', 'hatpins'. Above the drawers, neatly folded upon shelves, were larger items – shirts, nightgowns, blouses, combinations and, right at the top, corsets.

Leonard stepped down from a small, rickety ladder and laid three corsets on the counter.

'I want whalebone,' said Ena.

He assured her that all three were boned.

She fingered the material and found traces of dust in the ridges. Leonard looked sharply at Miss Bull, who pretended not to notice and fiddled with a display of shoelaces.

'Look at the state of that,' said Ena, thrusting her finger under his nose.

He stepped back and nervously pushed his glasses up his nose before stuttering, 'We – we – oh dear – it will have been with the bomb that dropped on Mawdsley Street. There was a great deal of dust.'

Ena pushed away the corsets. 'I'm not 'avin' them, they're damaged stock. There's a law against selling damaged goods as new. You want to be careful no one lets on to the bobbies. A man with your criminal record could go down for summat like this.'

Leonard flinched at the reminder of his humiliation after running Albert down in the van in the blackout.

'Of course,' continued Ena, 'these items should really be offered at sale prices.'

She didn't have long to wait for his answer. He knew from memory the corset's retail and wholesale prices and nodded. 'Twelve shillings.'

'I doubt if you need full coupons for reduced goods,' said Ena.

Again he nodded. 'Twelve shillings and two coupons.'

Ena placed a ten shilling note and a half-crown on the counter while Leonard bent to wrap the corset.

Vi was eager to call on Elsie and see how she was coping, but knew she couldn't just walk out on breakfast. It was two days since the abortion attempt had failed and Elsie had worked herself into a bad state. Having seen it all before, Vi feared for her friend's sanity.

Jim scraped back his chair and wiped his bread round his bowl.

Jack looked up from his breakfast and spoke to his son through a mouthful of oats. 'You're in a hurry, ain't you?'

'I'm goin' out.'

'Where to?'

'What are you?' asked Jim, aggressively. 'Me flamin' sergeant major?'

Vi watched the door close behind her son and started to clear away his plate and cup. She'd already swilled out at the abattoir and cleaned the Rovers ready for the Walkers' return. The rest of the day would be given over to finding food for the family's tea. She'd used nearly all the week's ration on feeding Jim and gave herself over to the inevitable queuing.

'What's up with our lad?' asked Jack.

''Appen it's because 'e's got to go back today. 'E 'asn't seemed right 'appy all weekend.'

'It'll be 'cos he 'asn't got his leg over.'

Vi carried the dishes into the scullery and called back, 'And 'ow would you know that? I've not seen you 'avin' any father-and-son chats. You've barely said two words to lad since he walked through door.'

'It's written all over 'is face. Pent up, that's what 'e is. I know for a fact that tart next door slammed bedroom door in 'is face. That ain't right. Lad comin' back expectin' a bit of comfort from his lass and she crosses 'er legs.'

'Elsie Tanner is not our Jim's lass. She is married, remember.'

Jack laughed. 'It ain't me who needs to remember. It's 'er. I've seen 'er walkin' past fellas in the street. 'Er backside's got a mind of its own.'

'Oh, aye? Makin' a study o' backsides, are you?' She turned the tap on full and waited until the water had reached the rim of the saucepan, then heaved the pan out of the sink and carried it to the range in the living room.

'Are you gonna sit there all day, clutterin' up the place?' she asked.

He glanced up from reading about the Germans' advance into Russia and watched Vi bend over as she placed the pan of water on the hob. He acknowledged ruefully that her backside had never swung like Elsie Tanner's. 'Right, that's me lot,' he said, pushing his bowl away. It was his second week of spending his nights fire-watching on the roof of Elliston's factory, and he was fast coming to the conclusion that he preferred night work to day. That way he avoided seeing most of his family and had the bed all to himself.

After Jack had removed his braces and started climbing the stairs, Vi had a few precious seconds to herself before Daisy came in from the parlour. She'd spent most of the weekend in the best room, concocting. She peered into Jack's discarded bowl and tutted as she found he'd eaten every morsel.

Walking back from the railway station, Jack and Annie Walker passed a queue of excited women outside Edwards'.

Seeing them, Vi called out, 'Mrs Walker, 'e's got cod!'

Annie smiled back and said smugly, 'I've had enough fish to last me a year. Blackpool's awash with it.' Then she sighed and gazed at the monotonous brickwork and lines of identical houses. 'I wish we could have stayed the week,' she said.

'So do I, love,' said Jack. As the train had pulled out of Blackpool he had become preoccupied with his return overseas later that day. He'd just time to walk Annie home, tidy himself up, kiss Billy then make his way back to the station. Still, it had been a grand leave.

Vi let herself into No. 11 and called out, 'Elsie? Are you in or out?'

'In.' The voice came from the kitchen.

Vi walked into the room and placed a small package on the table. 'I bought you some cod.'

Elsie's swollen eyes looked up and her lips attempted a smile but faltered.

It had been the same the day before, tears and more tears, Vi thought. 'Are you feelin' any better, love?' she asked.

Elsie blew her nose on a sodden handkerchief. 'A bit,' she said, in a small voice.

'Have you had anything to eat?'

Elsie managed a laugh. 'I can't stop eating. Must be tryin' to soak up all that gin. What a waste, eh?'

'Do you want to try again?' asked Vi. 'Sometimes it works second time round.'

'No. I'm not puttin' meself through that again. If the little bugger 'ung on after all that I reckon 'e wants to be born.'

'He?'

Elsie laughed again. 'Has to be 'e, doesn't it? Only a bloke would give me such a 'ard time.'

Vi bent over her and gave her a hug.

'I'll be all right, you just see. I'm a flamin' good mother to our Linda, and this one won't go short of love either.'

The sound of the front door opening caused both women to look up in alarm.

'Who is it?' demanded Vi.

'Mam? Is that you?'

Jim's voice sent Elsie into a flap. She pulled her cardigan around her exposed chest and rubbed the back of her hand across her eyes. 'I can't let him see me like this!' she hissed.

Vi ran across the room and intercepted Jim as he opened the living room door.

'What you doin' 'ere, Mam?'

'I could ask you the same question. Lettin' yerself into other folk's houses as if you owned the place.'

'I wanted to see Elsie, I called at factory but they said she were off sick. I want to say goodbye.'

The sight of him in his uniform, his hands twisting his cap, made Vi's heart leap. Her boy was going back to face God knows what. 'She's poorly, love. I were just fetchin' some fish for 'er dinner.'

'Can I see 'er?' he asked.

Before Vi could answer, the door behind her was tugged open and Elsie stood in the doorway. She smiled at the soldier. ' 'Ello, Jim.'

He gave a start at the sight of her blotchy face and said in concern, 'Elsie, you look bloody awful.'

'I've felt better.'

He didn't know what to say. He'd had a terrible weekend, traipsing through town looking for a bit of skirt. When he'd found a willing tart he'd dumped her before unbuttoning his flies. His heart hadn't been in it and he'd realised Elsie had been wrong: he hadn't just wanted sex, he'd wanted to spend his weekend with her. The whole of it, not just bed hours.

As if she sensed what he was thinking Elsie said, 'I'm sorry, love. You picked the wrong weekend to come back.'

'Will you write to me?' he asked hopefully.

'Course I will,' she said, knowing she'd never get round to it.

Vi watched as he leant forward and kissed Elsie's cheek. It tasted salty from her tears.

'So long, soldier,' Elsie said, and saluted him.

Vi took his arm and guided him out into the Street. Elsie watched them leave before she wandered back to her chair and sank into it to cry afresh.

Albert had lived through one of the worst weekends of his life. All over Weatherfield pubs were either closed or had notices stuck to their doors: 'No Beer'. It was a terrible thing. Reports had arrived from further afield, from Manchester and Oldham. It was the same everywhere. Albert noticed that the lack of beer was starting to have an effect on the behaviour of his friends and neighbours. Tempers were short and moral was sinking. Albert was no exception and in reply to a knock at his office door he found himself barking, 'Who is it?'

The door was pushed open slowly and Albert was surprised to see his wife. She stood uncomfortably in the doorway and looked round at the room in which Albert spent most of his day: it was small and dusty, with a high ceiling and piles of paperwork and files. It was dark, too, the only light coming from a small taped window. It wasn't the centre of bureaucratic industry Albert had led her to believe.

'What's to do?' he asked anxiously.

She took a few steps into the room and handed him a letter, complete with the King's profile. 'It came this morning. I couldn't wait for you to come 'ome. I'm worried.'

He shared her concern. Their address was handwritten in regular, sloping letters. The envelope was made of thick paper. He slipped a finger under the flap and opened it. He pulled out a sheet of writing paper, embossed with an address at the top right corner. He glanced at Bessie, cleared his throat then scanned the page. It was short and to the point. His mind stumbled over a few of the words and Bessie waited patiently while he read it a second time. Then he lowered it and looked at her, his brow creased.

'Well?' she asked.

'It's from that woman who's lookin' after our Beattie.'

Bessie bit her lip. 'Is she ill? Is it bad news? Oh, it must be bad news.'

'It's stuff an' nonsense, that's what it is,' said Albert, throwing the letter on to his desk. 'She says Beattie was upset by us tellin' her to come 'ome and she wants us to know as 'ow she's grown fond of Beattie and wants to adopt 'er as 'er own daughter.'

'But she's *our* daughter.'

' 'Course she is. Folk can't go round adoptin' other folk's bairns just as the fancy teks them.'

Bessie looked worried. 'She can't keep Beattie, can she? Not when we don't want 'er to?'

Albert attempted a reassuring smile, but his uncertainty showed through. 'Don't be daft,' he said, 'of course she can't. Beattie's our daughter and that's that. I'm goin' down to that school at lunchtime to 'ave a word with headmaster. 'E'll know what to do.'

244

Bessie felt better. Albert was right. Headmasters were like doctors and policemen: they always knew best. The matter would be safe in his hands.

Annie withdrew from kissing Jack and brushed his shoulder with her hand. He bent down and tousled Billy's hair while she dabbed her eyes with her handkerchief.

'Look after yerself, lass,' he said affectionately.

She waved him away with her hand. 'Off you go.' Her voice was croaky as she struggled to avoid making an exhibition of herself, 'Go on, or they'll be sending the MP for you.'

Jack lifted his kit-bag on to his shoulders. He shouted down the street to where Vi was tucking a bag of sweets into Jim's longcoat pocket. 'Come on, Todd, shake a leg!'

'Yes, sir!'

Jim pecked Vi's cheek and ran down the cobbles. The two men turned and waved before they disappeared down Rosamund Street. Annie shivered as they went.

'Back to normality, eh, Mrs Walker?' called Vi.

'Hardly,' replied Annie. 'My pumps are still dry.'

Vi went into her house and Annie turned to enter the Rovers but was stopped by the appearance at her elbow of the bent frame of Daisy Todd.

Annie gave a gasp of surprise. 'Mrs Todd. I'm sorry I didn't see you there.'

'I 'ave business to discuss,' said Daisy secretively, drawing her shawl over her face.

'I beg your pardon?' said Annie, following the woman into the pub.

Daisy moved her shawl and produced a green bottle, which she placed on the bar. Annie eyed it suspiciously. 'Whatever is that? I don't give deposits on full bottles, Mrs Todd.'

'I'm not after no deposit. That's beer is that.'

Annie raised an eyebrow.

'Made it meself from a recipe that's been 'anded down. My great-great-grandfather were at Waterloo an' 'e got the recipe from a Frenchie. There's not many as knows 'ow to mek beer when you've no 'ops an' barley. There's plenty more where that came from.'

245

Annie looked at the murky liquid in the bottle. 'What's it made of?'

Daisy drew in her breath. 'Secret, that is.'

'Where did you get it? You say you brewed it yourself?'

'All weekend I've been locked away.'

'Mrs Todd, this can't be beer if you've only just made it this weekend. Beer has to be brewed for weeks, months.'

'Not this sort,' said Daisy confidently. 'You start serving this an' you'll be tekkin' money 'and over fist. All the other alehouses round here are closed.'

Annie thought. She was right. If this stuff was as good as she said, Annie would be swamped by demand. She'd have to be careful that the brewery didn't find out but there were ways round that. The door swung open and Thomas Hewitt stuck his head hopefully round the door. 'Ale back on yet?'

Daisy shot Annie a look.

Annie delayed answering and instead invited Thomas to come in. 'I wonder if you could help me in a little experiment, Mr Hewitt.'

'Oh aye?'

Annie walked round the bar, produced a glass from behind the counter, uncorked the bottle and poured some of the contents into the glass. It was a cloudy, weak tan colour.

'What's this, then?' asked Thomas.

'Something new. I've heard it's very good. A French ale.'

'Beer?' His eyes widened in delight. He picked up the glass and gulped down the liquid.

Annie watched him carefully and waited for his reaction. He smacked his lips.

'French you say? Not bad. A bit weak, but not bad. Fill glass up again.'

Annie poured more from the bottle. As Thomas drank she moved away from him and whispered to Daisy, 'How much of this do you have?'

'How much are you willing to pay?'

'A penny a pint?'

'Twopence.'

Annie nodded.

Daisy spat in her hand and offered it to Annie, who screwed up her nose and said, 'My word is my bond.'

The news spread throughout the Street, from home to home, with residents keeping the precious information to themselves: the fewer people who knew, the better all round. Annie bolted the pub doors shut and those in the know let themselves into her backyard and gained admittance to the public bar via her hall. Daisy supplied twenty-six bottles, each holding over two pints of the beer. She calculated her profit and smiled toothlessly to herself.

The evening was spent with the residents forgetting their troubles and downing the wonderful brew. The jollity within the locked pub brought a visit from a policeman who, finding the doors bolted, used his initiative and wandered round to the back. Annie secured his silence by pouring him half a pint and he removed his helmet so as not to offend the Crown.

Albert detected a slight sharpness in the beer while Ena complained of a bleach-like smell but on the whole the residents supped cheerfully.

'What a shame Jack Todd's on night patrol,' said Albert, in mock concern. ''Appen we should save him a pint or two.'

'Give over,' said Thomas. ' 'E'd not do same for you. In situations like this it's every man for himself.'

In the snug, Bessie was filling in her friends on the letter. 'Albert took it to Bessie Street and talked to the headmaster.'

'Can you do that, then?' asked Martha in amazement. 'Just turn up and speak to 'im?'

' 'Course you can, 'said Ena, ' 'e's not God, is 'e? You want to ignore her, she knows nothing. What did he say?'

'Albert said he took it very serious and said he'd get in contact with the 'eadmaster at the school where Beattie's been going to. See if he'd have a word with the woman.'

'I've seen this 'appen before,' said Ena. 'Folk talk about the gypsies carryin' kiddies off but this sort of thing's more common. Folk wi' money think they can buy anything. Remember the strikes of nineteen eleven? We were that desperate for money 'cause our dad didn't get strike pay that me and my sister Alice cut our hair off an' sold it on Plank

Lane market to a man who made 'airpieces for the bigwigs in Oakhill. I had 'air down to my 'ips before that day. Skriked me eyes out for days.'

Martha nodded in agreement. 'There was a woman who rode down Rosamund Street in a carriage, not that long since, and she'd stop when she saw a mother with children and 'ave her footman ask if the kiddies were for sale.'

'She doesn't want to buy Beattie,' said Bessie. 'She just wants to keep 'er.'

'And she's not offerin' you nothin' for 'er?' Martha was amazed.

'That's not the point,' said Ena. 'Money don't come into it. It's the principle of these folk thinking we're so stupid and desperate that we'll agree to anything.' She turned to Bessie and said, 'You want to get down to the police station with that letter. Get them to fetch Beattie back on the next train and throw that evil-minded woman behind bars.'

'My mother always threatened to sell me to the gypsies,' said Minnie.

The others looked at her.

'I can just see you with a big 'ooped earring, selling lucky heather down Deansgate,' said Ena. 'And how come you're not drinking this stuff like the rest of us?' she demanded.

Minnie fingered her glass of lemonade nervously and said, 'I've a delicate stomach.'

Police Constable Ernest Longswaite made certain his helmet was firmly in position before leaving the Rovers and proceeding in a westerly direction along Rosamund Street. His ten-minute detour into the Rovers had brightened his spirits and he whistled 'When You Wish Upon A Star' as he strolled along the empty streets.

Since Newton and Ridley had stopped delivering to their public houses the streets of Weatherfield had been deserted at night. Residents spent their evenings in their own homes, and since there had been no air raids for a couple of weeks, neighbours had seen little of each other.

Ernest turned into Mawdsley Street and continued

whistling as he walked past the dark terraced houses. Half-way down, the row ended in a jagged mess of brickwork and rubble. Looking through it Ernest could clearly see the back of Coronation Street. There was a chink of light shining through a gap in some curtains and he could make out the unmistakable shape of Elsie Tanner as she rocked her daughter to sleep. He smiled at the domestic scene and, crossing the street, made his way up the rest of the terrace back towards Rosamund Street. At the corner he continued on, past the shops on Queen's Parade. As usual he put out a hand to check that each door was securely fastened.

Walking past Swindley's Emporium he thought he heard a noise but, after checking the door, he carried on to the wool shop. Glancing back he caught glimpse of light inside Swindley's. Whoever was inside wasn't stock-taking. He went back into Mawdsley Street and cut down the ginnel running to the rear of the shops. He located the back of Swindley's by counting off the shops in his head – Piggott's butchers, Edwards' fishmongers, Swindley's drapers. The back gate was open. He eased himself in and pulled his truncheon from his belt. He considered his options, but before he could decide on what to do the sash window in Swindley's stockroom was pulled up with a squeak and a pair of legs appeared, lashing out in an attempt to make contact with the overturned fruit box that stood under the window. The legs stopped moving when Ernest's heavy hand grabbed the seat of the trousers and pulled the body through the window.

Ernest shone his powerful torch into the startled face. 'Well, well, if it isn't Tom Hayes. What's up, lad? Run out of bootlaces, did you?'

Tom blinked in the glare of the light and dropped the bag containing Leonard Swindley's day's takings of three pounds seven shillings.

Rose Hayes had been free of tablets long enough to deal with the policeman's arrival without Esther's help. Her daughter stood on the staircase in her dressing-gown as her mother's shrill voice echoed around the hall. Ernest Longswaite blinked at the stream of incoherent words that rattled off Rose's tongue. '. . . evil ways, nastiness, jewellery boxes, I can't do wi' it, wash your hands as well as your feet . . .'

Esther ventured down the stairs, one at a time, and placed a hand on her mother's sleeve.

Rose stopped talking and glared at the policeman. 'I don't care!' she shouted.

Ernest looked to Esther for guidance. 'Esther, perhaps if you could come down to the station.'

Esther thought of her brother waiting in the cells at Tile Street and felt certain he'd rather have her looking after him than their mother.

'I'll just put some clothes on.' She turned to climb the stairs, but Rose stopped her.

'No. Esther, don't go.' Her voice was calm and she continued, 'We can't do any more for him.' She looked at Ernest and said, 'Thank you for letting us know, but I think it's best if the magistrate decides what should happen now.'

'Mother, you don't mean –'

Rose's voice changed again as she howled at her daughter, 'Don't tell me what I mean! I don't care! I don't care! Lock him away. Evil. Evil!'

Ernest gave Esther a sympathetic look and put his helmet back on. Rose was the lad's mother, and if she wasn't willing to take responsibility, the matter would have to be dealt with by the magistrates. 'We'll keep him overnight. He'll go before the bench in the morning. If that's what you want?'

Rose nodded, once again seeming in control of herself.

Esther sank down on the stairs and closed her eyes. 'Will I be able to go to the court?'

'Aye. Call at the station first thing and I'll get someone to talk to you.' He paused and looked at Rose. 'I could have let him off with a caution, you know. Just this once.'

'No. I can't control him. He's best off being dealt with. It's these pills I've been takin'. Perhaps if my head was clearer . . .' She ran her fingers through her hair and wandered off down the corridor into the living room.

Ernest glanced sympathetically at Esther and left.

*

Thomas Hewitt woke in the middle of the night, a sharp pain cutting into his stomach. He struggled to sit up and twisted in agony over the side of the bed before vomiting into his chamber-pot.

Ena clutched her stomach and hobbled slowly back into the vestry. Alerted by the noise of the toilet flushing, Vera stirred in bed. Ena made to join her but a pain in her abdomen caused her to cry out and she doubled over.

Albert hopped from one foot to another as he waited outside the toilet door. Inside, Bessie complained, as he rattled the door, 'Go and use Hayes' lav. I'm not budging!'

Esther dropped an egg on the shop floor and burst into tears. Mrs Foyle came quickly to her rescue by wrapping a fresh egg in a paper bag and handing it across the counter to the customer, who paid and left the shop, wondering at the terrible waste of a broken egg.

Esther mopped up the mess and offered to pay for the egg, but Mrs Foyle refused and made a cup of tea for them both. She knew, without asking the cause of the trouble. She'd been lucky in her experience of the magistrate's court with just the fine. Tom had been sentenced to a year in a juvenile prison. Like Esther and Ernest, Mrs Foyle was certain he'd return more of a hardened criminal than the led-astray lad he now was.

Esther dried her eyes and wished she could take something to stop her mind turning over and over the problems of her life: father dead; mother mad; brother in prison. She was the one meant to keep them all together, and all she could do was remember the happier times: Christmas carols around the piano in the front parlour, birthday cakes with burning candles and melting icing, Whit walks when relatives pressed shilling pieces into her gloved hand and admired her new white dress as she paraded with the other chapel girls through the streets of Weatherfield. Innocent pastimes and innocent days, now smeared with the dark stains of death and deceit.

*

Ena's ashen face was the first thing Annie saw as she opened the pub for airing. Vi Todd hadn't turned up for work but the bar smelt of bleach. Annie let the sun in and was shocked by Ena's appearance.

Ena lifted a finger and pointed it accusingly at Annie. 'Florence Maybrick got the death sentence for what you did to us last night.'

Annie blinked. 'I beg your pardon, Mrs Sharples.'

'Poisoner! Assassin!' The flow was stopped as Ena bent double and clutched at the door for support. 'I'm 'avin' the law on you!'

Annie stared after her and ventured out of the door to witness her staggering across the cobbles to seek sanctuary in her vestry.

Ernest Longswaite was back in Coronation Street for the third time in twelve hours. He'd had a disturbed night with stomach cramps, which was unusual for a man who prided himself on an iron constitution. His four visits to the lav hadn't been pleasant but, since donning his uniform, he'd felt better and ready to face the world.

His first task of the day had been to follow up a couple of complaints of attempted murder, both of which had led him to a bemused and indignant Annie Walker of the Rovers Return Inn. She was now at his side as he knocked on the door of No. 9 Coronation Street.

There was the thump of feet on stairs and the door was pulled open by Jack Todd, who frowned at the intruders. 'Ernie, whatever's to do? I've only just got me head down. I've got the wife puking up and I've had no supper!'

'Mind if we come in, Jack?'

The unlikely trio walked into the living room, Annie casting a disdainful eye over the mess and clutter. She noticed that the dirty pots were still in the scullery sink and tried to identify the pungent odour that assaulted her nostrils.

'Is your mother about, Jack?' asked Ernest, removing his helmet.

'Don't ask me, she's probably skulking around somewhere. Why? What's the daft old bat done now? More nickin'?'

'I'm here investigating a string of mysterious illnesses. You say your Vi's not well? Was she by any chance in the Rovers last night?'

Annie nodded.

'Seems we've another victim to add to the list. That's fourteen so far.'

'What's to do?' asked Jack in concern. 'Nowt catchin' is it?'

'Only if you sup the brew like the rest of them.' Ernest produced one of the green bottles he'd taken from the Rovers' bar and placed it on the table. 'I was hoping your mother could shine some light on whatever she's been putting in these bottles.'

Jack's throat dried as he looked at it. Hesitantly he asked, 'Where . . . where did you get that?'

'It's one of two dozen your mother sold to Mrs Walker. It contained a form of ale, brewed by your mother over the past weekend.'

Jack sank into a chair and muttered, 'The stupid old bat.'

'Obviously I'd like to talk to Mrs Todd as soon as I can regarding the contents of her ale.'

'Nettles.'

'Pardon?'

'It'll 'ave been nettles. It's a good brew, always works.'

'But does it always poison, Jack?'

Jack sighed. 'You're barking up wrong tree, Ernie lad. It's not the brew that's to blame, it's the bottles. Two dozen, you say? She must 'ave been nosin' around the allotments. They're all mine. The bottles. I keep them in my shed.'

'For what purpose? There is a shortage of glass at the moment. If you had any bottles you should have brought them to the station. They could have been used for war work.'

'They *are* used for war work!' Jack flinched under Annie's stony glare. 'They're bottles we experimented wi' in Home Guard. We used 'em to make SIP grenades.'

'SIP?' asked Annie.

'Self-ignited something or other,' said Jack. 'We filled them with some chemicals that ignited when you broke glass.'

Ernest nodded grimly. 'Phosphorous.'

'They weren't any good as you 'ad to drop the bottles from eight foot up to get the stuff to ignite so we threw it away. I kept the bottles in case we needed 'em again. Ma must've nicked 'em to put her brew in.'

Annie stared in horror at the bottle. 'Mrs Sharples was right. I've poisoned all my regulars!'

CHAPTER FOURTEEN

1 April 1942 Women who refuse to do war work face tribunals. The Street's women face a different sort of trial when a telegram arrives.

Six months had passed since the Great Poisoning, as it came to be known. During that time the war had spread all over the globe. Moscow became a battleground between the Russians and the Germans, the British lost Singapore and the United States finally entered the War after the Japanese bombed Pearl Harbor. Dot Todd's heroine, Carole Lombard died in a plane crash, the government called up all unmarried women in their twenties, rationing extended to cheese and canned fish, and Elsie Tanner remained manless. It had taken the residents days to recover from the poisoning, and Daisy had been ostracised by the community. The police disposed of the bottles and Annie had been thankful when the brewery started delivering beer once more. Under guidance from Manchester's breweries she divided her weekly supply into nine; she sold two-ninths on Fridays and Saturdays and one ninth on the other days of the week. This way beer was available every night for a limited period only and, despite the rise in price to tenpence a pint, there were few complaints. For this Annie was pleased: her holiday in Blackpool had left her pregnant and she was in no mood for annoying customers.

Being pregnant meant that Annie was pushed to the front of any queues, although she had competition at Mrs Foyle's shop as both Elsie Tanner and Ida Barlow shared her bulging state.

Elsie had hoped that her second delivery might be as speedy as her first, but was sorely disappointed in the twenty-two-hour labour. She'd shrugged off Ena's offer of help, not having forgiven her for writing the letter that had landed her in this state. Instead, it had been Vi Todd who tended her on the Tuesday that ended March before delivering the baby boy on Wednesday morning. Elsie named the wrinkled, bawling fellow Dennis. Vi hadn't attended many births but understood why Elsie had wanted her involvement. Afterwards, while tucking sheets around Elsie, she'd beamed down at the little chap.

Elsie gave her a smile in thanks then closed her eyes, nestling the back of her head into a freshly pummelled pillow.

Vi stroked the baby's face with her finger. He grasped it tightly.

'Will you leave the poor sod alone,' murmured Elsie, her eyes still closed, 'I know you're still there, prodding at him.'

'I can't help it. He's so bonny!'

'Takes after his mother, that's why. 'E's a little Grimshaw, this one.'

Vi slowly pulled her finger free and stroked Elsie's forehead. 'No regrets, then?'

'Ask me again in a month's time when I've had no sleep and me nipples feel as if they're gonna fall off.'

Bessie Tatlock was a shadow of her former self. Even Albert, with his mind on his office job by day and his ARP duties by night, couldn't fail to notice that the colour had gone from her cheeks and the glint from her eyes. She had always sought pleasure from her family and food and for nearly two years had been denied an abundance of both. Rationing was a drag. She couldn't kid herself otherwise. Albert had always appreciated her cooking but the dishes she had served had been traditional fayre and easily made with the right ingredients. Now, everything was different and the newspapers and the wireless urged her to find new and exciting ways of serving what was available. These dishes took time to prepare, and she found that her heart just wasn't in oatmeal mince,

bortsch or mock apricot flan in which carrots were passed off
as the fruit. She saw no point in spending ages preparing
these dishes when both she and Albert sat down to eat with
heavy hearts. Instead she cooked the vegetables from the
allotment as she always had and served them with whatever
pieces of meat she could lay her hands on. She'd always been
plump. 'Homely' was how Albert referred to her. He liked her
that way and so did she. Now she'd lost so much weight her
pinnies hung on her and she had to fasten her skirt with a
nappy-pin borrowed from Ida Barlow – otherwise it fell down.

The worry of Beattie's adoption hung over her like a dark
cloud. In the six months since receiving the letter everyone
had told her not to concern herself, that Beattie would soon
be home, that things would be back to normal. She believed
what she was told by the teachers and people at the town hall
because they wore suits and ties and spoke nicely, and she'd
always been brought up to respect her betters. So why was
Beattie still in Blackpool? Why were her letters never
answered, her presents never acknowledged? Albert didn't
seem as affected by it as she was, and she started to question
his feelings for their only child. What she didn't see was the
anguished look that crossed his face at least once an hour
when he remembered the little lass who had bounced on his
knee. He worked in local government and understood
bureaucracy, but that didn't stop him feeling frustrated by
the red tape tied round a wealthy woman's demands to adopt
a little girl from what she considered to be the slums of the
inner city.

Unable to face her mother over lunch more than three times
a week, Esther Hayes had taken to eating her sandwiches in
North Cross Park, overlooking the allotments and St Mary's
churchyard. She sat on a park bench and threw crumbs of
bread to the three remaining ducks on the pond. It was
surrounded by allotment plots, whose users drained its water
on a regular basis to water their produce. It was little more
than a large puddle now and the ducks wallowed in the mud.

Esther had been to visit Tom every second Sunday and was

pleased to find he seemed to enjoy the regimented life he led behind bars. Rose's mental state had picked up after she'd shaken off the effects of the sedatives but her body had declined. The week before Christmas she'd taken to her bed and, despite the doctor saying he couldn't find anything wrong with her, she'd remained there ever since.

There was certainly nothing wrong with her appetite: Esther trudged up and down stairs carrying trays of food that Rose bolted while criticising her daughter for using too much or too little salt, for undercooking or burning, being mean or extravagant. Esther took all the complaints in good heart, never objected to all the trips to empty the chamber-pot and bore a pained expression whenever she contemplated her mother.

She shook off the last of the crumbs from her skirt and stood up. As she did so the heel of her shoe slipped in mud. She gave a cry and waited to land on her behind but was saved as a man grasped her arm and supported her. She recovered her composure and found herself looking into the face of a ginger-haired man in his late twenties. His nose was freckled and it twitched as he asked, 'Are you all right?'

She laughed and was suddenly aware that her teeth were too large for her mouth. 'Yes, thank you. Thank you very much.'

He offered her his hand as she stepped gingerly across the grass and on to the path. 'My name's John,' he said.

'Esther – Esther Hayes.'

They shook hands.

'I'm very pleased to meet you, Esther. I wonder, would you think me awfully cheeky if I offered to buy you a cup of tea? I'm killing time and I'd consider it a frightful honour if you would accept.'

She knew she had half an hour to go until the end of her lunch break and, despite her natural reservations, found herself nodding. 'Yes, I should be pleased to join you. There's a tea room next to the bank.'

They walked off across the park, she wearing a headscarf and sensible shoes, he dressed in the uniform of a sergeant in the 7th Cheshires. That evening, while sitting before her dressing-table mirror and brushing out her hair, she'd rebuked herself for being so daring as to have accepted John's invitation. She decided it must have been the confident manner in which he'd held out his hand to her. She'd allowed him to take control. He'd chosen where they'd sat in the tearoom, ordered for her and had led her in conversation that was aimed at bringing her out of herself. She knew she'd acted out of character. Shy little Esther who wouldn't say boo to a goose, sitting with a handsome soldier, not stuttering or blushing. Looking back, she couldn't recollect what they'd spoken of and the time had sped past, resulting in her returning fifteen minutes late and receiving the sharp side of Mrs Foyle's tongue. But she hadn't minded. It had been worth it.

The day had delivered another surprise, in the shape of her sister Ada who had returned to Bessie Street School and No. 5 after an absence of fifteen months. Before she'd left, Ada had been the one who ran the house, had taken care of Mother's tantrums and calmed the domestic waters. Ada was aware of a new atmosphere in the house. It was colder and still, but the peace seemed forced, strained. It was as if the house had taken on Esther's emotions and was waiting to snap and lose control.

Over tea that evening, just after Ada had unpacked her bags, the sisters had eaten their steamed fish roll while listening to the news on the wireless. Upstairs, Rose had sucked at the cod, rejected the crust and fidgeted in an attempt to get comfortable. She wasn't happy with having Ada back on the scene as she feared the routine into which she'd fallen with Esther would now be spoilt.

Ada wondered at Esther's uncomplaining attitude. Letters had prepared her for her mother's physical state but after only an afternoon in the same house Ada had found it hard to keep a civil tongue when Rose had called her up the stairs for the twelfth time in an hour.

'And the doctor says there's nothing wrong with her?' she said, sipping her tea.

'Nothing that he can find,' replied Esther, 'and he's done several tests. He got quite excited three months back when he thought it might be her blood pressure and he sent some blood off to be examined. It didn't amount to anything. He hardly bothers now, just comes in, looks her over and goes out again.'

'How much is he charging for that?'

Esther smiled ruefully. 'Don't ask. The most important thing is his visits tend to give Mother a boost. She's on top form for the next couple of days – like now. He came yesterday and she's right as ninepence.'

Ada stared at her in disbelief. 'You mean this is her at her best?'

'Oh, yes,' said Esther. 'She's quite chirpy today.'

Ada looked at her sister with admiration. The shy, overlooked fourteen-year-old had turned into a young woman much put-upon but still able to smile. Ada thanked her stars that threat of bombs had got her away from the house during such an awful period. She drained her cup and started to clear away the dishes, telling Esther to stay where she was for a change.

'Oh, I can't. I've got to get changed.'

In answer to Ada's quizzical look, Esther continued, 'I hope you don't mind, it being your first night home and all, but I've said I'd meet someone in town.'

'What sort of someone?' Ada knew that a flushed face and twinkling eyes could only mean one thing.

'Just someone I met today at the park. I agreed to go out to the cinema.'

'The Bijou?'

'No, the big one in town.'

It was a treat for Esther to venture into Manchester at all, let alone visit the cinema. John met her, as arranged, on the steps of the central library. She was relieved to see him, having convinced herself during the fifteen-minute tram journey into town that he would have forgotten all about her. People tended to do just that and she was thrilled that Sergeant John Brown hadn't. They greeted each other clumsily and he handed over a quarter-pound box of Paradise Fruits. There was time to kill before the film so they sought out a café to share their second pot of tea that day.

Esther felt self-conscious when John asked her questions about herself and her home life. In her natural modesty she played down her enormous contribution to the smooth running of the house and she explained that Rose was 'delicate' after Sid's death. She decided against bringing Tom into the conversation, and in turn asked John about his background.

He was the son of a solicitor and had been brought up in Marple, a leafy, picturesque village in Cheshire. Hearing this, Esther immediately felt intimidated but, sensing her panic, he assured her he was a simple soul and much more interested in personality than background.

They talked of the action John had seen in Greece and of Esther's shelf-stacking techniques, which had revolutionised the corner shop, and discovered a mutual admiration for the music of Chopin. They talked for so long that they missed the film and, instead, opted for an evening stroll through the bombed-out heart of Manchester.

Esther returned home at a quarter past eleven and found Ada waiting up for her. She slipped off her coat, hung it on the peg by the front door and appeared surprised at the lateness of the hour.

'Where on earth have you been?' demanded Ada. 'I've been worried sick.'

'We went for a walk. It seemed a shame not to, it being such a lovely evening.'

Ada got out of her armchair and picked up the glass of water she'd placed on the table nearly an hour before. 'Well, now you're home I'm going to bed.' She felt frustrated that Esther hadn't told her who her new friend was or what they'd talked about.

As if reading her sister's thoughts, Esther spoke quietly, her head bent as she toyed with her watch-strap. 'Ada, I've something to tell you.'

Ada waited for her to continue. 'I'm ... going to be married.'

As she finished brushing her hair Esther realised she had done the impossible. She hadn't fallen in love, but she was

261

confident that would come. No, she'd put in motion her escape route. Out of Coronation Street and away from Rose.

Six days after Dennis Tanner had announced his arrival in the world with a healthy howl, another resident's screams filled Coronation Street. It was seven thirty in the morning and the munitions workers were getting ready to march in to work together. Ena criticised Vera for letting the milk for her porridge boil over and was pulling on her coat when she glanced through her window and saw the lad arrive on his bicycle. His ill-fitting uniform gave away his mission as he parked his bike against the Todds' front window, knocked and handed the white slip of paper to Vi. She'd already cleaned at the abattoir but still had the Rovers to see to and she was annoyed to be disturbed at her between-jobs cup of tea. She had to read the typed words a couple of times before their meaning sank in. She staggered in the doorway and when the lad asked if there would be a reply she shook her head numbly.

Dot appeared at her mother's side and pulled the telegram from her hand. 'Oh, my God!' Dot's shout echoed around the house and brought Sally to her side.

'Whatever's the matter?'

'It's Jim,' wailed Dot. ' 'E's dead.'

Sally grabbed the piece of paper. 'We regret to inform you . . .'

Dot slumped to the floor and covered her mouth as she cried. Vi stood with her back to the front door, her fingers clenched around the lock. She wasn't aware of the voices around her, of Jack pounding down the stairs, demanding to know what was going on, of Daisy's ashen face as Sally broke the news to her. She stood and stared straight ahead, her brain frozen.

And then she screamed.

She pulled open the front door, staggered out on to the cobbles and roared. The noise flooded the Street, running from wall to wall. The neighbours appeared at windows and doorways.

Instinctively Ena knew what had happened and rushed

from the vestry to throw her arms around Vi, and hold her in a vice-like grip.

Elsewhere, Bessie clutched Albert and buried her head against his chest, Martha's hand reached for Percy's, and Annie pulled Billy to her.

Elsie, ready for her second day back on the machine bench, opened her front door and walked straight into Sally and Dot as they stood clutching each other, wailing in competition with their mother. Sally handed her the telegram and her throat tightened as she read it.

Vi crashed to her knees in the middle of the Street, still with Ena holding her in silent comradeship.

Jack watched his wife uselessly. His bare arms hung limply at his sides, his mouth gaped and his eyes stared blankly ahead.

Ada Hayes moved down the pavement, planning to offer Jack some comfort, but as she drew close the sight of him made her draw back. It was as if he needed to be alone, as if the touch of another human would make him explode.

Vi stopped screaming and shouted, 'Why 'im? Why my boy? Why take my boy?'

Ena rocked her, saying, 'Let it go, love, let it all out.'

Vi needed no encouragement. 'For God's sake, why my Jim?' She looked up and saw Elsie standing on the pavement. She thrust out a hand to her. ' 'e's gone, Elsie, my Jim's gone!'

Elsie blinked back tears. She took a few steps forward and grasped Vi's outstretched hand. Vi's fingers enclosed hers. 'You loved 'im Elsie, didn't you? You loved 'im like I did, didn't you? 'E thought the world of you, Elsie. 'E adored you. You did love 'im, didn't you?'

'I did, Vi. 'E was a wonderful man.'

' 'E was, wasn't he?'

Vi's eyes opened wide and shone under the sheen of tears.

Suddenly Jack broke free of his trance. He marched into the house only to emerge seconds later with his rifle. Martha gasped in wonderment as he set off with purpose, still only half dressed. Vi took no notice of him but Ena urged Albert to follow him.

Albert caught up with his friend at the entrance to the

park. He tried to get him to stop walking but Jack carried on. Reaching their allotment plots he raised the rifle and fired into the chicken run. He uncocked the smoking barrel and reloaded the rifle, firing off another shot at the birds. Albert sank back and watched as Jack moved around the plots, seeking out any livestock and blasting anything that moved.

Jim Todd's death, brought about by a bullet shot from an Italian gun during a battle in Malta, brought the war into the living rooms of Coronation Street. Marjorie Barlow's death, along with Madge Mason's and Sam Burgess's, had all been shocking, but the three had been outsiders. Likewise, Sid Hayes had never been considered part of the community, even if he had lived at No. 5 for over thirty years. Jim was different: he had been Coronation Street born and had grown up playing under everyone's feet. He would be for ever the cheeky little scamp who stole apples from the shop and chalked on front doors. His death was as effective as the blackout in putting out the lights in the Street. The residents gathered in small groups to grieve quietly and remember. They all agreed that the loss was made worse by the denial of a funeral. At a funeral service you could centre your grief on the coffin, then toast the lad on his way, but there would to be no funeral, no wake, no grave to lay flowers on.

The priest at St Luke's called on the family, and Vi sat in silence as he urged her to seek consolation in the Bible. Ena, too, pressed on her Good Book, and quoted liberally from Psalms and the New Testament. Vi listened to it all but heard none of it.

A week after the arrival of the telegram, another knock at the door heralded the arrival of a familiar face. Walter Greenhalgh, with his condolences. The sight of a young man wearing a uniform identical to Jim's seemed to bring Vi out of her daze. Before the lad had chance to take off his cap she was shooting questions at him.

What had happened?

Had he been with Jim at the time?

Had he suffered?

Where was he buried?

What had been his last words?

Had he received the letter she'd sent him?

Walt did his best to reassure Vi, having been forewarned by the Army chaplain as to what the expected answers to such questions might be. Yes, Jim had received the letter, he'd told Walt how much his family meant to him, especially his mother. He hadn't stopped talking about his weekend on leave, he'd bored all his friends with tales of his father's exploits, boasted of his mother's cooking, and swore no girl was as good-looking as his sisters. The family swallowed every word, not for one second believing Walter but accepting the words as representing something that might have, could have, should have been.

Walt himself was obviously upset at the death of his best friend, and Vi was touched when he embraced her and asked if she would mind if he wrote to her sometimes. Dot showed him out and was surprised when he kissed her on the cheek. He made to walk away but she pulled the door shut behind her and called him back.

'Why did you kiss me?' she asked.

'Because I wanted to.'

'Why?'

'Because I think you're very pretty.'

She was uncertain if he was playing with her or not. Either way she wasn't going to let him walk away without putting him straight. 'Look, Walt, I'm flattered but don't think you can push your way in like this.'

'Like what?'

'You know, comin' round, sayin' the things me mam wanted to hear. Askin' to write 'er a letter, then kissin' me. I don't need your sympathy. My brother's dead.'

'I know. It wasn't sympathy. I just . . . wanted to kiss you.'

She felt her cheeks burning and knew she was working herself up into a state over nothing but couldn't stop herself. 'Well, don't do it again, because I don't want you to. I 'ave plenty of fellas kissin' me, but only if I want them to. I don't need you to kiss me.'

'I'm sorry.' He tried to win her round with a smile. 'It was just a kiss.'

'Whatever.'

He shifted uncomfortably on the pavement and asked, 'Could I write to you? As well as your mother?'

'Why?'

'I'd like to. That way we could get to know each other better.'

'Why would we want to do that?'

'We could see where it led.'

She laughed in surprise. 'You're serious, aren't you? Oh, Walter, I'm sorry, I thought you was just feelin' sorry for me but you really do mean it!' She laughed again.

He looked hurt. 'Is it really that funny? The idea that I should find you attractive and want to get to know you better?' he demanded indignantly.

'No. It's just . . .'

'Just what?'

'Well, you're just not my type.'

He felt himself getting angry. First she had laughed at him and now this. 'What is your type, then?'

'I'm sorry Walt, but I just don't find you . . .' She looked at him and realised there was so much she didn't find him – tall enough, good-looking enough, charming enough, rich enough – but settled on the one she thought would hurt him least. '. . . I don't find you interestin' enough. I'm sorry but I'm not attracted to you.'

He opened his mouth but no words came out. He closed it and walked off down the Street.

Dot returned to her family to find Vi looking lovingly at the photograph of Jim that Walt had given her. It had been taken in Africa and Jim had a monkey perched on his shoulder. 'I'll get a frame for this in the morning.'

'You do that, love,' said Jack.

'He can stand next to the clock.'

Dot perched on the arm of Sally's chair and said, 'Do you wanna 'ear summat funny?'

'Go on.'

'Walt's just given me a kiss and asked if he could write to me.'

She was surprised that no one else understood the joke.

'What's funny about that?' asked Jack. 'Apart from fact 'e must need 'is eyes seein' to.'

'Ha ha,' said Dot, picking up a biscuit and nibbling it. She swung her leg and munched.

'He's a nice lad,' said Vi, 'and it was kind of him to come and see us. He didn't 'ave to.'

'Sounds like 'e wanted to see our Dot,' said Sally.

'So? She'll not do much better.' As far as Vi was concerned, being Jim's best friend made Walter Greenhalgh a prince among men.

'You what?' Dot squawked. 'Do me a favour. I'm not that desperate.'

The slap took her completely by surprise. She hadn't seen her mother dart round the table and raise her hand until it was too late. She gasped and her face burned. 'What was that for?' she demanded.

'There's nowt wrong with Walt. He's a good, hard-working lad. You should be grateful he's shown an interest in a slut like you!'

Dot jumped off the chair and shouted, 'Well, I'm not grateful! He's short and fat, and his hair's goin', an' I wouldn't be seen dead wi' 'im! You only think he's any cop because he said Jim died in his arms! You just want me to fancy 'im because you want to keep his arms in the family. Give you something to stroke and light candles for!'

She saw the second slap coming, hopped out of the way and tried to march out of the room. But Vi flew after her and walloped her across the back of her head. Dot shrieked and ducked, only for Vi's boot to make contact with her shin.

'You no-good slut!' Vi roared, continuing to hit out at her.

'Get off me! Get 'er off me!'

Jack and Sally looked at each other, unsure what to do. Neither wanted to tackle Vi while she was so fired up and both felt Dot deserved some form of punishment for what she'd said. Dot staggered to her feet, shielding her face from Vi's hands as they struck out, again and again. Vi lunged at her neck, caught at her top and pulled at it, ripping it across the seam. Dot escaped and ran into the parlour where she locked herself in and listened, panting, as Vi banged on the door.

As soon as their mother had run upstairs to her room,

Sally knocked on the parlour door and told Dot it was safe to come out. Dot unlocked the door and fell into her sister's arms, sobbing.

Then Vi reappeared at the top of the stairs and flung down a suitcase. It landed with a thud at the front door.

'Get out of this house!' she yelled from the landing.

Dot's eyes were wide with terror as her mother started to descend the stairs. She made to escape into the living room but Vi caught her arm in a vicious grip. She dragged Dot back through the hall and, with her free hand, opened the door.

Dot called to Sally to help her but the ferocity of Vi's attack had left Sally numb.

Vi propelled Dot out into the night. The suitcase followed and the door slammed in her face. Dot stared at it through the strands of hair that hung down across her forehead. She grasped the handle of the case for support and looked about her. The curtains hanging in the vestry had been pulled back by Ena's heavy hand and Martha Longhurst's bedroom light had come on. Determined not to give the neighbours the pleasure of seeing her discomfort, she began to walk down the street. Her feet moved automatically but her brain had no idea where they were carrying her.

CHAPTER FIFTEEN

26 July 1942 Sweets are rationed but the Yanks arrive in Weatherfield with plenty of gum.

The sun shone down at the start of a new day and in the houses on Coronation Street most of the residents slept through their normal rising time, enjoying the luxury that was Sunday morning. Ena Sharples was not one of those residents: for her, Sunday was the most important day of the week and she had to be up and about earlier than usual. Two services and the Women's Bright Hour in the afternoon meant a steady flow of Mission users throughout the day, starting with the 8.30 a.m. meeting.

The Mission of Glad Tidings had served the community since it first opened its doors on Christmas Eve 1902. Over the years the size of the congregation had diminished, and with most of the men fighting overseas, those still attending tended to be older married couples, widows and mothers clinging to prayer to protect their absent sons. Ena had attended the Mission's Sunday school and had played the harmonium since the 1920s. Ever since taking over as caretaker, she had regarded the whole building as her own responsibility and property. The Mission circuit sent a lay preacher each week to deliver a sermon but they operated on a rota and it was Ena's presence that provided continuity to the forty-odd regular attenders.

After sweeping the hall floor, Ena set out the folding wooden chairs in rows, then turned her attention to the stage area. Vera, woken by the clatter, appeared at the vestry door-way and, without being asked, started to polish the brass goblet that Ena had already placed on the centre table. Like Ena, Vera enjoyed routine, and could be found every Sunday morning rubbing Brasso into it.

'Who's the preacher today, Mam?' she asked.

Ena pushed her broom across the stage and, without paus-ing, said, 'Swindley.'

'Senior or junior?'

'Junior. Old Thomas Swindley's gone in the 'ead. They won't be gettin' 'im to do any more preachin' from this stage, not after 'e were caught swiggin' the Sacrament after preachin' on the evil o' drink.'

'Is drink evil?'

'When some folk sup it it is. I'm glad to say I've never 'ad any trouble with the odd glass I 'ave across at the Rovers, but then I believe in moderation in all things.'

Vera's finger was turning black from the small circles she was making as she rubbed. She looked up from her task and asked, 'Does Elsie Tanner go into the pub much?'

Ena stopped sweeping and eyed her daughter with suspi-cion. 'Why do you ask about Elsie Tanner? What's she to you?'

'I were just wondering, wi' me never 'avin' bin in the Rovers, on account of you sayin' it's not a suitable place for young ladies.'

'And so it's not. I only go in meself to keep Martha Longhurst company, and you know what an ale-hound she is. If I wasn't there to keep an eye on 'er she'd drink 'erself under the table every night and a Black Maria would be sent for to stop 'er smashin' the place up. It's a rough hole, that Rovers. If it wasn't my Christian duty to save Martha from 'erself I wouldn't cross threshold.'

Vera looked longingly into the goblet and wished she could experience the evil that lurked behind the pub door. It was true that she'd never been a bright child but Ena exaggerated her lack of mental ability. Vera had thought it was her mother's way of protecting her but since working in muni-tions she'd come to the conclusion that it was because Ena needed someone to control and she was an easy victim.

She was no longer a child. Her twenty-first birthday was only weeks away and the munitions work had given her a glimpse of a world she was missing out on. Girls of her age, and younger, could do anything they wanted. They spent evenings going to dances and to the cinema. Vera had never swung under a glitter-ball and was only allowed to see films after Ena had sat through them and granted her seal of approval. Vera longed to see what all the factory-floor fuss was about Tyrone Power. She'd heard Elsie talking about a dream she'd had in which bare-chested Tyrone had fought off hordes of pirates to save her from a fate worse than death. If Elsie, with her exotic lifestyle, rated the actor then Vera was certain he was something extraordinary.

After being thrown out by her mother, Dot Todd hadn't moved far. She now rested her curls just feet away from her old bed, on the other side of the wall that adjoined Nos. 9 and 11. Elsie had taken her friend in, thinking the family rift would soon heal. She'd been mistaken: Vi had spent the last three months ignoring her younger daughter. Dot pretended not to mind.

She stretched out on Elsie's lumpy spare bed and looked out of the window towards the back of Mawdsley Street, or what was left of it. Sunday morning in back-street Weatherfield wasn't the most glamorous of locations and she closed her eyes, transporting herself to Hollywood, where a movie mogul who looked like Robert Taylor would discover her, declare her to be the most beautiful girl in the world, and launch her career.

Elsie broke the fantasy by barging into the room and throwing a pair of stockings in her face. 'You've bin wearing my last pair of stockings and don't deny it!'

Dot flicked them off her nose. 'If I 'ad a pair you'd be welcome to a lend.'

'I were saving these for summat special. You must 'ave had a good root through me drawers to find 'em!'

'I didn't think you'd mind.' Dot sat up in bed and attempted to look contrite.

Elsie couldn't be bothered to keep the argument going and

sighed. 'I 'ate Sundays,' she said. 'Everything's shut, there's nowt on wireless, and all you can 'ear is Ena pounding away on that piano thing.'

'Me mam always makes a Sunday roast,' said Dot nostalgically.

'I've got a tin of Spam in the cupboard,' said Elsie.

Dot shook her head. 'It's not the same as meat and two veg with apple crumble for afters.'

'It's better than nowt.'

'I'm fed up with better than nowt, make do and mend. This war's draggin' on too long. Sometimes I think it'll never end and we'll be eatin' Spam for the rest of our lives.'

Elsie grimaced at the thought.

'Tell you what,' said Dot, brightening, 'why don't we go out for the day?'

'Where? Everything's shut.'

'Countryside isn't. We could take a number sixty-three tram at the depot, go up into the moors. It's a lovely day, Linda could 'ave a run-round.'

'What about Dennis? I don't fancy pushin' his pram over fields.'

'Get me mam to look after 'im. Yer know how much she dotes on 'im.'

Elsie was warming to the idea. It would certainly make a change, get them out of the Street for a while. 'All right, then,' she said. 'Yer on.'

Vi proved the ultimate in a good neighbour when she volunteered to look after Linda as well as Dennis. Elsie didn't need much persuading to leave her daughter behind and before the second service started at the Mission she and Dot had left Coronation Street far behind. They chatted and giggled like truant schoolgirls all the way to the depot.

The arrangements for Esther's marriage were carried out in the most proper manner. An announcement of the engagement had appeared in the *Evening News*, Esther had visited John's parents and won their approval. All this had happened without John being present as, the day after proposing to Esther, he had returned to active duties. He was a conscientious letter-writer, while Esther spent most evenings penning diary-like letters for him so that he would be informed of all her activities. Their communications could never have been called love letters, but they were affectionate and, for her part, coy. However, the contents mainly concerned dreams for the future: their home together and life after the war. The closest they came to mentioning sex was their admitted desire to have children one day.

Observing her sister's happiness, Ada felt pangs of jealousy as she contemplated her own future with bedridden Rose. At Esther's happy news, Rose had suffered a relapse and accused her of abandoning her responsibilities. Esther had pointed out that Ada would be on hand to look after her, and had assured her that she wasn't going to rush into marriage. Even if she had met John only hours before agreeing to marry him, she intended to wait six months to test their feelings and be certain she wasn't making a mistake. Now, after three months, Esther was convinced that John was the right man for her. His caring and considerate personality shone through in his letters, and it was with a happy heart that she worked at the sewing machine, making her wedding dress, as and when she had coupons to buy the precious material.

After she had attended the first service at the Mission, Esther worked on the dress at the living room table.

In the scullery, Ada peeled potatoes and listened as Esther hummed. She hated herself for begrudging Esther her joy, but it was like a light shining in darkness, illuminating grime and dust. Ada felt as if she wanted to shield her face from it and was forced to recognise the void it revealed as her inheritance.

'What did you think of the sermon?' Esther called.

'I'm spoilt for sermons,' said Ada, 'Dad was always so clear and concise. Everyone else seems to waffle and drag on so.'

Esther agreed. She'd felt embarrassed for Leonard Swindley as he'd fumbled for words and lost his place in his notes. Afterwards he'd congratulated her on her engagement and asked if she'd be getting married at the Mission. She'd skirted round the question, rather than say she'd opted for St

Mary's because she felt the nineteenth-century church would look nicer in the photographs. The service was the last of her worries anyway. The most pressing thing was how she'd get Rose to attend.

It had been a fluke. Elsie and Dot had boarded a bus believing they were heading off to Saddleworth but instead had travelled west to Warrington. Disappointment and frustration had turned into thrilled delight when other girls on board had informed them of the new arrivals to the region.

'Yanks. Hundreds and hundreds of 'em,' said a young woman with sharp features. 'They've been arrivin' for a couple of weeks. They're everywhere, all of 'em gorgeous. My friend Beryl's goin' steady with one and her mother's horrified because 'e's black. But 'e's got the most gorgeous eyes and 'e's so polite. Not at all like the savages you see at the flicks.'

Another girl joined in the conversation. 'They've got loads of cash and nowt to spend it on. Honest, you only 'ave to look at them and they're chuckin' chocolate and ciggies at you.'

Dot beamed in anticipation but Elsie was more wary. 'What are they 'ere for?' she asked.

'To 'elp us win the war,' said the first woman. 'We're allies, aren't we? And Mr Churchill's always sayin' as how we should be more friendly towards our allies. That's me all over is that, friendly.' She giggled, sat back in her seat and started to sing: '"I don't want to set the world on fire, I just want to start a flame in your heart . . ."'

The rest of the bus joined in. Dot nudged Elsie in the ribs and grinned at her. 'Better than borin' moors, eh?'

Elsie couldn't help feeling she would live to regret the outing.

Oliver Hart was nineteen. Having spent all his life on his father's cattle farm in Kansas, his skin was bronze, his muscles were hard and his blond hair was crew-cut. He was cleaning his teeth, and next to him his new-found best friend, Arnie Haptner, was using the mirror to practise his repertoire of smiles. He fixed his mouth in position and nudged Oliver, who glanced at him.

Arnie broke the smile and said, 'That's the winner. Shows my dimples off. The girls go wild for dimples.'

Oliver shook his head in disbelief. In the ten days he'd known Arnie his mountainous ego had known no limits and now, with a foray into town in the offering, it took on a life of its own.

The two men shared a Nissen hut along with ten other GIs from the US Army in a converted field adjacent to Burtonwood's aerodrome. The site was full of soldiers and their more glamorous brothers in the US Air Force.

It was the first time Oliver had been overseas, or even away from home for more than one night. At first he'd suffered pangs of homesickness but since his arrival in England he hadn't had a chance to dwell on what he was missing. Having been brought up in open spaces, where the nearest neighbour was twenty-six miles away, the industrial north of England took some getting used to. As did sharing his corrugated-iron home with eleven strangers. The men had been forced to accommodate each other's presence and sought comradeship from each other when faced with meeting the locals.

Oliver had ventured out of the camp one evening, eager to explore one of the public houses his guidebook told him about. He'd been issued with the book, which was meant to serve as an instruction to how he and his fellows were to behave while in Britain. Others had flicked through it, laughing at the contents, especially concerning the difference in language, but Oliver was keen to learn all he could about the country. He attempted to memorise all the dos and don'ts at the back – don't make fun of British speech or accents, don't tell the British that America won the last war, don't show off and, most importantly, the one rule written in bold, NEVER criticise the King or Queen.

He'd entered the first public house he'd come across and sampled British beer for the first time. Disappointed by the taste and disillusioned by the wary glances he received from the locals, he'd been puzzled by the name of the pub. The barmaid told him that the King's Head commemorated the execution of King Charles I. Oliver considered this a gross criticism of the monarch.

Tonight's outing would be different though. He was going out with the rest of the hut and they intended to have a wild time.

Elsie and Dot climbed down from the bus and were caught up immediately in the rush of excited, chattering girls who propelled them forward into the heart of town. Almost straight away, Elsie caught a glimpse of her first American uniform. She gasped at the sight of the well-fitting brown fabric, which looked so much smarter than the khaki Jim had worn. She pulled Dot into a shop doorway and checked her appearance in the window. 'Right, what's the plan?' she asked.

Dot shrugged. 'I don't know. Just follow the rest, I suppose.'

'Are you kiddin'? There must be hundreds of girls out there all after the same thing. There's no point millin' around the place. Besides, the best-looking ones will 'ave been taken by now.'

'Well, what should we do then?' asked Dot.

'This needs some thinkin' about, does this,' said Elsie.

'Well, don't think too long, else there'll be nothin' left.'

' 'Ave you ever been to Warrington before?'

' 'Ave I 'eck.'

'Right, well, imagine you're an American, out of camp for the day. Where would you go?'

'Walk in the park?'

'Maybe . . .' Elsie poked Dot with her finger. 'I've got it! You'd be 'omesick, wouldn't you? You'd want to go somewhere that reminded you of 'ome.'

'What? In Warrington?'

Elsie grabbed Dot's hand and pulled her out into the road.

'Where are we goin'?' asked Dot but Elsie didn't answer. Instead she darted in and out of the crowd, glancing from side to side. After a while she found what she was looking for, and slipped down a moderately quiet street. 'Here we are.'

They were outside a small cinema. Unlike the Bijou on Rosamund Street, this one opened on Sundays. Dot looked at the poster outside the ticket office and let out a sigh of annoyance.

'*Bad Men of Missouri*! I saw that months ago! I 'ate westerns.'

'Not today you don't, love. Today you love 'em so much you'll be 'appy to sit through this again.'

Ten minutes later the girls were being walked down the darkened aisle by a uniformed middle-aged woman with a torch. She shone it in the middle section of the stalls and said, in a hushed voice, 'There you go.'

Elsie led the way through the sea of knees and settled down in the middle of the row of seats. Dot sat next to her.

While Dot watched the newsreel intently, Elsie closed her ears to the narrator's cultured tones and tried to home in on any accents from across the Atlantic. She was shocked to hear one directly behind her.

'What did 'e say?' The voice was deep and masculine.

'I don't know. Something about a race with an egg.' The second was as deep as the first and Elsie snuggled into her seat with a shudder of delight. It came as a shock for her to realise she'd been without a man for nearly a year.

She decided she'd wasted enough time and turned round to smile at the soldier behind her. 'It's an egg-and-spoon race. You put your egg on your spoon and you run as fast as you can. My name's Elsie and this is my friend Dorothy, but everyone calls her Dot.' She froze when she realised there were not two soldiers sitting behind her, but a row of twelve.

'Hi there, Elsie. I'm Arnie and this is Oliver, that's Jake, Harry, Ray, Vic, Al, Max, Cliff, Mario, Harlan, and at the end is Ginger.'

Elsie gulped and nudged Dot. 'Say hello to the nice gentlemen, Dorothy,' she said, undoing the top buttons of her blouse. ' 'Asn't it got rather 'ot in 'ere all of a sudden?'

Back in Weatherfield, Ida let Kenneth play in the backyard in the afternoon. She laid out a rug on the flagstones for him but he refused to sit still. Instead he wandered about, pulling the heads off the dandelions that grew between the cracks in the paving. The new baby, David, lay asleep in his pram. Ida sat on a stool and closed her eyes under the heat of the summer sun.

'Hello, love.'

It was Bessie's voice, and Ida let out a deep sigh, knowing she'd be forced to natter throughout this most precious time when David was sleeping.

'Hello, Mrs Tatlock,' she said, forcing herself to smile as Bessie's face appeared over the back wall.

'Lovely day, isn't it?' said Bessie. 'I've hung some washing out. Goodness knows what my old ma would say, hanging washing out on the Sabbath. I hope Ena doesn't see! Oh, look at Kenneth, isn't he getting big? He's such a bonny lad, isn't he? Would he like a humbug?' Without waiting for Ida to reply, Bessie dug into her apron pocket, located one and threw it over the wall towards Kenneth. He picked it up and stuffed it into his mouth.

'Have you seen that notice she's put up at the corner?' continued Bessie, oblivious to Ida's strained expression. 'Half a pound of sweets to last a month! Me and Albert get through half a pound in a night. I never expected sweets to be rationed. We'll be havin' coupons to breathe fresh air next!'

She carried on talking without any encouragement from Ida. Talk, talk, talk. Ida found herself staring at the front wheel of Frank's bike. It rested where he'd left it years before, against the wall. The piece of tarpaulin he'd covered it with must have fallen down. Ida had forgotten all about it bike and seeing it again reminded her of Frank. Her eyes misted over.

Bessie carried on talking.

The jeep roared round the corner into Coronation Street and came to a noisy stop outside the corner shop. Alerted by the screech of brakes, Ena and Martha both stared out of the vestry window as Arnie leapt down and put out a hand to guide Elsie on to the pavement. She stumbled and fell into his open arms, giggling. 'My, what strong arms you've got, soldier,' she said, as coyly as she could.

'I can halt a stampeding bull,' he replied proudly.

'I bet you can,' she said, eyeing him up and down. 'Only trouble is, we don't have many bulls round 'ere. What we do 'ave plenty of is nosy neighbours.' She shouted across at the

Mission, 'You want to be careful, Mrs Sharples. Arnie 'ere can stop a stampeding bull, so I don't reckon 'e'll have much trouble with a nosy old cow!'

The curtains twitched furiously, and Elsie laughed.

Arnie looked about the Street in amazement. 'I've never seen anything like this place. These houses are so tight. How do you breathe?'

'We take deep breaths,' said Elsie, demonstrating.

Arnie stared at her breasts as they rose and fell, straining the material of her thin blouse. 'Which one's your house?'

'Right behind you. Dot's stayin' with me at the moment . . .' The mention of her friend's name caused Elsie to look into the jeep for her.

Dot was sprawled out in the back, sandwiched between Cliff and Ginger. At the wheel, Oliver followed her gaze and laughed. 'Seems like quite a party back there, fellas.'

'You bet!' came the reply.

'So, this is Manchester,' said Oliver, smiling at Elsie.

'Well, a grubby little corner of it. Weatherfield's what we call a district of Manchester. That's if we were trying to impress. Normally we'd refer to it as a stinkin' hole.'

'Pardon me?' said Oliver. He found Elsie and Dot's accent hard to follow and had spent most of the afternoon asking them to repeat themselves.

'It's a dump,' said Elsie in explanation, pulling a face.

'Yeah,' said Dot, emerging from the jeep somewhat rumpled. ' 'Itler should do us all a favour and flatten the place.'

At the appearance of a dark-haired young woman in a tight, knee-length skirt Oliver's attention shifted from Elsie. He whistled and asked, 'Who is that?'

Dot looked up and sighed. 'It's me sister Sally.'

Oliver stood up in the jeep and opened his arms wide, calling, 'Helloooooooo, Sally!'

Sally wandered over to the group. 'Hello, yourself. Where have you all sprung from?'

'The US of A, Sally,' said Arnie with a leer.

'That much I'd guessed.'

'We found them wandering, like little lost sheep,' said Elsie.

'Yes, that's right,' said Dot, staring hard at her sister. 'We found them first.'

Ginger and Cliff appeared at Oliver's side to see the latest attraction. Sally raised her eyebrows and said to her sister, 'Two each? Don't you think that's being just a little bit greedy?'

'Oh, Sally,' said Arnie, 'there's plenty of us to go round. Don't you worry your pretty head about working it out.'

Sally looked up at the jeep and said, 'You're not playin' fair, soldier. You know my name but I don't know yours.'

'Oliver Hart, ma'am, from Kansas.'

'Well, Oliver Hart from Kansas, I'm very pleased to meet you.'

Dot saw the way they looked at each other and fumed. It was Jean all over again. It wasn't fair, the way they took one look at Sally and forgot all about her.

Across the Street, in the Mission vestry, Ena scowled. 'That Elsie Tanner, she's at it again! Bringin' them in by the carload now, she is.'

'It's disgustin',' said Martha, ogling out of the window.

'Don't tell me,' said Minnie. 'If anything's carryin' on I don't want to know about it.'

'Well, neither do I,' said Ena, 'but I can't ignore it when it's carryin' on under me nose, can I? Will you look at that one with the ginger hair? He's got his hand round Dorothy Todd's waist!'

'In broad daylight, too,' piped up Martha.

'Who are they, Ena?' asked Minnie, her curiosity getting the better of her. 'Are they foreigners?'

'Worse than foreigners,' said Ena grimly. 'Them's Americans!'

CHAPTER SIXTEEN

August 1942 1,000 Allied sailors killed by Japan in Solomon Islands. A hut full of US servicemen conquered by Elsie Tanner.

In a district of New Orleans, his home town, Sergeant Irvin Masterson was considered king of the keys whenever he played the honky-tonk piano. Now, miles from his roots, Irvin was making another joint swing, the Rovers Return Inn, Weatherfield.

A bunch of enthusiastic Americans had wheeled the piano out from its usual place in the select bar, and complaining Albert had been unceremoniously shifted out of the way to make room for it. Annie had made a point of having the piano tuned regularly in the hope that her pre-war application for a music licence would eventually be granted. Like much other red tape the lack of a licence didn't seem to matter in wartime when the authorities realised people needed to utilise whatever they could to take their minds off the situation. In recent years the ivories had been played by either Mrs Foyle or Ena but neither of those ladies had given them the hammering Sergeant Masterson was treating them to.

While Albert retired to a distant corner to join Jack Todd and Thomas Hewitt's game of dominoes, Sally slipped behind the bar to give Annie and Martha a hand in keeping the beer flowing. The arrival of the GIs for the evening had led Annie to break into her emergency barrel of best bitter, although she had been delighted to accept the four bottles of whisky brought by her new regulars from Burtonwood. She was glad of Sally's help as, from time to time, she had to keep darting into the hall, listening out for any stirring from five-month-old Joan, who lay asleep in her cot upstairs.

Martha finished serving a soldier with a pint and a whisky chaser. He held out a palmful of money and she selected the correct change. He beckoned her to come closer across the bar and, while whispering in her ear, slipped another coin into her hand. She giggled and moved across to the till, glancing back over her shoulder at the American.

'You want to be careful, Mrs Longhurst. These blokes take no notice of weddin' rings,' said Sally, enjoying teasing the blushing woman.

'Get on wi' you,' said Martha. 'I'm a respectable woman.'

'Well, I'm glad I'm not,' said Sally, smiling across to where Oliver Hart stood playing darts with his friends. He caught the smile and winked back.

Annie spoilt the moment: 'Sally, Mrs Sharples wants another bottle of stout.'

Sally moved across to the snug and produced a bottle from behind the counter. 'I'd go easy if I were you, Mrs Sharples. There's not many bottles left.'

'When I want your advice I'll ask for it,' said Ena. 'You barmaids should know your place and not overstep the mark.'

Sally laughed. 'I'm only 'elpin' Mrs Walker out, you know. I do 'ave a job or 'ad you forgotten? I 'aven't, but perhaps that's because I've 'ad to stare at your ugly face all day!'

Ena scowled and dropped her sixpence on the bar. She'd been furious when the sections at the factory had been mixed up by a manager keen to leave his mark. As a result she, Minnie and Martha had been sent back to their original bench with Elsie, Sally and Dot. Thankfully Vera had ended up at a nearby bench run by a strict Methodist, who monitored her section's conversation.

Sally crossed the floor to Martha and pulled a face. 'I don't know how you put up with 'er breathin' down yer neck all the time.'

Opportunities to criticise Ena were rare so Martha made the most of this one. Making sure Ena couldn't hear her, she said, 'It's 'er Vera I feel sorry for. What sort of life is that for a young woman? You know Ena drove 'er other daughter to run off with that gypsy? That were 'er Madge. Course, that was when they lived in Inkerman Street so you wouldn't 'ave known her. Big girl, like Ena. Face as 'ard as our backyard wall. And 'er 'usband, Alfred, 'e didn't 'ave much of a life. My Percy says it must 'ave been a relief for 'im to die when 'e did. Was the only way 'e could escape 'er naggin'. 'Ee were a good lookin' man. I were surprised when 'e married 'er – she's always bin ugly as a cracked pot.'

Elsie Foyle tapped out the rhythm of the piano beat on the table top where her gin danced around in its glass. She swayed her shoulders and shook her platinum curls to the delight of the New Jersey serviceman on whose lap she sat.

Bessie Tatlock craned her neck as she gave Ena a commentary on the shopkeeper's decline into depravity. 'They're singin' together, now.'

'I bet they are,' said Ena, 'and it won't be Handel's Messiah, either.'

Ena sat with her back to the public bar but had positioned Bessie and Minnie at angles so they had the bar covered for her.

Minnie gasped.

'What now?' demanded Ena.

'Martha's just waved to that one with glasses that you said reminded you of Buster Keaton.'

Ena sucked in air between her teeth. 'Remember that Australian she met on Armistice Night?' she said. 'I'm sayin' no more.'

'It's only a wave,' said Vi. She sat apart from Ena and her colonels, on the bench beside the bar. Daisy sat next to her, sucking her way through a packet of crisps.

'I might 'ave known you'd see nowt wrong with collaboration,' said Ena, glaring at Vi.

'Give over. It's only a bit of fun.'

'Some people turn a blind eye to too much if you ask me,' said Ena to Minnie, 'even when it goes on under their own roof.'

'Are you referrin' to me, by any chance, Mrs Sharples?' asked Vi, raising her voice.

'All I'm sayin' is I'm glad my daughters haven't brought shame and damnation upon my house. That's all I'm sayin'. Don't you agree, Minnie?'

'Nay, Ena,' said Minnie, shifting uncomfortably in her chair, 'don't drag me into it.'

'Personally, I'm glad my daughters can have a bit of fun,' said Vi. 'At least I don't keep 'em locked up like prisoners. At least I'm not afraid to let them spread their wings in case they shoot off and never come back. How is your Madge, Mrs Sharples?'

Ena flushed but she didn't retaliate. Instead she wiped her nose on her sleeve and said to Bessie, 'Ignore 'er. She's common.'

The gentility of the snug was disturbed when the door flew open and a couple of tan uniforms appeared.

Ena was affronted by the intrusion. 'Get out! Men by invitation only!'

The men looked at each other and laughed. One walked in and whistled. He eyed Minnie up and down and held out a hand. 'Would you care to dance, ma'am?'

Despite Ena's icy glare, Minnie giggled and waved the man away.

Ena looked about for support and shouted into the bar. 'Annie Walker, I don't think much of your establishment when decent women are molested in the safety of their own bar!'

The Americans turned to each other. 'What did she say?'
'Search me?'

Albert approached the men and tapped one on the shoulder. 'Excuse me, but I think you're botherin' these ladies.'

Dot called across the bar from her place by the piano, 'Come on, lads, leave the biddies alone. They're too old for you!'

'Don't be so cheeky!' shouted Vi, getting to her feet. She linked her arm through a soldier's and walked him into the public.

Ena watched them go, then smirked to herself. 'See what I mean? Common.'

Jack Todd looked up from his dominoes to see Vi and Dot dancing between the tables and grunted his approval. At least they weren't disturbing him with their rowing any more. Mother and daughter had made peace, although Dot had opted to remain in residence at No. 11 for the time being.

Albert shuffled back into his place. Thomas looked up from laying a domino on the table, removed his pipe, and said, 'Saw them off, then, did you, Albert?'

'Just told them what's what.'

'Good on you.'

Albert glanced at his dominoes, looking for his double three to place. It was missing. He looked about him on the floor around his chair.

'What's up?' asked Jack.

'I've lost a tile.'

'You can't have,' said Jack.

'I 'ave, I tell you. I 'ad it 'ere ready to lay. Now I can't go!'

'You'll 'ave to knock, then, won't you?' said Thomas, carefully covering the double three with his leg.

'If I knock, you'll win,' complained Albert.

'Will I?' asked Thomas innocently. 'Fancy that.'

The mood changed in the bar as Sergeamt Masterson left his post to relieve himself of the pints of bitter that had been bought for him. Elsie Foyle slipped on to his stool and, encouraged by her neighbours, played a slower piece, singing along, '"You are my sunshine, my only sunshine . . ."' Dot and Vi joined her at the piano and took up the song.

Hearing a wail upstairs, Annie disappeared into the living quarters, leaving Martha and Sally to man the bar. Sally herself broke ranks when she grasped Oliver's hand and joined in the song:

> 'The other night, dear, as I lay dreaming,
> I dreamt that you were by my side.
> Came disillusion when I awoke, dear,
> You were gone and then I cried.'

Oliver leant across the bar and whispered in her ear, 'I shan't leave you alone tonight, sweetheart.'

They kissed across the pumps, causing Oliver's friends to raise a cheer.

' 'Ey up,' said Ena, getting to her feet, 'they've started. I'm not 'angin' around 'ere to see the rest of 'em at it. Minnie, get your bag.'

Minnie looked as if she was about to protest but, seeing Ena's grim expression, she rose from the table. The two women pushed their way through the crowded bar. Seeing them go, Martha called out 'Night, Ena,' only to receive a cold glare in return.

Once outside the pub, Minnie sighed despondently. 'I suppose I should get back to Mother,' she said forlornly.

'Yes, you do that. Never mind all that carryin' on in there. You want to think of your poor mother sat alone in your draughty house, all alone with 'er thoughts.'

'You're welcome to come back with me, Ena. Mother likes you. I could make some cocoa.'

'No. I'd best not. Someone 'as to keep an eye on the goings-on in the Rovers. No, I'll just sit by the window and keep watch. It's a thankless job but someone 'as to do it.'

The women started off down the Street but stopped when Ena pulled up short and beckoned Minnie to keep quiet.

'Whatever's the matter?'

'Ssh. Look at 'er, Elsie Tanner.'

Minnie followed her friend's gaze and saw Elsie walking towards them, sandwiched between two tall, dark-headed men in dark brown uniforms. 'Who are they?' she asked.

'Well, they're not Laurel and Hardy, that's for certain.'

Elsie saw her observers and laughed. 'Well, lads, I told you I'd show you the sights and 'ere's one of our old monuments now. Forget the Tower of London and Big Ben, 'ere's Ena Sharples.'

One of the men tipped his cap and smiled. 'Hello, Mrs Sharples.'

'Don't waste yer teeth on me, lad, you'll not find all of us as easy as 'er.'

Ena made to walk off but Elsie called, 'Don't go yet, Mrs Sharples, I've got a riddle for you. How do you get change for a shillin'?'

Ena ignored her.

'Don't you know? I'll tell you then. Two Tanners! I'm Elsie Tanner and this adorable 'unk just so 'appens to be called Steve Tanner!'

Ena eyed the young man up and down. She supposed he was good-looking, and the way he'd raised his cap had impressed her. He seemed to have more manners than the rest of his kind. She felt it would be impolite to ignore him and smiled. 'Good evening. This is my friend, Mrs Caldwell.'

Another tip of the cap. 'I'm very pleased to meet you both. This is my good pal Greg Flint.'

The other American didn't tip his cap. He looked longingly down the Street to the noise coming from the Rovers.

'I've not seen your uniforms before,' said Minnie. 'Are you in the Army police?'

Steve laughed, showing off his perfect teeth. 'No, ma'am. Actually we're both in the Air Force.'

'Bit of a coincidence, don't you think, Mrs Sharples? Us both being called Tanner!' said Elsie, giving Steve's arm a squeeze. 'I bet there aren't any Sharples in America.'

' 'Appen not,' said Ena, 'but I were born a Schofield and I know for a fact there's at least one of them there. My brother Tom. 'E went over in nineteen twelve. Lives in Connecticut. Perhaps you've met him?'

Steve shook his head and said, 'I'm from Boston, ma'am.'

Ena said, 'Well I'll drop 'im a letter and see if 'e's heard of you. Goodnight.'

Elsie pulled Steve away from Ena, who watched them walk towards the Rovers, then shouted down the street, 'Who's lookin' after yer bairns tonight? Or 'ave you left 'em all alone!'

Elsie carried on smiling and said, 'Ignore 'er, she's had a drop too much.' Reaching the Rovers she pushed open the door and said, ' 'ere we are, best welcome in Weatherfield.'

She pushed her way to the bar through the crowds of singing uniforms and dresses, and became aware of the hostile looks her party was receiving. While waiting to be served she whispered to Steve, 'You're not a wanted criminal, are you?'

'It's because we're fliers. These guys all seem to be Army.'

'Oh, right. I suppose it's like a class thing, like with the RAF.'

'Not really. It's just that having the more exciting job we tend to steal all the girls from them.'

Elsie basked in his smile and thanked her lucky star for having crossed their paths. Since meeting Arnie and Oliver in Warrington she had taken most of their hut to bed, but Steve Tanner had a quality that made her want to keep him close to her. He was charming, wonderfully handsome and, to her surprise, seemed genuinely interested in her.

Greg Flint clapped his hands and shouted across the pumps to Sally, 'What does a fella have to do to be served round here?'

'Say please,' said Sally. 'What's your fancy?'

'You, sweetheart, on a piece of rye bread with pickles and some mozzarella.'

'Well, I'm afraid I'm not on offer. Best or mild?'

Greg shrugged. 'Whatever. It all tastes like gnat's pee.'

Returning to the bar, Annie caught the remark and bristled. 'I can assure you,' she said, 'that I keep the perfect pint. It may not be as strong as it ought to be but that is because there is a war on. We all have to make sacrifices.'

Elsie jumped in to assure Annie that her guests didn't mean to cause trouble.

'Two pints of bitter, please, Mrs Walker, and I'll have a gin.'

'I'm afraid I'm out of gin,' said Annie.

'It's okay, Elsie,' called Oliver from the dart-board. 'There's plenty of whisky behind the bar.'

Annie pulled a face. Whisky was definitely not a lady's drink.

'Cheers, Oliver!' Elsie introduced him to the airmen, and Sergeant Masterson started thumping the keyboard again.

Mrs Foyle was lifted on to a table and started to dance, tapping her shoes. The men around her started to jeer and clap.

The sight of the shopkeeper's skirt flaring up distracted Jack Todd from his dominoes. He gazed lustfully at her legs and envied the serviceman who ran his fingers up and down her calves. 'Bloody 'ell,' he muttered.

Albert was also gaping at the view.

Thomas used the distraction to take a look at Jack's dominoes and settled back to change his strategy.

Bessie watched her husband ogling Elsie Foyle's legs. Poor Albert didn't get many pleasures in his life. Why shouldn't he gaze at a well-turned ankle? She just wished he didn't look so gormless.

Sally finished her shift behind the bar and said goodnight to the revellers. She waited outside the pub until, as arranged, Oliver could join her. Silently she took his hand and led him round the back of the Rovers and into the ginnel that ran between the backs of the houses on Coronation and Mawdsley Streets. She intended to take him into her old nesting-place, in the ruins of her grandmother's old house, but he was too impatient and pinned her against the wall of the Tatlocks' outhouse.

He kissed her neck and she allowed herself to go limp under his weight. His smell, of whisky and aftershave, aroused her and she ran her hands over his backside. He moved his mouth across her face and explored her lips with his tongue. She closed her eyes and sighed, as he whispered in her ear, 'Fancy a wall job?'

She murmured approval so he started to unbutton her blouse. She moved her hands round to the front of his trousers and, unzipping them, thrust her hand into the warmth of his groin. He pulled up her skirt around her waist and she wrapped her leg around his hip.

Albert sat in the closet, and he was startled by the grunting coming from the other side of the brick wall. He decided to leave as soon as he could and cursed under his breath as he realised the hook from which the newspaper squares hung was empty.

CHAPTER SEVENTEEN

December 1942 Britain's VD epidemic hinders the war effort but the women of Coronation Street carry on as normal.

Inside No. 5 Coronation Street, Ada and Esther sat before the unlit fire attempting to put the finishing touches to Ada's matron-of-honour dress. John's family had dug deep into their pockets: they wanted their only son to marry in style. Esther had been embarrassed by the gesture but grateful too as her family had made no provision for her wedding and she had hardly any savings to her name. She was pleased to have Ada's support as Rose was ignoring the whole venture, as if by denying it it would go away.

Tom was due home in time for the wedding, and Esther was nervous about her in-laws meeting him. He had shown no repentance during his time in prison. She realised he was no longer her little brother, whose boisterous behaviour was explained away as boys being boys. He was sixteen years old and the enforced exercise behind bars had turned his scrawny body into a powerful one. It had also given him more confidence, as if he needed it.

Although it was two doors away from the pub, the sound of singing carried into the Hayes living room.

'Mrs Tatlock said the Rovers is full of Americans, these days,' said Esther.

'Yes.'

'You don't have to spend every night keeping me company. You could go out if you wanted to. The girls who come into the shop say the Americans are very generous.'

Ada shook her head. She wasn't interested in men in the way her acquaintances were. In the past she'd longed to go out to the cinema or to a dance, but that was because Sid had forbidden it. Now that she was free to do as she pleased she found she had no desire to do anything but sit at home. At the back of her mind was the fear that if she did venture out she'd unleash something wild within her that she'd been suppressing all the years. Once released, she might never be able to tame it again. Much better never to let it out of the box.

The bridal gown had been finished three days before the wedding. It hung from a padded hanger on the wardrobe door in the cramped room Esther had shared with Ada all her life. The room had grown up with them, the double bed making way for two singles, Sunday-school certificates for picture postcards from friends lucky enough to see far-flung places. It was a beautiful dress, a perfect copy from one Esther had admired in *Picture Post*. She'd lost count of the number of clothing coupons she'd used in buying the fabric, having gone through all the family's rations along with generous friends'. It was a full-length white creation, with pale pink roses embroidered around the hem. Ada's dress was in pink to match the roses. Ada had insisted on being called matron-of-honour because, at thirty-two, she refused to be bridesmaid to her younger sister. It was the only time she'd allowed her jealousy to surface and she hadn't been proud of herself for doing so.

There had been a great deal of debate as to who should give the bride away and in the end Esther had asked Albert Tatlock to do the honours. Albert, bursting with pride, took his duties seriously and struggled gallantly to compose a speech on the merits of someone he had always thought to be a stuck-up wet Nellie. Sadly the residents of Coronation Street never heard the speech, or even caught a glimpse of the bridegroom as tragedy struck Esther's young life once more.

The day before the wedding, she was interrupted when cooking the evening meal by a sharp knock at the door. She removed her apron and rushed to admit the caller. It was John's father. 'Mr Brown!' she exclaimed in surprise.

He looked tired and pale, and as he removed his trilby his hand shook. She offered him a cup of tea but he declined, saying he had much to do that night. She knew from his tone that it was bad news. Hoping to spare him anxiety she attempted to give him an opening. 'Something's the matter, isn't it? With John? Please tell me outright, Mr Brown. Has his leave been cancelled?'

'No. No, but you're right, something terrible has happened.'

She sat down and gestured for him to take the comfortable chair but he remained standing and, after shuffling his feet, blurted out, 'I'm so sorry Esther, but I'm afraid John is dead.'

A laugh escaped her. It had to be a joke, but the man's face told her it was anything but.

'How?' she asked quietly.

'He was coming home for the wedding. You'll remember he wrote saying the major had granted him special leave? He'd been given four days. Well, he left for England this morning but over the North Sea . . .' he broke off, choking on a sob.

'What happened? Did the plane crash?'

'Shot down by enemy fighters. It crashed into the sea. No survivors.'

Her hand rose automatically to her mouth. She wanted to vomit. First her father, now her fiancé. What was the point of a blasted war that blew people up, flattened cities and ruined the lives of ordinary people like her? People who just wanted to live in peace, not harming anyone, not taking up too much of the earth's space.

Mr Brown fumbled with the brim of his hat. Neither could think of anything to say so they remained in silence, each sharing the other's grief.

Ada's arrival home broke the tableau. At the sound of her cheerful voice, Esther fled the room. She raced past her bewildered sister and out of the house. Ada moved to follow her but Mr Brown laid a hand on her arm. 'She's had some bad news, I'm afraid.'

Outside in the cold street, Esther leant against the back wall of Elliston's and took in short, sharp gulps of icy air. Her head was spinning. She didn't want to return home to face John's father, Ada's sympathy or her mother comparing her grief to her own at losing her husband. Alone and frightened, Esther remembered another time when she'd fled No. 5, in fear of Sid's punishment after spilling ink over his sermon notes. Then, as now, she'd stumbled into the Street and had found help from an unlikely source. Wanting to turn the clock back, Esther ran up the street towards the Mission. A light was on, burning through the black-out curtain at the window. Cautiously, she knocked at the door.

Ena heaved a heavy sigh and pushed herself up off the sofa. She'd only just come in after a gruelling twelve-hour shift and her fingers ached from turning the tiny pieces of metal into bolts. Iron-filings were embedded in her skin and she longed to soak her feet in water. Now someone was knocking on her door. She pulled it open and barked into Esther's pale face, 'Yes, what do you want?'

Ignoring the ferocity of the greeting, Esther saw only the kindly face that had produced the toffee tin when she was twelve and in need of help. 'I need help, Mrs Sharples.'

Ena stopped herself from shouting a retort. Esther Hayes was an unusual caller. She could be found every Sunday in the third row on the left in the congregation but Ena couldn't think of a time when the lass had called at the Mission. At least, only the once. She stood aside, to let Esther in, and said, 'I've no toffees to offer you but if a weak cocoa'll do you're welcome.'

Esther smiled with gratitude then burst into tears. Ena made no attempt to stop the flow, just stood with her arm around the girl's shoulders. She had all night, if necessary. Esther apologised for the tears, sniffed and said, in explanation, 'I've just heard my John's been killed in a plane crash.'

Ena had seen so many die young. It didn't surprise her any more but she mourned them just the same. Over the next two hours she worked to patch Esther's broken heart. She talked to her plainly and simply about loving and losing, of her own experience of bereavement, of Minnie's husband taken in his prime, of Dinky and Madge Low, the original occupants of No. 1, who had shared only one night of married happiness before he was slaughtered in the trenches and she died in childbirth. Of her love for handsome Harry Moss, and her own wedding plans, before he, too, was killed on the Somme. She talked of the waste of young men and women whose lives were crushed by fate and of those who were left behind to mourn and question God's motives. She had no answers and, as she said, she'd been asking questions for over thirty years. She could only pass on what she'd learnt, that God had his own plans and that mercifully he used time to heal the wounds. When Esther returned home to anxious Ada, her heart was still heavy but her mind was clearer. John was dead and so was her chance of escape.

Elsie Foyle rubbed the soapy lather into her face then splashed water from a bowl decorated with roses on to her cheeks. Despite having access to much beyond the means of the ordinary housewife, it had been quite a few months since she'd managed to get her hands on any soap. Of all the things taken for granted and now looked upon as a luxury, it was soap that had bothered her most about the war.

She checked her reflection in the mirror and gave herself a mark of approval. Forty-two and she still had all her own teeth. There weren't many of her customers who could say the same. She glanced over the rest of her body, much of it encased in a corset, and straightened out a seam on one of her new nylon stockings. The three inches of flesh between her panties and her stocking top wobbled as she ran her hand down her calf. Telling herself she'd still be a knock-out on the stage, she attempted a high kick. It was a mistake and she doubled up on the bed to get her breath back. Then it was back to the trio of mirrors on her dressing-table for the application of cherry-red lipstick. Not too much, just a Cupid's bow. Her hair was perfect – it always was – but her eyebrows needed a pluck. She reached for the tweezers and grimaced in anticipation of the pain. Needing something to see her through the agony she leant across to the bedside cabinet and reached for a chocolate from her box. Orange Creme. Her favourite. She popped it into her generous mouth and enjoyed teasing the almost liquid centre out of the shell.

The chocolates, together with the soap and the nylons, had

been a present from a thirty-year-old American sergeant with roving eyes and dimples called Ted. He'd been paying court to her for two months, had embarrassed her by his attention, ignored her protestations that she was too old for him and had broken down her defences to such a degree that tonight she was preparing to succumb to his tactical manoeuvres. She yelled in pain as she removed the first hair.

One by one the residents had been charmed by the friendly allies. Vi Todd had become a surrogate mother to the men in Oliver's hut while Elsie Tanner's living room was treated as a home from home. At first she'd attempted to cover up the existence of Linda and Dennis but now they had been accepted as part of the Anglo-American set-up. Dennis was passed round to be fed and burped by paternal types while Linda was fed chewing gum and was developing a Southern twang. The same visitors showed a polite interest in Albert's map of the conflict in the Middle East, plotted each night while listening to the news, and were taught the art of playing the spoons by Thomas Hewitt. Bessie started knitting to order, and Percy Longhurst opened up a card school in the front parlour, using the lid of May Hardman's precious piano as a drinks table. Martha enjoyed having the house full of GIs, she smelt the smoke from their expensive cigarettes and thrilled to the winks they gave her over their hands of cards. That was until she discovered that her daughter Lily was getting more lustful looks than she was.

Martha had always kept Lily in the background, taking as her example the way Ena treated Vera. Lillian Margaret Rose Longhurst, however, was no Vera Sharples and had constantly fought back. On leaving school she had refused to work in munitions and had taken a job in a Manchester department store as a sales assistant and sometime mannequin. Ena had had plenty to say on the subject of models, reminding Martha of the girls at the Windmill Theatre in London who entertained by 'modelling' in the altogether. Martha had urged Percy to put his foot down and order Lily to give the job up but she'd always been the apple of his eye and all it took were some crocodile tears to have him assuring her she was in the right job. Besides, as he told Martha, it wasn't every girl who was glamorous or pretty enough to be a mannequin.

The Americans arrived in Coronation Street, as they usually did, mob-handed. Oliver Hart jokingly said it was the only way they dared to arrive: individually they might be devoured by Ena the Medusa from the Mission. The jeep turned into the Street at eight thirty and for once the vestry curtains weren't instantly pulled across. Friendships had grown up between the Americans, as well as the residents, during their visits and it was a mixture of uniforms that descended from the jeep. Oliver made his way to No. 9, Steve Tanner and Greg Flint knocked on Elsie's door, while Ted Cooper sauntered down to bang on the shop knocker.

Sally stood on the living room table while Vi carefully drew a line up the back of her legs. 'Is it straight?' asked Sally, panic in her voice.

'I think so.'

'Well, don't stop. Hurry up or he'll see.' She groaned in dismay as the knock sounded at the door and pleaded, 'Gran, will you get it?'

While Daisy scurried off into the hallway, Vi carried on with the line. 'How far should I go up?' she asked.

'All the way.'

Vi raised an eyebrow, and behind his newspaper Jack grunted.

'It's only for show, Mam, for when me skirt flies up when he throws me over 'is shoulder.'

In the hall, Oliver greeted Daisy. 'Is she ready for me?'

'She's ready for owt, lad,' cackled Daisy.

Sally just had time to leap down from the table before he walked into the living room. She welcomed him with a kiss.

'Hello, Mrs Todd,' said Oliver, presenting Vi with a packet of Lucky Strikes.

She made sure Jack wasn't watching, and tucked them away in her apron pocket. 'Have you time for a cuppa before you go?'

'No, thanks, Mam,' said Sally quickly. 'We've got to get the others yet.'

From behind the paper Jack cursed.

'Bad news, Mr Todd?' asked Oliver politely.

'What? No, lad, I'm just trying to do this blasted puzzle.' He looked up into the room and asked, 'Anyone got a rubber?'

Oliver was stunned. His father had always told him the English weren't as stuffy as they were portrayed in the movies but to be so upfront amazed him. 'Well, sir,' he began, 'I have got a packet . . .'

Sally kicked Oliver's shin and said, 'Cross it out and start again, Dad, it's what you usually do.'

Before Oliver could embarrass her further she grabbed his jacket and pulled him out of the house.

Vi slipped out of the back door and let herself in to No. 11's scullery to report for babysitting duties. She stopped short when she came across a couple entwined on an armchair. He was in uniform and, from her angle of view, Vi couldn't work out who the girl was. She coughed loudly and the American looked up. He had smudges of lipstick over his cheek and looked sheepishly at her. His girlfriend was Dot.

Vi took off her coat and said, 'You two carry on as if I weren't 'ere. Evenin', Greg.'

Greg Flint jumped up from the chair and straightened his shirt. 'Evening, ma'am.'

'I must say,' said Vi to her daughter, 'it's a relief to see you've finally settled for Greg. I never did take to that Ginger.'

'Mam!' Dot cried.

'What's the matter with you? I'm only sayin' I'm pleased. I like Greg, reminds me of an old sheepdog me auntie 'ad on 'er farm. Lovely creature with big soppy eyes. You don't mind, do you, Greg?'

'No, ma'am.' He eyed Vi with caution, not understanding if she liked him or not.

The hall door opened and Elsie and Steve entered, laughing. They held hands but their fingers moved apart when they found Vi had already arrived.

'They're both flat out up there,' Elsie said.

Vi nudged Dot out of the chair and settled into it herself. 'Good. I've got a sweater I want to finish for Sally's Christmas present.'

'I've no more coal in the scuttle,' said Elsie apologetically. 'It's this bad weather.'

'That's all right, love. Our 'ouse is as cold as Piggott's freezer. Which is the best place for my Jack. You've never seen 'im in the altogether 'ave you Elsie? Just like one of them pigs 'angin' up by its trotters.'

Dot muttered under her breath in embarrassment but Elsie was amused by the vision.

'Bet you've not got much fat on you, Steve,' said Vi, with a sly look.

'All muscle, ma'am,' he said.

'I bet.'

'I've 'ad enough o' this,' said Dot, grabbing Greg by the hand. 'Are our Sal and Ollie out yet?'

Vi nodded. The two couples pulled on coats and rushed out of the house, calling goodbye to Vi. She waited for the door to slam then laughed to herself, wishing she'd been born into a different generation. She'd have shown those Yanks a thing or two.

After having supplied Esther with a shoulder to cry on, Ena felt in need of creature comforts. The next day would be Saturday and, since her section had the day off, she decided to treat herself to a night out. Minnie had been nagging on about a singer from Newcastle who was packing them in at the Spread Eagle on Palmerston Street. Ena wasn't keen on singers – none had a voice to compare with hers, but she had been intrigued to hear that this particular chap had entertained the Royal Family at Buckingham Palace. She decided to grant him an audience and, seeing as how pub landlords had become fussy about serving non-regulars, remembered to put a glass in her bag, wrapping it carefully in a scarf to keep it safe.

Vera, returning home from lates, found Ena stood by the mirror, putting on her best hat.

'Are you goin' out?' she asked, disappointedly.

'I am.'

'I thought we could play crib.'

' 'Ave you nowt better to do wi' yer time? By 'eck, it's true what they say about the devil and idle 'ands.'

'I've been lookin' forward to a natter.'

'Well, you'll just 'ave to talk to yerself, won't you? It won't be first time.'

Having satisfied herself that she looked suitable, Ena opened the door to leave, letting a blast of cold air into the vestry. 'Don't wait up.'

'I won't,' said Vera. ' 'Appen I'll go out meself.' It was out before she could stop it. That little ounce of rebellion.

Ena stared at her then laughed.

The door closed but Vera could hear the laughter continue as Ena walked past the vestry window and disappeared under the viaduct arch. Vera watched her go, her cheeks flushed with anger. How dare she laugh? A movement across the street caught her attention. A group of people were climbing into a jeep. Elsie Tanner was one of them.

Vera didn't stop to think of the consequences, even to question what she was doing. With Ena's mirth still ringing in her head she grabbed her coat and ran out into the Street.

'Elsie!' she called. 'Elsie, wait!'

Oliver was just driving the jeep away from the kerb when Vera darted in front of it. He braked sharply, causing the passengers to jolt forward. Greg let out a loud complaint but Dot told him to be quiet as she stretched her neck to hear what Vera and Elsie were saying.

'Whatever is it, love?' asked Elsie, concerned.

'Elsie, can I come wi' you?'

Dot giggled at the idea but Elsie sensed that Vera needed to escape the Street, even if only for one night. She moved up closer to Steve and invited Vera to sit next to her. Without giving the Mission a backward glance, Vera climbed aboard and the jeep sped off.

During the journey to the camp, Elsie took charge of Vera. As the miles mounted so did Vera's fear of what she was doing.

299

She had second, third and fourth thoughts about the wisdom in defying her mother, who had forbidden her so much as to pass the time of day with an American. What would she say about her dancing with one? That was another thing she hadn't thought of. Dancing! She'd heard enough on the munitions floor to realise that her experience of leading her mother in the waltz during chapel fund-raisers was not going to stand her in much stead.

Elsie tried to calm her nerves while, behind her, the Todd girls kept bursting into hysterics at the thought of who their travelling companion was. Elsie produced lipstick from her handbag and did her best to improve on what Nature had blessed Vera with. Nothing could be done about the heavy work dress she had on, but Elsie backcombed her hair to give it volume. What she was most concerned about, though, were the thick socks bunched around Vera's ankles, exposing her bulky legs. She wasn't the only one aware of the problem.

Steve produced a packet from his inside pocket and gave it to Elsie. 'It was meant to be for later as a thank-you but I guess your friend needs them more than you.'

Elsie unwrapped the stockings and kissed his cheek.

The service base at Burtonwood consisted of a series of huts, lined up domino fashion, along a stretch of airfield. At one end of the camp stood huge hangars where the engineers worked on the magnificent aircraft that were parked on the grass alongside the airstrip. The first Americans to arrive in the camp, Oliver among them, had been delivered by cramped trains to an empty field where the hangars were still being erected and fields of tents waited to be occupied.

As Oliver had stumbled over guy-ropes on his way to the latrines, he couldn't believe what he'd volunteered for. The camp had been built around the tents, starting with the officers' quarters. After a few weeks engineers had erected the Nissen huts that now housed the servicemen. Compared to the tents they were spacious, but the novelty had soon worn off. Each contained six double-decker bunks, with hardly any room for personal effects, and a small metal bar connected to the wall by each bunk for hanging clothes. Two crews, each of six buddies, were assigned to each hut. Oliver was an easy-going guy, but if he hadn't been he would have been forced to become so in an environment where you were never alone.

The main hangar had been decorated with streamers and balloons especially for the dance. A glitter-ball had been borrowed from the local dance hall and it turned slowly, high above the floor, sending reflections of light shooting over the room like a miniature, jewelled, sun. A stage had been built on one section of the floor and the 8th Army band belted out 'In The Mood' as the Coronation Street party entered the room. Dot didn't have time to look around as Greg rushed her on to the dance floor and she disappeared from view among a sea of gyrating bodies.

Elsie Foyle glanced around at the young men and excited girls, and told herself she must look ridiculous standing in such company. Ted squeezed her arm, called her 'baby' and told her he'd find them some drinks. She slipped on to a vacant chair, glad to be out of sight of all those in the hall. She should never have come. Who was she trying to kid? Herself? Ted? Mutton dressed as lamb, that was her. She looked enviously at the couples dancing and watched the young women swinging around their partners' bodies. They didn't need to rely on whalebone for their curves.

Vera sat next to Mrs Foyle and smiled, weakly, at her. The music was far louder than she'd anticipated and the rushing crowd on the dance floor made her feel claustrophobic. She was nudged in the back by a passing man and apologised for getting in his way. He took no notice and she inched her chair towards the nearest table, wishing she could just crawl under it and wait until the dance was over.

'Hi honey, how about it?'

It took a few seconds for Vera to realise that the thick-set man with the greased-down hair was talking to her. He stood, staring at her, waiting for a response so she asked, 'Sorry?'

'Do you wanna hit the floor?'

It was difficult to hear over the sound of the trumpets, but from the way he was gesturing he was interested in dancing with her. The idea appalled her.

'I don't . . .' she started, but he smiled encouragingly and pulled her to her feet. She looked around wildly, hoping Elsie Tanner would see her plight and rescue her, but she was nowhere to be found. Almost at once they were on the dance floor. He grabbed her hands and started pumping. She moved her feet slowly and swayed gently from side to side. Under her breath Vera counted, 'One two three, one two three . . .'

Oliver's hand grasped Sally's buttock and gave it a firm squeeze. She tightened her grip on his hand and blew a strand of hair out of her mouth.

'You're gorgeous,' he shouted at her, over the blare of the music.

'I know,' she shouted back.

'I've got to fuck you tonight,' he yelled.

'You'd better!'

Dot had never found ballroom dancing to her taste. Too straight-backed and formal. Jiving and jitter-bugging were far more to her taste and she'd practised her footwork under the bench at the factory while her fingers fiddled with bolts. Greg was a fantastic dancer and Dot was thrilled to be his partner, especially when she saw the lustful looks other girls gave him. She untied the scarf round her neck and stuffed it into his breast pocket. 'There, that's better. Now you'll stand out from all the other uniforms.'

Queuing for the toilet, Elsie Foyle was poked in the face by the bony elbow of the woman in front of her.

The woman turned and smiled apologetically. 'I'm sorry, I've bin in such a rush to get 'ere I forgot I still 'ad me curlers in!'

Mrs Foyle smiled at the sight of her as she fumbled with the three rollers protruding from under her turban.

'I'm all thumbs tonight,' said the woman, a hairpin stuck between her teeth.

'Here, let me.' The shopkeeper's dainty fingers released the woman's hair. She made quick work of it and said, 'Now all you need is a comb through.'

They moved up with the queue and the woman smiled her

thanks. 'I'm Hilda,' she said, 'Hilda Crabtree. From Manchester.'

'Elsie Foyle, I'm also from Manchester.'

'Whereabouts?' There was a trace of Liverpool in her accent.

'Weatherfield.'

'Never!' Hilda's mouth opened in surprise. 'Oh, that's fate! So am I! Kitchener Street. Do you know it?'

'Yes. I've a little shop on Coronation Street, opposite the Mission of Glad Tidings.'

Hilda was impressed, 'Coronation Street, eh? I've 'eard tell folk from that side of town are a bit hoity-toity. You've got bay winders, 'aven't yer? An' yer own lavs? Thought so. Well, you've done me a service. Ta ever so. I can look my Ralph in the eye now. That's if I can find him!'

On the dance floor, Sally started to regret covering her legs with gravy powder: as she danced and sweated amid the hustle and bustle they were sticking together.

The short man smiling into Vera's bosom said his name was Mario, and he lived in New York, although his family hailed from Sorrento in Italy. Wanting to be encouraging, Vera had said she liked ice-cream, and had struck the right note as he immediately spouted lists of his favourite pasta dishes. They'd been dancing for some time before Vera realised she had stopped concentrating on her feet and was enjoying herself. They still hadn't been able to synchronise their steps but he had attempted to spin her round at one point. The move had nearly succeeded but his cufflink had caught up in her hair and the spin had been abandoned as she struggled to free herself.

Gliding past in Steve's arms, Elsie gave Vera a thumbs-up. They had danced non-stop for over an hour and when the music changed from 'Don't Sit Under The Apple Tree' to 'Kalamazoo', Elsie stopped and held her hands up in protest. 'These shoes are diggin' into me ankles summat awful,' she shouted.

'Drink?' he suggested.

They pushed their way off the dance floor and headed towards the bar. Elsie stood by and watched, admiringly, as

Steve secured the bartender's attention before others who had waited longer and was soon carrying two large whiskeys over to her.

She took the glass and bellowed, 'Is there anywhere we can go for some peace?'

He forged a way through the crowd for her and within minutes they were standing under the night sky. Elsie looked back towards the hangar where Military Police stood guard and where every foot of the side wall was occupied by kissing couples. She linked her arm through Steve's and together they strolled off across the tarmac. 'Want to see some bombers?' he asked.

She nodded, her ears buzzing from the loudness of the music.

As they wandered around the airfield he told her about how he had always wanted to fly and how, frustrated by his own country's lack of involvement in the war, he had crossed the border and joined the Royal Canadian Air Force. He had met Greg during training and they had won their pilot's wings on the same day. Now in England, they were both eagerly awaiting instructions to bomb Hitler, and were growing frustrated with sitting about taking part in practice drills.

She listened to every word, loving every minute of his company. It wasn't just that he was the most good-looking man she'd ever seen, or that he was considerate and caring. She looked upon him in a way that wasn't just sexual. For the first time in her life, Elsie Tanner was in love. She was glad he was stuck here drilling. The last thing she wanted was for him to fly off in his bomber and be shot down out of the sky. She hugged his arm tightly.

'Hey, that's a strong grip you've got there!' he said, in mock protest.

She snuggled against him.

'What's the matter?' he asked.

'You'll think me daft.'

'Daft?'

'Stupid, silly.'

'No, I won't. Tell me.' His voice was soft, enticing.

'I'm just worried about you, getting . . .'

'Killed?'

'Don't say it. It might be a jinx if you say it. I've known fellas, seen them laughing in the Rovers one weekend, the next . . .' She shivered and stopped walking. She looked up at his bronzed face and said, 'Kiss me.'

He bent his head and tilted her face towards him. Their lips came together and held. His arms wrapped round her and pulled her close. Unlike Oliver, or Jim Todd, or Arnie, or all those other men, he didn't grope her breasts or backside. He kept his hands on the small of her back and she felt protected.

'I think I love you,' she said, not knowing how vulnerable the words would make her feel once they were out.

He kissed her forehead and smiled. 'If you love me half as much as I love you, then I'll be happy.' It had to be a line from a Bette Davis film – it was too smooth to be real life – but his eyes bored into hers and she felt certain he couldn't be lying. He knew he didn't need to. One word from him and she'd strip naked and let him have her on the tarmac. She was convinced he was aware of how he made her feel and was confused in that he didn't lunge at her like all the others. She supposed it came down to the fact that he respected her. The thought frightened her. No one had respected her before. What did he see in her that was different from the others?

He stroked her hair and whispered in her ear, 'If only you weren't married . . .'

She drew back from him, not wanting him to see the tears forming in her eyes. 'Is it me kids?' she asked.

'No. No, I think they're a swell pair. I really do, Elsie.' His voice was sincere. She knew he wasn't lying.

'I'm only married in name, you know?' she said. 'Arnold and me, well, there's no future for us. If we both survive this war it'll be divorce straight away.'

'You can't be sure of that. There's Linda and Dennis. They need their own father.'

' 'E'd be no good for them. 'E'd sell 'em, given half the chance. We only married because I was caught wi' Linda. I was sixteen, mad keen to get away from home. I kidded meself it would be all right.'

'But you've not had time to live together, to settle with each other.'

Why was he finding excuses? Was it because he didn't really want her and was trying to throw up obstacles to stop them getting together? Was he trying to distance himself from her? Why did he have to care so much? She started to sob.

Appalled by her tears, he hugged her and kissed her again. 'I'm sorry. I shouldn't have spoken about your husband. I had no right.'

'You had every right!' she shouted at him, shaking his hands off her shoulders. 'You mean more to me than he ever did or ever will. I can't bear to think of him anywhere near me again! It's you I want. I don't care about Arnold. I'll divorce him tomorrow. I want you. I want to leave this hole of a country behind and live in America with you. As your wife.'

He stopped her talking by kissing her hard. His tongue teased her lips apart. She pressed herself to him and ran her fingers through his hair. 'I want you inside me,' she said, 'but not 'ere, not like the rest of them. We're different.'

'Next Friday,' he said. 'Christmas Day. I'll bring presents for the kids.'

She loved him. She really loved him.

Vera's head was spinning from the two vodkas Mario had slipped into her orange juice. She felt sick and rested her head on the corrugated sheeting behind her. Her chin knocked against Mario's hair as he lapped at her nipples and fumbled with her belt. She felt nothing but he was obviously enjoying himself as between slurps he muttered, 'Yeah, baby, oh, baby.'

He had had more to drink than her and his reflexes were slow. Frustrated at being unable to unhook her belt, he tried to yank her skirt up. She resisted, pushing her hem down and trying to shift away from him. Although he was shorter than her he was muscly and weighed more. She couldn't squeeze from under him but the force of his body pressing against her was too much. With a sudden groan she lurched forward and vomited over his hair and down his back.

Back in Weatherfield, Ena walked down Jubilee Terrace and headed towards the viaduct arch. She tried to calculate what the landlord of the Spread Eagle must have taken in the evening. It was the first time in her life she had had to pay just to enter a pub, and having done so the rest of her time had been spoilt as she refused to believe the singer worth the sixpence entrance fee.

'I've 'eard tom cats wi' more of a song about 'em,' she'd complained to Minnie Caldwell. At least she'd taken her own glass: she saw one poor soul trying to sup his pint out of a saucer. She'd read of some pubs charging for the use of glasses then giving the deposit back when they were returned, as if they were pale ale empties. She'd made certain she'd put the glass back in her bag before leaving. She knew there'd be no confusion over which was hers: there couldn't be many in the pub engraved with 'A Present from the Isle of Man'.

She pulled her scarf round her neck and walked against the wind as it shot through the viaduct. Once in Coronation Street, she hurried to her vestry door and let herself in. The room was quiet so she assumed Vera was tucked up in bed. Pulling off her mittens, she decided to have a cup of cocoa and lit the two-ringed stove in her tiny kitchen area. Above the sink hung a sampler she had sewn in her last year at St Mary's Sunday-school. The tiny crosses read 'Thou God Seest Me'. She smiled as she read the familiar words and nodded as she accepted the wisdom of the teacher who had instructed her on what to sew. The knowledge that God saw everything she did had kept her feet on the straight and narrow, and her battles had been fought in the certain knowledge that He saw and supported.

There was just enough milk to make half-and-half cocoa and, leaving it to boil, she wandered around the room. The curtain was pulled across the bed but she made no attempt to quieten her actions, not bothered if she woke Vera or not.

She settled down on the sofa, placed her mug on a side table and closed her eyes. Three hours later she woke with a start, her neck aching. She'd fallen asleep and the draught blowing in under the door had attacked her bones. She stumbled off the sofa and shuffled across the room towards her bed, roughly pulling aside the curtain as she did so. The sight of the empty bed woke her. She spun round to look at the clock on the ornate bookcase. Half past three in the morning. The bed hadn't been slept in. Vera wasn't there and hadn't been there all night. Ena stood by the bed and cursed her thankless daughter. Where on earth was she?

CHAPTER EIGHTEEN

December 1942 Goodwill to all men, especially Steve Tanner.

The ring of the shop bell caused Elsie Foyle to grimace. If she was going to survive the morning she'd have to muffle it with a dishcloth.

'What's up with you?' demanded Ena. 'I've laid out corpses looking more lifelike than you.'

Mrs Foyle put a hand up to steady her thumping head and smiled weakly. 'Yes, Mrs Sharples, what can I get you?'

Ena dumped her basket down on the counter and barked, 'A dark blue dye, small mustard, a bottle of HP, and some bakin' powder. I'm restocking me shelves.'

Mrs Foyle moved slowly around the shop, gathering the goods.

'I don't suppose you've seen owt of my daughter, 'ave you?'

The question took Mrs Foyle by surprise and her face betrayed her. Ena's sharp eyes saw her struggle to compose her features. 'I see. Don't deny it. I want to know where she is. I've been lyin' awake all night imaginin' all sorts so don't hold back or, I'm warnin' you, know that the Good Lord will be jottin' down what you say in the Book of Life. Thou shalt not bear false witness.'

Mrs Foyle placed the tin of Colman's mustard on the counter and sighed. 'She's over twenty-one. Surely she can do as she pleases.'

'Not when she shares my eiderdown she can't. Now, where is she?'

There was no point in pretending she didn't know. 'She came out with a group of us last night.'

'Oh, yes, now we're gettin' somewhere. Clark Gable on at the Bijou, was 'e?'

'No. We went dancin'.'

'You did what? Does your 'usband know you go dancin' behind 'is back? I bet you went into Manchester as well, for all the world to see. 'Ave you no shame!'

'Don't come in here lecturing me, Mrs Sharples. There's nowt to say that a body can't have a bit of fun. I've done nothing to be ashamed of and if you go round saying any different I'll have you up in front of the magistrate.'

'You wouldn't dare,' said Ena, scornfully. 'He'd remember you for what you are, Elsie Foyle, a black marketeer.'

'Get out of my shop!'

'Don't worry, I'd sooner do without me bits and pieces than give you me 'ard-earned money. But don't think I've finished with you, madam. A group of you, you say? Well, where there's a dance in the offin' Elsie Tanner will've bin involved or my name's King Dick!'

The bell jangled violently, causing Mrs Foyle to cradle her throbbing head as Ena stormed out into the Street.

She marched down the terrace and hammered on Elsie Tanner's door. 'Open up! Open up, I say! I want a word wi' you!'

She continued to bang on the door until the upstairs front window shot up and Elsie stuck her bleary-eyed head out into the air. 'What on earth's goin' on!'

Seeing Ena she shouted down, ' 'Ave you finally gone pots-for-rags, Mrs Sharples? Am I goin' to 'ave to call for a little yeller van?'

'Come down 'ere,' shouted Ena. 'I've got words to say to you!'

'Say 'em from there. I'm not decent.'

'No, and you never will be decent either, you painted trollop!'

'Oh, change the record, Mrs Sharples. If you just want to call me names . . .'

'I want my daughter, that's what I want!'

Elsie bit her lip. She'd forgotten about Vera's night out. She withdrew her head and closed the window.

Ena started banging on the door again.

The commotion caused Martha Longhurst to appear at her own front door. Seeing her friend attacking Elsie's paintwork she joined her. 'What's to do?' she asked, keen to establish as many details as possible.

'I've caught a rat and I'm goin' to skin it,' said Ena.

The bedroom window at No. 9 shot open and Jack Todd's head and shoulders appeared. 'What the bloody 'ell's goin' on down there!' he demanded. 'Some of us are tryin' to get some kip!'

'Get back to yer pit, Jack Todd, this is no concern of yours!' yelled Ena, carrying on with the knocking.

The door next to Elsie's opened. 'Don't you go bawlin' at my 'usband,' Vi said.

'I might o' known you'd stick your twopennyworth in. I bet your girls were involved in all this as well!'

'All what?' asked Vi.

'Yes, Ena,' said Martha. 'What's up?'

Ena's knocking came to an abrupt stop when Elsie opened the front door. She pulled her dressing-gown around her but managed to reveal more than she hid. 'Mrs Sharples, could you stop makin' so much noise, please? I've a baby asleep upstairs.'

'Just answer me this. Where is my daughter?' Ena felt weary from the knocking and her eyes pleaded with Elsie to give her a plain answer.

Elsie felt a pang of guilt. 'I don't know –' she began.

'Don't you lie to me, you little madam,' interrupted Ena. ' 'Ave you the bare face to stand there and tell me you and your pals didn't drag her off to some den of iniquity?'

'I was goin' to say,' continued Elsie, 'that I don't know where she is now. Last I saw of 'er she were dancin' with an Italian.'

Ena's face felt as if it had been struck. '*An Italian!*'

Elsie softened her voice and stepped forward. 'Mrs Sharples, if I knew where Vera was I'd tell you. And, for what it's worth, we didn't drag 'er. She insisted on comin' with us and, in case you're wonderin', I think she 'ad a good time.'

'I'm not interested in 'ow much she enjoyed it,' spat Ena. 'She's a decent, well-brought up girl –'

'Woman,' said Vi, from her doorstep, 'She's a woman.'

Ena glared at her. Faced with Vi's hostility and Elsie's defiance she felt outnumbered. She backed off the pavement and pointed a finger at Elsie. 'If anything's 'appened to my Vera I swear I'll make you regret the day you ever set foot in this Street.'

'Mrs Sharples, I regret it every time I look at your face!' And with that Elsie slammed her door. Vi sniggered at Ena's discomfort then withdrew into her own house.

'Tek no notice, Ena,' said Martha, placing a hand on her friend's sleeve. 'I know you're worried about Vera. 'Ave you tried the police?'

'Fat lot of use they'd be. They'd say same as that scabby lot. She's twenty-one, she can do as she pleases. They don't know 'ow she can't cross a road on 'er own, or be trusted to light gas stove. They've not 'ad to look after 'er all these years, puttin' 'er first. It's just a game to them. Summat to laugh at!'

Martha had only ever seen Ena cry once before, at her husband's graveside when the coffin was lowered. She was shocked into silence by the tear that ran down her cheek. Not wanting to be seen crying in the street, Ena ran into the vestry, leaving Martha to marvel at the pity of it all.

Tom Hayes stuffed the brown paper parcel containing his change of clothes under his arm and climbed through the cut-out doorway in the huge prison door. He looked about himself and smiled in recognition as Esther waved to him.

'Hello, Tom,' she said, awkwardly, looking him up and down.

'Hi, Esther,' he said, giving her a peck on the cheek.

She was at a loss for something to say but luckily he wasn't. 'Smell that air! Great i'nt it? Freedom that is, bloody freedom.'

'If it's that sweet you'd better make certain you keep smelling it and not go back to those ways,' she lectured.

He nodded solemnly, as he had before the governor just half an hour ago. Yes, he assured them both, he would be a model citizen. His life of crime was firmly behind him.

'Ada not with you?' he asked.

'She's at 'ome with Mother.'

'Oh. 'Ow is Mother?'

'Same as ever.' It had been a year since Rose had ventured out of her room and Esther now viewed her as part of the bedroom furniture, as permanent as the double wardrobe with the mottled mirror.

They walked in silence down the road towards the bus stop.

'Shame about your fella.'

'Yes.'

'Bloody Germans.'

He hadn't sworn so much when he'd been sent away, thought Esther. Still, the rough edges were bound to rub off.

Linda Tanner sat at the table crayoning on an empty cereal packet. Elsie looked over her shoulder and asked, 'What's that?'

'It's the 'ouse we're goin' to live in in America.'

'Who said we were goin' to live in America?' asked Elsie in surprise.

'We are. When you marry Uncle Steve.'

Elsie was bemused by her daughter's reasoning. She was about to say that things weren't that simple when she was startled by a cough in the scullery. She spun round and found Vera Sharples standing sheepishly by the sink, her hand on the back door. 'Vera!'

'It wasn't locked.'

'What 'appened to you? Where 'ave you been?'

Vera smiled broadly and said, 'I've 'ad a wonderful time, Elsie. I tried to find you but you'd all gone.'

'We didn't know where you were, and Dot thought you'd come 'ome.' It was a lame excuse but Elsie was too ashamed to admit how bad she had felt leaving her behind.

'It's all right,' Vera assured her. 'I've bin up all night with a lovely man.'

Elsie closed her eyes and cringed at the implications. 'Was it that Italian?' she asked.

'Oh no,' laughed Vera, ' 'E were awful. I didn't see 'im again after I were sick all over 'im.'

Elsie pulled a face.

'He disappeared, and then I met Ronnie.'

'Oh, yes?' said Elsie, warming to the story.

'Oh, Elsie, he's gorgeous. Tall with dark green eyes.'

'Go on.'

'Well, he finds me standing at the back of this hut, sorting meself out after Mario had pulled me about a bit, and he picks up me scarf, because I'd dropped it on grass. Then he said he'd look after me.'

'And did he?'

Vera blushed and looked coy.

Elsie asked Linda to check on Dennis, and as soon as she was out of earshot gestured for Vera to join her at the table. 'Vera, love, we're friends, aren't we? Pals? Mates?'

'Are we?' asked Vera in delight. 'I didn't know.'

'Of course we are,' said Elsie. 'Now, friends tell each other everything. So, what happened between you and this Ronnie?'

Vera looked blank. 'How do you mean?'

'Did he do anything to you? Did he kiss you?'

Vera blushed and put her fingers to her face in embarrassment.

'Did he?' pressed Elsie.

Vera nodded.

'Did he touch you anywhere? Anywhere private? Did he take your clothes off?'

Vera smiled fondly at Elsie and said, 'We made love.'

Elsie placed a hand over Vera's. 'Are you certain? Did it hurt?'

'A bit, but he said it was all right because he loved me. I love him as well.'

'Vera, did he use anything? Any precautions?'

'Oh, yes. It was damp on the grass so he took his mac off and let me lie on top of it. He was very kind.'

'No, love, you're not understanding me.' Elsie bit her lip, unsure how to ask what needed to be asked. She cursed the randy Yank who had taken advantage of Vera's simple nature. 'When he took his pants down, did you see his cock? You know what a cock is don't you? The milkman's 'orse has got one.'

'It wasn't as big as Neddy's,' said Vera.

'No love, they never are. But you saw it? That's good. Now did he put anythin' on it, like a little raincoat?'

Vera's eyes widened and she chortled at the thought. 'Don't be daft.'

'He didn't, did he?' said Elsie, feeling sick.

'Oh, Elsie,' Vera's eyes danced with happiness, 'I've never felt like this before.'

'Make the most of it, love.'

Leaving Vera to keep an eye on the children, Elsie crossed the cobbles and knocked on the vestry door. Ena opened it and stared at her. 'I've not come to fight,' Elsie said quickly. She looked past Ena's shoulder, to where Minnie and Martha sat, trying to see who the caller was. 'I've got news concerning Vera. I think you'd rather hear it in private.'

Ena weighed up Elsie's words then turned to her friends. 'Right, you two, I've got business with Elsie and I'd be grateful if you'd shift.'

Martha opened her mouth to object but Minnie hurried to her feet and pulled on her coat. 'Come on, Martha,' she said, 'Rovers will be open.'

Elsie waited for the women to leave before she sat on the sofa.

'Well?' asked Ena, standing over her.

'If I tell you where she is, you're not to go mad at 'er.'

'Don't start lecturin' me on 'ow to deal with that wilful madam,' said Ena.

'Mrs Sharples, there's folk round 'ere think you treat Vera like a skivvy and a slave. I prefer to think you protect 'er from 'erself. Am I right?'

'You are, but that still doesn't give you the right –'

'Mrs Sharples, it's Vera I'm worried about, not you. I know you don't think much of me and the life I lead but it's because of that life that I can see what you're doin' to Vera. You're suffocatin' 'er, keepin' 'er locked away like a tiny baby. I know she's not all there in the 'ead but she's not as daft as you mek 'er out to be. All she needs is some encouragement and she'll be fine.'

'Encouragement? Is that what you call lurin' an innocent girl away from 'ome?'

315

'Will you just shut up and listen for one minute?' Elsie's tone was harsh.

'Don't suppose I 'ave much choice,' grumbled Ena.

'Right. In the first place, it was Vera who asked to come wi' us, not t'other way round. Second, I admit I didn't look after 'er as well as I should but, to be honest, I thought she were old enough to tek care o' 'erself. Now, she's just turned up at my 'ouse and she's told me what she's bin up to. I could come out with a story to cover for 'er but, despite what you think of me, I'm not one for deceiving folk. We went to a dance at the camp. The American camp.'

Ena opened her mouth to comment but Elsie raised her hand and carried on, 'From what I can work out some low-life got 'er tiddly and, to cut a long story short, she's spent the night with some fella who's told 'er his name is Ronald Reagan. Of course, if you'd let her go to pictures once in a while she'd have seen right through that one. She says they made love and from what I can gather 'e didn't use anything. I'm sorry, but them's the facts an' it's no use me tryin' to fancy them up for you. She thinks she's in love.'

Ena sat in silence.

'Mrs Sharples, she's frightened to come 'ome in case you 'it her.'

'She's some sense, then!' said Ena.

'It wasn't 'er fault she was taken advantage of. You know what fellas are like.'

'I do not! Not the sort of men you're talkin' about. I've only ever known one man in my life, and Alfred Sharples always treated me with respect.'

'Well, you've been very lucky,' said Elsie, with feeling, 'because most of the men I've bin with 'ave just bin after what they could get.' She paused, feeling sorry for Ena as the implications were sinking in. 'Don't be 'ard on 'er Mrs Sharples. I know you mean 'er well by protectin' 'er, I see now that it's for 'er own good, but she 'as to 'ave some freedom. Some life of 'er own. And if I were you I'd get down on yer knees and pray nothin' comes of last night. When are 'er monthlies?'

'I don't know.'

'Well, find out. She's a good girl and doesn't deserve a kid on top of everythin' else.'

Ena felt suddenly out of control. She was always the one giving the advice, the one taking charge of people's lives. She resented Elsie's intrusion, telling her what she should or shouldn't do with her own daughter. But she was also grateful to her for caring enough to speak on Vera's behalf. She sighed and said, 'You'd best fetch 'er over.'

'You won't 'it 'er?'

Ena shook her head.

There was a fire roaring in the grate at No. 3 and on the wireless a man with a soothing voice was reading from St Luke the Apostle.

Bessie presented a bundle to Ida Barlow, saying, 'It's only a mitten and bonnet set. I 'ad some wool left over from makin' Beattie's Christmas cardigan.'

Ida took the garments and thanked Bessie. 'Can you stay for a cup of tea?' she asked, glad of the company.

'Oh, that would be champion,' said Bessie, easing herself into a chair beside the fire. David lay on a rag rug in front of the hearth, gently cooing to himself. 'I love Christmas,' she said, ' 'specially when you've children round you.'

Ida wandered into the scullery to fetch the tea caddy and said, 'I'm not very fond of it, really. You know, it's two years to the day that Marjorie died.'

'Is it really?' said Bessie, in surprise. 'It don't seem possible.'

'I went to lay flowers on her grave this morning.'

'You must miss her,' said Bessie, sounding sympathetic.

'I do. But I miss Frank more.'

'Ah, love.'

'Me father died in last war, you know. Mother always said it was the waitin' for news that was worse than knowin' for sure.'

'Still nothing?'

Ida spooned tea into the pot. 'Not a word.'

'Don't fret, love,' said Bessie. 'You never know what's round corner. He turned up out of the blue last time, didn't he? What's to say he'll not do same again?'

'It's different this time. He'd been writing to me every week for months. Suddenly the letters stopped coming.'

There was a rhythmic knock on the door, causing Ida to look up in alarm.

'I know that knock,' she said fearfully. 'You get it, I don't want to see him!'

Alarmed by Ida's reaction, Bessie got to her feet and wondered what to do.

The knock came again. Ida picked up David and hugged him to her.

Bessie ran to the door and opened it. At the same time, Albert opened the door of No. 1. They both looked at the telegram boy with trepidation.

'Hey,' said Albert, 'aren't you Sydney Roberts's youngest?'

'That's right,' replied sixteen-year old Alf.

' 'Ow is yer dad? I've not seen him since ARP meeting last summer. He said you'd joined GPO. Right proud of you, 'e was.'

'Albert!' objected Bessie. 'Lad's 'ere on business!'

Alf smiled at her and asked, 'Mrs Barlow?'

'No,' said Bessie, 'that's to say yes, right 'ouse but I'm not Mrs Barlow. She's busy. What is it?'

'Telegram needs signin' for.'

Bessie looked in horror at the piece of paper. It was fate, laughing at them because they'd been talking about Frank. Alf offered a pencil but Bessie backed away from it.

'Can I sign?' asked Albert.

'Suppose.'

Albert quickly wrote his name and said, 'Tell yer dad Albert Tatlock were askin' after 'im.'

'Will do. Take care, now.'

Alf Roberts cycled off, leaving the Tatlocks staring at the cable in Albert's hand.

'I don't want to read it,' called Ida, from the living room.

The Tatlocks walked through to join her. Albert held out the paper but she refused to touch it. 'You read it,' she said. 'I don't want to hear if it's bad news.'

Albert slowly opened the telegram and ran his eyes over the typed message. 'It's from the War Office . . .'

Ida clutched David and gazed into the flames in the grate.

'. . . and it says Private F. Barlow has been captured by enemy forces and is interned in a prisoner-of-war camp . . .'

'Where?' asked Bessie.

'It don't say.'

Bessie eyed Ida with alarm as she let out a moan and staggered.

'Not dead! He's not dead!' she said.

'That's right, love,' said Albert.

'Oh, thank God! Thank God! I thought . . . after all this time he must be dead!'

Albert held out the telegram and she lowered David to the ground before taking it from him to read the wonderful news herself.

Christmas Day was heralded by Minnie, Vera and Martha standing in the middle of the Street, wrapped in their warmest clothes singing 'Hark The Herald Angels' while Ena knocked on the front doors and rattled a collection box under the noses of the residents. 'Support the War Orphans' fund,' she challenged each one, and watched carefully to make sure they submitted legal tender.

In the scullery at No. 1, Bessie rolled out the crust for the rabbit pie that was to be the family's Christmas dinner, and mumbled to herself about how she wished the Tatlocks were following Thomas Hewitt's example and eating at the communal canteen that had opened up in Bessie Street School for the festive season. She'd put the idea to Albert but he'd refused to consider it, saying that no one else knew how salty he liked his food and he wasn't going to eat in public as he'd feel he wouldn't be able to let his braces down. Instead he passed Christmas morning listening to the wireless and sucking sweets while she prepared lunch for five, as she'd agreed to pool resources with Ida. Bessie would cook the pie while Ida tackled the vegetables and they were going halves on the pudding and mince pies.

Vi Todd's scullery was a blur of activity. Sally stood at the sink peeling potatoes; Dot cut up Brussels sprouts and Vi herself stirred the bread sauce. In the oven the turkey (brought over the night before by Oliver dressed as Santa Claus) roasted in its own juices, and Elsie Tanner ironed napkins borrowed from Annie Walker. Jack rolled a cigarette and delighted Linda by performing disappearing tricks with his matches. Dennis lay asleep in the parlour and Daisy opened the sherry.

'Anyone for a drop?' she asked.

Four voices shouted, 'Please,' while Jack asked for a beer.

'You can't 'ave one yet, not till the men 'ave arrived,' said Vi.

'I'm a man, I've arrived, I want a beer.'

'Well, you can't 'ave one,' repeated Vi, 'I've only got four bottles in and if you 'ave one now there won't be enough to go round at dinner.'

'Go on, Dad, 'ave a sherry, might make you frisky. You wanna watch yerself, Mam, he might pinch yer bum,' said Dot.

'He'd get a thump across 'ead if he did,' retorted Vi.

'Oh, will I?' said Jack.

'Yes, you will, so think on. Keep yer 'ands to yerself!'

'What?' said Jack, getting up and waving his hands in the air. 'These 'ands? These 'ands 'ere?'

Vi squealed as he chased her round the table. 'Jack! Stop it! Stop it!'

Sally and Dot laughed at the sight of their parents frolicking about.

Jack caught Vi and tickled her. She lashed out at him with a wooden spoon, flicking bread sauce over his face. She giggled as his fingers sought out her vulnerable spots and laughed so much her sides ached. At last he stopped and straightened up.

'Blimey, Jack, I didn't know you 'ad it in you,' said Elsie.

'Fancy a bit, do you?'

Vi got up from where she had ended up, on her knees under the table flap, and said, 'Don't spoil it Jack. I might be a pushover but I'm sure Elsie could run rings round you.'

The back door opened and Sally was pushed out of the way

by a walking fir tree. The needles brushed against her bare arm and she cried out in protest. 'Watch it!'

'Where on earth did you get that?' Elsie asked Steve, as his grinning face appeared round the side of the branches.

'Saw it in the park. Didn't take long to chop down.'

'You didn't!'

Steve guffawed. 'It's from our hut. Didn't seem much point keeping it there today of all days.'

The tree was walked into the living room and placed in a corner. Although no more than four foot tall, it dominated the room.

'We've nothing to put on it,' said Dot, but was silenced when Oliver threw a box at her.

'Tinsel and baubles.'

Linda's eyes were wide with excitement as Dot pulled silver tinsel from the box and started to drape it around the tree.

Greg struggled into the house under the weight of a wooden box, which he dropped on to the table with a sigh of relief.

'Whatever's in there?' asked Vi.

'Whisky, chocolate, couple of tins of peaches . . .'

'Peaches!' shouted Sally in delight.

The tins turned out to be catering size, provided by one of Greg's friends in the army cookhouse. Each one was meant to feed twenty men.

Oliver reached into his pocket and pulled out a branch saying, 'And I have brought some mistletoe, which my good friend Steve here assures me is just the thing I need to kiss the hostess.' He clasped Vi to him and kissed her lips.

From his chair Jack muttered, 'If you fancy 'er you must be desperate.'

Oliver released Vi and held out the mistletoe to Sally. She joined him in an embrace and their lips met, causing Greg to whistle and Dot to stick her fingers down her throat.

Daisy smacked her shrivelled lips and said, 'Me next!'

Amy Carlton sat on one of the folding chairs from the Mission hall and watched Ena carve the chicken. 'I only like white meat,' she said. 'Dark makes me heave.'

'So you say,' said Ena, gritting her teeth and regretting the charitable side of her nature, which had issued the invitation that included Amy.

'Can I 'ave the parson's nose?' asked Martha hopefully.

'I thought your 'usband wanted it,' said Ena, wishing the lot of them would shut up and leave her to the carving.

'Did you ask for it?' Martha accusingly asked Percy. 'You know I like it. Why are you bein' so awkward?'

Percy adjusted the party hat on his thinning hair and said, 'I'm not. I didn't know you'd want it. You don't normally.'

'How do you know? When was the last time we tasted chicken? You're mixin' me up with Bessie Tatlock or Violet Todd. *They*'ve 'ad chicken time and again. Sick of it by now, I bet they are. And why? I'll tell you why. Because their 'usbands look after them. Their 'usbands think about them and 'ave allotments to provide food for the larder. Not like you. You just sit around waitin' for me to fill that 'ollow pit you call yer stomach!'

Percy closed his eyes, as if by doing so he'd shut out his wife's voice. He'd only agreed to share his Christmas dinner with her friends because she'd lured him by saying Ena had bananas.

'Have you finished?' asked Ena, waving the knife at Martha. 'Some of us want to 'ave our dinner in peace.' She placed slices of meat on a plate and handed it to Minnie saying, 'Pass that to Lily. Help yerself to spuds.'

Fourteen-year-old Lily spooned a couple of roast potatoes on to her plate and reached for the vegetables. Next to her, Vera smiled to herself.

'What you lookin' at me like that for?' challenged Lily.

'I'm 'appy,' said Vera, hugging herself.

'Oh, right. You're easily pleased, aren't you?' Lily speared a carrot with her fork and lifted it to her mouth but before she could put it in Ena stopped her.

'Aren't you forgetting something Lily Longhurst?'

'Cranberry sauce?' Lily asked hopefully.

'Grace!'

As her guests lowered their cutlery and contritely bowed their heads, Ena towered over them and prayed, 'Thank you for this humble table, Lord, and may your peace be upon each one of us, especially Martha, Amen.'

Albert pushed away his plate with a sigh of contentment. 'Now it's as far away as it ever was,' he said.

'There's more sprouts,' said Bessie.

'Nay, lass, I couldn't eat another mouthful.'

Ida stared at her plate and said, 'I wonder what Frank's 'avin' for his Christmas dinner.'

'Bound to be something tasty,' said Albert. 'Christmas is always special in wartime. I always remember in trenches, Christmas nineteen sixteen, we all stopped shooting each other and sang carols, just for the day, then we started up again at midnight. That were the day Ralph Thackery got his brains blown out. We'd been friends since school.'

'Really, Albert,' objected Bessie. 'Today of all days!'

'It's because it's today I'm tellin' tale,' said Albert.

'You'll 'ave to forgive him, Ida,' Bessie said, apologetically. 'He always gets maudlin at Christmas.'

'Its all right Mrs Tatlock, I don't mind. I'm just glad I know where Frank is. Mr Tatlock's right. I'm sure he's being well looked after. I wrote him a letter yesterday, sent it to the Red Cross. I don't mind him not being able to send me one back, just so long as he knows I'm not worrying any more.'

'I hate Brussels sprouts!' declared Oliver.

'You're not alone there, son,' said Jack, 'but you get used to them.'

'Like warm beer?' asked Steve.

'And the rain?' added Greg.

'Back home,' said Oliver, 'we have fields of corn, waving in the breeze. Juicy corn, ripe and tender and ready to be picked and boiled.'

'Sounds wonderful,' said Sally.

'Oh, it is. I love Christmas on the ranch. Pa kills one of the head and we have huge fat steaks on the bone. Medium rare with Ma's potatoes and pickles.' He smacked his lips at the thought.

'Well,' said Vi, 'I 'ope you've had enough to eat.'

'Heck, Mrs Todd, I didn't mean anything by it, I was just saying what it's like back home. I didn't mean any offence.'

'Don't worry, Oliver, none was teken.'

She rose and started to gather up the empty plates.

Elsie and Sally also made to help but Oliver put out a hand and stopped Sally. 'Mrs Todd, would you mind waiting just a minute?'

Everyone looked at him. He stood up and cleared his throat. 'I'm not very good at saying the right thing. You've probably guessed that by now.'

They laughed.

'But I would like to say thank you, to all of you, for making us so welcome.'

'Hear, hear,' said Steve, clapping.

'I'd also like to say something else. I know you don't have Santa Claus here but he's always been a hero of mine and I'd like to give Sally her Christmas present now, if that's all right?' He reached into his pocket and produced a small box, which he handed across the table to Sally. Her hand shook as she took it from him and opened it to reveal a diamond ring.

Elsie and Sally gasped as Oliver asked, 'Sally, will you marry me?'

She pushed herself away from the table, ran round to him, and flung her arms around his neck.

Greg cheered while Vi burst into tears.

'Yes! Yes, I'll marry you,' shouted Sally. He hugged her close and they carried on kissing while being slapped on the back.

Daisy took advantage of the uproar to dip her fingers into the bowl of peaches and slip a slice on to her tongue.

Four hours later, after the peaches, the Christmas pudding, the whiskey and sherry, the parlour games and the singing, Elsie lowered a sleeping Dennis into his cot. She stroked his head as he snuggled into the mattress then turned to where Steve stood cradling Linda in his arms. 'Where shall I put her?' he asked quietly.

Elsie lifted an empty stocking from Linda's tiny bed and pulled back the covers. He bent down, laid her on the sheet, covered her and kissed her forehead. They left the room, closing the door behind them. In the landing she looked into his eyes and smiled. 'Thank you for making it so special for them, and for me.'

'You're the one to thank. If it wasn't for you I'd have spent the day playing checkers in the mess.'

'No, you wouldn't. You'd have been with some other girl.'

'Would I?'

'Yes, you would.'

She took his hand and led him across the landing to her bedroom. He stopped her opening the door by putting his hand on her shoulder and asking, 'Are you sure?'

By way of an answer, she pulled him through the open doorway.

Inside her bedroom she crossed to the bed, sat down, then slowly started to undo the buttons that ran down the front of the floral print. The dress fell from her shoulders, exposing her naked breasts. He walked to her and started to kiss her neck. She closed her eyes, and gave herself up to the mounting pleasure. It had never felt like this before. Ever.

CHAPTER NINETEEN

March 1943 The Allies step up the war on Germany. Sally Todd prepares to step down the aisle.

Oliver and Sally's wedding was to take place the next morning. They'd wanted to marry in January but regulations stated that two months had to pass after Oliver had informed his CO of his intention to take an English bride. Major Harris did all he could to discourage his men from getting tied down with local girls, viewing them as free-loaders just interested in gaining access to the greatest country in the world. However, he was an honest man and, unlike many of his rank, didn't bury marriage applications under mounds of paperwork. He went on the assumption that if a soldier was brave enough to voice his intentions against his own well-known views then that man shouldn't be hindered. Oliver's application was unusual in that Sally wasn't pregnant. The usual enquiries, checking for Communist sympathies, were made into her background, and Oliver had to supply a letter from his father confirming that he had a job to return to and that the Harts were prepared to support their new daughter-in-law if necessary.

For Sally, the most daunting part of the procedure had been when she'd been called in to face Harris across his desk. She'd tried not to be intimidated by his brusque manner and booming voice, and had answered his questions carefully, wary that he might lead her into a trap and declare her unfit to marry an American. Jack and Vi had stumbled their way through form after form, giving permission for the wedding

326

to take place and swearing that their daughter was of sound mind and body. In all, fifteen documents were filled in, signed and countersigned. By early February Sally felt as if she were marrying into royalty.

Oliver's grandmother's wedding ring was sent across the Atlantic and Elsie, Dot and Sally amused Vi by dieting, while the matter of the wedding dress hung over No. 9. Even pooling everyone's coupons the dress remained elusive. That was until, walking home from work one evening, Sally had been invited into No. 5 by Esther Hayes.

Sally had never been inside the Hayes' home before, and was instantly jolted by the peace. No. 9 was never like that – even when it was empty the walls seemed to vibrate their own noise.

'I hope you don't mind,' said Esther, leading her into the living room, 'only I've been brought up to hate waste. That's probably why I'm so good at making do and mending.' It was a feeble attempt at humour but, like all people with strong personalities, Sally intimidated Esther just with her presence.

The dress she had lovingly made throughout the autumn of 1942 was hanging from the picture rail. Sally eyed it, not daring to hope.

'It seems a terrible waste to have it hanging in the wardrobe. I overheard your mother telling Mrs Foyle you were struggling to get one of your own. Please don't feel insulted but I thought maybe you could wear it. I'd love you to have it. I think we're the same size . . .'

Esther was astounded when Sally squealed and threw her arms about her. 'Oh, Esther, it's beautiful. I never 'oped to get married in such a wonderful dress!'

It was a perfect fit. It was full length and slender around the hips. The bodice was fastened up the front with the tiniest of buttons. Long puffed sleeves came in tightly at the wrists. It was a miraculous sight in a world of coupons.

While Oliver spent his last night of bachelorhood getting drunk with his countrymen, Annie Walker gave the select an airing for Sally's women-only party.

Martha and Minnie were the first to arrive but were disappointed to find the buffet hadn't been laid out yet. 'I've had instructions,' said Annie smugly. 'Not until nine o'clock.'

'Nine o'clock!' complained Martha. 'I'll 'ave fainted by then.'

'I can get you a packet of crisps,' suggested Annie.

'Go on, then.'

They sat at a table near the open fire. Minnie lifted her glass to her lips, and sipped her shandy.

Martha looked scornfully around the room, taking in the balloons floating at half mast and the shabby banner that read 'Good Luck Our Sal'. 'Not much thought gone into this do,' she said. ' 'Course, in our day we didn't 'ave 'en parties. Only dancin' we got was at reception after ceremony. I 'ad my reception at the Balmoral Rooms.'

'We didn't 'ave a sit down,' said Minnie, 'just 'am and tongue in me mother's front room.'

'That's right, I remember. There were cat 'airs in the sandwiches.'

'That was our Peg. She moulted summat terrible towards the end.'

'I were married twice, you know,' said Martha proudly.

'Were you? I don't remember.'

'Yes. Once for real and then eleven years later when 'e got fed up with 'avin' no photographs to remember us 'appy day. I still fitted my dress,' she said smugly. 'I've 'ad the same waist measurement since I were sixteen.'

'So 'ave I.'

'You 'ave not. Minnie Caldwell. 'Ow can you sit there and tell such a bare-faced lie? You've ballooned!'

' 'Ave I? Perhaps it's my shoe size that's the same.'

Martha shot Minnie a bewildered look and was grateful when the select door opened and Ena bustled in.

'Evenin', Ena. If you've come to 'ave first pickin's you've 'ad it. It's not comin' through till nine.'

Ena snorted. 'I've had a nice bit of cod for my tea, thank you very much. This war's not made me a cadger.'

Albert followed Ena into the room and hovered at her arm. She turned. 'What are you waitin' for?'

'Your drinks order.'

'You what?'

'I'm 'elpin' out. Waitin' on.'

'By 'eck, Annie Walker doesn't miss a beat, does she? Well, I'm tellin' you now, whether you take my order or not, I'm not payin' select prices. I'm 'ere to give a neighbour 'er send off. Not because I choose to be. Tell Annie Walker I'm payin' snug prices or I'm suppin' nowt.'

Albert scurried off to seek guidance while Ena inspected the room.

Watching her eyes move, Martha said, 'Not much is it, Ena?'

'Oh, I don't know,' said Ena, not wanting to agree with Martha. 'I think Annie Walker's excelled 'erself.'

The door opened again and Albert appeared.

'Well?' demanded Ena.

'Snug prices for them who normally pays them.'

'Right, I'll 'ave a light bottle.' Ena settled down on a stool with her friends. 'Right, ladies, what are we talkin' about?'

'Shoe sizes,' said Minnie. 'Mine's a five, but I used to take a two in a clog.'

'Tek no notice of 'er, she's in one of 'er moods,' said Martha. 'Actually we were remembering us own weddin' days.'

'Well, I remember both of yours an' neither of them were owt to brag about. She 'ad us trudgin' through the streets because her daft husband 'ad bought her a couple of kittens and she wanted to see them as soon as register 'ad been signed, and 'alf of guests went down wi' food poisoning at your do.'

'That wasn't my fault!'

'Still, that's what comes of 'avin' yer reception at a dump like the Balmoral. I've 'eard the strays won't even eat from their bins.'

Ena's drink arrived along with the bridal party. The Todd women pushed their way into the room and greeted the others. 'I might 'ave known you'd be first 'ere,' said Vi.

Ignoring the hostile welcome, Ena used her sweetest smile on the bride-to-be and said, 'Much 'appiness, Sally. I know I speak for all the ladies in the snug when I say I hope you'll be as 'appy in your marriage as we've been in ours.'

'Thank you very much,' said Sally and then, because she felt it was expected of her, continued, 'Will you have a drink with me?'

Vi shook her head at her daughter's naïveté while Ena said, 'That's very kind, isn't it, ladies? I'll 'ave a port and lemon.'

'Brandy,' said Martha.

'Can I 'ave a Sidecar?' asked Minnie.

'A what?' said Martha, staring at her.

'A Sidecar. I once saw Joan Crawford order one in a film and I've always wondered what they tasted like, only the occasion's never arrived.'

'I don't think Mrs Walker's got any Sidecars,' said Sally. 'She's got cherry brandy miniatures, though.'

'Oh, well, perhaps I'd better 'ave another shandy.'

'You were born in wrong town, you,' said Ena, looking at Minnie. 'I can just see you done up as one of them gangster's molls in Chicago, a big feather boa round your neck. You've got the eyes for it. Sly.'

'Oh, count me in,' said Dot, 'wrapping me arms round the neck of James Cagney, watchin' him playing cards then movin' round the table, spyin' on them playin' against him.' As she talked she moved round the trio sat at the round table, her arm draped over Martha's shoulders, pretending to look at her hands. 'I'd tip him the wink,' she leered at Minnie, 'and later, when he'd won thousands, he'd buy a bottle of champagne and he'd drink it out of me slipper.'

'Get you,' said Vi. 'Nearest you'll ever get to champagne is a bottle of pale ale with a twopence deposit on it.'

'Are we 'avin' music?' asked Daisy.

'Yeah, course we are,' said Sally. 'I want a good old knees-up.'

'Well, piano's over there,' said Vi, 'but who's goin' to play it?'

'Ena'll play, won't you?' asked Martha.

'I might be persuaded,' said Ena.

'Another port and lemon for Mrs Sharples,' said Vi to Sally. 'But think on, Ena, we don't want no 'ymns or funeral marches. We want good tunes, summat to kick yer 'eels to.'

Ena crossed to the piano, lifted the lid and ran her fingers along the keys before thumping out the notes to 'It's A Long Way To Tipperary'.

In the Rovers' bar, Annie reached up to the top shelf of her display unit for the cherry brandy. She grimaced as Ena hit a wrong note and looked around for the right glass to use for a miniature. 'Honestly, Mr Tatlock, I shan't have a piano left, the way Mrs Sharples pounds at it. Someone ought to tell her she's not kneadin' bread. It'll be me who has to fork out if any keys need replacin'. It's a thankless job bein' a publican, it is, really.'

'Aye, it's opened me eyes I 'ave to say, and I only started 'alf-hour since. Do you know, as soon as them women in there knew I were waitin' on they came over all superior, lookin' down their noses at me?'

'I know exactly what you mean,' said Annie. There was a time when being in the licensed trade gave you some standing in the community.' She sucked in her breath through her teeth and continued, sourly, 'Not any more. They treat this pub like a public convenience.'

'Well, I tell you this, Mrs Walker, you've gone up in my estimation, you 'ave, really.'

'Thank you, Mr Tatlock, that's very kind of you. You've always struck me as a very decent man. Very decent.'

The pair smiled at each other in mutual appreciation. On the other side of the bar, Thomas Hewitt banged on the counter with a coin.

'Oy, stop canoodlin' and give me some service. Stood there like a couple of lovebirds! Keep yer courtin' to when towels are on pumps. My throat's as dusty as our coal shed.'

'See what I mean,' said Annie, giving Albert a meaningful look.

By the time Esther and Ada made their way tentatively into the select, Martha and Vi were linking arms and lifting their skirts while Elsie sang along to Ena playing 'Roll Out The Barrel'. Daisy Todd lifted her skirts to show off her red petticoat and opened her mouth wide as she roared with laughter, treating everyone to the sight of her gums. Mrs Foyle had borrowed Minnie's beret and was doing her impersonation of Mrs Mop, shouting, 'Can I do yer now, sir?' at the top of her voice, while Bessie Tatlock was screeching at her to stop, saying, 'Give over, do, or I'll wet meself laughin'!'

It was their introduction to the Rovers and the Hayes sisters were amazed by the sight. They felt completely out of place. Sally saw Esther and beckoned her over, calling for the room to quieten down. 'Bit of 'ush, please, can I 'ave some 'ush? 'Cos me mate's 'ere, our Esther, who 'as treated me like blood, so she 'as.' Two gins and three pale ales were taking their toll as Sally slurred her words and clutched at an embarrassed Esther. 'She's saved my life and I want everyone to know 'ow much I love 'er. I love you, Esther, I really do.' Having said that she burst into tears.

'Yes,' echoed Vi. 'Three cheers for Esther and 'er wonderful weddin' dress'.

As those around Vi joined in the cheering, Ena leant across to Minnie and whispered, 'Good job 'er fella died, i'nt it? Otherwise Sally Todd would be walkin' up the aisle in her knickers.'

'Oh, Ena, you shouldn't say things like that.'

'Why not? I speak my mind without fear or favour. Anyroad, me and Esther 'ave an understandin'. She wouldn't mind me sayin' owt.'

Politely refusing alcoholic beverages, Esther and Ada opted for cordials. Ena beckoned for them to join her, and made it clear to Minnie that she should vacate her stool in their favour. 'You took yer time arrivin', didn't you?' she said. 'Mind you, you've not missed much, apart from me on piano.'

'It all seems very jolly,' said Esther, glancing around.

'They're a rough lot, the Todds, but they're simple folk and don't mean no 'arm by it, least roads Sally and Dorothy don't. Vi's always bin ready for a fight. She was a Makepiece, and they were *known*, if you follow me. They were gonna name a wing at Strangeways after the Makepieces.' Ena dried up when she realised she wasn't going to get any gossip out of the Hayes sisters. She changed the subject, 'How's your mother, the poor soul?'

Esther exchanged a guilty glance with Ada before saying, 'She's no better.'

'I don't recall seein' you two in 'ere before,' said Ena.

'No,' replied Ada, 'we've never actually been in. Silly, really, what with it being just a few doors away but Father had us sign the pledge when we were young and there's never seemed much point . . .'

'Oh, I know what you mean. I only come in myself to keep my friends company. Do you know Mrs Caldwell? She lives with her mother and that woman is an evil soul, keeps at her day and night. The doctor called on me a few years back and pleaded with me to keep Minnie company of an evening, fearing she'd snap and take the bread knife to the old hag. It's been known to happen – just look at the Hewitts. There's still blood on the cobbles outside number seven from when she 'ad 'er turn. It's nice to get out every now and again.'

Esther listened as Ena carried on her one-sided conversation, seemingly without drawing breath. She knew that Ada felt as uncomfortable as she did about sitting in the select while their mother lay alone in the house. Any bravado they'd felt in joining the party had been replaced with worries about Rose needing help, wanting food or having a relapse with no one nearby to help. It had never entered their heads to ask Tom to spend a night in for a change.

Two streets away, standing in the dark of the railway viaduct, Tom Hayes' face was illuminated as he struck a match and lit a cigarette. He took a long puff then handed it across to his companion. Her small fingers took it and she smiled bravely, glad that the darkness covered the flicker of doubt that crossed her face. She'd inhaled enough cigarette smoke at home but this was the first time she'd ever tried one herself. Gingerly she drew on it then coughed into her hand.

Tom laughed. 'You'll get the 'ang of it soon enough.'

'What? You reckon this is me first?' asked Lily Longhurst indignantly. 'Just a different brand to me normal, that's all.' She drew on the fag a second time.

'It's all right if it is yer first time. I like that. Me showin' you what to do.'

'Do you, Tom?' She looked up at his face, making out his eyes in the shadows. He leant down and pressed his lips to hers in a rough kiss.

She smelt the smoke on his breath and closed her eyes, wanting to drag out the experience.

He broke from her and, supporting himself with one hand on the brickwork of the viaduct, used the other to stroke her face. 'How old are you?' he asked, although he knew full well she'd been two years below him at Bessie Street and had only been saved from evacuation because she'd had measles in September '39.

'Sixteen,' she lied.

He smiled and said, 'You know I think you're a real beaut, don't you?'

She simpered with delight. He was the first lad ever to show an interest in her and she lapped up every word he said.

'I reckon you'd like to try something else for the first time, eh? Something better than smoking.' She giggled nervously and asked, 'What's that, then?'

'I'll show you.' He kept looking into her eyes while pulling at the buttons on his trousers. They dropped to the floor and he pulled his underpants down to join them. The air brushed between his legs and the sensation added to his excitement. He grasped Lily's hand and pulled it towards him. 'Now, 'ave a stroke of that,' he said.

She knew she wanted to keep him with her, knew that she wanted to prolong the night. If she didn't do what he said he might go off and find someone who would. She reached out and allowed him to guide her fingers.

'Now,' he said, his voice quiet, 'get down on to knees. Don't worry about the cobbles, they won't hurt you.'

Obediently she slowly lowered herself down, half fearful and half excited as to what was to happen next.

Annie broke up the party at eleven, well past her normal closing time, and refused to allow anyone to linger. She turned on all the lights in the pub and locked the piano lid. The guests left in small groups, singing as they went and calling into the night. Emerging into Coronation Street, Elsie Tanner walked straight into the lamppost and shouted at it: 'Why don't you look where you're going?'

The bride-to-be was the last person out of the pub, supported by her mother. Vi draped Sally's arms round her and dragged her along the pavement to No. 9.

'Lift yer 'eels, will you? Just along 'ere an' then you can drop dead in yer bed. Till mornin' when it's your weddin' day.'

'I don't want to get married!' Sally shouted, then burst into tears.

' 'Course you do, everyone wants to get married. I married yer dad, didn't I?'

'I 'ate me dad.'

'So do I,' said Vi, 'but I married him. And if I married 'im you can marry your Ollie.'

'But 'e wants me to live in Kansas and I don't know how to ride an 'orse!' Sally slipped from Vi and fell in a heap on the pavement, sobbing.

Vi swayed and carried on walking. Reaching a door she pushed on it but it failed to open. 'Open up,' she shouted, banging at it. 'Jack, open the door!'

Sally crawled towards her. 'I can't ride an 'orse! He won't want to marry me when he knows I can't ride an 'orse!'

'Open up!' shouted Vi, pounding on the door. She fell forward as it opened suddenly, and ended up with her face flat against Thomas Hewitt.

'What you doin' in my 'ouse?' she demanded. 'I'll 'ave the bobbies on you!'

Thomas shoved her away and said, 'You live next door, you stupid cow!'

Twelve hours later, the mother of the bride sat on one of Ena's hard folding chairs and tried to compose herself. She kept bolt upright to compensate for the fact that her head was spinning. To her left, Ena played the harmonium with, it seemed to Vi, far more gusto than was necessary.

Martha turned a page of the music and bent to whisper in Ena's ear. 'Vi Todd still looks pickled.'

'Them that can't 'old it shouldn't sup it,' said Ena sanctimoniously.

Martha listened to a few bars of 'Dear Lord And Father Of Mankind,' and smiled to herself. 'Three hymns, then? That's how it should be.'

'Oh, I insisted. She were all for a quick rush through Handel's Messiah but I told her it were her duty as an Englishwoman to have traditional hymns. Let them Americans see they're not the only ones who can swank it. I thought we'd 'ave 'Fight The Good Fight' after they exchange vows.'

Oliver fiddled nervously with his sleeve and hissed at Steve Tanner, 'You've got the ring?'

Steve said, 'Relax.'

Oliver glanced around the congregation. He'd been disappointed at Sally's decision to have the ceremony in the draughty old Mission hall, having looked forward to a country parish somewhere near Warrington. He'd given way quickly, not wanting to appear stubborn over such a small issue. So long as the place didn't seem too weird in the photograph he had promised to send home. According to his mother, half of Kansas wanted to see the face of the girl who had stolen the heart of the town's most eligible bachelor.

He caught the eye of Annie Walker, who beamed at him. He smiled back and quickly looked away. 'The pub woman's smiling at me,' he said to Steve.

'Smile back.'

'I have.'

'Good.'

Oliver glanced at his watch. 'Five minutes to go.'

Arnie leaned over and tapped him on the shoulder. 'Wanna make a run for it? I've got the jeep outside.'

'Don't put ideas into his head,' laughed Steve. 'He's just fool enough to take you up on it.'

Albert pulled at his collar and grumbled, 'It's too small.'

'I told you to get down to Swindley's for another,' said Bessie. 'But, as usual, you knew best. Well, you can just stop fiddlin' with it. Folk are watching.'

'I wish she'd get a move on, I want the lav.'

Bessie crunched on her boiled sweet.

Lily scraped the side of her shoe along her chair leg and scratched the back of her head. A piece of red brick fell into her hand. Percy looked at it and frowned.

'What's that?'

'I dunno. Bit of dirt. Probably fell from the lav ceilin'. You know Mam's been gettin' at you to see to it.' She looked over her shoulder, searching the faces in the congregation.

'Will you keep still?' complained Percy. 'You're not too old to 'ave yer legs slapped, you know.'

I'm old enough for more than you'd guess, she thought smugly. She glanced at him out of the corner of her eye and wondered if he and her mother ever . . . No, it wasn't worth thinking about.

The two Elsies sat together. Foyle offered Tanner a humbug and gestured down the rows to where Annie sat in front of them. 'Have you 'eard the latest? She was round at my place last night asking my opinion of her hair. Full of herself. Bursting to let on what the excitement was. Turns out she's got the lead in one of those operatic affairs she goes in for. Amateur, of course. I'll work on her and find out when it's on. Be a good laugh.'

'Can she sing?' asked Elsie, amused at the thought.

'Can she heck! They'll have been desperate to take her on. Her big part'll probably amount to her walking on stage carrying an urn.'

Sheltering from the rain under the entrance porch, usher Harry Hewitt cupped his hand round the end of his cigarette and peered into Viaduct Street, craning his head round the corner awaiting his cousin's arrival.

His younger cousin, Dot, slouched against the other side of the porch and dragged at her cigarette. She eyed Harry up and down and was surprised to see how well his uniform fitted him. 'Bit of a coincidence, your leave fallin' this weekend,' she said.

'Aye.'

'Is it funny bein' 'ome after all this time?'

He could have said how much he hated it and that it had only been Sally's wedding that had brought him to

Weatherfield, having spent all his previous leaves in Bridlington with his sister Alice. Not a man to speak much, he opted for a grunt instead.

As if cued by his thoughts, Alice Burgess bustled into the porch from the hall and tutted when she saw Dot. 'Get away from that wall – you'll ruin the dress.'

Dot looked scornfully at the full-length green creation Vi had found for her at the exchange shop set up in the town hall. It had to be thirty years old and, despite three washes with Rinso, still smelt of mothballs. She'd had designs on the matron-of-honour outfit Ada Hayes had made for Esther's wedding but Ada had altered it into an evening gown for herself.

'She's cutting it fine,' said Alice, peering out into the rain.

At that moment Jack Todd ran round the corner, holding a raincoat over Sally's head as she rushed to keep up with him. They exploded into the porch and Alice sought refuge as rain-drops shook from their garments.

'It's an omen, isn't it?' wailed Sally. 'Rain on yer weddin' day means summat!'

'Don't talk daft,' said Harry affectionately. He gazed at Sally as she emerged from under the raincoat and, with Dot's help, started to sort out the folds of her dress. Esther's roses peeped in clusters from the hem and a thin gold chain hung around Sally's ivory neck. 'You look beautiful,' he said in admiration and kissed her cheek.

'What do you think, Dad?' Sally asked.

'We'd best get it over with, I want some o' that pork pie Ollie promised to bring wi' 'im.'

Ena struck up the Wedding March and Mrs Foyle shivered. 'It always gives me goose bumps,' she said to Elsie.

'Always makes me feel sick,' replied Elsie, looking into the aisle as Sally and Jack slowly walked down it, followed closely by Dot.

Oliver and Steve took their positions at the front of the hall, and received a smile of encouragement from the Reverend Mr Fisher.

Sally gripped her father's arm and hissed through her veil

at him, 'You could at least smile! Look as if you're 'appy for me!'

Minnie sniffed and blew into her handkerchief. Sitting next to her, Amy Carlton said, with more volume than necessary, 'Pull yerself together! Yer mekkin' a fool of yourself as usual.'

'I can't 'elp it, I always cry at weddin's.'

'You know why that is, don't yer? 'Cause they remind you of day you married that useless lump. I can tell you, *I* cried at your weddin'. Saw right off what a waste of space 'e was. No backbone, idle and shiftless. Talk about a match made in 'eaven!'

Amy became aware of the hostile looks she was receiving from those sitting near her. She didn't care: it was a free country and she spoke her mind.

As the happy couple were exchanging vows, Army Staff Sergeant Joe Scharl couldn't tear his eyes off the beautiful blonde across the aisle. He caught her eye and blew her a kiss. His neighbour, Sergeant Ted Cooper, saw it and glanced across to where all the women sat on the bride's side. 'Which one do you fancy?' he asked.

'The beauty sitting next to your shopkeeper.'

'Oh, Elsie Tanner.'

Joe raised an eyebrow and tried out the name for effect, 'Elsie Tanner. I've heard of her. She's the tart who went through the whole of Hut C in a week, isn't she? I didn't think she was blonde though.'

'Was a redhead. Must have dyed it.'

Elsie nudged Mrs Foyle and whispered, 'Don't look now but there's a Yank over there keeps leering at me.'

'It'll be the hair. I told you it would give you a boost. These lads go mad for blondes.'

'I only 'ad it done because Steve spent whole time we sat through *Johnny Eager* goin' on about 'ow wonderful Lana Turner looked.'

'It suits you.'

'I should 'ope it does, considerin' what you charged me to do it.' She shot a look across the aisle and was disturbed to see the soldier still looking at her. She felt uncomfortable under his gaze.

The reception was meant to be in the select but as all her regulars were guests, Annie allowed the party to flow over into the public. Having proved his abilities the night before, Albert was pressed into service again to help Annie cope with the number of thirsty Americans. She was thankful that they'd brought a barrel with them from Burtonwood, as well as the bottles of whisky that had become the normal offering. It cut down on the profits but at least it prolonged the drinking and gave the pub a pre-war atmosphere.

Annie poured herself a sherry and raised her glass in thanks to the bald New Yorker who had insisted she'd kept his change. 'Your very good health,' she said.

The man moved off towards the select, balancing five full pint glasses on a tray decorated with a painted view of the New Forest. He manoeuvred his way through the chairs but as he approached the door it swung open towards him and Thomas Hewitt barged through. The soldier managed to keep the glasses upright, although plenty of beer was spilt on to the tray and down his uniform. 'Hey, watch where you're going!' he cried.

'Oh, go 'ome, Yank,' muttered Thomas, continuing his journey to the bar.

'Yes, Mr Hewitt?' asked Annie, with disdain.

'Free ale?' he asked.

'The first pint is. I believe you've 'ad that already.'

Thomas pulled a face and fumbled in his pocket for change. 'Give us a pint of best.'

'I've only got mild.'

'What do you mean? That Yank 'ad bitter in them glasses.'

'That is correct, but our American guests brought their own barrel out of consideration for my supplies.'

'Blimey,' said Thomas. 'It's comin' to something when you can't even get a pint in yer local cause some bleedin' Yanks have nabbed the whole barrel.'

'Mr Hewitt, I'd rather you didn't use bad language in here. There's no need.' Annie placed his beer on the counter and held out her hand. 'That'll be tenpence.'

He threw the money on the bar and took his pint into the select, cursing all things American as he went.

In the select, Mr and Mrs Hart stood behind the two-tiered wedding cake and posed as Mrs Foyle snapped their photograph. As soon as she'd finished Vi lifted the cardboard cake off the table to reveal the real thing: a short fruit cake with a six-inch diameter, which had used up three months' worth of the family's butter and sugar rations.

The guests applauded it and raised their glasses to toast the happy couple.

Ena settled down on the piano stool, ready to start playing, but before her fingers could touch the keys she was interrupted by Irvin Masterson, who slid down next to her and said, 'Hope you don't mind, ma'am, but Ollie's requested some honky-tonk.'

Ena glared at him indignantly but he took no notice and started to pound the piano.

With a yelp of delight, Sally grabbed Oliver by the hand and rushed him on to the floor. The guests pushed chairs and tables out of the way and started to clap as the newly-weds danced.

Sitting in a corner, Minnie watched Sally as Oliver flung her around his body and sighed. 'I were never any good at the Black Bottom.'

'It's not right,' said Martha, in disgust. 'It's not decent to show that much of 'er legs in public. Percy 'as never seen that much of my legs and we've been married twenty-three years come May.'

'It must be nice to be able to dance,' said Minnie wistfully.

'Excuse me, ma'am,' said a tall American, standing next to their table, 'I'd be happy to dance with you. There's really nothing to it, just go limp and follow my lead.'

'Oh,' said Minnie, delighted. 'I couldn't possibly. My husband tried to teach me the Charleston once and I got into a terrible pickle. No, I'll finish my drink and then I'll go and check on Mabel.'

'Mabel?' he asked politely. 'Is that your daughter?'

'Oh, no,' laughed Minnie. 'Mabel's my pussy. Do you have pussies in America?'

Steve Tanner drained his whisky and, wanting a dance, looked round for Elsie. She was nowhere to be seen. 'Dot,' he called, 'seen Elsie?'

'She's in public, getting us a couple of gins,' said Dot, as she danced by with Greg.

Steve pushed through the guests and made his way out of the room. His head was feeling the benefit of three whiskys and he decided to call it a day after a fourth. He walked into the Public and immediately saw Elsie. She was standing at the bar, having paid for her gins, but was being halted in her attempt to leave by a burly soldier with stripes on his arm.

'Come on, let me pay for them for you,' said Joe Scharl, his words slurring.

Elsie smiled but said firmly, 'No thank you.' There was no way she wanted to be beholden to this Yank. The way he had kept looking at her throughout the service had disturbed her and she'd tried to avoid him during the reception. 'Could you let me pass, please?' she asked.

'Stay with me for a while,' he said, pressing himself against her. 'Come on, I know all about you. I've read what you can do on the walls of the toilets. Why don't we nip outside?'

She pushed him off and said, 'No, thank you, I want to get back to my friend.'

'Bring her with you. She can watch.' He reached out and groped her breast.

Instinctively Elsie threw her gin in Joe's face, and he jerked back. She tried to get past him but he recovered and grabbed her shoulder. 'You bitch!'

Albert hurried across the bar but before he could reach Joe, Steve had appeared by Elsie's shaking side. 'Apologise to the lady,' Steve commanded.

'What lady? No lady here, just this whore –'

The punch took him by surprise and sent him sprawling across the bar. He leapt up and threw himself on Steve. Elsie screamed.

'Mr Tatlock, get help,' ordered Annie, and watched as Albert scurried into the select.

Glasses broke as Joe and Steve rolled around on the floor

together, raining blows on faces and stomachs. Joe broke free and staggered to his feet, levelling a kick at Steve's groin but Steve saw it coming and dodged it. He clambered up in time to see Joe raise a chair over his head and send it smashing down on the bar, just missing him.

Elsie's screams, rather than Albert's presence, alerted the wedding guests to the fight and they piled through the door to observe.

Oliver jumped on Joe's broad back and tried to hold him while Steve aimed a blow into his stomach.

'Go on, hit the bloody Yank!' shouted Thomas Hewitt.

'They're all Yanks,' said Percy Longhurst.

'I know,' said Thomas. 'Good to see them knocking seven bells out of each other.'

'Watch it, Pop, or it'll be your turn for a good hiding,' warned Ted Cooper.

'I'd like to see you try,' said Thomas, squaring up to him.

The second fight broke out there and then, and Bessie Tatlock was knocked sideways as Thomas was sent sprawling against her.

Percy Longhurst had never liked Thomas, but the assault on a countryman couldn't be tolerated and he thumped Ted in the mouth.

'Ted!' screamed Elsie Foyle, rushing forward.

Before she could get to him, Ted had retaliated and Percy's upper teeth shot across the room.

As relations between the Americans and British worsened, Steve finally got the better of Joe with a left hook, which sent him flying across the bar, over the counter and left him in a heap at Annie's feet. She looked on in horror as the brawl spread among the guests.

In the select, Ena reclaimed the piano and, as she played 'There'll Always Be An England', started to sing:

> 'Red, white and blue,
> What does it mean to you?
> Surely you're proud,
> Shout it aloud.
> Britons awake . . .'

Later on that evening, as Oliver sat on the Todds' double bed, he flinched as he removed his shirt. Sally made a fuss over the bruise that was already forming across his ribs. 'I 'ope they're not broken,' she said.

'I don't think so.'

He stood and dropped his trousers, flinching again as he shook them free of his legs, unable to bend to pull them off.

'Does it 'urt much?' she asked.

He attempted to smile through his bloody mouth. His swollen eye distorted his vision and he couldn't make out if she was annoyed with him or not. 'Sorry,' he said.

'It's all right,' she said, stroking his arm. 'I could do wi' an early night.'

The next morning, Sally crept out of bed without disturbing her husband. The bruises on his torso were a different colour now and she couldn't help but admire the way they blended in with his tan. Whenever she was bruised, her skin went shades of green and yellow and looked like mould.

She pulled on her dressing-gown and quietly left the room. It had been the first night she'd spent in her parents' bed and, with Oliver having to return to the camp later in the day, it would probably be the last.

Downstairs Vi was sipping a cup of tea. She looked up in surprise when Sally entered. 'You're up early. I wasn't expectin' to see you till lunch.'

Sally joined her at the table and yawned. 'I need to talk to you.'

'Go on, only if it's owt about your wedding night I don't think I want to know.'

'I'm pregnant.'

Vi looked at her daughter in amazement. 'Don't be daft, love. Eh, there was me thinkin' you knew all there was to know about that sort of thing. You can't know you're pregnant love, not yet. It takes a few weeks.'

'I'm three months' pregnant Mam. I just didn't want anyone to know until after weddin'.'

'And there were me thinkin' 'ow proud I was of you, the first one in family for years not to 'ave to get married.'

'I didn't 'ave to, Mam, I wanted to.'

'Do you want it?'

'Mam!'

'I'm only askin', 'cos if you don't I can 'elp you out there.'

'Mam,' said Sally, 'I want it. I'm very 'appy. I've got an 'usband and a baby on way. You should be pleased for me.'

Vi put down the cup and reached across the table to grasp her daughter's hand. She looked at the ring on her third finger and smiled at her. 'I am pleased for you, love. And don't fret, I'll 'elp you all I can.'

'I should 'ope so. After all, it's your grandchild we're talkin' about.'

Vi's smile faded at the realisation that she was to be a granny.

CHAPTER TWENTY

May 1943 The Dambuster squadron wreck the Ruhr dams. Uncle Sam wrecks Elsie's war.

Ena's munitions bench had progressed from bolts to welding machines. The transition had been a long time coming and, as Elsie said, saved their sanity. They could all drill bolts without looking now and the thrill of operating different machines had kept them chattering excitedly for days. The machines were positioned close together so it was still possible to maintain a conversation with the woman on either side.

Minnie Caldwell pulled on her lever and remembered the question she'd been saving up all day to ask her friends, ever since that morning's newspaper. 'Ena, how do they make a bouncin' bomb? I've never 'eard of one before. It can't be like the one they dropped on Mawdsley Street because if that had bounced it would have ended up in Coronation Street.'

'How should I know?' said Ena. 'I'm not a member of the Brain's Trust, yer know.'

'No, but you generally know things.'

'It spins,' called Martha, from Minnie's left, pleased to know something that Ena didn't. 'It's shaped like a barrel and it spins so it bounces on water.'

'How do you know that?' asked Ena, surprised.

'Oh, I know a lot. I've always been inquisitive, ever since a girl.'

'You mean nosy,' said Ena.

'No, I don't. I mean I 'ave an enquirin' mind.'

'Aye, and a long nose you keep pokin' into other folk's business,' said Ena, determined not to allow Martha the chance to crow over getting one up on her.

Martha waited until Ena had bent again to her work then stuck out her tongue. She shifted her weight from one foot to the other and complained, 'I miss me stool.'

'You want to be like Sally, then,' said Ena. 'Get pregnant again.' She jerked her head at where Sally operated her machine, from a tall stool.

'I fancy a game of cards at lunch. Are you interested?' Martha asked.

'I like Snap,' said Minnie.

'Well, I don't,' said Ena. 'I like dominoes. My brother Tom was a champion domino player. 'E had medals for it, that and barrel-jumpin'.'

'It's not a sport you 'ear of much these days, barrel-jumpin',' said Minnie.

'Oh, it's a dyin' art,' said Ena sadly.

Martha agreed. 'You don't find many clog-dancers either, and when were last time a fella came round to grind yer knives?'

'I do me own wi' a stone. Always 'ave,' said Ena proudly. 'You want to be careful, Martha, you're beginning to sound like yer mother, always 'arkin' back to the good old days. You're not fifty yet, are you?'

'Fifty!' said Martha indignantly. 'You know very well I'm forty-six. I may be a few years older than you, Ena, but there's no need to be spiteful.'

Minnie sighed. 'I wonder if the Rovers will 'ave a crowd in tonight. It were very quiet last night.'

Standing next to Ena, Elsie leant across and said, 'What's the matter, Mrs Caldwell? Missin' our American friends? Don't worry, they'll be in tonight.'

'Give over pinin',' said Ena. 'You can't expect it to be buzzin' like the 'Ollywood canteen every night.'

'It seems quiet when they're not around.'

'Costs more an' all,' muttered Martha, 'But say what you like about Americans, they're very generous.'

'Aye, with their 'ands as well as their money. I saw the way that dark fella was pawin' you last Friday night.'

' 'E was not pawin' me!' said Martha indignantly. ' 'E were readin' my palm. 'E 'ad gypsy blood in him.'

'I don't 'old wi' fortune tellers. I agree with the Almighty where they're concerned. Look at the Witch of Endor.' Ena grimaced.

'He were only lookin' at me lifeline.'

'I'm surprised 'e could find it with the amount of wrinkles on your 'and,' Ena held up her own to the light and continued, 'I used to 'ave lovely smooth 'ands. Now look at 'em, cut and raw.'

'Aye, that's what comes of workin' 'ard all yer life,' said Martha.

'It's this weldin', I reckon. They should give us gloves,' said Ena. She would have said more but her conversation dried at the sight of Vi Todd appearing at the factory door. Vi searched the room for her daughters.

' 'Ey up, whatever's she doin' 'ere?' wondered Ena, as Vi rushed through the benches to reach them.

Sally stopped working and jumped down from her stool in concern. 'Mam, whatever's the matter?'

Vi caught her breath. 'I've run all the way,' she panted. 'It's terrible news, love, they're packing the camp up!'

There was no need to ask which camp. As far as the women were concerned there was only one.

The colour drained from Sally's face and she asked, 'When?'

'Now. The news is all over the place, Army and Air Force are both on the move. Every man in the place is packin'.'

'What'll we do?' asked Sally in alarm. 'They won't send them off without sayin' goodbye, will they?'

'Course they will,' said Ena. 'It's the forces, not *Worker's Playtime.*'

Elsie tore off her overall and flung it on the floor by her machine. 'Well, I'm not 'angin' around. If Steve's goin' I'm seein' him off!'

'You can't,' said Martha. 'We've only just had us tea break. What'll foreman say?'

'Stuff the foreman. I'm goin' to see Steve! Sally? Are you comin'?'

Vi helped Sally out of her overalls and hugged her. 'Go on, love. You go with Elsie and find yer man.'

Hesitantly, Sally looked around the factory. How would they get to the camp? Was there any point in going? The men might have left by the time they arrived.

Elsie grabbed her hand and pulled her through the benches.

Back at the section, Dot stopped work and went to untie her apron.

'Where do you think you're goin'?' demanded Vi.

'With Sal and Elsie.'

'Oh, no, you're not. You've not got a man to see off. That Greg fella dumped you, didn't he? Well, don't waste yer time on him. You stay 'ere and show me 'ow to work this machine.' She slipped Sally's overall over her head and tied the belt round her waist.

Martha stared at her. 'You can't work that. You need months of training to learn it!'

'Give over,' said Ena. 'A monkey could operate it. Just position yer butt and pull yer lever – you'll soon get the 'ang of it.'

'It's excitin' isn't it?' said Minnie. 'Do you think Sally'll get to see her 'usband?'

'I 'ope so,' said Ena. 'It's bad enough when they march off to war and you wave them off, but to go without sayin' good-bye, that's a terrible thing.'

'It'll seem very quiet without 'em,' said Martha.

' 'Ark at you,' said Ena. 'You did nothin' but moan about 'em when they first arrived. Now look at you, one of 'em reads yer palm and you're bosom buddies.'

'How can you say that?' demanded Martha indignantly. 'It was you called 'em summat rotten. Treated 'em like they'd invaded us. I remember the way you took yer 'andbag to that little chap who pinched yer bum!'

'I was only doin' what any decent woman would do. I'm not goin' to stand by and be interfered wi' in the middle of the street, am I? Mind you, I don't know why I'm askin' you. You wouldn't put up a struggle. Oh, yes, these last few months 'ave opened my eyes as far as you're concerned, Martha Longhurst. I've seen you doing your Tallulah Bankhead bit, lookin' through yer eyelashes and laughin' yer daft little laugh.'

'My laugh isn't daft!'

'It is. Sounds like an 'en bein' strangled!'

Martha stared at Ena in outrage. She turned her back on her and dropped her lever too quickly, narrowly missing her fingers.

'Was Tallulah Bankhead in *Forbidden Paradise* or was that Gloria Swanson?' asked Minnie, frowning as she tried to remember. 'I liked the silent films best because you could guess what they were sayin' and the 'ero always won in the end.'

'Aye,' said Ena sadly. 'It don't always follow in real life, does it? In my experience the 'ero dies of pneumonia an' it's the villain who ends up smellin' of roses.'

'I 'ope the 'ero wins today,' said Minnie. 'I like Sally's Oliver. 'E's a nice boy.'

Elsie and Sally stood outside the factory wondering which would be the best way of getting to the camp.

'Train?' suggested Sally.

'When's the next one? It'll tek too long!'

They spun round, looking up and down the road for inspiration.

'We can't just turn up at the camp,' wailed Sally. 'There'll be 'undreds there by the time we turn up and they won't let us see them!'

Elsie refused to be negative and grabbed Sally's hand. 'Let's get into Manchester, there's bound to be buses or trucks goin' that way. Someone'll give us a lift.'

They set off to the bus stop as fast as they could.

All around them pandemonium had broken out as the news of the Americans' departure spread through Weatherfield. Girls and women poured into the streets from houses, shops and factories and ran in the same direction. The same thought occupied all their minds.

Elsie and Sally had a head start on their Weatherfield

sisters but even so, as the train pulled into Warrington station, they found themselves surrounded by anxious women, none of whom seemed to know where they were going, just all following each other. Out of the corner of her eye, Elsie saw the familiar green of an Army truck setting off outside the station. She pulled Sally with her and pushed through the women into a side street. Calculating which road the truck would take, she tore in the same direction, shouting behind for Sally to keep up. Her heart pounded and she heard the blood pumping in her ears but pushed herself to run faster. At the end of the back-street she jumped into the road, startling the soldier behind the wheel of the truck. He braked hard and swerved to avoid her. As soon as he had stopped Elsie wrenched open the passenger door. 'Are you going to the camp?' she demanded.

The driver nodded.

'Please take me and my friend. We've got to see her husband.'

'I can't, I'm sorry. It's against regulations.'

'Bugger regulations!' cried Elsie. 'My friend's pregnant. If she runs to the camp she'll probably have a miscarriage and it'll be your fault!'

Sally caught up and, assessing the situation, pleaded with the driver with her eyes.

'Are you really married?' he asked.

She flashed her ring at him.

'All right, but you'll have to crouch down and I'll drop you off just before we get there.' The women climbed into the cab and Elsie kissed the soldier's cheek and said, 'Thank you.'

The truck's progress to the camp was hindered by the number of women running along the road. As the camp gates approached Elsie and Sally jumped out and joined the tide. The gates were firmly shut and the women crowded around the perimeter of the camp, clinging to the wire and shouting names of boyfriends in the vain hope that they'd be heard.

'This is ridiculous!' Sally moaned. 'We'll never find them!'

Inside the camp, everything was happening in a rush. Soldiers hurried about, loading trucks and jeeps, the screams of the women sounding in their ears. They threw cigarettes and chocolate bars into the air and watched, some laughing, as the women fell over each other to grab the precious items.

Elsie pushed Sally through the crowd, towards the direction of Oliver's hut. She knew from past journeys that it was on the outskirts of the camp, the last one in a row. As she fought through the women she saw a familiar face. 'Arnie! Arnie!'

She waved and whistled as he turned, his arms full of blankets. He recognised her and rushed over to the fence. 'Hiya, sugar, come to see us off?' he asked.

'Arnie, where's Ollie and Steve? Sally's got to see Ollie. Can you get him?'

Arnie glanced behind him and shrugged. 'I guess. You hang on here and I'll fetch him.'

Sally wanted to cry with relief. It was going to be all right, after all. She hugged Elsie and rested her head on her shoulder. 'If I can only just say goodbye, tell him I love him.'

'He knows you love him,' said Elsie, with a smile. While happy for Sally she knew Steve would be at the other side of the camp, where the planes stood.

They waited for what seemed like hours until Arnie reappeared. 'Sorry, sugar, can't find Ollie anywhere. No one's seen him all day.'

Sally clutched Elsie's hand and closed her eyes in despair.

'Are you sure?' demanded Elsie. 'What about the others in the hut?'

'It's empty, we cleared it out this morning. They've been driving guys out in trucks for hours. I'm sorry, it looks like you've missed him.'

'What about the airmen?' Elsie asked.

'They were the first out. Like I say, you've missed them.'

Vera Sharples waited by the clocking out machine as normal at the end of the day. Ena punched her card and took her coat from Vera's hand. In the shift-around on the factory floor Vera had found herself on a bolt bench near the factory gates and it had become her task to fetch the coats each evening, saving Ena precious minutes. They walked out into the evening, taking deep breaths of air.

Since attending the dance at Burtonwood, Vera's life had expanded under a new relaxation of Ena's rules. Elsie had told her to be more assertive when dealing with her mother, reminding her that she was a grown woman and that, if Ena ever got too much to cope with, there was a bed waiting for her at No. 11. Vera had blurted this out to Ena the next time she crossed her and, after her initial fury, Ena had been forced to adapt the way she dealt with her. It was one thing to have a daughter walk out, another to see her living across the Street with Elsie Tanner. She knew the neighbours would have a field day with that so she wisely bit her tongue

Ena had been thankful that nothing had come of Vera's liaison with 'Ronald Reagan', and realised she should act quickly to ensure the risk didn't arise again. It was then that she'd decided it was time her daughter settled down with a suitable young man and started casting her net around the locality. Her quest was hindered, of course, by most of the eligible bachelors being at war. After contemplating those on offer, Ena had settled upon Leonard Swindley as the most suitable: he was a sober, hard-working lay preacher, whom she felt certain she could dominate.

However, fate had taken matters out of her hands when Vera announced she'd found an engineer called Bob Lomax whose work in the boiler room at the munitions factory kept him from fighting overseas. Ena interrogated the slow-witted man over Sunday tea and, after watching the pair bumble through the meal, gave Vera her blessing. Confident that here was a man who wouldn't take advantage of Vera's placid nature, Ena encouraged him to propose marriage and instructed the young couple to settle for a long engagement, hoping she could spin it out until after the war. Bob was happy to go along with Ena's plans as he enjoyed having his life controlled for him. After Ena had given him, through Vera, instructions on the value of chastity, he made no sexual demands on Vera. The engagement ring on Vera's finger gave her more confidence and made her feel more in control of her life. Everyone seemed happy.

'I saw Bob at lunchtime,' she said, as they walked home.

'You'd 'ave a job to miss 'im, seein' as 'ow he 'angs round canteen door for you every day.'

Vera was delighted by Bob's attentiveness. 'He's asked me to the cinema tonight. You don't mind, do you?'

'Me? Why should I mind? Whenever 'ave I stopped you doin' anything? You do as you please, I fancy an early night.'

They walked on in silence, each full of their own thoughts, Vera with the thrill of sitting next to her fiancé sharing a bag of sweets, Ena with Sally and Elsie. She hoped they'd found their men. Who knew when they'd get a chance to see them again?

Elsie collected her children from Ida and let herself into No. 11. She hated coming back to an empty house each night, starting a fire in the grate and going through the motions of making a meal for them. Her spirits were low, and her feet ached from all the running she'd done. Linda ran round the room, pretending to ride a horse.

'Is Uncle Steve coming tonight?' she asked hopefully.

'No, love.'

'Oh, I want to see him and show him my horse.'

Elsie watched her daughter canter out of the room then sank into a chair. She reached for a cigarette packet, but it was as empty as she felt. Stuck into the frame of the rainbow-edged mirror hanging over the sideboard was a snapshot, taken at Sally's wedding. Elsie looked at the blonde girl clinging to the arm of the beautifully dressed airman and remembered Steve's words as the picture had been taken. 'Wait till I show the guys back home my very own Lana Turner.'

Looking at her reflection in the mirror, her eyes red from crying, her hair now two-toned blonde and natural red, she was all too aware that the only film star she resembled was Lassie. Perhaps it was a good thing she hadn't seen Steve, that he'd always carry a picture of how she was, how he wanted her to be. He'd been stunned when she'd gone blonde – not because she looked that good but because she'd done it for him. He'd told her that she didn't have to change anything about herself, that he loved her just the way she was. For her to have thought that much about his feelings had meant so much to him.

All her life Elsie had been undressed by rough, urgent

hands, her body pummelled and pulled by brutish selfishness. She'd been an object not of desire but of lust. It was down to the way she was built and the way she had taught herself to act. It had taken just one look at the hairy-chinned crones and the haggard women aged by childbirth, eyes deadened with hopelessness, for her to stick out her hip, undo her top buttons and wink at the boys. She'd used what God had given her to escape the slums of Back Gas Street, but the last few months had given her a fresh hope, of life beyond Coronation Street.

The war had opened up the world to her and she was restless. She'd heard exotic accents, learnt new expressions, and been allowed a glimpse of what her future might be. Steve loved her. He was kind and gentle, a considerate lover and a man with whom she knew she would always come first. She'd dared to believe America would welcome her as much as he had. Elsie Grimshaw, Stateside. Only now it wasn't going to happen. She didn't even know where he lived. Unlike Sally, she didn't have the security of the ring and the child growing inside her. All she had was a photograph of a woman who didn't look like her any more.

Thomas Hewitt stood outside the Rovers at closing time and cursed. He was loath to go home and be embraced by its emptiness. Instead he decided to nip to the Tripe-dressers' Arms to see if he could get service there. As he turned the corner into Rosamund Street a jeep passed him and drove past the Rovers.

'Bloody Yanks!' he shouted, waving his fist.

The jeep pulled up outside No. 9 and a man jumped out.

Sally heard its arrival and opened the door in a hurry. Her face registered her disappointment when she saw it wasn't Oliver.

'Mrs Oliver Hart?' The voice was American and authoritative.

'Yes.'

'US Military Police, ma'am. We're looking for your husband. He left camp this morning and hasn't been seen since. Have you seen him at all?'

Sally stumbled over what the man was telling her. Oliver missing? 'I've not seen him,' she said, 'We went to the camp but they said he'd already left . . .'

'We?'

'My friend came with me. Her boyfriend, Steve Tanner, was my husband's best man.'

'Oh, yes. Pilot Tanner. He's also disappeared. Do you mind if we take a look inside the house, ma'am?'

As the officers entered No. 9, Sally banged on Elsie's door.

It was dark when Vera said goodnight to Bob and started for home. She decided to take the short-cut from the back of the Bijou, down Victoria Street and into Viaduct Street, along the side of the Mission. It was a quiet route: most people stuck to the main roads where the blacked-out streets seemed more familiar. As she came near to the Mission porch she stumbled into a dustbin left on the pavement and sent the lid crashing to the ground.

Inside the porch, his trousers about his ankles, Tom Hayes looked over his shoulder into the darkness.

Lily Longhurst tensed and grabbed his shoulders. 'Who's that?' she whispered urgently.

'It'll be a cat,' he said.

Lily had her back to the Mission door and his body was pressed against hers, his buttocks clenching as his groin thrust backwards and forwards. It was the same position they used every night. They had taken to meeting in the porch when Lily had put her foot down over the rough brick-work under the viaduct. No one ever wandered round the side of the Mission at night and, apart from Ena having to deal with the used johnnies in the morning, Tom was confident no one would ever discover his love-nest. Lily didn't enjoy the nightly rituals as much as Tom seemed to, but she couldn't bring herself to object to them. The one time she'd told him he was hurting her he'd slapped her across the face and cursed her for putting him off his stroke. She'd been surprised by the slap but afterwards he'd apologised and told her she was his girl. To make amends he'd given her a packet of nylons, which she'd hidden under her mattress.

Vera grovelled about in the dark, located the lid and put it back on the bin. When she passed the porch, she heard the grunts and paused. 'Who's there?'.

'Bloody hell!' Tom disengaged himself and pulled up his trousers.

Vera shone into the porch the little torch Ena always made her carry. Lily blinked in the light and pulled her clothes around her.

'What are you doin'?' asked Vera.

'Go away!' shouted Lily.

Before Vera could shine the torch on him, Tom knocked it out of her hand and pushed past her roughly. She didn't have time to react and fell against the wooden bench, which ran the length of the porch. She gave a cry then lay still.

'Oh, God, Tom, what've you done to her?'

'Nothin'. She must've slipped and fell. Come on, we'd best scarper. I don't need no trouble.'

'But we can't just leave her here,' said Lily, frightened by Tom's harsh voice and the way he'd struck out at Vera.

'Come on,' he said, pulling her arm. 'Serve the stupid cow right, interruptin' us like that.'

'But she might be hurt –' Lily broke off as Tom hit her across the face. She gasped and burst into tears.

'Stop crying!' he hissed and pulled her out of the porch.

She followed him as he ran round the corner into Coronation Street. 'Tom, wait for me!' she cried, but he took no notice. He went straight home, furious at his ruined evening. He slammed his front door shut and, ignoring Esther's greeting, rushed up the stairs. He paused outside his bedroom and then, changing his mind, opened the door to Rose's room. She was in bed, asleep, just as he'd hoped she would be. He slipped in the room and crossed the floor to the dressing-table that stood in front of the window. He opened the drawer and put his hand in among the handkerchiefs and garments. He felt the shape of a small oval box and withdrew it. He'd been planning this for weeks, having finally decided that Coronation Street was too small for him. He couldn't breathe in the atmosphere, aware that his every move was monitored by either Esther or Ada. The problem with

Weatherfield was that everyone knew him and suspected his every move. He was sick of living under scrutiny and despised the woman who snored in the bed behind him. She was like a leech, living off her daughters, and he was determined to escape her.

The box's contents – her engagement ring and her mother's gold wedding ring – would easily convert to enough cash to get him to London. He had mates there from Strangeways who he knew would put him up. He was disgusted with himself for having to fumble around in porches with a little tart like Lily. Vera Sharples had done him a favour, only she was too thick to realise it.

He walked towards the door and looked down at Rose's sleeping face. He hated her for never giving him the attention or love he'd sought, growing up under Sid's hard rule, and he hated her for what she had become. Carefully he lifted a pillow from the side of the bed and, grasping it firmly, lowered it over her face.

'Tom!' It was Esther. 'What do you think you're doing?'

He flung the pillow aside and stormed out of the room. 'What is it with you?' he demanded. 'Why do you have to watch every fuckin' move I make?'

Tom was used to giving out slaps, so Esther's took him completely by surprise, as it did her. 'Don't you dare swear at me.' Her voice was shaking and she fought against the tears of rage that sprang into her eyes. 'Who do you think you are? That's your mother in there. She thinks the world of you!'

'She put me away, let that copper walk off with me. She never lifted a finger to help.'

'And what about you? Stealing from the neighbours, out all night goodness knows where. Have you any idea what you've put her through? Or me?'

He glared at her in defiance. 'You've turned into a right sour old maid, haven't you?'

She enjoyed delivering the second slap. 'Get out of this house before I call the police and have you done for attempted murder.'

He looked into her face and knew she meant it. He thrust the box into his pocket, bounded down the stairs and out. He would never return, he told himself, setting off down the Street. In the morning he'd catch the first train to London and be free of Coronation Street for ever.

Parked in their jeep under the viaduct, the two military policeman watched Tom disappear, content that he wasn't one of the pair they were looking for.

Annie Walker had just finished washing up the last of the evening's glasses when the stillness of the closed pub was disturbed by the rattling of the front door. She walked round the bar and pulled the black-out curtain to one side. 'We're closed.'

'I'm not after a drink.' The voice was sharp and recognisable.

Annie wondered what Mrs Sharples could possibly want from her. If she'd come to cause trouble she'd picked the wrong night: the beer and the customers had run out at nine and she was in no mood to be neighbourly. She shot back the bolt and opened the door. Ena furtively slid in.

'Your country needs you,' she said mysteriously.

'I beg your pardon?'

'You've been doin' dramatics, 'aven't you? Well, time's come to show 'ow good an actress you are. Yer neighbours need yer 'elp.'

Nine minutes, and a hurried explanation later, Annie changed into her oldest blouse and purposefully ripped one sleeve so that it hung off her shoulder. She sat in front of her bedroom mirror and, instead of putting in her usual curlers, ran her hands roughly through her hair. Then, after applying fresh lipstick, she smudged her lips, and smeared some on to her cheek. The finishing touch was to kick off one of her shoes before leaving the pub. She noted that Ena had already over-turned a couple of chairs.

She stumbled down the street, her eyes wide, her hands shaking. The jeep was exactly where Ena had said it would be and she flew at it, calling out to the occupants. 'Oh, help me, please help me.' She flung herself on the jeep and started to sob.

Watching from the vestry window Ena worried that she was overdoing her performance and decided never to waste good money on paying to see her on the stage.

'What's the matter, ma'am?' The policemen were out of the jeep and attempting to comfort the distraught publican.

'Two men – Americans. They forced their way into my hostelry and were brutish towards me!'

The policemen pricked up their ears. 'Americans, you say? Where are they now?'

'In my cellar, helping themselves to my spirits.'

'Don't worry, ma'am, you're safe now. We'll take care of them for you.' They set off at speed towards the Rovers, leaving Annie to limp after them as fast as she could with only one shoe on.

Unaware of the commotion in the street, Elsie and Sally sat at the living room table inside No. 11 and shared a packet of cigarettes. The hands on the clock seemed frozen as the women waited impatiently.

'They've got to come, 'aven't they?' asked Sally for the third time.

'Why else do you think we've 'ad police turnin' the place inside out? Why else would they both disappear like that? I've told you, they're comin' to see us, I know it.'

'Why don't they 'urry up, then?' asked Sally.

Vi eased herself out of the armchair and offered to make a pot of tea.

'No thanks, Vi, I'm awash wi' it as it is,' said Elsie.

' 'Ow about I put the wireless on?' suggested Vi. 'You've got to do summat to tek yer minds off it.'

'Not the wireless,' said Sally. 'Suppose they knocked at the door but we couldn't 'ear?'

'What if Dot's nipped to lav? She wouldn't 'ear 'em if they knocked next door,' said Elsie, in a panic.

'Give over,' said Vi. 'If they got no answer there they'd come 'ere. If they're smart enough to escape the bobbies this mornin', they'll find a way to see you, don't you fret.'

The sound of the front door opening sent the three women to their feet. They stared at the living room door as it slowly opened. Sally groaned.

'Mrs Sharples!' shouted Elsie. 'What do you think you're doin' scaring folk like that?'

'Oh, is that what I'm doin', is it? Scarin' folk? There was me thinkin' I'd come neighbourin'.'

'Nosyin' more like,' retorted Elsie.

'I must admit I was curious to see them fellas at your door earlier on. From the look of 'em I'd say they were bobbies, American ones at that. Am I right?'

'Well done, Mrs Sharples. Your powers of observation are as sharp as ever. Like your ears, you old bat!' Elsie glared at her and continued, 'Satisfied now, are you? Now you've bin proved right. Yes, we've 'ad the bobbies in, turnin' our 'ouses inside out, and before you go and pick over the bones with the rest of the vultures they weren't after black-market nylons.'

'Oh, I know that,' said Ena. 'They'd 'ave been lookin' for them that brought the nylons in first place.'

'Exactly.'

' 'Course, they wouldn't find them 'ere. Not when they're sat in my vestry drinkin' cocoa.'

Sally and Elsie stared at Ena. Elsie walked round the table and looked into Ena's eyes. 'If this is a joke . . .'

'No joke,' she said. 'Just the truth.' Her tone changed, becoming more serious. 'Get your coats and follow me. Hurry! I've got Annie Walker doin' 'er Scarlet O'Hara bit but I don't reckon it'll fool the bobbies for long.'

Vi remained at No. 11 to look after the children while Ena led Elsie and Sally across the cobbles. Elsie noticed the jeep hidden in the shadows and tried not to look suspicious. Ena ushered them into the vestry, which looked empty. Suddenly the bedroom curtain was pulled across and the wonderful figures of Steve and Oliver raced across to their women.

'We've not got long,' said Oliver, hugging Sally to him.

'Mrs Sharples,' said Elsie, 'thank you.'

'Don't waste your time thankin' me, these two did me a service earlier on. They found Vera bleedin' to death on me own doorstep. But for their quick action I dread to think what might 'ave 'appened.' She crossed to where Vera lay in bed and smoothed down the blankets.

'Is she all right?' asked Elsie.

'She'll be fine. It's not first bang on head she's had in her life, I dare say it won't be last.'

Elsie drew Steve away from the bed and pressed herself against him, whispering, 'We went to the camp but you'd gone.'

'I couldn't leave without seeing you, Elsie. I love you.'

The tears stung her eyes as he wrapped his strong arms around her. The weariness and upset of the day dropped from her shoulders as she allowed herself the luxury of feeling him, smelling him. She urged herself to remember everything about him: his square jaw, his bright eyes, the way his Adam's apple danced when he laughed, his smell, the exact colour of his hair.

The plan had been to lure the policemen down into the cellar then for Annie to lock them in. However, she was dismayed to find that when she'd arrived at the pub they'd already established that the cellar was deserted.

'Perhaps they're upstairs,' she suggested.

One took the bait, but to Annie's frustration the other moved towards the front door. 'Where are you going?' she demanded.

'We've a radio in the jeep,' he said. 'I'll call for back-up. These men are obviously more dangerous than we thought.'

She couldn't stop him but told herself she'd done her bit. Which, considering her customers' attitude towards her, was more than many in her position would have done.

The policeman ran along the street towards the jeep but, as he crossed Viaduct Street, was brought up short by an unsteady voice demanding, 'Halt and identify yourself!'

Jack Todd stood near the jeep, his rifle in his hand. He'd been nearing the end of his Home Guard patrol when he'd stumbled across the unattended jeep. He knew from the markings that it wasn't an English make and that was all that was needed to panic him into believing the Germans were about to storm his town.

The American eyed the older man with amusement and raised his hands in mock surrender. 'Hi, Pop.'

Jack lowered the rifle. 'Another bloody Yank,' he muttered.

'Suppose it were you I saw earlier on with your mate. Carryin' Vera Sharples home. Drunk, was she? You won't 'ave got far wi' 'er. She ain't got the sense to know what you're after.'

'Vera Sharples?'

'Aye, over at the Mission.' Jack gestured to the building. 'It's funny 'cos I thought one of you was Oliver, our Sally's fella. Reckon I need glasses . . .'

The American didn't stop to listen to any more. He pushed past Jack and made towards the pub.

Two minutes later the sharp sound of knocking on the vestry door broke the spell of happiness for the four lovers sheltering inside. Ena opened the door into the Mission hall and beckoned for the couples to escape through it. They rushed out through the vestry and she locked the door behind her.

The knock sounded again. 'Who is it?' she asked.

'Police. Open up.'

She pulled back the curtain into place across the bed and opened the door slowly. 'Whatever's the matter?' she asked innocently.

'Stand aside, ma'am.'

'I certainly will not. You're not the police.'

'Military Police, ma'am.'

'Well, I'm a civilian and I'm not doin' what you say. What do you think you're doin'? Knocking on folk's doors at this time of night.'

'We have reason to believe there might be servicemen on the premises, ma'am.'

Ena drew herself up. 'How dare you? How dare you suggest such a thing? I'm a widow, I'll 'ave you know, and I've a daughter in bed ill. I don't know what you're used to but we're decent women round these parts!'

Behind the policeman, across the Street, Vi opened Elsie's front door and called across to Ena, 'Havin' trouble, Mrs Sharples?'

'Bein' insulted, Mrs Todd. Insulted in me own 'ome, me who lives in a place of worship, who plays harmonium twice every Sunday as folk gather for prayer and teachin'. I've a good name round these parts. You ask anyone! How dare you suggest I've got servicemen in 'ere wi' me?'

Jack joined his wife in the street and was about to tell her about his encounter with the Americans when to his surprise she ran across the street and prodded one of the policemen in his chest. 'You ought to be ashamed of yourself, upsettin' Mrs Sharples. I'll vouch for her. She's a good and decent soul. Keeps 'erself to 'erself, never 'as a cross word to say about anyone. 'Ow dare you come round and say such wicked things about a God-fearin' woman?'

'For the last time, ma'am, will you stand aside and let us in?' demanded the policeman.

There was nothing left to do but pray. Ena's subconscious muttered a silent entreaty while she continued to block the policemen's path. As soon as she'd said Amen, the piercing sound of the air-raid siren cut through the night. It alarmed the men and gave Ena the chance she needed to gather her wits. 'Right, I'm on duty now,' she said, and slammed the door in their faces.

The men hammered afresh but broke off when they realised they were no longer alone. Out of every doorway on Coronation Street appeared men, women and children, clutching blankets, jewellery boxes, family albums and Thermos flasks. Albert, his tin hat firmly in place, arrived at the double and rushed to the side of the Mission to lead the way to the front entrance.

'Evenin',' said Martha, to the policemen. 'Nice night for a raid. Very clear. You want to take cover. Come with us, if you like, you'd be very welcome.'

'You want to watch them,' said Vi, clutching baby Dennis to her chest. 'They were trying to force themselves on Mrs Sharples earlier.'

'Ena?' said Martha in disbelief.

'Yanks are like that,' said Dot, holding Linda Tanner's hand and joining her mother. 'Randy sods. Anything in a hair-net.'

The residents continued on their way towards the shelter. As she went Vi continued to shout abuse at the men. Daisy Todd, tagging on behind and totally in the dark as to her daughter-in-law's attitude, picked up the theme out of a sense of loyalty and jeered at the men, waving her fist at them.

'Remember nineteen eleven!' she cried in defiance, referring to the highlight of her life when she'd unseated a mounted policeman during a march for jobs.

'I've had enough of this place,' said one policemen to the other. 'They're all mad.'

'Half-wits,' agreed his colleague. 'They're probably all related to each other. Why don't we head back and say Hart and Tanner never came near the place?'

'Sure.'

The residents filed into the Mission, with Albert at the door handing out the coloured chalk. As they sought cover in the cellar, no one noticed the shadowy figures huddled together at the far end of the hall. Helped by Percy Longhurst, Ena led a subdued Vera out of the vestry and into the shelter below, where she was received by Elsie Foyle who, without asking any questions, made her comfortable on a bunk. Breaking from her mother's side, Lily Longhurst knelt by Vera's side and clasped her hand. 'You all right?' she asked. 'I'm sorry 'e 'it you. I tried to stop 'im . . .'

Albert waited for all of the regulars to arrive out of the cold night air then pulled the big oak doors towards him. Just as they were closing, Annie Walker appeared, a fur coat hanging over her shoulders.

'Hello, Mrs Walker,' he said in surprise. 'You don't usually join us. Where's the bairns?'

'Is Mrs Sharples here?'

Ena appeared and looked at Annie in alarm. 'What's to do?'

Annie broke into a smile. 'It's all right. I've just seen them drive off down Rosamund Street.'

Ena turned into the hall and called, 'It's the all-clear. They've given up!'

Albert looked on bemused as the four youngsters appeared from the dark recesses of the hall. Elsie hugged Steve and allowed him to pull her to his chest. 'You'd better go, they may come back.'

'She's right,' said Ena. 'We've held 'em off all we can. At least you've 'ad chance to say goodbye.'

Annie looked enviously at the two couples, so much in love. She wished Jack was next to her with his arms round her as Steve had his around Elsie.

Sally clung to Oliver until Elsie had to pull her away from him. Cherishing the sensation of Steve's last kiss, Elsie put her arms protectively around Sally's shoulders and promised Oliver to look after her. 'Write every day,' she urged Steve.

'I will.'

'Where are you going?' asked Sally.

Oliver shrugged. 'Wherever we're needed. Probably down to the south coast then over to France and Germany, but who knows?'

'How will you get back to the base?' asked Annie in concern.

'We'll catch up with the truck on Ashton Road. One of our buddies is going to fix it so it breaks down.' Oliver smiled down at his wife and kissed her forehead. 'We'll have to run, though.'

'Just go!'

Oliver ran to the door and turned to wave one last time, whispering, 'I love you, Sally.'

Steve's fingers lingered on Elsie's cheek, then he pressed his cap badge into her hand. 'Till we meet again,' he said and saluted her. She closed her eyes tight, not wanting to see him disappear into the night.

They were gone. Sally and Elsie embraced, Sally sobbing, Elsie stroking her hair.

Vi emerged from the shelter and opened her arms as an invitation for her daughter. Sally ran into them and Vi patted the back of her hair.

'He loves me, Mam.'

'I know, love.'

'You were smashin', Mrs Sharples,' said Elsie.

Ena sat on the edge of the stage. 'By 'eck, I never thought I'd see the day when I'd 'elp you 'ave a kiss and a cuddle with one of your fancy men.'

'Steve's more than that, Mrs Sharples.'

'I know, lass. We've all got someone out there. I were lucky enough to find mine first time round. 'Appen wi' some folk it teks a bit longer.'

'That's very true, Mrs Sharples.' Elsie laughed. 'I never thought I'd be agreein' wi' you, either.'

'I suppose that's what war does. Makes you think twice about yer beliefs, what you think's right and wrong. Brings folk together more.' Ena took Elsie's hand and squeezed it. For the first time she admired the spirit in the younger woman's eyes. At the back of her mind she'd always thought Elsie reminded her of someone. Now she realised who it was. Herself.

Elsie looked beyond Ena, to the door leading out on to Viaduct Street. She was confident that Steve would outrun the police. That he'd make it to the waiting truck and that all would be well. If she'd been a religious woman she'd have thanked God for letting them have the chance to say goodbye and even though she wasn't she still uttered a silent prayer. She held Ena's hand tightly and leant against her sturdy shoulder. Hostilities ceased. For the moment.

Albert put his hand on Annie's shoulder and asked, 'Would you mind tellin' me what's goin' on?'

'Not now, Albert,' said Ena, getting to her feet. 'While we've all been mitherin' on that siren's wailed it's 'ead off. We'd best go downstairs.'

Annie pulled her coat closer and pushed open the door. 'See you all in the morning,' she said.

On the Mission step she almost bumped into Minnie Caldwell as she rushed up to the door calling, 'Mr Tatlock, don't shut me out!'

Minnie entered the hall, clutching a bundle wrapped in a rug. A cat peered out at the strange surroundings. 'I'm sorry I'm late but I couldn't find Mabel anywhere and Mother had already gone to the shelter.'

'You're not bringing that moggy down into my clean basement!' said Ena.

'Oh, I must. She gets very frightened.'

'Just 'urry up, will you?' said Albert. 'I've not 'ad me tea yet and Bessie's got sandwiches down below.'

Minnie made for the stairs, but before she went down she

turned and smiled brightly at Ena and Elsie. 'I've not missed anything 'ave I? You 'aven't started the sing-song yet, 'ave you?'

Ena and Elsie exchanged a smile.

'No, Mrs Caldwell,' said Elsie, 'you've not missed a thing.'

The Way to Victory

CHAPTER ONE

Summer 1943 Mussolini overthrown.

'Sodom and Gomorrah,' announced Ena, with feet splayed and eyes flashing as she stared at the poster stuck on *her* noticeboard outside the Glad Tidings Mission Hall. She had a broom in one hand so she stuck that under her arm and tore down the offending item. 'Sodom and Gomorrah,' she repeated.

A voice from behind startled her. 'What's to do, Mrs Sharples?'

She turned swiftly. 'Oh, it's you, Albert Tatlock. You wouldn't think there was a war on in Weatherfield, would you?' She didn't give him time to answer but thrust the offending poster in front of his nose so that he had to take a step back to see it properly. 'It's a disgrace, that's what it is, a bloomin' disgrace.'

Although his eyesight was poor and his glasses were thick he could easily see the can-can dancer's red bloomers. 'Oh, aye.'

'Is that all you can say – "oh, aye"? Don't you think it's a disgrace? All this lot in Coronation Street think about is dancing and someone from round 'ere has dared to stick it on *my* noticeboard.'

Albert shrugged. 'My dancin' days is over, Mrs Sharples. I'm on me way to join a queue.'

'What for?' she asked, suddenly interested.

'Who knows? But I did read in the paper as 'ow someone's seen a banana.'

Mrs Sharples propped her broom by the noticeboard, rolled up the poster, which advertised a dance next Saturday night at the church hall, and stuffed it under her arm. 'I'll find out who stuck this 'ere if it's the last thing I do. I'm the caretaker 'ere, after all. We can all manage without bananas but pictures showin' – showin' everything is a different matter.'

'Aye,' repeated Albert. 'You comin' to join the queue?'

To Ena, finding the culprit came before queuing – there was always a queue to join. 'I'm seeing Elsie Tanner first. She's behind this. People round 'ere are getting lax. Only last week there was a dance and when the siren went off only four people left and came to my shelter.'

'Right then, I'm off,' said Albert. 'Mrs Foyle might have summat tasty on sale.'

Ena watched for a moment as Albert walked off to join the queue at the Corner Shop, then she picked up her broom, put it back in the cupboard, removed her apron and stomped down the street. First stop, No. 11 – young Elsie Tanner's.

At Elsie's Ena knocked hard enough to disturb half the Street. A few curtains twitched but the residents were well used to the regular stand-up barneys between Ena and Elsie. It was nine o'clock in the morning and the sun was shining, but Elsie's curtains were still closed. Ena gave up knocking and yelled through the letterbox, 'Elsie Tanner! I know you're in there! I want a word with you.'

There was still no answer. 'Lazy madam,' muttered Ena. By now she'd begun to think again about the queue. She had her ration books tucked in her apron pocket and nothing much in her larder. And she needed soap. Elsie Tanner would have to wait. 'I'll be back,' she shouted. Then she laid the poster over her shoulder as if it were a rifle and marched off to join the queue.

Elsie Tanner lay in bed smoking a Woodbine. She'd no idea why Ena Sharples was on the warpath and she didn't care. Like the bombers, Ena always came back. All Elsie thought about in quiet moments was Steve Tanner, her American GI. One letter – that was all she'd had. He was on the move, he'd said, he'd write again when he knew where he'd be based.

Twice a day the postman delivered mail but there was nothing from the USA. She pushed to the back of her mind the idea that he might have found someone else. After all *she* had scarcely seen a man since Steve had left in May.

She puffed on her fag and watched the smoke-rings. The room was dark because of the blackout curtains but at least the kids weren't screaming yet. She'd spent most of the night in the basement shelter of the Glad Tidings Mission Hall and her Dennis was teething – he'd screamed the place down. Poor little bugger had nappy rash too. Was it the kids Ena had come about? She was always saying they were pasty-faced and would get rickets if Elsie wasn't careful. Voice of doom, Ena could be, but she had done Elsie some favours in the past – one of which had been tricking the Military Police so that she could say goodbye to Steve. She could still remember the feel of his lips, her head snuggling into his shoulder that last time. He'd stroked her hair and said he loved her. What a difference there was between him and her old man Arnold! He'd rip her knickers off without a by-your-leave – just a grunt and "I love your bum".'

The trouble with Arnold was that she'd married him. At sixteen. She'd had to – her Linda was on the way. She was three now, and bright as a button. Her Linda and Arnold's Navy pay were the only things to recommend him. Arnold had got her pregnant on his last leave. At least she was *sure* it was him. Some women weren't too certain who had fathered their children. In wartime no one asked too many questions about the timing of leave. At least, not to your face. Behind backs there was always gossip. Even about those women who daren't look at a man for fear of getting pregnant.

The Americans, in Elsie's opinion, had been well prepared for wartime Britain. They had lovely muscled bodies, nylons, cigarettes, chocolates and johnnies. If it weren't for some self-control and the johnnies many a GI would have left behind more than fags and nylons.

'Mam . . . Mam,' whined Linda, as she walked into Elsie's bedroom with a snotty nose and a bare bum. 'I've wet the bed, Mam.'

'You always do, pet,' Elsie said, as she pulled back the bedcovers and the little girl with her cold bum got in beside her.

'I love your bed, Mam.'

Elsie smiled and lifted her arm up so that Linda could snuggle down. 'Go back to sleep, love.'

One more Woodbine later Dennis began bawling and a Saturday of washing sheets and nappies stretched before her.

Ena joined the 'blind' queue. Folk called it that because the queues were so long you couldn't see what was being sold. She usually barged to the top and waylaid someone who'd just been served, then she'd announce the purchase to the rest. Some women left the queue immediately, perhaps a bit put out that they didn't need that particular item, but most stayed because anything you bought that you didn't want you could always swap or sell on. Today she didn't do that because Minnie Caldwell was at the back end.

'Hello, Ena,' she said. 'It's a nice day. What's for sale?'

'Never mind the weather, Minnie Caldwell. And how would I know? I've just joined the queue. It'll give me time to simmer down.'

'What's wrong, Ena? Who's upset you?'

'This,' Ena took the poster from her shoulder, unrolled it and held it up. A few in the queue turned round to look. 'Mind your own business,' said Ena loudly, and they turned back.

Minnie smiled. 'Ooh, Ena, it's lovely and bright,' she said.

'Lovely and bright, Minnie Caldwell? Is that all you can say? My Mission Hall is lovely and bright. This is . . .' she searched for the word '. . . rude.'

'If you say so, Ena. But I like paintings.'

'It isn't a bloomin' paintin', it's an advertisement. Sometimes, Minnie, you can be as slow as our Vera.'

'She's not slow, Ena. Not now . . . not now she's grown-up.'

'In my eyes, Minnie Caldwell, she'll never be grown-up.'

'That's as maybe, Ena, but—'

'Don't go off the subject, Minnie,' said Ena. 'I reckon Elsie Tanner's responsible for this. She'll be over that namesake of hers, Steve Tanner, by now and want to be out gallivantin'.

And if she asks you to keep an eye on 'er kids, say no. She's always palmin' off those kids on all and sundry. And I'm sure she only feeds them on chips and bread and marge.'

'What's that got to do with the poster, Ena? I didn't know Elsie could paint.'

Minnie had a point and Ena paused, but only for a second. 'I'm sure she's only good at one thing and you know what *that* is. But she'll be behind it and when I've finished standin' 'ere gettin' varicose veins I'll be along to Number eleven to 'ave it out with 'er.'

'Yes, Ena,' said Minnie, with a little smile.

It was nearly eleven when Ena returned to do battle at No. 11. This time Elsie was up and dressed, wearing bright red lipstick, her cheeks rouged with the same colour. For a moment Ena forgot her mission. 'If you took as much trouble over your own kids as you do paintin' your face, Elsie Tanner, they'd be a lot healthier.'

'Is that it, Mrs Sharples? I'm young and I want to look nice. That's not a bloody crime, is it?'

'No, but this is,' said Ena, producing the poster from behind her back.

'Well, you'd better come in, Mrs Sharples, before you make an exhibition of yourself on my doorstep.'

Sometimes, but not often, twenty-year-old Elsie got the better of Ena Sharples, and this was one of them. Not for the first time Ena realized that she and Elsie had something in common. She couldn't condone Elsie's loose morals but the girl had spirit and, grudgingly, she admired that. 'Right, then, I'll come in,' said Ena, trying to sound as if it had been her idea.

Dennis lay on his back, kicking his legs in the middle of the back room on an old blanket, wearing only a grey-looking vest. Linda was playing with some cards and from the scullery came the smell of boiling nappies. Suddenly Ena's irritation began to disappear. Elsie wasn't a good housewife but she tried – and, after all, being married at sixteen and losing her mam and dad in an air-raid must have been terrible for her.

'Take a seat,' said Elsie. 'Get it off your chest, Mrs Sharples.'

Ena's hackles rose at Elsie's cocky tone. 'It's this,' she said, unfurling the evidence.

'That's nowt to do with me,' said Elsie, taking more notice of the place and date than of the can-can dancer. 'Never seen it before.'

'Aye, well, you would say that.'

Elsie fixed Ena with a hard stare. 'I may be a lot of things in your opinion, Mrs Sharples, but I'm not a liar.' Before Ena could answer, Elsie carried on, 'And I don't think there's anything wrong with that poster. We all have legs and we all wear panties – some bigger than others. Even the Queen.'

Ena was outraged. 'How dare you! The Queen wouldn't flaunt herself.'

'I'm not sayin' she would. I'm just sayin' she's got legs and wears bloomers, and I don't know nothin' about your poster.'

'It seems I've come to the wrong place,' said Ena stiffly.

'You certainly have. You're only peeved because the church is puttin' on the do, not your miserable old Mission Hall.'

At that moment Dennis, beginning to bawl, rolled over on to his front. Ena's sharp eyes couldn't fail to see the sight of his blistered bum. She had a soft spot for babies, had delivered dozens as the unofficial local midwife – she had even brought Elsie's kids into the world. Which was why nothing would stop her if she had something to say about the welfare of 'her' babies.

'Poor little mite,' she said. 'You should be ashamed of yourself, letting him get in this state.'

'He's teethin', and I forgot to take a clean nappy with me in the raid last night.'

Ena looked across at Elsie as she lit a cigarette. It wasn't smoke bringing those tears to her eyes. She softened her tone. 'You're doing right,' she said. 'Let the air get to 'is bum and make up a paste with some starch and water and put that on. And in future remember I always 'ave a few spare nappies. Lovely and soft they are too.' Ena cooed at the baby for a while, and although she sniffed at the sight of Linda with the playing cards, she played Snap with her while Elsie made a brew.

'What are you feedin' these kids on, Elsie?'

'They don't go 'ungry.'

'Are you tekkin' them to the clinic?'

'I get what's goin' for them.'

'Your Dennis looks as if he never sees the sun.'

Elsie stood up and folded her arms. 'Thanks for the advice, Mrs Sharples. Perhaps you'd ask the Almighty for an extra sun ration for my kids – and while you're at it, ask Him to put a stop to the war so that us women can have a bit of a break.'

'It's a pity your Arnold isn't—'

'It's a pity my Arnold was ever born, Mrs Sharples.'

They stared at each other for a moment. But Mrs Sharples had to have the last word. At the door she said, 'At least you 'ave a good chance of seein' 'im again. More than can be said for that fancy piece Steve Tanner.'

Before Elsie could respond, Ena had slammed the front door shut.

'Mam – Mam!' called Linda.

'Oh, shut up,' said Elsie, 'or I'll put you through the mangle with the nappies.'

'Mam, I'm 'ungry,' whined Linda, pulling at Elsie's skirt.

Elsie patted her head. 'We won't let that silly old moo get us down, will we? I'll do you some bread and marge with a bit o' Spam.'

CHAPTER TWO

Autumn 1943 Allied Invasion of Italy begins.

The Rovers smelt of damp clothes and rough tobacco. Saturday night was the busiest of the week. Outside it was raining pailfuls and Annie Walker admonished those who came through her portals with wet feet. 'Please be kind enough to wipe your feet, ladies and gentlemen.' Then she added, for good measure, 'Remember where you are.'

'You're right, Mrs Walker,' said one of the ARP wardens on his rounds. 'This *is* hallowed ground, but just make sure you observe the blackout.'

Annie, hand on pump as she drew a half-pint of mild for Albert Tatlock, said archly, 'I always do. I'm very fussy about observing the regulations.'

'Worse than a sergeant major,' someone muttered, but Annie didn't see who had said it so she carried on serving Albert, who had come in for a game of dominoes and a bit of warmth.

In the Snug Ena had taken off her damp coat but she still felt cold. 'You'd think Annie Walker could keep the place warmer than this,' she said loudly to Martha Longhurst, who sat staring into her glass of milk stout. 'What's up wi' you?' asked Ena.

'Nothin' a hot summer's day by the sea wouldn't put right.'

'Well,' said Ena, 'when the war's over they'll tek all that barbed wire down and we'll go to Blackpool for the day.'

'Will we really, Ena?' said Minnie Caldwell, lifting her glass. 'That would be lovely.'

'I've just said we would. There's nowt to do now but get on with it.'

'I 'ate the winter,' said Martha.

'You 'ate all the seasons of the year, Martha Longhurst. It's no good you sittin' there with a face like a busted cabbage. Think yoursel' lucky.'

'Lucky? I've got nowt to feel lucky about.'

'You've only got yoursel' to worry about. Your Percy's soft as soap and your Lily loves nothin' better than a bit o' housework. You can do what you like when you like. And you've got a little job charring. No responsibilities. Thank the Almighty for that. Some poor women round 'ere are really strugglin'.'

'You're right, Ena,' said Minnie. 'There's lots worse off.'

Ena gave her a scathing look. 'You was one of them I was thinkin' of.'

Minnie thought about that for a moment. 'What do you mean, Ena?'

'I mean,' said Ena, 'that mother of yours runs you ragged.'

'She's right poorly, she can't 'elp that.'

Ena sniffed. 'Lazy, more like. Just lays abed with you scurryin' around like a frightened rabbit.'

'I like looking after my mam,' said Minnie quietly. 'And I've got my Mabel.'

'I reckon you go without food to feed that cat of yours.'

'No I don't, Ena. I don't get any thinner, do I?'

Ena cast a glance over Minnie's rounded little body. 'Can't expect to at our age. A woman gets fat in her forties.'

'Martha doesn't.'

Ena shrugged. 'I reckon Martha Longhurst lives on fresh air and misery.'

'What yer blatherin' about?' said Martha.

'Your brain's gettin' addled,' said Ena. 'There's none so deaf as those that can 'ear.'

Martha, with her most animated expression since the outbreak of war, pointed a finger at the window. 'Nothin' wrong with my brain. I was lookin' at that blackout curtain.'

Ena gave the floor-length curtains a glance. They *were* moving. 'We'll see about this,' she said, and marched over to the window.

'Ena always has to be first,' commented Minnie. 'I do admire her.'

'Don't be so soft,' said Martha. 'It'll be nowt but a cat or summat.'

Startled, Minnie stood up. 'It could be my Mabel – she might 'ave followed me in.'

Martha grabbed Minnie's arm to pull her back down. 'Let Ena deal with it.'

By now Ena was the centre of attention. 'Come out,' she boomed, 'and show yoursel'.' The curtain twitched but Ena could wait no longer. Wary of breaking the blackout, she kicked at the lump.

'Ow!' Out came a fair-haired little boy.

'Billy Walker, what *are* you doin'?'

In his hand he held a nearly empty half-pint mug. Beer foam was round his mouth and some had dribbled down his pyjamas.

Annie Walker nearly fainted on the spot. She had never felt so mortified in her whole life. When she *did* find her voice she sounded as if someone had strangled her. 'Billy, get to your room – at once!' He scampered out, grinning, with Annie behind him.

'That took that smell-under-her-nose look off her face,' said Ena, as she sat down. 'I'll be 'avin' words with 'er about young Billy.'

'The trouble with you, Ena,' murmured Minnie, 'is that you and Annie Walker both think you're better than anyone else.'

Ena's withering look would have rotted compost but Minnie didn't seem to notice. Both Ena and Annie were proud. It *was* a sin, Ena knew, and the good Lord knew it, but she'd been made that way and she couldn't change. All she could do was pray. 'That's as maybe,' she said, 'but I don't put on airs and graces.'

'That's true enough,' said Minnie. 'You're always Ena.'

When Annie Walker finally emerged she put on a brave smile, saying, 'Just a minor misdemeanour.'

Albert Tatlock, waiting for a third half, said, 'That's what Chamberlain thought before 'Itler invaded Poland.'

'Mr Tatlock, I'm surprised at you. My Billy is good as gold.

It's because he's going to Bessie Street School now. All sorts of ideas they've given him. He only started in September and already he's the best reader in the class.'

'Oh, aye,' said Albert, hand outstretched for his beer.

Ena came up behind him and said, 'I expect 'Itler was a good reader, Albert Tatlock. What do you think?'

He clutched his ale and took a swig. 'Aye, 'spect 'e was.' He moved away sharpish, knowing a skirmish was ahead.

Ena leaned over the bar and fixed Annie with an icy stare. 'A word of well-meant Christian advice, Mrs Walker.'

Annie squared up to her full height of five foot three. 'Yes, Mrs Sharples. I thought you might want to have your say.'

'There's no need to take that tone wi' me, Mrs Walker. I'm just bein' friendly. With your Jack away, you want to do what's best, don't you?'

'Of course. Boys will be boys.'

'Aye, but you expect more of your Billy don't you?'

Annie Walker's shoulders relaxed a little. 'Yes, of course I do. I want him to be different.'

'I suppose by that you mean – not like the lads round 'ere.' Annie nodded.

'Well, in that case you can't run an alehouse and look after young 'uns, 'specially your Billy.'

'What are you suggesting, Mrs Sharples?'

'You need a body to 'elp you. Make sure 'e stays in bed of an evening. Play wi' 'im for a bit and keep 'im out of mischief.'

'What sort of helpful body?'

'Go down the school and find a school leaver to live in. Some young lass would be grateful for a job wi' bed and board.'

Annie let the idea sink in. 'I don't know if I could afford a . . . nanny.'

'You can afford a few shillings a week, Mrs Walker. A woman like you 'as a bit stashed away for a rainy day. The lass could stay till your Jack comes home for good.'

'A nanny,' murmured Annie. It was music to her ears. Why hadn't she thought of it before?

'Don't make the poor lass a skivvy within a week,' warned Ena, wagging her finger. 'You overwork her and she'll be tailin' it down to the munitions factory as fast as some 'ere sup their ale.'

'I'll think about it, Mrs Sharples. Thank you for your advice.'

'Don't just think about – do summat!'

Ena walked back to her seat, smiling.

'There you are, Martha, I win,' Minnie declared.

'What's bin goin' on?' asked Ena, looking from one woman to the other.

'I had a little bet on and I've won,' giggled Minnie.

'What have I told you about the evils of gamblin'? You should be ashamed.'

'Well, I'm not this time, Ena. Martha's gettin' the milk stouts, aren't you, Martha?'

Martha stood up, looking grim, and walked to the bar.

'Come on, Minnie,' said Ena, the thought of a free drink easing her disapproval. 'What the 'eck were you bettin' on?'

Minnie's round, pretty face smiled. 'I bet you'd 'ave the last word with Annie Walker. Well done, Ena.'

They'd only just started their drinks when the siren sounded. Ena thrust her ARP helmet on immediately. 'Right,' she said. 'Follow me.'

No one moved. 'Come on, you lot,' she called out, 'war's not over yet.'

Still no one moved. Eventually Minnie said timidly, 'We're going into Mrs Walker's cellar for this one. She's got some lovely Glenn Miller records.'

Ena bristled with annoyance, reminding Minnie of a cat with its fur on end. 'Next you'll be tellin' me you lot are tired of "The Old Rugged Cross" and "Abide With Me".'

'The war's been on a long time, Ena,' said Minnie. 'We need a change.'

As Ena walked off, only Albert Tatlock followed her. He, too, was an ARP warden so he didn't have a choice. Ena was aware that Annie Walker's eyes were on her back and that she was feeling she'd won some sort of victory. So she turned and stared the landlady in the eye. 'Never forget,' she said in a loud voice, 'the lads round 'ere may be rough round the edges but they all went to Bessie Street School and they're 'eroes – 'eroes every one of them.'

Churchill could have taken lessons from me, thought Ena, as she strode off into the dark with the sirens still blaring. Annie Walker might have thought she'd bested Ena on this one but defeat wasn't a word she knew. By 'eck it wasn't.

The raid was a short one, over by midnight, and Annie Walker was glad to have her cellar empty. It had been a long day and although the cellarman had done the heavy lifting she had been constantly on her feet and there were always Billy and Joan to keep an eye on. Even getting a char was difficult these days. The wages in the munitions factories were good and single women had joined the services in huge numbers. If she'd been single Annie would have wanted to entertain the troops. Her voice was as good as Gracie Fields's, and anything in that line would have been better than being stuck at the Rovers with only rough types to talk to. The trouble was, none of them wanted to better themselves. Even her Jack didn't have much ambition. To him, running the Rovers was the pinnacle of success. He'd told her he wanted a quiet life after the war, get to know young Billy and baby Joan, who was just beginning to toddle about and in her fourteen months had only seen her father twice. Annie wanted more. Other women, the young ones anyway, had been out to dances and enjoyed themselves – married or not. She had been stuck wiping up slops and trying to keep an air of decorum in the bar. From morning to night she was like a mole, rarely seeing daylight. She tried to make the best of herself, but why bother? Folks in Coronation Street thought she was a joke just because she had standards.

As she lay in bed that night the thought of having a nanny cheered her. Billy wouldn't get into mischief again and everyone round here would see that *her* children were far superior to the likes of the Tanners – all snotty-nosed and ill-bred.

Tomorrow, she thought, I'll be down that Bessie Street School to find a nice refined girl to look after the children. The war will soon be over. Jack will be back and then everything will be better. Perhaps the amateur dramatic society will start up again. Even better was the thought that they could move to the country, live among more genteel people.

For now, though, a nanny would have to do. Royalty had nannies, didn't they? And look how well *they* turned out.

At No. 1 Albert Tatlock banked up the fire with more wood. His wife Bessie had made a brew, and although it was the middle of the night they didn't want to go to bed. The bedroom was like an icebox, and many a night they sat at either side of the fire talking, mostly about Beattie, their daughter, who had been evacuated to the countryside at the start of the war aged five. Bessie held her cup with both hands to get a bit of warmth into them. 'The war might be over soon, Albert,' she said. 'Did we do the right thing in lettin' 'er go away?'

'We didn't 'ave much choice, did we? An' she's 'avin' a good life there. That woman who took her in 'as treated 'er like her own.'

Bessie nodded and stared into the fire. 'Too much so for my likin'. All that trouble we 'ad when she wanted to adopt 'er.'

'Aye, but she didn't, so it's no good frettin' about it now, is it, hen?'

He patted her knee, and Bessie's eyes filled with tears. 'Last time I saw her she seemed to 'ardly know me. And toys and lovely clothes – I didn't know there were such things.'

'She'll settle down when she comes back to us,' said Albert, giving the fire a good poke.

Bessie sighed. 'She talks so posh now they'll tease the life out of 'er at school.'

'She'll soon talk as rough as the others.'

'Yes, Albert, but will she like it?'

'She'll have to lump it, won't she?'

Bessie fell quiet then, for Albert's mouth had set like concrete. Best humour him, she thought.

'At least Ida Barlow, and young Kenneth and David need me.'

'Aye,' said Albert. 'With Frank away, I don't know 'ow she would have managed wi'out you.'

'Is that true? 'Cos I don't know 'ow I'd 'ave managed without them.'

'There you are, then. All sorted. How about another brew, or 'as the kettle bust?'

Bessie smiled. Albert was back in a good humour, and as she busied herself in the kitchen brewing tea and spreading some pork dripping on toast she felt a lot brighter altogether. Her Albert loved his food, and she always managed to make something tasty. You had to count your blessings, she told herself. One was knowing her Beattie was safe and well fed. The other was her Albert. He was a rock in times of trouble. You're a lucky woman, she told herself. And the war was coming to an end, so the papers and the Pathé News said, so it must be true. After the war everything would be easier, she was sure of that.

CHAPTER THREE

Autumn 1943 Italy declares War on Germany.

Annie Walker powdered her nose lightly and applied lipstick carefully. She wanted to look smart and she still had a few good frocks from before the war. She'd shortened them to be fashionable, and now as she looked at herself in the mirror she felt satisfied. The added white collar above the powder pink frock made it look brand new. She slipped on her grey overcoat with its fox-fur edging, and felt grand enough to meet Bessie Street Senior's headmaster.

Martha Longhurst was keeping an eye on Joan and Billy was at school. Although the new cellarman, Ned Narkin, had a shifty look, he seemed to know what he was doing and would be on the pub premises until she got back. Her world was organized, and as Annie walked towards Bessie Street she felt cheerful, in spite of the drizzle and the drab houses. With so many men away the women had neither time nor money to deal with decorating: the paint on most doors was peeling and the window-frames would barely last another winter.

Bessie Street School was an old Victorian building with iron railings and windows so high that the children couldn't see out of them. Inside it smelt of Izal and damp shoes, and it reminded Annie of a public lavatory. Her footsteps echoed on the shiny wooden floors, and as she made her way to the headmaster's office, she passed quiet classrooms where children sat dipping their pens into inkwells as they copied work from the blackboard. She remembered her own schooldays and how she had always striven not to make any blots and how if she

386

did make the odd mistake she got very upset. So far she hadn't seen a soul, save for an elderly caretaker with a mop and bucket who pointed her silently in the right direction.

When she knocked on the office door a deep voice boomed, 'Come in,' and just for a moment she felt a little nervous.

When she entered the headmaster's sanctum she *still* felt that way. John Barnstable was a tall, handsome man in his early forties, with striking brown eyes and thick wavy hair. She'd always liked older men and his refined accent impressed her, so much so that her legs felt wobbly. 'I'm so grateful for a few minutes of your valuable time,' she said.

Smiling, he shook her hand. 'Do sit down, Mrs Walker,' he said. 'My secretary is away at the moment. The house next door to hers was bombed last night. Otherwise she would have been here to make you a cup of tea.'

Annie did not take her eyes off his face. 'I wondered, Mr Barnstable,' she began. 'if you had a suitable school leaver who would be interested in being a nanny to my two children. Someone refined and respectable, you understand. I'm a businesswoman, you see, and my husband is away so I want the best.'

'Of course you do, Mrs Walker. May I say that you look too young to have children. The responsibility has rested on you lightly.'

Annie felt herself blushing. His eyes were twinkling and she remembered how Jack had looked at her in the early days of their courtship.

'I do have one or two girls who would fit the bill,' he said, 'but of course, these days they have so many choices. Let me just check their record cards.' He walked to a cupboard, took out several brown envelopes and began reading through them. 'Do you have any preferences?'

'Preferences?' she queried.

'Religious preferences.'

She shook her head. 'Not at all. As long as the girl is well-spoken, reliable, clean, tidy and good with children, I shall be happy.'

He smiled at her again. 'You seem to be a young woman who knows what she wants.'

'I do,' said Annie. 'My ambition is to live in the countryside away from all this.' She waved her hand towards the grimy window.

'Likewise,' said John Barnstable.

In that moment Annie sensed she had found a soulmate.

'Would you like to peruse these report cards,' he asked, 'while I find us a glass of sherry?'

There was nothing Annie would have liked better. By the time she had drunk her sherry she knew that he was single, enjoyed concerts and poetry, that he'd enlisted, but a problem with his Achilles tendon had precluded him from active service so he'd joined the Home Guard.

When she disclosed her address he said, 'You don't look tough enough to be running a public house on your own.'

Annie smiled. 'I'm tougher than I look.'

He would write, he said, when he'd made arrangements for her to interview the girls she'd deemed suitable.

As she was leaving he shook her gloved hand and seemed to hold on to it for ages. 'Perhaps one evening,' he said tentatively, 'with your husband's permission, of course, we could attend a concert together.'

When she paused, he added. 'My mother could come too, which would be . . . more proper.'

Annie didn't know whether to be glad or sorry about his mother. 'That would be most acceptable,' she said primly.

On the way back to the Rovers she smiled at the idea of getting Jack's permission. The post was so unreliable that she would have been to the concert before he received a letter. Anyway, she rarely went out, and if his mother was coming with them that made it respectable. Didn't it?

At the Rovers Martha Longhurst greeted her: 'I was wonderin' where you'd got to.'

Annie smiled. Today even the Martha Longhursts of Weatherfield couldn't dampen her spirits.

As Martha slipped on her overcoat, woollen mittens and black beret she noticed Annie Walker looking in the mirror above the fireplace smiling at her own reflection. 'Everythin' all right, Mrs Walker?'

'Everything is fine, Mrs Longhurst. Thank you for asking.'

Martha hurried along the street to the Mission of Glad Tidings. She'd never seen Annie Walker so cheerful before, but she knew Ena would know what to make of it.

At No. 3 Ida Barlow looked at the clock on the mantelpiece. It was time to collect her Kenneth from school. He'd started in September at Bessie Street Infants and although his teacher said he was doing well he often seemed tearful when he came home. David, who was only two, sat on the floor stacking empty cotton reels, every so often toddling towards her, arms outstretched, for a cuddle. Ida had found David easier than Kenneth: he had a sunny, easy-going nature while Kenneth was always quiet and serious.

Ida walked to the school with David, and smiled at the few mothers who were waiting. Many of the five- and six-year-olds walked home alone – there was little traffic and always someone to look out for them.

When Kenneth came out of the school door she could see him looking for her anxiously. When he finally caught sight of her he ran towards her and grabbed her hand tightly. 'Did you have a nice day, pet?' she asked. He didn't answer, just lowered his head and watched his feet. He always avoided the cracks in the pavement, saying it was bad luck to step on them.

On the way home he hardly spoke. David was trotting along, chewing at one of his mittens. Ida smiled indulgently with a son on each side. Her little men.

'He's always doing that,' said Kenneth, pulling his brother's hand from his mouth.

David screeched.

'Now look what you've done,' said Ida. 'Leave our David alone!'

Once they were home she made fingers of toast with treacle but Kenneth refused to eat. David ate the lot, and before Ida had a chance to stop him had smeared sticky fingers on one of his brother's books.

'He shouldn't run round eating,' said Kenneth, snatching back his book and looking angry. 'It's not right.'

Ida sighed. Kenneth sometimes sounded like a little old

man. Everything will be all right when Frank comes home, she told herself.

'Can I go out, Mam?' asked Kenneth a little later.

'You mean next door?'

He nodded.

'Well, don't be a nuisance and don't be long.'

The Hayes family lived at No. 5. Ada was a teacher at Bessie Street School, and Kenneth seemed happier with her, which made Ida wonder what she was doing wrong. He still wet the bed at night, which worried her, but Ada Hayes said most children did it because of all the disturbed nights they'd had. But it was all right for *her* to say that when she had no children of her own. It was getting the sheets dry in wet weather that was the problem. Ida stared across at the clothes-horse by the fire. It was always up, and David loved to drag the wet things on the floor.

It was Friday night. Bath night. Ida began to fill the kettle and a few saucepans. She prayed there wouldn't be a raid before they'd finished.

Elsie Tanner's Friday night treat was going to the pictures. The kids were in bed and she sat smoking and reading the local paper. There were several cinemas to choose from; the Ritz was showing *In Which We Serve*, but she didn't see the point of watching war films these days. On at the Bijou was *Gone with the Wind*, which was more her cup of tea. She'd seen it before but anything with Clark Gable in was worth seeing ten times. If only, she thought, there were men like him in Weatherfield but since the GIs had gone it was mostly young lads and granddads who were left and the odd service-man on leave. Girls didn't have much choice now.

She looked at the clock. Half past six. Her friend Dot Greenhalgh (Dot Todd that was, before her marriage) would be knocking for her at seven and Vera Sharples was due at half past to keep an eye on the kids.

The tin bath was ready in front of the fire but Elsie still shivered as she took off her work clothes. She'd just soaped herself with her last bar of Lifebuoy when she heard a noise from the scullery. Her back door was always open but she wasn't expecting Dot for another fifteen minutes at least. Sod it! she thought. If anyone comes in now they either wash my back or take a running jump. No one did appear and the slight scrambling sound worried her only for a moment – just a cat on the scrounge.

She was out of the bath and half dressed when Dot yelled, 'Hiya,' as she appeared in the back room. Elsie, Dot Greenhalgh and her sister Sally Hart worked together. They all had men in their lives, but not in Weatherfield, and their attitude was that they were young and what their men didn't know couldn't hurt them. Dot had just married Walt Greenhalgh, a factory fitter now overseas, but she didn't pine for him. 'It's like 'e's on the back-burner,' she once said to Elsie. 'And that's where 'e'll stay till 'e comes 'ome for good.' Sally had married Ollie Hart, a US serviceman, in the summer and had been three-months pregnant then. Now she was blooming.

Dot began humming and did a little dance with her hands behind her back as she watched Elsie slipping on her blouse. 'It worked,' she said.

'What did?' asked Elsie.

'The notes we sent.'

The week before they'd hidden notes in the pockets of the uniforms they machined at Elliston's. It relieved the boredom and they liked to outwit the chargehand. 'Wotcha got?' asked Elsie, noticing now that Dot was hiding something.

'Close your eyes, Elsie, and 'old out your 'ands.'

Elsie laughed. 'It's not summat 'orrible, is it?'

'Well, it's not a dead rat.'

Dot put the parcel into Elsie's hands. Excitedly Elsie tore it open. 'Bloody 'ell,' she said. 'Nylons and butter. I've not tasted butter in ages. What's 'is name, then?'

Dot shrugged her shoulders. ' 'Ow should I know?'

'What? No note?'

Suddenly they were both laughing so much that Elsie nearly fell back into the still full tin bath. They were still laughing as they emptied it down the drain in the backyard.

When Elsie tried to share the treasures, Dot shook her head. 'The notes were your idea. What a bloody nerve you've got, askin' for little luxuries to be left at your back door. The bloke who left this little lot is probably a lunatic. Perhaps you should bolt your back gate.'

'Nah,' said Elsie. 'Who locks anything round 'ere? 'E was just a sex-starved sailor.'

'Or a soldier or an airman. We put in nearly as many notes as stitches.'

'Look, Dot, share and share alike – you 'ave 'alf this butter.'

'You keep it,' she insisted. 'Give it to the kids. Sally gets stuff from Ollie, and 'e earns more than your Arnold.'

Elsie sat down and pulled up the nylons, fixed the suspenders, then slipped on her highest heels. 'I'm in the mood to meet some lads tonight,' she said, doing a twirl. 'Then they could take us all dancin' tomorrow night.'

'Don't forget Sally's a married woman, and she looks pregnant now.'

'She 'asn't let that worry 'er so far,' said Elsie, as she admired the length of leg she was showing in her shiny nylons. 'As far as my 'usband's concerned, I 'ope I never clap eyes on 'im again.'

Half an hour later, Vera Sharples arrived looking flustered. 'I 'aven't told me mam I'm 'ere 'cos my Bob's coming round. Is that all right?'

' 'Course it is,' said Elsie, slipping on her coat. 'Don't go doin' owt I wouldn't do, will you?'

Vera nodded solemnly.

'And 'elp yourself to bit of butter, pet,' said Elsie, at the back door.

'Where did you get that from?' asked Vera, wide eyed.

'A secret admirer,' said Dot.

'Oo, eh,' murmured Vera.

'You've got your Bob,' said Elsie. ' 'E's like a secret admirer.'

'I s'pose 'e is,' murmured Vera thoughtfully. 'Ta-ra then.'

Outside it was perishing cold but they hardly noticed. 'That Vera's a cartridge short of a gun load,' said Dot, as she linked arms with Elsie.

'She's all right. Just a bit soft. Ena tried to stop her growin' up so she's a bit young for her age.'

Dot laughed, 'Not like us, is she?'

Elsie grinned back. 'No, but I'm doin' me best with 'er.'

The queue, mostly of young lads, was moving quickly. 'You girls gonna sit with us?' one asked.

'Nah,' said Elsie. 'Thanks, lads, but we're fixed up.'

'Are we?' asked Dot.

Elsie had seen a couple of soldiers join the queue. One had winked at her. 'Not yet, but we soon will be.'

The cinema was nearly full, and in the darkness Elsie and Dot became separated from their quarry by a pretty usherette with a torch. Soldiers came before civilians and they were given the best seats near the back. The girls peered into the darkness and eventually found two side seats near the front. 'Too bloody close to the screen,' complained Elsie. 'I'll 'ave neck ache in the morning.'

'You'll 'ave your throat cut if you don't be quiet,' said an irate voice behind them.

The film was already half-way through, and during the interval, as Elsie queued for a cup of squash, one of the soldiers whispered in her ear, 'Fancy a drink later, sweetheart?'

Elsie looked him up and down. He was tall, pale and skinny. She preferred his mate, who was stockier and had a cheeky grin. 'Just a quick one then. Our mams are expecting us home.'

He looked slightly disappointed but winked at her. 'See you out front then – ten o'clock.'

They came out at five past ten to find the lads waiting in the foyer. 'I'm Ted,' said the tall thin one. 'And he's George.'

Before Elsie could blink she was walking arm in arm with Ted, and he was trying to nibble her ear. 'Give over,' she said, irritated that she'd ended up with the skinny one. 'I said we'd 'ave a drink with you but I didn't say owt about chewin' me ear.'

Ted wasn't easily put off. 'You're the best-lookin' girl I've seen round 'ere. Me and George are goin' back to base tomorrow and then we're off to God knows where. I think you should try and be nice to us.'

Elsie didn't like him or his tone, and now they were outside it was as dark as a coal shed and she began to wonder if she hadn't made a mistake. Coronation Street seemed a long way away and she could hear that Dot was having trouble.

'If you must know,' she was saying loudly, 'I'm a married woman.'

'Don't worry me, love,' said George. 'Means you've 'ad a bit of experience. I like a lass who knows what she's doing.'

Elsie tried to think of a plan of action but Ted was fumbling with her coat buttons. 'It's bloody freezin',' she yelled. 'Don't do that!' She slapped his hand away but he took that as a playful invitation and tried to grope her breasts. As they turned into Rosamund Street she remembered that someone kept an Alsatian in a kennel in their yard.

'Come down 'ere,' she said, pulling him into the back alley, 'but keep quiet.'

Elsie wasn't sure which yard held the dog but at least she was expecting it and Ted wasn't. Suddenly the dog heard them and barked ferociously. Ted was thrown off guard and Elsie kneed him hard between the legs then added a kick on the shins for good measure. She wasn't sure where Dot was in the dark but she screamed, 'Run, Dot, run!'

She ran, the dog carried on barking and then the air-raid siren sounded. Dot caught up with her in Coronation Street and they carried on running until they reached No. 11, breathless and laughing. The siren wailed on but just as Elsie got out her key the all-clear sounded.

They were still laughing when they got inside. 'You two look as if you've 'ad a good time,' Vera said. 'Thank God the all-clear's sounded.'

'Yes,' said Elsie, still laughing. 'Thank Gawd for that.'

CHAPTER FOUR

Autumn 1943 The island of Corsica is taken by the French Resistance.

Business at the Rovers had been brisk. A few Weatherfield servicemen had managed to get forty-eight-hour passes and the single men had spent their wages at the Rovers, for which Annie was grateful. She was also grateful for the help of young Teresa Dakins – her new nanny. According to Ena Sharples, she was 'thinner than a stick of liquorice'. Annie had insisted Teresa wore a navy dress with a white apron, which made her look more like a waitress than a nanny. 'I'll look upon it as a penance, Mrs Walker,' she said, in her soft Irish accent.

Teresa had her own room at the Rovers, which she'd decorated with religious pictures. She went to Mass on Sunday, never asked for time off, and Billy's behaviour had improved so much that Annie was both amazed and delighted. How Teresa had managed it Annie didn't know. When she asked, the girl's thin little face lit up and beneath her thick glasses her brown eyes twinkled. 'Just one of God's little miracles,' she said. 'He performs them all the time, even when we don't see them.'

Now that she had help with the children Annie's life improved. She'd been to a concert and to supper with John Barnstable. Both times his mother had been there. Annie had found the old lady difficult. She was short and round with sharp eyes, deaf when it suited her and she talked in a loud voice. Once when John had gone to fetch their coats Mrs Ivy

Barnstable had leaned across and said loudly in Annie's ear, 'You're not a patch on his last girlfriend. She had real class. You just run a nasty little pub.'

Shocked, Annie said sharply, 'My public house is certainly not nasty. It's a pleasant refuge – and I'm not your son's girl-friend, I'm a married woman.' As the old woman stared at her Annie added primly, 'We are just friends. I can promise you that.'

'Aye,' said Mrs Barnstable. 'And Hitler signed a piece of paper promising not to invade Poland.'

Annie wrote to John telling him that in view of his mother's attitude it might be better if they didn't see each other again. He wrote back saying his mother was jealous of any friends he had, male or female, and he didn't want to lose her friendship. Would she meet him on Saturday for lunch in Manchester? His mother would not be there. He would wait for her at the railway station between twelve and twelve thirty.

It was Thursday and still Annie didn't know what to do.

Ena Sharples was first in the Snug. Rain was falling in torrents and she was glad to see a roaring fire. 'I'm glad to see you braved the weather, Mrs Sharples,' said Annie.

'Couldn't do owt else. I've got a bone to pick with Martha and Minnie.'

'What have they been up to?' asked Annie, as she poured Ena's milk stout. Normally Ena would have waited until she'd given her friends a dressing-down but since they weren't here she told Annie Walker. 'The Mission committee,' she explained, 'wants me to run a mother's group in the evenin' for hymn practice and Bible readings and suchlike. So I gets everythin' ready and not a Christian soul turns up.'

'Oh dear,' murmured Annie.

'You don't sound surprised.'

Annie looked round her near-empty pub. 'It's inclement weather, Mrs Sharples, and most mothers are very busy.'

'They shouldn't be too busy for the Lord. And I know for a fact there's two who promised to come and didn't.'

'I think this is the pair of them now,' said Annie, with a nod.

Ena turned towards the door as Minnie and Martha, soaked through, walked in. 'I want words with you two.'

'It was all my fault, Ena,' said Minnie, as she shook her coat over the old newspapers Mrs Walker had provided around the coat stand. 'There's no need to blame Martha.'

'You're both grown women, although sometimes, Minnie Caldwell, I think God forgot to help you grow up like He did my Vera.'

'Well, I think He's 'elpin' her now,' said Martha.

'What the 'eck do you mean by that, Martha Longhurst?'

'You're always sayin' the Good Lord moves in mysterious ways.'

'And what if I am? Explain yerself.'

Martha shrugged. 'Just that your Vera's been seen goin' in and out of Elsie Tanner's at all times of night. And I've 'eard said that Bob Lomax has been with her.'

'How dare you! My Vera's a good girl. She may be slow but she's been brought up in a good Christian home.'

'Well, it seems she prefers Elsie Tanner's heathen ways.'

Ena plonked herself down and sipped her milk stout as if it had the medicinal qualities of brandy.

'Don't upset yourself, Ena,' said Minnie. 'Martha and me was plannin' to come to the mission but I've got a bit of bother at home.'

'Don't talk in riddles, woman. What's all this got to do with my Vera?'

'Nothin' at all, Ena. As you said, Vera's a good girl. But I asked Martha to listen for me.'

Ena's glance at Minnie would have withered an irate camel but Minnie carried on nervously. 'As I said to Martha, if anyone can sort this out it'll be Ena.'

Ena's expression softened. 'Stop goin' round 'ouses, Minnie, and tell me what's up.'

Minnie eased herself to the edge of her seat. 'Ena, I've bin 'earin' noises for days now. I thought I'd gone doo-lally. Mam didn't 'ear anything.'

'Your mam is as deaf as a tin 'elmet.'

'Please, Ena, let me finish. My Mabel 'ears things no one

else does and 'er 'ackles and 'er fur kept goin' on end. So I asks Martha to come in the 'ouse and listen for me.'

'And?'

'She didn't 'ear anything. We 'ad to wait, you see. The noises seem to come at night. And I reckon it's . . . I reckon it's a ghost.'

'You're barmy, Minnie Caldwell. Your Armistead would be ashamed of you. Some daft ideas you do come up with. And 'ow come you didn't 'ear anything, Martha Longhurst? You could 'ear a whisper of gossip in an empty barn.'

Martha sniffed. 'I've never known *you* to refuse to listen to a bit of gossip.'

'That's as maybe,' said Ena, glaring at her. 'But Minnie 'ere is vergin' on going "up top road" so we'd better do summat before they come to take her away.'

The local mental hospital was 'up top road' and by now Minnie was near to tears. 'Call yourself a Christian woman, Ena?' she said. 'I'm right worried an' all you can do is mek fun of me.'

'You're always worried over summat, Minnie Caldwell, so take that look off your face or you'll turn the beer.'

Minnie muttered, 'I'm not stayin' 'ere to be insulted. I 'eard what I 'eard.' Then, with a glower at both Ena and Martha, she stood up, walked to the coat-stand, grabbed her coat and walked out without even putting it round her shoulders.

'That was right nasty, Ena,' said Martha. 'If you won't 'elp her, what's she goin' to do?'

'I didn't say I wouldn't 'elp her. I'll manage another milk stout and then get meself round to Minnie's for a vigil. I shall stay all night or until I 'ear summat. Ghosts! I've an idea the only ghosts she's got is a bird in the attic or mice under the floorboards.'

'I 'ate mice,' said Martha, shuddering.

'Don't expect they'd want to share your billet, Martha Longhurst. You wouldn't 'ave enough scraps to feed a cockroach.'

Twenty minutes later Ena was banging on Minnie's door. 'There's no need to knock so 'ard, Ena,' said a flustered Minnie, as she opened the door. 'Bangin' like that won't frighten ghosts away.'

'There's no such things as ghosts, and well you know it.'

'You'd better come in, Ena,' said Minnie, looking tearful. 'And I do believe in ghosts. What about angels and the Holy Ghost? I tek it you believe in them?'

Ena marched into the back room and surveyed the scene. Minnie kept a clean and tidy home. She was fond of lace, and there was a lace runner on the drop-leaf table and lace anti-macassars on the two armchairs. Although the lino was worn she'd made two rag rugs to cover the worst bits and for Mabel to sit on in front of the fire.

Ena slipped off her coat and handed it to Minnie. Then she sat in the chair nearest the fire. 'The Holy Ghost isn't a *real* ghost, Minnie,' she said. ' 'E's a good spirit, not a lost soul frightenin' folk to death.'

Minnie hung up Ena's coat and shook a few more lumps of coal from the scuttle on to the fire.

'You'd best put kettle on, then,' said Ena, picking up the poker to give the coals a helping hand. 'We'll see if your ghost wants to come out to play tonight.'

Minnie wondered if a ghost could be scared, like mortals. Because she had a feeling that Ena had it in her to scare anyone dead or alive – even 'Itler.

An hour later Minnie hadn't heard a sound. 'I've got a feelin' you may 'ave done the trick, Ena.'

'Too soon to say that, Minnie Caldwell. At first light we should bloomin' well know.'

'Are you stayin' up all night Ena?'

'Yes by 'eck, and you're stayin' with me.'

Minnie sighed and walked towards the door. 'I'll get some blankets, then.'

'And pillows. May as well be comfortable as we wait for our ghostie.'

'I do wish you'd take it seriously, Ena.'

'I'm 'ere ain't I? And God's on our side.'

'If you say so, Ena.'

At No. 11, Elsie had planned to get some ironing done but it was nearly ten o'clock and she hadn't even started. Once she'd got the kids to bed she'd sat down and fallen asleep. It had been a rotten day at the factory, the boiler had packed up and they'd had to work in their coats.

Dot had said she'd pop round at about ten so Elsie had planned to do some ironing before she came, but all she'd managed to do so far was heat up the flat-iron.

This time when she heard a noise she was quick, but not quick enough. All she could see in the dark outside was the twinkle of raindrops on the back of a tall man as he disappeared through the yard door. On the back step he'd placed three brown-paper parcels. She gathered them up, put them on the table and waited excitedly for Dot to turn up.

Within seconds Dot had appeared. 'Did you see him?' asked Elsie.

'See who? What are you talkin' about?'

Elsie pointed to the parcels on the table. 'Oh, my Gawd,' said Dot. 'Has he just been?'

' 'E probably passed you in the street.'

'Must be a bloody phantom then 'cos I didn't see a soul.'

Elsie could wait no longer. ' 'Ere, you open one,' she said, handing the biggest parcel to Dot. 'It might be more butter.'

Dot began tearing at the brown paper. 'It's better than Christmas, this is.' Inside was a small bottle of brandy, a bottle of 'Evening in Paris' perfume and a jar of Pond's Cold Cream. Elsie's packages contained a huge hunk of cheese, a bottle of Camp coffee and a two-pound bag of sugar.

'Gawd, Elsie, this must be black-market stuff. We'd better be careful.'

'Who's gonna find out about it? We 'aven't even seen 'im.'

Dot fondled the brandy bottle. 'There could be more than one bloke. And in this life you never get owt for nowt. He just wants to get into your knickers.'

'Well 'e'll find enough room,' laughed Elsie. 'All me knickers need new elastic.'

Dot looked serious. ' 'E doesn't know you, does 'e? I mean, nothin' gets left at my door.'

'Nah. 'Ow would he know me? 'E just thinks 'e's on to a good thing. 'E must be desperate.'

'Or just a barmy bugger.'

'Well 'e must 'ave some brass to buy this lot.'

For a few moments they stood silently contemplating their treasures until Dot starting sniffing. 'There's an 'orrible smell in 'ere, Elsie.'

'Oh bloody 'ell – it's me iron. It's been on the gas for ages.' She ran into the scullery and grabbed a tea cloth. The iron looked black on the bottom and it was red hot. 'Time for a drink, Dot. Sod the ironin'. 'Ow d'you fancy a cup of Camp with brandy?'

'Elsie, I haven't 'ad a brandy in years. Sounds smashin' to me.'

They sat and drank until the brandy bottle was empty and everything they said made them laugh. They laughed most about Ted and George. 'You should 'ave seen 'is face, Dot, when I kneed him in the nuts. I don't know what surprised 'im more, the dog barkin' or me 'armin' his essentials.'

'I don't reckon their essentials were up to much, do you, Elsie?'

Elsie laughed again. 'We'll never find out now, will we?'

'No, thank Gawd. Ugly beggars, weren't they?'

'It were too dark to see.'

'Just as bloody well.'

As she staggered home Dot was still smiling. She caught a glimpse of a man's shape ahead of her in the darkness but she didn't take any notice. The rain was still falling but she didn't take any notice of that either.

Tucked up under blankets Ena and Minnie slept in snatches. When Ena woke she made sure she wasn't alone. 'Minnie Caldwell, I 'aven't 'eard as much as a breath of wind in the bloomin' chimney.' Minnie, half-asleep, only grunted. With Ena for company she'd relaxed, believing any ghost would keep his or her distance.

It was nearly three a.m. when Ena woke again. She'd been dreaming of her dead husband Alfred and she felt bleary-eyed and not quite awake. But she'd heard something, and she would have sworn on the Bible that the gas lamps flickered at the same time as she heard the footsteps and a low moaning sound. 'Minnie, wake up. I've 'eard summat.'

'What's 'appened? What's to do?' Minnie sat bolt upright, rubbing her eyes.

'I'm not sure where it's coming from.'

Minnie couldn't help noticing the slight change in Ena's voice.

'You're not scared, are you, Ena?'

'Don't be so daft. I'm scared of nowt. But your Mabel's 'eard something.'

The cat was crouched on her haunches wide-eyed with terror. Minnie eased herself up from the chair and approached Mabel, but she was too fast and leaped away to cower under the table. 'Ooh, Ena, what are we going to do?'

'We'll keep our 'eads, that's what we'll do.'

'You've gone ever so pale, Ena, as white as Mabel's paws.'

'Stop mitherin', Minnie Caldwell, and listen.'

They both listened. The dying fire crackled in the grate and the gas lamps hissed softly, but otherwise the noise had stopped. 'It wasn't mice I 'eard,' said Ena, 'or even bats.'

Minnie shuddered. 'It is a ghost, Ena, isn't it? I've got no 'oles in me slates and me attic 'as only got a tiny little trap door. Nobody could get through it.'

'I don't want to say you're right, Minnie, but that wailin' noise didn't sound 'uman.'

'You think it *is* a ghost, then?'

Ena shrugged. 'There's more in 'eaven and earth than folk like us know about. I'm thinkin' we might need someone who'd know more about it than we do.'

'Who are you thinking of, Ena?'

'Mr Swindley. 'E'll know. 'E may not be much of a preacher but 'e'll 'elp us on ghosts. 'E'll say the right prayers and sing the right hymns.'

Minnie shook her head. 'I think we'll need a proper vicar for this with a dog collar and everythin'.'

'A chapel man is what we need, Minnie. We'll 'ave no hoity-toity church vicars in 'ere.'

'If you say so, Ena. What will Mr Swindley *do*?'

'I've just told you that. Now, let's get back to sleep. If it is a ghost it ain't goin' to ravish you in your sleep. Ghosts don't 'ave them sort of ideas.'

Minnie snuggled down beneath the blankets. 'I'd never thought of that, Ena.'

'Well, you wouldn't, would you, Minnie? Now, go to sleep and stop mitherin'.'

During the last few weeks Sally Hart had grown and grown, and her mother, Vi, had let out as many of her clothes as she could. 'I never showed at all till I was seven months gone,' Sally said to Dot, as they sat in the kitchen of No. 9, 'but now I feel like I've got a bag of cement up me jumper.'

'You're like a barrage balloon,' said Dot, laughing, 'but you're near your time so you'll be doing no dancin' for a while.'

'You will stay with me, Dot, if there's a raid, won't you?' said Sally, grabbing her sister's hand.

'Give over, Sally. Mam and me won't leave you for a second if the bombs are as near as Rosamund Street and falling like ruddy confetti.'

Sally managed a weak smile. She'd got terrible backache and she fidgeted on the hard wooden carver chair her dad usually sat in.

A few minutes later Vi came in with a loaf of bread and a pound of liver under her arm. 'That's grand, that is,' she said irritably, 'you two doin' nothin' while I've been queuing for hours. Get the irons on the stove. There's enough ironing to keep you two goin' all evenin'. I've got tea to cook and a pile of mendin' and since neither of you can thread a bloomin' needle . . .'

'Don't go on, Mam,' said Dot. 'Sally looks a bit peaky.'

Vi cast a quick glance at Sally. 'She's not due yet,' she said, as if Sally wasn't there. 'I reckon she's got 'er dates wrong. She don't look near big enough to me. I bet the 'ead's not down far enough yet.'

While Vi peeled potatoes and chopped cabbage Dot set two flat-irons to heat up. 'Don't forget to rub a bit o' soap on them,' said Vi. 'I don't want them iron marks on my clothes.'

'You're not ailin', Mam, are you?' asked Dot. 'You look ever so tired.'

Vi smoothed back some stray grey hairs from her forehead.

'What yer mean is I'm in a bad mood. Well, I am. Someone I know 'ad a cot for sale in Rosamund Street and when I got there it'd gone.'

'Never mind, Mam, we'll manage,' said Dot. 'We've got the drawer emptied from the press so we can mek do.'

Vi sighed. 'That's all I've ever done, mek do. I was 'opin' my first grandchild would at least 'ave a cot.'

'Mam,' Sally's plaintive voice came from the back room, 'I've got a bit o' backache.'

'So 'ave I, pet,' said Vi. 'You get on with the ironin'. It'll tek your mind off yer back.'

Sally struggled to her feet and soon had to admit that Vi was right. Standing up she did feel a bit better. Dot gave her a few hankies to iron while she folded sheets, and Vi grumbled in the scullery about the quality of the liver. ' 'Urry up, you two,' Vi called, after they'd been ironing for half an hour. 'I want to get tea cooked an' on the table.'

Dot rolled her eyes. With Vi in this mood they just couldn't win.

Once the ironing had been put away Dot laid the table and Sally resumed her place in the carver chair. ' 'Itch yerself up,' said Dot, as she slipped a cushion on the seat. Sally smiled with relief at the comfort. Vi had dished up liver, mashed potatoes and onions with gravy so thick it would have plugged sinks. Sally looked at her plate and felt sick. Her mother was a terrible cook. Blood was oozing from the liver and mixing with the lumpy gravy.

'Tek that look off your face, Sally,' said Vi. 'You needs to keep up your strength.'

Sally picked up her knife and fork and started on the cabbage. She looked across at Dot and winked at her. Dot knew what to do. 'Mam, is there any bread?' she asked.

'There's always bread, Dot,' said Vi, 'as you well know, but don't you go cuttin' it. You cut bread like a lumberjack. I'll do it.'

Once Vi had left the table Dot grabbed a piece of old newspaper destined to be torn into squares for the privy, wrapped the liver in it and thrust it into her handbag. Sally smiled with relief. When the bread appeared she ate a slice and said, 'That were nice, Mam, but I'm full now.'

Vi looked disapprovingly at the left-over vegetables. 'You eat too much bread, Sally, but you can mek a bit o' space for a nice rice pudding.'

Sally felt like crying – her stomach was gripping and gripping and her back hurt like someone was punching her. She heaved at the thought of her mother's rice pudding – she always got the skin and she hated that brown burnt bit.

Then, just as Sally thought she couldn't feel worse, she felt a gush of warm water trickle down her leg. The shame of it. She hadn't known she wanted to go, she'd had no warning. Mam would be cross about the cushion. Perhaps if she stayed put Vi need not know what had happened.

Sally struggled through a few mouthfuls of rice pudding, then Vi went out to start the washing up and Dot finished the rest.

'I've wet meself,' Sally whispered to Dot. 'I can't seem to stop going.'

'I'll 'ide the cushion,' Dot whispered back. 'You go and sort yerself out.'

A few minutes later Sally came back, looking ashen. 'I'm bleedin',' she said, as she sat down in her dad's chair. Then she gripped the arms as a spasm of pain took her breath away.

'Mam! Mam!' yelled Dot. 'Our Sally's bin tekken poorly.'

Vi rushed in, took one look at her daughter and knew. 'Our Sally's not poorly. It's her time.'

At that moment the air raid siren wailed. Sally clung to Vi's arm. 'I'm scared. Don't leave me, will you?'

Vi laughed. 'We'd like as leave you as a pigeon fancier would shut his birds out. Now then, Dot, you can put kettle on.'

'What for, Mam?'

'A brew, what do think? We'll be a good few hours yet.'

Sally refused to leave the chair for her bed. 'I don't want to lie down, Mam. If we get bombed I'll 'ave to try to mek it to the shelter.'

'You won't be able, pet. You just concentrate on 'avin' this baby.'

'I wet meself, Mam,' admitted Sally. 'On your best cushion.'

405

'Yer didn't wet yourself, pet,' said Vi, patting her daughter's hand. 'That was your waters breakin' – don't yer know nowt?'

Sally relaxed in the chair. Her mam seemed to know what she was doing and she felt a lot better now she knew she hadn't disgraced herself. The pains began to come every ten minutes or so but Vi got Dot to rub her sister's back hard with the heel of her hand right at the base of her spine and that helped.

An hour or so after the air raid warning they heard low rumblings in the distance. 'Nothin' to fret about,' said Vi. 'That's Manchester gettin' it. I've a feelin' in me bones it won't come Weatherfield way tonight.'

'I 'ope you're right.'

Sally was still in labour when the all-clear sounded at midnight. Dot felt near to tears on her sister's behalf. Sally was sweating and red in the face, and sometimes she cried out with the pain in her back. ' 'Ow much longer, Mam?' she asked.

Vi looked at her younger daughter sternly. 'A babby takes nine months to grow and they don't shell like peas whatever you 'ear 'bout women who only tek a couple of hours. Our Sally's goin' sure and steady and that's the best way. Too fast, and it's bad for the babby. Now, don't start shrikin', get that drawer out and put best towels on the bottom and a hottie underneath with a little vest, nightie and nappy warmin' up on it.'

Dot filled the stone hot-water bottle and took it upstairs. When she looked at the makeshift cot she found it hard to believe that perhaps by morning a new little person would be lying there.

When she came downstairs things had changed. Sally was grunting and trying to swear at the same time and now she was lying on the floor with her skirt up, no knickers and her legs wide open. 'There's nowt dignified about 'avin' a baby, is there?' said Dot, who had only the vaguest idea about childbirth.

'Yer dignity's the last thing to worry about,' said Vi. 'Now, Dot, you 'old her shoulders and I'll deal with other end.'

Sally could hardly think now. Something sharp was stabbing at her back and she knew she was making grunting noises. She couldn't go on, she was convinced of that. 'When I see the 'ead you can push, pet,' said Vi. 'You're doin' reet well now. It won't be long.'

Dot, holding Sally, had pins and needles in her feet, and every time Sally moaned she wanted to moan too. It seemed to go on and on.

'I can see the 'ead, our Sally,' encouraged Vi, who now had beads of sweat on her forehead. 'Nearly there, love.'

Sally pushed and grunted and grew redder in the face. An hour passed. Vi began to frown. 'Dot, I'll 'old 'er while you fetch pillows and towels and get a saucepan on the boil.'

Vi took over Dot's position and Dot stood stamping her feet to get rid of her pins and needles. 'Not bloody Christmas – now!' yelled Vi. Dot looked anxiously at her mother. Until now Vi had seemed confident but Dot sensed something had gone wrong and with a final worried glance at her sister she ran upstairs and began grabbing pillows and towels. In her hurry she nearly fell down the steep stairs. 'Don't break yer neck,' said Vi. 'I might need yer to find a doctor.'

Vi banked Sally up with pillows, placed the clean towels under her bottom and one across her belly, then gave her some water to drink. Dot put a saucepan of cold water on to boil then stood awaiting instructions. Sally, meanwhile, was groaning and seemed weak. 'You 'ang on Sally,' shouted Dot.

'There's no need to shout at 'er. She can still 'ear.'

'Mam, help me,' said Sally weakly.

'I'm goin' to, pet. Not long now.' Vi stood up, pushed Dot into the scullery and whispered, 'Get a doctor 'ere – quick!' She pressed a torch into Dot's hand. 'Look where you're going. It'll be black as a coalman's boot out there.'

And it was. The dark engulfed Dot. She half ran, half walked, hoping to see an ARP warden or a policeman but the street was deserted. She ran on to the Glad Tidings Mission Hall and banged several times on the door.

In moments, Ena Sharples appeared wearing a man's dressing gown and with curlers in her hair. 'By 'eck, Dot Greenhalgh, you're a noisy one.' Then, seeing the girl's expression, Ena asked, 'What's 'appened?'

'It's our Sally – she's 'avin' baby and summat's wrong. She needs the doctor.'

'You get back 'ome. I'll get doctor. There's a fire on the outskirts of Weatherfield and 'e'll most likely be there.'

Dot hesitated.

'Go on, girl. Run! You tell your mam I'll get 'im if I 'as to drag 'im there by 'is braces.'

Dot arrived home breathless. She took one look at her mother's face and then at Sally. 'She's gone all pale, Mam.'

'Where's the doc?'

'Ena Sharples is goin' for 'im. She says 'e's at a fire.'

'I'll wait no more than fifteen minutes. Our Sally's been pushin' two an 'alf hours.'

'What do we do, Mam, if doctor doesn't come?'

Vi put a finger to her lips and whispered. 'I'll do summat, don't you worry.'

'Oh, gawd, you're not goin' cut 'er belly open?' cried Dot in horror.

'Don't be daft, girl, and keep your voice down.'

Dot really didn't want to know *what* her mother was going to do. She felt sick.

'Give our Sally a little warm water and sugar and a drop of brandy in it.'

Dot found the emergency half-bottle of brandy in the front-parlour sideboard and took a swig herself before mixing Sally's drink. Then she sat on the floor and put the cup to Sally's lips. The brandy seemed to give her more strength and during the next pushing session she shouted out, 'Never again! I'll 'ave nowt to do with a man ever again.' When the pain passed she lay back exhausted on the pillows and murmured. 'I want my Ollie.'

'Now, listen 'ere and listen good, our Sal,' said Vi firmly. 'The doc ain't arrived so you've got to do what I say. You pushes when I tells you and not before. Dot 'ere will 'old yer legs. If yer wants to 'oller you can.'

'What are you goin' to do, Mam?' murmured Sally.

'I'm going to 'elp you, that's all yer needs to know.'

'I wish my Ollie was 'ere,' said Sally again.

'Thank Gawd 'e isn't,' said Vi. ' 'E'd be as much use as a torch to a blind man.'

Vi washed her hands carefully with Sunlight soap, picked

up a pair of scissors then took a deep breath. She was scared witless. She knelt on the floor and saw the expression on Dot's face. 'You just tek care of our Sal and tek no notice of me.'

Dot closed her eyes and Vi wished she could close hers too.

When the next contraction came it was fierce and Sally screamed out, 'Oh, Gawd, Mam! Oh, Gawd!'

'Start 'ollering, pet,' she said. 'You can push now for all you're worth.'

Seconds later Vi breathed, 'Thank Gawd for that.' She knew now the next push would do it. 'Come on, my sweetheart, nearly there.'

Sally pushed as if her life depended on it. Then, gloriously, the pain was over and she raised her head in time to see her baby's face just as the little mouth took its first gasp. She sank back. 'Oo, Mam,' she murmured.

Vi laid the baby on Sally's chest and covered him with a towel. 'What is it, Mam?'

Vi laughed. 'Oh, 'eck. I forgot to look.' She lifted the towel to check. 'It's a boy, and 'e's bloody perfect.' Vi could feel the tears of relief and joy running down her cheeks. It was the best moment of her whole life.

Sally smiled in tired contentment as the baby rooted for her breast.

Neither she nor Vi noticed that Dot had fainted.

Moments later an elderly doctor they had never seen before came in with Ena Sharples leading the way. He cut the cord. 'Grand job you've done, Mrs Todd. I couldn't have done better myself.' Vi swelled with pride, and after she'd paid him five shillings, he left. They quickly washed 'our Clark' and dressed him in his white nightie and cardigan. Ena made a brew and hot toast with dripping, and after three slices and hot sweet tea Sally's colour returned to normal.

'You don't mind 'im bein' called Clark, do you, Mam?' asked Sally drowsily.

'As long as 'e's not called Adolf,' said Vi, 'I'm 'appy.'

Her grandson soon nestled and fell asleep beside his proud mother and Vi added brandy liberally to her tea, Ena's and Dot's.

Dot still felt a bit shaky and was sorry to have missed the birth, but she was thrilled that Sally looked more like her old self – and as for 'our Clark' she could only look at him in wonderment. 'He's champion, Mam,' she said. 'Look at his 'air and 'is little fingers.'

'Aye,' said Vi. ' 'E's smashin'. I'm right proud of our Sal for bein' so brave.'

'It was you what 'elped her, Vi,' said Ena. And then, feeling she had to add a touch of realism to the event, said, 'Your Sally will 'ave her work cut out now.'

But nothing Ena Sharples said at that moment could alter the sheer happiness of the Todd family. 'A beautiful baby boy,' said Vi proudly, before swigging back a neat brandy. 'And he's my grandson.'

CHAPTER FIVE

Winter 1943 First major daylight raid on Berlin.

Ida Barlow read and re-read the letter. She'd had a postcard at Christmas from Frank, a standard issue POW card telling her that he was well. But now she had a letter and every word was precious. He was keeping busy, was glad the winter was nearly over and he was grateful for the Red Cross parcels they received. He said how much he missed his family and that he was sure the war would be over soon. She was to be brave and keep her chin up.

Bessie was as excited as Ida about the letter. 'That's lovely for you, pet. Just you look on the bright side – at least as a POW 'e won't be fightin' any more. 'E'll come 'ome to you safe and sound.' Somehow that didn't cheer Ida up. What would he be like when he came home?

'Now, come on, Ida,' said Bessie briskly, 'tek that face off yer. I've got some lovely bottled fruit for you. That'll cheer you up.'

Ida managed a smile as she hugged Bessie. 'I feel as if I'm always taking food from you and Albert.'

'Albert don't go short. You can tell that by the size of 'im.'

Ida smiled. ' 'E's a fine figure of a man – 'e's like Mr Churchill.'

' 'E'd like to run country, that's for sure.'

Bessie made a pot of tea while Ida woke David from his nap in the armchair. He snuggled, eyes still closed, on her lap. ' 'E's a little angel, isn't he?' said Bessie, as she laid down the tea tray. 'Let me 'old 'im for a while. You pour the tea and 'ave one in peace.'

Ida sat at the table deep in thought and drank her tea. 'You look worried, pet,' said Bessie. 'What's up?'

'It's Kenneth. He's a strange little lad. When I talk about his dad he doesn't look a bit pleased.'

'And you don't know why?'

Ida shook her head.

' 'E's jealous.'

'Of his own dad?' queried Ida, in amazement.

Bessie nodded. 'I've seen it before in the first war. Eldest boys like your Kenneth forget they're nowt but babes and start actin' like little men. 'Ow many times have you called 'im "your little man"?'

Ida thought about that. 'I s'pose you're right, Bessie.'

'I'm right,' said Bessie firmly. 'And I bet both the babbies sleep in your bed at night.'

Ida nodded. 'They don't sleep well on their own, Bessie. They start off in their own beds but what with the raids and everything they get scared.'

'You're not the only one who sleeps with their kiddies,' said Bessie. 'It's only natural in times like these. But then one day out of the blue a big stranger in uniform comes and 'e gets in bed with their mam. What must they think?'

'But e's their father.'

'That's as maybe, but they don't know each other, do they?'

Ida stared into her teacup as David struggled from Bessie's lap and toddled across the room to join her. 'What do I do about it, Bessie?'

'Nowt you can do, really. When your Frank does come 'ome 'e'll be jealous too. 'E'll want you all to 'imself and 'e'll want a bit o' peace.'

Ida looked even more worried now.

'Stop your frettin',' said Bessie. 'On Frank's first night back we'll 'ave the kids – give you a chance to be with Frank on yer own. And let's 'ope that day won't be far away.'

'Won't Albert mind?'

Bessie laughed. 'He loves those two as if they were 'is own, so don't you worry about that.'

Ida brightened as she imagined the day Frank would return, and how it would be to cuddle up in bed with her man once more. The only niggle of doubt she had now was that he might seem like a stranger to her too.

Betty Preston's job at Earnshaw's munitions factory had come as a shock to her. The boiler-suits they wore didn't flatter her buxom figure and it didn't suit her face to have her curly hair scraped back under a headscarf. Some of the women wore curlers under their scarves and didn't care how they looked. Betty wasn't as pretty as some but she did think being presentable was important, and she always tried to look well groomed. She had expected the work to be hard but the women were even harder.

Gradually she was getting used to the bad language and their continuous chatting about dancing and the men they'd met. It upset her that the married women seemed the worst. With their husbands away fighting, they all acted as if they were single again. Every week someone was to be found crying in the ladies' because they had been 'caught'. Most often they said their babies were premature, and with a little luck their husbands would never find them out, but one woman wasn't so lucky. Her husband had come home on leave unexpectedly and found her not only pregnant but with her boyfriend. It had nearly come to murder and both husband and boyfriend had been arrested. Betty had found it quite distressing but the women she worked with seemed to take it in their stride.

Betty had never had a boyfriend. Her father Harold was a strict God-fearing man and she'd been happy to live by his rules, but she had a mind of her own and now, at eighteen, she wanted to do what *she* wanted, not what her father thought she should do.

One Saturday evening she asked her sister Maggie to go to the pictures with her. Harold and their mother Margaret had fallen asleep by the fireside so they whispered together in the scullery. 'Come on, Maggie, it'll be a good film. You'll enjoy it.'

Maggie looked worried. 'What if 'e finds out?'

' 'Ow should 'e find out? We'll say we went to see a friend.'

Nothing Betty said could make timid Maggie change her mind. 'I'll go on my own, then. You can tell him I'm baby-sittin' or summat.'

'Lyin's a sin, Betty.'

Betty shrugged. 'Well, goin' to the pictures isn't. It's our patriotic duty to watch the Pathé News.'

'Who says?'

'I do,' said Betty.

'What about Mam?'

'What about 'er?'

'What'll I give 'er to eat?'

'There's always bread and drippin'. You know she'll eat anything.'

Betty crept out of the house and into the fresh night air. She didn't mind the cold – she was well padded enough – and it was a relief to be away from the stifling atmosphere at home. Although she was sure she loved her mam and dad, it wasn't easy.

Betty could just about remember her mother being different. She'd been a child then and she could remember her mam laughing and playing hide-and-seek with them or taking them to the Red Rec and pushing them on the swings. Then, as the years went by, she got quieter and took to eating. And she just got fatter and fatter. When the war started Betty thought she would lose weight but she didn't. Harold had insisted that both girls gave up their sugar ration for Mam, and he always seemed to find extras for her. He ate very little himself and most of his food found its way to their mother's plate.

Betty knew the neighbours called him 'Holy Harold', and he looked like a crow with his bent back and his black coat-tails flapping behind him. As for her mother, few people knew she was even alive. She hadn't left the house in years and Betty had realized as she got older that that was what her father wanted. Her mother was the queen bee who had to be fed and her dad was a worker bee who had to keep her sitting in the hive. It wasn't right, Betty thought, but what could she do?

Once she joined the cinema queue she put her family out of her mind. She wanted to enjoy herself even if she was on

414

her own. It didn't bother her that there were mostly couples standing outside the Bijou. She was just glad to be out of her Tile Street home and mixing with folk who just wanted to enjoy themselves.

The long queue was slow-moving and people got bored. Someone started singing 'It's A Long Way To Tipperary' and she soon found herself joining in. She had a good voice – she'd even sung in the church choir before the war and she was enjoying herself so much she didn't notice the man in uniform edging nearer to her. When he began singing, too, she did notice him. He had a fine deep voice and he could sing in tune. Betty was so impressed she turned to look at his face. His face was as handsome as she'd expected from his voice, and she turned away as she blushed. When they'd finished singing he tapped her shoulder. 'You have a lovely voice.'

To Betty's ears he sounded posh. He was from down south she could tell. 'You sounded champion too,' she said.

'I'm Ted Farrell. Corporal. I'm stationed in Manchester. All on my tod and looking for a pretty girl to share the evening with.'

'You're a bold one,' said Betty, and giggled.

'Fair maiden was never won over by a chap who didn't breach the front line.'

'You talk ever so posh,' said Betty. 'You're not from round 'ere are you?'

He smiled. 'Yeah, I'm really posh. I say "barth" and "parth" and "bus". I can't quite say "boos" like the locals do. I'm from Portsmouth where they speak proper English.'

Betty couldn't let that go. 'There's nowt wrong with the way people round 'ere speak.'

'Did I say there was? Now I've met you the north is improving by the minute. It would get even better if I knew your name.'

'Betty Preston.'

'Well, pretty Betty Preston, now we've been properly introduced perhaps we could sit together to watch the picture.'

No one had ever called Betty pretty. 'Oh, all right,' she said, suddenly shy and a bit unsure. When they got to the box office he insisted on paying.

Betty could hardly concentrate on the film she was so conscious of the handsome soldier sitting beside her. Most of the Weatherfield lads were too rough for her and those who knew her wouldn't come anywhere near because of 'Holy Harold'. She resolved there and then to lie about where she lived. Since she'd worked at Earnshaw's she'd learned more about the world and she realized that if her dad had his way she'd turn out like her mother. She had a feeling that Corporal Ted Farrell was going to become very special to her, and Betty wasn't going to let anyone come between them.

That night Ida Barlow and Bessie Tatlock were in the cinema. Bessie had asked Albert to baby-sit because Ida hadn't been out in the evening for weeks and she was definitely looking peaky. During the Pathé News there was a little feature on 'make do and mend' and forming neighbourhood sewing groups.

'We could do that,' whispered Bessie.

Ida didn't answer. She was thinking about Frank's last leave and wishing she could turn the clock back. Was he getting enough to eat, she wondered. He was fussy about his food and thought foreign food was ' 'orrible'.

'What do you think, Ida?' Bessie persisted.

'Aye. It's a good idea.'

On the way home Bessie talked non-stop. 'We could put a little notice in Mrs Foyle's shop. There's those that can't sew in the Street – the likes of Elsie Tanner for one. She might like some of her clothes altered, and Mrs Walker, she likes to be fashionable. We could charge them just a little.'

Ida nodded. She wanted to get home as quickly as possible. She wasn't used to being out after dark, socializing. She was only used to rushing to the Glad Tidings Mission Hall shelter and she had a strange feeling in the pit of her stomach – as if she was about to hear bad news.

Bessie carried a tiny torch but it was only as bright as a match in the dark. In the alleyway leading to the back door she stumbled first against a dustbin and then, in Ida's yard, her toe hit a flower-pot. They both laughed nervously. 'Do be careful, Bessie. Albert will think you've had a drink.'

Bessie chuckled. 'I can't remember last time I 'ad a drink. I reckon that was Christmas 1939. I don't like the taste of the stuff.'

Ida was about to answer when she heard a creaking sound. It was the privy door opening. 'Oh, Lor'!' shrieked Bessie, as a man appeared. In the darkness all either of them could see was a sailor's uniform. Just for a moment Ida stood open-mouthed, thinking by some miracle it was Frank. Then he spoke and she realized he was a stranger.

'Sorry, ladies,' said the sailor, moving nearer to them. 'I've been in the Rovers drinkin' with me mates and I got took short. I saw your back gate was ajar and I was desperate, if you know what I mean.'

'Where are you off to now, then?' asked Bessie.

'I'm 'oping to find a mate in Manchester. 'E'll give me a bed.'

'I bet you've missed the last bus,' said Bessie. 'You can stay with us, if you like.'

He paused, but not for long. 'That's very good of you, missus. It'd be a treat.'

Ida gave him a shy smile, 'What's your name?'

'Ron – Ronald Feathers. They call me Duck in the Navy.'

Albert Tatlock looked up in surprise as they entered with a sailor in tow but he stood up and shook his hand. 'Are you hungry, lad?'

'I'm always 'ungry,' Ron said. 'Me mother couldn't cope with me appetite. I reckon that's why she wanted me to join up.'

Albert tapped out his pipe. 'That's one thing about the services, they do try to keep you stoked up. You can come next door if you like, my missus'll give you summat tasty.'

'No, I'll do it,' said Ida eagerly. 'It's nice to cook for a bit of company.'

Ida went into the kitchen with Bessie and began peeling potatoes. ' 'E's a nice-lookin' lad,' said Bessie. 'My Albert loves a chat with a serviceman – 'e'll keep the lad up till the early hours.'

Ida only had a little bit of cheese, bread, two slices of ham and some rice pudding in the larder. She sliced the potatoes thinly and fried them in a little square of lard. Bessie cut some bread and spread it with margarine then made a pot of tea.

Ron seemed well pleased with the food, and Ida watched him eat with satisfaction. It was a treat to cook for a man but she wished he was her Frank.

Once the Tatlocks and Ron had left, the house seemed very quiet. Ida reread Frank's letter and when she went to bed that night she kissed his photo. 'You'll soon be 'ome, pet,' she said aloud. 'Where you belong.'

Betty and Ted Farrell walked out of the Bijou into the dark and the wailing of the air-raid siren. 'It won't be much,' said Ted.

Betty laughed. ' 'Ave you got 'Itler's word on that?'

Ted took her hand. 'Come on, Betty, it might only be one Luftwaffe plane but it could still finish us off. Let's run.'

'Where to?' asked Betty, out of breath after a few hundred yards.

He stopped. 'You tell me. I'm lost.'

'The Glad Tidings Mission Hall on Coronation Street – it's nearby.'

'I'm not doing any praying,' said Ted, squeezing her hand.

When they arrived Ena Sharples was already playing the harmonium. She was singing 'Onward Christian Soldiers' at the top of her voice.

Betty looked round nervously. She'd never been the subject of gossip but she might be now if one of Earnshaw's girls saw her. She knew a few people by sight but now the raids were shorter and fewer the numbers flocking to the Mission cellar had dwindled. Ida Barlow sat on a mattress with her two children, who were half asleep. Betty thought she looked as if she'd been crying. Martha Longhurst, Ena's friend, was making cups of tea and handing them round. In all there were only about eight people. Betty knew that most sheltered now under heavy tables or a Morrison shelter in their front rooms. Her own mother didn't move from her chair and Harold, believing the Lord would protect him of all people, sat beside her, praying loudly so that God would hear him above the drone of the Stukas.

Ted found a spare mattress and they sat down together and joined in with the singing. He put an arm around Betty's shoulder and she didn't mind a bit.

She felt quite sorry when the all-clear sounded half an hour later.

CHAPTER SIX

Winter 1943 The Russians enter Romania.

'Minnie Caldwell's ghost is summat like the war,' Ena said, as Martha placed a half-pint of milk stout on the table in the snug of the Rovers. 'It lies a bit quiet for a while but doesn't bloomin' well go away.'

'What you going to do about it, Ena?'

'I've already done it. Mr Swindley's goin' to exercise the 'ouse in the mornin'.'

'Exercise, Ena? You mean flappin' your arms about and doin' knee-bends? What good'll that do?'

'Don't be so daft, Martha Longhurst.'

Martha wasn't put out. 'You've got the wrong word, Ena, and I'm goin' to ask Annie Walker. She knows nowt but long words.'

Annie Walker smiled graciously at Martha's question. 'The word is *exorcize*, not exercise. Is this Minnie Caldwell's ghost, by any chance?'

Martha nodded.

'I believe,' said Annie, 'that exorcism is best performed by the Church of England. They do follow a prescribed ritual.'

Martha's mouth dropped open. There was something different about Annie Walker these days. She was even more snobby than usual . . . but there was something else and it irritated Martha that she didn't know what it was.

She returned to the Snug deep in thought. 'Are your corsets too tight for you, Martha Longhurst?'

'What are you on about, Ena?'

'Your face.'

'It's *exorcize* not bloomin' PT.'

Ena shrugged. 'I'm sure that's what I said.'

'By 'eck you didn't – and you know it.'

'I'm not 'ere to argue, I'm 'ere to make sure you turn up at Minnie Caldwell's in the morning. She's twitchin' and twitterin' like an 'ungry sparrow. She'll need 'er friends.'

'Like as not I'll be there.'

Ena sighed. 'There's something on your mind, Martha. I know you too well. What's up?'

' 'Ave you noticed owt different about Annie Walker?'

Ena folded her arms. 'Out wi' it, Martha. She's bin botherin' you for a while so it's 'bout time you told me what's on your mind beside your usual misery.'

'I reckon Annie Walker's got an admirer.'

Ena leaned forward. 'You're like Sherlock 'Olmes you are. Who's got 'is eye on 'er, then? Whoever 'e is 'e must need his 'ead testin'.'

'Some 'ould say she was a good-lookin' woman.'

'No one round 'ere,' said Ena. 'Mind, if she didn't open her gob there might be a few blokes who'd give 'er a second glance.'

'Maybe 'e's not from round 'ere.'

Ena thought about that. 'You keep your ears open, Martha. If she is messin' with a fancy man then Jack Walker should be told.'

'Ooh, Ena, you wouldn't.'

'Wouldn't I? Jack Walker is a gent, and if she's messin' around it's my duty to warn 'im so 'e can put things right.'

'Who says it's your duty, Ena?'

Ena pulled back her shoulders and stared at Martha. 'As caretaker and resident of the Glad Tidings Mission Hall I'm specially placed to do God's work. And in the marriage vows what does it say?'

'Which bit, Ena?'

'It says, "Let no man put asunder".'

'Does it, Ena – us under what?'

'Asunder,' repeated Ena. 'Don't you know owt? Go and ask

Annie "Long Words" Walker. She'll tell you. And get in another couple of milk stouts while you're at it.'

That night the siren sounded just as Annie Walker got into bed. It'll be a false alarm, she told herself. She waited for a while to see if Teresa woke up, but she didn't, and Billy and Joan both slept on. She heard low rumbles a long way away so she listened but didn't move from the warmth of her bed. If the bombing came nearer she could gather up the children and be in the cellar in less than a minute. When the all-clear sounded half an hour later she snuggled down again and had just started to drift off to sleep when she heard noises. That silly idea of Minnie Caldwell's about a ghost must be playing on my mind, she told herself. First she heard a click, then a slight thump.

'Teresa, is that you?'

There was no answer. 'Billy?' she called.

Still no answer.

When the bedroom door handle moved, Annie sat bolt upright in bed with her breath caught in her throat and her heart thumping as hard as a beer barrel on cobbles. The door opened slowly with a whining creak. Annie picked up the torch she kept on her bedside table and shone the beam at the door.

'Annie, love, it's only me,' said Jack, as he stumbled into the room.

'Jack, whyever didn't you let me know you were coming home?'

'Didn't know meself. I've only got twenty-four hours. So give us a kiss, Annie.'

Annie sensed there was something different about Jack. It was only when she did kiss him that she realized what it was. 'Jack Walker, you're drunk!'

'Correct!' he said, saluting and staggering at the same time. Annie helped him on to the bed and undressed him. 'I met some mates of mine,' he said, as she took his socks off, 'and we only 'ad a couple of pints.'

Before Annie could think of a suitable reply Jack had turned on his side and was snoring heavily. Annie lay awake miserably listening to her husband. She had never known him to be drunk before. He'd always been a gentleman, a cut above the other men in Weatherfield. Now he was like all the rest. John was a *real* gentleman. Jack had changed. She didn't know him any more and worse than that was that, just then, she didn't really care.

Minnie Caldwell hadn't slept a wink since the all-clear. She hadn't left the house because she couldn't leave her mother alone. Amy was only in her sixties but rheumatoid arthritis had crippled her and she was deaf too. The doctor had long since given up on her condition, recommending only splints and aspirin. Amy refused the splints but took the aspirin, and although Minnie found her mother hard work she loved her dearly. Amy had little appetite, and Minnie thought herself lucky that she had extra coupons and that she had an excuse for not leaving the house for every air-raid. 'I'm more than 'appy to die in me bed, Minnie,' Amy would say, 'so you get to a shelter and leave me in peace.'

When Minnie tried to argue, Amy would look up to heaven and say, 'When your number's up, it's up, and it's the Good Lord that decides, not that ruddy 'Itler.'

Minnie tossed and turned the rest of the night as every noise in the house magnified. When she heard her back door open she began to shake. She pulled the eiderdown over her ears and prayed that she was imagining things.

'It's only us,' came Ena's voice, followed by heavy footsteps. Minnie looked at the clock – it was half past eight. Most days she was up by six. Hurriedly she slipped on her dressing-gown and slippers and walked downstairs, feeling so shaky she had to hold on to the bannister. 'I locked the back door,' said Minnie. ' 'Ow did you get in?'

'Since we know you leave the key under the flower-pot, Minnie Caldwell, it wasn't difficult,' said Ena, as she sat down. 'And, by 'eck, you look a sight – I've seen back end of a skinned pig lookin' better than you do now.'

'Leave her alone, Ena,' said Martha, straight-faced. 'You might spook 'er.'

'Go on, laugh at me,' said Minnie. 'You won't laugh when you 'ear the wailin' and the moanin'.'

'The Good Lord will see you right, Minnie,' said Ena. 'I *'ave* been prayin' for you.'

'It's done nowt to 'elp me so far.'

'I think,' said Ena, 'you should get dressed first then we should 'ave a pray 'stead of doing nowt but frettin'.'

'Yes, Ena,' said Minnie.

'Well, don't just stand there, Minnie, like Lot's wife! Get a move on.'

Minnie came down minutes later, hoping that Ena had made a brew, but tea wasn't on Ena's mind. 'Kneel down, you two,' she said, 'we 'ave to do it right.'

The three knelt on the floor and Ena began praying: 'Dear Lord, our poor friend 'ere, Minnie Caldwell, 'as been 'avin' problems with an uneasy spirit. We know you're looking down on us but we'd be ever so grateful if—' She was interrupted by a loud knock at the front door.

Minnie gasped in surprise. 'Calm down, Minnie,' said Ena rising to her feet. 'It's not the Second Comin', it'll be Mr Swindley.'

He was a slim, dapper man whose sermons, according to Ena, 'roused as much fire in the belly as a bowl of blanc-mange'. But he had offered to try his hand at exorcism for a fee of half a crown, and Ena had found out that a Church of England vicar cost twice that.

Mr Swindley wandered around the room, listening at walls and muttering to himself. 'I sense there is a presence,' he said, 'but the Lord is here too.'

'Praise the Lord,' said Ena loudly.

'Yes indeed,' said Mr Swindley. 'You say the sound comes from above, Mrs Caldwell?'

Minnie looked upward fearfully. All eyes followed hers. 'Lord,' Mr Swindley called loudly, 'Lord hear our prayer for the soul in torment. We are kneeling before you—' He broke off. 'Kneel down, everyone, close your eyes and think of the Lord.

'Lord,' he began again, 'if this poor soul has sinned in a previous life—' He broke off to clear his throat. 'And we have all sinned. She is sorry now and begs forgiveness . . .'

'Is it a woman?' whispered Minnie.

'That's nowt to do wi' it,' said Ena. 'Shut up and pray.'

If Mr Swindley heard, he didn't let it put him off. 'Cast her out, Lord, of this 'umble 'ome, set her free to be beside the still waters. The Lord is my shepherd, he leadeth me beside the still waters, he restoreth my soul . . .'

By the time they had finished the twenty-third Psalm and sung 'Guide Me O Thou Great Redeemer', their knees were aching and their throats were parched. They were all getting to their feet when they heard a thump from above.

'Hallelujah!' shouted Mr Swindley excitedly. 'The Spirit moves. Praise the Lord.'

Minnie didn't look convinced but all was silent as they listened for more noises from above.

'There,' said Mr Swindley. 'We can be sure that the good Lord's word 'as been 'eard. You'll be troubled no more. That'll be two shillings and sixpence.'

It was only an hour after everyone had left that Minnie heard weeping from above. This time she didn't put her faith in the Lord. She cried out in despair, 'Oh, Ena, what am I going to do?'

Harry Battersby and Hilda Crabtree were at the Tripe Dressers Arms and Harry had ordered the drinks. He handed Hilda hers and at first sip she thought her port and lemon tasted strange. ' 'Ave you put gin in this?' she asked.

He shook his head. 'Nah, don't be daft. Just sup up, 'Ilda, and be grateful.'

Hilda looked round for somewhere to deposit the drink and in the corner of the Snug noticed a wilting aspidistra. Harry began talking to the men standing at the bar and she found herself ignored. After she'd fed two drinks to the plant Harry lurched towards her. There was no doubt about it: he couldn't hold his drink and she didn't like the look in his eye.

'I'm off to powder me nose, 'Arry,' said Hilda.

' 'Urry back, lass. I'll be walkin' you 'ome soon.'

It sounded like a threat, and Hilda retreated to the ladies' lavatory to think through her escape plan. The back window was a bit small, even for her, and she couldn't face the indignity of getting stuck. She tidied her thick dark hair, reapplied her lipstick, pulled her shoulders back and walked out to the bar. Harry Battersby, you're not going to get the better of me, she said to herself.

He was still surrounded by a rowdy group of soldiers, but he was slumped against the bar looking as if his legs had turned to jelly. At nineteen Hilda hadn't had much experience of men but she knew that Harry no longer posed a threat. ' 'Arry, I'll tek you 'ome,' she said, grasping his arm.

Someone laughed. 'You be gentle with 'im lass – 'is wife'll 'it 'im with a saucepan when 'e eventually gets in.'

Hilda was shocked at this but she was too proud to show it, especially to a group of drunken men.

She half dragged Harry out into the darkness, fished in the pocket of her jacket, found her torch and shone it low on the ground. The fresh air rallied Harry and he managed to walk with only a slight list towards Hilda. 'I thought you was stayin' with yer mam,' she said. 'You should 'ave told me you was married.'

'My missus don't like me much. But you, 'Ilda, are my sort of lass.'

'That's as mebbe, 'Arry Battersby, but I'm a respectable girl and I don't go drinking with married men.'

'Does that mean,' slurred Harry, 'that I won't be seein' you again, 'Ilda?' My sweet little 'Ilda.'

'I tell yer somethin', 'Arry, if 'Itler ever rides a bike to your front door I'll 'ave a drink with yer.'

'That's a no, then, is it?'

'You're 'ome,' she said, as she propped him against his front door. 'Ta-ra.'

She'd just got to the corner of Gladstone Terrace when the siren sounded. She hesitated for a moment – which shelter? The glue-factory cellar was too smelly and she couldn't bear the warden at the Glad Tidings Mission Hall – bossy old bag. She began running down Upper Edward Street – she could run like a whippet but she'd got her best shoes on and they cramped her toes and her running style. She'd nearly made it to the Crimea Street shelter when she heard Stukas overhead. She shone her torch upwards as if that would help her judge if one of the bombs were coming her way. 'Put that light out!' boomed a loud voice from nowhere. In her confusion she dropped her torch but carried on running until she made out the shape of the Co-op. She'd just rounded the corner when her foot hit something solid. She and one of her shoes went flying.

'What the flippin' 'eck!' The fall had winded her and the mound she'd tripped over moved. Big hands helped her to sit upright. ' 'Ello, chuck.' In the dark, Hilda struggled to pull down the skirt of her favourite green suit and find her shoe. 'What the 'ell are you doing sittin' there like a big dozy dog?' She didn't give him the chance to reply. 'The Stukas could come back this way. You should be in a shelter. Now, where the 'ell is me shoe? I've already lost me torch.'

'I've got mine, love.'

'Well, don't just sit there bein' gormless, 'elp me find me shoe – and don't you "love" me. My names 'Ilda Crabtree – Miss.'

'And I'm Stanley Ogden – Private 84265517.'

He took his torch from his khaki trouser pocket and shone it in her face. She snatched it from him and shone it back in his face, but in those few seconds Stanley had seen big bright eyes and a tumble of dark hair. She looked just like his favourite aunt Cissy.

Hilda's first glimpse of Stanley surprised her. He was clean-shaven with a fine, squarish head, and as he helped her to her feet she noticed he had good strong arms. He wasn't Clark Gable but he was the nearest she'd find to him in Weatherfield. 'If you 'elp me find me shoe and me torch you can see me 'ome – if you're not too drunk.'

'I can 'old me drink,' he said. 'I just came over a bit tired like. It's me first day back in Blighty.'

'Well, it's your lucky day then, Stanley. Because if you 'adn't come over tired, like, we'd never 'ave met, would we?'

'The all-clear 'asn't sounded yet, 'Ilda.'

'Well, we'll just pretend it 'as 'cos I ain't 'oppin' on one leg to a shelter.'

'I could carry you,' said Stanley.

427

'Plenty of time for that, Stanley Ogden. We 'ave to get to know each other first.'

Somehow Stanley didn't doubt that Hilda Crabtree would do just that.

Now that Hilda had set her sights on Stanley Ogden she wasn't going to let him rejoin his unit without a ring on her finger.

They'd been to the pictures and Stan wanted a beer. They went into one or two pubs but didn't stay long.

'Let's go somewhere all quiet and private, like,' he'd suggested.

Hilda held tight onto his arm as they walked back to Kitchener Street. 'I know what you're after Stan. I'm doin' nowt wrong and takin' chances so you can think again.'

'I've got to be back soon 'Ilda. You might not see me again.'

'Best not to do summat I might regret, then.'

'I thought you liked me. You said I was a fine figure of a man.'

'There's nowt wrong wi' you but if I gets caught who'll look after me then?'

'If yer gets in trouble I'd 'ave to marry yer, 'Ilda.'

'Would yer, Stan?'

He shrugged. 'Yeah, why not?'

'That's settled, then.'

'What is?'

'Us getting wed.'

Stan's thoughts floundered. Eventually he sorted something out. 'I meant I'd wed yer if we got caught.'

'What if I was to say, Stan, that I knew somewhere we could go tonight?' She squeezed his hand and moved closer to him. Stan smelt her *eau-de-Cologne* and was defeated.

' 'Ilda?'

'What?'

' 'Ave you been with a man before?'

She dropped his hand as if it were a hot pie. 'Stanley Ogden, 'ow dare you? I'm only nineteen and no man 'as ever as much as seen me stockin' tops.'

Stanley breathed a sigh of relief. He didn't want to admit he was still as pure as an unfired rifle. Her expectations wouldn't be that high, and he felt so excited at the mention of her stocking tops he thought getting wed was a small price to pay. After all, when the final push came in Europe he might not make it home and, if so, he would never know the pleasure of Hilda's legs with or without her stocking tops.

'All right, then, 'Ilda.'

'All right what?'

'We'll get wed. Now, where's that place we can 'ave a kiss and a cuddle?'

'When?'

'When what?'

'When can we be wed?'

'I dunno. Soon.'

'It'll 'ave to be soon 'cos you're due back. Tell you what, Stanley, we could get a special licence.'

' 'Ow long does that take?'

'Three days.'

Stanley had thought about it for a few minutes. It would mean going AWOL but the thought of being alone with Hilda was overwhelming him. 'Right, then, you arrange it, 'Ilda, and we'll be wed in three days.'

She took his hand. 'Thank Gawd you've seen sense, Stanley Ogden. I'll tek you to that place I knows now.'

Stanley could hardly wait but as they walked towards the Red Rec he began to get suspicious. 'There's nowt round 'ere, 'Ilda.'

'It's not a bloomin' palace but we'll be on us own.' Hilda took Stanley's spade-like hand and, with her own torch, led him across the allotments that now took up all the space on the Red Rec. Each allotment owner had built his own little shed out of bits and pieces of wood and Hilda had already decided which one it was to be – her dad's. She knew where he put the key and that it was clean and tidy inside. 'This is it, then, Stan. The key's under the flower-pot.'

'Give us the torch – I can't see a ruddy thing.'

Stan lifted the flower-pot that stood to the right of the shed and stared down in the torchlight. 'There's nowt 'ere.'

429

'Give us that torch, Stanley. You're useless.'

Hilda shone the beam in every nook and cranny surrounding the shed. There was no key. She couldn't believe it.

'I reckon,' said Stanley, 'you've bin tryin' to lead me on. There's nowt 'ere for us. I'll tek you 'ome.'

'You'll do no such thing, Stanley Ogden. I can't abide a man who gives up easy. We'll try the other sheds – there'll be one open.'

It was wet and muddy underfoot and a light drizzle began to dampen Stanley's ardour. After finding four locked sheds he said, 'I've 'ad enough of this.'

'Shush, Stanley,' whispered Hilda. 'I can 'ear summat.'

Stanley couldn't hear a thing at first but then he caught a shuffling noise and what sounded like a woman giggling. ' 'Ide yerself, Stanley,' said Hilda, giving him a little push. They crouched down by the side of the shed and listened.

It was quiet for a while and Stanley's right leg went into spasm. 'I'm gettin' ruddy cramp.'

'Keep quiet,' urged Hilda. 'Give it 'ere. I'll rub it.'

Stanley tried to alter his position but sprawled across Hilda instead. A man's voice from behind them said, ' Shed's free now, mate. You two will get nowt but piles on wet ground.'

Hilda, mortified, scrabbled quickly to her feet. She heard the woman laughing but already the couple were just vague shapes in the dark.

'Did you see who it was?' she asked.

'Give over,' said Stanley, rubbing his calf muscle. 'I can't see through me arse.'

'No need for swearing, Stanley Ogden. At least now we can go inside in the dry.'

Once they were inside with the door closed there was standing room only. The shed smelt of compost and damp and Hilda hardly gave Stanley time to get his bearings. She clung round his neck, nibbling at his ears and saying, 'Oh, Stanley, we're alone at last.'

Twenty minutes later they emerged. He felt like he had when he'd got away from Dunkirk – relieved, happy and a bit shell-shocked. Hilda had told him what to do and he'd done

it. His major disappointment was that it had been too dark –
he still hadn't seen her stocking tops.

'Not bad, Stanley,' said Hilda, as they made their way
across the allotments. 'We'll soon be wed and then you'll learn
to do it properly.'

'I've 'ad no complaints before.'

'That's as maybe, Stanley, but some girls are 'appy with
owt.'

All the way back to Kitchener Street he tried to work out
what she meant.

Stanley Ogden and Hilda Crabtree were married at
Weatherfield Register Office by special licence. Hilda wore her
green suit and a green felt hat with an added half veil. Stanley
wore his Army uniform and wished he could have sunk a few
pints before the ceremony. He confessed as much to Hilda.
'Never mind, Stanley,' she said. 'After we're wed we can 'ave a
drink in every pub in Weatherfield.'

Stanley was grateful that the ceremony took less than ten
minutes and he only felt happy after he'd had his first pint in
the Tripe Dressers Arms. At each pub they went into they
proclaimed they'd just got married and there was always a
well-wisher to buy the next drink. Stanley felt happier and
happier as the day passed.

In the evening they had a fish supper, then made their way
to the Rovers.

Martha was getting in the milk stouts when they came in
and she heard Stanley telling everyone he'd just got wed.

'Ena, 'ave you seen that couple at the bar?' she said, as she
placed the drinks on the table.

Ena craned her neck. 'That's 'Ilda Crabtree and Stanley
Ogden – they 'aven't known each other five bloomin' minutes.'

'Special licence,' said Martha. 'I 'eard them say that.'

'I think that's romantic,' said Minnie.

'You would, Minnie Caldwell,' said Ena. 'I say, "marry in
'aste repent at leisure".'

'I didn't wed in 'aste,' said Martha, 'and look what 'appened
to me.'

'Your Percy 'as no stayin' power,' said Ena.

'He hasn't much with me but he managed right enough with that barmaid,' Martha said regretfully.

'Some men like trollops,' said Ena, 'and no one could accuse you of owt like that.'

Martha sighed and sipped her milk stout.

CHAPTER SEVEN

Spring 1944 Sevastopol is liberated by the Red Army.

Elsie Tanner was running out of coal, and even though it was supposed to be spring her house always seemed cold. On her way to work she'd seen women taking prams and wheelbarrows to coal collection points but she couldn't afford it anyway. Two shillings was all she had in her purse. And she was also down to her last packet of Woodbines. She'd put some wood on the fire and her last three measly lumps of coal, and watched as they smoked briefly and then went out. She took a sheet of old newspaper, held it to cover the grate, and was just about to give up when a flame burst into life. Before she could remove the newspaper it had caught fire. 'Sod and damnation!' she shouted, as she beat the life out of the paper with her brass coal shovel. Blackened bits of paper had settled on her old rug in front of the fireplace and now she needed the dustpan and brush to sweep up the mess. Now it was finally burning, the fire gave out as much heat as a bundle of matches, so she was determined not to stay in and freeze to death.

Dennis and Linda were fast asleep upstairs. It would do no harm to leave them for a couple of hours, although if she was lucky Minnie Caldwell might agree to check on them. There was a dance on at the church hall on a Wednesday evening, and although it didn't have a licence she reasoned that she and Dot might meet a couple of servicemen with money to spare for a few drinks and a bag of fish and chips.

She smoked a Woodbine from a fresh packet she'd bartered

for sweet coupons and lit the oven so that the heat warmed up the scullery. Then she put on a kettle to boil so that she could have a strip wash. It was lucky she'd still got a pair of nylons left because she'd run out of gravy browning. Lots of girls her age now wore trousers but she had good legs and full hips so she had convinced herself they didn't suit her. Tonight she was going to wear a tight black skirt that came just above her knees, and a white blouse, low-cut and a bit see-through — enough, she thought, to have eyes out on stalks.

She stared in disgust at her last sliver of Lifebuoy soap and added it to the metal soap-saver with the other pieces then swished it round in the water until it went cloudy. She was just taking off her bra when she heard a commotion in the backyard and an 'Oy, you!' She lifted the kitchen blind a fraction but she couldn't see anything so she carried on washing. She'd just started towelling herself dry when the back door opened. Len Fairclough, blood streaming from his nose, staggered through the door.

They stood open-mouthed in surprise at the sight of each other. 'What the 'ell are you doin' ere, Len?' Before he had a chance to reply, Elsie added, 'And you can shut your gob — you've seen tits before.'

'Not like yours I 'aven't,' he said, wiping his hand across his bloody nose.

'Sit down and I'll get you cleaned up,' ordered Elsie, as she slipped into her dressing-gown, then pushed Len on to a stool. 'Put your 'ead back — that'll stop it bleedin'. And then you can tell me what you're doin' 'ere.'

' 'Aven't you got a clean 'ankie?' he asked, as the blood dripped on to his shirt.

'You come in 'ere,' she said, as she lifted his chin back, 'bleedin' on my floor, interruptin' me wash and now you want an 'ankie?' He grinned at her and she patted his cheek. She'd met Len at Dot's wedding and they'd been to the same junior school for a short time, but any friend of Dot and Walt's was a friend of hers so she didn't feel put out.

Upstairs she found a packet of two handkerchiefs she'd had as a Christmas present. She took one out, got to the bedroom door and rushed back for the other.

It didn't take long for the bleeding to stop once she squeezed his nose for a few minutes. 'What 'appened?' she asked. 'Did you trip over me mangle?'

'Not your mangle, yer ruddy boyfriend. 'E was bendin' down puttin' somethin' on your back step and I never saw 'im in the dark. I was 'ead first in the concrete and 'e just run off. This leg of mine is a bloody nuisance.'

He pulled up his baggy grey trousers to reveal a plaster cast. 'What 'appened?' asked Elsie.

'I tripped,' said Len. 'Goin' down to the ship's boiler room. The doc says it'll take weeks to heal, mebbe months. I'm out of action for some time.'

'Some would say that were a bit of luck.'

'Not if they felt the pain,' said Len.

'So what was you doin' creepin' round my back yard?'

'I saw this strange bloke 'angin' around in the alley so I kept an eye on 'im and he came in your backyard so I followed 'im just in case 'e were up to no good.'

'Do you fancy a brew?' asked Elsie.

'Don't get me off the subject. Who is 'e, then?' asked Len, wiping the blood from his chin.

'I dunno. 'E's not me boyfriend, though – 'e just leaves me things.'

'What are yer talkin' about, Elsie?' said Len sharply. 'I 'ope you're not doin' owt stupid.'

'It's none of your business, Len Fairclough, so don't take that tone with me.'

Len said quietly, 'I want us to be mates, and I don't see why you've got strange blokes leaving things on your back step.'

Elsie stiffened. 'If you must know, Dot and I put little notes in the RAF uniforms with our addresses and I've been left little presents.'

'What about Dot? Is 'e leavin' little presents for 'er too?'

'Nowt I know of.'

'Don't you think that's strange – that 'e picked on you.'

' 'Appen I didn't think about it.'

' 'Appen you should, then.'

'What are you gettin' at, Len? There's no 'arm. I haven't even met 'im. I 'ardly know you, so mind yer own . . .'

He was staring at her. 'Just you think on, Elsie. I'm staying around 'ere for a while. Vi's puttin' me up at the moment and Dot said I should keep an eye out for you—'

'She's got a bloody nerve!' interrupted Elsie. 'I don't need the likes of you, Len Fairclough, breathin' down me neck and you can tell 'er that from me.' She resolved to tell Dot exactly what she thought of her interference.

Len made no move to leave and Elsie's impatience grew. 'There's that saying,' said Len, ' "Beware of Greeks bearing gifts".'

'Was 'e a Greek?'

' 'Ow the 'ell could I tell?'

'Was 'e tall?'

' 'Appen 'e was.'

'And you didn't see 'is face?'

'Your yard is as black as a coal-'ole. I couldn't see me 'and in front of me.'

Elsie took a close look at Len's nose. 'It looks a bit swollen but it's stopped bleedin',' she said. 'You can go back to Dot and tell 'er to get round 'ere. I want words with 'er.'

'What about me tea?' asked Len.

'Get Dot to make you a brew.'

Len limped out to the backyard and before he'd opened the back gate Elsie had retrieved the package. She couldn't wait to open it. When she did she couldn't believe her luck: Player's cigarettes – hundreds of them. She didn't hear Len's return.

'Couldn't wait, could you?' said Len from the open back door. 'You just smoke your ruddy fags. But don't think they're for nowt. 'E'll be back. 'E's after yer body.'

' 'Ere, catch!' she called, throwing a packet towards him. 'And you listen to me, Len Fairclough. I admit my body's been 'ad a few times, me 'usband being the worst cos 'e left me reminders. But I'll tell you this much – I'd 'ave enjoyed meself a ruddy sight more if I'd 'ad presents like this bloke leaves.'

'You know what you are?' yelled Len. 'Nowt but a tart!'

'Get out, Len,' Elsie shrieked, 'and bloody well don't come back! Think on this – there's worse things than being a tart. At least I gets pleasure, which is a ruddy sight more than I ever got with my Arnold.'

'I'm off,' said Len. 'You're as stubborn as a ruddy mule. You need a man to take you in 'and. You've got no coal, the 'ouse is bloody freezin' and all you want to do is get yer knickers down for a few fags.'

Elsie picked up the frying-pan and clenched her fist. 'Just mind your own business and sod off, Len, or you'll be 'avin' another bloody nose.'

As a final gesture Len threw the cigarettes back into the kitchen then slammed the door.

Elsie sighed as she picked up the packet, opened it and lit a cigarette. She inhaled deeply. After two drags she felt calmer. This is me, she thought. I'm not going to smoke Woodbines for ever more. I'm a Player's girl now.

Next time she'd be waiting for her mystery man because, whoever he was, he was a good provider. And that was more than could be said for a few men she'd been in the sack with, Steve Tanner being the only exception. He'd been in a different league altogether.

An hour later Dot peered round the kitchen door, looking sheepish. 'Do I need a white flag or shall I wave me knickers in the air?'

Elsie tried not to smile. 'What makes you think I need the likes of Len Fairclough keeping an eye on me?'

'Elsie, you've no 'usband worth speakin' of, no dad, no brother and no boyfriend. You need someone to rely on.'

'I rely on meself, Dot Greenhalgh, and don't you forget it.'

'I see you've got some fags,' Dot observed.

'Yeah, but if you say owt else to Len I'll stop sharin' with you.'

On their way to Minnie Caldwell, who was always soft enough to say she'd look in on the kids, Elsie said, 'Anyway, Len with a peg-leg wouldn't be much 'elp to me.'

'Don't take the mick, Elsie. According to a letter I've 'ad from Walt, Len was a real 'ero. Did 'e tell you he slipped?'

Elsie nodded.

'Well, he slipped 'cos their ship was bombed and his leg got smashed, but he teks no notice of the fact 'is bones is pokin' through his bell bottoms and manages to haul three blokes up from the flooded boiler room. And if 'e doesn't get a medal 'e bloody well should.'

437

'I've always thought he was a good bloke,' said Elsie, ashamed of herself. 'But I still don't need 'im to spy on me.'

At home in Jubilee Terrace Minnie Caldwell was a disappointed woman. Her mother wouldn't settle and the noises were worse than ever. Even more worryingly, half a pork pie and half a loaf of bread had gone missing from the pantry. And it wasn't the first time food had gone missing. At first she thought it was just her memory going and she'd eaten it herself. But now she knew. Someone had been in her house. She'd never ever locked the back door, there had been no need, and since she'd lost the key she couldn't lock it now. It was probably a hungry tinker, she thought, and she hoped he had needed that pork pie and bread more than she did. She'd only had a slice of bread and marge with treacle for her tea but since the noises had started she'd lost her appetite.

She'd just put some soda in her washing-up water when a knock came at the back door. She jumped in surprise and the box flew out of her hand, soda crystals spreading all over the scullery floor. 'By 'eck!' she muttered as she opened the door. 'Oh, it's you. You can come in.'

All dressed up, Elsie entered, followed by Dot. 'Did we startle you?' asked Elsie. Minnie didn't answer, she just got down on her knees and began scooping up the crystals. Elsie and Dot joined in. 'What's up, Mrs Caldwell?' asked Elsie, seeing that she looked close to tears and wasn't her usual self at all.

Minnie told her about her ghost, the nightly noises and the visit from Mr Swindley. She also told them about the missing pork pie, and finally admitted that other food had been taken.

'Ghosts don't need food,' said Elsie. ' 'Ave you looked in yer loft?'

'The openin's too small for a body to get through.'

'Let's 'ave a look anyway,' suggested Elsie – the sooner Minnie was sorted out the more likely it was she'd look in on the kids.

They trooped upstairs to look at the twelve by twelve inches of the loft hatch.

'It's not likely to be a German parachutist,' said Elsie. 'They eat too much to be that small.'

'German prisoner-of-war?' suggested Dot.

Elsie shook her head. 'They get better fed than we do.'

Minnie said, in a whisper, 'We ain't never goin' to find out, are we?'

'Aye, we will, so don't fret,' said Elsie.

'My mam's got a ladder,' said Dot, 'and Len Fairclough's staying and 'is 'ead ain't twelve inches square so at least 'e can 'ave a look.'

'What about Ena?' asked Minnie.

'What about 'er?'

'She'll want to be 'ere. She'll think I've gone behind 'er back.'

'Is she in Rovers?'

'Aye, more than likely,' said Minnie ruefully.

'You get round there and get her, then,' Elsie said, giving Minnie an encouraging push. 'Dot, I've got nowt to say to Len, so you go round and ask 'im to bring 'is little ladder.'

'We'll never get to the dance at this rate,' said Dot, looking disappointed.

'The blokes 'ardly mek a move till last dance,' said Elsie, 'so we'll still manage that and a fish supper if we're lucky.'

Once they'd gone Elsie sat on the floor and listened. A few minutes later she heard a scrabbling noise. 'Oh, my Gawd!' she said aloud, as the thought sprang into her mind that it might be rats.

Ena Sharples, Minnie and Martha turned up seconds before Len and his ladder. With six people on the tiny landing it was shoulder to shoulder and Len had to raise his voice. 'Come on, you lot, stop mitherin' and move out me way.' There was some shuffling about. 'Well, get on wi' it, lad,' said Ena, peeved at the idea of Elsie Tanner taking the initiative. 'We've got milk stouts waitin' on us at Rovers.'

With the ladder in position Elsie murmured to Len, 'Are you sure you can do this with your leg? I can go up there as long as I tek me shoes off.'

'You just 'old the ladder, Elsie. I'll be slow but I'll do it.'

Len inched up the ladder, dragging his plastered leg

behind him. Eventually he made it to the loft hatch. 'I can't see 'owt,' he said. 'I'll need a torch.'

'Minnie Caldwell – torch!'

At Ena's command Minnie rushed downstairs. Martha stood silent, her face set in its usual sombre expression. Dot giggled nervously and Elsie hoped the whole episode would soon be over and she'd either be dancing or in the pub with some nice-looking bloke with money in his pocket.

Once Len had the torch they waited for his verdict, staring upwards in silence. 'There's nowt I can see,' he said, 'but there's an 'orrible smell.' He carried on scanning with his torch for some time until Ena grew irritable. 'Good thing you're not an ack-ack man, Len Fairclough,' she said. ' 'Ow long is it goin' to take you to realize there's nothing up there?'

'You're wrong, Mrs Sharples. There *is* something up 'ere.'

That shut Ena up and again they waited.

'Come out, whoever you are,' Len shouted. Then there was a sound they couldn't fail to recognize: someone was sobbing. 'We won't 'urt you. Come on – show yerself.'

After a few moments Len gasped. 'Ye gods!'

'What is it?' they all shouted at once.

'It's a little lad, an' 'e's in a bad way.'

' 'Ow could 'e get up there?' asked Minnie, amazed.

' 'E 'ad 'elp, of course,' said Ena. 'Come on then, Len, tell 'im to come down.'

'Come on, lad,' said Len gently. 'You need 'elp. Come towards me. Don't be scared.'

He switched off the torch. 'I'll go back down,' he called into the dark of the loft, 'and you 'ave a little think.'

Len came down the ladder painfully slowly, his face grim. 'He's scared to death. I don't think he's goin' to budge. Got any ideas?'

It was Ena who spoke first. 'He might come out for another little 'un.'

'Who do you suggest, Mrs Sharples?' said Len. 'A bloomin' tooth fairy?'

'There's no need for cheek,' said Ena sharply. 'What about Kenneth Barlow? 'E's a bright lad and not an 'aporth of fat on 'im.'

440

'He'll be asleep in bed. Ida won't like it.'

'Don't argue with me, Len Fairclough. That lad's in and out of 'is bed like a yo-yo during the raids. She'll let 'im come if you ask 'er proper.'

Len went off immediately. Now that the loft was open they could clearly hear the boy's quiet sobbing. 'I can't stand 'ere doin nowt,' said Elsie. 'I'm goin' up. Dot, you 'old the ladder for me.' For once Ena kept quiet. No one was going to see *her* bloomers.

Elsie shone the torch on what she thought at first was a pile of old rags, until they moved and a little head raised itself. Eyes half closed, he squinted at the beam of light then his head sank down again. 'It's all right, pet. You can come down. Honest.' There was no response.

Ten minutes later Kenneth Barlow turned up holding Len's hand. He wore a coat over blue-striped pyjamas and wellington boots. He looked a little scared and still had a crease mark of sleep on his face.

'Will you be all right on the ladder, son?' Len asked.

'I think so,' said Kenneth solemnly, as he slipped off his coat.

'I'll be right behind you,' said Len, 'so you've got no worries. Once you're through I'll 'and you the torch.'

Kenneth went up without looking down and easily squeezed through into the loft space. They could hear him talking but not the response. After some time Kenneth's face appeared. 'He thinks you're Nazis and you'll take him back.'

'Back where?' asked Len.

'To a place where they were cruel to 'im.'

'You tell 'im,' shouted Ena before Len could reply, 'that we'll look after 'im.'

'I'll 'ave to pull him along,' said Kenneth. ' 'E says 'e can't stand.'

'Do your best, Kenneth, lad,' urged Len.

Shortly afterwards they heard thumping noises and whimpering, and then eventually Kenneth's wellies appeared. Len moved down the ladder two rungs as Kenneth emerged. Finally they saw the face of their 'ghost' – a little white face, eyes half closed with yellow pus, hair matted. 'Come down backward, lad, like Kenneth,' Len encouraged him. 'You just look up, not down.'

Kenneth smiled broadly as his feet reached the floor. 'You're a little 'ero,' said Minnie, and gave him a hug. By now Len had grabbed the boy to stop him falling from the last two rungs. He scooped him up in his arms and stared down into the ashen face. The lad was soaking wet, filthy, and weighed no more than a bundle of sticks.

'Don't just stand there, Len Fairclough!' yelled Ena. 'Get that baby downstairs by the fire.'

'The sergeant major's in charge now,' whispered Elsie to Dot, as they followed Len to the back room.

'What was that, Elsie Tanner?'

'Just sayin' you'll know what to do, Mrs Sharples.'

' 'Appen we'll all 'ave to do our bit.'

Len watched the boy's face worriedly. 'E's in a reet bad way, Mrs Sharples.'

'Nowt that a bit o' warmth, a sup of tea and some food won't put right,' she replied. 'Minnie, fetch blankets and towels. Elsie, put the kettle on. Dot, get the tin bath down from 'ook.'

'No orders for me, Mrs Sharples?' asked Len.

Ena fixed him with her most withering look. 'You take young Kenneth 'ome, and tell Ida he did a champion job.' She patted Kenneth on the head, slipped sixpence into his hand, then held out her arms. 'Pass the baby over, Len, and tell no one about this. Kenneth, you don't want to end up in 'ell do you?'

'No, Mrs Sharples.'

'Well, say nowt except to your mam and tell her to say nowt to anyone. I'll be in to see 'er in the morning.'

It took some time to half fill the tin bath with hot water. It was placed in front of the fire and Ena gently undressed the child when everything was ready to her satisfaction.

' 'E stinks something awful,' said Dot.

'So would you,' said Ena 'if you'd been in a loft for weeks.'

Minnie had brewed tea and made a bowl of bread and milk for the boy. 'Put plenty of sugar on it, Minnie – and, you two, off you go.'

Elsie and Dot needed no second telling, but as they got to the back door Ena shouted, 'Elsie Tanner, if you've left those kids of yours alone, think on this baby and get yourselves off 'ome.'

'Mitherin' old bag,' muttered Elsie, knowing their night out was ruined. Neither of them could forget that pathetic little scrap. 'Mebbe I should go 'ome,' she said then, uncertainly.

'Aye,' said Dot. 'I'm not in the mood for dancing either. I'll come with you.'

'How's your Sally's baby?' asked Elsie.

Dot smiled. 'Our Clark's grand. Sally's still a bit tired but me mam 'elps 'er ever such a lot.'

'I wish I 'ad a mam to 'elp me,' said Elsie, as she linked arms with Dot. They both shivered in the frosty night air and hurried along, their breath visible in the dark.

In the back alley Elsie said, 'Do you fancy a fish supper?'

'I fancy some chips.'

'Right, then,' said Elsie, 'chips it is,' and they set off for the fish shop.

CHAPTER EIGHT

Spring 1944 U-515 and U-68 sunk by US.

Now that Annie had help with Billy and Joan she had a little more time to herself. The Rovers closed at two o'clock on Sundays and didn't open again until seven. Annie had found John Barnstable the ideal companion for Sunday afternoons. Their only problem was finding somewhere to go that was well away from Weatherfield. Occasionally John borrowed a friend's Ford motor car and brought a picnic tea. Then he drove to the Peaks and they ate their sandwiches and drank a flask of tea. Sometimes, if it wasn't too cold or wet, they walked. Annie found that she didn't mind a bit when John held her hand.

Teresa had Mondays off and an evening in the week. She went to early Mass on Sunday morning and afterwards spent time with Billy reading him Aesop's fables or Bible stories. Annie's only concern was that she had found Billy once with rosary beads, but she consoled herself with the thought that he was much better behaved now.

Occasionally Teresa asked awkward questions. 'Where will you be off to today, then, Mrs Walker?'

'I'm seeing my friends in Manchester again.'

'You've been visiting them a lot lately,' Teresa said, as she bent down to pick up Joan.

Annie didn't like the expression on the girl's face. It was as if the little madam *knew*.

'They *are* very good friends,' said Annie.

'You're lucky, Mrs Walker. I don't have any friends.'

Annie wasn't surprised: there was something a little too pious about the girl but at least she didn't drop her Hs like most people in Weatherfield.

'I'll be back for opening time,' said Annie. 'If there's a raid you know what to do.'

'Of course, Mrs Walker.'

Outside it was drizzling and the sky was grey. Annie pulled up her fur collar and walked briskly to Bessie Street School. It was risky meeting John there but she reasoned that if anyone saw them she would say that he had offered her a lift to her friends in Manchester.

As she sat beside him in the car Annie realized that part of her excitement stemmed from their meetings being so clandestine. She truly liked John but her heart was Jack's. Even so, when she hadn't seen Jack for months and months she could hardly remember his face. His last unexpected leave had been short and miserable. He'd been hung over the next morning and had spent most of the day in bed. He'd been morose and had taken little interest in the Rovers or the children and he had ignored Teresa. He wasn't the Jack she had known of old. Occasionally she wondered if she was keeping John in reserve in case Jack didn't come back at all. Every week she heard of some poor woman who'd had the dreaded telegram. John Barnstable was her war insurance policy.

'You're looking lovely, Annie,' he said now, as he patted her gloved hand.

To Annie compliments were like the cream on strawberries – delicious and essential. John made her feel young and desirable, even though they had only kissed and held hands. For Annie that was enough.

As he drove through empty streets and out towards the Peaks, the rain turned to sleet but they barely noticed. Once they were into open country John stopped the car and they ate salmon sandwiches, a real treat, and talked about their week. They hardly noticed when the sleet turned to snow.

'We'd best be getting nearer town before it gets dark,' said John. Annie felt disappointed the time had slipped by so quickly. She was happy just to be away from the Rovers for a few hours, and she felt quite intoxicated by the hand-holding and kissing.

He started the drive back under darkening skies. Dense grey clouds gathered ominously and driving snow beat against the windscreen. A few miles on, the snow became a blizzard. John stopped the car in a country lane. 'We can't go on,' he said, 'until this clears somewhat.'

By now it was five o'clock and dark. Annie shivered and he put an arm around her. 'We'll just have to snuggle up,' he said, as he gave her a playful squeeze. Annie giggled. There was plenty of time to get back to the Rovers.

Ena Sharples stood outside the Rovers in the snow at just after seven and was shocked to find the door locked. The pub had once run out of beer but she'd never known it not open on time. Soon a few others joined her, Albert Tatlock and Tom Hewitt from No. 7, and finally Martha Longhurst. 'Well,' said Ena, 'we'll achieve nowt standin' 'ere stampin' our feet and gettin' frostbite. I'm goin' round the back.'

'She keeps it locked, Mrs Sharples,' said Albert.

Ena glowered at him as though he were responsible somehow. 'There's that lass who's got "nun" written all over 'er face – she'll unlock it.'

'If there's anyone there at all, Ena,' said Martha. 'It seems reet quiet and deserted to me.'

'Martha, this isn't the *Marie Celeste*, this is the bloomin' Rovers.'

'Aye. But it seems a bit strange, don't it?'

Ena thought it seemed very strange indeed, but she wasn't going to admit it. 'I'm goin' round the back. You lot please yerselves.'

Eventually Teresa answered the back door. 'What kept yer?' asked Ena.

'Mrs Walker told me not to open the back door to anyone.'

'And where might Mrs Walker be at this moment?'

'She's visiting her friends in Manchester.'

'Didn't know she 'ad any friends.'

'She often sees them on Sunday afternoons.'

'That's as mebbe but she'll want the Rovers to be tekkin' brass so stand aside and let me through.'

Behind the pebble glasses Teresa's eyes widened. 'Oh, I couldn't let you in. Mrs Walker would never forgive me.'

'She'll never forgive losin' good beer money, so you can let me pass.'

'Jesus, Mary and Joseph,' murmured Teresa.

'Did Jesus turn water into wine, lass?' asked Ena.

She nodded. 'Well, think on me as God's right 'and at the Mission. 'E's called on me to turn water into wine.'

Teresa thought about that for a moment. 'But that was at a wedding.'

'And this is wartime, girl. Out of my way.'

Teresa shrank back as Ena Sharples barged past. Then she crossed herself for luck and ran upstairs to guard her charges.

Once the door was opened Ena designated Albert Tatlock barman and Tom Hewitt cellarman. They didn't argue, and soon Albert was taking orders and working the pumps as if he'd been doing it all his life.

'It's funny Ned ain't 'ere either,' said Martha. 'You don't think Annie Walker's with 'im, do you, Ena?'

'Sometimes, Martha Longhurst, you amaze me.'

'Why's that, Ena?'

'Because you're such a blitherin' idiot. Annie Walker may be a lot of things but she's not blind, deaf or daft. If she'd've 'ad a choice between 'Immler or Ned Narkin, she'd 'ave chosen 'Immler.'

Martha pursed her lips. Maybe Ned Narkin was a long shot but Annie Walker *was* seeing a man, of that she remained sure. And one day she'd find out who it was, just so that she could tell Ena Sharples and see her surprised. For once Martha would be first in line with a bit of news.

Time went by and there was still no sign of Annie Walker. More people came in, stood at the bar and waited while Albert Tatlock used the pumps with slow deliberation. Hilda Ogden walked in and pretty soon was announcing in a loud voice at the bar, 'I'm tellin' yer what I saw and it's God's 'onest truth. I *did* see Mrs Walker in a car with a man. They looked . . . friendly, if you knows what I mean.'

In seconds Ena was behind her. 'I've 'eard of you, 'Ilda
Ogden. There's nothin' you like better than a bit o' gossip but
don't you come in 'ere spreadin' lies and causin' trouble.'

Hilda bridled. 'I don't 'ave to stay 'ere to be insulted.'

'That's true,' said Ena. 'You could be insulted anywhere.'

Hilda stuck her chin in the air. 'I wouldn't 'ave another
drink in 'ere if it was the last pub in the world,' she said, and
with a clatter of high heels she left the Rovers.

When Ena had sat down in the snug, Martha said, 'I
thought you didn't even like Annie Walker and there you are
standin' up for 'er like a good 'un.'

'I don't like 'er, Martha Longhurst, but I'll be blowed if I
lets a little madam like 'Ilda Ogden start gossip mongerin'.'

'Want to do it yerself, do you, Ena?'

Ena frowned. 'There's nowt wrong wi' Annie Walker as a
landlady. She keeps this place better than most.'

'Didn't I tell you she was carryin' on with someone? Didn't
I tell yer first but yer didn't believe me?'

When in doubt Ena ignored what didn't suit her. 'Sup up,
Martha. Let's get round to Minnie and see 'ow the little lad's
doin.'

' 'E's said nowt and 'e's bin with Minnie for days.'

'Aye,' said Ena. 'Minnie's the right one to care for 'im, though.
'E's come on gradely since she's bin feedin' 'im. 'E'll talk in 'is
own time.'

'Where's 'e come from, though, Ena? They'll want 'im back.'

Ena fixed her friend with a steely look. 'That lad will go
nowhere but where 'e wants. I'm tellin' you that now so
don't you forget it. I like kids and I 'ate those that are cruel
to 'em.'

'What about the authorities? They'll come after 'im.'

'We'll 'ide 'im. The whole bloomin' street will 'ide 'im. Do
you 'ear me?'

'Minnie can't keep 'im for ever,' said Martha, adjusting her
beret. 'What about 'is ration books? What about 'is schooling?'

Ena shrugged. 'Ada Hayes is a teacher. She'll know what to
do.'

They were just putting on their coats when the siren wailed,
and soon they could see smoke rising over Manchester.

'Good thing there's no full moon tonight,' said Ena. 'There's nowt I 'ate more than them Stinkers.'

Martha walked on, nodding in agreement. She hated them too. On the night of a full moon, drums of oil were moved into the middle of certain streets in Weatherfield and one of the ARP came round and lit them. Great black clouds of smoke rose up and no one could see a hand in front of them. 'It's me winders and me blinds I 'ate cleaning the next day,' said Martha, 'and I've 'eard some parts of the country don't bother.'

'That's 'cos they've got better shelters than us,' said Ena, as they approached Minnie's house. 'Now, stop mitherin' and let's get on wi' it.'

When the siren sounded Minnie Caldwell had placed pillows and blankets under her heavy table. Amy had said, 'Leave me be – it won't be owt,' so Minnie had made a brew and helped her mother drink it from an invalid's cup.

Since he'd been staying with her the boy hadn't spoken to her, but he had spoken to Amy and Mabel, the cat, although Minnie knew he spoke too quietly for her mother to hear. She'd found out this evening that his name was Dieter Holliman. He'd refused to go to bed upstairs and she'd made him up a bed between two armchairs near the fire. His arms and legs were matchstick thin and the bedrooms were unheated so Minnie had been glad to keep him by the warmth of the fire.

Just before the siren had sounded Minnie was in the scullery and he'd been stroking the cat on his lap. 'Your name is Mabel,' he'd said, in his precise way, 'and I am Dieter Holliman.' Minnie noticed he had an accent but she didn't know what it was. His name could have been German but she didn't care – he was such a poor little scrap. However, even in the short time he had been with her Minnie had seen great improvements. She'd bathed his eyes every hour with boiled warm water and a pinch of salt for two days and now they were clear. Even his cheeks seemed plumper. She noticed that he tried to hide food under cushions or in his pockets so she gave him extra, saying, 'You save that for later, pet.' And when he smiled for the first time, Minnie was so pleased she thought she'd burst.

The sirens worried him but not so much as someone knocking on the door. It was then that he trembled in fear.

'Come on, Dieter, you snuggle down with me under the table,' said Minnie. 'Bring Mabel with you.'

Minnie was so tired that she fell asleep and slept through the raid and the all-clear.

Ena's voice woke her, though. 'Minnie Caldwell, the street could be reduced to bloomin' ashes and you wouldn't know a thing about it.'

Minnie crawled out from under the table as Ena and Martha stared down at her. 'Ooh, it 'asn't 'as it, Ena?'

'No, Minnie – yer daft bat – it's still standin'. Manchester got a right 'ammerin', though.'

'Poor souls,' murmured Minnie.

'How's your other poor soul?' Ena asked, pointing towards the sleeping boy.

'He's champion, Ena. Good as gold, 'e's been. He spoke to Mabel tonight. He says 'is name is Dieter Holliman.'

'Sounds foreign like.'

'I think 'e's German,' said Minnie.

' 'E looks German,' agreed Martha.

'Who asked you, Martha Longhurst? What do you mean, 'e looks German? I don't think 'e looks a bit like 'Itler or 'Immler or Goering.'

'Aren't Germans supposed to 'ave fair 'air and blue eyes?'

'Them three I've just mentioned 'aven't.'

Peeved, Martha sat down and folded her arms. 'You just 'ave to be *right* about every blessed thing.'

Ena smiled. 'That's because I'm not wrong 'bout most things. Now, Minnie, you put kettle on. We 'ave things to talk about.'

'What sort of things, Ena?'

'For one, what are we going to do about little lad, and two, 'ow do we keep Annie Walker on the straight and narrer?'

'What do yer mean, Ena?'

'You mek a brew, Minnie, and I'll tell yer.'

CHAPTER NINE

Spring 1944 No civilian casualties in May.

Elsie Tanner stopped at the fish and chip shop on her way home from work. It hadn't been a good day: her machine had gone wrong three times and Dot hadn't been there to have a laugh with – she had the flu. There was a long, slow-moving queue, her feet ached and her admirer hadn't left her a gift since Len Fairclough had fallen over him in the dark.

'What'll it be, Elsie?' asked Joe Jackson, the fish-shop owner. Joe had a big, round, permanently red face and he wrapped his fare faster than the eye could follow.

'Roe and chips, please, Joe.'

'Cheer up, it might never 'appen,' he said, giving her a wink, which meant he'd given her extra for the kids. 'When are yer comin' dancin' with me, darlin'?'

Elsie forced a smile. 'When yer wife gives me permission.'

He shrugged and wiped the sweat from his forehead. 'You go careful, Elsie – you're one of me best customers.'

She was tempted to eat a few chips on the way home but it was raining so she walked as fast as she could, holding the warm package in her hands. She was soaked by the time she got home. The house was in darkness and just for a moment she'd forgotten where she'd left her kids. She was turning on the gas lamps when she remembered – a girl in Gas Street had them, a sister of Amy Clutterbuck who worked at the factory. She'd promised to walk them back at seven. It was ten to now.

She ate her roe and a few chips, then read the newspaper they were wrapped in. The news had been mainly good lately – but if it was that good, she thought, why wasn't the war over yet? Allied bombers had destroyed Cassino in Italy. She wondered if Steve had been sent out there – she hoped so: she'd heard Italy was a warm country. 'Not like this freezing 'ole,' she said aloud.

Once the fire was lit and roaring, she took off her coat. Then she put the rest of the chips in a low oven and sat down to smoke one of her last Player's cigarettes.

Minutes later Amy Clutterbuck's sister arrived, a sour-faced woman in her thirties.

'Your Dennis 'as got a scurvy 'ead, sticky eyes and his bum's sore,' she said, as she propped him, still asleep, in an armchair.

Elsie shrugged. 'Our Dennis 'as always got somethin'. What about Linda?'

'She wet herself twice.' Linda hung her head and ran to her mother.

'She's scared of the outside privy. Someone 'as to go wi' 'er.'

'That's as maybe, Mrs Tanner, but she's too old to wet 'erself.'

'I'll tell 'er that. 'Ow much do I owe you?'

'That'll be two and six.'

'Aye.' Elsie rooted in her purse. 'I've only got two bob. I'll 'ave to give you the other sixpence tomorrow. I'll give it to your sister.'

When Frozen Face had gone Elsie muttered, 'I'll 'ave to borrow it from your sister first.'

'Mam,' said Linda, pulling at her skirt, 'I don't like 'er. She's like a witch.'

'You won't 'ave to go there again, pet. I'll find someone better.'

'You always say that, Mam.'

'It's the war, our Linda. Would yer like some chips and a cuppa?'

Linda put her arms round Elsie's neck. 'I think you're the best mam in the world.'

'What you anglin' for?'

'Can I sleep in your bed, Mam?'

'Aye. If you promise not to wet it.'

Linda pushed her little face towards Elsie and kissed her cheek. 'Mam?'

'What?'

'That Mrs Clatter said you was a tart. What's she mean?'

Elsie might have felt insulted if anyone else had said it but the woman did have a prize face – ugly as a box of frogs. 'It means, our Linda, that the old bag doesn't like men and they don't like 'er.'

The explanation was beyond Linda. 'Can I 'ave me chips now, Mam?'

Later, with both children asleep in her bed, Elsie did some washing and listened to Glenn Miller on the wireless. She felt bored to tears and was planning to go to bed early. She'd just stripped to her underwear for a wash by the fire when there was a knock at the back door.

'Come on in, then,' she called out, glad to have a visitor. 'I've nowt on so if you're a fella close yer eyes.' It was a joke, of course. She thought it might be Dot having dragged herself out of her sick bed or Sally wanting a break from baby Clark. She didn't expect a complete stranger holding a bottle of whisky and a bunch of flowers. 'Oh, Gawd,' she said, grabbing her cardigan and covering herself.

'Bella! Bella!' he said.

He was tall with thick black hair and dark brown eyes. He was also the best-looking man she'd ever seen in Weatherfield. And she'd always preferred the RAF blue. 'No, I'm not Bella,' she managed to say. 'I'm Elsie.'

He smiled, showing perfect white teeth. '*Bella* means beautiful and you are.'

'You're not from round 'ere, are you?'

He shook his head. 'Born in Manchester – my dad was Italian – Antonio Bartolini at your service.' He bent to take her hand, lifted it to his mouth and kissed it slowly. Then he looked deep into her eyes and Elsie was lost. She guessed that Antonio Bartolini could teach her a thing or two, especially after she'd had a whisky or three.

Antonio didn't rush. He poured the drinks, sat opposite her

and told her about his family's ice cream business and how he'd been interned on the Isle of Man for a few weeks. When he'd been given clearance he'd joined the RAF and now he was a flying instructor. He'd found her note and liked the sound of her. 'And now I've met you, Elsie. And I mean it when I say you're like a goddess.'

Elsie had never met such a man before. His voice was as deep and warm as a hot toddy and he had class. Steve had been classy, too, but even he didn't quite have Antonio's easy charm. And when Antonio kissed her he didn't ram his tongue straight down her throat like some men, he nibbled a little at her lips then whispered in her ear that she was not only the most beautiful woman he'd ever met but the most exciting. Elsie was old enough to know better but she still liked to hear such things.

They'd drunk two whiskies and Elsie was beginning to regret letting the kids sleep in her bed. Antonio was showing her how to dance the tango when a little voice at the door said, 'Mam, Dennis is cryin'.'

Elsie sighed with disappointment, but Antonio smiled broadly at the little girl. 'Hello,' he said, taking her hand and kissing it. 'You're as beautiful as your mother.' Linda giggled.

'I'll go up to 'im,' said Elsie. 'Come on, Linda, back to bed.'

'Leave her for a while,' said Antonio. 'I like *bambini*. Let's see what I have in my coat pocket for a pretty girl.'

Linda's pudgy hands clutched at the bar of chocolate he produced and she'd torn the paper off in seconds. 'And some Du Maurier for the lady,' he said, laying four packets on the table.

Dennis settled quickly enough with a nappy change and his dummy, and when Elsie came downstairs Linda was sitting on Antonio's lap with her face covered in chocolate. 'Gerroff, pet,' said Elsie irritably. 'You'll get chocolate on 'is lovely uniform.'

'It's all right. I've got to go now, anyway,' Antonio said.

Elsie couldn't contain herself. 'Don't go yet. Linda's off to bed after I've washed her face.'

Antonio kissed the top of Linda's head and put her on the floor. She'd eaten all the chocolate and was now licking her fingers. 'I have to be back at the base, Elsie. I'm flying tomorrow.'

As he was leaving, the thought crossed Elsie's mind that maybe she wouldn't see him again. Her kids put off a lot of men. But then he kissed her hard and gently squeezed her left breast, murmuring in her ear, 'I'll take you dancing tomorrow night.'

'Aye. If yer like,' she answered trying to sound nonchalant. She washed Linda's face and laid her alongside Dennis in the double bed. Then she came downstairs and poured herself a whisky. She picked up a packet of Du Maurier and held it for a moment. Du Maurier was a lady's fag. They didn't taste as good as Player's but, like Antonio, they had class. It was then that she noticed the folded slip of paper. It read – 'Elsie, make me a happy man and buy yourself something nice with this.'

Elsie picked up the crisp white five-pound notes. A tenner! With a tenner she could do so much. A little voice in her head said, 'You can't take that.' But a louder voice said, 'With that much money you could take a few days off work and still buy something.'

'Sod it,' she said aloud. 'I'm 'avin' it.' She smiled to herself – 'avin' it in more ways than one, but at least this time the man knew how to treat a woman and he looked like a film star. She'd given others her all for nowt, so why not enjoy herself now?

Ida Barlow and Bessie Tatlock had spent the evening surrounded by old clothes. A few other women had shown interest in a make-do-and-mend group but no one had turned up. 'Folks round 'ere are always slow to catch on to summat new,' said Bessie. 'We'll just 'ave to do what we can with our old stuff.' So they unpicked seams and Ida sketched a few ideas on brown paper.

' 'Ow's Minnie Caldwell gettin' on wi' little lad?' asked Bessie.

'Our Kenneth's been round to see 'im. They seem to be getting along like an 'ouse on fire.'

'Your Kenneth needs a little mate.'

Ida nodded. ' 'E seems 'appier since 'e's met him.'

'It's a wonder Minnie Caldwell can afford to feed a young lad.'

'She can't,' said Ida, as she sucked the end of her pencil. 'I've been sendin' 'er a few rock cakes and some scones. Minnie says he's so 'ungry he'd "eat a scabby 'oss between two slices o' bread".'

Bessie laughed. 'I've got some bottled fruit and pickled eggs that'll 'elp 'er out, but she can't keep 'im forever, can she?'

'Kenneth said 'im and two older boys ran away from an orphanage in Manchester. The lad's Jewish.'

'Poor little mite,' said Bessie. 'If 'alf what we've bin 'earin' about is true I bet 'e 'asn't got a soul left.'

Ida put down her pencil and gazed at her designs. 'Kenneth said 'e escaped from Germany before the war with 'is mam, but you know what kids are like – full of daft stories.'

Bessie nodded. 'Let's 'ave a look at yer drawings, then.' She picked up the sheet of brown paper and studied it carefully. 'By 'eck, Ida, you are a clever girl. If you colour 'em in with some of Kenneth's crayons I reckon we're in business. A few bob 'ere and there would 'elp you out.'

Ida nodded, but what was more important to her was the designing. Both Bessie and she could sew and if she could make stylish clothes from nothing she reckoned she was suddenly part of the war effort and she had a new interest. For the first time since the war began Ida felt she could cope.

Betty Preston was in love. The day after she had met Ted she was doing some soldering, wearing her protective goggles, and she looked up to find all eyes were upon her. She liked to gossip herself and she knew immediately that they'd been talking about her. Because making munitions was noisy, all the girls became expert lip readers, and she saw one of them mouth, 'You're a dark 'orse.' It didn't bother her that they talked about her. But how did they even *know*?

In the canteen above the noise of *Worker's Playtime* she

456

asked the ringleader, a girl called Hazel Perks, 'Why 'ave you bin talkin' about me, Hazel?'

Hazel grinned. 'You knows reet well. You was seen with a bloke last night. Smashin'-lookin' by all accounts and you 'adn't let on to anyone.'

'I likes to keep my business to meself. And who told you?' Betty glanced around the canteen tables, and there sat skinny Hilda Ogden trying not to grin. Betty stood up and walked over to her. ' 'Ilda Ogden, if you saw me last night why didn't you say 'ello?'

Hilda's mind didn't work quickly enough to answer that one.

'You're like an old woman, 'Ilda,' said Betty. 'All wind and gossip. Say nowt about folk if you don't want them to say owt about you.'

Hilda shrugged. 'At least I've got meself a husband.'

Hazel Perks laughed. 'Gawd, 'Ilda, you're priceless. Is that all you care about?'

'Bet he wears specs, then,' one of the girls said.

' 'E does not. 'E's right 'andsome and 'e's good to me.'

'What does that mean, 'Ilda? That 'e bought you a shandy and asked before he took yer knickers off?'

Hilda was off her chair and across the room faster than a rivet from a gun. 'You dirty bitch!' she screamed, as she flew at the girl who'd insulted her. In moments they were on the canteen floor in a heap of arms and legs and a torrent of insults that made Betty cover her ears. No one tried to stop the fight even when Hilda grabbed her opponent by the hair and began banging her head on the table. 'My Stan's an 'ero,' she shrieked, 'and don't you forget it.'

In the group watching, one quiet voice said, ' 'E'd 'ave to be a ruddy 'ero to marry 'er.'

The fight only broke up when the klaxon sounded for them to get back to work. Betty smiled to herself. A bit shy, she was glad that she was no longer the centre of attention. At least now, though, she felt more like one of the girls than she had before. And Ted had done that for her. You've gone daft, she told herself, when she felt all excited just at the thought of him. He was the reliable type, the sort of man she wanted to marry, and she was seeing him again tonight. Nothing was going to stop her – not her father or her poor mother. Ted was her priority now.

CHAPTER TEN

Spring 1944 Resistance blows up hydroelectric station at Bussy.

In her flat at the Glad Tidings Mission Hall Ena was perusing the local paper. Tucked away on the second page she read, 'Missing boys cause concern.' Three boys had run away from a children's home in Manchester. The youngest, Dieter Holliman, aged nine, was thought to be in the Weatherfield area.

Ena slipped on her coat, picked up her umbrella and marched out into the drizzle. When she arrived at Minnie's, Dieter was doing a jigsaw on the floor. The weeks he'd been with Minnie had transformed him, and he looked more like the nine-year-old he was than the six-year-old he had appeared to be when they first met him. 'Hello, Mrs Sharples,' he said. 'Can you do jigsaws? I'm stuck.'

'I'll 'elp you in a minute, lad. After I've 'ad words with Mrs Caldwell.'

Ena pushed Minnie into the scullery and closed the door. 'It's in the papers,' she said in a whisper.

'What is, Ena?'

'About the lad, you daft cluck.'

'No need to be rude, Ena. I do 'ave feelin's.'

'Aye, but I'm right mithered. It says in the papers 'im and two other lads are missin' from an orphanage. It says they're concerned – mind you, they've done nowt about it till now. 'As 'e told you what happened?'

' 'E's still scared, Ena. 'E thinks the Nazis will come to take us both away if they find 'im.'

459

'Don't you fret about that, Minnie Caldwell. 'E'll tell us nowt till 'e thinks it's safe. Don't you forget in all this we've got the Lord on our side.'

'I think I'll just rely on you, Ena.'

'Aye. Well, put kettle on and I'll 'ave a talk wi' the lad.'

'Don't you frighten 'im, Ena,' warned Minnie.

Ena's eyes flashed bright as coal in snow. 'Now, you look 'ere, Minnie Caldwell. If that lad ran away from a bloomin' orphanage he 'ad good reason. And, as I live and breathe, 'e won't be goin' back. I reckon 'e's suffered enough.' She took a breath. 'We just 'ave to work out a plan.'

'I do 'ope so, Ena. I love 'avin' 'im 'ere.'

When Ena returned to the back room Dieter looked at her warily. 'Now then, lad,' she said, getting down on the floor with him. 'Let's see if I can 'elp you wi' this jigsaw.' She managed to find two pieces before she said, 'Did they 'ave jigsaws in the 'ome?'

He looked up sharply. 'Did Kenneth tell you?'

Ena shook her head. 'Nay, lad. It's in papers.'

'They're looking for me?'

Ena nodded. 'It's up to you, lad. Do you want to stay in Weatherfield?'

He stared at her, his blue eyes full of fear. 'You won't send me back, will you?'

Ena patted his shoulder. 'Why don't you tell us all about it, lad?'

Dieter stared down at the jigsaw. 'They said I was a bad lot at the orphanage,' he muttered. 'The matron kept locking me in my room. I didn't mind that – I was used to hiding and being on my own.'

'What did you mind, lad?'

'I wet the bed at night and she made me wash the sheets and called me "Dirty Dieter", and then everyone made fun of me. Then she said I was stealing food. I wasn't, Mrs Sharples, honest I wasn't. I only saved bread and put it in my pocket. She hit me with a ruler for that. She said I was a German Jew thief and no one should trust me. There were two other boys she didn't like – big boys – and we decided to run away. They helped me get into the loft and they'd bring me food. I don't know where they are now but I wouldn't tell if I knew. It's a horrible place, that home, and it's nice here. Mrs Caldwell lets me save bread and I don't wet the bed any more.'

Ena ruffled his hair. 'What's her name, this matron?'

'Mrs Makins.'

'Well, pet, I don't think you'll be seein' 'er again. There's just one more thing I wants to know, lad. How come you speak such good English?'

His lower lip trembled. 'My mother spoke English and I've been in England since I was three.'

Ena longed to ask what had happened to his mother but she could see tears in his eyes and guessed she was dead. 'Where did you live before the orphanage, Dieter?'

He looked down. 'In London – the East End.' Ena lifted his chin and smiled at him. 'Can I stay here for ever?' he asked.

'As long as you want to. Weatherfield folk will see you right.'

Minnie came in with some bread and jam and tea, and placed the tray on the table. She'd been listening at the door and her insides were twitching like an eel on a plate.

' 'Ave you come up with a plan, Ena?' she asked.

'Aye. I'll be payin' that 'ome a visit.'

'You won't cause a row, will you?' asked Minnie nervously.

'Row?' said Ena. 'I tell yer this, Minnie Caldwell, that Mrs Makins is going to rue the day she was born. The fear of God is what she'll know. As I've said before, I can't abide them as is cruel to kiddies and them who think they can take advantage of folk who're different.'

'Don't you get yerself in trouble, Ena.'

Ena sipped her tea thoughtfully. 'Don't fret, Minnie. Trouble is comin' *their* way, not mine. Just you wait and see.'

Minnie smiled across at Dieter. She was still worried but she put her faith in Ena. She loved Dieter already, and if Ena needed help then she was more than willing to give it. 'When you go and see that Mrs Makins, Ena, can I come with you?'

There was a long pause before Ena said, 'You 'ave a 'eart of gold but I can't see you bein' much 'elp.'

'Why not, Ena? Two of us would be better.'

461

Ena thought about that. 'Minnie Caldwell,' she said, 'sometimes you're a bloomin' inspiration.'

'Does that mean you do want me 'elp, Ena?'

'You stay on the 'ome front, Minnie, where you belong,' said Ena, slipping on her coat. 'What we need for this is a bit of brawn. The man who's got it don't need brains. I'll do the thinkin' and 'e can look tough.'

The only trouble with Ena's new plan was that she couldn't think of anyone who quite fitted the bill.

Annie Walker had only just recovered from her mortifying experience of being late for opening time then getting caught in a raid. She'd been in a communal shelter twice now. She hated the smell, the snotty-nosed children, and the never-ending gossip, even the forced cheeriness of the communal singing. There were times in the Rovers when she could forget the war was on. Being with a smelly crowd in some dingy shelter *was* the war for Annie. At least, it felt like a battleground. And the gossips at the Rovers had had their field day too. No one had said anything to her but she knew, by the whispers and glances, that they suspected something. She'd written to John and told him that perhaps they shouldn't meet for a while and at long last he'd replied. It had been Teresa who picked up the post that morning.

'Letter for you, Mrs Walker, from . . .' and then she'd smiled in her sly way. Annie's stomach did the polka. She sat down to read the letter. He was missing her. She was his ideal woman and he would do anything to make her happy including leaving Bessie Street and finding a new post in the country. He had enough money for a little house and he would happily take on Annie's children. When she was divorced from Jack they could marry. The word divorce shimmered in front of her eyes. *Divorce*. People like her didn't get divorced. She'd made vows that couldn't be broken.

The letter and Teresa's knowing look unnerved Annie all day, and that evening in the bar she felt particularly tetchy.

'Please wipe your feet and show some consideration,' she exhorted her customers. When Elsie Tanner came in, flaunting her new boyfriend, she felt even more irritated. A trollop like Elsie Tanner could do what she wanted yet Annie couldn't get back late just once without rumour and gossip.

Elsie and her new man sat together, holding hands and laughing, and Annie felt jealous.

'What's up wi' you, Mrs Walker?'

Ena's voice broke into Annie's thoughts. 'Your usual, Mrs Sharples?'

Ena nodded.

'Is it true what I hear?' asked Annie. 'That you've taken in a young runaway that the authorities are looking for?'

'That's as maybe but it's of no interest to you, is it, Mrs Walker?'

'I'm interested in the welfare of children, and if he's run away he's probably a real troublemaker.'

Ena tried to keep her temper. 'Annie Walker, I'll say nowt to you now but I'll be round for a chat wi' you before opening time in morning. Till then I should say nowt to anyone or you might regret it.'

'Is that a threat, Mrs Sharples?'

Ena paused. 'Aye.'

Annie's hand trembled as she placed Ena's milk stout on the bar. Some of it spilled and Ena glared at her. 'I like a full measure, Mrs Walker, as I'm reet sure you do.'

'What's that supposed to mean?'

'You wouldn't want me to say anythin' 'ere, would yer?'

Annie topped up the glass and moved on to her next customer. Her legs were shaking so much that she thought her knees would give way. She realized that Ena Sharples knew something that might give her a hold over Annie – *for ever*.

Elsie Tanner finished her third gin and orange and squeezed Antonio's knee. 'I'm 'avin' a lovely time,' she said. 'I aven't been so 'appy for ages.'

'I've got a surprise for you, Elsie.'

'You've given me nowt but surprises. What's it this time?'

'I've got two days leave.'

Elsie was delighted. 'You'll stay at my place, won't you?'

'Elsie, darling, where else would I stay?'

'It did cross me mind that an 'andsome bloke like you might 'ave a little Italian wife hidden away.'

He laughed. 'Italian women aren't so little. But I don't have a wife – yet.'

' 'Ave you got plans, then?'

He took her hand. 'When a certain beautiful woman is free, who knows?'

'Pity there's nowt I can do about my Arnold, then.'

'After the war you can.'

'This ruddy war that we're supposed to be winning goes on and on.'

'Soon it will be over, my Elsie, and then you and I . . .' He kissed her hand and stared into her eyes.

'Stop it,' she said. 'You make me spine tingle.'

'Don't worry, you'll soon be—' He couldn't finish because a man approached their table.

'I thought you and the Todds were meant to be friends,' said Len Fairclough.

Elsie, a little drunk, merely laughed. 'What's the matter, Len? Someone locked you in the privy?'

Antonio stood up. 'I'm with this lady. What's the problem?'

'That's no lady – that's Elsie Tanner.'

Elsie stood up too. She was angry now. 'What the 'ell 'ave I done to upset you?'

' 'Ave you bothered to go round and see Dot?'

'Flu's catchin'. I don't want to give it to my kids, do I?'

Len stared at her. 'You don't mind leavin' them alone while you go out with yer Eyetie boyfriend.' At this Antonio gave him a hefty push. Len staggered on his good leg but didn't fall. 'You bloody foreigner!' he shouted. 'Why aren't you fightin' on yer own side?'

Antonio pushed aside a chair and advanced towards Len, who now had his fists raised. 'I thought you Eyeties were meant to like kids,' bellowed Len. 'It's all right for 'er to leave 'er kids screaming in the dark, is it, so as a neighbour 'as to come in to them.'

Antonio stopped in his tracks. 'Is this true, Elsie?'

Elsie looked ashamed. 'Dot couldn't 'ave 'em and they were asleep.'

Antonio raised his palms to Len. 'Sorry, mister. I'll take her home now.'

Len lowered his fists.

'Elsie, put your coat on,' said Antonio.

'I 'aven't finished me drink yet.'

'Yes, you have.'

'No, I 'aven't.'

He picked up her glass and downed the gin. 'I say you have.'

Elsie lunged at him. 'You've got a bloody nerve,' she screamed. He grabbed her wrist and began pulling her to the door. Elsie kicked him once or twice but he seemed not to notice. As they left, the Rovers erupted into cheering.

Annie Walker, relieved that no damage had been done and that Elsie Tanner had got her comeuppance, gave Len a pint on the house.

'Mrs Walker hasn't done owt like that since 1938,' said Albert Tatlock. 'They must be right – war *is* nearly over.'

Elsie's high heels clattered up the street as Antonio dragged her along. Once in the back alley she shouted, 'You're not me bloody 'usband. And you're 'urtin' me arm.' She didn't care if the neighbours heard.

'Good,' said Antonio, as he pushed her through the back door. 'No wife of mine would leave her children alone. That bloke at the Rovers was right and you should be ashamed of yourself.'

A flustered Bessie Tatlock stood up from a chair. 'I'm just going,' she said. 'They've both gone back to sleep now. Screaming fit to bust, they was.'

She rushed away, leaving Elsie with arms akimbo and Antonio's eyes flashing like a pair of searchlights.

'What I do with my kids is my business,' said Elsie, who had sobered up now. 'Not yours or Len Fairclough's.'

'Perhaps you don't care what happens to them.'

'That does it!' she said, snatching up Dennis's bottle and throwing it at him. He ducked. Then she threw a salt cellar, followed by a bottle of vinegar. Each time they missed. The vinegar bottle smashed against the door, which incensed her more. She threw cushions at him and finally her right shoe.

'Caught you, you sod,' she screamed, as the shoe hit the side of his head. She felt a lot better then, but as Antonio sank slowly to the floor, fear took a grip. He lay on the floor behind an armchair. She rushed to kneel beside him. 'Oh, Gawd, Antonio, wake up! Come on! Speak to me. It were only a shoe.'

There was no sign of a wound but he lay, eyes closed, unmoving. She shook him by the shoulders but there was still no response. She put her ear to his chest to see if his heart was still beating but she wasn't sure if it was her own heart hammering away that she could hear. Just as she lifted her head from his chest his hands grabbed her face, his eyes flicked open and he was staring at her. Elsie's mouth was half open in surprise but not for long. He pulled her to him and began kissing her passionately. She struggled at first but then relaxed as relief mixed with desire flooded through her. Then he rolled her over so that he was on top of her with her arms pinned down and he began to laugh. 'Elsie Tanner – the only woman I know who can throw like that is my mama and she throws like an Italian. I always knew you were the woman for me.'

He kissed her again and Elsie didn't resist this time. Nothing could stop her enjoying herself now – not the kids, not the war, not even her memories of Steve. Nothing mattered except the pleasure. And Antonio was proving he could supply a lot more than fags.

CHAPTER ELEVEN

Spring 1944 Rome falls to the Allies.

Annie Walker had waited for Ena Sharples's visit with real trepidation. When the knock came an hour before opening time she told Teresa to take Billy and Joan out for a walk. One thing she didn't want was any of her conversation being overheard.

'Do take a seat, Mrs Sharples,' she said. 'Would you like some tea?'

Ena was in no mood to be polite. 'I'll mek me point and then I'll be off.'

'And what is your point, Mrs Sharples?'

'I'm not one to make owt of molehills, Annie Walker, but I'd say you've been cutting your privet a bit close to the edge.'

'There's no need to talk in riddles, Mrs Sharples.'

Ena put a hand on her hip and stared at Annie. 'You've been seen,' she said. 'We've all 'ad our suspicions and we know you've got a gentleman admirer.'

Annie wasn't surprised and she decided her best form of defence was to go on the attack. 'Who I see is none of your business, Mrs Sharples. I do have a gentleman friend, and that's all he is. A true gentleman. I've done nothing to be ashamed of.'

'Your Jack is a real gent, Mrs Walker, don't you forget. 'E's fightin' for you and yours while you're seein' your fancy man.'

Annie, well used to keeping her temper under control, said evenly, 'I can see I have to repeat myself. It's purely my business and I have nothing else to say on the matter.'

'I mek it my business when you start openin' your big gob about that little lad.'

'I was only thinking,' said Annie, 'about what was right and proper.' As soon as the words had left her lips, Annie realized she'd given Ena all the ammunition she needed.

'Right and proper, is it, to send a lad back to a 'ome where 'e was badly treated?' snapped Ena. 'Right and proper, is it, to see a man behind your 'usband's back? Right and proper, is it, not to open Rovers on time? Right and proper . . .'

Wearily Annie put up her hand. 'You've more than made your point, Mrs Sharples. What is it you want me to do?'

Ena folded her arms across her chest. 'I'm goin' to get that orphanage sorted,' she said, 'but if anyone comes lookin' for 'im you say 'e was in Weatherfield but 'e's gone now. Do you understand? And if we can't get coupons for the lad we might need 'elp to keep feedin' and clothin' 'im.'

'But surely Mrs Caldwell can't plan to keep him for ever?'

'These things 'appen in wartime,' snapped Ena. 'If we can't look after the kiddies there's no bloomin' 'ope for us.'

'Very well, Mrs Sharples. Is there anything more?'

'Just your Jack. I won't be writin' to 'im now, but think on about what's right and proper. You're not Elsie Tanner – she's a trollop and she never did care for that Arnold of 'ers. Your Jack is a good man and 'e deserves an 'ero's 'omecomin', not findin' out his missus 'as been pantin' like a bitch on 'eat for another man. You save your breath for your Jack.'

Tight-lipped, Annie said, 'Thank you so much for your advice. I'd be grateful if we never spoke of this again.'

Ena turned to go. 'Don't think because I'm a widow I don't know nowt about animal passions. I put me passion into servin' the Lord and you'd do well to do the same.'

When Ena had gone Annie Walker went into the bar and had a quick swig of brandy. She rarely drank alcohol but today she needed a stiffener. The trouble was, she knew that Ena Sharples was right. She'd tried to end it, wanted to, but John was persistent. Too persistent. He had come round after hours and tried to persuade her that her future lay with him. He'd begun writing to her every day. It was easy enough for

Ena Sharples to dispense advice but she had a feeling John Barnstable just wasn't going to take no for an answer.

Betty Preston was running out of excuses for going out in the evening. As she walked home from work she realized that a third evening of 'baby sitting' might make her father suspicious, and if Holy Harold found out she had been to dance halls and pubs there would be a holy war. Betty hadn't even told her mother.

When she arrived home her mother was sitting in her armchair looking pale and breathless. 'Are you all right, Mam?' asked Betty.

'I've been movin' about too much. Tried to get the rugs up so I could give 'em a good beatin' in the yard.'

'I always do that, Mam. Just leave it to me.'

Her mother's plump hand grasped Betty's arm, and Betty was shocked to see that Margaret's hair was turning white. She hadn't noticed before. 'You do far too much, Betty,' she said breathlessly. 'Your father only wants to feed me and Bible thump. You won't be here for ever.'

'What do you mean?'

'You know what I mean, my girl. I know you've got a boyfriend.'

'How'd you know?'

'Maggie saw you with 'im.'

'Trust 'er to open her big mouth. If she tells Dad I'll swing for 'er.'

'I'm sure your dad would like you to get married.'

'Oh, yes, Mam. A holy Joe and then a life like—'

'You can say it. A life like mine. I don't want that for you, Betty. Is 'e a nice lad?'

Betty nodded. 'He's perfect, except 'e's a southerner and 'e's no church-goer.'

Her mother sighed. 'That'll give your dad a heart attack. Best keep it quiet.'

Betty made Margaret a cup of tea, beat the rugs in the garden and began peeling potatoes. Should she stand up to Harold? What could he do? Clip her ear? If he did that she could run out of the house in a huff. Maybe, she thought, she could say he was from Manchester way, which wasn't a complete lie, and that he was a regular chapel-goer, which was a downright lie.

When her father came in he took one look at Margaret and began blaming Betty. 'Look at the state your mother's in! She should be in bed. Have you given her anything to eat?'

'I'm just getting the tea ready.'

'Well, leave that and get your mother to bed.'

'I don't want to go to bed, Harold,' said Margaret. 'I'm feeling better now.'

'And I know what's best for you. Betty will 'elp you.'

'She's all right, Dad,' protested Betty 'She was a bit breathless but there's nowt wrong now.'

'I'll be the judge of that. Now do as you're told.'

Betty stared at her father defiantly. 'No.'

'What did you say?'

'I said no, Dad. Mam doesn't want to go to bed.'

Harold advanced towards her menacingly. 'A child doesn't argue with its parents.'

'I'm not a child, I'm a woman.'

'You live under my roof and you'll do as I tell you.'

'Stop it, Harold,' cried out Margaret. 'I can manage on my own.' Harold turned his head to watch his wife lumber to her feet. Her bulk seemed to fill the room but Betty knew that inside the huge frame was a small frightened person. And it was Harold who had made her so.

Margaret made her way slowly up the stairs. Betty stared at her father and for once he looked away. Then she said, 'I'll go up and see to Mam and then I'm going out.' He didn't answer and at that moment Maggie walked in.

'Maggie, go up to Mam,' Betty said. 'She needs 'elp gettin' into bed. I'll see to the tea.'

Maggie looked daggers at Betty but she didn't argue.

Just before Betty went out she looked in on her mother, who lay propped up on several pillows, her face white and beads of sweat on her forehead. She seemed to be asleep, the remains of a plate of liver and onions on the table by her bed. Just as Betty turned to go, her mother's eyes flickered open and she said, 'Whatever 'appens to me, pet, mek sure you leave this 'ouse.'

'Aye, Mam.'

'Promise me.'

'I promise.'

Margaret sighed and murmured, 'You're a good girl.'

Betty met Ted outside the Rovers with a heavy heart and a worried expression.

'What's the matter, Betty, love?' he asked.

'Me mam's not well.'

'Let's 'ave a drink, then, and you can tell me all about it.' He put an arm around her and Betty sensed that if there was one person she could trust with her family secrets it was Ted. And it made her realize that not only did she trust him, she really was in love with him.

When Antonio had left after his leave Elsie Tanner felt that the sunshine had gone with him but at least he'd promised to write to her. She received few letters and sometimes she doubted that Arnold could even write. Antonio's letters would make her feel she was more like the other wives who waited for the postman. She guessed that his family must be rich because most servicemen only earned enough for beer and the odd night out but Antonio always had money.

Elsie had been to the Todds' and gave Sally as much help as she could. The flu had left Dot weak and depressed, but now she was rallying and it was Vi who was giving cause for concern. There was a rumour that she'd got tipsy on a night out with some old friends and had fallen into the canal during the blackout. She'd denied it, saying she'd just got soaked in a downpour. Either way, Dot had sent for the doctor twice but all he could suggest was aspirin and cough linctus. Vi had taken to her bed looking ill and feverish and coughing up blood.

'She won't die, will she, Elsie?' Sally had asked her.

'Your mam is as strong as an ox,' said Elsie. 'There's nowt a bit of a rest won't cure.' But when Elsie went upstairs to say goodbye and saw Vi pale and slack-mouthed, with her chest sounding like a bubbling cauldron, she wasn't so sure.

It was Friday, late afternoon, and Elsie had finished work early. Orders at Elliston's had slackened off and word was

that now that the Allies were planning a final push in Europe
the workers might have to go on short time. Elsie could just
remember the Depression, and with her bit of extra money in
her old teapot she felt more secure. She'd paid a girl who used
to work at Elliston's to have the kids till Saturday morning
and she'd used her clothing coupons to buy a new dress with
a low-cut white collar and she wanted Dot to see it. 'Come
back with me, Dot, and I'll show you me new dress.'

Dot looked anxiously at Sally. 'Will you be able to manage
Mam and your Clark for a couple of hours?'

'Go on, you 'ave a break,' said Sally. 'Mam's asleep and
Clark's quiet for once and you 'aven't been out for ages.'

'You've turned into a right little mother hen, our Sal. I'm
proud of yer.'

On the way to Elsie's, Dot's worries about Vi surfaced.
'Should I let me dad know?'

'I reckon 'e might get leave,' said Elsie, 'and that might be
the tonic she needs.'

'Yeah, you're right Elsie – I'll do that.'

Elsie couldn't wait to show Dot her dress and she stripped
off straight away, put it on and waited for Dot's admiration.

'It's reet glamorous, Elsie, shows your figure off a treat.
Where did yer get the brass for that?'

Elsie smiled. 'Antonio sends me a bit now and again.'

'Where does 'e get it?'

'There's no need to put that expression on your gob, Dot.
I'm always givin' you a share of me food and fags.'

'Aye, and I'm grateful, but it makes you wonder, don't it?'

Elsie shrugged. ' 'Is folk are in business so they see 'e's all
right.'

Dot lit the cigarette that Elsie offered and began to cough
at the first puff.

'You're still coughin' for England, Dot. You should pack up.'

'Don't try and gerroff the subject, Elsie. You told me they
was in the ice-cream business and I've seen no ice-cream
since war began.'

'That's what 'e told me.'

'Well, he wouldn't say owt about black market would 'e.'

Elsie thought about that for a moment. ' 'Ave you noticed

'ow folk moan about black marketeers but if anything comes their way they pay up and say nowt?'

'Aye. You're right. Bloody 'ypocrites, they are.'

'Anyway,' said Elsie, 'I 'eard from 'im this morning and 'e's got what 'e calls a little "business proposition" for me.'

'What is it, then? Nothin' against the law I 'ope.'

Elsie shook her head. 'No, it's nowt like that. 'E says as 'ow a lot of his mates 'ave nowhere to go when they're on leave. They get a couple of days and they're stuck at the base. So 'e says could I offer them bed and breakfast? They'd pay me the going rate.'

Dot said thoughtfully, 'Are you sure there's nowt else they'd want?'

'What yer tryin' to say?' asked Elsie suspiciously.

'Don't get me wrong, Elsie, but 'ow would you cope with young 'andsome blokes walking about in their vest and pants?' Dot asked.

'Are you sayin' I've got no control?'

'Well, you ain't exactly a nun, are you?'

Elsie tried to keep a straight face. 'Neither are you, Dot. I don't see as 'ow I'd 'ave a problem.'

'You would if you'd 'ad a few gins.'

Elsie laughed. 'That's not a bad idea. Do yer fancy one now?'

'Does 'Itler need his cronies?'

After two gins Elsie broached the subject of the kids. 'See, Dot, if I 'ad three payin' guests then what would I do wi' kids?'

'You mean, would I 'ave 'em?'

'Or yer mam, and we could give 'er a few bob.'

'Only when me mam's on her feet again. Could be a bit o' fun for us, Elsie. Any road, I'll give you a 'and wi' the washin' and be your chaperone.'

Elsie chortled. 'Three gins, Dot, and you're worse than me. Some chaperone you'd mek.'

'I need a bit of fun, Elsie. I 'aven't heard from Walt in weeks. Sometimes I think I'll never see 'im again.'

'All I 'ope is I never see my Arnold again ever.'

'Not likely is it?'

Elsie grimaced. 'It's about as likely as Ena Sharples tekkin up with Len Fairclough.'

Elsie poured them both another large gin and half-way through they realized she was in no condition to go out. 'Never mind, Dot – soon lads will be comin' to us. We won't 'ave to go far for a dance, will we? I might even get a gramophone.'

Dot giggled. She hadn't felt as good as this since she first set eyes on Sally's baby. At last life was looking up.

Suddenly, an hour later, Sally was banging and screaming at the front door.

Elsie opened it. 'Quick – quick! Get Dot!' Sally shouted, tears streaming down her face. 'Mam's dyin'!'

As the three of them ran, Elsie called, ' 'Ave you sent for the doc?'

Sally was too choked to answer but she nodded.

In the bedroom Len sat holding Vi's hand. Her face was sunken, her nostrils thin and waxy-looking. Her breathing was loud and strained, and every so often it stopped, to start again with loud gasps. Dot and Sally stood by her bed, crying.

'She can't die,' sobbed Sally. 'I needs 'er. My Clark needs 'er.'

Len stood up stiffly. 'You girls come and sit by your mam and 'old 'er 'ands. I reckon that's what she's waitin' for.'

Elsie and Len left the room. Elsie was in tears too. She couldn't believe Vi was dying. She'd always been so strong and full of life.

An hour later Sally and Dot appeared, red-eyed but a little calmer. 'She's gone, Elsie,' said Dot. 'She's left us.' There seemed to be nothing Len or Elsie could say to comfort them. 'I wish me dad 'ad been 'ere,' said Sally, picking up her sleeping baby and rocking him backwards and forwards. ' 'E'll blame us – I know 'e will.'

'It's no one's fault,' said Len. 'You did your best. And you were with 'er. That's what matters.'

Ena Sharples sat alongside Martha in the Rovers. ' 'Ave you bin to that orphanage yet, Ena?' asked Martha, with a touch of suspicion in her voice.

'Not as yet. There's bin no sign of anyone searchin' for the lad. An' I'm lookin' for a man to go wi' me.'

'Not scared to go on your own, Ena?'

'Don't talk dafter than usual, Martha. I'll tell you summat. If 'Itler 'imself walked in 'ere now I'd be owt but frightened. I'd go for 'im soon as look at 'im.'

' 'It 'im with your gas mask, would you, Ena?'

'Martha Longhurst, I'd probably pick you up and use you as a bloomin' batterin' ram.'

Martha sipped her milk stout unperturbed. 'You've still not told me owt 'bout this fella you're looking for.'

Ena looked around the bar. 'I've 'eard this Mrs Makins 'as got a big 'usband. She might not let me 'ave my say.'

'By 'eck, Ena, I can't believe that.'

'Are you bein' funny, Martha Longhurst?'

'It's not in my nature to be funny, Ena.'

'Aye. You never said a truer word. Now, where was I afore you poked your oar in?'

'Mitherin' about not 'avin your say.'

'I need a man,' said Ena, casting Martha a glance that would quell a Zulu warrior, 'as'll do as 'e's told but can act tough if needs be.'

'Sounds like a lot of blokes round 'ere. Not much between their lug-'oles but fists the size of pig's trotters.'

'That's as mebbe. Show me one then.'

Martha looked round the Rovers and found she couldn't prove her point. Albert Tatlock and Tom Hewitt and one or two old boys of the Home Guard were in but not one had muscles bigger than a pigeon's egg. And then the door opened and in walked Stanley Ogden and Hilda.

' 'Im,' said Martha.

Ena looked around. 'Where?'

Martha nodded in the pair's direction. 'Over there, by the door.'

Ena stared at the pair of them. ' 'E might do,' she murmured. 'Why didn't I think of 'im before? 'E's easily led if you ask me.' After a few seconds' deliberation she stood up. 'I'll get us another milk stout and see just 'ow much persuadin' 'e'll need.'

Annie Walker smiled frostily as Ena ordered the drinks. 'This gentleman is first, Mrs Sharples.'

Ena looked Stan up and down. He was tall and broad and he didn't have a pretty face. 'Well, a big fella like you won't barge in front of a poor widow like me, would you, son?'

'No, missus. You go first. I ain't in no 'urry. Me an' 'Ilda are still celebratin' gettin' married.'

'Well, in that case,' said Ena, 'I'll buy you both a drink.'

'No need, missus. Let me buy you one.'

Ena smiled. 'Aye, lad. You do that. I might just 'ave a little job you can 'elp me with.'

He grinned, and Ena knew she'd found her man.

CHAPTER TWELVE

Spring 1944 Stalin declares: 'The wounded German beast must be pursued and finished off in its lair.'

On the day of Vi's funeral Jack Todd arrived home on compassionate leave and the hearse arrived early to wait outside the front door. The undertakers, in black top hats and tails, carried Vi's coffin out of the house. Jack, with his daughters, walked behind the hearse. Other family and friends fell into step behind them and the slow procession made its way past the occupants of Coronation Street, who stood in silence by their front doors, the men removing their caps, the women nodding their respects.

After the funeral service and the burial, Dot and Sally served tea, ham sandwiches and Madeira cake to the crowd of mourners. Jack drank most of a bottle of whisky and stared morosely into space until he fell asleep.

Dot, now dry-eyed, murmured to Elsie, 'I don't feel young any more. Me mam bein' gone 'as changed everything.'

'I know, pet.'

'I'll do me best for Sally and our dad.'

'I know you will,' said Elsie. 'And I bet your mam is lookin' down from 'eaven at this very minute feeling reet proud of you both.'

'I do 'ope so.'

'What was it she used to say when you 'ad a moan?'

Dot smiled. ' "If there's nowt you can do then you just 'ave to put up and shut up." '

'You can't argue with that, Dot,' said Elsie. 'Shall we 'ave a proper drink now?' She pushed Dot nearer to the sideboard, where there was a bottle of port and a half bottle of gin. 'A toast for your mam,' she said.

They toasted Vi with gin and orange squash. 'Mam did love a gin,' said Dot.

'We'll 'ave to 'ave a few more, then,' suggested Elsie.

Dot smiled. 'Any excuse, Elsie Tanner!' and suddenly they were both laughing. And Dot knew, sure as sure, that somewhere peaceful her mother was laughing with them.

'Nice 'ere,' commented Stanley Ogden, as he and Ena stood outside The Gables Orphanage on the outskirts of Manchester. The detached house, with neat lawns and apple trees on both sides, was a big contrast to the cramped terraces of Coronation Street.

'There's nowt nice about this place,' said Ena. 'Now, remember, Stanley Ogden, you say nowt but keep your face set, like there were 'ordes of 'Uns comin' at yer.'

'Aye. I'll do me best, Mrs Sharples.'

As they stood on the porch Ena said, 'You've bin on a long leave, Stanley. When are you goin' back exactly?'

Stanley looked at his feet and mumbled something Ena didn't catch.

'You've gone AWOL, you daft beggar, 'aven't yer?'

'Aye,' he said. ' 'Ilda wanted to get married.'

'Your 'Ilda's not the one in the army, is she? Now, you get back to where you're supposed to be today or the MPs will come for yer.'

'What about 'Ilda?'

Before Ena had a chance to reply, the front door was opened by a girl of about fourteen, wearing a floral apron. She didn't say a word, just looked them up and down and beckoned them in. Inside the door there were two lines of hooks and dozens of coats of different sizes. Underneath were children's boots and shoes. The hall floor was covered in brown linoleum and the walls were a dull green. There were two paintings of mountains and not a sound of a child.

The silent girl led them to a waiting room and pointed to

the chairs. A door with a sign, saying *Mrs Makins, Matron* faced them. Ena didn't speak; she was rehearsing in her mind what she was going to say.

A little girl of about two toddled in and walked across to Stanley, looked at him briefly, said, 'Daddy,' and climbed on to his lap. The silent girl appeared suddenly from nowhere to scoop up the child, who began screaming loudly enough to shatter glass. The girl didn't seem to notice.

Mrs Makins appeared then. She was tall and thin with straggly grey hair, and wearing a white overall that made her look like a butcher. Ena also noticed she looked exhausted, the black rings under her eyes and sallow complexion suggesting that she never saw any sunshine.

Ena wasted no time in telling her why they were there. 'It's about Dieter Holliman. You've bin lookin' for 'im.'

Mrs Makins managed a smile. 'Thank goodness for that. I was beginning to think he'd never be found. We heard he was in Weatherfield but no one there could tell us anything.'

'Goodness has nowt to do with it.'

'What's that supposed to mean – and who are you anyway?'

'I'm the caretaker of the Glad Tidings Mission Hall, Mrs Ena Sharples, and this 'ere is Sergeant Stanley Ogden.'

'You'd better sit down and tell me what all this is about.'

Matron Makins sat behind a desk in a wing-back chair. Ena sat stiffly on an upright chair and the newly promoted Stanley stood to attention by her side. 'We might know where young Dieter is,' said Ena.

Mrs Makins seemed pleased. 'That's wonderful. I'll get someone to collect him at once.'

'You'll do no such thing,' retorted Ena. 'Dieter is reet 'appy where 'e is. There's nowt could even drag 'im back 'ere.'

'Why ever not?'

' 'E says you were cruel to 'im.'

'What absolute nonsense!' snapped Mrs Makins. 'Everything I did was standard procedure.'

'I bet that's what the Nazis say when they're killin' folk.'

'Don't be so ridiculous.'

Ena stood up slowly and deliberately, walked over to the desk and planted her hands firmly on it. 'Don't you call me ridiculous!' she snapped. 'You ill-treat a Jewish kiddie who's probably escaped from who knows what and you've got the bloomin' cheek to call me ridiculous.'

'I wasn't aware that I was mistreating him.'

'There's nowt as stupid as those who 'ave a bit of power.'

Mrs Makins stood up. 'This is getting us nowhere. I think you should leave *now*.'

'We'll leave when we're ready, Mrs Makins,' said Ena. 'Stanley, guard the door.'

Stanley marched to the door and stood blocking it. His face was expressionless.

'I want that lad's papers and his ration books,' demanded Ena.

'Mrs Sharples, you can't possibly have those. It's against the law.'

'Is cruelty against the law?'

'We're going round in circles. I shall be forced to fetch the police.'

'Aye. Mebbe that's a good idea and then we could ask the kiddies 'ere how you treat 'em. I reckon you could be sacked.'

At the mention of being sacked, Mrs Makins's face paled and she slumped back in her chair. She muttered, 'I may have been wrong about Dieter but he was stealing food and bed-wetting. There are thirty-five children here and they have all had terrible experiences. If they all stole food and wet the bed, how would we cope? It's hard enough as it is. I can't get staff. Some young women have joined up and the others work in munitions for half-decent wages. Sometimes I'm here on my own. The girl who let you in works here now. She's been struck dumb ever since her parents died when their house was bombed. That was in 1941.'

Ena's indignation lessened as she began to recognize that this woman was a nervous wreck. 'How come these kiddies can't be evacuated to the countryside?'

Mrs Makins sighed deeply. 'They aren't wanted – they have too many problems. Some were evacuated but they were sent on here. I do my best but I don't think I can carry on.'

For once Ena fell silent. After a few moments she said, 'Young Dieter's very 'appy where 'e is. He's put on weight and 'e wants to go to school. But we need 'is papers. If you write something down about 'im being evacuated to Weatherfield then there'll be nowt for anyone to worry about.'

Mrs Makins rubbed a hand wearily across her forehead and said, 'Very well. But I would appreciate it if you brought him to see me so that I can see he's well.'

'Aye, if and when 'e's willin'.'

While Mrs Makins searched in the filing cabinet for his papers and ration book, Ena said, ' 'Ow did he get here, any road?'

Mrs Makins paused in her search. 'It seems,' she said, 'his mother worked as a translator as her English was so good. She managed to get out of Germany before war broke out. Her husband, a doctor, planned to follow her later. She took Dieter to the East End of London and they stayed in a house with relatives of hers. The house was bombed – they usually went to a shelter but someone was ill so they stayed at home. Dieter was the only survivor. He was in severe shock for weeks and they kept him in hospital. He only said one word – 'Manchester' – so the authorities presumed he had relatives in the city. We had a vacancy so they sent him here.'

'Poor little mite,' muttered Ena.

'They're all poor little mites,' said Mrs Makins, handing Ena the ration book. Then she took up a pen to sign the evacuation order. She paused, 'I do hope this is the last I shall hear of these allegations.'

'Just sign the bloomin' thing and we can be off.' Ena held out her hand for the order, then tucked the papers in her handbag. 'Mebbe this is the last you'll 'ear of us, Mrs Makins. Depends on 'ow you go on. If you 'its a child again or meks their life a misery you think on this. The good Lord is watchin' yer and I meself could come back 'ere wi' Stanley and set about *you* wi' a ruler.'

Mrs Makins said nothing.

'Come on, Stanley,' said Ena, 'tek that look off yer face. You look as if you've got a poker up yer bum.'

On the way home Ena felt well satisfied with her efforts. It had been a good morning's work but the other orphans worried her. ' 'Ow many more will there be after this war is over, Stanley?'

Stanley stopped in his tracks. 'More what, Mrs Sharples?'

'Never mind, Stanley. There's nowt you can do. You'll just do yer bit and 'elp to mek more widows and orphans.'

'Aye,' said Stanley. 'I just does as I'm told.'

Ida Barlow and Bessie Tatlock's make-do-and-mend group now included Minnie Caldwell and Martha Longhurst. Minnie had sorted out some old clothes that had belonged to her late husband, Armistead, that she hadn't had the heart to get rid of. Now, with his trousers and jackets cut down and remade, Dieter had some new clothes. Martha could sew, but her main aim was not to make do and mend but to collect gossip and recycle it.

Elsie Tanner's appearance late one Thursday afternoon was a surprise to them all.

'I wonder if you could 'elp me, Ida and Bessie,' she said. 'I've 'eard you can do wonders with a needle and cotton.' They expected a bag full of clothes but Elsie placed a bag of bedding on the table. 'It's sheets, pillowcases and counter-panes,' she explained. 'I was wonderin' if you could turn the sheets sides to middle and patch me pillowcases, and there's a couple of Arnold's shirts that need the collars turnin'.'

Martha Longhurst was quick off the mark. 'Your Arnold comin' 'ome then, is 'e?'

' 'E'd be as welcome as ruddy snow in August,' said Elsie cheerfully. 'I'll pay you, of course. I can't sew a button on without 'elp so you'll save me life if you freshen up me sheets.'

'Aye, we'll do that,' said Ida. 'Take us two or three days.'

'That'll do grand,' said Elsie. 'I don't need 'em till Monday. Can't stop. Thanks. Ta-ra.'

'Well,' said Martha even before Elsie had gone through the back door, 'what do you mek of that?'

'Spring-cleanin', that's all,' said Ida.

'Elsie Tanner, spring-clean?' sneered Martha. 'She's the sort of woman who does 'er washin' on a Sunday.'

'She does go to work,' said Bessie.

Martha began to undo the bundle of bedclothes. 'These

sheets 'ave seen nowt like starch since she got 'em. Does she call them white? And they got more 'oles in 'em than a colander.'

'We'll do a bit o' patchin',' said Bessie 'and give 'em a good boiling and a bit o' starch and they'll be as good as new.'

'What I'd like to know,' said Martha, 'is who she wants to impress. I reckon she must 'ave a new man.'

'You always think the worst of people, Martha,' said Minnie quietly.

Martha squared her shoulders. 'Chamberlain thought the best of 'Itler and look what 'appened. 'E invaded Poland.' She continued the unpicking she'd started but her heart wasn't in it. 'I shall 'ave to go – I've just remembered summat.'

'What might that be, Martha?' asked Minnie.

Martha frowned at her. 'Just a bit of private business, Minnie Caldwell. I'll catch yer later.'

Martha made her way direct to the Glad Tidings Mission Hall, where she found Ena polishing the chairs. 'Guess what, Ena, I've got a bit o' news.'

'So 'ave I, Martha Longhurst. You put kettle on and I'll tell yer.'

'But—'

'You can tell us in a minute, Martha. Put the kettle on.'

Martha did as she was told, mumbling, 'Are you sure you're not related to someone in Berlin?'

Ena didn't hear. She had troubles of her own.

At the Rover's, Annie Walker and Ned Narkin were clearing up and washing glasses.

'You lock up at the back, Ned,' Annie said.

'I allus do,' he said sullenly.

Annie was wiping the bar when she heard footsteps behind her. She assumed it was Ned but when a voice said, 'Annie,' she almost jumped out of her skin.

'John! You nearly gave me a heart-attack. Did Ned see you?'

'Come out from behind the bar where I can see *you*.'

'You shouldn't come here after hours, John,' said Annie,

walking towards him. 'It's not right, and that Ned is a sly old beggar.'

'Ned's gone home now. We're all alone. Perhaps I could have a drink while I'm here.'

Annie poured him a whisky and herself some sherry and as they sat together in the Snug, John took her hand. 'Please, Annie, I know we could be happy together. Why won't you even consider leaving this place?'

'I'm always thinking about it. I haven't heard from Jack in weeks. He may even have been taken prisoner.'

'You'd have heard if he had been.'

Annie shrugged. 'These things happen. We're meant to be winning the war but I don't see any sign of it.'

'I'm trying to win you over, Annie,' he said, stroking her hair, 'and I don't see much response.'

'I'm sorry, John. You mustn't come here again. Too many people know. I've already been threatened.'

'Who by?'

'An old harridan called Ena Sharples. She says she'll write to Jack if I divulge something I know about.'

'What do you know?'

'I'd best not say.'

'If it's about that German lad,' said John, 'he's now a pupil at Bessie Street. He's officially an evacuee staying with a Mrs Caldwell.'

Annie breathed a sigh of relief and at long last smiled at John. He put his arm around her and began kissing her.

'John, you mustn't. No,' she protested. But he continued to kiss her and his hand found her knee. 'No, John,' she said again but it was such a weak protest he didn't hear.

Neither of them heard Teresa walk into the bar and then towards the Snug. 'Mrs Walk—' The girl's mouth dropped open in shock. Hastily Annie rearranged herself. 'What on earth is it, Teresa?'

Teresa glanced away, her face as flushed as Annie's. 'It's the children, Mrs Walker. They've got lice.'

CHAPTER THIRTEEN

Summer 1944 Allied bombers wreck coastal fortifications between Cherbourg and Le Havre.

Elsie Tanner staggered slightly as she made her way upstairs. She'd been out dancing with Dot but had spent most of the time drinking. The kids were staying overnight with Sally, and Elsie was looking forward to a quiet night. She'd just got into bed when someone started banging on the front door. She leaned out of the front window to see two sailors and a soldier on her doorstep. 'What the 'ell's goin' on?' she yelled.

'Mrs Tanner,' yelled one of the sailors. 'Your 'Tonio said you'd put us up.'

'Oh, Gawd,' muttered Elsie, grabbing her housecoat and rushing downstairs.

She opened the door and saw one or two curtains twitching. 'Sorry we couldn't let you know, love,' said the taller sailor. 'We didn't know ourselves until three hours ago. All hush-hush but it's to do with the invasion plans.'

'Come on in, lads,' said Elsie, 'and mek yerselves at 'ome.'

The arrival of her paying guests had sobered Elsie up, and as they put down their rucksacks and sank into her armchairs she realized just how much room they were going to take up. 'What's yer names, then, lads?' she asked.

'I'm Jack,' said the sailor who had spoken to her at the door. He had blue eyes and thick dark hair. 'This is Eddie Barnes, me shipmate, and in the corner is Jimmy Lawrence

485

from bonny Scotland.' Eddie smiled shyly. He was young, only about twenty, but already he had tired eyes and a worried frown. Jimmy, the soldier, was broad with a wide face and a broken nose. He'd opened his rucksack and now produced a bottle of whisky. 'Ha'e you got some glasses, lass?' he asked, with a grin.

Two doubles later, Elsie remembered she had no sheets on the beds and it was far too late to disturb Ida Barlow. 'Dinnae worry, hen,' said Jimmy. 'A few more wee tots and we'll no' need sheets. We'll sleep like bairns where we sit.'

Jack laughed, 'And Eddie 'ere could sleep on a hammock during action stations if he's 'ad enough to drink.'

Eddie smiled again at Elsie. She couldn't help noticing that he kept glancing at her then looking away.

They talked until the early hours. Eventually Jack and Jimmy fell asleep in the armchairs while Elsie and Eddie continued smoking, drinking and chatting. 'I think you're lovely,' he said suddenly. Drunkenly Elsie ruffled his hair. 'I've never 'ad a girlfriend,' he murmured, 'never 'ardly kissed a girl. I don't suppose I will now. I've lost so many mates who were the same as me. They never 'ad no time either. Now we're goin' to start the invasion and I bet I miss out altogether.'

'I'll give you a kiss,' said Elsie.

'Will you?'

'Aye. Why not?'

She kissed him and afterwards he sighed deeply. 'That were lovely,' he said. 'That's the best thing that's 'appened to me since I joined up.'

Elsie smiled. 'You come with me, lad,' she murmured. 'I can show you summat better than that.'

She took his hand and led him to her bed. 'Your boat's just come in, Eddie,' she whispered in his ear, 'and a reet safe 'arbour it's found.'

Early Saturday morning Ena Sharples joined the queue at the Corner Shop hoping to buy sugar. Martha was way ahead of her in the line but she left her place to join Ena. 'Have you 'eard, Ena?'

'I've 'eard nowt, Martha Longhurst. What are yer on about?'

'Elsie Tanner.'

'What's she bin up to now?'

'I'm surprised you haven't 'eard, Ena.'

'Martha Longhurst, do you keep that beret on your 'ead to keep your brain warm? 'Cos if yer do it's doin' yer no good.'

'Do yer want to know or not?'

Ena shrugged. She was always annoyed when Martha got hold of a bit of news before her and especially annoyed when she made a meal of telling her. 'Just tell us and be done wi' it.'

'Men,' said Martha. 'Servicemen. That's why she wanted 'er sheets patched up.'

'Do you know, Martha Longhurst, you could mek a bloomin' mystery of the Second Coming? You know reet well that men and Elsie Tanner is as common as a bit o' drippin' on toast.'

'They're stayin' there,' announced Martha loudly. 'The three of 'em. Two sailors and a soldier. I reckon they're payin' guests.'

'Payin' guests? Payin' guests! Were you born, Martha, or did you creep out from under a bit o' rhubarb? If she's got men stayin' there she's running a brothel.'

'Do you think so, Ena?'

'I've just said so, 'aven't I? You can stay 'ere and get me sugar and some barm cakes. I'm off to see Elsie Tanner.'

Martha opened her mouth to protest but Ena was already marching off in the direction of No. 11.

She banged hard on the door. 'Elsie Tanner,' she yelled, 'I want words wi' you.'

The door opened suddenly and Ena was faced with the hairy chest of a man otherwise naked but for socks and a towel. 'Och, woman, there's no need to break down the door,' said Jimmy.

'Where's Elsie Tanner?'

'She's away in the Land of Nod, missus. We 'ad a bellyful last night.'

'Aye, well, give 'er a message from me.'

'Aye, I will.'

'You just tell 'er 'er Arnold will 'ear of this.'

'Who's Arnold?' asked Jimmy.

'Arnold is 'er 'usband.'

Jimmy shrugged. 'Nae harm's done, woman. Be off wi' ye or I'll show ye what I keep under ma sporran.'

Ena left hurriedly. She knew only too well that the curtains of Coronation Street were twitching as fast as a chicken with its throat cut. And she wasn't prepared to be a laughing stock. There was no doubt that she had to do something, not tomorrow or the next day but this instant.

Back at the Mission she put pen to paper – twice. She had a duty to the children. It was best men knew what was going on on the home front. It would give them a chance to put things right. It was her Christian duty and nothing would deter her.

Elsie Tanner woke up with a start. She opened her eyes and stared at the fair head on the pillow beside her. Who the hell are you? she wondered, until her memory came flooding back. She had no regrets – he'd told her it was the best experience of his life and he'd always be grateful. Then he'd gone to sleep like a baby and still slept although it was past ten.

It was Jimmy who changed her contented mood. 'Some old biddy came round,' he told her, 'threatenin' to tell your 'usband.'

Elsie drank a cup of scalding tea and dressed quickly. She powdered her nose, used her lipstick as rouge and put plenty on her lips. Only then did she feel ready for the battle. She strode towards the Glad Tidings Mission Hall and hoped the neighbours saw her. In fact, she'd rather Ena came out into the Street for the row just so that everyone could hear what she had to say.

Disappointed to find the door open, she walked in and found Ena with a brush in her hand. 'Just flown in on yer broomstick, 'ave yer?'

'I'm glad you've come, Elsie Tanner. I was at your place today but you didn't 'ave the brass neck to speak to me. I suppose as usual you 'ad nowt on.'

Elsie advanced towards her. 'So 'elp me, Ena Sharples, I'll bloody swing for you.'

Ena pointed the broom handle threateningly. 'Don't you come any closer. I've no scruples about clobbering yer wi' this.'

'What exactly is your gripe wi' me?' demanded Elsie.

Ena lowered the broom slightly. 'There's nowt so sly as a painted Jezebel and that's what you are. You're a married woman with kiddies and every week you're at the post office collectin' your 'usband's wages and now you're—'

'I'm what? Come on, it's not like you to beat about the bloody bush.'

Ena took a deep breath. 'You're a . . . prostitute and you're runnin' . . . a brothel.'

Elsie stared hard at her adversary then burst out laughing. 'I wish I'd thought of that, Mrs Sharples. You see, I don't sell meself, I gives it away for nowt.' She carried on laughing and Ena grew red in the face.

'You've got no shame, woman,' she bellowed.

Elsie stopped laughing and glared defiantly. 'You're right, Ena "Holier than Thou" Sharples. I enjoys meself, which is more than can be said for you. I reckon your Vera is the result of an Immaculate Conception.'

'Don't you bring my Vera into this. She's a respectable girl.'

Elsie laughed. 'Aye, she may 'ave been innocent once but she's not married yet.' Vera was Ena's Achilles heel and Elsie knew that, just as Ena knew that Arnold was Elsie's. All's fair, thought Elsie, especially in war. Love didn't come into it.

'If my Vera's up to owt I wants to know,' said Ena in a calmer voice.

Elsie sensed she was getting the upper hand. 'If I was you I'd get 'er and that Bob Lomax down aisle as soon as you can.'

'She's not. . . ?' Ena couldn't bring herself to say the word.

'She would be if I 'adn't told 'er what's what.'

'If you ask me,' said Ena, 'it was you who led 'er astray.'

'Don't talk ruddy daft, Ena Sharples. It was me who found 'er on Red Rec allotments in one of the 'uts. If it weren't for me your Vera would be goin' up aisle fit to bust 'er dress.'

'It was 'im, then, who took advantage of 'er.' said

Ena, her voice wavering. 'He looks as if butter wouldn't melt if he bloomin' sat on it.'

'Aye,' said Elsie. 'But 'e's still a man. And your Vera is woman enough to 'ave 'ad 'er wicked way with 'im.'

' 'Ow dare you, Elsie Tanner? My Vera wouldn't—'

'Don't kid yerself,' said Elsie. 'Your Vera isn't a frigid old busybody like you. And I'd be grateful if you didn't write to my Arnold. 'E's quite 'appy and you know 'ow much trouble it caused last time you stuck your oar in.'

' 'E 'as a right to know.'

'The man is an animal. Don't forget 'e's a soldier and 'e's more than up to killing me and the kids. He raped me and beat me up. 'E could 'ave killed me then. If you write to 'im, anythin' that 'appens will be on your conscience till the day you die.'

Ena could feel the colour drain from her face. 'There's summat you should know,' she mumbled. 'I've already sent the letter.'

'You stupid old cow!' screamed Elsie, flying at Ena, pulling her turban off and slapping and kicking for all she was worth. Ena fought back and they struggled together on the floor of the Mission Hall. They rolled over and over, not seeing the bucket of dirty water with which Ena had washed the floor. Rolling in the water made no difference, hands clutched at wet hair instead of dry. Elsie managed to slap Ena around the ear and bang her head on the floor.

'Stop it at once.' The weak voice of Mr Swindley caused barely a pause in the fight. When he got no response he ran out of the Mission Hall to get reinforcements.

He came back with Len Fairclough. Len hobbled over and grabbed Elsie's arm. She lashed out at him. 'I'll land you one, Elsie, if you don't stop,' he yelled.

The anger in his voice finally got through to her. 'Let me go, Len. Let me 'ave one last swing at 'er.'

'You're comin' 'ome now,' said Len, pulling her towards the door. 'You've not changed since you were at school,' he said. 'You got into as many scraps then as a drunken sailor.'

Elsie, wet and breathless, said nothing. She could hear Mr Swindley berating Ena for besmirching the Mission's good

The Way to Victory

name. The last words Elsie heard were, 'You should be thoroughly ashamed of yourself, Mrs Sharples.'

Ena didn't answer. Elsie considered she'd had a victory because if Len hadn't pulled her away she'd definitely have won.

But by the time Len had marched her down the Street, Elsie's bravado was weakening, and as she approached her front door she was near to tears. The thought of Arnold returning to create havoc was a real worry. Elsie hadn't exaggerated when she'd told Ena Arnold could kill when he was drunk. He was a nasty piece of work and he was the one person in the world who scared Elsie.

Ena sat in the vestry her head in her hands. When she took her hands away little clumps of hair fell out. That didn't worry her. It was what she'd done that worried her. The letters had gone – it was too late to change that – and now she was full of apprehension and regret. Act in haste, she thought, repent at leisure. If anything happened to Elsie's children she'd never forgive herself.

CHAPTER FOURTEEN

6 June 1944 The D-Day Landings.

Like everyone else, Dot Greenhalgh and Elsie Tanner had known that some sort of invasion was planned but they hadn't realized the effect it would have. Overnight, it seemed, servicemen disappeared from Weatherfield. There were no dances and paying guests were a thing of the past, while most factories stepped up production.

Dot and Elsie went to the pictures to catch up on the news, but the cinemas were nearly empty and they were forced to buy their own drinks in the Rovers afterwards. On the night of the D-Day landings even Ena Sharples was absent from the Snug.

'Just as well she's not 'ere,' said Elsie sipping her port and lemon. 'Mood I'm in I'd be ready for another go at 'er.'

'It's only 'cos you're mithered about your Arnold,' said Dot. 'With any luck 'e'll 'ave copped it on one of them beaches in Normandy.'

Elsie looked at Dot's expression to see if she was joking. 'I don't wish 'im any 'arm,' she began.

'I know that,' interrupted Dot, 'but there's a lot of women 'round 'ere who've got mixed feelings 'bout which bloke they wants to see come 'ome.'

'You for one, Dot.'

'Aye,' she said. 'I 'aven't seen my Walt for so long I've forgotten what 'e looks like. The couple of leaves 'e's 'ad 'aven't been so grand. 'E slept most of 'is last twenty-four-hour leave.'

'There'll be no leave for a while and not much going on,' said Elsie, looking at the few old men in the bar. 'What'll we do?'

'Gawd knows,' laughed Dot.

As Elsie was buying another drink a tall man wearing a black overcoat came to the bar. 'Excuse me,' he said to Annie Walker, 'I'm looking for Mrs Ena Sharples.'

'She's not come in yet,' said Annie.

'Are you expecting her?'

Annie looked at him carefully. He was clean and well dressed, although the black overcoat looked strange in summer. He wasn't local, that was for sure, for his accent sounded foreign. Annie was wary. Ena Sharples might have been a thorn in her side but she *was* local and it was always best to be wary of strangers. 'She'll probably be in soon. Would you like a drink while you wait?'

'No, thank you.'

Annie wanted to question him but he smiled and left.

Elsie was intrigued. 'I wonder what 'e wants with Ena Sharples,' she said to Dot.

'I thought 'e looked like the ruddy Grim Reaper,' her friend replied.

Elsie chuckled. 'There's nowt like a bit of 'ope, is there?'

Ena didn't appear that evening and it was two days later that she came in with Martha and Minnie.

'Mrs Sharples,' said Annie, eager to see her reaction, 'there's been a strange man looking for you.'

'Did he want owt?' snapped Ena.

'I really couldn't say. He just asked for Mrs Ena Sharples.'

' 'E must 'ave said more 'an that.'

'No, that's all, but I had a feeling he might have been from the orphanage.'

'Oh, you did, did you Annie Walker? Dieter is stayin' with Minnie Caldwell, all legal, like, and we 'ave papers to prove it.'

Standing alongside them with an empty half-pint glass in his hand, Albert Tatlock overheard every word. ''E was in Corner Shop two days past. 'E said as 'ow 'e was looking for the little lad. Mrs Foyle lied like a trooper and said there were no spare little lads in Weatherfield.'

'Well,' said Ena. 'I'm glad someone round 'ere 'as got some sense.'

'I reckon 'e's gone now,' said Albert. 'I 'aven't seen 'im since.'

Ena breathed a sigh of relief. 'I 'ope no one says owt about this to Minnie. She dotes on that lad.'

Back in the Snug Ena swore Martha to secrecy. She nodded solemnly and then dropped a bombshell of her own. 'Is it true, Ena, your Vera's getting married in a church?' Ena nearly choked on her milk stout. 'Whoever told you that, Martha Longhurst, is an out-and-out liar. My Vera will be married at the Mission and very soon.'

Martha was silent.

'Well?' demanded Ena.

'Well what?'

'Who told you?'

Martha stared into her glass. 'I 'eard it in a queue. Didn't recognize the voice. Just said she'd 'eard she was 'avin' banns read.'

Ena stood up, threw her tin helmet over her shoulder and said, 'You finish me drink. I'm goin' 'ome to wait for my Vera and see if she's got owt to say for herself.'

Mrs Stanley Ogden stared out of the window of the room she'd shared only four times with her husband since their wedding. Her dad had let them have the front bedroom, but Hilda had soon realized that she couldn't afford to keep Stanley for long: he couldn't use his ration books here and, anyway, being AWOL he wouldn't get paid. With the D-Day invasion starting she was sure the war would be over in a couple of months.

Hilda thought back to Stanley's last morning with her. She'd woken at about six, with Stanley fast asleep and snoring beside her. She'd snuggled down beside him, resting her cold feet on his calves. But she couldn't sleep. 'Stanley? Stanley, are you awake?' she'd asked. He fidgeted. 'Are you awake, Stanley?' she'd repeated.

'I am now. Can't you let a man rest?'

'It's time you went back to your barracks. War's nearly over.'

Stanley had opened one eye. 'Who told yer that?'

'Everyone's sayin' it. Now we're over there the Germans will just give up.'

' 'Ilda you're talkin' out of the top of your 'ead. Now let me get some kip.'

'You'll 'ave to get a job then.'

'Do give over, woman. 'Ow can I get a job? I've got service papers. I'd be caught in a day.'

'Me dad says we can't afford to keep yer much longer – you eats too much.'

Stanley groaned and sat up in bed. 'I'll stop eatin' then.'

'Don't talk daft. There's no need for that. You'll just 'ave to give yerself up.'

'Aye,' said Stanley, with a deep sigh, 'but there's nowt you know about the glasshouse. It's bloody 'orrible. Up at six, march everywhere at the double, bread and water if you do owt wrong and I'd be there months and bloody months.'

'No need to swear, Stanley.'

'Sometimes, 'Ilda, you're enough to make a saint swear.'

'You can't lay low for ever, Stanley.'

' 'Ilda, I've 'ad a thought.'

'What?'

'I'll join the French bloody Foreign Legion if you're so keen to get rid of me.'

'It's not that, pet, it's me dad.'

Stanley sat on the side of the bed. 'It comes to summat when yer new bride wants yer out of the road.'

Hilda was about to disagree when banging had started on the front door. She had jumped out of bed, run to the window and seen three burly Military Policemen standing on the front door step. 'Run! Stanley, run!' she'd shouted in panic. Stanley paused for only a second and began looking for his trousers, but Hilda gave him no chance. 'Quick – out the back and over the fence,' she said, giving him a shove. Stanley, in vest and underpants, had made it only to the back gate. He was stopped by an MP as wide as the back gate itself.

'I think you're improperly dressed son,' he'd boomed, 'especially for the glasshouse.'

Stanley was led back inside and allowed to get dressed. Hilda glared at the policemen. 'My Stanley was 'ere lookin' after me and if you big lugs 'urt 'im you'll 'ave me to reckon with.'

'Ooh, missus, I'm all of a tremble,' said one.

Hilda wasn't deterred. 'I'm a pregnant woman, and Stanley 'ere was 'avin' to stay with me as I was reet ill.'

'Regular little paragon, ain't 'e?' he said, smirking at Stanley, then added, 'Get your mouth closed, Ogden, and your boots on.'

'Did you 'ear me?' Hilda demanded.

'Now, look 'ere, missus, keep your lip buttoned. You don't look much fatter than a wax taper so with a bit of luck your man 'ere will be out of the glasshouse by the time it's born.'

' 'Es my 'usband,' said Hilda indignantly.

When one of the policemen laughed at that, Hilda felt like crying, but she didn't give into it. 'I 'ave a right to kiss 'im goodbye.'

'You've got no rights, sweet'eart, but you can. Make it quick.' Hilda kissed Stanley, who was now dressed in his khaki uniform and standing to attention. 'Be brave, pet,' she whispered in his ear.

'Right, Ogden. You know the drill,' shouted the MP with stripes on his arm. 'Left, right. Left, right, left, right.'

It had been a whole two weeks before she had heard any more from Stanley. He was given a month's sentence and was then to go straight back to his unit. 'You're a wonderful woman, Hilda,' he wrote. He also said he was 'behaving himself' but he missed his beer. 'See you soon, chuck,' were his last words.

Hilda left her bed and stared out of the window. It was a pity, she thought, that he hadn't gone AWOL for longer. He was much safer in the glasshouse. Anything might happen to him once he got back to the front.

Albert Tatlock prided himself on being the Weatherfield war correspondent. As an ARP warden he considered it his duty to be well informed on the war's progress. He read the newspapers avidly and listened to the BBC news on the wireless. He took some of the gung-ho propaganda with a pinch of salt but on 13 June, when the first V1 rockets hit London, he felt a real need to talk it over with somebody other than Bessie. She was convinced the war would be over in weeks and then Beattie could come back to them. Albert felt that unless the RAF could find and bomb the rocket sites then the V1s would be a major setback.

'What do you think, Tom?' he asked Tom Hewitt in the Rovers at lunchtime.

'Blowed if I know. But I feel sorry for the poor beggars in London.'

'Strikes me,' said Albert, 'these doodlebugs can't get up 'ere – not enough fuel.'

Tom, who'd seen the carnage in the First World War and had learned to take nothing for granted in, both war- and peacetime, said dourly, 'The Krauts are clever sods. Them rockets are too fast for radar to pick 'em up and the ack-ack guns too bloomin' slow. You mark my words, this war is far from over. There'll be thousands killed yet.'

Albert had a feeling he was right. ' 'Ow's your 'Arry doing?' he asked, to change the subject. 'I don't 'ear that often,' said Tom. 'When 'e does come 'ome on leave 'e's as miserable as sin. 'E 'ardly leaves the 'ouse, says the girls don't want to know the local lads, they only want the Yanks.'

Albert nodded. 'They want their nylons and chewing-gum any road. When war's over and Yanks 'ave gone it'll be a different story.'

'I 'ope so,' said Tom. 'I'd like to see our 'Arry settle down before I peg it.'

'There's nowt wrong with you, is there?'

'War weary, that's what I am, Albert – war-weary. And this summer we've 'ad nowt but rain. Worst summer I've ever known.'

'Aye,' said Albert. 'At this rate we'll be lookin' forward to a bit o' drier weather in the winter.'

The rain was depressing Ida Barlow too. She sat in her front parlour patching some of Kenneth's clothes while Bessie cut out a pattern on the table. They had made a small profit from their make-do-and-mend activity. Few women wanted to join them but many happily left their mending and alterations to be done. Ida kept her share of the profits in an old teapot and took pleasure in how proud Frank would be when he came home to find a little nest-egg.

David was having an afternoon nap, Kenneth had just gone back to school after his lunch and she and Bessie had just eaten beetroot sandwiches followed by a cake made with dried eggs and a bit of lard. 'I'm fed up with eatin' animal innards,' said Ida, out of the blue. 'I've tried 'em now – sweet-breads, chitterlin's, tripe, kidneys and liver. There's nowt could make me eat 'earts and brains.'

Bessie, scissors poised, said, 'Reminds me of the depression years and they was a treat then.'

'Well, I don't know where the butcher gets 'em all from,' said Ida. 'He's never got any good cuts left but he'll always say, "I've got some lovely offal, love." '

'A nice stuffed slow-roasted 'eart is what Albert likes. A few vegetables with that and it goes down a treat.'

Ida began to feel slightly queasy and wanted to change the subject. 'It's the poor kids I feel sorry for.'

'Eatin' offal?'

'No,' said Ida, smiling at long last. 'This bloomin' rain. Kenneth 'ates the rain and 'e 'asn't been out to play with Billy Walker for ages. For some reason Annie's stopped him playing with Kenneth.'

'E's 'ad a very short 'aircut, that Billy,' said Bessie, as she paused for a long faultless cut through the cloth. 'I reckon e's got nits. I bet Annie Walker's blamin' everyone and keepin' him away from other kiddies.'

Ida began scratching her head immediately. 'I'd better check my two,' she said. 'You'd think we 'ad enough to worry about without nits, wouldn't you?'

'Aye, pet, but things could be worse,' said Bessie. 'At least 'Itler's gettin' his comeuppance now.'

' 'E doesn't 'ave to eat offal though, does 'e?'

' 'E's a vegetarian,' said Bessie.

' 'E never is.'

'My Albert told me. 'E knows ever such a lot. So you stop frettin', Ida dear, 'cos 'Itler will be eating nowt but 'umble pie soon.'

Ena Sharples waited up for her showdown with Vera but she fell asleep and it had to wait until morning. It was only six a.m. and Vera was hardly awake.

'What's this I 'ear, my girl?' demanded Ena.

Vera, trying to wash her face at the sink, mumbled under the towel. 'About what, Mam?'

'Don't you act the innocent wi' me. I know about your weddin' plans.'

'It's Bob's family. They want a church do.'

'Take that towel off your face and look at me.'

Vera did as she was told, sheepishly. 'Sorry,' she mumbled.

'Sorry?' yelled Ena. 'Sorry? You will be sorry, my girl. This Mission has given you an 'ome all these years and now you turn your back on us.'

' 'Is mam says she won't come to some back-street chapel and they'll pay for everything, so—' Vera broke off, intimidated by Ena's expression.

Ena could feel her chest nearly explode with fury. 'Backstreet chapel? How dare she? This chapel has provided shelter for 'undreds. Clean blankets and towels and cups of tea. What's St Mary's ever done? Nowt, that's what! And you, yer great puddin', couldn't even stand up for yerself. I bet you said, "Yes, Mrs Lomax, no, Mrs Lomax," like a bloomin' parrot.'

'I did try, Mam,' interrupted Vera.

'I did try, Mam,' mimicked Ena. 'You've got no backbone, girl. Sometimes I wonder if I wasn't given the wrong baby at the 'ospital they 'ad to take me to. You were trouble, Vera, even before yer was born.'

Vera began to cry and wiped her eyes with a corner of the towel. There was nothing she could say, her mother just wasn't going to listen.

'And you can stop that skrikin', that'll do yer no good. You just get round to the Lomax 'ouse and say you'll 'ave marriage service 'ere.'

Vera looked up, her eyes full of tears. 'No,' she said, in a wavering voice.

'What do yer mean, girl, no?'

'Bob and me 'ave decided and that's an end to it,' said Vera, jutting out her chin defiantly.

Ena had never heard that tone in her daughter's voice before but she guessed Vera would give in in the end. She softened her voice. 'Now look 'ere, Vera. I shall be right proud of you on the day. I can do a nice little tea for you 'ere. It'll be a grand day.'

'No,' said Vera, still defiant. 'It's my day and I'll do as I want.'

'Well, I'll not be comin' to see you wed in a church,' said Ena, her mouth set in grim determination.

'Aye, Mam. Do as yer please.'

Ena opened her mouth but Vera was already slipping on her jacket and walking to the back door. She turned as she put her hand on the latch. 'It's next Saturday, Mam, at two thirty.'

Ena's emotions seesawed between anger, surprise and misery. But it was pride that won the day. 'You'll be on yer own, then,' she said.

Vera left without another word and Ena recognized at long last that Vera was now grown-up and that she had lost control.

For some time Ena sat and prayed. Of one thing she was sure. God was on her side.

CHAPTER FIFTEEN

Summer 1944 Sustained attacks by V1s over southern England.

Minnie Caldwell rarely got letters and when one did land on her mat it always made her slightly anxious, especially if she couldn't immediately recognize the handwriting. She'd picked up the letter and stared at the postmark. It was local, but no one in Weatherfield would write to her and her bills always came in plain brown envelopes. This was pure white and now that she realized she couldn't guess the identity of the sender she tore it open. It was from Bessie Street School. Would she please see the headmaster as soon as possible, at her convenience, to discuss a matter relating to Dieter Holliman?

Minnie's first reaction was to take the letter straight to Ena. She'd already slipped her coat on but at the back door she took a deep breath and decided that if Dieter had been misbehaving at school no one else need know about it.

All the way to the school Minnie tried to work out what Dieter might have done. At home he was always well behaved and polite. Had he been fighting or checking the teachers? Minnie couldn't believe he would do such things. It was more likely that the others were picking on him.

By the time Minnie was ushered into the office she was as nervous as any child on their first day at school. Mr Barnstable, with his handsome face and kind eyes, instantly put her at her ease.

'Do sit down, Mrs Caldwell,' he said. 'I deliberately didn't mention any reason for wanting to see you about Dieter.

501

First, let me say that he is a credit to the school – he's bright and diligent, polite and attentive, and he gets on well with the other children.' He paused. 'I don't want to worry you, Mrs Caldwell, but it's been reported to me that a man has been asking questions about Dieter.'

'What sort of questions?' asked Minnie anxiously.

Mr Barnstable smiled. 'Please don't be too worried. He hasn't approached Dieter. It seems this man asked another child to point Dieter out and then he stood and watched him in the playground.'

Minnie nibbled her bottom lip. 'Did 'e wear a long black coat?'

'Yes,' Mr Barnstable said. 'You know about him, then?'

Minnie nodded. 'I 'ad 'eard 'e were asking around Weatherfield some time back.'

'I'm sorry to say that I've only just heard about this. It seems he first appeared some weeks back but this visit was just two days ago.'

'Oh dear,' murmured Minnie. 'I think 'e must be someone from the orphanage.'

Mr Barnstable shook his head. 'I rang the orphanage but the new matron knew nothing about Dieter and nothing about the man.'

Minnie fiddled nervously with the handles of her shopping-bag. 'What should I do, then?' she asked.

'All I can suggest at the moment,' said Mr Barnstable, 'is that you collect him from school each day.'

'Aye,' said Minnie, standing up. 'I'll do that.'

Minnie couldn't get away from Bessie Street School fast enough. Now she *did* want to see Ena. She'd know what to do. And she'd have to warn Dieter.

Ena was polishing the Mission chairs when Minnie arrived. 'Well, Minnie, you look as if you've lost sixpence and found a ha'penny.'

'I've bin to Bessie Street School. That bloke's bin watchin' my Dieter.'

'The black-coat man?'

'Aye. 'E's bin round this week.'

'Well, Minnie Caldwell, I'll 'ave to pay another visit to that orphanage, won't I?'

' 'E's not from there – the 'eadmaster checked.'

Ena sighed. 'Best put kettle on then, and work summat out.'

Ena had always kept a photo of Vera on the mantelpiece in her flat. Minnie noticed it had gone. Since Vera had got married and moved away, Ena hadn't been herself at all. For a while she stopped going into the Rovers and had taken instead to playing the harmonium and singing hymns all on her own. She'd lost weight too.

'Are you all right, Ena?' asked Minnie. 'You 'aven't been quite yerself since your Vera left.'

Ena's eyes sparked. 'Minnie Caldwell, I'd rather you didn't mention that name to me. She's no daughter of mine. I've cast her out.'

'But it says in the Bible—' began Minnie.

'Don't you tell me owt about the Bible, Minnie Caldwell. I knows the Bible. "Honour thy father and mother", that's what it says. And she didn't. Now let's talk about lookin' after young Dieter. There's nowt to be gained by talkin' about the cross I 'ave to bear.'

Minnie noticed that Ena had perked up no end at the thought of a new challenge.

'We don't want to frighten 'im away, Minnie,' said Ena, as she measured out the tea-leaves.

'We don't?'

'I've just said we don't. We need to catch 'im red-'anded.'

' 'Ow will we do that, Ena?'

'We'll tek it in turns to be at Bessie Street School at play-times and dinnertimes and we'll catch 'im.'

' 'Ow?'

'What do yer mean, 'ow?'

' 'E'll run off, won't 'e, Ena? And I can't run and I've never seen you run.'

'I'll 'ave you know, Minnie Caldwell, I won the egg-and-spoon race and the three-legged race when I was at school.'

'That was a long time ago, Ena, and it won't 'elp if 'e puts up a fight.'

'I'll tell you summat,' said Ena. 'We wouldn't be winnin' this war if Winnie were Minnie. You'd throw your 'ands up if one single Nazi did a goose-step down Coronation Street.'

'I would not!'

'That's as mebbe, but you've got to keep your wits about you. We don't know who this bloke is or what 'e wants.'

' 'E could be a spy,' suggested Minnie.

'I shouldn't think there's owt Dieter could tell 'im.'

'You never know, Ena. 'E did get out of Germany so mebbe this bloke 'as been sent by 'Itler to find out 'ow 'e did it.'

Ena squinted at Minnie. 'Sometimes,' she said, 'you surprise me, Minnie.'

'Why's that, Ena?'

'Because you talk nowt but bloomin' tosh. You know Dieter and 'is mam got out before the war even started. Sometimes I think you're as deaf as yer own mother.'

Elsie Tanner had two letters that morning. She recognized the handwriting on both: one was from Steve, the other from Antonio. She didn't need to waste time choosing which to open first. Steve would always be the winner.

Her hand trembled as she opened the letter and she felt a wave of disappointment at its length and that it had taken three weeks to arrive. He apologized for not writing before, said how much he missed her and that he was thinking about her all the time. He was in France but he couldn't tell her exactly where. His final lines were the best: 'I meant what I said, Elsie. However long it takes I'll be back for you and we'll be married. That's a solemn promise. All my love and kisses, honey, your ever-loving Steve.' She read it again and again and felt a mixture of hope and fear: hope that he meant what he said and fear that either he wouldn't come back or that something or someone would come between them.

Antonio's letter was longer, contained a crisp five-pound note, and he talked about the last time they had made love, how beautiful she was and how he wished his hands could reach out and touch her breasts, and how each night she should place her own hands on her breasts and think of him. 'You silly sod,' she said aloud, but secretly she was delighted that two good-looking men desired her. Surely *one* of them would come back for her when the war was over. She'd heard nothing from Arnold so maybe he hadn't received the letter from Ena Sharples. With any luck he might have decided by now that he couldn't care less about her and the kids.

There was a postscript to Antonio's letter – 'Christmas is coming. Any room at the inn for some mates to stay? I might be lucky and get a bit of leave soon. *Ciao.*'

Elsie hummed to herself as she walked towards Dot's. She and Sally quite often had Dennis and Linda to stay overnight. In fact, every Friday now she took them round and Dot bathed them, gave them cod-liver oil, syrup of figs and Virol. The Virol was the only thing they liked. When they were peaky or just not eating well, she gave them Parrish's Food. It tasted like iron filings but they didn't seem to mind. The wet summer was past now but even without much sun Dennis and Linda had lost that 'air-raid shelter' grey complexion that most children seemed to have.

She'd just reached the back alley when she saw a telegram boy cycle by. The postman was always welcome, the telegram boy never. Someone was just about to get the worst sort of news. He stopped his bike on her side of the road and she was just wondering who it might be when she realised the lad was knocking on *her* door. She ran, as fast as she could – Please don't let it be Steve, please don't let it be Steve, she kept saying to herself. Breathless, she almost snatched the telegram from the boy's hand. She tore it open to read: WE REGRET TO INFORM YOU ABLE SEAMAN EDWARD ROYSTON HAS DIED IN ACTION FROM INJURIES RECEIVED. LETTER AND EFFECTS TO FOLLOW.

'Any reply, missus?' asked the telegram boy.

Elsie shook her head. It had taken her a few seconds to realize that Edward Royston was her Eddie, the lad who'd taken a real shine to her and her to him, although on her part she'd known he was just passing by and that he'd been too young for her. Poor Eddie, she thought, but why had *she* got the telegram? They were usually sent only to the next of kin.

Dot was coming towards her. 'Where the 'ell 'ave you been? We'll be late for work.'

'I 'ad a telegram.'

'Oh Gawd,' said Dot. 'Who's copped it?'

'That Eddie'

'That fair-'aired lad who couldn't tek his eyes off you?'

' 'E must 'ave put me down as 'is next of kin.'

'Poor little beggar,' said Dot. ' 'E was a 'andsome lad.'

'And a nice fella. I could 'ave fallen for 'im if I'd put me mind to it.'

'Elsie, my old mate,' said Dot, putting an arm around her, 'you could fall for a gorilla if 'e was good to you.'

'That's not true. I'm quite fussy.'

'Aye,' laughed Dot. 'Two gins, and to you all men look like Clark Gable.'

They walked to Elliston's, and Elsie told Dot about the letters from Steve and Antonio. 'I've got me doubts about that Antonio,' said Elsie thoughtfully.

'Why's that, then? Do you think 'e's in the Mafia?'

' 'Is letter was postmarked Manchester. Now, if 'e's in the country why 'asn't 'e bin to see me lately?'

'Mebbe he got a mate to post it for 'im.'

Elsie thought about that. It did seem a possibility. He had lots of mates. ' 'E did send me a fiver, Dot, so I'll treat you tonight – nice fish supper and a few drinks at the Rovers.'

Dot smiled. ' 'E might be a bit of a mystery man, Elsie, but 'e is good to yer.'

Elsie had to agree with that, but when she got to work she found the only person she thought about was Eddie. He was the sort of bloke who would have given her the moon. He'd been just nineteen. At least he'd found his manhood with her. He had deserved that at the very least.

Ena had made a list of 'school watchers' so that no one was overburdened with the task. Albert Tatlock, Bessie and even Tom Hewitt and Ida Barlow were on the team. Day after day they kept watch on the school playground, but there was no sign of the man in the black coat.

'It's bin three weeks now, Ena,' said Martha when they met in the Snug of the Rovers on Friday night. 'Don't you think it's time to pack it up?'

Ena sipped her milk stout thoughtfully. ' 'Ow long 'as this war been goin' on, Martha Longhurst?'

'Five years.'

'Doesn't that tell yer somethin'?'

Minnie, who was sitting quietly watching the other customers, said, 'We are winnin' the war, aren't we, Ena?'

'Who asked you, Minnie?' said Ena crossly. 'I was talkin' to Martha. And of course we're winnin' the war. Don't you know owt?'

'I only 'eard,' said Minnie undeterred, 'that 'Itler's new rockets, them V1s, are killin' 'undreds in London. 'E could win the war with them. They don't 'ave pilots, do they?'

Ena gave Minnie her sternest look. 'I can see you've bin readin' your squares of newspaper in the privy again.'

'I 'ave not,' said Minnie. 'I 'eard it from Albert Tatlock and 'e 'eard it from the wireless.'

'Well, 'e's no business filling your 'ead with doom and gloom. There's enough of that round 'ere without 'im spreadin' all them Lord Haw-Haw lies.'

'Mebbe Lord Haw-Haw's right,' said Minnie, with a touch of defiance.

Ena leaned forward. 'Minnie Caldwell, if you was a German you'd be taken out and shot if you talked owt about defeat.'

Minnie frowned. 'But I'm not a German.'

Ena shook her head despairingly. 'Talkin' to you, Minnie, is as 'ard as rubbin' two wet sticks together to mek fire. Now, are we goin' to talk about your Dieter or not?'

'Yes, Ena.'

' 'Bout time. Any road – scare stories or not – we carry on. This bloke may know we're watchin' school and 'e may just 'ave to tek a chance one day.'

'Chance for what, Ena?' asked Martha.

'A chance to snatch Dieter away.'

'Why would 'e want to do that?' asked Martha.

' 'Ow the 'eck would I know?' said Ena irritably. 'Mebbe 'is family's important or summat.'

'Mebbe 'e's a prince,' suggested Minnie.

' 'E may be a prince to you, Minnie Caldwell, but I don't think Germans 'ave princes, do they?'

Neither Minnie nor Martha had an answer to that.

'So it's decided, then. We all agree,' said Ena. 'We keep watch on the school.'

'If you say so, Ena,' said Minnie.

'Aye,' murmured Martha.

It was two days later that the parcel was delivered to No. 11. Elsie thought at first that it was from Antonio but when she tore off the brown paper and saw inside she realized it was not. There was a letter, a wristwatch, a fountain pen, a penknife, a compass and a Bible – she recognized the watch as Eddie's. Seeing his few possessions laid out before her on the table made her legs feel wobbly. She sat down to read the letter:

Dear Mrs Tanner,

My name is Daphne Harold and I am a Navy nurse. Eddie was not well enough to write this letter himself so he has dictated it to me. As you probably know by now, he designated you his next of kin so by now you have his effects. Sadly Eddie died of his wounds a few days ago. He was very brave and he did so want you to have this last letter. These are his own words and they do show how much his stay with you meant to him. May I offer my sincere condolences.

Hello Elsie,

Nursie here is writing down everything I say. I'm being well looked after and I'm not in any pain but I've well and truly copped it.

I think about you all the time. I know you thought I was a bit young for you but I was very old in my head. The stay I had at your place was the best time I've ever had. I can't remember any family – my mam abandoned me. Just having a place to go for my leave was smashing and you were so good to me. You gave me the best night of my life and I don't think I'd be dying so happy if I hadn't met you. I hope little Linda and Dennis are well. I've enclosed my life savings inside my Bible. It's not much but I hope you treat yourself and the kids.

I do hope you'll say a prayer for me. Perhaps one day we'll meet up on the other side. All my love, Eddie.

Elsie opened the Bible and took out the four five-pound notes. Then she burst into tears. Not only had a lovely lad died but he might have been a man who could have loved her just for herself, the man who, in bleak moments, she doubted she would ever find. 'God bless you, Eddie love,' she whispered, as she slipped on his wristwatch. I'll never forget you, she thought, not as long as I live.

CHAPTER SIXTEEN

Winter 1944 V2 kills 271 in Rex Cinema.

Ida Barlow had begun sorting out her box of Christmas decorations in late November. All she needed now was the tree, some crêpe paper and paper chains. She'd saved some dried fruit and sugar and she had a tin of ham and another of salmon put by. Bessie had given her two jars of mincemeat and some bottled fruit, so apart from little presents for Kenneth and David she was organized.

Bessie had called in that morning to suggest they join forces for Christmas dinner.

'We'd love to 'ave you, Ida,' she said. 'Albert's getting a 'uge turkey for his Christmas bonus, I've got sherry and port put by and I know Albert's been whittling away mekkin' wooden toys for your Kenneth and your David.'

Ida gave Bessie a hug. 'We'd love to come – only you must promise me you'll come to us on Boxing Day.'

'Aye, that'll be a treat,' said Bessie. 'Christmas is nowt like the same without kiddies.'

'Your Beattie will be 'ome soon,' said Ida. 'This time next year it will all be over.'

Bessie nodded. 'I do 'ope so. The trouble is our Beattie 'as settled in so well in the country she's all but forgotten us. She's found a new life, see, and we can't offer 'er the same things.'

'You're 'er flesh and blood,' said Ida. 'That's what matters.'

'Aye,' murmured Bessie. 'I 'ope you're right.'

'Your Beattie is like Dieter – in a strange place but quite 'appy and well looked after.'

Bessie smiled. 'Talkin' of the little lad, I thought Minnie might like to join us all for Christmas dinner.'

'That's a nice idea,' said Ida. 'Our Kenneth will 'ave a bit of company – but what about Ena?'

'What about 'er?'

'I think she goes to Minnie's on Christmas Day on account of Minnie's mother.'

'Oh, aye,' said Bessie, 'We'll work summat out.'

When Bessie left, Ida got to work. She was making Bessie a dress as a Christmas present from some material she'd had left over and forgotten about. There was only just enough and she hadn't got a pattern but she'd sewn up the side seams and all she had to do now was fit the sleeves and hem it. It was as she was putting in the second sleeve she remembered that she hadn't written to Frank for three days. It was even more of a shock to realize that she hadn't even thought about him since she'd last written.

Annie Walker always decorated the Rovers on 1 December. The Christmas tree had to wait until the fourteenth but this year she had Teresa, and Annie had to admit that her help was invaluable. Teresa had already made a Christmas cake and the pudding and was suggesting she would also cook the Christmas dinner. Annie had drawn the line at that.

Her main problem this year was what to do about John. He'd remained persistent and still visited after closing time. Annie couldn't resist him: she had no real friends – couldn't mix with other women in the day and her customers she kept at arm's length. John was a lifeline and he opened up the worlds of books, music and even politics to her. He promised even more after the war – a country cottage, trips abroad, visits to the theatre, an end to the routine of life at the Rovers. Annie tried to keep alive the memory of her love for Jack but she hadn't even had a letter for weeks and his last visit had been an unmitigated disaster. She didn't want to admit it but Jack was fast becoming someone in the past, someone for whom she felt fondness but nothing more. It was John now who stirred her physically and mentally. With him she could be the person she wanted to be. Mrs John Barnstable, headmaster's wife, she thought, was far more her natural self than Mrs Jack Walker, publican's wife.

She had already bought and wrapped Christmas presents for Billy and Joan. Their stockings would contain an orange, a few sweets, some Plasticine for Billy and a small doll for Joan. What to buy John was a problem, but she'd finally decided on cuff-links and a Thomas Hardy book. She hadn't forgotten Teresa either: she'd bought her a new Bible, some soap and a tin of talcum powder.

All things considered, Annie was looking forward to Christmas. She hoped that Teresa would want time off but she hadn't broached the subject yet. Her talk of cooking Christmas dinner had come as a surprise. The idea of John sitting down on Christmas Day with Teresa there wasn't what Annie had in mind. Would he want to bring his mother along too? Maybe it would be a case of the more the merrier, but Annie wasn't convinced. She would have preferred Christmas dinner with John as the only guest.

Elsie Tanner looked at her front room and wagged a finger at the three servicemen who had descended on her a few days before Christmas. One had ebony skin and the best physique she'd ever seen – his name was Tyrone Kingston and he sang gospel songs in a voice as rich as the black treacle, or molasses, as he called it, that he liked on his porridge. He was in the American Army and recovering from injuries received in the Normandy landings. The other two, Norman Jenkins and 'Chalky' White, were both sailors with nowhere else to go. They seemed puny compared with the massive Tyrone, yet they were more aggressive, always arguing among themselves, and they were untidy.

'Now, look 'ere, lads,' said Elsie, trying to sound stern, 'I've got things to do and I can't do 'em with you lot sprawled all over me floor.'

Chalky, who had been listening to the radio lying on his back by the fire, struggled to his feet. 'Shall we go down the pub, Elsie?'

'Aye,' she said, 'that's a good idea. And don't come back till closing.'

'I'll go with them, ma'am,' said Tyrone. 'Keep an eye on them.'

As they were leaving Tyrone said, 'If you like, ma'am, I'll cook supper for you tonight.'

Elsie laughed. 'That's the best offer I've 'ad in a long time. I'd invite Dot and Sally but I've done nowt about doin' any messages.'

'Messages?' he queried.

'Larder's empty,' said Elsie. 'I haven't 'ad time to join the ruddy queues.'

'You leave the provisions to me, ma'am. I know where to go.'

Her guests had left at midday. By seven there was no sign of them. At seven thirty she'd put Dennis and Linda to bed after she'd given them Bovril sandwiches and hot milk, and once she was sure they were asleep she crept out of the house to buy herself a fish supper. On the way back she peeped into the Rovers, not only to see if they were there but to have a drink. She was about to approach the bar when she saw Len Fairclough drinking on his own. She wasn't sure if he'd seen her but she made a hasty exit, nearly tripping over in her high heels in the process. She'd only gone a few yards when she heard footsteps behind her. 'Elsie, 'ang on a tick.'

She turned to see Len's face looming towards her in the darkness. ' 'Ello, Len. You back on leave again?'

'I only lasted a few weeks – me leg played up. They 'ad to resct it and I'm in plaster again.'

'Look on the bright side, Len. At this rate you could still be 'ere when the war ends.'

'I'd rather be back at sea – I 'ate 'anging about wi' nothing to do.'

Elsie looked at her watch. 'Any road, I can't stop to chat – I've left the kids asleep in bed.'

'No need to be sarky wi' me,' he said with a grin. 'I'll walk you 'ome.'

'I 'ad to 'ave a look in Rovers to see if my lodgers were there,' she explained. 'They went out at dinnertime and I 'aven't seen them since.'

'What do you expect?' he said, falling into step beside her. 'They'll be drinkin' Weatherfield dry.'

'They're good lads,' said Elsie. 'One of 'em was goin' to cook for me tonight but I was starvin' so I've bin down the chippy.'

'I can smell 'em.'

'You can 'ave some,' said Elsie, 'so as you know I don't bear you any grudge.'

Elsie didn't bother with plates, just shared out the fish and chips in the newspaper it had been wrapped in and added extra salt and vinegar. She handed Len his parcel. 'If they come back steamin' drunk,' he said, 'and you can't 'andle 'em, Elsie, you get round to my place and I'll sort it out for you.'

'I'll manage 'em, Len. They'll only want to sleep it off.'

'Elsie?'

'What?'

'I do care what 'appens to you, you know.'

'I know you do, Len – you're a good mate.'

Len looked uncomfortable and rubbed his hands nervously. 'I want to be more than just a mate.'

'What do you mean, Len?'

'Do I 'ave to spell it out? Don't act like you're no sharper than an 'orse's bum.'

'There's no need to raise your voice to me, Len Fairclough.'

'You'd know it if I raised me voice.'

Elsie stood up from the table and crumpled up the remains of the paper from their fish supper. Then she smiled and threw the balls of paper at him. 'You don't frighten me, Len Fairclough.'

'I don't want to frighten you, Elsie – I want to woo you.'

'Don't talk so daft, Len. Mates is mates. Anyway, if you and I got together you'd want me to be respectable. And I don't want to be respectable. I want to 'ave fun. You'd want slippers by the fire, a home-made pie in the oven and me darnin' ruddy socks as I listened to Arthur Askey on the radio.'

'That sounds all right to me,' said Len. 'What more could a man ask?'

'See, Len, that's just my point. That's what a lot of men want—'

'Most men,' he interrupted.

'Aye, and most women want summat different. Look at the girls round 'ere – the married ones with their 'usbands away. They may work 'ard and not 'ave much money but they've made their own fun, found new friends. The men will come back, the women will lose their jobs and they'll be lucky to get a shandy on a Saturday night once a month.'

Len looked at her thoughtfully. 'You sound as if you don't want the war to end.'

'Mebbe I don't,' murmured Elsie. 'Even if Arnold came back a changed man I wouldn't want 'im. I know now there's men who know 'ow to treat a woman.'

'I suppose you're sayin' I'm not one of 'em.'

Elsie patted Len's cheek. 'There's no need to look like that. There's a girl for you somewhere – even with your gammy leg.'

Len stared at her for a moment. Then he said, with a grin, 'You know 'ow to butter up a bloke, don't you? My leg won't be in plaster for ever, then I'll come chasin' yer. You're the only one for me, Elsie Tanner, and one day you'll realize that.'

When he'd gone Elsie lit a cigarette and stared into the fire. Len was a decent bloke, hard-working, reliable, and he had a sense of humour, but underneath all that she sensed he wanted to control her. The thought that he might be a man who *could* was what frightened her.

Elsie dragged another chair across the room and rested her feet on that. She slipped her coat over her shoulders as she noticed the fire was nearly out, smoked one more Player's and fell asleep.

She woke up at the sound of the back door opening. 'About ruddy time,' she said without opening her eyes. She waited for sounds of drunken revelling but there was only a shuffling and a faint groaning noise. Her eyes sprang open and there stood Chalky, blood dribbling from his mouth, one eye half closed, supporting Norman, who was covered in mud and blood, had a bleeding nose and a large swelling on his forehead.

'What the 'eck's 'appened?' she said, springing up to help
Chalky support Norman and guide him to a chair.

'We was set on,' said Chalky, wiping the blood from his
mouth with the back of his hand.

'Where's Tyrone?' asked Elsie.

Chalky looked at Norman, who looked away sheepishly.
'We did our best, Elsie, honest we did. There was too many of
them. They chased us down by the canal.'

'What the 'ell's happened to Tyrone?' demanded Elsie.

Norman, whose eyes were beginning to close, peered
through the slits to say, 'We lost 'im.'

' 'Ow could yer lose 'im?' yelled Elsie. ' 'E's six foot four and
built like a tank.'

'We've bin looking but it's pitch dark out there,' said
Norman. 'It was 'im they were after. We took 'em on but there
was too many of 'em. We 'ad to do a runner and we thought
Ty was behind us but 'e wasn't.'

'Did you go back to look?'

'Aye, but there was no sign of 'im.'

Elsie grabbed her coat and a torch. 'You two clean yourselves up and get to bed. I'll get 'elp and go and find 'im.' As she
went to the back door she said, 'I'll talk to you two in the morning. At this rate you won't survive till bloomin' Christmas.'

As she rushed along to Len's she realized that some paying
guests were more like schoolboys and she was sounding like
their headmistress. She banged loudly on Len's front door,
not caring who she woke up in the Street. 'Len, wake up, I
need your 'elp,' she shouted.

He came to the door with his one good leg in his trousers
the other trouser leg at half mast over his plaster. 'Do you
want to wake the whole bloody Street, Elsie Tanner?'

'It's Tyrone. The lads 'ave been beaten up and Tyrone's
missing.'

'Where?'

'By the canal.'

'Right – you knock up Albert Tatlock,' said Len, 'and then
go 'ome. We'll find 'im.'

'I'm not goin' 'ome, I'm comin' with you. With your leg you
might not be much 'elp.'

'Elsie, don't argue. Just get Albert.'

Elsie had no intention of arguing: she was going with them and that was that. When he answered the door Albert already had his tin helmet on. Elsie waited while he put some clothes on over his pyjamas and wondered if he *ever* took his helmet off.

Len looked daggers at Elsie but said nothing until they got near the canal. Then he said, 'If you fall in, Elsie, I'll do nowt to fish you out.'

The canalside was dark and deserted. It began to rain, and the only sound they could hear was the faint hoot of an owl and rain on the water. They yelled Tyrone's name as they walked and shone their torches back and forth. Elsie was squinting as the rain whipped at her face, but she'd seen something in the water. 'Over there,' she shouted, pointing.

Len hobbled over to investigate. 'Elsie, you stay back,' he called out.

'Oh, Gawd,' Elsie heard him say, followed by, 'What the 'eck?'

'What is it?' she asked, trying to move forward, but with Albert hanging on to her arm trying to pull her back.

Len was limping towards them with a large round object in his hand. 'I thought it was 'is ruddy 'ead,' he said.

Elsie laughed in relief. 'That's a pumpkin. Steve told me about pumpkin pie. Tyrone must be 'ere somewhere. 'E must've been plannin' to cook it.'

Albert, impatient to get out of the rain, walked on ahead. Len and Elsie followed at a slower pace. Elsie's teeth were chattering with cold, and when Len put his arm round her she was grateful for the warmth of his body. They walked on and on. Elsie's shoes were letting in water, and as the ground got wetter her heels sank into the mud. She had never walked this far along the canal and she was surprised to see a lock.

Albert saw Tyrone first – he couldn't miss the big man, straddled precariously over the side of the lock gate.

' 'E's not dead, is 'e?' yelled Elsie.

Albert felt for his pulse. 'His heart's still beatin'. But 'e's out cold.'

Between them they heaved and tugged the huge man on to the ground. ' 'E's eaten too much pumpkin pie by the weight of 'im,' said Albert, trying to catch his breath. Once they had Tyrone flat on his back he groaned a little. Elsie felt his face: it was icy cold. He'd gone out in a thick black jacket with a fleecy lining; now he wore only his underpants and a vest with his shoes and socks.

'We can't carry 'im back,' said Len.

'We 'ave to keep 'im warm,' said Elsie, taking off her coat and putting it over him. Len knelt down with difficulty and began shaking him and slapping his face. 'Don't 'urt 'im,' said Elsie, pushing Len aside.

'*You* bring 'im round, then, Elsie. He's passed out. I bet a bloke like 'im could drink a barrel of beer on his own. He could be out cold till mornin'.'

'Let's get 'im on 'is feet,' suggested Albert, 'and then you and me, Len, can see if we can drag 'im along.'

'Shall I run and get some 'elp?' asked Elsie.

'No. We'll need you to 'elp us,' said Len.

Albert took off his woollen scarf and tied it round Tyrone's neck. Only one arm would fit into Elsie's coat but it was better than nothing. Then the two men hauled him upright and crouched down to fix his arms over their shoulders. 'One, two, three – *up!*' called out Albert.

Tyrone's legs dragged lifelessly along as they began the slow walk home, and Len's leg hurt under the strain. He hoped he'd make it back to Elsie's house without doing even more damage to it. Soaked to the skin and struggling to walk, Elsie took off her shoes and stuffed one into each of Len's jacket pockets.

Half-way home, both Len and Albert were exhausted and had to pause for a breather.

'I'll take over for a bit, Len,' said Elsie. 'You want to watch out for that leg.'

'Don't fuss, Elsie,' Len said. 'I just need a bit of a rest. Why don't you take over from Albert for a bit?'

'Will you let me, Mr Tatlock?'

Albert looked uncertain. 'If you're sure you can manage.'

'It'll keep me warm,' she said.

'Aye,' he said. 'It'll do that all right.'

The sheer weight of Tyrone came as a shock to Elsie and she felt as if her whole body was being pressed into the ground. After a few yards she felt exhausted. Then, through the rain, she saw torchlight and shapes. 'It's the ruddy cavalry,' shouted Len. Elsie couldn't speak – she had no breath left.

The 'cavalry' came in the form of Chalky and Norman. Only an hour or so earlier they had been near to collapse. Now they had revived, and although they could hardly see through their swollen eyes they took Tyrone from Elsie and Len, who leaned his arm across Elsie's shoulders, 'To take the weight off me leg,' he said, and winked at her mischievously.

When they reached No. 11 they managed somehow to get Tyrone up the stairs and on to the bed. Elsie gave him a brisk rub with a towel, which made him groan. She took that to be a good sign. When he felt warmer Elsie went downstairs to read the Riot Act. ' 'Ow could you let 'im get in that state?' she stormed. ' 'Ow ever much did 'e drink?'

Len was making tea, Albert had gone home, and Chalky and Norman had stripped off and were rubbing themselves down with towels. Chalky started to answer but Len interrupted, 'You tek them wet clothes off, Elsie, or you'll catch your death.'

For once Elsie agreed. 'I'm near perished but not as bad as poor Tyrone. Why didn't you two keep an eye out for 'im?'

'We did, Elsie,' said Chalky. 'It wasn't—'

'Elsie, get that wet kit off,' interrupted Len.

'Aye-aye, Captain,' said Elsie, giving him a mock salute.

When she came downstairs again, Chalky and Norman, wearing towels, were fast asleep and snoring.

'You've got to give this lark up,' said Len. 'You'll get a reputation you'll never live down.'

'Good,' said Elsie. 'I don't give a damn what people round 'ere think of me.'

'I'm warnin' you, Elsie. It'll all backfire on you. I know you've been skivin' off work, sayin' you're poorly. Elliston's will only put up with so much. You'll lose your job, and then 'ow will you feed the kids?'

'My kids won't ruddy starve. I'll feed 'em 'owever I 'ave to get the money.'

Len picked up his wet coat. 'One day, Elsie, you'll be standin' on a street corner, with a short skirt and a freezin' bum. You'll still be young but you'll look old, and you'll wonder why you didn't listen to me.'

'Bugger off, Len.'

'I'm goin', but think on, Elsie. That Eyetie of yours isn't all he seems.'

'What do you mean by that?' she asked, hands on hips, more than ready now for a scrap.

'You'll tek no notice of what I say, Elsie, you're too bloody stubborn. You'll find out.'

Before she could answer Len walked out. 'Well, bugger you, Len Fairclough,' she shouted after him. 'I don't need 'elp from anyone – or your bloody advice.'

In the armchair Chalky opened one eye and said, 'What's up?'

'You can shut your trap too, Chalky White. I've just about 'ad enough for one day.'

CHAPTER SEVENTEEN

Christmas Eve 1944 V2 Rockets bomb Manchester. Hundreds killed.

Ena Sharples wasn't best pleased that Minnie Caldwell was going to Bessie Tatlock's for her Christmas dinner. Ena had hoped to hear from Vera, but although she'd sent her daughter a Christmas card she hadn't had one in return.

Minnie had seemed excited at the thought of spending Christmas surrounded by children. Ena had taken round a pot plant, a colouring book and some crayons for Dieter, but although Minnie gave her tea and cake, Ena could see she was getting in the way of the marathon bake of mince-pies. As usual, Minnie had been apprehensive: 'The Germans won't mek war at Christmas, will they, Ena?' she'd asked. 'I mean they did 'ave a sing-song in the trenches in the first war.'

'They 'ad a bit of lull over Christmas one year,' said Ena, 'but they didn't 'ave 'Itler then, did they? And this war is nowt like the first one.'

'Aye,' said Minnie. ' 'Fore I forget, I 'ad a message for you from Martha. She says she wants you to 'ave your dinner with 'er.'

'Oh she does, does she? Well, you tell 'er I'll be with our Vera.'

'Will you, Ena? That'll be nice.'

That Martha's invitation had come the day before Christmas Eve, forcing Ena to tell a fib, irritated her but Ena wasn't going to have any one feel sorry for *her*. She did say sorry to God in her prayers but she was convinced He knew that some little white lies were justified.

Today was Christmas Eve and there was a midnight service, so Ena planned to do a bit of baking herself. She wasn't going to let Minnie's mince-pies outshine what she could provide, and she reasoned that she'd have more worshippers if she could provide a bit of a spread after the service.

As for tomorrow, she'd bought a scrawny little chicken and Minnie had given her a Christmas pudding, so she wouldn't starve. But she knew that after the Christmas Day service at eleven o'clock she wouldn't see a soul. Even the Rovers closed on the evening of Christmas Day.

It was still early but Mrs Foyle's Corner Shop opened at five thirty for the newspapers so Ena decided to be first in the queue for whatever was going. She'd heard a rumour that some chocolate might be off ration for a few days but she'd heard things like that before and been disappointed.

Ena was also disappointed at the size of the queue. A fine drizzle had set in, umbrellas were up and word was soon passed down the queue that there was plenty of bread but no chocolate. 'That just about sums up this war,' said a grey-haired woman standing in front of her. 'Plenty o' bread and scrape, but nowt tasty like a bit o' chocolate.'

'You should be grateful to 'ave what we do,' said Ena, unable to resist a little pontificating. 'You're old enough to remember the Depression years. This isn't owt like as bad.'

'Who asked you? I wasn't speaking to you, you nosy old bag.'

Ena would have replied, but as the woman turned to her she realized she was much younger than she thought, barely twenty-eight. And now Ena remembered that she came from Kitchener Street. Her name was Alice Fallows: her husband had been on leave and he'd died in his sleep on his first night home. The doctor said it was a heart-attack. A day later Alice's hair had gone grey. Ena decided to put Alice Fallows on her prayer list.

Tyrone had made steady progress and was easy to look after. He hadn't ventured out since being found at the lock. 'I'm not a coward, ma'am,' he'd told her the next day, as they sat having breakfast. Elsie had her usual three cigarettes and three cups of tea. She was on the third when Tyrone explained what had happened. 'I only asked a girl if she'd like a drink and next minute two guys were calling me names – buck nigger and worse. I wasn't planning to get sore about it and I guess I hoped I wouldn't have to fight them, but suddenly there were six of them swearing and blaspheming, and Chalky and Norman waded in and all hell broke loose.'

'Were you drunk, pet?' asked Elsie, who had a soft spot for him. His only fault, as far as she could see, was that he wanted four sugars in his Camp coffee and she was fast running out of sugar.

'No, ma'am. I've signed the pledge. I've never drunk alcohol.'

'So then what happened?'

'We fought, ma'am, and we fought good, but others joined in against us and Chalky said, "Let's make a run for it," but I was slow and they caught up with me. I don't remember being by the canal.'

'Tyrone, you're lucky to be alive.' She touched his huge biceps. 'Must be all that muscle.'

'I owe you, ma'am.'

'Just call me Elsie, for Gawd's sake.'

'Yes, ma'am, Elsie. And I still owe you some of my cooking. Allow me to buy a turkey and cook it US of A style.'

Now it *was* Christmas Eve and Elsie had the biggest turkey she'd ever seen and a man who insisted he was cooking the whole meal. Elsie just knew she and the kids were going to have a good Christmas. Nothing could go wrong now.

It was just after midday when the siren wailed. Elsie shrugged her shoulders. Hitler's army was in retreat everywhere. It was just a false alarm.

Twenty minutes later they heard bombers overhead. 'Hey, ma'am,' said Tyrone, 'don't you think we should get to a shelter?'

'On Christmas Eve?' exclaimed Elsie. 'Mince-pies are in the oven all over Weatherfield. I don't know of anyone who won't just tek a chance.'

Tyrone went out on the front step and saw the tail end of

dozens of bombers. 'Jeez,' he murmured. 'And we're supposed to be winning.'

He'd just closed the front door when they heard the noise – a great roaring sound as if a locomotive had passed through Coronation Street. Then another and another. Elsie had snatched up the screaming Dennis and Linda. Tyrone threw his arms round all three of them and Chalky White lived up to his name.

Elsie knew this was no ordinary bombing raid. They'd heard Manchester being bombed many times. This was different and the noise was terrifying.

'They're V2s,' shouted Tyrone, above the roaring. 'Come on, let's get out of here.'

It seemed that all the occupants of Coronation Street were on the move at once. Women just picked up their children and ran without coats towards the Mission Hall. Elsie was amazed to see Annie Walker running, with Joan in her arms, closely followed by Teresa. 'Billy!' Annie was calling frantically, 'Billy, answer me.' She was grabbing anyone she saw, saying, 'Have you seen Billy?' Most people were shrugging her off. Elsie noticed, so she handed her two to Tyrone. 'Take 'em to the Mission, please, love.'

'Anything you say, ma'am. I'll take good care of them.' He sang quietly as he ambled off, and both children stopped screaming to listen.

'Where did you last see 'im?' asked Elsie, taking hold of Annie's arm to stop her running round like a headless chicken. Annie turned to Teresa and the girl muttered tearfully, 'He was just outside the back playing with a whip and top and I looked again about two minutes later and he'd gone.'

'There's nowt you can do 'ere. You get to the Mission,' said Elsie. 'I'll get the lads to look for 'im.'

Another huge explosion silenced them and in the distance they could see a pall of black smoke rising. Annie Walker seemed rooted to the spot and Elsie tried to push her along, to no avail. Minnie Caldwell rushed up, her bottom lip trembling. ' 'Ave you seen my Dieter? 'E went out 'alf an hour ago and I 'aven't seen 'im since.'

Elsie didn't have time to answer as a bomber came into view and someone shouted, 'Down!' They all flung themselves to the ground. The bomber seemed to slow overhead and begin a silent descent. Acrid smoke from the rear of the plane filled the air. This is it, thought Elsie. We've all 'ad it. The deafening noise that followed seemed to confirm that, but then a shout went up – 'It's 'it the Red Rec.' Everyone struggled to their feet and began to run in that direction.

By the time Elsie and everyone else arrived the plane's cockpit was on fire, the fuselage was in pieces and the tail plane had smashed down several potting sheds. Albert Tatlock was shouting for people to get back but everyone stood watching the inferno in dumb horror and fascination. The sound of fire engines joined with the crackling noise of the burning plane, and the sound of collapsing sheds.

A few members of the ARP were pushing people back behind the gates. 'Look at that,' shouted someone. 'Near the cockpit. It's the pilot.' Now the smoke had lifted they could make out the shape of a man crawling away. Elsie was inside the Red Rec when, above all the noise, she heard a cry. At first she thought it was the pilot moaning, but then realized as she ran nearer to him that he was making no sound. He was hideously burnt. She looked down at him and, even though his face was badly burnt, she could see he was very young, only a boy. He said one word: *'Mutter.'*

Albert Tatlock knelt down to him, then got up and pulled her away. ' 'E's dead, Elsie. We can't do anything for 'im.'

'The poor little sod said *"Mutter"*, Mr Tatlock. What does that mean?'

Albert sighed. 'He was asking for his mother, Elsie.'

The fire brigade arrived and word soon spread that people had been killed and many injured in Manchester. Above the noise Elsie again heard a cry. 'Shush,' she yelled. 'There's two kids missing and I can 'ear somethin'.' Suddenly there was a collective silence and, apart from water sizzling on hot metal, nothing.

As the all-clear sounded it seemed the entire population of Weatherfield converged on the Red Rec. Norman and Chalky and Len Fairclough were among them. Tyrone appeared with

the children and a distressed Annie Walker. Once Ena
Sharples appeared on the scene, however, she tried to take
charge. 'I don't know what you're all gawpin' at,' she shouted.
'You should all go 'ome and let the professionals get on with
the job.'

'You 'aven't 'eard, then, that little Dieter and Billy Walker
are missin', 'ave you?' said Elsie.

'I did 'ear, but they're not 'ere on the Red Rec, are they?'
she said, glancing at the chaos and confusion all around. 'It's
like ruddy Armageddon,' she muttered.

Elsie didn't know Armageddon from Blackpool but she was
worried. 'I thought I 'eard cryin' a few minutes ago.'

Ena's face took on a determined look. 'Well, that's different
– why is no one doin' owt?'

One of the firemen stomped towards them. 'You can't 'ang
around 'ere. We don't think 'e was carryin' a rocket 'cos you
silly beggars would 'ave been blown to kingdom come if 'e
had.'

'There's two kiddies missing and there's been cryin' 'eard
somewhere round 'ere,' said Ena. The fireman looked across
at the expanse of smouldering wreckage and at the sheds in
varying stages of collapse. 'The crew's busy, so you'll 'ave to
get a few men to form a search party.' Then he added, 'And I'm
moving out all the women and children – they'll catch their
deaths.'

Ida Barlow put an arm around a weeping Annie Walker
and led her away.

All the men who owned sheds and plots tried to identify
their own bits of debris. Elsie saw that some had tears in
their eyes. The loss of their land and produce was a big blow.
The allotments were their pride and joy. Albert Tatlock's was
in the park but he was upset for Tom Hewitt and the other
men. Ena, who had no intention of leaving with the other
women, said, 'Don't just stand there like a couple of pansies,
Tom and Albert. Look for them kiddies. You can always grow
more bloomin' sprouts.'

Still-standing shed walls were torn down, tools placed in
piles, rubble and peat shifted but there was no sign of the
boys. Elsie began to think she'd imagined the cry because

since that second sound she'd heard nothing. Then, to her relief, Len Fairclough shouted, 'Quiet! I 'eard something.' Everyone stopped talking and listened but now the dark clouds that had been hidden by smoke opened up and the rain came down in torrents.

The search continued and then suddenly came a weak 'Help. We're down here. Help!'

The voice came from somewhere beneath the ground and everyone crouched down low. Len called out, 'Hang on, lad. Keep shoutin'.'

It was a few minutes later as Len was hobbling across the flooring base of a shed with no sides that he heard another weak 'Help!'

He began lifting the loose boards and there, wedged together, were the dirt-covered faces of Dieter and Billy. Everyone gathered round to see Len try to ease out Billy's head. But it wasn't easy. Billy tried to speak but began to cry instead. His head was firmly stuck. 'We'll have to dig 'em out,' Len said. Albert immediately grabbed a spade. 'With our bare 'ands,' added Len. 'We might 'urt 'em usin' a spade and they might sink further down.'

The earth was soft and damp and both boys whimpered in fear. 'Somebody sing to 'em,' suggested Tom Hewitt. Tyrone, who was digging alongside Len, began singing 'Jingle Bells' in his deep bass voice, and after two choruses Len shouted in triumph. 'Billy's comin' out.' In seconds he was free, closely followed by Dieter. Both boys were wrapped in bits of old sacking and Len and Tyrone couldn't resist hoisting them in the air in triumph. A loud cheer went up.

'Praise the Lord,' said Ena. 'Someone run and tell Annie Walker and Minnie they're safe.'

It was a tired, wet, exhausted group that began walking out of the Red Rec. Billy Walker fell asleep in Len's arms and Dieter explained tearfully to Tyrone, 'We were digging our own shelter. When we heard all the noise we jumped in the hole and covered it up with the planks of wood but then we couldn't get out.'

They'd just reached the gates when a man in a long black coat approached Tyrone. Ena Sharples ran forward instantly and grabbed his arm. 'Caught you!' she cried. 'You've got a bloomin cheek, comin' 'ere again.'

'You do not understand,' he said.

'Aye,' said Ena. 'But the police will.'

CHAPTER EIGHTEEN

Christmas Day 1944.

Annie Walker's Christmas wasn't one she'd ever forget. Billy had been subdued after his rescue but unhurt, and after food and drink he'd fallen asleep clutching his teddy bear.

The Rovers had been full on Christmas Eve, from opening until Annie was forced to eject the last stragglers. By midnight she was still clearing up and putting the bar money into the safe. She felt exhausted and was longing for her bed. Her one last job was to fill Billy and Joan's stockings, then she could finally get off. She was just locking up when she heard a noise outside. Her heart sank. If that was John she would just have to send him away. She unlocked the back door and looked outside. The yard was empty, apart from some barrels and crates. She told herself she was imagining things when suddenly from behind a barrel she caught a glimpse of red. 'Who's there?' she called. 'Come on out.' She advanced towards the barrels. Just as she got there Father Christmas popped up, complete with a long white beard, red coat and white cuffs. She jumped back in surprise. 'John, what are you playing at? You frightened me half to death.'

'John?'

'John?' she repeated uneasily.

'It's Jack,' came a cold voice she hardly recognized. 'So it *is* true.'

'Jack, why didn't you tell me?' she said, in a voice hardly

above a whisper. She wished the ground would swallow her up. If he replied, she didn't hear. Her knees felt weak, her head was spinning. Father Christmas was ripping off his beard. He was not full of Christmas cheer.

Betty Preston was first up on Christmas morning, not that anyone would have known it was Christmas. There was no tree, no paper chains and the three cards they had received Harold had torn up. 'Jesus Christ never 'ad paper chains 'anging in his stable and I'll 'ave none in mine,' he'd said.

Betty stayed at home purely for love of her mother but she'd had to make her own strategies for coping. One was to use a box number for Ted's letters, another was to go out as much as possible.

She'd slept badly: the rocket attack on the Manchester area and the plane crashing had really frightened her. 'God will protect us,' Harold had said, refusing to let Margaret leave the house. Her mother had wept, saying it wasn't fair that her daughters were placing their lives at risk. 'I *want* to go to a shelter,' Margaret said. 'I'd be fine if Betty 'elps me and steadies me a bit.'

'If you fell,' said Harold cruelly, 'who could pick you up?'

And so it was settled. During the V2 raid Betty and Maggie had clung to their weeping mother and Harold had knelt and prayed. For the first time in her life Betty faced up to the fact that her father wasn't just domineering, overbearing and a religious zealot. He was mad – a madman who had deliberately fattened up his own wife so that she could never leave him.

Margaret had been so upset by the raid that she had refused to go to bed, saying she would rather die sitting upright. Now she sat pale and puffy, covered with crocheted blankets. Her eyes were closed but Betty knew she wasn't asleep. She filled the kettle and lit a taper to fire the gas ring. Nothing happened. 'Mam, there's no gas,' she called.

'The fire's nearly out too,' Margaret called back.

Betty set to straight away, raking out the embers then pulling out the metal ash pan under the grate. It was still fairly hot so she carried it out gingerly to the backyard. There she tipped the embers into the metal dustbin outside that stood next to the pig-bin. Not that the pig-bin ever saw many leftovers in the Preston house. Betty filled a bucket with coal and placed a bundle of wood on top, then struggled back into the house.

'What are we going to do with no gas on Christmas Day?' asked Margaret wearily.

'I don't know,' said Betty. 'I'll get this fire going and when it's nice and 'ot we can put the kettle on top. We could 'ave toast usin' the toastin' fork and we could roast chestnuts.'

'We can't cook a ten-pound turkey, though, can we?'

'Not unless the gas comes on soon.'

'Your father will go mad,' said Margaret.

Betty raised her eyebrows but said nothing. She arranged the coal and the wood, then she folded some newspaper into strips and wove it between the coals.

Even with a brisk fire the kettle seemed to take ages to boil and by then Harold and Maggie had appeared. Harold wouldn't believe there was no gas and had to try it for himself. He even tried the gas lamps, but of course they didn't work either.

Suddenly Betty couldn't bear to be in their dark, dreary house any longer. She slipped on her coat and went out. She didn't often cry, but the shock of the raid had upset her and soon tears were welling. All the houses were in darkness and in Coronation Street the only lights she could see were at the Mission. It seemed like an omen and the door was open so she walked inside. There was a small Christmas tree in the entrance and in the chapel area a nativity scene had been placed in one corner. Betty sat down on one of the chairs and cried.

Ena Sharples knew Betty by sight and she knew Harold Preston too. She watched Betty for a while from the back of the Hall then sat down quietly beside her. 'What's up, Betty? It's Christmas Day. You shouldn't be sittin' 'ere skrikin'.'

Betty wiped her face with the back of her hand. 'Gas is off. I think it's off in the whole of Weatherfield.'

'There's no need to break your heart about that, is there?' said Ena, giving her an awkward pat on the back. 'We'll

531

work summat out. Folk will 'ave to do their best with open fires. Or they can find someone who's got electric and we can share the food around – 'ave a party 'ere. Some can bring sandwiches and 'ave their proper Christmas dinners when the gas comes on.'

Betty was silent for a while. She'd never spoken about her family situation to anyone, but now she couldn't stop herself. 'My mam 'asn't left the 'ouse for years, Mrs Sharples.'

'Why's that, then?'

'She's too fat.'

Ena let Betty talk, and the girl told her everything. How her father treated them, how he stuffed Margaret with food and didn't encourage her to do anything for herself, how he kept her in the house during raids. Eventually she stopped.

'I reckon,' said Ena thoughtfully, 'you and your mam and sister need a bit of 'elp from someone. A bit of Christian charity.'

'My dad doesn't believe in charity.'

'I don't mean that sort of charity. Now, dry your eyes, girl, and we'll go and get your mam out of there for the day.'

'She won't come out – 'e won't let 'er.'

Ena smiled grimly. 'Betty, your dad's built like a string bean. 'Ow's he goin' to stop us? Besides, I've got somethin' to say to 'im.'

Ena led the way back to No. 6 Tile Street. Betty walked slowly behind her, dreading that Ena would make things worse rather than better. Her father wasn't going to let Ena Sharples into the house, of that she was sure.

'You go round the back,' said Ena. 'Tell 'im I'm 'ere and I want words with 'im.'

' 'E won't come out.'

'You just tell 'im I've got a memory like a bloomin' elephant.'

'Aye. But I know he won't speak to you.'

' 'E will. You'll see.'

Nervously, Betty gave her father the message, at which he glared furiously. 'What 'ave you bin sayin', girl? She's a terrible, evil woman, and you bring 'er to our doorstep – may God forgive you.'

To Betty's great surprise he went to the front door and slammed it shut behind him.

'Well, 'Arold Preston,' said Ena, resting her hand on the doorframe, 'it's a long time since I've seen you.'

'What's all this about, Mrs Sharples? What right 'ave you to interfere with a God-fearin' family?'

'You 'aven't always been God-fearin', 'ave you, 'Arold?' said Ena slyly.

Harold opened his mouth like a dying fish then closed it again.

'You 'ad trouble findin' yourself a wife, didn't you, 'Arold? Let me think who there was ... There was Lily and Cissie and Phyllis. All left you, didn't they? Too much spirit they 'ad. I remember poor Lily best. You was the one who got 'er in the family way, weren't you? Killed 'erself, didn't she?'

'I offered to marry 'er, as God is my witness,' Harold blustered. 'I even bought 'er a ring.'

'She must 'ave realized that life with you was goin' to be a bloomin' misery. I'm not sayin' as 'ow she was right to tek 'er own life but she was a good girl 'fore you got your 'ands on 'er.'

'I've tried to mek amends for my earlier misdeeds,' said Harold. 'I've served God as best I know 'ow.'

'Aye,' said Ena. 'Bein' a tyrant and feedin' that poor wife of yours so as she's the size of an 'ouse. Are you plannin' to kill 'er off like you did poor Lily?'

'You're a wicked woman, Ena Sharples. I love my wife. I look after 'er.'

'Don't talk rubbish, man! If that's your idea of lookin' after someone then you've no more sense than an organ-grinder's monkey. 'Ow you can afford to buy 'er enough food I'll never know. People round 'ere are gettin' thinner, not fatter.'

The look on his face told her the answer.

'You've bin stealin', 'aven't you?'

His silence was answer enough. His face had paled and his thin shoulders sagged. 'Food made 'er 'appy,' he said finally.

'A bit of freedom would 'ave made 'er even 'appier, 'Arold Preston,' snapped Ena, jabbing him in the chest with her finger. 'You've been a wicked, wicked man. You lost three girls, and then poor Margaret comes along, wants to get away from 'er unhappy 'ome and she's bloomin' putty in your 'ands. I suppose you thought by mekkin' 'er fat she'd never be able to leave you like the others did.'

He shrugged miserably. 'What are you goin' to do?' he asked.

Ena knew she had him in her power. 'I'm doin' nowt. It's you that 'as got to do summat.'

'What can I do?'

'You tell your Margaret she's comin' to the Mission for the day. Bring your turkey with you and we'll find a way to cook it. I'll ask no questions about 'ow you got it. By God's good grace you might be forgiven one day, but only if you change your ways.'

Harold's chin sank towards his chest. 'I'll do my best.'

'You'll do more than that, 'Arold Preston. If you backslides I shall 'ear about it and your stealin' will come to light. You'll be behind bars 'fore you know what's 'it you.'

Harold sloped back into No. 6 with his head down and with a lot of thinking to do.

When Ena got back to the Mission the news of her party had spread, and most of Coronation Street and beyond seemed to be clamouring on her doorstep. 'Give me a chance to open the door,' she said. 'You're all welcome.'

She stood at the front of the Mission. 'Just bring what food you've got that doesn't need cookin', like a bit o' cake and some mince pies—'

Some wag from the back shouted, 'And then you can feed the five thousand!'

Ena was not deterred. 'I want some big strong lads to set trestle tables up and get chairs round and us women will supply the food.'

'What about beer?' asked Len Fairclough.

'There'll be no drinkin'. I 'aven't got a licence to sell beer.'

Ena failed to notice the little murmur that went round. She also failed to notice that Len Fairclough and a lad called Percy Sugden left the mission immediately for the Rovers.

Much to Len's surprise it was Jack Walker who answered

the door at the Rovers. 'If you can carry a barrel of beer, lads, you can 'ave it with pleasure. My way of saying thanks for savin' our Billy.'

'Well, thanks, Jack,' said Len, 'and a merry Christmas to you and yours.'

Percy suggested a wheelbarrow, and as the allotment holders had collected their belongings there was no problem in borrowing one from Albert Tatlock.

'We'll 'ave to keep the barrel outside,' said Len. 'If Ena Sharples finds it there'll be 'ell to pay.'

They pushed the wheelbarrow to the Mission and hid the barrel behind the dustbin.

'The women won't want to drink beer, Len,' said Percy. 'And what will we do about glasses?'

Len laughed. 'We'll 'ave to drink it from tea cups and the women will 'ave to bring their own drink.'

By one o'clock the tables were covered in white sheets and women were carrying in baskets of food and laying the tables. Excited children ran around, but no one minded.

Having organized everyone, Ena began playing carols on the harmonium. There was no sign of Mr Swindley, who was to have preached at the Christmas Day service. His sermons were often dull so Ena had never felt happier. She could choose the carols to suit herself. This was her kingdom and she was in charge.

Margaret, with Betty on one arm and Maggie on the other, made slow, nervous progress towards the Glad Tidings Mission Hall. Harold's contribution had been to joint the turkey and start frying the pieces on the open fire. 'I've no idea 'ow long it will take,' he said, as smoke billowed around the room. 'I needs to pray,' he told his wife. 'I'll come along later.'

Betty had been amazed by her father's changed attitude since Ena had spoken to him. He was subdued but he'd patted Margaret's arm and told her to enjoy herself. Betty feared that her mother wouldn't, that people would stare or make fun of her, but when they arrived there was such a jolly atmosphere and Bessie Tatlock said, 'Nice to see you all.

Would you ladies like to 'elp with putting the paper serviettes round?' Betty was even more amazed when her mother joined in with the carol singing.

Ida Barlow brought home-made Christmas crackers for the children and some decorations for the table. Bessie had been delighted with her dress and had worn it for the day. When she received compliments from Dot and Sally, and told them Ida had made it, they praised Ida's flair and asked if she could make dresses for them too. Ida was delighted: she was good at something and she couldn't wait to tell Frank.

After a short time Betty and Maggie stopped worrying about their mother. She had to sit on two chairs but Bessie and Minnie took her under their wing and they could see that she was happier than she'd been in years. Sally let her cuddle little Clark. 'Doesn't that look pretty?' she said, holding up the baby so that he could see the table decoration of twigs stuck into a flower pot covered with green crêpe paper, each twig strung with silver milk-bottle tops. 'I just wish your gran could 'ave been 'ere to see it.'

Elsie Tanner, Tyrone, Chalky and Norman arrived after everyone else. Tyrone was the only sober one. Elsie deposited her children near the Hayes sisters, who seemed more than happy to look after everyone's offspring and were showing the older children how to make crêpe-paper hats. Out of the corner of her eye, Elsie saw Len signalling her and Dot towards the back door. Dot preferred to stay with the lads. 'You go, Elsie,' she said, giving her a little push. 'He probably wants a kiss under the mistletoe.'

'Fat chance,' said Elsie, laughing.

Outside, Elsie stared at the beer barrel in amazement. 'Who the 'eck gave you that?'

'Jack Walker's 'ome on leave. 'E did.'

'I've brought me own booze,' said Elsie. 'And I'm goin' to slip some vodka into Ena Sharples's squash. We'll be doin' the conga and the 'okey-cokey before she knows what's 'it 'er.' Then she laughed. 'If we sing "Roll Out The Barrel" don't, for Gawd's sake, do owt daft, will you?'

Len smiled. 'Elsie?'

'What?'

'Give us a kiss.'

Elsie pushed him away, laughing. 'You find some mistletoe and I might just oblige, but only one. I 'aven't kissed any of my boys yet.'

Len turned away to refill his cup from the beer barrel. He didn't want Elsie to see how disappointed he was.

Two turkeys cooked in pieces arrived burnt, the Brussels sprouts turned to mush, the potatoes were as hard as iron but no one cared. Only the arrival of a policeman with the man in the black coat caused a hush.

Ena left her harmonium, wondering why she felt a little unsteady.

'Mrs Ena Sharples?' queried the policeman.

'What's 'e doin' here?'

'His name is Ruben Holliman and he's Dieter Holliman's uncle.'

Ena stared at the tall gaunt man. Now that she looked at him closely there was a slight resemblance. 'The lad doesn't seem to know owt about you,' she said suspiciously.

'He doesn't remember me,' said Ruben Holliman. 'But let me explain. I've changed. The war has changed me. I begged my brother to get out of Germany in 1938 but he was a doctor and he wanted to stay. He encouraged his wife Irana and Dieter to leave for England before war broke out.'

'Why didn't you speak up before, man?' asked Ena. 'You've got a tongue in your 'ead.'

'I tried, Mrs Sharples, but when I saw how well and happy Dieter seemed, I thought it best to let him stay where he was. I believe a Mrs Minnie Caldwell is looking after him?'

'Aye, and she loves 'im like 'er own, so you tread carefully with 'er.'

'I am so very grateful, Mrs Sharples,' he said. 'Dieter is the only family I've managed to trace. My brother and sister are somewhere in Poland in one of the camps.'

'I'll be off, then,' said the policeman, 'as it's all sorted now.'

'Oh no you don't, lad,' said Ena sternly. 'You stay awhile and 'elp yourself to whatever you want.'

'A few minutes then, missus,' he said, taking off his helmet.

'As for you, Mr Holliman, don't stand around like a stick of rhubarb, go and mek yourself known to that nephew of yours. And don't go upsettin' Minnie Caldwell.'

Elsie Tanner and her friends made sure Ena played all their favourites. They danced the conga along Coronation Street and Tyrone even persuaded Ena to do the hokey-cokey with him and managed to kiss her on both cheeks. She'd supped enough vodka-laced squash to enjoy it. 'It's the best Christmas I've ever 'ad,' she said.

Elsie, in her own haze of alcohol, looked around the Glad Tidings Mission Hall with its balloons, paper-chains, laughing children, and even Martha Longhurst joining in, and thought most people would say it was their best Christmas ever. Except, of course, that so many loved ones were not there to share it.

'To absent friends,' said Albert Tatlock, raising his cup of beer.

'To absent friends,' everyone chorused.

CHAPTER NINETEEN

Winter 1945 Dresden destroyed by Allied air power. City burns for seven days and eight nights.

Annie Walker knew she would never forget Christmas 1944. Jack's leave had been a disaster. And, in Annie's opinion, it was all due to Ena Sharples.

On Christmas Day Jack had paid John Barnstable a visit. He never told her what was said, and she didn't ask, but Jack was as cold as ice and John hadn't contacted her since. Jack had also taken an instant dislike to Teresa. 'I reckon,' he'd said, 'that she was the cause. If she 'adn't been around to look after the kids you wouldn't 'ave been able to get up to owt.' Annie vehemently denied any wrongdoing but Jack refused to listen or speak to her. She saw a side of him that she'd never seen before and she supposed the war had hardened him.

As he left, two days after Christmas, he'd said, 'The war will end soon, Annie, and when I get back I want you to get rid of Teresa. I want things to be as they were. If you get up to owt I shall 'ear about it and, believe me, there'll be real trouble.'

Annie nodded wordlessly. Jack was never one to rant and rave or even raise his voice, but she found his cold, deliberate tone far more frightening. He'd always had a stubborn streak and while before the war she had always been able to get her own way, now she realized it wouldn't be so easy. Her dreams of living in the country with either man were

shattered. And it was all due to the interference of Ena
Sharples. Jack had mentioned a letter but hadn't said who'd
sent it, but there was only one person it could have been. It
had taken her weeks of resentful thinking but she'd decided
that an eye for an eye was a Biblical reference that Ena
would understand.

Ena's job and her home at the Glad Tidings Mission Hall
were, of course, dependent on her good behaviour. Providing
alcohol on the premises was strictly forbidden and Annie
reasoned that if she told the Mission authorities someone
had stolen a barrel of beer and Ena had appeared to be drunk
then it would be goodbye Ena. The small fact that Jack had
given Len Fairclough the beer, Annie reasoned, wasn't important. Jack wasn't around to put his side of the story and who
would believe Len Fairclough?

It had taken weeks for Annie to decide on this course of
action but the fact that she hadn't heard from either John or
Jack since his leave had fuelled her desire for vengeance.
She'd sent the letter three days before. So now was the time
to tell Ena. Annie was going to have the pleasure of her
revenge – tonight.

After Elsie Tanner's paying guests had returned to their
units Elsie was left hoping that others would turn up, but no
one did. Sally and Dot seemed content to stay at home more
now, especially since fog, sleet and snow made going out at
night such an effort. The winter and the war wore on, queues
got longer, rations were cut and coal was in short supply.
Elsie was now on short time at Elliston's and the munitions
factories no longer offered overtime. Most people had no
spare money and few GIs were to be seen these days.

Elsie had seen a bit more of Len Fairclough but they
usually landed up arguing, mostly about trivial things. This
time it was her curtain rail: Len kept saying it needed doing
but she quite enjoyed irritating the ARP wardens. 'Oh, all
right, Len,' she agreed eventually. 'Just stop mitherin' me. You
can do it tomorrow.'

'Best if I do it tonight,' he said. She was about to argue
when the ARP wardens knocked on her door and when she

didn't reply, yelled through the letterbox. Elsie was outraged and had yelled back, 'Don't you know the bloody war is near over? You're power mad, you lot.'

'I told you,' said Len. 'I'll do it now before you get fined. Me leg's improvin' all the time, if that's what's botherin' you.'

'We 'aven't 'ad a bombin' raid since Christmas,' said Elsie, 'but if it meks yer 'appy yer can fix it and I'll mek yer a corned-beef sandwich for yer trouble.'

'It's no trouble,' said Len. 'I like doin' things for you.'

Elsie noticed the look in his eye. 'Give over, Len, or I'll change me mind.'

After he'd fixed the rail they sat drinking tea, smoking and chatting. 'What are you goin' to do after the war, Elsie?'

Elsie shrugged. 'I don't think that far ahead.'

'Well, you ought to – the war will end this year. What will you do if Arnold comes marchin' 'ome?'

Elsie laughed. 'I'll 'it 'im over the 'ead with a frying-pan.'

'What about your Eyetie friend?'

Elsie tensed. 'What about 'im? I do wish you'd call 'im by his name. Anyway, I 'aven't 'eard from 'im since before Christmas and I haven't seen 'im in months.'

Len stubbed out his cigarette in the brass ashtray and said cautiously, 'Elsie, 'as it ever crossed your mind 'e might be married?'

Contrary to Len's expectations, Elsie wasn't riled. 'I know a married man from five paces. 'E 'ad nicely darned socks but 'e said 'is mother did 'is mendin'. Anyway, 'e 'ad too much money to be married.'

'What if 'e comes marchin' 'ome and wants you to divorce Arnold and marry 'im?'

'I dunno. I know I'd do a lot for 'im but I wouldn't darn 'is socks.'

'A man wouldn't marry you for bein' owt like an 'ousewife.'

Elsie stared at Len. 'Is that supposed to be a ruddy compliment?'

'Tek it 'ow you please. I just wish you'd tread carefully.'

Elsie began to get irritated. He was always warning her about something. 'Look 'ere, Len. I'm not sixteen any more. I've seen a bit o' life—'

541

'No, you 'aven't, Elsie,' he interrupted. 'All you've done is seen a lot of men and made a bit of cash out of it.'

'You've got a bloody cheek,' she exploded. 'What gives you the right? You come 'ere pretendin' you're me best mate when all you really want is me body same as other blokes.'

Len jumped up from his chair. 'That isn't true, you stupid woman,' he shouted. 'I want to *marry* yer not bloody *buy* yer.'

'Well, I wouldn't marry you, Len Fairclough, if you was the only man without a wooden leg in the whole ruddy world.'

Len made for the door, then turned. He was calmer now. 'I'll tell you this, Elsie, love. You and me was meant to be together and all your life you'll 'ave regrets because you'll never find another man who'll think as much of you as I do.'

'Wanna bet on that one, Len?' she said defiantly.

He didn't answer. He knew he was right. Where Elsie Tanner was concerned he was always right.

Betty Preston walked to work in the rain. She hadn't heard from Ted for a while but things at home had improved. Her mother was losing weight, she went out for short walks and she had started doing a bit of housework and shopping. But just as Margaret seemed to be blooming, Harold was fading. He still read his Bible but he was much quieter and he seemed to get thinner and greyer. All in all, though, Betty was happy. She was convinced that Ted would come back for her soon. He'd promised he would.

When she arrived at Earnshaw's to clock in there was a message for her. The supervisor wanted to see her. Hilda Ogden had had the same message and they stood side by side waiting for the supervisor to appear.

Once the klaxon had sounded they could hear the sound of heavy metal clanging and the factory coming alive. Betty grew restless and Hilda, whose swelling stomach never looked the same two days running, patted her bump. After a while Betty asked, ' 'Ow's your Stanley?'

'Champion,' said Hilda. ' 'E's a prisoner-of-war in Italy.'

'I'm sorry to 'ear that.'

'Don't be,' said Hilda. ' 'E says 'e's quite 'appy and it's better than bein' in the glasshouse.'

'Is 'e pleased about the baby?'

Hilda smiled. ' 'E's real 'appy. I'm ever so proud of 'im. When 'e was in the glasshouse they said 'e was a model prisoner so I know 'e'll keep out of trouble in Italy. 'E says 'e 'ates the food there but 'e's always bin fussy. 'E says I should move in with his mam, but I dunno – I don't think she likes me much. She thinks I talk a lot.'

'Aye,' said Betty, trying to keep a straight face. 'I wonder why.'

The supervisor turned up then, looking grim. 'I expect you know why I want to see you.'

'No, I don't,' said Hilda. 'I've done nowt wrong.'

'I'm sorry, but we 'ave to lay the two of you off. Last in, first out, I'm afraid that's the policy.'

Both Betty and Hilda stood there in a state of shock. The supervisor looked at Hilda and said gently, 'In your condition, 'Ilda, you wouldn't 'ave bin able to carry on much longer anyway.'

Hilda, determined not to cry, wasn't going to leave without some sort of protest. 'You could 'ave kept us on till the end of the war.'

'The war's nearly over, 'Ilda,' she said. 'They won't need munitions any more.'

'They could mek something else,' said Hilda. 'Just cast-offs, that's all we are.'

'I'm sorry, there's nothing I can do. It's a fact of war.'

Betty slipped her coat back on. It was a blow but she realized it wasn't anybody's fault. 'Come on, 'Ilda, let's go 'ome,' she suggested.

Hilda wasn't prepared to go without having her say. 'Us women 'ave kept this war bloomin' going. It ain't right.'

'I can't stand 'ere all day, arguing,' said the supervisor, taking envelopes from her pocket. 'The bosses want you to go today, so I've got you a week's pay and a week extra. I couldn't do better than that for you.'

Hilda snatched her envelope. 'Well, thanks for nothing. You can 'ave this while you're at it.' Hilda reached a hand inside her skirt, pulled out a cushion and threw it on the floor. 'And I'm reet glad to be rid of that and yer rotten job.' She flounced to the door.

Betty and the supervisor stood, eyes fixed on the cushion on the floor. They couldn't have been more surprised if a baby itself had been lying there.

Two grim-faced senior members of the Mission Hall's board of governors arrived at Ena's flat at just after ten a.m. They came straight to the point. 'We've come about the serious business of you supplying alcohol on Christmas Day,' said Archie Barnes. Ena had known Archie for years: he was an assistant bank manager, unmarried, nearing fifty with sparse hair and a sparse body that needed large braces to hold his trousers up.

'I never did,' protested Ena. 'You know I'm a stickler for the rules, Mr Barnes. Christmas Day we only 'ad tea and lemonade and orange squash.'

'That's as maybe, Mrs Sharples,' said Cecil Adcocks, a bachelor nearing retirement, who Ena thought had a face as bland as a dumpling and a personality to match. 'We've had a report, you see, concerning a stolen barrel of beer and much drunkenness.'

'As God is my witness,' said Ena, 'I don't know what you're talkin' about. I saw nobody who was drunk and I would 'ave noticed. There isn't much that gets past me,'

'We do know you're diligent, Mrs Sharples,' said Adcocks, 'but the fact remains that this is what we've heard.'

'Well, you've 'eard wrong, Mr Adcocks. And I'd like to know where you 'eard this malicious gossip.'

'We can't divulge that, Mrs Sharples.'

Ena stared at both men. She would have liked to rant and rave at them, but her job and home depended on their relying on her to run the Mission properly.

'I can mek a good guess as to who 'as told you this pack of lies,' she said. 'It's someone who's 'oldin' a grudge against me. If you leave it wi' me I'm sure the culprit will admit they've been doin' nowt but mekkin' mischief.'

Both Adcocks and Barnes looked undecided. 'Will you excuse us a minute, Mrs Sharples?' said Archie Barnes. 'We need to talk this through.'

Ena stood outside the vestry door trying to eavesdrop, but

she could hear nothing until they raised their voices slightly and even then she couldn't make out any individual words. It seemed ages before they reappeared, unsmiling. 'We've decided,' said Archie Barnes, 'after a lot of heart-searching, to allow you three days to write us an account of the events of Christmas Day. If, as you say, this is merely malicious gossip then maybe the person in question would be willing to retract the allegations.' He paused to cough nervously. 'There's nothing we can do to save your job, Mrs Sharples, if you can't satisfy us that you were unaware of the situation. And we shall inform the police about the stealing of a barrel of beer from licensed premises.'

Ena swallowed and took a deep breath. 'You'll 'ave it down in writing and I can promise you that the owner of the evil tongue will repent 'er ways. I'm one that believes God is on the side of the righteous and I'm a God-fearin' woman.'

'You have three days, Mrs Sharples, to prove that,' said Cecil. 'Let's hope you're right.'

When they'd gone Ena could hardly contain her temper. She'd sort Annie Walker out if it was the last thing she ever did – she'd sort the snooty bitch out if she had to face tanks or fire-throwers or even a barrage of V2s. 'I'll deal with her,' she said aloud. Then she got down on her knees to ask the Lord God for guidance on retribution. She only spoke to Jesus when she was in a good mood. The God of the Old Testament was the one she needed now.

Elsie Tanner sat with her feet in a bowl of mustard water and her eyes and nose streaming. Both Dennis and Linda had got whooping-cough and none of them was getting any sleep. Now Elsie was trying to cure her cold. She'd taken aspirin and hot toddies but she didn't feel any better. The day before she'd squashed both children into the pram and taken them to the gasworks again to let them breathe in the fumes. She'd tried it three times – it was supposed to cure the whooping-cough but it hadn't worked so far and most of the time they lay weak and listless on her bed.

She was drying her feet when she heard the back door open. 'We've got the plague 'ere so you've been warned.'

' 'Ello, Elsie.'

In her shock at the sound of Arnold's rough voice she jumped and knocked the mustard water over the rug. She ignored the pool of water, pulled her dressing-gown around her and tried to keep her voice level. 'What are you doin' 'ere, Arnold? I thought you said you was never coming back.'

'I've bin wounded. Some shrapnel in me chest. Where else would I go to but me own 'ome?'

'I don't want any trouble, Arnold.'

Even as she spoke Elsie could see he didn't look capable of trouble. He'd lost weight, his face was grey and his eyes sunken. 'I'm dog tired, Elsie,' he said. 'Will you mek me a brew and then I'll get me 'ead down.'

Elsie felt unnerved by such a subdued Arnold. She made him tea and used the last of her butter to make him a potted-meat sandwich. 'I 'ear you've bin enjoyin' yourself,' he said, as he sipped his tea.

'You've 'eard wrong, then, Arnold. I've 'ad payin' guests, that's all.'

'More bed than breakfast, I bet,' he said smiling. 'You always were a lousy cook.'

Elsie stared at him. At fifteen she'd thought him tall and handsome. Now she saw a sad, broken man and she felt herself warming towards him. She'd never love him like she loved Steve but Arnold was still her husband and she should try to make the best of it.

'Lovely sandwiches, pet,' he said. 'I'll get meself off to bed now. 'Ow are the kids?'

'They've 'ad the whooping-cough – they're still asleep.'

'I won't wake them, then,' he said.

After an hour Elsie went upstairs and peeped in on Arnold. He'd folded his uniform neatly and hung it up. He lay on his back, his hair and face clammy-looking. At that moment he reminded her of Dennis when he was poorly. He seemed to be a changed man, and Elsie felt a real wave of optimism that once the war was over Arnold might prove a good husband – if that was what she wanted.

Arnold stayed for nearly two weeks. He gained weight and the colour came back to his cheeks. He played with Dennis and Linda, and only went to the pub three times on his own. Even though he got a bit nasty he didn't threaten her, and Elsie's optimism grew.

On the day he left to go back to sea Elsie offered to go with him to the station. He shook his head. 'You stay put, Elsie, love,' he said, kissing her. 'I want to remember you waving me off from the front doorstep.'

With Dennis and Linda in her arms, she waved until Arnold was out of sight.

Elsie felt near to tears. She had enjoyed having him home and so had the kids. It was only later when she went to the teapot where she kept her savings that she found he'd taken half the money. 'You sod!' she said aloud. But later, when she'd calmed down, she realized he could have taken *all* the money. Her Arnold did have a conscience, after all. And he was her husband, she told herself, so he was entitled to half.

CHAPTER TWENTY

Spring 1945 Hitler and Eva Braun commit suicide. Tuesday 8 May. VE-Day. Victory in Europe.

Ena Sharples had walked with head held high and shoulders back towards the Rovers for her showdown with Annie Walker. In her own private war she'd been determined that, like Germany, she would have Annie Walker signing a peace declaration. But Annie's signing would be immediate.

She'd seen Annie's wary glance as she entered the Rovers and she ordered a half of mild and said nothing. She'd just stared. It was when she was ordering her second half that Annie had asked, 'Is anything wrong, Mrs Sharples?'

Ena waited until her beer was poured before saying through gritted teeth, 'Nowt that an announcement to all your customers wouldn't solve.'

'What are you talking about, Mrs Sharples?'

Ena ignored her question. Annie Walker knew full well what it was about. 'Mind you,' said Ena, in a loud voice, 'after I've said my piece to everyone 'ere I doubt you'll 'ave any more customers.'

Annie looked flustered, much to Ena's delight. 'I think,' said Annie, 'it might be better if we talk in private.'

Ena looked at her milk stout. 'I'll drink this first,' she said. 'It'll give you time to have a serious think about the sin you've committed.'

Annie raised her eyebrows but said nothing. There were far too many people around and they were beginning to take an interest.

Ena rejoined Minnie and Martha in the Snug. 'What did she say, Ena?'

'I 'aven't said owt yet, just that she should think on 'er sins. I reckon she's as rattled as Lord Haw-Haw.'

'Do be careful, Ena,' said Minnie. 'You don't want to mek things worse.'

'Worse? Don't be so daft, Minnie Caldwell. 'Ow could things be worse? I'll lose me job and me 'ome if I can't get Annie Walker to tell the truth.'

'There *was* beer being drunk,' said Martha, 'and you did look as if you'd 'ad a drink or two.'

'Who asked you, Martha Longhurst?'

Martha sniffed. 'I'm entitled to me opinions.'

'Not while I'm 'ere suppin' ale you're not,' said Ena, glancing over to where Annie was trying to serve several people at once. 'If you've got nowt useful to say don't bother to open your trap.'

'There's no need to get nasty with us, Ena,' said Minnie. 'We're only tryin' to 'elp you.'

'I don't need 'elp. And your 'elp is as much use as a penn'orth of soap to wash an elephant.'

Both Minnie and Martha fell silent. Talking to Ena in the mood she was in was a waste of their breath.

Once Ena had finished her drink she stood up and walked over to Albert Tatlock. 'Albert, I've got to 'ave words with Annie Walker. Tek over the bar, will you?'

Albert nodded. 'Aye. You're not up to owt, are you, Ena?'

Ena shook her head. 'Nowt that that woman 'asn't brought on 'erself.'

In Annie Walker's parlour the two women faced each other sitting at either end of the dining-table with a lace runner and a spider plant between them.

'So, Annie Walker,' said Ena slowly, 'your plan is to mek me lose me job and me 'ome by tellin' downright lies to me gaffers.'

'You had beer on the premises,' said Annie. 'And I heard you were drunk.'

'I was 'eck as like. I drank orange squash all day. You're just doin' it out o' spite because I wrote to your Jack.'

'Are you surprised, Mrs Sharples? After all, you tried to break up my marriage.'

Ena was indignant. 'I did no such thing. For a woman who thinks she's well above 'er station in life you can be as dim as Minnie Caldwell. I was tryin' to keep a family together. Do you think any stepfather is goin' to think as much of your kiddies as their own flesh and blood?'

Annie didn't answer so Ena repeated herself. 'Flesh and blood and the sacred oath you made Jack, that's what matters.'

Annie's lower lip dropped slightly and Ena could see that she was fiddling with her wedding ring.

'Now, I've 'eard as 'ow I was tricked about the beer,' continued Ena, 'but I didn't *know* they 'ad it outside and that meks me an innocent party.'

'Well, you *should* have known,' snapped Annie. 'The Mission was your responsibility.'

'We all mek mistakes, Annie Walker, but your main mistake was in sayin' Len Fairclough stole that barrel of beer. He could've gone to prison but 'e went to see Adcocks and Barnes and they agreed not to tek any further action until Jack 'imself could be contacted.'

'Oh, my God,' murmured Annie.

'You might well call on God, Annie Walker. When your Jack comes 'ome for good I reckon there's some questions 'e'll want to ask you 'imself. And I know Jack. 'E might be a gentleman but 'e's got some passion in 'is soul and knowin' what war does to people, 'e'll be a different man from the one you remember.'

Annie stared ahead, then at the floor. Ena Sharples was an old witch but she was right. Jack had already changed. She had no choice. 'What do you want me to do?'

'You can send a letter explainin' you told a lie and as 'ow you've lived to regret it. You can also say I knew nothin' about the beer.'

There was only a short pause before Annie muttered, 'Very well, Mrs Sharples.'

As Ena left she fired a parting shot. 'You think you're better than any of us, Annie Walker, but you're a woman who 'as morals to suit 'erself and one who doesn't know when she's well off.' Ena paused and opened the door into the pub and said loudly so that everyone could hear, 'You're worse than that trollop Elsie Tanner – only at least she don't pretend to 'ave any morals. She might sell 'er body but you'd sell your ruddy soul.'

Having had her two halves and a pound of flesh, Ena signalled to Minnie and Martha that it was time to leave. They walked out together, Ena with her head held high. She would have felt as proud as any prize-fighter, except that she'd scored a knockout in the first round and victory had come too soon for her to really relish the moment.

Ida Barlow and Bessie Tatlock heard the news of Hitler's death on the wireless on 1 May. Bessie came straight round in case Ida hadn't heard it.

'At long last he's done for himself,' said Bessie.

'About time too,' agreed Ida, putting on the kettle for a celebratory cuppa. 'It *is* nearly over *now*, isn't it?'

'Course it is, love. Albert says only a few more days. Mind you, there's still the Japs to worry about.'

'I've got used to the war,' murmured Ida. 'It's like it's never been any different.'

Bessie smiled. 'One day we might look back on these years and say they were the best years ever.'

Ida didn't believe that, but she'd managed without Frank, and, thanks to Bessie, she'd found a new talent. When the children were older, she decided, she'd look for a job outside. She hadn't really known the meaning of ambition before but now she had visions of her own little dress shop. It was a dream that kept her going. She was sure Frank would be delighted that she could now help out with the housekeeping money. She'd got a little bit put by and she'd treat Frank to the best meal he'd ever had. She just knew that as soon as the war was over the shops would be bulging with meat and cheese and butter.

'It'll be grand, won't it, Bessie?'

'Let's 'ope so, love.'

Since Arnold's visit Elsie had been in the doldrums. Money was tight now. Dot and Sally had rallied round, bringing scones and vegetable pies to cheer her up, but there had been no more paying guests. One blessing was that Elliston's short time had ended when they landed a large contract for demob suits so at least Elsie had full wages. Another blessing was that Dennis and Linda had fully recovered from whooping-cough.

On evenings when she didn't go out and the kids were asleep and the house was quiet, Elsie sat smoking and wondering what the end of the war would bring. She tried to pin her future hopes on Arnold, but Steve Tanner was often in her thoughts and dreams. She still longed to see him one more time, but deep down she doubted she would. What man in his right mind would want a woman with two young children in tow and no money? Steve would have to rebuild his life, but she couldn't believe he'd manage that with the three of them. Anyway, for all she knew he was a prisoner-of-war in Europe or, worse, fighting the Japanese.

As for Antonio, she'd heard nothing from him. Like a few other men in her life, he had become a fond memory. Just have to keep hoping for something better, she told herself. She was sure of one thing: one day her prince would come.

Betty Preston wasn't used to idleness. Margaret had resumed most of the housework and the cooking, which left Betty either standing in queues at the shops or at the labour exchange. Now that the war was almost at an end, Betty's hopes of Ted writing diminished. She had another admirer, though – a lad from Weatherfield who had been conscripted to work in the mines. He lived in Rosamund Street with his gran, his name was Joe Pattishall, he was twenty-four and she'd been to the pictures with him twice. He was quiet and shy, and when Betty had said no to being kissed he hadn't minded.

'I can wait,' he said. 'Me gran says a good girl is worth waitin' for.'

As Betty stood in her second queue of the day at the labour exchange, listening to an elderly lady with a voice like a foghorn shouting 'Next!', she realized what was wrong with Joe: his opinions were all his gran's. He had none of his own and if Betty didn't agree with his dear old gran then he got sulky and defensive. He takes me to the pictures, thought Betty. I don't have to marry him. Although Betty would have liked children she'd seen too much of her mother's marriage to risk marrying the wrong person.

'Next!' came the shout. 'Next!' the woman repeated.

Betty, startled, moved to the counter. 'Here's one might suit you, Miss Preston – usherette at the Bijou.'

'That'll suit me grand,' said Betty. Now she wouldn't need Joe or his gran's opinions ever again. She smiled sweetly at the woman with the foghorn voice and was given details of the hours and the pay. If she went to see the manager she could start whenever she liked. The money was poor but it was a job, and she'd get to see all the latest films.

On her way home she caught a glimpse of her father, black tailcoat waving in the breeze and the sun glinting on his ivory-handled walking stick. He seemed to be moving more slowly than usual so she easily caught up with him. 'I've got a job, Dad,' she said cheerfully.

He stopped and took a deep breath. 'What doing?'

'Usherette at the Bijou.'

He didn't answer but carried on walking. They had just turned into Tile Street when he stopped. Betty had noticed how pale he'd grown of late but now he seemed ashen and grey and his upper lip was beaded with sweat.

'Are you all right, Dad?' she asked anxiously.

He struggled to answer her and when he did it was in a whisper. 'Fetch your mother.'

Betty ran the few yards to No. 6 and her mother tried to hurry out to Harold – but by the time they reached him he'd collapsed on to the pavement. Margaret knelt clumsily beside him and put an ear to his moving lips. Betty stood looking on, hardly able to believe what had happened. Someone called an ambulance, but by the time it arrived Harold Preston was dead.

Betty and her mother walked slowly back to the house. Neither of them cried. Once they were indoors Betty asked, 'What did he say, Mam?'

Margaret gave a wry smile. 'That he was on his way to meet his Maker.'

At the sight of Betty's face Margaret said, 'Don't fret too

much, pet. He never did live in this world – he was always half in the next.'

In the days that followed Betty often wondered if learning of her job at the Bijou had killed her father, but then she remembered his slow decline since Ena Sharples had spoken to him at Christmas. Whatever had she said to him?

On her way home from work Elsie marvelled at how Coronation Street had been transformed. Bunting and balloons had been strung up, trestle tables opened in readiness for the day that had finally come – VE-Day. Victory in Europe. Somehow the sight of the decorations waving in the breeze meant more than all the speeches and the long-winded negotiations since Hitler's death. Tomorrow really was the war's end.

Elsie paused at her back door. A parcel wrapped in brown paper had been placed on her back step. Antonio. She picked it up, guessing by its weight that it contained cigarettes, and was just about to go indoors when she heard a creak. She turned to see Antonio appear from the privy.

'Elsie, my lovely,' he said, as he swept her into his arms and carried her indoors.

Although she was pleased to see him she wasn't going to be swayed by his romantic gesture. 'Why 'ave I 'eard nowt from you before now?' she asked.

'It's been difficult. But I've thought about you every day.'

She noticed now that he was unshaven and the civvies he wore were creased and looked as if he had worn them for some time. 'What's up?' she asked.

'I need a drink.'

She gave him a whisky, and he drank it neat in one go. 'Are you goin' to tell me what's wrong?' she said, offering him a Woodbine.

He took a deep drag. 'They're after me, Elsie.'

'Who are?'

'The police, the family. Quite a few people.'

'What for? What 'ave you done?'

'I've been a naughty boy. Will you help me get away?'

'Have you killed anyone?'

'No, Elsie. On my mother's life I haven't killed anyone.'

'Tell me what you've done then.'

He stood up and stroked her face. 'I will, my lovely, in time but now all I want is to hold you in my arms and sleep beside you.'

Elsie thought, but only for a moment. Already he was kissing her and she wanted him. 'You'll need a shave first,' she said. 'I'll be blowed if I'll sleep with a man whose face is as rough as a sow's arse.'

Antonio laughed. 'Elsie, my darling, I've missed you.'

The morning of VE-Day Elsie woke to find Antonio up and dressed. 'What's the rush?' she asked, still only half awake.

'Do you have any money?'

'About a quid, that's all,' she said, still half asleep.

'What 'appened to all the money I sent you?'

Elsie raised herself up on one arm. 'I didn't realize I was meant to be savin' it for you.'

'I just hoped you'd got some left,' said Antonio, as he sat beside her on the bed and stroked her arm.

'I would 'ave,' she said 'but my 'usband came back and nicked it.'

'Arnold's a devious sod,' he said.

Elsie sat bolt upright. 'You know 'im? You never told me.'

'How do you think I came knockin' at your door? I got your note but you could 'ave been an old bat. Arnold told me you were a looker.'

'Where did you meet 'im?' she asked suspiciously. 'He's in the Navy and you're in the Air Force.'

'In the Naafi.'

'Oh,' said Elsie. She had other questions to ask him but Dennis wandered into the bedroom, saying that Linda was wet, so Elsie knew her day had begun in earnest. 'It's a street party today, pet. War's over.'

Dennis grinned happily and yanked at his falling pyjama trousers but he was far too young to know what a street party was and the war was all he'd ever known.

Minnie Caldwell wet-combed Dieter's hair and pulled his jumper down. 'You 'ave scrubbed up well, pet. You'll 'ave a lovely time today.'

'Will there be cakes and ice-cream?' he asked.

'There'll be cakes. Everybody's making summat. Don't know about ice-cream, though.'

If Minnie was honest she didn't want the war to end. Dieter's uncle Ruben was planning to make a home for his nephew, possibly in Weatherfield so that Dieter could stay at Bessie Street School. Since Christmas he had visited several times and Minnie realized that soon it would just be her, Mabel and her mother, who now slept both day and night. Dieter had brightened Minnie's life and she prayed every night that he wouldn't forget her.

'Time to go, lad,' said Minnie. He slipped his small hand into hers and Minnie fought back her tears. Plenty of time for that when 'e's gone, she told herself. 'Let's go and listen to what Mr Churchill 'as to say.'

'Will he be in our street, Auntie?'

Minnie smiled. 'Only 'is voice. It's coming over the loudspeaker at three o'clock.'

Elsie had rushed around all morning. Finally Linda and Dennis looked presentable and they ran round excitedly, knowing that something different was going to happen.

'Aren't you coming out?' she asked Antonio.

He shook his head. 'I've got to lay low.' He patted the children's heads. 'If something should 'appen, Elsie, sweetheart, remember you're my one and only and I'll be back.'

Elsie blew him a kiss. How many women had heard that routine? Antonio wasn't the man she had thought he was. He seemed smaller, shabbier and poorer, somehow less foreign and exotic. But last night he had said he loved her. And that meant a lot to Elsie.

Today Coronation Street lived up to its name, thought Elsie, all brightened up for a real celebration, with tables laid with cakes and trifles and sausage rolls and sandwiches, bunting, balloons and Union Flags, and excited children screaming and laughing. The adults, including servicemen, stood around silently waiting for Winston Churchill to speak. They all knew it was a moment they'd never forget.

It was at about ten to three that Elsie saw the police car

stop at the top of the road. They had come for Antonio, she was sure of that. With any luck they'd wait till the speech was over. She grabbed Len Fairclough by the arm. 'Len, you've got to 'elp me. Get a few lads in uniform into my 'ouse. I want them to 'old up the police for a while.'

'Who is it you're 'idin'?'

'Antonio.'

'I might 'ave known. You're a bloody fool, Elsie.'

'Don't argue, Len. I've got to warn him.'

'He'll get caught. If not by the civilian police, the MPs will get 'im.'

Elsie dashed through the crowd and into No. 11. 'Antonio, you've got to get out – police are 'ere.'

Antonio grabbed his small suitcase and began throwing in the few clothes he'd brought. Then he started to kiss her. 'There's no time for that,' she said, pushing him towards the back door. 'Just get going.'

As he opened the door two burly policemen rushed in. Within seconds he was handcuffed. 'What's 'e done?' asked Elsie, hanging on to the policeman's sleeve. ''E's a flyin' instructor.' The policeman smiled grimly. 'Is that what 'e told you, love? Truth is 'e worked as a Naafi supervisor and robbed it blind in the process.'

Elsie couldn't resist it. She gave Antonio a stinging slap across the face. 'I love you, Elsie,' was all he said and he was still shouting, 'I love you,' as they dragged him away.

Elsie wondered how she could have been so easily deceived. Then she took a deep breath and resolved to go out into the Street with her head held high.

Len was nowhere to be seen, and Antonio was being bundled into the police car and all eyes were on her.

'Len Fairclough, I want to speak to you,' she yelled into the crowd.

But the crackly sound of the loudspeaker stopped everyone in their tracks. Even the children were quiet to hear Winston Churchill's speech. His resonant tone reached all of the crowd in Coronation Street. The war with Germany was officially over, he told them, and a great cheer went up as he finished. Ena Sharples began singing 'Rule, Britannia' at the top of her voice. Everyone joined in, and even Elsie forgot Antonio's abrupt departure as two soldiers linked arms with her.

Later, as darkness fell, a bonfire was lit on the Red Rec. They burnt effigies of Hitler and sang everything from 'Roll Out The Barrel' to 'It's A Long Way To Tipperary'. Everyone danced, and Elsie Tanner collected several soldiers and kissed them all. She'd eventually found Len with Dot and Sally so she didn't say much except, 'You wait till tomorrow, Len Fairclough, I want words with you.'

He'd had a few drinks and he'd grinned at her. 'Elsie, love, I'm tremblin' in me boots.'

Ida Barlow stood next to Bessie and Albert Tatlock, thinking about Frank. Ena, Martha and Minnie came to join them. 'The men will be 'ome soon, won't they?' Ida said, to no one in particular.

'Don't 'old your breath,' said Ena. 'It'll tek time.'

'It'll be grand when they come,' murmured Ida.

'Aye,' said Ena. 'Things will change.'

Minnie looked towards the lights of Weatherfield. 'It's champion to see the lights on again.'

They stood, for a moment, enjoying the sight of Weatherfield lit as brightly as a Christmas tree. 'And did you 'ear Mr Churchill's speech?' Minnie said. 'It fair made me spine tingle. What did 'e say at the end, Ena?'

Ena smiled. 'Trust you not to remember, Minnie Caldwell. 'E said: "Advance Britannia. Long live the cause of freedom. God save the King."'

'Ooh, Ena,' said Minnie. 'Even when you say it, it meks me spine tingle.'

'Don't be so daft, Minnie Caldwell. How about a chorus of "Abide With Me"?'

'Do we 'ave to, Ena?' asked Minnie plaintively.

'Aye. Just because war's over doesn't mean we can forget our Maker.'

Ena began to sing and nobody minded. Slowly everyone joined in, their voices rising up, sombre yet happy.

In a rare moment of silence after the hymn, Ena looked at the happy crowd and gave a thought to those faces that were missing. Some would never return. Others would come back

changed. In her eyes, Weatherfield's war was the only one
that counted and Weatherfield had come through to Victory.
Advance, Britannia. Long live the cause of freedom. God save
the King. Minnie was right. It *did* make her spine tingle.